MAEVE
BINCHY

MAEVE BINCHY

Light a Penny Candle

The Lilac Bus

Bloomsbury Books
London

This edition published in 1994 by Bloomsbury Books,
an imprint of Godfrey Cave Group,
42 Bloomsbury Street, London WC1B 3QJ

1 3 5 7 9 10 8 6 4 2

Incorporating:

Light a Penny Candle
First published 1982
Copyright © Maeve Binchy 1982

The Lilac Bus
First published 1984
Copyright © Maeve Binchy 1984

ISBN 1 85471 455 4

Printed and bound in Great Britain by
Mackays of Chatham PLC, Chatham, Kent

CONTENTS

Light a Penny Candle

Page 7

The Lilac Bus

Page 455

Light a Penny Candle

It had been very dull and matter-of-fact in the coroner's court. No great raised bench with wigged judges, no dock, no uniformed police calling down the corridors for the next person to appear. It was actually quite like an ordinary office; there were books in glass-fronted cases, and lino on the floor – at one corner it had definitely been nibbled or chewed by something.

Outside, the world was going on normally. Buses passed by, no one stopped to see them. A man in a taxi read his newspaper and didn't even raise his eyes as the little group came out on to the street.

Both the women wore black, but then they would have worn black anyway if they had been going somewhere formal. Aisling wore a black velvet blazer over a grey dress. It was an outfit that made her copper hair look even more coppery than usual. Elizabeth wore her good black coat. She had bought it at a January sale two years before for half price and the sales woman had said it was the only genuine bargain in the store. 'It'll take you anywhere, my dear,' she had said, and Elizabeth had liked the sound of that . . . it reminded her of a magic carpet.

Although the rest of the world took no notice, the little group watched them for a moment. Elizabeth, putting her hand up over her eyes as she turned the corner, came out on to the steps leading down into the street. Aisling stood on the steps already. They looked at each other for a long time – probably only seconds, but that can be a long time . . .

Part One

1940–1945

I

Violet finished the library book and closed it with a snap. Yet again, a self-doubting, fluttery, bird-brain heroine had been swept away by a masterful man. He would silence her protests with kisses, the urgency of his passion would express itself in all sorts of positive ways . . . *He* would organise the elopement or the wedding plans or the emigration to his South American estates. The heroine would never have to make all the arrangements herself, standing in queues at the travel agency, the ticket office, the passport office. Violet had to do everything herself. She had come back from an endless morning of standing in shops to beat the shortages. Other women seemed to enjoy it, to think of it as a game of hunt-the-thimble. 'I'll tell you where there's bread if you tell me how you got those carrots.'

Violet had been to the school and had a highly unsatisfactory discussion with Miss James. Miss James was not going to organise any evacuation for her class. All the parents so far had friends or relations in the country. There was no question of the whole class decamping and continuing their education in some rural setting with safety from bombs and plenty of good country food. Miss James had said quite tartly that she was certain Mr and Mrs White must have friends outside London. Violet wondered suddenly whether they had friends anywhere, city or country. She felt very dissatisfied with Miss James for forcing her to face this possibility. George did have some cousins in Somerset, near Wells. But they had lost touch. Oh yes, she'd read all the heart-warming stories of long-lost families having been brought together over the evacuation of children . . . but somehow she didn't think it would happen to George. Violet had no relations to speak of. Her father and his second wife were in Liverpool, separated from her by a feud too long-lasting to dream of mending. To heal would be to open the wound, examine it and forgive. It was so long ago it was almost forgotten. Let is stay that way.

Elizabeth was so timid, so unsure of herself, she would not be an easy evacuee. She had inherited her father's awkwardness, Violet thought regretfully. She seemed to expect the worst from every situation. Well, perhaps it was better than having expected great things and having got so little. Violet suspected that Elizabeth and George might be the lucky ones; to expect defeat and conflict and being relegated to second best meant freedom from shock when it happened.

It was no use whatsoever discussing it with George. These days George had only one thing he could discuss – the kind of country which would accept a man for military service who hadn't a brain in his head, and refuse a man like George who could have been of some real assistance in the war ... It had been bad enough to see all those younger, brainless men do well in the bank, move into different aspects, get preferment, buy motor cars, even – that had been galling. But now, when their land was threatened and their nation was in danger, George had been told that some services were essential to the country and that banking was one of them.

They had found no terminal disease at his medical examination, just a series of inadequacies. He had flat feet, he had a whistling chest, he had sinus trouble, he had varicose veins, he was slightly deaf in one ear. His offer to lay down his life for his country had been met with a series of insults.

From time to time, Violet felt an old, familiar surge of affection for him, a sharing in his outrage, but mainly she felt he brought a lot of it on himself. Not his deafness, not his veins, but his rejection and his disappointment. He went out half-way to invite it.

So the problem of what they were to do with Elizabeth would, of course, be Violet's and Violet's alone. As were so many of the problems.

Violet stood up and examined her face in the mirror. It was a perfectly acceptable face. It had nice colouring, according to what the magazines advised; and her hair was blonde, naturally blonde. Her figure had always been good. Even before the drawing in of belts that had become associated with patriotism and this dreadful war, Violet used to watch what she ate. Why, then, did her face have no sparkle? It wasn't a lively face. It looked flat somehow.

Of course it looked flat, Violet thought with a surge of resentment. Anyone's face would look flat had they been dealt such a poor hand in everything. The chap that had said her eyes were violet like her name had turned out to be a confidence trickster, and had swindled everyone in the neighbourhood. The fellow who had said she should sing professionally had only meant her to sing to him in the bath while he poured her sparkling wine. The eager young banker who told her that together they would rise in London society so that everyone would know her name and envy her distinguished husband his luck, was at this moment with his flat feet and varicose veins, picking his teeth and making excuses down at the local branch of the bank where he would stay forever.

It had all been so different, so dull. It had all been so unfair and so flat. No wonder her features had blended into the background.

She looked at the cover of the library book. Under the transparent library binding a masterful man leaned on an old gnarled apple tree with his riding crop in his hand. Violet wondered whether people should be prosecuted for writing novels like that.

Elizabeth came home from school slowly. Miss James had said that

Mother had been in to discuss things. She had said not to look so anxious, there was nothing to worry about. Elizabeth had looked doubtful. No, really, Miss James had assured her, Elizabeth's Mummy had only come in to discuss what would happen when the children all went off to the country to stay in quiet places by the seaside or on farms. Elizabeth wasn't fooled by Miss James's way of describing what lay ahead. She knew it was something dreadful, something spoken of with dread by parents . . . as if it were torture. They tried to make light of it, but it was no use.

Elizabeth had thought it was 'vaccination' when she had heard of it first. It was another long word with dangerous associations. Father had laughed and put his arms around her, and Mother had smiled too. No, they assured her, evacuation was being sent to the country in case bombs fell and hurt children. But why couldn't parents come to the country too, Elizabeth had wanted to know. Father had said he had to work in the bank, and Mother had sniffed; and suddenly the nice smiling bit, the short happy bit when she had mixed up the words was gone. Father said Mother could go to the country, as she had no job. Mother had replied that if she had a job she wouldn't have remained on the bottom rung of it for fifteen years.

Elizabeth had run off pretending that she had to do her homework, but she just took out an old doll and unpicked it, stitch by stitch, while she cried and wondered what she could do to make them smile more, and what she had done that made them so angry all the time.

Today she had another fear in her heart. She wondered if Mother had fought with Miss James about something. Mother had thought Miss James was silly before, when she had taught them to sing nursery rhymes in harmony. 'Big girls, ten years old, singing silly nursery rhymes,' Mother had said, and Miss James had answered her pleasantly. But a lot of the fun went out of it after that. . . .

Elizabeth found it hard to know when Mother would be happy. Sometimes she was happy for days on end, like the tim they had gone to the music hall, and Mother had met an old friend and he had said that Mother used to sing better than anyone on the stage in London. Father had been a bit put out, but what with Mother being so cheerful, and even suggesting they all have a fish supper, he cheered up. Mother didn't usually suggest anything so common as a fish supper. When they had fish at home, it was little bits of fish, with lots of bones and funny knives that weren't really knives to eat it with. Mother loved those knives. They had been a wedding present and she warned everyone not to let their handles go into the water when the washing-up was being done. Elizabeth didn't like the fish that Mother cooked, with the bones and little bits of egg and parsley on it, but she was glad to see it because the knives always made Mother so good-humoured.

And sometimes when she came home from school, Mother would be singing: that was always a very good omen indeed. Other times, Mother would come and sit on Elizabeth's bed and stroke her fine, fair hair and tell her about her childhood and how she had read books about men who did brave deeds for beautiful women. Sometimes she told Elizabeth funny stories about the nuns in the extraordinary convent school where everyone had been Roman Catholics and believed the most amazing things, but Mother had been allowed to go for walks during the religious instruction classes because it had all been quite so amazing.

The terrible thing was that you never knew when Mother would be happy or when she would not.

Today she was writing a letter, which was unusual. Elizabeth thought that it was a complaint letter, and she prayed that it wasn't about Miss James. She approached nervously.

'Are you busy, Mother?' she asked.

'Mm,' said Mother.

She stood there, a thin little ten-year-old; her short, fair hair – almost white it was so fair – was pulled back from her face with an Alice band, but when she was fussed – like now – little wisps of it escaped, standing up like spikes. Her face was red and white at the same time; the parts around her eyes and nose ashen, while the crimson high up on her cheeks moved like a red shadow.

'Oh,' she said.

'I'm going to send you to Eileen.'

Eileen was a name on a Christmas card, it was a name associated with a small, cheap toy on her birthday. Last year, Mother had said she wished Eileen would drop the birthday gifts, it was silly to keep it up and *she* couldn't possibly be expected to remember all the birthdays of Eileen's dozens of children.

'It seems the only possible solution.'

Elizabeth's eyes filled with tears. She wished she knew what she could do to be allowed to stay. She wished hard that she could be the kind of girl that parents didn't send away, or that they'd come with her.

'Will you come with me?' She looked at the carpet hard.

'Oh, heavens, no dear.'

'I was just hoping. . . .'

'Elizabeth, don't be so silly. I can't possibly go to Eileen's, to the O'Connors, with you. . . . Darling, they live in Ireland. Who would go to Ireland, Elizabeth, for heaven's sake? It's out of the question.'

Thursday was always a busy day because the farmers coming in for the market brought their lists into the shop. Sean employed a boy, Jemmy, who wasn't 'all there', to help carry out the supplies from the yard. He didn't want the children cluttering up the shop on a Thursday, he had said so a dozen times. He wiped a weary forehead with a dusty hand in annoyance when he saw Aisling and Eamonn escaping from the ineffectual grabs and shouts of Peggy and running into the shop.

'Where's Mammy, Da, where's Mammy?' shouted Aisling.

'Where's Mammy, where's Mammy?' repeated Eamonn.

Peggy, running and giggling, was just as bad.

'Will ya come here, you brats,' she laughed. 'I'll tan the backside offa you, Aisling, when I catch you. Your father's after saying a hundred times, he'll have yez locked up if you come in here on a Thursday.'

The farmers, busy men who hated having to take any tie at all away from their deals and discussions on beasts, laughed at the sideshow. Peggy, hair escaping from a bun, filthy apron stained with the last twenty meals she had served, was loving the sensation she knew she was causing, Sean looked at her helplessly as she darted here and there, making even more of a game of it than the children were, with her bold winks at the farmers and the come-on glance giving encouragement to any of them that might want to come back and find her at the end of the market when the pubs were making them feel like powerful men. Jemmy stood open-mouthed and delighted, with the planks in his hands that should have been loaded on a trailer.

'Get those bloody bits of wood outside and come back in here,' roared Sean. 'Now, Michael, ignore these antics, I'll deal with that lot later. How much are you going to need for the plastering? Are you doing all the outhouses now? No, no, of course you're not. Far too much to take on at one time.'

Eileen had heard the commotion, and in small quick steps she came out of her little office and down to the shop. Her office, with its mahogany surrounds and glass windows on all sides, looked like a little closed-in pulpit, Young Sean had said to her once. She should really preach a sermon to everyone in the shop, rather than fill in books and ledgers. But if Eileen didn't fill books and ledgers, there would be no shop, no house, no luxuries like Peggy, and Jemmy, who got a few shillings on a Thursday which made him important again in his family.

Her face was set in a hard line when she met the excited children and the flushed Peggy. Taking each child in a most uncomfortable place, just under the shoulder, she marched them firmly out of the shop; and after one glance from the Mistress, Peggy lost a lot of her bounce and followed quickly with her eyes down. Sean sighed with relief and got back to what he knew about.

Up the stairs of the house in the square, the children squealing and wriggling, Eileen was unwavering.

'Put on some tea, please, Peggy,' she said, her voice cold.

'But Mammy, we just wanted to show you the letter.'

'With the picture of a man on it.'

'It came by the afternoon post. . . .'

'And Johnny said when he was giving it that it was from England. . . .'

'And the man was the King of England. . . .'

Eileen ignored them. She put them sitting on two dining chairs opposite her and faced them.

'If I've told you once, I've told you a million times, on Thursday, on market day, your father doesn't want to see hide nor hair of you in that shop and neither do I. As it is, he's over there waiting on me to come back and do the bills, and write up the books for the farmers. Have you no idea at all of obedience? Aisling, a great, big girl of ten years of age? Do you hear me?'

Aisling hadn't heard a word. She wanted her mother to open the letter, which she vaguely thought was from the King of England because of what the postman had said.

'Aisling, listen to me!' shouted Eileen, and seeing that she was getting nowhere, she reached out and slapped the bare legs of the two of them. Hard. Both began to cry. At the sound, Niamh woke up and began to cry in the cot in the corner of the living room.

'I only wanted to give you the letter,' wailed Aisling. 'I hate you, I hate you.'

'I hate you too,' echoed Eamonn.

Eileen marched to the door. 'Well, you can sit here and hate me.' She tried not to raise her voice, since she knew that little Donal would be sitting up in bed, listening to every sound. Just thinking of his little face made her heart move suddenly, so she decided to run upstairs to see him just for a few seconds. If she went in and said something cheerful he would smile and go back to his book. Otherwise she might see his face pressed anxiously to the bedroom window as he watched her crossing from the house to the shop. She peeped in at his door, knowing well that he was awake.

'You're to try and sleep, pet, you know that.'

'Why is there shouting?' he asked.

'Because that bold sister and brother of yours came into the shop caterwauling on a Thursday, that's why,' she said, adjusting the bedclothes.

'Have they said sorry?' he asked, begging to be reassured.

'No, they haven't – yet,' said Eileen.

'What's going to happen now?'

'Nothing too bad,' she said, and kissed him.

Back in the living room, Aisling and Eamonn were still mutinous.

'Peggy called us for tea, but we're not going,' said Aisling.

'As you wish. You can certainly have my permission to sit here for as long as you like. In fact you can sit here for a long time. Because neither of you two will get to have a lemonade this Thursday evening after your behaviour.'

The faces were round-eyed with disbelief and disappointment. Always on a Thursday, with his order-book full and his cash-box bursting, Sean O'Connor took his wife and children down to Maher's. It was a quiet place. There would be no farmers with manure on their boots scaling bargains in there. Maher's was the drapery as well as having a pub and Eileen liked looking at the new jackets or boxes of cardigans with Mrs Maher. Young Sean and Maureen liked sitting up on high stools reading the notices behind the bar and looking like grown-ups; Aisling and Eamonn loved the way the fizzy lemonade went up their noses, and how Mr Maher would give them a biscuit with icing on it, and their father would say they were spoiled. The Mahers had a cat which had just had kittens. Last Thursday the kittens' eyes hadn't been open, so this week, for the first time, they would be allowed to play with them.

And now it was all cancelled.

'Please, Mammy, please, I'll be good, I'll be very good . . .'

'I thought you hated me?'

'I don't really hate you,' said Eamonn hopefully.

'I mean, nobody could hate their mother!' added Aisling.

'That's what I thought,' said Eileen. 'That's why I was so surprised you both forgot that, the way you forgot about coming to the shop . . .' She gave in. It was the only time in the week when Sean relaxed properly, that hour in Maher's with the children nicely scrubbed and neat playing peacefully with cats or rabbits or caged birds. She picked up the letter and went into the kitchen.

'I've the tea wet, Mam,' said Peggy nervously.

'Pour me the large mug, please. Keep those children in the living room and see to the baby.' In a moment, she had her tea and, letter in her pocket, was striding back to the shop. It was an hour before she had time to open the letter.

In Maher's that night, Eileen passed it to Sean to read.

'My eyes are so tired I can hardly see it,' he said. 'Anyway, that writing's like a spider half-drunk getting out of an ink-pot.'

'That's italic script, you ignoramus, that's the way the nuns in St Mark's taught us to write. Violet remembers it, I don't, that's all.'

'That Violet has little else to remember,' said Sean. 'Life of ease over there, she has.'

'Not since the war started,' Eileen pointed out.

'No,' Sean agreed into his pint. 'No. Is her man out in the trenches? I suppose he'd be an officer, being in the bank and all. That's the way the British Empire does things. If men have good accents they get good jobs and they get to be officers.'

'No, George isn't in the army at all, he had something wrong. I don't know what, anyway he was medically unfit.'

'Too cushy a life in the bank, I suppose he didn't want to leave,' said Sean.

'Sean, it's the child, it's Violet's child, Elizabeth. They're all being sent out of London for fear of the bombs . . . you know, we read it in the papers. Violet wants to know will we have her here?'

17

'This isn't the country ... they're not evacuating them to Ireland, this is our country. They can't make us join their bloody war by sending us all their children and old people ... haven't they done bloody enough already . . .?'

'Sean, will you *listen* to me!' Eileen snapped. 'Violet would like to know whether we would take Elizabeth for a few months. The little school she's in is closing down because all the children are being evacuated. George has relations, and so has Violet, but they ... they asked if she could come here. What do you think?'

'I think it's a bloody liberty, a bloody cheek and typical of the British Empire. Unless you can be of some use to them they've no time for you, they don't want to know you, not a letter, barely a Christmas card. Then when they get themselves into this stupid war they're fawning all over you. That's what I think.'

'Violet is not the British Empire, she's my friend from school. She was never a letter-writer, even this one is jerky and full of ... I don't know, brackets and inverted commas. She's not used to writing to people, not twenty or thirty letters a day, like I am. That's not the point. The point is will you have the child in the house?'

'That's not the point, the point is she's got a bloody neck to ask.'

'Shall I say no, then? Will I write tonight and say I'm sorry, no. Reason? Because Sean says the British Empire has a bloody neck. Will that do?'

'Don't be all bitter. . . .'

'I'm not being all bitter. I've had just as exhausting a day as you have. All right. Of course I think Violet has a bloody neck. Of course I'm insulted when I think she hasn't much time for me, if she doesn't bother to write unless she wants something. That goes without saying. The point is, do we have the child or not? She's Aisling's age, *she* didn't declare war on Germany, or invade Ireland, or attack De Valera or whatever. . . . She's only ten, she's probably lying there at night wondering will a bomb fall on her and blow her to bits. Now, do we have her or don't we?'

Sean looked surprised. Eileen didn't usually make speeches. And it was even more unusual for her to admit to a hurt or an insult from her precious friend of schooldays.

'Will she be too much trouble for you?' he asked.

'No, she might even be a friend for Aisling. And what can one child eat more than we all eat already?'

Sean called for another pint, a port for Eileen and more lemonades. He looked at Eileen, smart now in her white blouse with the brooch at the neck, her brown-red hair pulled up at the sides with combs. She was a handsome woman, he thought, and a strong partner in everything he did. Few people, seeing her in her navy office coat, working out the credit and the cash for the growing business, would know what she was like underneath. A passionate wife – he had always been amazed that she should respond to him as eagerly as he turned to her – and a loving mother too. He looked at her warmly. She had such a heart it could include more children than she had herself.

'Send for her, it's the least we can do to try and keep a child away from all the madness that's going on,' he announced. And Eileen patted him on the arm in a rare display of public affection.

The letter from Eileen arrived so quickly that Violet believed it was a refusal. In her experience, people who were about to make excuses and justify their actions always wrote quickly and at length. With a heavy sigh she picked it up from the mat.

'Well I expect we'll have to smoke out your father's relations after all,' she sighed as she brought it back to the breakfast table.

'Does this mean she says no . . .?' began Elizabeth. 'Maybe she says yes inside. . . .'

'Don't speak with your mouth full. Pick up your serviette and try to behave properly, Elizabeth, *please*,' said Violet mechanically as she slit the envelope with a paper knife. George had already gone to work and there were just the two of them. Violet thought that if you let standards fall you were on the way to destruction, so the toast was served with the crusts cut off in a small china toast rack, and all three of them had their napkin rings into which the folded napkin must be replaced after every meal.

Elizabeth nearly burst waiting for Violet to read the news. It couldn't have been more irritating. She would read bits aloud and then mutter.

'My deal Violet . . . delighted to hear from you . . . emm . . . umm . . . very concerned about you and George and Elizabeth . . . emm . . . umm . . . many people here think that we should be in the war too . . . do anything we can . . . children very pleased and excited. . . .'

Elizabeth knew she had to wait. She screwed her table napkin very tightly into a little ball. She didn't know what she wanted to hear: it would be a relief not to have to go across the sea to another country, a place that Father seemed to think was just as dangerous as London and a place that Mother dismissed as somewhere you couldn't go except in dire circumstances. She didn't want to go and stay in *an awful dump with dozens of children, and in a town full of animal droppings and drunkards* which was how Mother had remembered Kilgarret. Elizabeth didn't want to be in a dirty place somewhere that Mother disapproved of. But still, Mother had said this was the best place for her to go. Perhaps it had got better. It had been years since Mother had visited it, long before she had married Father. She had said she would never go back again – she couldn't understand how Eileen had been able to stand it.

But it was this place with all its dangers and dirt, or else it was more trouble and anxiety and looking for Father's cousins.

After a long time, and two pages, Violet spoke.

'They're going to take you.'

Elizabeth's face went its bright red and white colour. Violet was irritated; she hated it when Elizabeth flushed in this vivid way over nothing at all.

'When am I to go?'

'Whenever we like. It will take time, of course. We have to pack, and I have to write to Eileen about school books . . . what you need. She's full of welcomes but little practical advice about what to take with you and what you'll need. Oh, and there's this note for you . . .'

Elizabeth took the single sheet of paper. It was the first letter she had ever got from anyone. She read it slowly to savour it.

Dear Elizabeth,

We are all so glad that you Mummy is lending you to us for a little while, and we hope you'll be happy here. Kilgarret is very different from London but everyone is looking forward to meeting you and making you feel at home. You will share a room with Aisling, who is exactly the same age as you, there is only one week in the difference so we hope you'll be great friends. Sister Mary at the school says you'll probably know far more than all the class put together. Bring any toys or dolls or books you want, we've plenty of room here, and we're counting the days till you come.

Auntie Eileen

At the bottom of the page in a section where someone had ruled lines to keep the writing straight, there was another note.

Dear Elizabeth,

I have left all the shelves on the left side of the room for you and half the press and half the dressing table. Be sure to come for Eamonn's birthday, there will be a party. The Mahers's kittens are sweet they have their eyes open. Mammy is going to get one for you and me to share.

Love, Aisling

'A Kitten to share,' said Elizabeth, her eyes shining.

'And nothing about school fees, uniforms, anything,' said Violet.

Donal's cough was worse, but Doctor Lynch said there was no need to worry. Keep him warm, no draughts but plenty of fresh air all the same. How on earth did people manage that, Eileen wondered. He was finding the excitement about the girl from England almost too much for him.

'When will she be here?' he would ask a dozen times a day.

'She's going to be my friend, not yours,' Aisling said.

'Mam said she'd be *everyone's* friend,' he replied, his face clouding.

'Yes, but mainly mine. After all, she wrote to me,' said Aisling.

This was undeniable. There had been a letter which Aisling had read out several times. It was very formal. It was the first proper letter Elizabeth had every written. It had words like 'grateful' and 'appreciate' in it.

'They must have a better educational system altogether over there,' commented Eileen, reading it.

'Why wouldn't they? With all the wealth they made off the backs of other people,' said Sean. It was Saturday lunchtime. He had come in for his bacon and cabbage lunch. The shop closed on Saturdays at half past one, and the afternoon was spent making up orders in the back yard, but at least it was his own time and he didn't have to be in and out every time the door clanged open and the bell over the doorframe rang.

'Now, I hope you won't be going on with that kind of thing when the child arrives,' said Eileen. 'Isn't it hard enough for her going to another country without having you running her down?'

'And it isn't even true either, Da,' said Young Sean.

'It is bloody true,' said his father. 'But your mother is right. When the child comes we'll all hold our tongues and put our real thoughts out of our minds for a bit. It's only fair on the little one.'

'I don't have to put my real thoughts anywhere out of sight,' said Young Sean. 'I don't have any of this constant bellyaching about the British to make me feel good.'

Sean laid down his knife and fork and pointed across the table. Eileen interrupted quickly.

'Will you listen to me, please. I was just about to say that when she comes it might be the opportunity for this family to improve its table manners. Like a lot of puppies you are, slopping food on the table cloth and speaking with your mouths full.'

'Puppies don't speak with their mouths full,' said Eamonn. Donal laughed and, hearing the laughter, Niamh cooed and gurgled in the pram beside the table.

'I'm sure she'll think we're very rude,' said Aisling. Eileen was surprised to have support from this source.

'We all talk at the same time and no one listens to anyone else,' continued Aisling disapprovingly. Something in the way she said it, something schoolmistressish about her tone, made everyone laugh. She didn't know why they were laughing and looked annoyed.

'What's so funny?' she said, 'what's funny?'

Donal was sitting beside her. 'They're laughing because it's true,' he said. Aisling felt better and laughed a little herself.

They would have to be at the station early to look for someone reliable to look after Elizabeth on the journey. It had been thought that Violet might go with her as far as Holyhead, but it seemed a waste because she would have had to turn around and come back again, and the trains took hours and hours with all the delays and the shortage of fuel, and then of course there was the whole matter of the fare – it seemed senseless to throw money away in these hard times. . . .

George had wondered whether they should pay the O'Connors for Elizabeth's board; but Violet had said no. Evacuees in England didn't pay the host families, it was all part of the war effort. George had pointed out that Ireland wasn't part of the war effort; Violet had sniffed and said they should be, they jolly well should be, and anyway, the principle was the same. She had given Elizabeth five pounds and told her to spend it *intelligently*.

At Euston, Violet looked around for respectable middle-aged women to whom Elizabeth might be entrusted. She wanted someone travelling alone. A woman chatting might forget to look after her charge. She had several failures. One was only going to Crewe. One was waiting for her gentleman friend, one was coughing so much that Elizabeth would surely catch some disease from her. Finally, Violet settled on a woman who walked with a stick. She offered Elizabeth's services as a runner of errands and a helper with luggage on the trip. The woman was pleased with the arrangement and promised to deliver Elizabeth into the hands of a young man called Sean O'Connor at Dunlaoghaire when the boat docked. The woman settled herself into a corner and said she would leave Elizabeth to say goodbye to her parents alone.

Mother gave her a kiss on the cheek and said to *try* to be a good girl and not to cause Mrs O'Connor too much trouble. Father said goodbye very formally. Elizabeth looked up at him.

'Goodbye, Father,' she said gravely. He bent to hug her, he hugged her for a long time. She felt her arms clasping round his neck, but looked at Mother and detected those early signs of impatience. She released him.

'You'll write lots of letters, write and tell us everything,' he said.

'Yes, but you're not to go asking Eileen for letter-paper and stamps, those things cost money.'

'I have money! I have five pounds!' cried Elizabeth.

'Hush! Don't let everyone in the station hear you! That's the way to get robbed,' said Violet warningly.

Elizabeth's face went red and white again, her heart started beating and she heard the train doors slamming.

'It'll be fine, it'll be fine,' she said.

'Good girl,' said Mother.

'Don't cry, now, you're a big girl,' said Father.

Two big tears ran down Elizabeth's face.

'She had no intention of crying until you mentioned it,' said Violet. 'Now look what you've started.'

The train moved out, and among all the other people waving on the platform stood Mother and Father. Stiffly. Elizabeth shook her head to clear away the tears and as the blur went she saw them standing as if each of them was holding their elbows close in to their sides for fear of touching the other.

II

Donal wanted to know had all Elizabeth's brothers and sisters died. Were they killed dead?

'Don't be silly,' Peggy had said. 'Of course they didn't die.'

'Then where are they? Why aren't they coming?' Donal was feeling left out because Aisling had appropriated the coming guest so firmly. It was a question of 'my friend Elizabeth won't like that' and 'when my friend Elizabeth arrives'. Donal hoped that there might be a secret cache of brothers and sisters he could adopt himself.

'There was only one of her,' said Peggy.

'There's never only one of people,' complained Donal. 'There's families. What happened to them?'

Eileen couldn't manage to elicit similar enthusiasm from the rest of them. Only Aisling and Donal were excited. Young Sean never noticed who was in the house anyway; Maureen said that it was going to be painful having someone else as silly as Aisling around. Eamonn said he was not going to wash himself for some awful girl he had never met, and anyway he *did* wash . . . enough. Niamh, cutting a tooth, was red-faced and angry and cried in long, sharp bouts. Eileen herself had a few moments' worry about Violet's little girl. The letter had been very stilted, the girl was used to a much more gracious way of living. If Violet's short, sharp and unhelpful glimpses into her life were accurate. . . .

She hoped the child wouldn't be a frightened pickaheen of a thing, afraid to open her mouth. Then it would really be out of the frying pan and into the fire for the girl . . . the blitz of London or the noisy O'Connors in full cry. It would be hard to know which was worse.

In any event, the child might bring her closer to Violet again, after all these years. Eileen wishes they could have kept in touch more. She had tried, Lord knows, writing often and giving little details about life in Kilgarret and sending Violet's only child little gifts on birthdays – but Violet only scribbled a card from time to time. It annoyed Eileen that their closeness had seemed to vanish into the air, because it had been a very real closeness based on the fact that they had both been in that convent school on a false premise. Violet, because her family (wrongly) thought that a convent school might give their girl a little polish; Eileen, because her family thought that a convent school in England would be a cut above any kind of a Catholic education in the homeland.

Still, she was going to be brought back into Eileen's life again and Eileen was glad of it. Perhaps, in a year or two, when this terrible war was over, George and Violet might even come to stay in Donnelly's Hotel on the other side of the square, and thank Eileen from the bottom of their hearts for putting roses back into the cheeks of their daughter. The friendship would blossom all over again, and Eileen would have someone to remember those long-gone days in St Mark's which she couldn't talk to anyone else about because they all said she was uppity to have been at an English school at all. . . .

She would liked to have gone up on the bus herself to meet the little girl. A day in Dublin would cheer her. No squinting over books and bills, she could collect Elizabeth in Dunlaoghaire when the boat got in – or Kingstown, as some people still called it, just to get a rise out of Sean – and then they could take a tram into Dublin. She could take Elizabeth to see the sights, maybe even climb Nelson's Pillar, something else she had never done. But this was fanciful. . . . She couldn't go, Young Sean must collect the girl. He had been so restless and ready to fight with his father over anything, Eileen thought a day off from the shop would be no harm. He was to go off that Tuesday after work, on the evening bus. He could stay with her cousin, who ran a small boarding house in Dunlaoghaire – half a dozen eggs would pay the compliment for giving him a bed in the sitting room for the night. He had strict instructions to be on the pier before the boat even berthed so that the child wouldn't fear that no one had come to meet her. He was to tell her his name when he saw a ten-year-old in a green coat, with blonde hair, and carrying a brown suitcase and wearing a brown shoulder bag. He was to be welcoming, and give her some buttered brack and a bottle of orange squash while they waited for the bus home. On no account was he to dawdle so they would miss the bus. Eileen knew well Sean's interest in collecting a ten-year-old girl from a mail-boat was minimal, but if he were to meet any group of young lads about to enlist in the British army, as he had done the last time he was in Dublin, his excitement would be enormous.

Eileen arranged with the Mahers to collect the new kitten on the afternoon Elizabeth arrived; she wanted to have plenty to distract everyone if the arrival was not a success. She also wanted them all to think of the coming of Elizabeth with that of a new, black and white furry bundle, which was guaranteed to be a success.

Mrs Moriarty was a very kind woman. She had a picnic of her own and shared some cold tinned peas with Elizabeth; they spooned them together out of the tin.

'I didn't know you were allowed to eat them cold,' said Elizabeth. Elizabeth's own little picnic was very dull in comparison; six small, neat sandwiches with the crusts all cut off, very little cheese in three and even less tomato in the other three. There was an apple and two biscuits, all wrapped in white paper – even a folded paper napkin as well.

'Mother said I must make two meals of this, supper and breakfast,' she said gravely. 'But please do have a sandwich now in exchange for the peas.'

Mrs Moriarty took one and pronounced it excellent.

'Aren't you a lucky little girl to have a Mammy make all that for you now?' she said.

'Well, I made it myself really, but Mother wrapped it,' said Elizabeth.

Mrs Moriarty told Elizabeth that she was going home to live with her son and his scald of a wife in County Limerick. She had lived since she was a widow in England, and she loved the place, the bigness of London did your heart good. She had worked in a vegetable shop and everyone had been very pleasant and friendly, but now, what with her arthritis, and the blitz and everything, they insisted she came home. Mrs Moriarty didn't like it a bit. She wouldn't feel the same when the war was over, the others in the shop would think she had run away. But there was nothing she could do, her son and his brazen strap of a wife had been writing every week – they had even come over to plead with her. Everyone in their street said they were heartless to let a mother be roasted alive by bombs in London, so they had demanded that she come back.

Elizabeth agreed that it was hard to make a journey when you didn't want to, and as Mrs Moriarty spooned out some tinned pears she told her about Mother's friends, the O'Connors, who lived in a dirty town in a house where everything was untidy and in a square where animals came and soiled the place. Mrs Moriarty said thoughtfully that maybe Elizabeth should keep her worries about the town being dirty to herself, that perhaps she shouldn't pass on her mother's views until she had had time to form an opinion of her own. Elizabeth flushed and said that she wouldn't dream of saying anything like that when she got to Mrs O'Connor's – it was only because Mrs Moriarty was a friend and had told her about the awful daughter-in-law. . . .

They ate a tin of condensed milk to seal their conspiracy, and Elizabeth fell asleep with her head on Mrs Moriarty's shoulder and didn't stir until they were all woken up and turned out into the cold night air in Holyhead, with porters shouting to each other in Welsh and great confusion as they waited to be called into line for the mail-boat.

'Will they speak like that in Ireland?' asked Elizabeth nervously. The place seemed to be very unsafe with people shouting and laughing in a foreign language. Mother would have said something very putting down about it; Elizabeth tried to imagine what it might have been, but failed.

'No,' said Mrs Moriarty. 'In Ireland we speak English, we've thrown out anything that was any good to us, like our language and our way of going on.'

'And our mothers-in-law,' said Elizabeth seriously.

'That's it,' laughed Mrs Moriarty. 'Well, if they're bringing back mothers-in-law, Lord knows what else they might revive,' and she leaned on Elizabeth's shoulder as the line started to shuffle off slowly to the mail-boat, which stood large and awesome in the night.

Sean hated people like Mrs Moriarty, people who clutched at your arm and whispered you confidences out of the side of their mouths as if you were in the know, and they were in the know, but somebody else was not in the know. He pulled away slightly as she started to hiss at him that the little girl was very tired and sick from the journey, and that her mother had a hard mouth, and that he and his family shouldn't mind too much what she said.

'I think those people are waving at you,' he said eventually, in order to escape. A middle-aged man and woman were shouting, 'Mam, Mam, we're here!'

Elizabeth looked up for the first time since she had agreed to Sean identifying who she was. She stared long and hard at Mrs Moriarty's daughter-in-law, who had a smile of welcome nailed on to her face.

'She doesn't look scalded any more,' she said clearly. 'Perhaps the burns have healed now.'

Sean offered Elizabeth brack and lemonade as they walked in the early morning sunlight towards the bus stop.

'Mam said you were to have this if you were hungry,' he said ungraciously.

'Do I have to?' she asked. Her face was paler than her hair, her eyes were red and her legs were like sticks. He thought she was a miserable specimen.

'No, indeed you don't, it was only Mam being nice. I'll eat it myself, I love brack,' he said, loyalty to his mother coming unexpectedly to the fore.

'I didn't mean. . . .' she said.

'No matter.' He unwrapped two huge doorsteps of brack with a lump of butter spread unevenly between them, and began to demolish them.

'Is it cake?' Elizabeth asked.

'It's brack, I told you it was brack, you said you didn't want it.'

'I didn't know what it was.'

'Why didn't you ask me?' He wondered what kind of child would never have heard of brack.

'I don't know.'

They walked in silence to the stop for the Bray bus. Her suitcase was heavy and it dragged her down; she wore her shoulder bag criss-crossed over her thin chest. She looked the picture of an orphan.

Sean's mind was full of the boy he had met last night in the guest-house. Terry was seventeen, too young to join up, but he said that you could always say your birth certificate went up in the Customs House fire. Nobody in England knew when that was. Terry was off on the very same mail-boat when it turned around. He'd go to the nearest recruitment centre and he'd be in uniform in a couple of weeks. Sean couldn't sleep a wink from envy. Terry had spoken of other friends who had gone a month ago. Earning proper salaries, real wages, training, drilling, handling weapons, learning all the skills needed; going across the sea soon, but it was all hush-hush. Terry, too, worked for his father, on a small farm. He knew what it was like to get no real money, only pocket money, and a so-called training. He knew what it was like not to be allowed to grow up, your mam asking if you had been to confession, your da asking you to do a bit around the house to help your mam. No life. No chance to get into a uniform. . . .

'What kind of uniform does your da wear?' he asked Elizabeth suddenly.

Her little white face became all flushed, as if someone had hit her with a strong hand and left the marks of a slap.

'He . . . isn't . . . doesn't . . . you see he didn't have to go to the war. He's at home.'

'Why was that?' demanded Sean, his slight and marginal interest in this new girl waning as she couldn't even provide him with information about the day to day business of war.

'He had to stay in the bank, I think . . . I think they needed. . . .' And Elizabeth's face was working with the effort of trying to explain honestly something she had never understood, but which she knew was something that made Mother and Father prickly with each other.

'I think they had to keep senior men with bad chests,' she said eventually.

Sean looked at her without interest, his mind back with Terry and enlistment. They waited in Bray for the Wicklow bus.

'Do you want to go to the lavatory before the bus comes?' he asked suddenly. In all her ten years, Elizabeth had never been asked such a direct and embarrassing question.

'Er, yes, please,' she said.

Young Sean indicated two public conveniences with a jerk of his head.

'Over there, don't be all day and all night, the bus'll be here in five minutes.'

Elizabeth scampered up to the two low buildings. But there was no 'Ladies' or 'Gents' written on them. She had found it adventurous enough to use a public toilet in London with Mother, who had always insisted that she use lots of lavatory paper to guard her from all the infections which lay in the seat, but here the problem was monumental. There only seemed to be sets of initials over the doors, no names. On had MNA, the other FIR. Elizabeth gave it some thought. She looked back at Sean. He already thought she was silly, what would he think if she ran back to ask him which convenience she should use? Think hard. M must be for males, F for females. Courageously, she walked into the Fir.

Four men stood with their backs to her as she walked in. She wondered whether they were painting the wall in front of them, or doing some kind of repairs, and hesitated before going past them to seek the entry to the Ladies'.

One of the men turned around, and to her horror, his trousers were undone. He was an old man, without many teeth, and his cap was on back to front.

'Get on out of here, girlie, go on home and don't be a bold little girl,' he shouted. The other men turned around.

'Get on off with you ... you'll see plenty of it when you're older!' shouted a young man, and the others laughed.

Scarlet, her heart pounding, Elizabeth ran out to where Sean was shouting at her to hurry as the bus had just come around the corner.

'Holy God, did you go into the Men's?' he asked, and before she could say anything he added warningly, 'Don't tell that to Mam or she'll beat the bottom off you.' Elizabeth's brown case was snatched and thrown on the roof rack of the bus.

'It says Cill Maintain!' she cried. 'It doesn't say Wicklow, this is the wrong bus!'

'Oh, Jesus, Mary and Joseph, will you get in,' said Young Sean, who had found it hard enough to have to travel with a normal ten-year-old, but one who was obviously mentally disturbed was proving even worse.

It began to rain just then, as the bus headed off, passing by the fields of green, each surrounded by a hedge of darker green; and Elizabeth stared hard out of the window willing the tears back into her head. She was also willing herself to hold on until the bus stopped at another convenience where someone might tell her the significance of all these initials. It seemed like weeks since she had left London, and she realised to her horror that it was less than twenty-four hours.

Eileen had left the shop early, just in case the bus arrived sooner than expected. She wanted to be sure that she was there to welcome the child. Peggy was screeching, Aisling tongue-tied, Eamonn truculent, Donal unintelligible. . . . This would be no way to start a new life in the country. She smoothed her skirt and tidied stray wisps of hair, wondering how Violet looked now: she had always had fine hair and a milk-white face. Perhaps the little girl would be the same, not covered with freckles like all the O'Connors.

The table had been laid with more than usual care. Eileen had sent back a cloth which was badly stained – Peggy was annoyed that standards were seeming to be raised. Aisling ran in.

'Since you're home, Mammy, will we go on up to Maher's and get the kitten now and have it ready for your one when she arrives?'

'Her name is Elizabeth, not your one,' snapped Eileen. 'No, the kitten is for both of you to share.'

'I know,' said Aisling unconvincingly. Eamonn had bounded in behind her.

'Two paws each,' he giggled. 'One lot for you and one lot for her.'

'I'll have the front paws,' said Aisling thoughtfully.

'That's not fair, then she'd only get the bottom!' Eamonn snorted at his own audacity.

'Don't say "bottom", Mammy will belt you,' retorted Aisling, looking sideways at her mother like a trouble-maker.

Eileen wasn't paying attention. 'Come here to me now Aisling and I'll brush your hair. It's like a furze bush. Stand still now.' The brush was always on the mantelpiece of the breakfast room by the clock and it was taken down on Saturday nights for a weekly assault. Maureen and Aisling hated it and squirmed away – the boys were usually able to rely on their father for rescue.

'Stop titivating them, Eileen,' he would say, 'sure aren't they men? Their hair is fine. Leave them alone now.' But he never had any salvation for the long curly hair of his daughters. Aisling pulled and resisted.

'It's worse than getting ready for mass,' she complained.

'Don't say anything bad about mass, that's a sin,' said Eamonn, delighted to have caught her out in a crime equal to his own. 'Mammy, she said she hated getting ready for mass.'

'No, she didn't, she said she hated having her hair brushed. Aisling wouldn't say anything bad about God's Holy Mass, would you, Aisling?'

'No, Mammy,' said Aisling, eyes lowered. Eamonn was annoyed. Usually any question of insulting Holy God brought great retribution on the head of the culprit.

Peggy was still in a bad humour and she felt that times were about to change for the worse.

'Will I get Donal up, Mam? He says he's mad to be down here when the one arrives and he knows there's a fire. He says he doesn't want the one to think he's. . . .'

'Peggy, Elizabeth White is called Elizabeth. She is not *the one*. Do you hear me?'

'Yes, Mam. I know, Mam,' said Peggy, alarmed.

The hair brush was put away.

'I'll go up for him now.' Eileen crossed the room, but as she did so she looked automatically out on to the square. The bus must have arrived. There were straggles of people coming across the square from Donnelly's Hotel, where the Dublin bus drew up each day. And there was Sean, walking ahead, kicking moodily at a stone. Her big, handsome, restless son, worried and unhappy about something. Eileen's heart skipped with worry about him, as it so often did.

And behind him, dragging her own heavy case, was a white-faced little girl. Smaller and thinner than Aisling with hair so pale that it didn't look like hair at all. The green coat made her look more pale and wan than ever. She had a school hat with elastic under her chin and one of her gloves, attached by elastic to her sleeve, flapped about.

There, in the square in Kilgarret, her eyes like two big holes burned in a blanket, stood Elizabeth.

Just as she had predicted, Eileen noticed that Aisling had become awkward and tongue-tied.

'No, you go down, Mammy,' she said.

'Is she there? What's she like?' cried Eamonn. He rushed to the window and saw the little figure.

'Is that her?' he cried in disbelief. Stung to hear her new friend attacked before she had even laid eyes on her, Aisling moved to the window. But she couldn't see her. Elizabeth and her case had moved into the house. There was a scream up the stairs from Peggy.

'Mam, she's here, Donal's after opening the door for her. He came out of his bed and we never saw. . . .'

Eileen ran down the stairs from the breakfast room on the first floor. In the big, shabby door, silhouetted against the light, was the frail shape of Violet's daughter. Donal had helped her drag her suitcase into the hall. He looked at her with delight. A new thing come into the house. A new person coming to live.

'They're getting the kitten because you came,' he said to Elizabeth. Eileen opened her arms out wide.

'Come here to me and tell me all about the terrible journey,' she said.

Close up, Elizabeth's eyes were even more enormous than ever. 'I wet my knickers,' she said. 'I'm very sorry.'

Eileen tightened her grip on the bony little frame.

'It doesn't matter, love, we'll have that sorted out in no time.'

Elizabeth started to cry.

'No, it's terrible. The back of my coat is wet and it's gone on my shoes. I'm so ashamed, Mrs O'Connor. I didn't . . . I didn't know . . . I couldn't. . . .' her shoulders heaved.

'Listen to me, child, this is a house where people are always wetting their knickers, come on upstairs with me, there there. . . .' and Eileen stroked the fine hair and brushed away the tears, taking Elizabeth's hand away from her eyes. 'Sure, aren't you here now, home safe and sound. Come on with me. . . .'

Sean came in. 'Hello, Ma. Ma, I met a man in Dublin, this fellow Terry. . . .'

Eileen turned on him. 'Carry that suitcase upstairs at once you big useless lump. Get a move on now. Shut your mouth about who you met. You couldn't carry the child's luggage for her, you couldn't get a sick child down here safely and with some kindness. You hadn't a brain in your head to ask her did she need a lavatory.'

'I did!' Sean was enraged by the injustice of it. 'I did and do you know, she went into the Men's.'

'You're a big ignorant lump,' Eileen said, and didn't even notice the tears of rage and misunderstanding well up in his eyes. Tight-lipped, he picked up the case and carried it upstairs. He opened the door of Aisling's room and flung the case in hard. He had suspected that this girl was going to cause trouble. He was right.

It only took Eileen ten minutes to get Elizabeth ready for her first meal in

31

her new home. There was a rapid unpack to unearth clean clothes. The contents of the case were flung on the bed with an abandon that would never have been known back in London. Mother didn't do things like that. Mother would have gone away and let Elizabeth cope by herself but Mrs O'Connor didn't seem to understand.

'Step out of these wet things, come on now, sure we'll throw them in the wash with everything else. Come on, now, there's a good girl, and into the bathroom there with you. Give yourself a bit of a quick wash and you'll feel fresh all over. I'll hang up these. Come on, now, that's it.'

Mrs O'Connor actually expected Elizabeth to go across the corridor in just her vest and carrying a towel. She couldn't mean it. Never in her whole life had Elizabeth left her bedroom without being fully dressed or wearing a dressing-gown. She made an ineffectual stab at her suitcase.

'Could I please take. . . .'

'Yes, pet?'

'My . . . er . . . dressing-gown. . . .' Elizabeth was scarlet.

'Surely. Aren't you a funny little thing.'

And then there was no escape. She had to meet the family. If they were all as horrible as the one on the bus it would be very frightening. But Mrs O'Connor was . . . well . . . very friendly, Elizabeth supposed. Not like Mother, not like anyone's mother but very . . . busy and easy-going. The bathroom was enormous, not like the one at home. It had plaster falling off, and the geyser over the bath was all rusty. There were a lot of face flannels all screwed up, not on neat hooks. There were two mugs full of toothbrushes – how did they know which belonged to which person, Elizabeth wondered. There was a knock at the door. Elizabeth held on to the basin for a moment. Right. She did feel clean and comfortable again, and hungry – a bit travel-sick but definitely hungry. Bravely she unlocked the door and came out. Eileen took Violet's child by the hand and led her down the stairs to the breakfast room.

Donal was sitting by the fire, wrapped in a blanket that Peggy had found for him. He jumped up at once and the blanket nearly went into the grate. Eamonn was playing with two china dogs, making them bark at each other. Young Sean was standing moodily at the window. Maureen had come in, as instructed, in time for lunch; she had a mirror and was examining her nose without much enthusiasm. Peggy was hovering, not knowing whether to bring in the pot of soup or wait until the mistress called for it. The master of the house was sitting in his shirt-sleeves reading the *Irish Independent*. Aisling was at a drawing book, writing furiously; she barely looked up when the door opened.

'This-is-Elizabeth-and-will-you-mind-that-blanket-,' Eileen said in one breath. Eamonn rushed and rescued it before it caught the flame. Sean put his paper down.

'You're very welcome in this house, child,' he said. Elizabeth shook

32

hands with him gravely. Maureen nodded and Eamonn giggled. There was a gurgle from Niamh in her pram. Young Sean's eyes never left the square, where the bus, now loaded with passengers and provisions, had just left again.

'Aisling, come here and say hello to Elizabeth – what are you doing?' asked Eileen crossly.

'I was making a notice,' said Aisling, with one of her huge enveloping smiles. 'For our door. It's very important.' In big, uneven letters, she had written:

AISLING AND ELIZABETH. PLEASE KNOCK. NO ADMITTANCE.

She showed it to Elizabeth proudly.

'Who'd want to go into your silly old room, anyway,' said Eamonn.

'I don't think anyone is seeking admittance,' said Maureen.

'Better to have it there all the same,' said Aisling, seeking approval from Elizabeth. It was an important moment.

'Much better, I think,' said Elizabeth as she took the notice. 'Aisling and Elizabeth. Please Knock. No Admittance. Super.'

III

Eileen was beginning her letter to Violet. Somehow the presence of Elizabeth in the house made Violet seem further away rather than nearer. For three days she had been with them with her pinched little face flushing when anyone addressed her directly, trying to answer and be polite and often finding the wrong words. If Eileen hadn't known better she might have thought the child had been reared in an institution.

'How will I explain all about Sister Bonaventure?' she asked.

'What?' Sean shuffled the paper. He was sitting by the fire with his socks almost in the grate.

'You know how bad Violet is at writing, she mightn't reply for a month and we'd be in all kinds of trouble.'

'Huh,' said Sean, hardly attending to her. Violet and her ways interested him hardly at all.

'Of course, years back in St Mark's, Violet never went to religious knowledge classes. We used to see her out of the window walking round the hockey pitch.'

'Well, then?' grunted Sean.

Young Sean was sitting by the window. He always sat by the window nowadays, as if he hoped to see some other kind of life through it, or so Eileen imagined.

'What do you think, son?' she called to him. He hadn't been listening, but he thought that Elizabeth should go to the catechism classes, or whatever else was on offer. No point in making her more different than she was already. Eileen was about to agree, when her husband rattled the paper at the fireside and said that the English people were atheists, and that the one thing they feared most in the world was the domination of the Roman Catholic Church. Better not give them any more grounds for complaint.

'I suppose I'll have to make up my own mind as usual,' sighed Eileen and took up her pen.

Dear Sister Bonaventure,
I have been in touch with Elizabeth's parents, both devout Anglicans, and they would prefer it if she spent the time reading her Bible while the rest of the children are having their religious instruction lessons. They are very grateful to the convent for making this arrangement.

She read it out to them, and both men laughed.

34

'I hope God will forgive me,' she said seriously.

'*I* hope someone will be able to find the child a Bible – you know, the one she's supposed to be reading,' said Young Sean, and for a moment, there was real family laughter between them.

The kitten had been named Monica after endless arguments between Aisling, Eamonn and Donal. Elizabeth had not joined in. As the battle had reached a crescendo, Aisling had turned to Elizabeth and demanded to know who her best friend at school in England had been.

'I didn't have a best friend,' stammered poor Elizabeth.

'Well, who did you like best?' shouted Aisling.

'At school . . . um . . . Miss James,' was the honest reply.

'You can't call a cat Miss James!' Aisling tried once more. 'Who did you sit beside?'

'Monica. . . .' Elizabeth began.

'Monica!' exclaimed Aisling. 'That's it!'

They all said the name. None of them knew anyone called Monica. Elizabeth was a little disappointed. She had never liked Monica Hart – a bossy girl who used to laugh at Elizabeth and pinch her sometimes just to make her jump. She wished the beautiful furry kitten were not called that. Something like Blackie or Sooty – names that kittens were called in books – but the O'Connors seemed to think entirely in terms of people's names; they had been debating Oliver and Seamus before Monica had been settled on.

And now it was Monica's eternal future that was worrying. Aisling had been very anxious to baptise the new kitten, but Eileen had arrived in time to halt the ceremony.

'But, God couldn't send Monica to limbo, could he?' Aisling had persisted.

'No, of course not,' said Eileen, who often got weary of filling in the gaps that appeared after the daily religious instruction classes.

'What's limbo?' Elizabeth asked fearfully. It sounded bad.

'Oh, it's full of babies – you know, dead babies that didn't get baptised.'

'There are no cats in limbo,' said Eileen firmly. She had noticed the large eyes in the small anxious face becoming even rounder and darker at the mention of a place full of dead babies. It seemed so natural in the convent, with Sister Mary and Sister Bonaventure to talk of unbaptised babies going to limbo because they didn't have the sactifying grace that would let them look at God. It seemed unnatural and macabre trying to explain this to Elizabeth, who knew nothing of the rules.

'You never see pictures of them in heaven, mind,' said Eamonn trying to disrupt the calm.

'They're all round the other side,' cut in Eileen. Then, as she saw the question forming on all their faces, 'You know, the bit they don't show in the pictures of heaven where all the animals and birds and all the creatures St Francis loved are all gathered.' As she spoke, she wondered did all other parents have to interpret religion so wildly for their children, and whether the Lord approved of her efforts.

Violet opened the letter eagerly. The house had been far emptier without Elizabeth than she would have believed possible. Already she had forgotten her constant irritation with the little face that reddened and whitened like the colours mixing in a painting box. She hoped that Elizabeth was not being too timid amid the undoubtedly boisterous family in Kilgarret. She had forgotten to warn her about keeping her money safely hidden or giving it to Eileen for safe-keeping in case the rough boys and girls took it from her. Two letters fell out. Violet picked up Elizabeth's first. Lines had been ruled on a page for her. More lines than were used.

Dear Mother and Father,
I am very well I hope you are very well. We have got a new kitten called Monica, it is only for Aisling and me. Its not for Eamonn but we are going to let Donal play with it. Aisling is not like Aisling its like Ashleen. It's an Irish name. I start school next week. Aunt Eileen has borrowed a big Bible from some people who are Protestants and I will take it to the school to read when the others are reading about the Virgin and the Saints. Peggy tells us stories every night.
Love from
Elizabeth

A wave of anti-climax flowed over Violet. Who was Peggy? What was all this about a Bible, a kitten, the Virgin? Was all this rubbish about Aisling to do with how you pronounced her name? Violet read the little note again. It seemed happy and preoccupied, she thought, that much at least was good. But no questions about home, no hint of missing anyone. Of course, this was only the second letter that Elizabeth had written in her life. There had been no reason for her to write letters home before.

Sighing slightly, Violet picked up the other paper. Normally Eileen's correspondence was so long and flowery that she skimmed through, but this time she was eager to read every word. But Eileen had decided to be brief too.

My dear Violet,
Just a word to tell you how delighted we are to have Elizabeth with us. She is a lovely child, very gentle and eager to please. I hope she doesn't find our brood too much for her. She was pale and weary after the long journey but has cheered up greatly and is eating well and bouncing around. I thought you would prefer her not to have

36

Christian Doctrine lessons so I arranged a Bible for her from some of Sean's customers who are C. of I. It's the right one, It has Authorised Version on it, I looked.

We'll encourage her to write to you every week and she can post these letters herself in the square and she can say what she likes so you needn't think they come through us. The same when you write to her. Nobody but Elizabeth will see it.

I hope you are all managing over there all right. Our thoughts are with you in this awful time.

As always,
Eileen

What *did* Eileen mean about Elizabeth 'bouncing around'? Elizabeth didn't *bounce*. And why all the fuss about Bibles and authorised versions? The Irish were indeed obsessed with religion.

Violet put the letters on the hall table so that George could see them, then she put her headscarf on and went out to join the lengthening queues in the shops. . . .

Young Sean was being even more of a trial than usual in the shop and his father's patience was extremely limited. Eileen could remember a time when they had all looked forward to Sean's serving his time in O'Connor's shop. Sean more than anyone. He had begged to be allowed to leave school after his Intermediate Certificate when he was fifteen, but his parents would hear none of it. The eldest of the family, he had to put the stamp of education on them all by doing his Leaving Certificate.

Now the examination was done and the results expected any day, but the promised excitement and manliness of joining his father in the family business had not materialised. Young Sean was moody and would flare up on any subject. 'Ah, leave him alone,' Eileen would sometimes say to her husband across the supper table when another list of complaints about the day's work began. 'Can't you see the boy's worried sick about his exam results . . .?'

Sean Senior would grunt. 'Can't imagine that any piece of paper will make him any more use in the shop, only more arrogant if he gets it.'

Young Sean, stung by the sudden and unfair lack of interest in all school work, would retaliate. 'Well, you had me working like a black man all the last years saying it was the most important thing on earth – why?'

'Don't speak to me in that tone of voice. . . .' the master of the house would say.

And, 'I won't speak to you at all then,' the son of the house would reply; and a scraping of the chair and a bang of the door and he would be gone. A second bang of the door and he would be out in the square and across to the library where he would sit and read the newspapers for hours on end with everything they had to say about the world where there was war.

He would be seventeen on 7 September. Eileen remembered so well the year he was born, with the Civil War still all around them, and how she had written to Violet about her hopes that her son would grow up in a land that would never go to war again. She couldn't remember what, if anything, Violet had replied. But now it was happening, in a distorted way, her son was grown-up and his land was not at war – and that *was* the problem. . . .

She had thought of having a party of some kind on his birthday. It would be the day the school reopened and so the horror would be taken out of it for little Elizabeth.

Eileen found herself more and more drawn to this odd little girl. There was something more gracious, less rude and heavy and rough about her than there was in any of Eileen's own children. It was as if the polish which St Mark's was meant to confer had skipped Violet and Eileen and landed on Violet's child. She was so willing to please, and so unlike any of the O'Connors in this that Eileen felt somehow wistful. Why hadn't she been able to give any of this gentleness to her own family? Only Donal had any trace of it and that was because he was delicate and not able to tear through the house, shove and push, shout and grab.

Yes, a bit of a party might cheer up her restless son. He might lose his strained look and even Sean Senior might mellow a bit in the light of birthday candles. She began to make a list, then felt a pang of guilt about the birthday parties in England where no child would have cakes or cream – but it passed. And perhaps he would bring over a few of his friends from school; that young Murray boy, or one of the Healys, or whoever it was he was friendly with these days. Funny that she didn't know. There was a time when he used to have the house full of his friends.

When he came back from the library and crept into the kitchen to eat something from the meat safe, she would talk to him about the party. It would cheer him up. Cheer them all up.

7 September. Donal was waved off to school – he didn't want to be accompanied any further, not by his mother and *two girls*; and he ran off on spindly legs, like a leaf, Eileen thought, comparing him to the stout twigs of boys who were already pummelling each other cheerfully in the yard of the boys' preparatory. Then, with a smile, she deposited Aisling and Elizabeth, trying not to notice Elizabeth's fearful glance at the huge statue pointing to its exposed and open heart. . . .

She returned to the house in the square. Peggy, who hadn't expected the mistress back so soon, was half-heartedly fending off the gropings of Johnny O'Hara, the postman. Johnny was drinking tea and eating bacon on his soda bread, and that annoyed Eileen more than the fumblings.

She had ruled that it was extravagant to have bacon for breakfast, and here it was being handed out to the postman. She took the letter from the speechless Johnny, brushed aside the protests and explanations from Peggy with a curt request that Niamh should be restored to her cot.

Then she read that Sean had failed his Leaving Certificate examination.

She decided that she would tell her husband before anyone else.

Then she found that Eamonn had already gone to the school when the list was being read out and had galloped back to the shop with the news.

Then she heard on the wireless that an almighty blitz had begun on London, and that people were huddling down in the Underground to avoid the bombs and the falling buildings.

Then a message was sent from the school to say that Elizabeth had been sick and that Aisling was being sent home with her.

And as she sat down to try to cope with all the day had brought, she realised that she had not had her period since the middle of July and that she was probably pregnant. Pregnant at the age of forty.

Most things had sorted themselves out, as most things do, after two weeks. Most, not all.

Donal seemed stronger and happier at school than he had been during the summer term. He came home with names of friends and stories of what Sister Maureen had said. And plans for the Christmas play, where he would be playing an angel.

Elizabeth was not quite so fearful, and seemed to clutch at Aisling for safety. Aisling, in turn, was pleased and proud to have a new responsibility. It was better than a sister if not quite as good as a best friend. She was now an object of great interest in her class. An English Protestant refugee from the war over there *and* a kitten called Monica.

Peggy was so contrite about the episode with the postman that she took it on herself to make amends. She scrubbed floors unasked, and even tidied out cupboards, unearthing the most extraordinary things.

Young Sean got over the disappointment of his failure. Several other boys had failed too. The Brothers couldn't understand it, although one told Eileen quietly that he thought a few of the lads had their heads stuffed with all this nonsense about going over and fighting a war, and they hadn't given their work or their books enough attention.

Sean O'Connor had taken his eldest son's failure much better than Eileen had hoped. He had had a man-to-man talk and told him that life was full of failures and problems, that Irish history had been one crisis after another . . . all had to be met, faced and solved. He arranged a regular wage and regular hours of work for Young Sean in the store, and saw that he had a smart dun-coloured coat to wear, which lifted him into a different category.

News from London was bad. Every night the bombers were coming over. Every night the Underground stations were full. There were stories of people leaving London again for another evacuation, but not nearly as many went as had gone before, the previous year. A message came from George and Violet, that they were managing. They had taken their beds down to the cellar and lined the walls with mattresses and padding. Eileen shuddered to think what it would be like, and managed to explain it all to Elizabeth in terms of fun. Elizabeth found it hard to think of her parents doing anything in a spirit of fun.

Eileen's period resumed before she had told anyone of its delay. For four evenings she had had very hot baths and a glass of gin. It was just a relaxing thing to do after a day's work. She didn't even think she would worry Father Kenny by telling him about it in confession. It wasn't a sin or anything, it was just something women did to get their bodies back to normal when they were a bit overstrained.

Maureen had seen pictures of nurses bending low over fevered brows and holding the hands of brave young men while reading temperatures and noting pulses and being generally indispensable. She had started writing to Dublin hospitals for details of training. She thought that there would be more brave young men languishing in Dublin than there were likely to be in the local county hospital which they visited whenever Grannie was taken in, which was every winter. Or when Donal had been there for his asthma.

Sometimes Young Sean discussed it with her, which pleased her. It made her feel grown-up to be talking about careers and futures with her elder brother.

He had tried to persuade her to train for war nursing; then they could both go together. There wouldn't be so much fuss if they both said they thought it would be a great opportunity. He had changed his approach: he had begun to realise that his father really didn't see the cause of Good and Honour being with Britain. He now brought the subject up in a purely practical way. . . .

'What other chance would ever be half so good . . . the pay alone is terrific . . . they'll train you, you know, for a career or a trade. I'd be a skilled man when I came out . . . I'd have a whole set of qualifications I'd never be able to get anywhere else . . . Did you not hear there's fellows already from Dublin, fellows with hardly any education doing great out there, learning and getting qualified. . . .'

It wasn't any better than other lines of persuasion. Ones about duty and wishing to defend our way of life. But at least when he and his father argued now it was about points of fact and not blazing ideological rows which Young Sean didn't really understand and always lost. . . .

'Tell me, boy, why we should lift one finger to help them, let alone lose our young men for them in their fight? Yes, it's their fight. What ever did they do for us except bring us torture and humiliation for eight hundred years. . . . Yes, and leave our country when they had to leave it . . . leave it in the state it's in . . . half the land still bitter about the Civil War and a good quarter of it they're still hanging on to. . . . When they give us back the North, which belongs to us by right, when they make some compensation for all they did, then I'd consider fighting in their wars. . . .'

Maureen tried out her hair in different ways with her friend, Berna Lynch, and wore lipstick and powder when she was out of the house. Sixteen was a tiresome age to be in Kilgarret. There was nothing for young people: instead they were watched with suspicion, as if they were on probation from the age of sixteen to twenty – and even longer if, by then, they hadn't settled into the role of 'walking out' decorously with a suitable person. There were no social occasions. Maureen and Berna were considered too respectable to go to the local dance, where messenger boys and maids went. Peggy went to the dance on Saturday nights, but she hated to be asked about it. It wasn't for the likes of Berna and Maureen, she kept saying. They'd hate it even if they managed to get there. They were too well born for the fun and glitter of a hot dance hall, but they weren't well born enough for the tennis parties and supper parties of the people in the big houses. There were the Wests and the Grays and the Kents, all with young people of Maureen and Berna's age, but they never met them. The children had been in boarding schools in Dublin; they came home at the end of term to the railway station three miles away, sometimes they arrived on the bus in the square with their lacrosse sticks and suitcases and blazers. Families in station-wagons met them with cries of excitement, but they never mixed in the life of the town.

Berna, as a doctor's daughter, could have been their social equal . . . but for all their gentility, it was known that her father had a problem with the drink. It was well hidden, but well known at the same time. So Berna missed her chance. Sweet little thing – such a pity about her father. Awfully good doctor, of course, but inclined to go off on his own and mixing with all kinds of rough people. Then into a nursing home in Dublin and after that he wouldn't touch the stuff for about eight months. . . .

They were bored at the convent, they thought the other girls silly and parochial. The time passed very slowly while they waited for Maureen to be called for interview to the hospital and for Berna to go to secretarial college in Dublin. Meanwhile, they sorted out their hair and their skin . . . and hoped that they would have *some* experience of *something* before they got to Dublin and everyone considered them real eejits.

Eamonn was having an unexpectedly bad term. He had looked forward to going back to school, for it held no terrors for a big strong eleven-year-old able to defend himself. But this term, everything was different. Brother John kept rapping him over the fingers.

'Concentrate, young Eamonn O'Connor . . . we don't want you flopping your exams like that big brother of yours. . . .' And Brother Kevin, one of the kindest Brothers who never said a hard word to anyone, was also coming at him and being annoying.

'Now, listen to me, Eamonn, like a good boy. Remember next year you'll have little Donal here, after he makes his first communion, please God. Now, he's not a strong little lad and you'll have to take care of him, you know, you'll have to keep an eye on him. . . .'

And at home, things weren't any better. Peggy was no fun; she was forever cleaning and looking nervously over her shoulder, as if she and Ma had had a row. But there had been no row. He couldn't understand it.

Niamh had begun to cut teeth, and oh janey, what an awful noise she made. She had a bright red boiled face and her mouth was always open and dribbling. Eamonn thought she looked revolting and couldn't understand why they were always picking her up and soothing her. Everyone cut teeth, he thought savagely. When he had lost his and got new ones there was no fuss and roaring.

And Father was in a bad humour, he'd fight with Sean at the drop of a hat. And then Ma would get upset and look away; she was very tired every evening and had no time to talk to him about school or anything. Even Maureen was never there any more, she was always up at Berna's house.

But the worst of all was Aisling. Aisling used to be all right. Someone to play with. A girl, of course, and a sister, but only a year younger, so not too bad. But since the arrival of this Elizabeth, there was no fun to be had out of her. When the two of them came home from school, it was a glass of milk and a bit of soda cake with currants in it and then up the stairs with the kitten. Stupid name, Monica. Up the stairs and the door with their silly notice on it would close with a bang. Aisling and Elizabeth. Elizabeth and Aisling. It would sicken you.

IV

Aisling had taken her responsibilities about Elizabeth very seriously indeed. Not everyone was given a foreigner of their own to look after at the age of ten. Admittedly there were compensations, like the beautiful Monica who had a white front and a purr like an engine and an endless capacity for running after bits of string and rubber balls. And another was that she could get away with lots of things by 'having to help Elizabeth'. She never had to help with the clearing of the table at home nor the washing-up on Peggy's half day. At school she could get out of extra homework.

'I can't Sister, I really can't, I have to show Elizabeth how we do things. Honestly Sister.'

And she thought she was doing a good job. Day by day Elizabeth began to appear more confident. That anxious upturned look was getting less frequent. Aisling noticed that she didn't say sorry so much. She still wasn't very forthcoming about secrets and confidences and though Aisling pressed her about a whole variety of subjects she seemed withdrawn.

'But go on tell me about school . . . tell me about Monica . . . the first Monica.'

'There's nothing to tell,' Elizabeth would say.

'Oh go on, go on. I tell you everything.'

'Well, she was Monica Hart. She used to set near me, that's all.'

'That's *all*?' Aisling was not only disappointed, she felt that Elizabeth was holding out on her. There must have been more.

Or about birthdays. What did Elizabeth do, who came to the house, what did she get as presents?

Elizabeth had got a cardigan last May when she had been ten, and a box of paints. Yes, that was all. No, no party. Yes, perhaps some of the girls at school had parties. No, not Monica Hart, Who did she miss most? Well Miss James. Miss James was very nice. Nicer than Sister Mary? Well different. Nicer in a way because she wasn't a Holy Sister. You know, more a real person. Yes, she missed Miss James most.

'Apart from your Mam and Dad,' Aisling added just to have the record straight.

'Oh yes. You said at school. Of course I miss my Mum and Dad.'

Aisling used to include Elizabeth's parents in her prayers.

'God bless me and make me good, and God bless Mam and Dad, and Peggy and Sean and Maureen and Eamonn and Donal and Niamh, and Sister Mary, and everyone in Kilgarret, and everyone in Wicklow, and in

Ireland, and in the world. And God bless Elizabeth and make sure that her parents, Auntie Violet and Uncle George, are safe during all the things that are happening in London.'

Elizabeth used to say thank you at the end of these prayers which were chanted from the end of Aisling's bed. But Aisling pointed out that she wasn't saying them to Elizabeth, just to God.

Sometimes Elizabeth wondered what Mother would do if Aisling ran up to her and called her Auntie Violet. She was sure that Mother would think Aisling and all the O'Connors very rough. Which, of course, they were. But she hoped that Mother wouldn't come over and see them just yet anyway. If Mother came now she might take Elizabeth away. Mother hated dirt, and really sometimes the house was very dirty.

Nobody ever cleaned the bathroom, and the kitchen had bits of food all over it, not just under nice food covers like Mother had. Mother would never understand sitting at a table where the cloth was full of stains, where nobody had their own napkin ring, where if something fell on the floor it was picked up and eaten as often as not. Mother had been here years and years ago and only remembered that it had been dirty. Elizabeth feared that it might have got even worse since those days.

Even in a few short weeks Elizabeth had become very defensive about her new home; she would hate to hear Mother criticise it, or Father to make a disparaging remark about the way they lived. When Sister Mary had corrected Aisling in class the other day Elizabeth's face had burned.

'Sit up straight child and tie that carroty hair back. Now do you hear me, Aisling O'Connor, don't come into this classroom tomorrow without a bow on all that streelish hair.'

Elizabeth had been offended on Aisling's behalf. To call her beautiful hair 'carroty'. It was a great insult. Miss James would never have said anything about a pupil's appearance. It just wasn't done. But funnily, Aisling hadn't minded at all; she had just shaken it back, giggled at Elizabeth and, when Sister Mary's back was turned, made a face at her retreating presence which made all the other girls stuff their hands into their mouths to prevent a squeak escaping.

The other girls were from farms near Kilgarret, or else their parents had small businesses in the town. It was all so different here from home. Hardly anyone's father went out to work at a place and then came home from it in the evening. There *was* a bank but there only seemed to be two people in it, not like Father's bank. Eileen had pointed it out to her one day, as she pointed out lots of things which had some kind of link with home.

The pupils in the convent welcomed Elizabeth as a novelty but because she was so shy and timid some of them lost interest in her fairly quickly. This in itself was a relief, as she hated being the object of their attention. Aisling, as her self-appointed knight-in-armour, was often more of a menace than a help.

When the girls asked her about her other school, Aisling would intervene on her behalf. . . .

'She doesn't know much about it. It was bombed, you see, in the blitz. Everyone dead and buried in the rubble. . . .'

Sometimes Elizabeth would protest afterwards.

'Honestly Aisling . . . you shouldn't say that, I don't think the school is all in rubble . . . it's not true.'

'Oh, it might be,' Aisling would say airily. 'Anyway, you talk so little about your life in London people think it's funny. It's better to have an excuse.'

Did she talk very little? Possibly. Mother hadn't encouraged long tales with no middles or end like Aisling, Eamonn and Donal related about their doings . . . Mother hadn't been interested to enquire about the other girls at school and had even been bored when she talked about Miss James. It was all so *different*.

Nothing had led Elizabeth to expect their passionate interest in her soul. It had been explained to the class that since she was of the Protestant faith she would read her Bible during catechism classes. Green with envy for a lifestyle that didn't include five hard questions of catechism each evening, the others pestered Elizabeth about her own particular route to God.

'But you don't go to church, not even the Protestant church,' Joannie Murray persisted.

'No I . . . Auntie Eileen said she would take me . . . but, no. It's a bit different you see,' Elizabeth stammered.

'But don't you have to go to some church even if it's only a Protestant church?' Joannie Murray hated things to be inconclusive.

'Well . . . yes if you can. I think.'

'Why don't you go to the Protestant church then? It's just beside you . . . it's nearer than our church and we all go up the hill to our church. Every Sunday and holidays of obligation. Otherwise we'd go to hell. Why won't you have to go to hell?'

Aisling was usually at hand.

'It's different for her. She didn't have the gift of faith.'

This satisfied some of them but not all.

'The gift of faith is only hearing about God, she's heard about God from us now.'

Aisling found this a hard one to deal with.

'Sister Mary said that Reverend Mother knows all about Elizabeth not going to church and says that for her her brand of Protestant religion that's all right. Not all of the types of Protestants have to go to church you know.' This was greeted with some doubt so she went on triumphantly, 'After all, for all we know she mightn't have been baptised.'

'Weren't you baptised?' Joannie Murray examined Elizabeth like a possible leper. 'Oh you *must* have been baptised, mustn't you?'

'Um,' said Elizabeth.

'Well were you?' Aisling the Defender lost her patience and forgot her role momentarily. Really there were times when Elizabeth was very vague. Imagine not knowing whether you were baptised or not.

'Christened do you mean?'

'Yes, of course. Baptism.'

'I did have a christening robe,' Elizabeth recalled. It was in a box between layers of paper, and smelling of moth balls. That seemed to settle it. She had been baptised. Now the knotty problem. As a baptised Christian, shouldn't she be going to a church of some kind? Aisling was at a loss. But only for a while.

'We have no way of knowing whether she was baptised properly,' she said firmly. 'If not, then it doesn't count.'

'We could do it ourselves,' said Joannie Murray. 'You know, pour the water and say the words at the same time.'

Elizabeth looked around like a rabbit caught in a trap. Her eyes pleaded with Aisling. Mutely she begged to be rescued. She was disappointed.

'Not now,' Aisling said authoritatively, 'she has to have instruction first. When she's been instructed in the faith then we'll do it. We'll do it at break in the cloakroom.'

'How long will it take to instruct her?' They were eager now, anxious for the adventure of baptising someone. Elizabeth was the first possibly unbaptised person they had met.

'She's full of original sin of course,' said one of the girls. 'If she died the way she is she'd have to go to limbo.'

'Wouldn't it be better for her to go to limbo than risk hell? I mean if we baptised her now and she didn't know what she should do she might go to hell. She's better off as she is until she knows the rules,' Aisling insisted.

'But how long will instructing her take?' Elizabeth too looked trustingly at Aisling. Instruction might only take ten minutes. It was hard to know with matters of faith.

'About six months I think,' Aisling said. They were disappointed and prepared to query her. 'Sure she doesn't even know a word of catechism. Not a word. There'd be no point in her being baptised until she knows it as well as the rest of us. It was just her bad luck that they didn't do a proper job on her when she was a baby.'

'Of course, they might have done it properly,' Elizabeth piped up without very much hope.

'Not a chance,' said Aisling.

'Probably didn't get the water pouring and the words being said at the same time,' Joannie said sagely. 'That's the important thing.'

Her first Christmas in Kilgarret approached and Elizabeth was a much stronger and healthier child than the one who had crept across the square. Her skirt was even a little too tight around the waist and the pale face looked stronger and seemed less like Dresden china. Her voice was louder too. You now knew whether or not she was in the house.

Each week she wrote a letter home; Eileen added a note and then gave the child the envelope to post. None of them knew whether the sparse replies were due to the terrible chaos of London during the blitz or to the normal inertia of Violet. The newspapers had been filled with stories of the blitz. The Emergency, as the trouble continued to be called, had reached very serious proportions. An average of 200 tons of bombs fell on London an hour. One night in October the bombing had been so intense that it was almost impossible to imagine that any kind of normal life could go on.

Eileen said repeatedly that Violet was welcome to come to Kilgarret herself, and each time she wrote it she said a small prayer that she would not come. Not now, with everything so unsettled between Young Sean and his father. Not until they had time to do up the house in the spring. Not until she had a chance to put some manners on her own pack. She hadn't realised how uncouth they must all be until she watched the dainty manners and considerate behaviour of Elizabeth. The child stood up politely when an adult came into the room, she offered her chair, she held doors open. Eileen sighed. It would take a large bomb to get any of hers out of their chairs unless they felt like getting up. She didn't question Elizabeth's decision to come to mass on Sunday, regarding it as a further part of belonging. It meant that she had to join the Saturday night inspection of clean shoes, clean socks. Berets, hats, gloves and missals laid out. Hair washed, clean necks, clean nails. It was the one day in the week when Sean and Eileen O'Connor could see some sense in what they were doing, working until their bodies ached. To admire five shining children at mass, a kind of reward.

Elizabeth tried to remember whether she had known any churchgoing on this scale at home, but she could not recall it. Mr and Mrs Flint were 'church types', Mother had said, but she hadn't known that it meant all this washing and shoe polishing and great masses of people walking to and from a building where you knew everyone.

The crib had been put up in the beginning of December. Great life-size figures of the Family in the stable and real straw. Aisling went to pray in front of it when mass was over, and put a penny into a big collection box which was covered in melted wax. This allowed you to light a candle and stick it with all the other lighted candles; apparently, if you did this you got a wish.

'Do you get a wish even if you haven't got the gift of faith?' Elizabeth whispered on one occasion. Her wish would have been to receive a long cheerful letter from Mother and Father.

'I don't think so.' Aisling considered the matter seriously. 'No, I've never heard that you do. Better not waste the penny, keep it for sweets in Mangans.'

Christmas Day, for Elizabeth, had always been an anti-climax; so much looked forward to, so much talked about, but when it came it always seemed to bring some disapproval, or some other cause for complaint which she would pretend not to notice. Last year it had been one long discussion about rationing and arguments about how they could possibly manage. Elizabeth thought that the Day with the O'Connors would be utterly perfect. She expected a story-book Christmas for the first time in her life.

For weeks they had all been making each other presents, and the cry of 'Don't come in!' arose whenever you went into a room unexpectedly. To Elizabeth's great surprise, Aisling talked enthusiastically about Santa Claus. Once or twice, Elizabeth had ventured a small doubt about him.

'Do you think that there actually might not be a Santa Claus, you know, the gifts might come from . . . somewhere else?'

'Don't be daft,' Aisling said. 'Sure, where else would they come from?' She had lit several candles asking God to remind Santa Claus of her requests.

Elizabeth had changed a great deal in her four months with the O'Connors. Once upon a time, she would have said nothing and just hoped that things would turn out for the best. Now, however, she felt able to intervene.

'Auntie Eileen?'

'Yes, darling?' Eileen was writing in the big household book she filled in every Saturday.

'I don't want to interfere but . . . you see, Aisling is praying to the Holy Family people in the church and asking them to tell Santa Claus that she wants a bicycle . . . and, you know . . . just . . . I thought you should know as well, if you see what I mean, just in case she doesn't tell you.'

Eileen pulled the child towards her affectionately. 'Now, that's very kind of you to tell me that,' she said.

'It's not that I'm asking you to buy expensive things like that, it's just that Aisling believes very strongly that what you tell Santa Claus should be a secret, and she mightn't tell you.'

'Well, I'll keep that information very carefully in my mind,' said Eileen solemnly. 'Run off with you, now.'

Christmas Eve was like a combination of Saturday nights with all the shoe polishing and neck washing, and the day of Christmas play at school, all feverish excitement. Even grown-up people like Maureen and her friend Berna were giggling, and Young Sean was happy and wrapping up parcels.

During the night Elizabeth heard the door open. She glanced worriedly over at Aisling's bed but the red hair out on the pillow never stirred.

Through half-closed eyes Elizabeth saw Sean place the bicycle, wrapped in brown paper and holly sprigs, at the end of Aisling's bed. And to her amazement she saw a similar shape coming to the end of her own bed. Two sharp trickles of tears began in her eyes. They were such a kind family, she would never be able to thank them. She must really try to explain to Mother in her next letter how kind they were. Please could she find words that wouldn't irritate Mother and make Mother feel that she was being criticised.

Then it was morning and there were screams of excitement as Aisling in pyjamas tore off the wrapping paper. As Elizabeth swung her legs out of bed, Aisling, her face flushed with happiness, came over and gave her a great hug. She forced herself to put her arms around Aisling too. Though this was a new experience and she was always nervous of something new. Up to now they had only linked arms when coming home from school. That had been the closest contact. But now it was a sea of affection and excitement and it almost drowned Elizabeth with its unfamiliarity.

But in no time there were shouts and calls, and squeaks and hoots on a trumpet, and more shouts. . . .

'Down here in two minutes or Christmas or no Christmas you'll feel the palm of my hand!'

It was still dark as they went up the hill to the church calling and wishing people Happy Christmas. Several people asked Elizabeth what she got in her stocking . . . and Doctor Lynch, Berna's father, pinched her cheek and asked her was an Irish Christmas better than an English one. His wife pulled him away crossly.

There were sausages and eggs for breakfast, paper table napkins on the table. Niamh sat up in her high chair and gurgled at them. There was more suppressed excitement since presents were going to be given afterwards beside the fire. The big things had come in the night but the individual ones would come now, and then the girls could go out in the square with their bicycles, Maureen could parade with her new jacket and matching beret, Eamonn with his football and boots, Donal with his scooter. Then it would be in again for the huge goose that was already cooking in the range.

There were oohs and aahs over the presents, the pincushions, the bookmarks, the dish painted as an ashtray for Da, the necklace made of carefully threaded beads. But there was the greatest applause for the presents that Maureen gave. For Mam there was beautiful soap, and for Da there was a proper man's scarf. For Aisling and Elizabeth big bangles with coloured glass in them; for Eamonn a big light for his bicycle; for Donal a funny furry hat, and even for the baby a rattle. She had given her elder brother two matching hair brushes like gentlemen used in picture books, and for Peggy she had a sparkling brooch.

Maureen had been the last to do the distributing. She had asked if she could be and it seemed a glorious end to the present-giving. The air was so full of gratitude and re-examination of gifts that none of them except Elizabeth noted the anxious glances exchanged between Auntie Eileen and Uncle Sean. She couldn't interpret them – it was as if they alone had seen some hidden disaster. Uncle Sean evidently had decided to let Auntie Eileen deal with it, whatever it was. Elizabeth's face was reddening with anxiety, she knew it was.

'Right everyone, clear up all the mess, paper into this box, string into that, and *don't lose anything*!' Eileen supervised a huge sweep on the room. 'Now all of you out in the square, yes, you too, Sean, get a bit of exercise . . . and Donal, of course you can child . . . wrap up well. No, leave your furry hat here, that's the boy.'

In minutes she had the room cleared of people and presents. Elizabeth's heart pounded because she knew something was very wrong. She went into the kitchen with Peggy and helped to fold the paper up into squares. Peggy kept up a monologue about how much there was to be done for the meal and how little help anyone gave . . . but she was only muttering, and didn't expect any answer.

The voices came clearly from the next room.

'No, Maureen, sit down. Come on sit down. . . .'

'I don't know what you mean Ma, what is it?'

'Maureen, where did you get the money to pay for these things . . . where?'

'Ma, I don't know what you mean. I saved up my pocket money like everyone else. . . . Of course I did Ma.'

'We're not fools Maureen . . . look at these things. They cost a fortune. That soap you bought your mother . . . it's fifteen shillings. I saw it myself in the chemist.'

'But Da, I didn't. . . .'

'Just tell us where you got the money child, that's all your father and I want to know. Tell us quickly and don't ruin the day for all the rest of them.'

'I never took any of your money Mam, you can look in your desk, I didn't take a penny. . . .'

'I didn't miss anything Sean.'

'And I didn't touch anything in your pocket, Da. . . .'

'Come on, Maureen, you get a shilling a week, you have pounds' worth of stuff here. Pounds and pounds. Can't you see your mother and I are heart-scalded over it. . . .'

'Is this the thanks I get for giving you nice Christmas presents. . . .' Maureen had begun to cry. 'Is this . . . all . . . you . . . say accuse me of stealing from you.'

'Well, the only other alternative . . . is that you stole them from the shops.' Eileen's voice was shaking as she voiced the suspicion.

'I *bought* them,' persisted Maureen.

'God almighty, those hair brushes you gave Sean, they're over two pounds!' roared Sean. 'You're not leaving this room till we know. Christmas dinner or no Christmas dinner . . . if I have to shake every bone out of your body, I'll find out. Don't treat us like fools. *Bought* them indeed. . . .'

'You'll have to tell us soon or later, your father is right. Tell us now.'

'I bought you Christmas presents to please you and this is all you say. . . .'

'I'm going to go up to Doctor Lynch's house and see whether their family got fine presents from that Berna of theirs. Maybe the two of you were in this together. Maybe Berna will tell us if you won't. . . .'

'No!' it was a scream. 'No Da, don't go. Please don't go.'

There were sobs from Eileen, and shocked noises and wailings from Maureen as well as her mother. There was the sound of great slappings and a chair turning over. Elizabeth heard Aunt Eileen pleading with Uncle Sean not to be so hard.

'Leave her, Sean, leave her till you calm down.'

'Calm down. Stealing from every other trader in the town. Into their shops with that brat of a Lynch girl. Five shops, five families who've done business with us for years and this brat goes in and steals from them. Jesus Christ, what's there to be calm about . . . you're going in to every one of them when the shops open. Every single one of them do you hear, every item will be returned. And the Lynches will be told too, mind that. They're not going to live in innocence over the pair of thieves we have stalking the town. . . .'

Elizabeth exchanged a fearful glance with Peggy as they heard another blow and another scream.

'Don't you be minding all that now,' said Peggy. 'Better not to poke your nose into others' affairs. Better to hear nothing and say nothing.'

'I know,' said Elizabeth. 'But it's going to spoil Christmas.'

'Not at all,' said Peggy. 'We'll have a grand Christmas.'

'Ah, Da you can't hit a girl like that, stop it, Da, stop it!'

'Go away, Sean, I don't want you here, get out, it's my business.'

'Da, you can't hit Maureen like that, Ma stop him, he's hit her on the head. Stop it, Da, stop it, you're too big, you'll kill her.'

Elizabeth fled from the kitchen and got her new bicycle. Round and round the square she cycled, trying to brush the tears out of her eyes. She didn't want the others to ask her what was wrong. She had no hope that they would even get together for the goose now. Aunt Eileen had probably gone to the bedroom, Sean gone off out after the row with his father. Uncle Sean might have taken the keys and gone back into the store, and Maureen – heaven knew what would happen to Maureen. It was all turning out badly like everything always did. It was so unfair.

Other children who lived in the square had bicycles too and tricycles and scooters; there were marvellous tales about how Martin Ryan had seen the leg of Santa disappearing up a chimney and Maire Kennedy had heard the reindeer coming into the square. Aisling had already learned how to do tricks on her new bicycle . . . she was swooping around where the bus would stop on a normal day with both hands spread out wide and her red hair flying behind her. She saw Elizabeth looking at her and pedalled over.

'What's wrong, you look sad?' she asked.

'No, I'm fine.'

'Are you thinking of your own family and being a bit lonely?' Sometimes Aisling got great fits of concern over Elizabeth's temporary orphan status.

'Well, a bit,' Elizabeth lied.

'You have our family now, and we'll have a grand Christmas,' she said firmly.

At that moment, the O'Connors were called from the top of the steps by Eileen.

'Come on my four. Wash hands and ready for Christmas Feast. . . .'

She looked quite calm again, Elizabeth thought, and then felt a little lift as being called one of her four. Unwillingly, Eamonn, Donal and Aisling gathered their gifts and left their friends. A cursory hand wash was done and all hands dried simultaneously on a wet towel. The table was all set and Christmas crackers criss-crossed between each plate. As they slid to their places, Aunt Eileen said almost casually, 'Oh, by the way, there's been a mistake about some of the presents, could you give Maureen back what she gave you; there was a mistake about some of the prices. It has to be sorted out.' There was a bit of a grumble, a demand for reassurance that he would still get his bicycle light back from Eamonn. But it was over. The crisis was somehow finished. Maureen's eyes were very red, and so were Young Sean's. But no comment was made, and they pulled crackers with everyone else.

And afterwards when there were records on the gramophone there was dancing. Everyone danced except Eamonn who said it was silly, but he was in charge of winding up the gramophone which was a great help.

And as Elizabeth saw Uncle Sean dance a waltz with Maureen and noticed her lean her head against his jacket and cry, she thought she would never understand them in a million years.

The new term began with cold weather and Sister Mary in a very bad humour. She had chilblains and wore mittens, her fingers seemed swollen and purple and she had a racking cough. Donal was wheezing again, and Eileen kept him at home.

Maureen had gone to each of the shops where the Christmas gifts had been 'bought'. In front of Eileen she had handed them back, saying that she had taken them by mistake during her Christmas shopping. Nowhere was she met with anything but kindness. As soon as she left the shop, face burning with shame, the shopkeepers softened the humiliation for Eileen by saying that it was all that young Berna Lynch's doing, a wild bold strap if ever there was one; of course, with all the trouble the poor mother had with the doctor it was hard to know who to blame. They said that poor Maureen had had enough punishment by having to face them and told Eileen to forget it.

Sean had asked the convent what time Maureen's classes ended each day and insisted that she be home fifteen minutes later. He asked her to come into the shop and present herself to him and then to return to the house and begin her homework. Berna Lynch was not to come inside their home again, and Maureen was not to enter hers.

Young Sean read that in England an Air Training Corps had been started for boys between the ages of sixteen and eighteen. He read it out to his father as proof that seventeen was a man's age already. His father said that he didn't care if the British Empire reached into playpens and took their own boys out to fight at the age of four, no son of his, no Irishman of any decency was going to go and fight with them in further attempts to conquer the globe.

Aisling, annoyed by all the efforts to make her less giddy and to extract more work from her, decided that she would organise a baptism for Elizabeth to liven up the term. They fixed the date for 2 February, the Feast of the Purification. Aisling had an instinct that they should keep the baptism a secret. This instinct was shared by the other girls in the class.

It took place on the stone floor of the Junior Girls' cloakroom, less attractive than the River Jordan where Jesus had his baptism, according to the nice picture in the school corridor. Water from four holy water fonts had been poured into a school mug. Joannie Murray and Aisling had the words of the Ceremony written out in case they forgot them . . . which Elizabeth thought added to the importance and magic of it all. She knelt, and then in front of all the class they poured the water and said, 'I baptise thee in the name of the Father and the Son and the Holy Ghost, Amen!' There was a silence; then they all clapped.

Elizabeth stood up. Her pale hair was stuck to her head, her shoulders were dripping. She didn't like to rub away the water, as it was holy water and was special. She squeezed Aisling's hand.

'Thank you,' she said.

Aisling put her arm around her.

'You'll find it all a lot easier now,' she said.

Her letters from Mother did not arrive every week. Aunt Eileen's explanation was always the terrible postal system.

'The poor woman is demented posting you letters, it's just that things are so bad over there it could take days to clear a post box.' And later there was the excuse of Violet's work. 'Now your mother must be worn out from all that war work. We've no idea here at all how desperate things must be for them.'

Violet had written just after Christmas to say that she had volunteered for the WAAFs but the ridiculous people were only taking single people or childless people or people under thirty. It was so foolish of them since Violet would have been much more suitable than these silly girls only interested in face powder and wearing a smart uniform. It was the same apparently with the Army and the Navy so Violet wasn't going to keep on offering. She was doing her bit with the WVS of course and it was fairly harrowing.

None of these initials meant anything to Elizabeth but she discovered an unexpected ally in Aisling's elder brother, Sean. He used to read the letters with her and explain what WAAFs were. It wasn't the same as being in the *real* Air Force, he assured her, but it was the best women could be. Her mother would wear a uniform, he told her, and do drilling and training and have her kit examined every day. This didn't seem at all likely. Elizabeth couldn't imagine Mother in a dark uniform like a policeman or a bus conductor. Mother wore cardigans and skirts. She couldn't get into rough clothes could she?

Sean, in his conversations with her, told her far more about London that Mother's letters did. He said that the Women's Voluntary Service wasn't just a lot of ladies doing charity things like Aunt Eileen had thought; they didn't make cakes and have coffee mornings, they were down there in the rubble on the streets finding bodies and feeding poor people and clothing them. He showed her articles in the papers about the evacuation and the finding of foster homes. He read to her that some families had turned out to be so poor and badly looked after that the children had slept on the floor and had lice all over them. Women in the WVS who had never seen such poverty were having to cope with it.

Sean's eyes almost shone as he talked about the heroism. Elizabeth didn't like to tell him that she felt sure her mother could not possibly have got caught up in such earthy work as delousing children. It was so unusual and unexpected to see him talkative that she listened and felt flattered.

His father would grunt when he heard the tales his son would tell. 'There's plenty of charity work goes on in this country too you know. . . .' When he heard of women training for war he laughed. 'Oh, we had women shoulders here long before they had them over in England . . . what do you think Countess Markievicz was doing?'

When Sean told Elizabeth about boys of his own age and younger joining an Air Corps recruiting scheme by the hundred every day . . . thousands within weeks . . . his father lost his temper.

'God, it would be a relief if you joined them some day, I tell you that, instead of all this bellyaching about what a great lot they are over there.'

Eileen the peacemaker, darning from the huge bag that was always beside her chair, looked up mildly.

'Ah, Sean, leave the boy alone, isn't he just praising the people for doing so much to defend their country . . . wouldn't we do the same here but thank God we don't have to. That's all he's saying.'

'That's all he'd better be saying,' Sean said.

On the first day of May Sister Bonaventure toured the classrooms in the convent to inspect the altars for Our Lady. May was Our Lady's special month and it was an act of love and daughterly respect to our heavenly mother to decorate a little altar in front of her statue. Children who lived out in the country had brought bluebells and primroses, fresh white cloths and clean vases everywhere. Sister Bonaventure was very pleased. As she was leaving the classroom that nice little English refugee who was staying with the O'Connor's held the door open for her.

'Settling in all right child?' she asked.

'Oh yes, Sister,' the child flushed politely.

Sister Bonaventure patted her on the head.

It had been no trouble at all taking in a non-Catholic, she thought with pleasure, she was very glad she agreed.

On the first day of May, Eileen opened a letter from Violet which had a ten-shilling note pinned to it. It was to buy birthday presents for Elizabeth and Aisling – there was only ten days' difference between them. Eileen thought ruefully of all the years that she had parcelled up some little trinket for Violet's daughter in England and that this was the first time that Aisling had ever been remembered. It must have been through Elizabeth's letters. Eileen hoped that the child hadn't asked too openly for a present.

'It's impossible to buy anything here, will you do it?' Violet wrote.

Everything is in chaos. I'm glad now that I wasn't accepted into the WAAFs, they've passed laws to stop you getting out . . . it's in for the duration like men. We've all had to register for mobilisation. I could be sent off to some munitions factory in the country, the Lord knows where. George is an ARP and he's out every night with the other wards . . . I think they quite enjoy it – they behave like schoolboys, and he brings the most extraordinary people back to breakfast sometimes. Really rough men.

This week the cheese ration goes down to one ounce . . . think of it, one ounce a week. Nobody has any clothes and we are living like paupers because everything is in short supply.

You are awfully good to look after Elizabeth for us. And to get her to write all those letters. It's very expensive on stamps for you . . . so I shan't mind if she misses a week now and then. George says to thank you too . . . he's very impressed that you should take in a total stranger . . . but then he doesn't understand the blood-brothership of St Mark's and all we went through.

Thank you again my dear. As ever, Violet

Yes, as ever remembering bloodbrothership to relieve her conscience but not remembering a card or a letter to the child. Eileen knew that this was it as far as the birthday was concerned. Her only child was going to be eleven years of age in a foreign country with no acknowledgement from her home.

On that first day of May, young Sister Helen, Donal's teacher, wrote a note to his mother saying that the little boy was flushed and became overexcited and wheezed whenever he was asked a question. Perhaps his asthma hadn't entirely cleared? Should she talk to the doctor again, because it might be something in the classroom that brought it on? Sister Helen said that the child was so eager to learn it was very distressing to see him held back by his wheezing attacks. She put the note in an envelope and packed it in his schoolbag.

'Is it about me, Sister?' he asked with his face reddening.

'There's not a bad word in it, Donal,' she said. 'I'm telling your mother that you're one of the hardest-working boys in the class.'

He reddened even more with pleasure and bit his lip with excitement over it all.

On that first day of May, Maureen got the letter from the hospital which said that if her examination results were satisfactory she could have a place in the hospital in Dublin. She wrote a note about it to Berna Lynch, since the two girls did not meet. But Berna had new friends now and didn't reply. Maureen decided that it didn't matter. She must work like a demon for the next six weeks and pass her exams.

On that first day of May, Aisling and Elizabeth went into the shop after school to deliver a message. Da was to come home please for a minute, Mam wanted to talk to him.

'Well, how can I come home?' Sean asked crossly. 'Who'll look after the place? That lout of a son of mine is too good to be in here apparently . . . he hasn't been seen since lunchtime. . . .'

'Mam said to bring you.' Aisling was swinging out on the handles of the door that led to the back yard. 'She said no matter what.'

'Is she sick or something?' Sean was irritated. He pulled Aisling off the door and she shied away.

'No, Uncle Sean, she's not ill, she's sitting at her desk up in the sitting room, but she said it was important.'

'Well, tell her to come down to me if it's that important,' he said, about to turn away. . . .

'She *said* no matter what.' Aisling put on a baby voice.

In one movement Sean pulled off his dun-coloured coat, picked up his jacket from a nail, and strode to the door calling over his shoulder, 'Come on you two, outa there. We've enough annoyance without the two of you breaking the tools in here.' He put the 'Back in Five Minutes' notice on the door. He had no one but poor Jemmy to help him today. Jemmy looked at him with dulled eyes. It never occurred to him that the master would let him look after the shop. He came out and stood in the street patiently.

The girls trotted home after Sean, arriving in time to hear the news. Young Sean had gone to Dublin on the lunchtime bus. He was taking the boat to Holyhead tonight. He had said to Mam that if they brought him back he'd just go again. They couldn't keep him from doing what everyone wanted to do, fight in the war.

'Let him go!' roared Sean. 'Let him go, God damn him and blast him to hell forever!'

V

Elizabeth never told Violet about Sean's leaving. She didn't know why. It seemed somehow disloyal to describe any unhappiness, any scenes in the household. It was as if she were telling tales. Anyway there weren't any words. Nothing could tell anyone who wasn't there what it was like, even if anyone wanted to tell. About the weeks when Uncle Sean had gone down three or four nights a week to Maher's and had come home very late banging doors and singing bits of 'The Soldier's Song'. Or other times when things seemed to be going calmly and someone mentioned the war or rations or the time when Germany invaded Russia. Then Uncle Sean would laugh; a horrible kind of sound that only looked like a laugh when you saw his face grinning but didn't sound like one; and he would say, 'Ah sure, they've no trouble nowadays, the Allies. Haven't they got bould Sean O'Connor from Kilgarret on their side and he's a big man. He'll be eighteen next autumn, mind. He'll be helping them plan their strategies out there. . . .'

There was no news, no word. Bit by bit Eileen stopped looking out the window in case he was getting off the bus in the square. Bit by bit Peggy stopped setting places for him at table and even moved a chair out of the room. Bit by bit his bedroom became a boxroom. Things that weren't needed ended up in Sean's room. Once Peggy called it a boxroom, and that day Eileen went up and cleared it out, distributing things all around the house and saying loudly that it was Sean's room and she'd thank everyone to remember that.

But soon it went back to being a boxroom again. People didn't ask for news any more. Elizabeth begged Aunt Eileen not to worry about having a party for her birthday, she never had one at home, anyway, she explained. Auntie Eileen had hugged her and cried and cried into her hair. 'You're a lovely little girl,' she had said over and over. 'That's what you are, a lovely little girl.'

Aisling's birthday, ten days later, was firmly celebrated. It was now four full weeks since Sean had left. Aisling had said to Dad that she was going to invite six girls from the class to tea, Mam had said she could. There would be a cake and games and if Da was going to spoil everything and make them all ashamed of him like Berna Lynch's father had done at one of her birthday parties then could he go off to Maher's early and not come back till they were finished. Elizabeth trembled when she heard this ultimatum but it turned out to be the right action. Uncle Sean didn't stop being bitter, and laughing those imitation laughs but he did stop shouting and banging doors and smelling like the smell you got when you went into Maher's through the back door.

58

By the time that Maureen had got her Leaving Certificate things had become normal enough for a real family celebration. Everyone ignored Sean's remarks about Maureen now being his eldest child. Nobody picked him up on it, not even Donal who had a very literal mind. They all went to Dublin to settle Maureen into her new life. All except Peggy and Niamh, and they had been given so many instructions and warnings by Eileen that even Sean had to laugh.

'You've set so many spies on her that she'll be unable to move.'

'She's a desperate eejit, you know,' Eileen had said unguardedly. 'She'd lie down on our bed for half of Kilgarret if I hadn't put the fear of God into her. Haven't we got enough to occupy us without Peggy producing another baby for us by spring?' This comment mystified Aisling and Elizabeth.

They went to Dublin in the back of a lorry which had seats put in it and rugs over the seats. Donal sat in the driving compartment with Da and Mr Moriarty who was giving them the lift. He had to go to Dublin to get medical supplies for the chemist so he got his petrol easily. There was rationing in Ireland too but not nearly as bad as back in London; even milk and eggs were rationed there, Elizabeth learned in her letters from home. Mother had got a job now as a book-keeper in a munitions factory. She couldn't say where the factory was in case any Germans read the letter and came and dropped bombs on it. Elizabeth wished she could have shown Sean the letter. He would have been very excited about it.

They bumped along the road from Wicklow, past the sea on their right.

'Your home is just over there, Elizabeth,' Eileen said once. She noticed that Elizabeth didn't respond as she normally did when someone brought her into the conversation. 'I mean your other home,' Eileen added hastily, and this time Elizabeth smiled.

Mrs Moriarty, all wrapped up, sat in the back of the truck with her two daughters, who were going to the same hospital. Tonight they would all see the three girls off into their nurses' home and meet the nuns who ran it; then the Moriartys would go to their relations in Blackrock and the O'Connors to stay in the guesthouse in Dunlaoghaire where Eileen's cousin, Gretta, did a good business. They had eggs, and butter for her, ham and a chicken. It would more than pay for the night for the six of them in two rooms. Gretta would be delighted with the country food; she had hinted more than once that they could even sell her food and make a handsome profit since so many people getting on the boat were anxious to bring a little extra across the water. Big turkeys had been known to travel to England plucked and well wrapped up in blankets and cooed over as if they were babies. Customs men didn't poke their noses too deeply into shawls containing babies.

But Eileen didn't want to get involved in the black market. She was happy to use the food to pay for the outing.

Maureen's hospital looked very forbidding. Elizabeth thought it looked a frightening place, Aisling said it was worse than school. But they were told to straighten themselves up and behave nicely and not to make a show of themselves.

The goodbyes were said; Maureen was to write every single week. Eileen had given her eleven stamped envelopes. That would see her up to the Christmas holidays. The two Moriarty girls were saying goodbye too. Donal looked as if he might cry, Eamonn looked as if he couldn't get out quick enough. Sean ended it with a formal note.

'It's always hard to see the first bird leave the nest but it's the way things are.'

The nuns and everyone else seemed to like this and it got people moving.

'Yes, this is our first *girl* to leave the nest,' said Eileen firmly to the nun who ran the students' home. And then they were out and getting back into the truck.

Mrs Moriarty was crying and sniffing into her handkerchief. Suddenly Elizabeth leaned over to her.

'Do you have any relations in Cork, Mrs Moriarty?' she asked. This was such an odd event that the tears ceased almost at once.

'No, child . . . no, why do you ask?'

'It's just that . . . oh, about a year ago when I was coming to live here, I met a Mrs Moriarty on the train, and she was going to her son and daughter-in-law in Cork . . . and you know I hadn't heard the name before . . . and I wondered, since everyone in Ireland seems to be related. . . .'

Elizabeth stopped. Everyone was looking at her. She had never spoken like that before.

'You talk like us now,' said Aisling, laughing.

'God help us, we'll have to get that out of you fast before the war is over,' said Eileen.

Violet got out of bed just as the hall door closed, and George came in from his night's work. Sleepily, she put on her lilac dressing-gown, brushed her hair and padded down the stairs to put on the kettle.

'What kind of a night was it?' she asked him. He looked very drawn and old. He looked fifteen years older than his forty-two years.

'All right, really,' he said.

'George, what does that mean? Does it mean that you were fire watching and there were no fires, or that you put them out?'

'No, I was shelter attendant,' he said wearily.

'But what did you do?' Violet leaned against the sink. 'You never tell me what it's like, what happens.'

'Well. It's like when we went to the shelters, you know, and they sort of took charge.'

'Do you mean just shepherding people in and out . . .?'

'Yes, in a way. . . .'

'Like a porter in a station . . .?' Her voice had a high cracked disappointed note about it.

'It's much more dangerous,' he said, hurt.

Suddenly her tense body seemed to soften and she looked at him with real concern. An old, tired man, just finished a night of fear. He could have stayed in their own 'shelter', a cellar which had always been considered a nuisance and now was padded with cushions and mattresses. But two nights a week he spent with a torch and a round tin hat guiding people, people with no shelters, up and down stairs, trying to sound authoritative and trying to sound calming.

Tears came to Violet's eyes and poured down her cheeks. George raised his tired head and half stood up. . . .

'What is it Violet . . . what did I say?' he began.

Her shoulders heaved.

'I didn't say *anything*. . . .'

'Oh, the pity of it . . . the stupid pity . . . if someone up in the sky were looking down at this pathetic house in this pathetic stupid life, what would they say? You've had no sleep, I've only had a little sleep. Other people are dead. There's nowhere to rest, no food to eat, you have to go to that silly stupid bank and I have to go off to this dreary, dull endless factory. Two buses there, two buses back, four sets of queuing . . . and what's it all for?'

The kettle whistled behind her and she took no notice.

'What are we doing it for, George, what on earth is the point? There's going to be nothing afterwards. It's going to be just as bad after the war. . . .'

'Oh no . . . after the war. . . .'

'Yes, after the war. Tell me, what will be so wonderful?'

'Elizabeth will be back,' he said simply.

'Yes,' she stopped crying. 'That will be something.'

George got up and turned off the kettle; he made a pot of tea slowly. Violet wiped her eyes.

'I must write to Elizabeth today,' she said. 'I might do it at my break at work.'

Aisling and Elizabeth were now the senior members of the family. It was even suggested that they might have separate rooms, since Maureen would not be needing hers, except for the holidays. Sean's room, boxroom or not, would never be offered to them. But the girls didn't want to change their ways, finding first one excuse and then another. Maureen's room didn't get such good light for homework. It was further up the stairs and away from the bathroom. Aisling clinched it, in a fit of kindness, when she said that it would be sad for Maureen if she didn't think her room would be there to come back to.

Eileen let it go. It would be nice to have a guest room in case they ever had any guests. She had often hoped, over the years, that Violet would come to stay. There had been that visit a long time ago . . . before Violet had married . . . it hadn't been a success. Probably because Sean had been a baby and Violet had been full of the bright young flappers and all the excitement of the twenties in London. Nobody had ever said that it was a failure, but deep down Eileen almost wishes that it had never taken place. Now? Well, now, of course, anything would be a treat for Violet and George after the miseries of Britain, the long queues, the black market, the endless waiting at night for the bombs to fall . . . In fact she should really write and suggest it. . . .

Elizabeth was distressed to hear that Eileen had asked Mother to come over to Kilgarret. She wished the invitation had never been sent. She remembered Mother saying the place was dirty – sudden visions of Mother's nose wrinkled up in horror at some of the habits in the O'Connor household made Elizabeth almost faint. If Mother did come, she wouldn't fit in and Elizabeth would be running from one side to the other. It would be like old times, when Miss James said one thing and Mother misunderstood, and then Mother would say something and Miss James would be offended. Here in this house, people didn't brood and wonder what other people had meant, they asked them, and they shouted at them and often they thumped them. Elizabeth's heart lurched again when she thought how Mother might react when she saw Aunt Eileen slapping things out of Eamonn's hands if he had picked up some food that he wasn't meant to have taken. Mother would be appalled at Niamh's nappies trailing as she toddled round, and at Donal's stained dressing-gown, which he wore as much around the house as he did in his bedroom. Elizabeth couldn't even bear to think of what Mother would make of Peggy and whether she would ever bring herself to eat anything that Peggy had touched. . . .

The prayers that were muttered kneeling in the bathroom – she didn't want Aisling to know what she was praying for – were answered. Violet wrote to say that it was quite impossible. She did envy everyone in Ireland eating butter and cream and meat. She thought that it sounded like a kind of paradise. There was little gratitude for the invitation, but much on how everyone in Kilgarret was faring better than those in London. Eileen showed the letter to Sean.

'You can't say she isn't making much of us now. She says it sounds like heaven here compared to what they have to endure.'

'Well, you can write back and tell her that Ireland doesn't have to endure all that because Ireland didn't go on like the British Empire, shadow-boxing and fighting other European people instead of minding its own business.' Eileen had no intention of telling her anything of the sort. She went back to the letter. It sounded more interested in Elizabeth than any of the previous notes and scribbles had been.

I suppose she's much taller now. They do grow between ten and eleven. A woman beside me at work asked me if I had children, and when I said I had a daughter of eleven she couldn't believe me. I told her I hadn't married until I was twenty-eight and she couldn't believe that either, but she said I didn't look like anyone who had children. Suddenly, right in the middle of work, I felt very lonely and I started to cry. I've been doing a lot of that lately – it's war nerves, people say. They tell me to take these nerve tonics – everyone takes them – but they're worse than useless. I think of Elizabeth a lot these nights. I'm glad she's well and out of reach of the blitz. But sometimes, when I've had a long day, I wonder whether there was any point to all we learnt at school. It means nothing now. There's no point in being able to run a gracious home with nothing to run it on. And all that history. They never told us that wars just went on and on. . . .

Maureen's letters arrived every week. Sometimes they had blots on them, and the lines were crooked, but neither Sean nor Eileen seemed to mind a bit, and read them out cheerfully to everyone. Una Moriarty, who was eleven months younger than Norah, was doing very well, but Norah was being homesick and silly. They had been given a late pass and they all went to the pictures in O'Connell Street, but it was the one night when the projector broke down and there was half an hour's delay, so they'd had to go home without knowing the end of the picture. There was an awful lot of bed-making. The way the beds are made at home is all wrong, they have no corners. Staff Sister Margaret is like a devil but Sister Tutor is very beautiful and glides around, seeming not to walk like other people. They'd all be home on the bus the day before Christmas Eve. Maureen was looking forward to sleeping on and on and on.

Doctor Lynch went on one of his batters the day the Japanese bombed Pearl Harbor. It had nothing to do with the event, in fact he didn't even hear of it until five days later when he was discovered by the Guarda in a sailors' public house in Cork, slumped over a table. This time the return home was less dignified and discreet than on previous occasions. This time, Doctor Lynch was handed unceremoniously to the Guarda van going to Dublin, and then to another on its way to County Wicklow. The family had been told to expect him. The Guarda left him in the square. Their custody of him had been entirely informal; they had abuse from him all the way to Kilgarret. . . . He was now sobering, but in deadly need of another drink. He ranted that he had their numbers and they would all be demoted for this. Unshaven, without his coat – which had been abandoned somewhere on his joyous journey south to Cork – his eyes narrowed at the sight of the O'Connor house. That was the bloody family which had dared to insult his position by refusing to let their red-haired brat play with Berna. Tears of self-pity came into his eyes. That thick, ignorant Sean O'Connor with his builder's yard and dirty shop, with his tinker's brood of children, had dared to forbid Berna his house. Had dared to apologise on *his* daughter's behalf for something . . . which had never been proved, mind you.

Doctor Lynch came slowly up the steps. Peggy let him in and stood back fearfully as he climbed the stairs. Donal, running down to see who was the visitor, met him on the landing between the kitchen and the sitting room.

'Doctor Lynch.'

'Yes. Which one of them are you? Which of Sean O'Connor's brats are you? You're in your dressing-gown. Are you sick? Have you been sick, boy, come on?'

Flattened against the wall, Donal stared up at him with huge eyes.

'I'm Donal,' he said. 'I'm seven. I've a touch of asthma. It's not bad. I'll grow out of it.'

'Who told you that?'

'Everyone says it. Mam says it.'

'What does your Mam know about it? Does she deign to take you to a doctor at all, or does she have medical skills herself?'

Aisling and Elizabeth heard the shouting and rushed to protect Donal.

'Well, has she?' Doctor Lynch was roaring.

'Go to the shop and get Mam,' hissed Aisling, and Elizabeth, round-eyed, slipped down the stairs.

'Who are you?' The man smelt awful and had stubble all over his face.

'I'm just visiting,' said Elizabeth, backing away. She didn't stop to get her coat, though it was freezing outside.

'Nice to know the O'Connors are still allowed some visitors. Who's her father, then – a duke? A doctor's child isn't good enough for Sean O'Connor. . . .'

'Her father works in a bank in England,' said Donal helpfully.

Doctor Lynch gazed at him. 'You've more than a touch of asthma, young fella, you have a chest that whistles like a kettle. A great pity your mother never took you to a doctor. I don't like the sound of it. . . .'

Aisling's face blazed. 'There isn't a thing wrong with Donal, not a thing. He's a touch of asthma, that's all, it gets worse in the bad weather. And Mam has taken him to a doctor, to Doctor MacMahon. And the hospital. And everything. So you're all wrong. You're not a proper doctor anyway.'

'Oh, Aisling.' Donal looked at her nervously, afraid that she had gone too far. People didn't say things like that. . . . Doctor Lynch drew himself up. Aisling's mind churned, but she saw that she had to go on. If she stopped now, Donal's faith would go. He would always believe he had a terrible disease if she backed down in front of Berna Lynch's awful father. Taking a big breath and putting her arm around her brother's shoulder, she continued.

'I know what I'm talking about. My father and mother don't approve of you, Doctor Lynch. They think you're unreliable. That's why none of us go to you when we're sick. We go right out to Doctor MacMahon's house.'

She didn't hear her mother bounding lightly up the stairs, summoned by Elizabeth in a few short sentences.

'Doctor Lynch . . . Aisling. . . .' She saw that Donal was terrified as the two faced each other – the shaggy, unkempt doctor and Aisling, her eyes bright and her red curls bounding.

'You'll answer for this, you impudent little brat,' he said, moving towards her. Donal, standing in the corner, raised his voice, but only a thin squeak came out.

'No, she didn't mean. . . .'

'But I did,' cried Aisling. 'It's wrong to come here, to come here all dirty and shabby and start frightening Donal and telling him he's not well. He's only got a touch of asthma, do you hear me? Everyone knows it . . . everyone. . . .'

Eileen stepped in. It was to Aisling she moved, and she put a hand on a trembling shoulder.

'Come on, Matthew,' she said calmly. 'Go home with you at once. If you want to call on us, come back when you're in better shape. I can't imagine why you want to come here bringing yourself down to the level of children. Come on, shoo.'

Her voice brought relief to Donal's face. She was treating the doctor like a bold child.

'High and mighty Eileen O'Connor,' he said venomously, looking round him. 'Too good for this town . . . educated in England . . . what did it get you? A house falling down for want of a coat of paint, a husband covered with dirt over in a yard and a lean-to, a crowd of children one more wild than the next. . . .'

'We have the best children in town,' said Eileen. 'Are you going now or shall I send one of them over for your wife?'

'The best,' he laughed. 'This one will be in the churchyard before much longer, you sent that Maureen away before she disgraced you, and what about young fellow-me-lad strutting about in a Tommy's uniform?'

Eileen forced herself to laugh. Once she heard the sound of it it encouraged her and her second attempt was almost a peal.

'My God, Matthew Lynch, isn't it true what they say about drunks! They weave more fairy tales and have more imagination than people who write books. Listen, will you get out of here before my Sean comes back and kicks you out. . . .' She wiped her eyes at the amusement of it all. The children looked at her amazed. Even Peggy, who had come to stand at the door with Niamh in her arms, smiled without quite knowing why. The doctor, deflated and unexpectedly defeated, began to leave. Eileen's laughter annoyed him more than he could believe. He had only said what was true, why was she laughing? The door slammed and Eileen sat down. Her mirth hadn't subsided. Cautiously the children moved towards her and Peggy advanced into the room. When the door downstairs banged, Eileen leapt up and looked out of the window.

'Look at him, the poor buffoon, heading for a few quick ones now to give him the courage to face the wife. Oh dear, there's nothing so desperate as a drunk man – whatever you two girls do, and you too, Peggy, and you Niamh little heart, for God's sake don't marry a drunk. . . .'

Donal felt excluded. 'Doesn't he know what he's saying? Is he really unreliable?' he asked anxiously.

'When he's like that he's only got old potatoes rattling around in his head, not brains. Poor fool.' His insults burned into her like a hot rod pushed down the back of her throat. But she was winning, she was managing to make him ridiculous. She didn't have to deny what he'd said about Donal if she laughed at everything he said. She watched him pick up a newspaper from a bench near the bus stop, and then he shouted something to her. The window was closed so she couldn't hear.

'He's saying something, Mam,' said Peggy.

'I'm sure he is,' she shivered. 'Come on, Peggy, since I'm home anyway let's all have a cup of tea.'

'He keeps pointing to the paper,' said Donal.

'Come on away and we'll close the curtains, it's dark almost.' Peggy scuttled out to the kitchen as Eileen opened the window slightly.

'That's cooked your goose . . . America's in the war now. . . . Your snot-nosed boy'll be sent to fight . . . it's getting worse, not better . . . you'll lose two sons you cackling old hen . . . your big Tommy of a son'll be mincemeat in no time now.'

Eileen closed the window quickly and joined the little group by the fire.

'What's he saying, Mam?' Donal, worried still.

'Oh, more rubbishing and rawmaishing out of him . . . the man doesn't know what day it is . . . he just goes on and on and on. . . .'

There were, of course, other mothers who didn't know if their sons lived or died, but Eileen got no comfort from thinking about them. For some reason which she couldn't quite explain to herself she had pretended to other people that she heard from him. When a well-meaning or even just curious friend or neighbour would ask, 'Any word at all from Sean in England?' she would nod brightly and say yes, she heard from him, he was fine. She said it with quick darting looks in the direction her husband might come from . . . just brief letters, you know, and people thought that the boy wrote to his mother but had fought with his father. In some convoluted way, Eileen thought that this made things more *right*.

At times she wondered should she write to Violet and enquire about how to trace a missing boy who had gone to sign up. How did you set the machinery in motion to get him back? Show his birth certificate? Prove he was neither British nor eighteen? Then she knew she would never do that; but she was still tempted to hunt him out, just so that she could write to him. She could even get him to write to her at the chemist's. The Moriartys were unusual in Kilgarret, in that they were able to keep secrets. She had also read somewhere that you could contact missing persons through the Salvation Army, but it made it very final, in a way, if you asked an organisation like that to hunt for him. While you left it, and hoped and hoped, it didn't seem too bad. It didn't actually define him as a runaway son, a missing person. Sean was still going to write some time soon. . . .

She read the paper on her desk and tried to work out from the reports in the *Irish Independent* whether her son might have been trained by now, or if he were still too young. She went dutifully through accounts of what Stafford Cripps had said, and Churchill had said and Beaverbrook had said and Harold Nicolson had said; but none of them ever said what happened to young Irish boys who went off on boats to join the war. And the paper always referred to it as the Emergency, which seemed less frightening. She followed the progress of events as they moved out to the Far East, and of simpler matters nearer home. She read of the austerity measures, gasping at the idea of onions being so precious they were offered as raffle prizes. She read these things privately and without discussing them with Sean, though she didn't hide her interest either.

She was utterly unprepared for young Sean's letter when it did arrive, ten months after he had left home. It was from Liverpool. It was very short. He hadn't wanted to write at all, he said, or at least not until he was properly in the army and couldn't be got out of it. But there was this woman, his friend's mam, she was very nice and she said he should write just a word to his own mam because she'd be grieving. *He* had said that there were plenty more at home to keep his mam busy, but Gerry's mam, Mrs Sparks, had said he should still write. So. He was fine and he was meeting a whole lot of very nice people. He had done this and that until September, because they wanted to know what age was he and they wouldn't take him until he was actually eighteen. He had sent to Ireland for his birth certificate. He got a copy from the Customs House. He was in a camp now doing basic training. It was very interesting. He often spent time off with Gerry Sparks who was his mate and with Gerry's mam who was very nice and used to cook very well before the war because nowadays you couldn't get anything.

He sent her no love, no enquiries, no excuses, no pleas for understanding. His writing was bad and his grammar and spelling poor. Eileen thought of the years with the Brothers; she remembered how she and Sean had always thought he was very bright because he was their eldest son; but this was the letter of a near illiterate. She read it again and again, the birth certificate and the Customs House and the basic training, and the tears fell slowly down her cheeks.

She didn't tell anyone about the letter. She kept it folded in her handbag, and she kept the next one and the next, and the fourth one in November when El Alamein was son. She replied almost lightly, raking her letters before she posted them for any hint of anxiety or grievance. She even found funny little things to tell him, about the day the goat got into the shop and knocked down all the boxes; about Maureen coming home from nursing school and practising bandaging so enthusiastically that she stopped the circulation in Eamonn's arms for ages and ages; about the play that Aisling, Elizabeth and the little Murray girl wrote and performed, which was meant to be a serious and inspirational account of St Bernadette, and was such high comedy that the audience was convulsed. She sent cheerful greetings to Gerry Sparks's mother and wished there was some way of sending her a few things; but perhaps some time if Sean came home on leave he might be able to take her back a couple of chickens and some butter and eggs?

The life-line to her son was so gossamer thin she didn't dare to break it. Even telling someone might put it in danger. . . .

Sean knew that there were letters, but he never mentioned them. He grew more silent in the shop; he worked just as hard as ever, but he smiled less and had no time for a chat on Fair Day. Sometimes, Eileen would look at him, bending down in the yard and trying to take the strain out of his back, and she would fill with pity for him. Since the Emergency, coal was almost impossible to get, so they had to fill their outhouses with turf instead. Turf took so much room to store; even the rooms over the shop which had been stacked with brooms and potato baskets, boxes of globes and wicks for the lamps, brushes for whitewash and distemper . . . they were now all full of turf. Eileen felt she was breathing it through her pores as it billowed out of the grate and covered everything with its flakes.

Sean looked older than a man in his forties should look. Perhaps, Eileen thought, he had the worst of all worlds: living in the country but without the countryside's healthy life; a father of six without a father's hope and pride in his eldest son taking over the business. He had always been the one with energy and drive; he had saved and hoarded to buy this small place . . . the year of the treaty. It had all been so symbolic. A new nation, a new business; and there they were, twenty years later and their son out fighting for that same country from which they had won their freedom. . . . And Sean himself, who had seen this shop as a life's dream come true, was out in the cold yard, rooting around behind the road signs for some spare plough-shares. It was raining, and his head was getting very wet. Eileen left her little glass cage and, a bag over her head, went out to help him.

She held the huge black and yellow road signs, which had been taken down during the Emergency to confuse any invaders, and made room for him to find the bits of machinery.

'We'll do a great tidy-up on this lot, one day,' he said, gratitude in his tone if not in his words.

'I know we will,' she said. She wondered, as she spoke, whether he knew or cared that his son was spending springtime fighting in North Africa. The excitement had been so great when his call-up papers had arrived that even Gerry Sparks had added a few more words to the letter. Gerry was going with him. Eileen still didn't know whether Sean ever read his son's letters. She often left her bag open so that he would see them; but he never made any mention of it and they never seemed to have been disturbed when she returned.

Donal had eventually moved to the Brothers', having been persuaded to spend another year at the convent after he had made his first communion. It wasn't usual for a boy to stay there until he was eight, but Sister Maureen had managed to convey that it was perfectly reasonable. She had said, privately, that they should give him one more year before he had to face the rough and tumble of the school yard down at the Brothers'. Another year might make his breathing easier, his anxieties less. Eileen, who would have been happy for Donal to be educated for the rest of his life with the kind Sister Maureen, agreed readily. But the day had had to come, and now her delicate child was coming home every day, clothes torn, face terrorised, lips sealed. 'I fell,' he said, every day. Eamonn was worn out defending him.

'You see, Mam,' Eamonn explained, 'the fellows pick on Donal because he's nearly nine, fellows of just eight, and they're too tough and then I have to go an' clout them, and then the other fellows come up to me and say what am I doing clouting fellows of only eight for when I'm fourteen. It's desperate, Mam. That's why my coat's torn again.'

Aisling and Elizabeth, cycling home from school – arms touching, dangerously sophisticated thirteen-year-olds, with no time for the bold rough lads from the Brothers' – saw a crowd gathered around someone lying at the side of the road. Together, they slowed down and curiosity made them get off the bikes to see what had happened. At almost the same moment they recognised Donal's scarf, a long multi-coloured one that Peggy had knitted from bits of spare wool. Peggy loved wrapping him up in it every morning and would turn him like a top until he was under three layers at least. At exactly the same moment they dropped their bicycles in the middle of the road and ran to him. The other boys were looking frightened.

'He's only putting it on,' muttered one.

'Look at his eyes,' said another. . . .

Donal lay on the side of the road gasping for breath, his hands flailing in the air; his scarf lay trailing in the mud, one end of it still caught in the top button of his coat. Aisling was on her knees beside him in a flash. Just as she had seen her mother do a dozen times, she loosened his coat and his shirt collar with a wrench, at the same time raising his head on her arm.

'Take your time, Donal, you've got all the time in the world. As slowly as you like. Don't fight it,' she murmured. Elizabeth was on her knees at the other side, helping with the support. Her pale hair was in her eyes, her lisle stockings wet and torn from kneeling on the ground, her up-turned bicycle forgotten.

'Your breath is coming, that's it, in, out, in, out, that's it, you've got it again. . . .'

Aisling stood up and faced seven boys, who were all just a shocked by the sudden swoop the girls had made as by the whites of Donal O'Connor's eyes.

'We didn't do anything,' said one.

'No, nothing, we were only playing, we never touched him,' and there was a gabble of voices all trying to be freed of blame and guilt and involvement.

'You listen to me,' Aisling shouted. She glanced over at Elizabeth; they understood each other well enough. Elizabeth started to whisper to Donal. She still had her arm around his shoulder and she bent closer to his cold ear.

Aisling was formidable. 'I know every one of your names. I know you all. Tonight my mam and dad will be down to the school. Brother Kevin will know who you all are and Brother Thomas and Brother John. All of them. They'll deal with you. You know Donal has asthma. You could have killed him. You could all have been standing down in the court-house if we hadn't come along. You could have been young murderers. You hit him, or you knocked him down. . . .'

'We only pulled his scarf off him.'

'Yes, and nearly choked him. The worst thing you could do. Choke him and stop air getting into his chest. You stupid, thick murderer, Johnny Walsh, if Donal isn't well you're the cause.'

'She's only letting them think that, she's only frightening them,' Elizabeth muttered urgently to Donal. 'She doesn't mean it, but just look at them!'

Donal looked. They did indeed look frightened of Aisling.

'Don't say anything. . . .' Johnny Walsh began in a whimper.

'Don't be such a coward! Don't be such a murdering coward! I'll not keep quiet and let you get away with it, murdering a boy with a bad heart and a bad chest!' Aisling had the taste of power and loved it.

'You haven't a bad heart,' hissed Elizabeth. 'It's for show.' In the darkening evening, under the light drizzle, seven young lads were terrified.

'He's older than us, he's fourteen months older than me. . . .' began

Eddie Moriarty, white with fear at the thought of what his parents would do to him when this came out.

'Yes, and Jemmy in our shop is older than you and Paddy Hickey, the blind man, is older than you and you don't torment them, you great eejit!' shouted Aisling.

'What are you going to do?' asked Johnny Walsh fearfully. Aisling had been thinking.

'Pick up those bicycles. Now,' she ordered. 'Pick them up and wheel them back to town. Johnny and Eddie and you, Michael, come into my Da's shop and tell him what's happened. And tell him that from now on you're going to look after Donal. No need to mention his heart, just tell him that Donal had a fall and that you seven are going to look after him and protect him until his chest gets better.'

It seemed like a glorious escape, but Johnny wanted to make sure he wasn't walking into a trap.

'What do we have to tell your father?'

'That you're going to see no harm comes to Donal. And you'd all better pray on your knees that Donal's heart doesn't give out during the night.'

Magnificent, like the leader of a procession, she marched in front of them back to the town and into the square, while Elizabeth and Donal followed. Donal's face was wrapped up again in the scarf so no one else would see the giggles, and Elizabeth had one had over her face. The other was holding Donal's hand.

It was the only high spot in what was otherwise a very long, very dull term. Aisling thought it would never end. She was as defiant as she dared be, staying just within the limits, and she gave no time at all to her work. She fell behind in her marks and slipped from seventh to eighteenth in class in three weeks. Elizabeth had managed a steady average of tenth or eleventh – which was considered very good for a child who had never studied the basics. There was an element of suspicion that outside an Irish convent very little could have been taught; and that any child who had emerged fairly educated through a non-Irish, non-Catholic system must be a very diligent child indeed. She now joined in the religious knowledge classes; it had seemed silly to sit in the library reading a big Bible full of words she didn't understand, when she could hear marvellous stories of apparitions and angels and sins and Jesus being so good to his mother. . . .

There had been some more worrying conversations about Elizabeth's conversion. Some of the class wondered whether they should arrange for her first communion, so that she should have the chance to confess all her sins and get forgiveness at confession.

'I don't have all that many sins,' Elizabeth had said innocently once, and everyone was horrified. She was riddled with sin, they all were, but Elizabeth was particularly bad because of all that original sin, as well.

'But I thought that the original sin had been washed away after all the baptisms?' Elizabeth had now been baptised four times. There had been doubt about the validity of the first one on the cloakroom floor. There had been an accusation that the water might not have flowed at exactly the same time as the words were being said. Then there was a long and bitter debate about whether the words should be said in Latin or English; one school of thought was convinced that lay baptisms were conducted in the vernacular. . . .

For no reason that was ever voiced, Elizabeth's conversion had never been made public. There was an unspoken feeling that, for all the nuns were exhorting them to go and convert all races and spend their pocket money contributing to the conversion of little black babies, there might be a different attitude taken to doing the job on Elizabeth. It was also feared that if Elizabeth's parents in England were to hear about it there might be great trouble.

Her mother's letters seemed to come from another world, not just another country. Elizabeth was pleased that she wrote more often and that her letters did not consist of a list of instructions: be sure to take your medicine, wear your gloves, thank everyone. . . . As the war went on, Mother seemed to have cheered up, despite the complaints. There was no soap – the ration was three ounces every month: fancy trying to live a normal healthy life on three ounces of soap a month. There was no white bread – Mother had forgotten what it tasted like. She had friends in the munitions factory where she worked and very often she stayed overnight with Lily because it was such a long journey home and somehow in this depressing war, it was nice to have a friend to laugh with. Mother had changed her hair-style, she had a victory roll now; it looked funny at first but people said it suited her. Once or twice she said that she missed Elizabeth. She always ended her letters saying she hoped Elizabeth was well and happy and that it wouldn't be long now until she could come home and they could all lead a nice normal life again.

Mother said very little about Father in her letters. And when she sent a pound for her birthday present, just before she was fourteen, Elizabeth realised with horror that she hadn't mentioned Father for months.

Eileen was at her desk when Elizabeth came to talk to her.

'Are you busy?' she asked.

Eileen smiled. None of her own family would dream of asking such a question; they all assumed that she was always ready and willing to listen, to help, to act.

'I'm not busy,' she said, pulling up a chair. On her desk she had a shoe box filled with the shop accounts, the bills overdue that had to be sent out with a personal note. No firm reminders on a printed form could be sent to a farmer who might take offence and buy from the next town. She had a letter she now knew by heart from Mrs Sparks in Liverpool, an awkward, stunted little letter from a lonely widow whose son was away and who felt she had an ally in Sean's mother. She wrote of her loneliness and her hopes that they'd be back soon, and how she hadn't heard anything for six weeks and how she wondered whether Mrs O'Connor might have. She had a letter to a specialist in Dublin, and she had to plan which day to take Donal. She had a note from Sister Margaret saying that it was time they have young Niamh at school as she was nearly five now and could they bring her down towards the end of term so that it wouldn't be so strange to her when she started in September. And, Sister Margaret said, wasn't it the blessings of God how well young Donal had settled in at the Brothers'? She had heard from all sides how the roughest young hooligans were all a great support to him instead of picking on him. The Lord worked in mysterious ways. There was a letter from Maureen wondering would Da ever let her have three pounds for a gorgeous dance dress and she'd pay him back out of her allowance, when they started to get an allowance in summer. She had a letter from the County Home that said that Sean's father was sinking fast and was very anxious to see them. They mustn't be put off by the fact that he might not recognise them; he kept saying that he wanted to see his son and his family.

'No, I'm not busy, child,' said Eileen.

'It's just that, I don't know how to say it, but, you know, there wouldn't be any danger, could there, that my father is dead?'

'*Dead*? Oh, God forbid it should be true – what makes you say that, child? Where did you get such an idea?'

Elizabeth produced a large envelope with a little sticker on it saying 'Mother's letters'. There were over fifty letters, each with the date they had arrived. She laid them out, picking up one from August 1943.

'This is the last time Mother said anything about Father. She says he was upset because of women striking for equal pay with men, that they shouldn't do that when there's a war on. And then not ever again. Not even at Christmas. She doesn't say Father sends his love. She doesn't say anything about his ARP work. . . .' Elizabeth's eyes filled with tears. 'Do you think something's happened and she's protecting me?'

Eileen rocked her in her arms, the soothing words and the denials, the positive statements tumbling out. Of course he was fine, of course they'd have heard, of course they would, it was that things had changed so much in England, and since Mother was going out to work she now had a much broader life and she didn't just write about home. And men were hopeless at writing letters, sure just look at Uncle Sean now, he was most concerned to know how Maureen was getting on up in Dublin, but did he ever put pen to paper to write to her? Never. And then people don't always keep mentioning the same things, after all when Eileen wrote to Sean she often made no mention of his father. . . .

It had slipped out.

'Do you write to Sean? Oh, I didn't know. Where is he?'

'He's in Africa, he's grand, he's got a lovely English friend called Gerry

Sparks. He often asks after you in his letters . . . now to go back to you and your worries. We'll go and ring up home for you on your birthday. We'll go into the shop tomorrow night and make a three-minute call. We'll even book it tonight. And you can tell them that it's their big, fourteen-year-old girl talking. How about that?'

'Will it be very expensive?' Elizabeth wondered.

'Not at all, and isn't it a birthday?'

'Thank you very much,' said Elizabeth, wiping her eyes on the back of her hand and her nose on a sleeve.

'Oh, Elizabeth, there's just one thing. . . .'

'I know, Auntie Eileen, they're your business, the letters to Sean. I know.'

The next letter that came said that Sean and Gerry had left North Africa. They had been in the Anzio landings and now were well into Italy. Sean wrote that the Italian countryside was beautiful and bits of it would remind you of County Wicklow. There was even less life in his words and he wished for the fighting to end. He was glad that everything was well at home. Gerry's mum had written about how you wouldn't recognise Liverpool after all the raids. It was strange to think that nothing had happened in Ireland. He wrote that they might well see Rome. When he thought of all he had learned about the Holy City at the Brothers' and now he was going to see it! He was telling Gerry about it but Gerry hadn't heard of anything and didn't know about the Vatican and St Peter's. He'd write a letter from Rome, a proper letter and Mam could take it down to Brother John and show him that a boy didn't need a Leaving Certificate to get to the Holy City.

But Sean and Gerry didn't get to the Holy City with the rest of the allies. A minefield in the Italian countryside that looked a bit like County Wicklow took both legs off Gerry Sparks from Liverpool, aged twenty-one; and twenty yards away killed outright his friend Sean O'Connor from Kilgarret who still had four months to go before he was twenty-one.

Private S O'Connor had listed his address as the small terraced house in Liverpool where Amy Sparks received the news. She sat in her dark kitchen and thought of her only son. She read the telegram over and over again, thinking that she should react more. Then she prepared herself to tell the mother of Gerry's mate that Sean O'Connor would not be coming back to Kilgarret.

The call came through to the shop, and Eileen took it in her little eyrie. She listened without tears as Mrs Sparks explained. She waited calmly until the sobbing of the woman she had never met ceased. She sympathised in a low voice over Gerry, she said she was glad to hear that he would recover. She agreed that it was a blessing that Sean had been killed outright, but that it was great that Mrs Sparks would be able to look after Gerry.

'You sound such a wonderful woman,' Amy Sparks sobbed. 'Sean always did say "My Mam is grand". That's what he called you, *grand*.'

'He didn't mean it in the English sense, like a grand lady,' said Eileen. 'I was at school in England, I remember it was used differently.'

'Perhaps, if you ever came over to see your old school, perhaps you could come and stay with me. Perhaps you could come and see Gerry when they bring him back....' The longing in her voice was clear. 'There'd be no restrictions on you travelling.'

Eileen didn't even pause.

'I'll come very soon. If Gerry is coming back the week after next I'll come too.' She heard Amy Sparks gasp down the telephone. 'If there had been a funeral for Sean I'd have come.'

For some reason that she couldn't explain to herself afterwards, Eileen didn't tell anyone for four days. In that time she went mechanically around her daily jobs, doing them with almost super-human energy. It was as if she had made up a game with rules: she mustn't cry. If she let herself go and cried it would be worse for Sean. She had to be strong. Otherwise his whole life had no meaning, going out to that terrible place and being blown up. It would just be meaningless if people at home just wept great tears for him.

She was very methodical. She left Peggy a great list of things to do; she arranged for Eamonn to work in the shop. She extracted a promise from Donal that he would rest and keep warm. She arranged for Maureen to come to Dunlaoghaire and meet her in a hotel.

Then she told them why she was going to be away.

She told Sean on a sunny June evening. She sat on an upturned drum and told him that their son was dead. She told him of Gerry and how his legs were gone and of the telephone call from his mother. She talked about the countryside in Italy and how they had been on the way to Rome. The noises of the shop came up from time to time as Sean tried to take it in.

They never touched each other or held each other as she spoke of the telegram that had come to the house in Liverpool, and of the details that would follow later about the grave. She spoke the way Amy Sparks had done, in slightly halting sentences about how it had been very quick, and Sean must have known nothing.

Then she listened. She listened while he ranted, she listened, still sitting on the upturned drum, while he sobbed. She couldn't hear what he said into his big blue handkerchief. She waited while the sobbing ended and was replaced by sighs.

'Would you like me to come to Liverpool with you? It's a kind of pilgrimage, isn't it? A sort of funeral?'

She looked at him gratefully. He had understood, after all.

'No, he'd prefer you to be here.'

And then she called the children together and told them their brother was dead. She made the telling full of words like 'peaceful' and 'heaven' and 'what he wanted to do'. She used words like 'brave' and 'strong' and 'proud' . . . then she said that they could help her and help Sean by being very strong.

The tears were coursing down Elizabeth's face and Aisling's was working in disbelief. He couldn't be. . . . How did you. . . . It's not fair. . . . Maybe. . . . What if. . . . Then she ran out of words and cried on Elizabeth's shoulder and Elizabeth patted her head and said that they must be brave. Eamonn rushed back to the shop, his big innocent face stained and red. Donal protested that Sean couldn't be happy in heaven, he hadn't intended to go there, it was the bloody Germans and Italians that sent him there. He had never said the word bloody before.

And Eileen told Maureen in the chilly lounge of a Dunlaoghaire hotel, where Maureen cried like a baby and rocked backwards and forwards in Eileen's arms until the manageress came and asked would they like to go somewhere more private. So they walked up and down the pier for two hours while Maureen cried while she thought of all the things that Sean would never do.

Then the pilgrimage began.

It passed in a blur; the rubble in the streets of Liverpool, the blackout, the queues outside every shop. There was the visit to the hospital, where Gerry had cried. She had been very strong and she had smiled. Then she had asked a young priest with an Irish accent to say a mass for Sean. It was at seven in the morning and Amy Sparks had been there. Eileen had worn her black hat and gloves and carried a bunch of flowers which she was going to leave in the church. It was as near as she could manage to a wreath.

But she cried as she sat on the boat back to Ireland and the tears ran down her face while she made no attempt to wipe them away. Her coat was stained with them as she sat looking out to the dark sea and crying at the waste. She stood up, the tears still falling and her shoulders heaving and walked to the rail of the ship. As she held on to the bar, her hat was whipped away by the night wind. It flew up in the air, hit the deck and was borne off. But the other passengers saw that the handsome woman in the black coat didn't even seem to notice it had gone. She was saying something over and over again. Praying, possibly.

76

Part Two

1945–1954

VI

Violet had never understood why they had agreed to Elizabeth finishing her summer term at that convent school. It meant she missed VE Day; she missed all the celebrations, the turning on of lights, the tearing down of the blackout curtains and the scenes of wild excitement, where American soldiers swung passing girls into crazy dances, where crowds marched back and forth up Regent Street and round Piccadilly mad with happiness, hooting on car horns and singing 'Bless 'Em All' with tears running down their faces. It had been a heady day, but Violet had felt very left out. She didn't have a man with a kit-bag coming home triumphantly with tales of battles won; she had George, moodier and more nervy than ever. He had taken now to muttering to himself about fellows with medals and ribbons coming back to civvy street for promotion and praise. She had no daughter to clutch proudly to herself like other women had; nobody she could hold and urge to remember this day for the rest of her life. Her daughter was finishing some exam and singing in a concert carrying an image of the Virgin Mary and wouldn't be able to travel until the holidays – or that's what Eileen's letter had seemed to say. Violet hoped with a great sigh that they had not done the wrong thing in sending Elizabeth away for the duration.

Her own work in the munitions factory was over now. There had been a chance to work in a tobacco factory – so great was the shortage of cigarettes that there were unheard-of working conditions now, with shifts around the clock. But Violet didn't want to get involved. It was one thing doing important war work, which had to be done; it was another sitting at a factory bench making cigarettes with hundreds of factory workers. A few of the girls from the munitions factory said they would try it – anything was better than sitting around at home all day, or standing in never-ending queues. But Violet did not agree. After all those years of early-morning buses and late-night buses; of standing in whatever the weather and of bending low and straining to see . . . she thought she deserved a rest.

Anyway, her fifteen-year-old daughter was coming home.

Anyway, her friend, Mr Elton – Harry – said that she should pamper herself a bit. Harry Elton knew instinctively how women felt at the end of this long war. They felt dull and grey and drab and they needed a little . . . well, pampering. Mr Elton had been marvellous about getting silly little things, like small bags of sugar and a few ounces of knitting wool. She had been a little worried when he had got her four pairs of silk stockings. To accept a pair of silk stockings meant you had to give something in return, however small. But Harry Elton had laughed and told Violet he only wanted to see her smile. So she had taken them and told George that everyone in the factory had been given stockings as a bonus.

Everyone had been given a month's notice in the ARP on 1 May, but George seemed reluctant to accept it. He still went around to the Wardens' Post and the First Aid Post, and so did one or two of the others. Together they shook their heads over the situation. Irresponsible decisions like closing the Tube stations at night! Suppose it happened again? How were people to trust the Germans – how could anyone trust anyone in the war? So long had George worried and so often had he muttered that Violet had begun to wonder whether he was right. After all, he had been out there at night. Perhaps he did know what he was talking about.

'Silly old buffers – not your husband, mind – but those folk who don't want to believe it's over,' Harry Elton had said. 'Can't bear to think they're not little tin gods in little tin helmets any more. Can't bear to think that it's all behind us and the fun and laughter are all ahead. . . .'

Violet always felt better when she talked to Harry Elton; he had visited the munitions factory a lot – he was something to do with installing radios and loudspeakers for them all to hear *Music While You Work*. And then he had had something to do with organising transport. Always something new, something different. Harry Elton had nothing but praise for the brave boys in the forces, he didn't run them down like George did. He didn't complain, or make excuses about why he wasn't at the front; he just followed their progress all the time as if he were cheering on his local football team. Harry Elton made everyone feel good. Violet was pleased that he liked her so much.

There was so much noise and bustle at Euston that Elizabeth was momentarily worried that something was wrong. What, she wondered, could have gathered so many people together? But then, she had thought that at Crewe, too, and it was only the normal business of a big railway station. All around there were greetings and welcomings. People stood in groups, waving to a young couple who were going off on honeymoon. The bride's little hat was perched at a dangerous angle and she waved enthusiastically until she and the train were gone from view. Elizabeth paused and changed her suitcases to the other hands. She always liked looking at weddings; she and Aisling used to go to the church to observe the brides and comment on them, usually unfavourably, to each other. None of them had looked as, well, as ordinary as this little girl in her navy serge suit and her red and navy hat.

Elizabeth was glad of the distraction as she walked towards the barrier. She was afraid. Afraid that they might not want her back, despite their letters. Afraid that she wouldn't know what to say. Afraid that there might be nothing to say.

She was apprehensive about the days and weeks ahead. Back in Kilgarret they had seen the newsreels showing some of the blitz in London, but the reality was still quite different. Here it looked as if everything had been destroyed. She had seen from the train, particularly during the last, halting approaches to Euston, whole blocks with wooden planks nailed across windows. Twice she had been able to read the words 'Danger – Unexploded Bomb', which had made her heart leap; but the two girls from Birmingham had said it didn't mean much, just that the authorities were still working on clearing the site. They seemed so unconcerned.

She walked up the platform with the crowd, wondering which side Mother would be. Would she be pressed up against the railings, or standing on a porter's trolley peering down? Perhaps she was late? Suppose Mother wasn't there – should she go home, back to Clarence Gardens? Or wait? Perhaps she should wait a while and see.

She smiled at her silliness, and her smile broadened as she imagined what Aunt Eileen would say. 'Always facing a thousand worries, my poor Elizabeth, long before one has come on the horizon.' She had added that the perfect state of mind was half-way between Aisling and Elizabeth; Aisling never saw worries or responsibilities even when she was surrounded by them. A perfect state of mind . . . what a funny phrase . . . And as she smiled, she met the eyes of a woman smiling back. A woman much younger than she remembered, with shining fair hair, and a smart suit and a little hat with three feathers in it. The woman was waving and calling 'Elizabeth! Elizabeth!' Her lipstick was very red. 'Elizabeth!'

It was Mother.

She smelled lovely as they hugged each other awkwardly, though some of the powder from her cheeks brushed off on to Elizabeth, who couldn't say anything for a while.

'You look like an advertisement, Mother, you look so young and . . . everything,' she managed at last. 'I thought you'd have got different.'

Violet had been going to say that she could hardly believe she had a grown-up daughter – a daughter with a waist and a small bosom; a tall girl instead of a trembling ten-year-old . . . but she was so taken aback by the compliments to herself that she tinkled a little laugh and said the first thing that came into her head. Sadly, it was a negative thing.

'Oh, darling, what a nonsense, and what *have* they done to your hair, your lovely hair? Did they cut it with a knife and fork? We'll have to see to that before we do anything else.'

She picked up one of Elizabeth's suitcases and they walked out into the late June sunshine. Election posters stared at them as Churchill and Attlee still sought the people's support. Elizabeth was fascinated; in Kilgarret there had only been ordinary notices describing dances or fairs or pilgrimages. Not instructions to keep mum. . . .

'Look, Mother,' she giggled, pointing to a big picture. Violet looked, wondering what had happened. 'Keep Mum . . . it's a pun. . . .' Her voice trailed away. 'Is your journey really necessary?' 'Careless talk costs lives.' Some of them flyblown and torn. Some newer and shiny. But none of them were new to Mother. Elizabeth could have spent hours reading them – what fun she would have had with Aisling. Together they would have memorised the phrases and recited them to each other. With a pang. Elizabeth realised she would be sleeping in a room by herself from now on and have no Aisling to talk to.

Outside the station some rebuilding had begun, but the street was still full of debris. Heaps of rubble on both sides of the road told Elizabeth more about the blitz than a hundred letters or a hundred newsreels had done. These had been houses and offices. Now they were bits of buildings. Odd, awkward-looking bits jutted up, door-ways remained standing in isolation.

Yet Mother walked past it all on the way to the bus stop, unperturbed, giving the little laugh she used to give when she was impatient.

As they scrambled on the bus, Elizabeth staring to see a woman conductor, Mother said, 'Your father's very excited about your homecoming – he's bought gulls' eggs. They were one and three each. We're going to have them tonight as a celebration. And a nice friend of mine, a Mr Elton, has got us some real cake. You know, with sugar and butter in it.'

Elizabeth looked at Mother with affection. She seemed so like a girl, more like Maureen and her friends than Aunt Eileen. And she did look lovely. Her belted, dark green jacket had big, military shoulders – she had such a tiny waist. Elizabeth touched her hair. It had been cut a week ago in Kilgarret by Maisie O'Reilly who ran the La Bella hair salon. Only very smart people went there, but Aunt Eileen had said that she must have a nice style and set before they sent her back to England. It had cost quite a lot but Aunt Eileen had said not to think about that; they couldn't send her back looking like a tinker. Aisling had tossed her own mop of red curls around in the salon and discussed long and loud what fashionable people would do if they had been unlucky enough to have been born with this dreadful colour of hair. It had been another funny-sad day with the end of her stay in sight. Aisling had said twice that maybe Elizabeth should make her home in Ireland and abandon the idea of going back to London. Aunt Eileen had been very short-tempered and said this was a selfish and infantile suggestion and she didn't want to hear it again.

Elizabeth looked out of the window; everywhere there seemed to be queues, and there were lots of people in uniform. It was all very crowded. She thought of Kilgarret. Aunt Eileen might at this very moment be writing a letter to her. She said she would write every week for a while, that Aisling would promise to write but would never put pen to paper. Aunt Eileen wouldn't promise that she'd come over to London, but said she'd think about it.

'Child, when you get back there you might be of a different mind,' she had said. 'I don't mean that you wouldn't want me, or any of us, but we're part of a separate life. Remember that you weren't at all displeased when your own mother didn't come over here. People have to have compartments in their lives.'

Mother was smiling at her. 'I can't tell you how good it is to have you home,' she said unexpectedly. 'It was a good long war. It's hard to have lost all those years of you growing up. But you've grown up very nicely. I hope I did the right thing. . . . I've always hoped that.'

'I liked it there, very much. It was different, but they were all very kind, all of them. . . .'

'I know, you always said that in your letters. That's another thing. You were a good letter-writer. Your father and I were delighted.'

'How is Father?' asked Elizabeth with her hands clenched tight until the knuckles stood out.

'He's very well, of course he is. I told you he got us some gulls' eggs, didn't I? He's been looking forward to your coming back for ages.'

Violet laughed again, and Elizabeth felt a flood of relief. It wasn't a cruel laugh, she wasn't thinking of Father as someone who was going to make her impatient and purse her lips. She squeezed her mother's arm happily.

'It's great to be back,' she said.

George had been looking at fifteen-year-old girls for three months. He wondered if Elizabeth would look like young Miss Ellison might have looked two years ago. Miss Ellison who came into the bank with her father was seventeen. He wondered whether she might look like the little princesses. He hoped that she would not have picked up too many Irish ways. The Irish were very unreliable, and from their irresponsible attitude towards the war which Mr Churchill had severely trounced them about, to their smuggling and black market tricks, they were very devious and knavish. He had wished that Elizabeth had never been sent there.

Admittedly she had written regularly and these friends of Violet's had been very kind to her. They had been remarkably generous, too, for people with no great income and a large family. It had all gone on far too long and he felt cheated of his child's youth. She would now be a grown-up girl, silly and female and wanting to talk about film stars and make-up. He would never be able to talk with her and show her things and explain how things worked. She would never come to him for advice or believe that he knew everything which is what daughters always did to their fathers.

This war had robbed everyone of what was their right. It had robbed him of his wife, too. Violet hardly knew whether he breathed or not. She was perfectly agreeable most of the time, but she seemed to live on a different planet. It was if she didn't even notice him. That's what the war had done to people like Violet, taken away their normal family feeling, taken away a sense of home. Violet didn't even cook or take a pride in what she could get from the shops like other women did. Everyone at the bank talked about the rationing, the shortages, and joked that if you stopped to talk to a friend in the street people would think it was a queue and would line up behind you.

But Violet barely cared, she read novels and she saw friends from the munitions factory from time to time. She was getting thinner too, all skin and bone, he thought.

'Mrs Simpson always said that you can never be too thin or too rich,' Violet would laugh if he said anything about it.

She hadn't even planned a special meal for Elizabeth's return. If he hadn't been able to get out yesterday and queue for gulls' eggs there would have been the usual powdered egg omelette or a tin of corned beef.

He hoped that Elizabeth would not have become very distant and giggly. He hoped she would be glad to see him and want to talk to him and ask him his views about things. He wanted to tell her about the war – properly, not the way the Irish would see it. He wanted to show her his maps of the world, and the charts he had made, with all the armies in different colours. She would question him about tactics and strategy, and he would look thoughtful and give her his considered opinion.

The gate clicked and they were there. Violet carrying one suitcase, the tall girl with the shining fair hair clasping the other. He cleared his throat as he opened the hall door. She was going to be a tall blonde stranger.

Aunt Eileen had said that she would probably find Clarence Gardens had got smaller when she got back, it was something that happened to everyone; they thought the places they knew when they were young were huge. Elizabeth had laughed at this, she remembered Clarence Gardens very well, she said, the blue and beige carpet, the hall stand, the front room where they only sat on *occasions*. This was the room which had the little corner cabinets with ornaments and where Mother used to sit and write her letters or read in the afternoons.

But how odd, the house itself hadn't got smaller, just the stairs, and the distance from the hall door to the stairs. She had thought it was quite a big hall, but in fact it was only a small passage. She hung up her brown coat, draping it over a peg, and moved quickly to take stock of her surroundings. Father went into the kitchen ahead of her. . . .

He was fussing now, touching things patting them, like an old woman, not like Father. He seemed flustered as if she was a visitor. Which of course she was in a way.

'Well well,' he said rubbing his hands, 'Well well well.'

'It's amazing to be back again Father,' she said.

'Heavens,' he said, smiling at her happily.

'Did you miss me a lot, it must have been a bit empty . . . I mean lonely or quiet. Quiet without me,' she said. She stumbled over the words, knowing that 'empty' was wrong, but not being sure why.

'Oh I missed you, all the time, a child growing up in a different country . . . very odd . . . very peculiar. . . .'

'Yes.' She wished Father had said something more extravagant. 'Of course I wrote a lot,' she said.

'Yes yes, but it's not the same.'

He was trying to be polite to her, trying to tell her how much he missed her, yet it sounded as if he was complaining.

'Well, I didn't start the war,' she said, laughing.

'No no, and you were so good, no complaints from you all that time . . . such cheery letters,' he said hastily.

'You never wrote Father, I wish you had.'

'I can't write letters, your mother is the letter-writer in this house.'

Elizabeth wondered why he couldn't write letters, he must have been taught to write them like everyone else. She said nothing.

'It's been so strange,' Father said, struggling. 'So strange, and now having you back, that's strange too.'

He echoed Elizabeth's own thoughts . . . but she wished he could have found a nicer word than strange. . . .

'Yes, you'll have to start getting used to me again,' she said, hoping that it might make him smile to hear her talking in that grown-up voice. But he must have missed the jokey note in her tone.

He seemed more anxious than ever to please her . . . he waved towards the oven . . . a big expansive wave taking in the whole kitchen. . . .

'We have a special supper tonight . . . great treat in your honour. . . .' he said. In the little hall, Mother was carefully rehanging her coat, fishing out the little loop at the top which Elizabeth had hardly ever done since she had got the coat. The O'Connors were not great for hanging clothes on hangers or using the little loop.

'It's all just the same,' Elizabeth marvelled. She did wonder whether they had got a new and smaller range, but no, it seemed exactly the same as the one that had been there. She saw the garden changed through the windows, the remains of the Anderson shelter . . . she remembered Mother had written about that. . . . She walked into the front room, it smelled cold and musty. Mother's little desk was still there, but there were a lot of boxes on top of it with a permanent look. The room felt damp and Elizabeth gave a little shiver. The antimacassars, the linen back on the dark red sofa and chairs, seemed crumpled and the room looked as if it hadn't been used for a long time.

Father was behind her.

'Perhaps we should have a cup of tea in here in your honour?' he said, eager to please and hoping that she wasn't disappointed for some reason.

Elizabeth shivered slightly again. 'Heavens no, Father, let's go back to the kitchen, it's just grand in there.'

'It's not really *grand* . . .' began Father.

'In Ireland they say "grand" when they mean good,' she said, linking him into the kitchen.

'What do they say when they mean grand?' Violet asked, bringing up the rear.

'I think they still say "grand",' said Elizabeth, and they all laughed and it felt like being at home.

There was so much that was new, so much to absorb and remember. Of course, Violet had written about the points system and rationing and the endless queues; but the reality was so mean and shabby, it was all so dispiriting. Sixteen points for this, two for that – and even when you had sorted out points and coupons, and queued for ages, there were still shortages. 'Waiting for further orders,' Elizabeth would be told, and then, from force of habit, 'Don't you know there's a war on?'

'Do you remember Monica Hart?' Violet wanted to know. 'She was a school with you. . . .'

'I remember,' laughed Elizabeth. 'Aisling and I called our cat after her. It's still there you know, a huge black cat called Monica. Niamh sort of thinks she owns it now, but it was Aisling's and mine for a long time. . . .'

Violet noted the dreamy note that came into Elizabeth's voice when she spoke all the strange Irish names of Eileen's family. She had never said she had missed them nor hinted that she was lonely. But Violet realised that it must be a huge shock, coming back to a house that was silent all day from one where there was constant companionship and apparently half the town passing through on some errand or other.

'They live just down the road now, the Harts,' she went on. 'I see Monica sometimes on her bicycle. Perhaps you could be friends. It would be nice for you to have a friend.'

'Yes.' Elizabeth was unenthusiastic.

'Before you go to school. Monica is at the grammar school, she can tell you what it's like and give you hints. . . .'

'Whatever you like,' said Elizabeth. She didn't like the thought of meeting Monica again, bossy Monica who used to pinch her during Miss James's class. Miss James was in hospital she had heard, she suffered from war nerves. Mother had met someone who had gone to visit her and Miss James was smoking a cigarette and making a basket and didn't want to talk.

'Good,' Violet was brisk. Elizabeth had been home for five days. She was very content to sit around, reading and writing an interminable letter to Ireland. She would stand placidly in queues, and once she had understood coupons and points had been very helpful with the shopping. But Violet wanted her to live a more normal life and not behave like a visitor in her own home.

Monica had become much less bossy, though, or at any rate she showed no desire to pinch Elizabeth any more. She was polite and rather silent when she came to tea. Elizabeth had to do most of the questioning. Violet seemed to think it was all going quite successfully.

'I'll leave you two to talk over old times,' she said, putting on her hat. 'I have to meet people from the munitions factory. We're going for a little drive.'

'Do the factory ladies have a car?' asked Monica with interest.

'Oh Monica, you'd be surprised what we factory ladies have these days,' said Violet with a tinkle and she was gone.

'Your mother's like a film star,' said Monica.

'Yes, I suppose so,' shrugged Elizabeth. Suddenly she remembered saying to Aisling, 'You've got the loveliest mother in the world, she's so strong,' and Aisling had shrugged too. Perhaps people don't ever appreciate their own mothers properly, she decided.

'What's your mother like?' she asked Monica.

'She's all right,' said Monica unhelpfully.

Elizabeth sighed. It was uphill work. Aunt Eileen would have known how to get the conversation going, and Aisling wouldn't have cared, she would have just chattered on happily about whatever interested her, and it would be up to Monica to join in or not as she wished. . . .

But Elizabeth wasn't able to do either of these things.

'Do you collect stamps?' she asked Monica desperately.

'No,' said Monica.

'Neither do I,' said Elizabeth, and for some reason that seemed funny to both of them, and they laughed until they had pains in their sides.

Monica was an avid film-goer. She knew all the details of the film stars' lives and was anxious to fill Elizabeth in on all she had been missing.

'Of course, you were away for all of this,' she would say forgivingly, as if Elizabeth had actually lost out on being part of the Hollywood scene because of her five years in Ireland. Monica had no time for Shirley Temple who had just had her first screen kiss with much publicity . . . Shirley Temple was strictly for adults to go ooh and aah over. No, Monica liked Deanna Durbin, and Hedy Lamar and Lana Turner and Ava Gardner, and she admired Judy Garland and Bette Davis though she didn't actually want to imitate them. She knew all about their marriages, their romances and which child was by which marriage to whom.

Monica suggested that Elizabeth wear her hair like Veronica Lake hiding her face, but it didn't work. The shock of blonde. almost white, hair looked odd and untidy when Elizabeth tried it. Elizabeth wondered what it would be like to kiss Clark Gable as she studied his photograph. Would his moustache tickle her nose and make her sneeze?

'I expect it would be just like kissing anyone with a moustache,' Monica said sagely.

'I expect it would,' Elizabeth agreed emptily. She felt so ignorant about the world of films; now she was going to be a non-starter in the world of kissing too. The only field where she had any superiority was having come from a land of plenty. From a place where there was as much to eat as you could ever want, and where nobody stood in queues for anything.

'What did they used to eat on Sundays, tell me again,' Monica would beg.

Elizabeth described the Sunday lunch; soup and home-made soda bread. Then a boiled chicken with white sauce and boiled bacon, and potatoes in their jackets, and cabbage cooked in the same water as the bacon so it tastes all flavoury. And apple tart and the top of the milk. And sometimes they had red lemonade and sometimes they had glasses of milk. Monica listened in a dream of gluttony, her mouth watering at the thought of it.

'And teas, tell me about their teas.'

Sometimes Elizabeth wished she wouldn't go on so about food because it made them all feel deprived. She told of the apple cake which Peggy made, and how it was like bread but there were bits of apple and sugar baked in it. or when they had black pudding spread on bread.

Monica said enviously, 'They must have had very good connections.'

'No, they didn't have any connections . . . you see there wasn't a war there.'

'Of course there was a war there, there was a war everywhere, and what about the Enniskillens and all those, they're Irish aren't they?'

'Yes, but it's a different part of Ireland. There was a war up in the North but not . . . not where I was. That's why I was there.'

Monica dismissed it.

'You missed lots of fun not being here, I tell you. You could see all kinds of famous people . . . they were all round the place keeping up people's spirits. I even spoke to Sarah Churchill once. You must know Sarah Churchill, she's famous. She has gorgeous red hair.'

With a pang Elizabeth thought of Aisling and how her face would light up if she heard someone talking about gorgeous red hair. She wished again and again that it was easy to write what you felt. Her letters to Aisling seemed so dull and Aisling's were very off-hand and breezy. If it weren't for Aunt Eileen she would think that nobody in Kilgarret even remembered her.

Violet wondered whether they should send some gift to Eileen's family to thank them for all they had done for Elizabeth. She had discussed it with George.

'You were the one who said that they wouldn't notice an extra mouth at the table,' he had grumbled. 'Anyway, where are we going to get some kind of proper present as you call it?'

Violet reflected.

'They were very generous, you know, they bought her a bike, and when she left they told her to sell it and keep the money because it was hers not theirs. They bought her clothes, you know, underwear too.'

'I thought we sent money for clothes.'

'We did, but not enough. I mean, Eileen always wrote to say she'd bought Elizabeth a new winter coat with the money we sent, but Elizabeth tells me that she got everything the other children did, you know, and Sean used to give them all money for the cinema or whatever. I suppose I'm just a little worried in case we took it all too casually.'

'You wrote and thanked them, didn't you?' George said in an aggrieved tone.

'Oh certainly, I wrote and thanked . . . but you know they did a marvellous job on Elizabeth. She's so grown-up and yet not changed at all. Did you know that she's going to be in a form with sixteen-year-olds? She's far ahead of what we had expected.'

'She's read quite a lot,' George said, pleased. 'She was telling me yesterday that she and Aisling used to read Wilkie Collins to each other at night. Only one of them could have the torch so they took it in turns to do the reading aloud.' He laughed at the thought of it.

Violet smiled too. 'I don't think she's lonely or anything, but it would be nice to keep in contact. The trouble is there's nothing for us to buy here. They're the ones who can buy things. I wonder if they realise it?'

'Why don't you write again and say when rationing's over we'll send them a gift to say thank you.'

'I'll need to say it tactfully,' Violet mused. Eileen was always full of pride, and stubborn. She was very much her own person, and you had to go fairly carefully not to offend her.

'Elizabeth was very fond of her. She doesn't say much about her husband, though,' George said.

'I suppose he was busy and not home much, he was always a very hard worker. Rather uncouth but a lot of get-up-and-go.'

'Not like some you could mention, I suppose.'

Violet looked at him. 'Oh George, my dear,' she had said gently. 'I wasn't thinking of comparing him with you. You've got all the get-up-and-go you want . . . or any of us wants. Really, I wasn't making a point. You must know that.'

George looked surprised and pleased. He grunted and left her sitting at her desk. She had decided then that she would ask Harry Elton what he thought. Harry always knew exactly what to do. He had a feel for that sort of thing.

Harry indeed had given it all some cheerful thought when he met Violet for a Saturday drink by the river.

'Let's treat it as a serious problem of state,' he had laughed. He had been delighted at the defeat of Winston Churchill in the election the month before. Labour had said they would build five million houses and they were the boys to have in power. Harry was as sunny about this as he was about everything else.

'Sorry for Churchill? Never. He was a great old geezer when we needed a bit of puffing and blowing. But now we need houses and jobs.'

He took everything that Violet said as being important and worth discussing. Harry Elton never grunted. He probably didn't know how to.

The classrooms were only a little like the convent classrooms. They had bigger and better blackboards and good maps on the wall, but there were no statues, no holy pictures, no little altar to the Sacred Heart of the Little Flower which someone would be in charge of each week.

Elizabeth found it very strange that classes did not begin with a prayer. She used to stand waiting for this to be said each time and then sit down quickly and shamefacedly.

'You mean they prayed before every class?' Monica was disbelieving.

'Well yes, a short prayer.'

'Before maths and history as well as RK?'

'Oh yes, just a quick Hail Mary for an intention.'

'What kind of intention?' Monica was fascinated.

'A sick nun, perhaps, or a happy death, or the conversion of China. . . .' Elizabeth said, feeling a hopeless interpreter of the ways of the convent.

She found the smell of chalk and disinfectant, the long dirty-cream-coloured corridors, more like a hospital than a school. It was a million miles from the incense-filled corridors around the chapel in the convent, the chapel where they dropped in almost every day to pray that Sister wouldn't ask for their history essays today, or that they'd know the answer if the bishop came and asked a catechism question.

'Was this Aisling more or less clever than you?' asked Monica as they walked home from school. Monica was very anxious to be allowed to go up West to see the crowds and the royal family going into the Royal Variety Command Performance. It was going to be the first for seven years. Her mother had agreed only if her school work improved, so now she had a serious interest in it.

'Aisling was much more clever, but she was very . . . I don't know . . . the nuns said lazy or careless. I think she was just bored by it . . . she hadn't time for it. It got in the way of all the fun. . . .'

'And did she get higher marks than you?' Monica was very annoyed at Elizabeth's success at school. Her years in a foreign land had not hindered her; in fact they had made her forge ahead. All Sister Catherine's patient work in the mathematics class had paid off, and she was top of her weekly tests in geography and grammar too. History and French were a little weak, but Elizabeth seemed to believe that if you were given homework you did it, if you were told you must learn a poem you learned it. . . .

'If she tried, Aisling could be top at anything. Sometimes we used to make a bargain. If she would learn her work for school I would go and make us midnight feasts. I had to do that because Aunt Eileen never minded if I came down to the kitchen for food, but she always said Aisling was up to no good.'

Monica walked moodily, kicking the heaps of leaves into the gutter. 'I don't know what my mother means by improve. I know more than she does already. How's she going to know whether I improve or not. . . .'

'I think you should just let her see you working . . . you know, have your school books out more than your magazines or film annuals. That would let her see you were improving.'

Monica screamed with laughter. 'Ooh you are deceitful Elizabeth White . . . I always thought you were really good. But you only pretend. . . .'

Elizabeth wasn't upset.

'No, I do work hard, I've nothing else to do . . . and in Kilgarret I worked hard because I didn't want to let Aunt Eileen down. But Aisling used to do that, she always pretended that she was working and she got away with it . . . she just liked laughing really.'

Monica said gloomily, 'That's not a bad thing. Lots of people like a good laugh.'

Elizabeth thought suddenly of her mother with her head thrown back. She never looked as young and happy as when she was having a good laugh. She seemed to be having more good laughs nowadays. And Aisling didn't appreciate all Aunt Eileen did . . . not even a little. Wasn't it funny how people often got the wrong mothers? Or the wrong daughters.

In December the good news was announced that the beef content of sausages was going to be increased from thirty-seven per cent to forty per cent.

'It doesn't seem very much,' Elizabeth commented to Father as they went for one of their Saturday rambles.

'Oh, you should have tasted a sausage when the rationing was at its height,' Father said. He loved telling Elizabeth about things she didn't know.

They had fallen into the habit of taking a Saturday stroll when Father would point out the various bombed sites, the condemned buildings and the streets which had had direct hits during the blitz. It was a catalogue of sadness, of disasters and near-disasters. Stories of Old Charlie, and Mr This and Mr That. There had been no laughter to remember, nothing very funny had happened. Nothing very dramatic had happened, like when Uncle Sean remembered things, where men were mighty and lads were brave. There were no tales of great kindnesses, or how well people had behaved to other people, like Aunt Eileen always remembered. . . . With Father it was all defeat, and opportunities missed, and good deeds being misunderstood.

'They must have been awful times Dad,' she said as they were coming home down the street. The afternoon was dark and it was nice to think of a cup of soup in the warm kitchen. Mother might be back too, she usually met her friends from the munitions factory on Saturdays, which made it a good time to go for a walk with Father. Or Dad. Sometimes she called him Dad, he seemed to like it. It was what the O'Connors used to call Uncle Sean. They used to laugh when she had mentioned Mother and Father. Fother! Fother! they had pealed, as if it was an odd form of address.

But Elizabeth felt she could never call Violet 'Mum' or 'Mummy'. That was what you called rounder, older people. She was Mother – or nothing.

'Perhaps Mother will be home,' she said as an attempt to cheer him up. His face had grown sombre in the telling of another gloomy story.

'No, Mother's going out, there's a reunion party for all her munitions people ... or some war workers, anyway. In a hotel. She said she wouldn't bother coming back, she'd go straight on.'

'Oh,' said Elizabeth. She didn't particularly mind. She was going to read anyway for the evening, and then when *Saturday Night Theatre* came on the radio she would make some sardines on toast and cocoa. Mother had done some washing that morning, it would dry near the fire and they would have to sit close in for warmth.

'We could play draughts,' Father said.

Elizabeth found draughts very boring. She wished that Father would learn to play chess. But chess and bridge were for intellectuals, he said. How could she convince him that it had only taken her half an hour to learn the pieces and the moves and then you knew it for life. She and Aisling used to play but Aisling was too impatient, she never cared about strategy or plans, she just exchanged pieces mercilessly until they were both left with hardly anything on the board. Elizabeth used to play with Donal – out of kindness because Donal wasn't really any good. He kept walking into awful trouble without seeing it coming. But she had played with him to be kind. Now she was playing draughts with Father to be kind. She wondered if Aunt Eileen would pat her on the head and say she was a great child if she were to see her playing draughts with Father.

The play turned out to be a historical one and Father said he couldn't bear all those play-acting ways of going on, calling people Thee and Thou, so when they had finished the sardines, he brought out the draughts board.

'Shall we take it in turns to be Black?' he asked, his face anxious.

'Do you mind Mother going out with Mr Elton and all the munitions people, Dad?' she said.

Father was very surprised.

'Mind?' he repeated. 'Mind? It's not a matter of minding. It's not a matter of going out with Mr Elton ... it's all of them going to a reunion.'

'I know Dad, but you know, that's all Mother likes doing. Don't you want her to like being at home, and being with us. . . .?'

'Heavens above, what are you saying? Of course Mother likes being at home with us, she's just gone out to one reunion party tonight. Just one night and you start saying that she's always out.'

Elizabeth looked down. She felt she had gone too far, but retreating was going to be just as bad. He would keep asking her what on earth she had meant, and he would go over and over the comforting clichés as if repetition made them more true.

'She's entitled to her night out like anyone is. She worked very hard during the war. Naturally she likes to meet her friends and talk about the times they had. . . .'

Elizabeth gritted her teeth. 'But you know what I mean, Dad, you do. You must notice that Mother only has half of her attention here with us . . . she's not really thinking about you and me. No Dad, it's true. We don't make the place fun enough for Mother, we're very boring you and I, we don't laugh and make jokes, I just read books and you read the paper, and I say "What did you say?" and you say "What's that?" when she speaks. We've got no bit of . . . I don't know . . . no bit of excitement in us.' She stopped. He was silent for a moment. His face worked slightly as if he were about to speak but was afraid he might cry.

Please, please God may he not cry. Please good kind Lord may I not have made him cry.

'Well. Em . . . well,' he mumbled.

Oh please God, I'll never bring the subject up again. I'm so sorry God, Elizabeth prayed. In her mind she saw the statue of the Sacred Heart on the landing in Kilgarret. The statue where Aisling would close her eyes and say, 'Please Kind Sacred Heart I'll give you anything if we don't have a test at school today.'

'No, you're right. I've got very little excitement in me. In fact I never had. But your mother always knew this. She wasn't misled, you know. She wants reliability and a nice safe harbour as well as a laugh and . . . what you call a little excitement. So everyone is what they are . . . you understand. Some of us are hard-working and reliable and provide the home and the hearth, other people provide the fun and excitement. That's the way the world is. Do you understand?'

'Yes, Father,' whispered Elizabeth. 'I see.'

'No, there's no need to apologise,' Father said, not noticing that she hadn't. 'No, you were quite right to say what you did. A person should be honest. You're a very good girl, Elizabeth. You are a great joy to me, and to your mother. We often talk about how lucky we are to have such a responsible little girl. Don't think we don't appreciate you.'

There was a hint of a snuffle in his voice. Elizabeth decided it must be headed off.

'Oh I'm not all that great,' she said. 'Come on, let me be Black first and we'll start the game.'

There was a present from every one of the O'Connors for Elizabeth at Christmas and a beret that Peggy had knitted, and holy pictures from four of the nuns, a calendar from Sister Catherine, and half a dozen Christmas cards from other people in the town.

Elizabeth was amazed as she unwrapped each gift. 'Look Mother, this is from Eamonn. Imagine Eamonn writing a card, and two butterfly hairslides. Aren't they lovely Mother, imagine Eamonn doing that! Do you think he went into the shop himself and asked Mrs McAllister? Oh, no, he couldn't have. Perhaps Aunt Eileen got them.'

Violet was sitting at the table helping her to open them and flattening out the paper and untying the string.

'Oh they are frightfully gaudy . . . but how sweet. Is Eamonn the delicate one, the invalid?'

'No Mother, that's Donal, Eamonn's the eldest boy, well, eldest now. I told you, he's going to work in the shop with Uncle Sean, he's nearly seventeen. . . .'

Every card had a proper message . . . and Aisling's enclosed a six-page letter which Elizabeth slipped into her pocket to read later.

'They're all frightfully holy, the cards. . . .' Violet said, fingering them.

'Well, you see, that's what Christmas is all about there . . . you know cribs and mangers . . . they go on about it a lot,' Elizabeth said. She felt a twinge of guilt now and then about having Lost Her Faith so easily on her return to England. She had tried to find the nearest Roman Catholic church, and visited it, but it was cold and damp, and very uninviting. But she felt sure that God (and Aisling's class at school) would understand, and regard it as a temporary lapse. Later she would take it all up again.

'What's this one?' A card in babyish writing fell from the pack. 'That's Niamh, she's sweet Mother, she's six. Were you not able to have any more children after me or did you just not want to? Or did they not turn up?'

'How funny you are, dear, er, there were complications and so that meant you couldn't have a sister.'

'But it didn't stop you sleeping in the same bed as Father? I mean could you still go on having . . . er . . .?' Elizabeth stopped uncertainly.

Violet looked taken aback. 'Eileen wrote to me that she had . . . explained all about . . . the facts of life and everything to you, she said she told you at the same time as Aisling . . . and that as far as she could see you seemed to have grasped everything satisfactorily. Now I'm not so sure.'

'What haven't I grasped?' Elizabeth wanted to know.

'Elizabeth, now I'm all for frankness, but there are some things you do not ask. People just don't talk about it. It's intimate, it's between the two people themselves. Eileen wouldn't tell you about her activities.'

'But it was different with Aunt Eileen, Mother,' said Elizabeth thoughtlessly. 'I mean, everyone knew that she and Uncle Sean loved each other anyway. Despite all the things they said, they were obviously very fond of each other . . .' her voice trailed away again as she looked at her mother's face.

Violet said nothing.

'Oh Mother, what have I said?' Elizabeth cried, stricken.

'Nothing dear,' Violet stood up. 'Nothing at all. Now, do they know in Kilgarret that there's been a ware here, and that we can't go around getting them gifts like this . . .?' her voice was brittle.

'Oh they know,' said Elizabeth. She had sent a letter to Aunt Eileen five weeks ago enclosing four pounds and a lot of ready-written Christmas cards asking her to buy things in Mrs McAllister's.

'That's all right then,' said Violet briskly.

'Mother I didn't mean. . . .'

'Gather up those things and tidy them away, won't you dear?' Violet said and she walked out of the room looking like people in films who've been deeply wounded and don't want other people to know.

Dear Elizabeth,

This is meant to be a happy Christmas letter, but I've never felt so fed up in my life. Mam's after saying that I should tell you all the news, but honestly there's nothing to tell. The place is so boring and I look so awful, I look so ugly, and there's nothing to do and everyone's in bad tempers like weasels. Sister Catherine's really a devil. I know you wouldn't hear a word against her, and she had a soft spot for you because you understood all those awful things, trains coming into a station and the platform half a mile long . . . but really she's the end. She has it in for me.

She called to the shop. *To the shop.* A nun coming all the way to talk to Mam at work. She said to Mam and Dad that I would have to be taken away from the school because I was a distraction and a bad influence on the rest of the class. I was getting one last chance.

Honestly it's not fair. I don't do nearly as much to disrupt her stupid classes as others I could mention. It's only because she never liked me, it's only because she can see me easily because of my hair. I wish you were here. You used to be able to make them see that things weren't serious. She said that as a favour, and *one last chance* I'll be taken back next term, but I'll be watched like a hawk. What's so new about that, I wonder? I'm watched like a hawk anyway.

I wish you could come here for Christmas and cheer us up. We never seemed to fight so much when you were here, or maybe we fight much more nowadays and it would still go on if you came back. But I don't think so. Mam said after the vicious, evil Sister Catherine left that you had the right attitude about work, you just put your head down and did it. I wish I could. I wish I could put my head down but it's so pointless. Seems so useless.

Maureen's doing a line with that stupid Brendan Daly, you remember him, they live in that place with the huge falling-down barn we used to pass cycling to school when we went round by the river. We used to say it was more of a barn than a farm. Anyway, he's serving his time in some food firm in Dublin and he met Maureen at a dance, and now they're going out together. Imagine going all the way to Dublin and having a life of your own and meeting someone from Kilgarret! Joannie and I say that when we leave and go into the world the first question we'll ask every single person is, 'Are you from Kilgarret?' Then we won't be in any danger of falling for someone from here.

Maureen's all silly and giggly and she actually calls him 'my Brendan'. You'd die laughing if you heard her. Daddy was asking her would she get the ring for Christmas, and Maureen got all annoyed and said she was twenty-one and could do what she liked. Daddy said he was only asking a civil question and when Maureen had gone off in floods of tears, Mam said to Dad that he should be more gentle because Maureen was obviously hoping for the ring but didn't dare to let us know that in case it didn't happen.

Honestly imagine marrying Brendan Daly and his awful sticky-out teeth! Imagine going to bed in the same bed as him and imagine being stuck with him forever and ever for the rest of your life.

Joannie thinks it's very funny, she keeps calling Brendan my 'brother-in-law', and whenever we're going to school she says, 'Will we ride past your in-laws' barn?' Joannie's very funny now, you'd like her more than we did last term, she's got more lively.

It's funny in your letters when you mention Monica. I always think of the cat. I never heard of anyone else called Monica. When you said you went to *Brief Encounter* with Monica I thought for a moment that you had taken a cat to the cinema. I saw it too, it came here two weeks ago for three nights. Everyone cried except me. I thought they were stupid not to go away together. I mean in England they can do that, there's divorce and everything and it's not against the religion. There was no reason for them to stay with their awful husbands and wives, except just to make a plot.

I said that the Mam and she said I had a lot to learn about loyalty and making a bargain and keeping it. Whatever I say or do it appears I have a lot to learn.

I have awful spots, on my forehead and on my chin. Joannie says that you can't see them much but when I asked Eamonn he said they were like lighthouses and that if people got lost they could see their way home by the red glares on my face.

Can you think of one single piece of cheering news to tell me? Like that you'll come and stay, or come back and live here. Or what am I to do to get that rotten, bad, half mad Sister Catherine off my trail?

Happy Christmas to you all, we couldn't get over that picture of you and your mother. Mam has it in her bedroom on the dressing table. Your mother looks like a beauty queen. Do you get on well with her these days? It must be funny going back and finding a new mother in a way.

Love from a very miserable

Aisling

Mother developed a bad flu just before Christmas. The doctor came and said she must build herself up more, that she had gone to skin and bone. Father and Elizabeth tried to give the doctor a picture of what Mother normally ate during an average day. She had no bread, no potatoes, no puddings. She just picked at things. She looked very pale and listless.

'I'm sorry to be such a trouble,' she kept saying. Father and Elizabeth had been preparing for Christmas in their own ways, making chains of paper, gathering greenery, holly and ivy from the common, making fancy place cards for the table, reading recipes for novel seasonal punches. Now Mother was ill and it would all be in vain. She refused to have her bed taken downstairs to where the one fire burned.

'That's out of the question,' she said faintly. 'Only invalids and old people have their beds taken down to the living room. I shall stay here until it's gone.'

Elizabeth offered to have the chimney in the bedroom swept and light a fire there, but Mother wouldn't hear of it. She wore mittens and had two hot-water bottles and that was fine. She lay uncomplainingly, her hair lank on the pillow. Father was totally unable to cope with it all. In the bedroom he stood wringing his hands saying, 'Violet, is there anything we can do?' in a hushed, death-chamber voice that obviously drove Violet to the limits of her patience with him. Downstairs he would rail senselessly at anything from current dieting fads, to the shortages in the war, to Mother getting colds going to meet friends from the munitions factory.

Monica's mother taught Elizabeth how to make broths and hot drinks and how to make a cold compress without drowning the patient and saturating the bed. On Christmas Eve the doctor assured them that there was no danger of pneumonia and that it was just a matter of a slow return to her old energy and her old self. Elizabeth, cheered greatly by the pronouncement, became impatient with Father who was still grumbling and muttering about doctors being know-alls and knowing nothing when it came to is.

'Father, do you never see any good in anything? Can you never see light at the end of the tunnel?' she snapped.

'Not really,' he said.

'But that's a dreadful way to live,' she said.

'In my experience, lights at the end of the tunnel tend to flicker out,' said Father.

Elizabeth thought of last Christmas as she prepared Mother's beef tea. Last Christmas Day, walking in the frost and early-morning darkness up to mass, shouting greetings at everyone, full of anticipation for the day ahead. Little Niamh had fallen and cut her knee. There had been enormous sympathy, dabbing with clean white handkerchiefs, taking her to a street lamp to examine the wound, but Niamh, more frightened than hurt, was roaring in great bellows.

'Oh Niamh, for goodness sake stop crying,' Aisling had said. 'Your leg isn't going to fall off. Don't spoil Christmas Day.'

'You can't spoil Christmas Day,' Donal had said.

Eileen had lifted the hefty five-year-old up in her arms. 'Tie a bandage on it Sean,' she had said briskly. 'Poor old warrior Niamh. But Donal's right, of course it won't spoil Christmas Day, nothing can spoil Christmas Day.'

Mother's hand was very thin. The soup spoon looked big and heavy when she held it.

'I'm sorry you're having such an awful Christmas, my darling,' she said to Elizabeth.

Elizabeth sat like a guard watching that she finished every mouthful.

'You can't spoil Christmas Day,' she said like an echo.

Violet looked at her. There was not a trace of irony in what Elizabeth had said.

Downstairs George was huffing and puffing with damp sticks to light a fire that wouldn't catch.

Tears came down Violet's pale face.

'It's all such a dreadful mess,' she sobbed. 'It wasn't meant to be like this. It's all such a hopeless mess. . . .'

'Mother, it's all going to be fine.' Elizabeth was distraught to see Mother's shoulders heaving like this. With her foot she closed the bedroom door in case Father should hear and come up to make things worse.

'No, it's all turned out wrong. There's no point in any of it. I couldn't be more sorry, but I can't think what else I could do . . . I tried my best, but I'm just not a good little housewife . . . I can't stand polishing up a house and cooking meals for nothing. . . .'

'But Mother, it's not for nothing, its for *us*,' cried Elizabeth. 'And we're very grateful, and when you're better we'll help you much more. I was saying to Father that we don't do enough for you. . . .'

Violet looked at her with swimming eyes. 'You still don't understand, you'll never understand. Oh God, it's such a hopeless mess.'

She turned her head on the pillow, and Elizabeth decided not to force any more beef tea on her. She sat there for a while but Mother said no more; her breathing became less agitated and then she slept or pretended to sleep. Elizabeth crept out.

Father looked like a big eager dog as he knelt by the fire with a newspaper hoping the draught would catch the flames. 'How is she?' he whispered.

Elizabeth paused. 'She's fine Dad, she's having a little sleep.'

She went back to the kitchen table which had been set for the festive meal. There were drawing of robins on cards, with holly in their beaks; Elizabeth had cut them out as shapes. There were three home-made Santa Claus figures propping up the table napkins. Bits of ivy and greenery had been criss-crossed across the table. Elizabeth sat down and looked at the plate of corned beef, and the three pieces of chicken. She had stood in a queue for four hours to get the chicken pieces; the corned beef was from a tin.

She felt fifty as she prepared the Christmas dinner.

Dear Aisling,

I meant to write, but everything was so confused and awful here, I couldn't take my mind away from it all. First about you . . . now remember the way you used to get away with everything by looking as if you were doing something? It worked before, why won't it work now; or is there any point in saying to Sister Catherine, let's have a truce? Or what about actually doing what they say and forgetting everything else except work for two terms? Then you'll be top of the class and they'll all be delighted and they'll leave you alone.

I don't think the first will work. Maybe we're all too old now to get away with things, or maybe the nuns are worried about exam results. In your place, I would make a truce with Old Catherine. Honestly, she was nice, but you'll never believe it. She was very lonely, she's much older than the other nuns. She lives for the pupils, and she'd feel so happy if you had a man-to-man talk, or a girl-to-nun talk. But you won't I suppose. So that leaves the last solution, work yourself to the bone as they say. You could regard it as a kind of a competition. You'll show them, you'll prove them wrong about you. I honestly think you could wipe the floor with the rest of the class. Monica (not the cat!) was asking me about you and I told her you were brighter than anyone here in Weston High, and she couldn't believe it, because she actually thinks I'm bright. And I'm not, I just put my fingers in my ears and learn.

Please let me know what happens. I wish you would write every day. I wish I could write every day. It all seems so far away sometimes, and then when I was reading your letter about Maureen and Brendan Daly – of course I remember him, he was awful – it all comes back. Did she get engaged, are they really in-laws now? I suppose we'll all have to be very polite and not say anything bad about them in case they become Maureen's nearest and dearest. Isn't it funny though that she likes him! You'd think Maureen could have anyone. . . .

I keep rambling on and on about Maureen because I want to put off writing the next part.

Everything is so frightening here at home. Mother was very ill over Christmas. She was in bed for ten days, it was a chest cold and flu but she was very weak, and she lay there like a ghost. But she was worried all the time about something, and I think that she's thinking about leaving us and going away. Now please, please, please, don't tell Aunt Eileen this, I may be wrong, it may have been just because she was so ill. But she kept apologising for things not turning out right, as if something was over.

I think Dad knows it too and won't admit it. Whenever I say that we might all do something, you know something cheerful that would please Mother, he just asks what's the point. If you knew how awful it is. They are both moving around the house apologising if they come into the same room as each other. No, don't laugh, that's what it's like. It seems impossible to try to place it in Kilgarret, with everyone running in and out of rooms all the time, but here there's only the three of us, and I sit reading and pretending not to be watching them.

Could you pray that it will be all right? I suppose you must know that I sort of gave up my faith. I never knew if I really had the faith anyway, since you wouldn't let me go to communion and confession, but whatever I had of it is gone. Just pray that Mother won't go away with Mr Elton, please Aisling, and ask people at school to pray for a special intention. I know you won't tell anyone. Mr Elton's very nice, it was he who took that silly picture, the present to you all, and he's always laughing and making jokes. And now that Mother's better and everything, she meets him a lot, and I'm so afraid he and she might be thinking of going off together. Sometimes when I come in from school and there's a note from Mother on the table saying she may be late, I'm almost afraid to read it in case it's saying more than that.

I may be wrong. Remember the time we all thought that Eamonn was drowned in the river, and he'd just gone home the other way? Well, that's the kind of fear I have now.

Love from

Elizabeth

Harry had said that no good came out of lies. Harry had said that there was nothing evil and wrong about falling in love, and now Violet must take the deception out of it by telling them. She must say it fair and square to George, she must tell Elizabeth. She must explain that there was no need for hurt or blame.

Violet wished it was as easy as that. Harry's wife, long gone from anyone's life and living in the west of England with her new husband, presented no problem. Harry had no children. He would be very happy to include Elizabeth in their household if she wanted to come. He was starting a new business, they would have a flat over the premises. There would be plenty of room for the girl.

Violet decided to tell them the day before Elizabeth's sixteenth birthday. But she knew that they both had seen it coming. The May sunshine fell on the table and on Violet's restless thin hands, which twisted and turned as she spoke.

Father didn't answer. He just sat there with his head bent. 'George, please say something,' Violet said.

'What is there to say? You've made up your mind.'

'Daddy, don't let is happen, say something to show Mother you want her to say,' begged Elizabeth.

'Mother knows I want her to stay,' said George.

'Oh don't be so weak Daddy, do something,' Elizabeth cried.

George lifted his head.

'Why am *I* the one who is weak, why am *I* the one who must say something, do something? *I've* done nothing. *I've* just done what anyone else does, plod along. This is what happens.'

'But George, we have to talk, we have to talk about arrangements.'

'Make whatever arrangements you like.'

Elizabeth stood up.

'If you have to talk about arrangements, like for a battle, you won't want me here. I'll go upstairs and I'll come down when you've finished.'

George had stood up also.

'No, there's no talk about arrangements. Do what you like Violet, set up whatever you want. I presume you want me to divorce you, you're not suggesting that I give you evidence or anything. . . .'

'No, of course. . . .'

'Fine, then whenever it's to be done get some solicitor to write a letter. . . .'

'But George. . . .'

'That's all, isn't it? I'm going out for a walk now. I'll be back at teatime.'

'But Daddy, you can't walk out now, you can't just go out of the room and not discuss it. . . .'

'George, what about Elizabeth, what will we do? Will you . . .? I mean. . . .'

'Elizabeth is a grown-up girl, she's almost sixteen years of age. She can go with you or stay here, or move between both houses . . . I presume you will have a house. Your friend isn't going to expect you to live in his van is he . . .?' George had reached the door. 'I'll be back for tea,' he said and closed it behind him.

Violet and Elizabeth looked at each other.

'I'm sorry Daddy was so weak, he's a bit afraid of you, that's it,' Elizabeth said.

'Oh . . .' Violet began to speak but she was choked with emotion. She moved over and held Elizabeth's hand. 'Do you understand, do you have any understanding?'

Elizabeth signed. 'Yes Mother, I do, I think I do. It's awful, but I think I do understand. And you'd better cheer up because if the point of going off with Mr Elton is to have more life and fun and zing and everything, there's no point in feeling guilty and wretched. . . .'

'It's not going off, it's only half a mile away. Will you come? Harry wants you to, and I do. Very much.'

'No Mother, I can't, who'd look after Father? But I'll come often to see you, honestly and I . . .' her voice broke.

'What darling?' Violet looked at her, trying to help out the words.

'I was . . . I was wondering, if it happened because I went away? If I had been here during the war, would you and Dad have been more of a family, you know? More to keep you together.'

'Oh my poor child,' Violet put both her arms around Elizabeth, she hugged her, and swayed as her voice was saying soothingly into Elizabeth's hair, 'My poor child, in all the useless years that your father and I have been pretending to get along like normal people, you were the one thing that made any sense out of it all. You've always been the only thing that made sense of years of wrong turnings, and George thinks that too. If you were to blame yourself that would be the last straw.'

Mother sat and talked for another hour, about loneliness and age and the fear that you might go to the grave not knowing any spark. She talked about the war and the blitz and about people making fresh starts. She said lamely that George might find a nice lady who shared his interests. And then to Elizabeth's horror she went upstairs to pack.

'You're going now, Mother!' she cried.

'Darling, you don't expect me to serve beans on toast and talk to your father normally when I've told him that I've committed adultery and am leaving him?'

'No of course not,' said Elizabeth.

VII

... Oh do stop apologising for blots and lines being crooked and not knowing what to say. I just want you to say *something*. You were always the one who told me that the important thing was to say *something*, not to wait until I knew what to say, and thought it was right. I've started doing it. But *you* must continue to do it.

If you knew what it was like here. If you had even just a small idea, I think you would be so studded that even you would be speechless. It's very kind of you to write and say perhaps they'll get over it, but it's not like that. It's not a bit like Uncle Sean and Auntie Eileen shouting at each other, because that was only for the evening at most. And anyway they always talked immediately afterwards, and then there was the whole family ... there were all of you, and the house, and the shop, and everything. Here there's nothing, there's only the two of them, and they keep telling me I'm grown-up.

I wish I wish so much I could have stayed in Kilgarret. Suppose I had got a job after school there, or helped Aunt Eileen with the accounts or in the house or something. Then they might have had to hold off until I came back. They could have said they couldn't have done anything serious until I was home. But, you see, the awful thing is that they both say to me that I'm so sensible and I'm so understanding ... but I don't understand anything. I'm *not* grown-up. I wish they could see that. Mr Elton keeps saying to me that he'd like me to call him Uncle Harry. I told him I was no relation and that, without wishing to be difficult, it was a bit artificial. That's what I said.

He said, 'You called those people in Ireland Uncle and Auntie and you'd never met them, and look at how well that worked out.' I said to him that that was totally different, that I had gone to live with you, I was part of the family. I told him I lived there for over a third of my like. (I just worked it out.) And then Mr Elton said, 'Well, Elizabeth, your mother and I hope you'll live with us a lot of the time, even most of the time too, so don't you think it's a bit formal to have all this "Mr" business? I don't call you Miss White, now, do I?'

I didn't know what to say, so I said nothing.

'Right, that's a good girl,' he said. He thought I was considering it. But I feel that if I *did* call him Uncle Harry it would be letting

Father down somehow. Giving in or something, letting Father see that the other side had won.

Father always calls him 'Your-mother's-friend-Mr-Elton'. She went to live in a boarding house. Well she calls it living there, but it's so odd. She only pays a little because she helps the woman run the place. I went in there on Tuesday and she was in this awful room with all kinds of dirty sheets with a frightful smell and Mother was sorting them for the laundry. It really smelled foul. I said to Mother I couldn't believe she was doing this, and she said that a woman had to have dignity, and that she couldn't sit at home and wait for Father to make up his mind about the divorce, while eating his food and living in lodgings he had paid for; she had to make her own way.

I said, why didn't she go and move in with Mr Elton if that's what she was going to do eventually. She said it was to do with disgrace and reputation. I said that Monica's mother knew all about it already and I hadn't said anything to Monica. She said there were legal terms like reputation and disgrace which I didn't understand.

Sometimes she talks as if her mind was gone, like poor Jemmy in the shop. But mainly she sounds like someone much younger than she is setting out on some kind of dangerous mission. I don't blame Father for thinking it will blow over, but it won't. Please write, I'll go mad if I make any more dreadful silent suppers for Father with nothing else to think about.

What does Aunt Eileen say?

Love,

Elizabeth

Dear Elizabeth,

I got your letter this morning. Mam gave it to me on my way downstairs. You won't believe it but the postman still goes in to the kitchen to start messing with Peggy. I mean, they're nearly a hundred, both of them, and he still thinks it's great fun. Mam keeps a beady eye on them. Anyway, she said, why not take this stamped envelope, I've a bit of a note for Elizabeth myself in it. Mam must be like the fortune tellers, she couldn't have known you said write back really quick.

I think you should call him Harry. Very suddenly. Cut out all the nonsense about Uncles and Misses, if they're making out you're so grown-up, act grown-up. That's one thing.

Secondly, you'll have to stop worrying about the two of them, they were never happy. Honestly, even when you were here you used to tell me about them going all cold and prickly with each other. It would have happened anyway. Dad was reading in the paper about half the English population getting separations and divorces because of the war.

And another thing, it's not even a sin for them. They were never properly married in a Catholic church or anything, so there's nothing to be undoing or renting apart.

And if your mother is looking and acting all young, well, isn't that great! Isn't that what people are trying to do all the time? Whenever Mam says she feel like a girl again it's always over something nice like a picnic or a run up a hill.

And, I know Mam said it in her letter because she didn't seal it so I know I was allowed to read it, why don't you come over here for a bit? We could chat about it, and it'll be the holidays soon, and I'd love to know you were coming. It's dead lonely here without you. I'm very friendly with Joannie of course, and she's much nicer than we thought last year. But it's not the same as when you were here, it's not living with someone and being able to say anything you like.

What about your friend Monica (I still think it's Niamh's cat)? Is she able to laugh like we did? I don't think she can be, otherwise you'd have told her and her mother all about the business at home.

Listen, try to cheer up. I mean in a way they're right. You are grown-up. We're sixteen and a bit, and if people aren't grown-up then when will they be?

Can you talk to your Da about other things? Like we do with Dad here when he starts complaining about things. No, I don't suppose that's really a good example. At least he doesn't complain about Mam going off with another man. It's kind of unbelievable.

But it must have been desperate. I'm very sorry. I'm not good at writing it, but it's awful and I can't find words to tell you how I wish and pray that it will somehow be all right.

In the meantime you should go right up to him and call him Harry. Be sure to tell me what he says.

Love,

Aisling

Dear Aisling,
This is just a short letter. Calling him Harry was marvellous. He said 'What?' I said, 'I said, no thank you, Harry.' 'Oh,' he said. 'You asked me not to be so formal,' I said. 'Quite correct my dear,' he said. But he was knocked sideways. Then I called him Harry in front of Father, and Father laughed. He said I was right, that's exactly what Mother's-gentleman-friend was: a real Flash Harry.

Mother is pleased too. She says that she always knew I'd get round to liking him.

It's the first day of holidays, I'm going to stay with Monica for a week. Aunt Eileen suggested that maybe they might find it easier to talk if I wasn't there. She said that there wasn't much hope they'd get back together but they might be able to get formal things worked out if they didn't have to keep looking at me. I think she's right.

Monica has this awful boyfriend, well he's sort of unsuitable but she's delighted. I'm coming to stay because it means we can all go out together and her mother thinks she's only going out with me.

Love to all of you. I'm sorry to hear from Auntie Eileen that Donal was worse, I hope he's all right.

Love,

Elizabeth

Dear Elizabeth,
Donal's fine again, he had extreme unction, do you remember what that was? Anointing the hands and feet with holy oil, you only do it when people are dying. But he turned a corner. Sometimes it cures people. It cured Donal, he's fine, he's sitting up again and laughing. He has a fire in his room even though it's July.

Joannie has a boyfriend too, he's David Gray, one of the Grays, a Protestant. He's super-looking, but nobody's meant to know. He writes her notes and says he thinks he'll be able to take us both to Wexford next week in his cousin's car. Wexford! In a car! With the Grays!

Aren't you sorry you didn't come to stay with us instead of with Monica down the road? Why didn't you come by the way?

Love,

Aisling

When Elizabeth came back to the house in Clarence Gardens after her week with Monica, the first thing she noticed was how dirty it had become. All around the little rubbish pail in the kitchen there were bits of food, and the cooker was stained and crusted with old food that had been allowed to burn into the enamel. There was a smell of sour milk. The ashes in the sitting room had not been cleared and there was a trail of dirt around the front of the fireplace as if they had been very carelessly cleared on a previous occasion. The linen basket in the bathroom was open and clothes tumbled out on the floor. There was a sour smell in the bathroom too, and damp towels were rolled up in the corner.

A tray with the remains of a breakfast was beside Father's bed. Wasps buzzed around the jam and the milk had soured in the jug.

Out the window Elizabeth saw the garden overgrown and unwelcoming; nettles and briars choked the plants that she had helped to plant in the spring. This was to be the first year that flowers were acceptable. Up to now only vegetables had had a right to grow in a garden.

Elizabeth looked at Father's pyjamas thrown on the floor. He had left her a note saying that he had gone to have a consultation with the firm of solicitors who did work for the bank. He said in the note that the manager had told him he must feel free to call on them in his personal capacity.

Imagine. Father had sat down at this filthy table in the kitchen, leaving the house like a shipwreck and written about solicitors and personal capacity. He hadn't put the dishes under the tap, he hadn't said he was glad to have Elizabeth back.

No wonder there was no light in his life nowadays.

A wave of irritation about Mother came over Elizabeth suddenly. It wasn't fair. It just wasn't fair. People had to stay where they were. Aunt Eileen didn't like a lot a things, but there was no question of her running off. She did not like the way Uncle Sean talked about the British and the war, she didn't like Eamonn's 'rough friends', as they were called. She didn't like the way Aisling answered back, or Maureen brought all her dirty clothes down in a bag from Dublin to be washed at weekends. She didn't like Peggy's hair falling into her eyes or the postman coming in to neck with Peggy when everyone was out. She didn't like Niamh acting the baby to get her won way. Aunt Eileen got very cross if Donal went out without his coat or scarf, or if anyone ever mentioned the folly of Irishmen who had joined up during the war. But Aunt Eileen was able to cope. Her mouth would go into a tight line, and she would just get busier and busier. And even Monica Hart's mother who was meant to have 'nerves' coped with things when they went wrong. There had been some trouble when Mr Hart came back but Mrs Hart hadn't just packed her bag and left. And remember that poor Mrs Lynch, Berna's mother, *her* husband was awful, really awful, he had come around to the house in the square and nearly frightened them to death and he had been found drunk in bus shelters and everything. And Mrs Lynch didn't get on the next bus out of town.

Mother was behaving very badly, and it was silly. Suppose things went wrong with Harry Elton? She couldn't keep running away all the time. She really should face up to things. The nuns had always said that life was not meant to be easy. God had implanted in us a sense of restlessness so that when we got to heaven in the end, we'd calm down, and know the meaning of peace. That might well be true, certainly the restless bit was, everyone had it. Why did Mother give in to it when other people were able to damp it down?

Elizabeth sighed and just as she was about to boil a saucepan of water and start to cope with the mess an even greater wave of irritation came over her. He didn't love her, any more than he loved Mother. Father was incapable of loving people, he had become so wrapped up in himself and his worries he didn't even seem able to see the fact that there were other people around.

Elizabeth put down the saucepan again. For months she had worried about him, she had tried to console him, she had played draughts with him, kept away from subjects that might upset him, steered away from danger areas and tried to keep an atmosphere of normality in the house. Things were not normal. He and Mother didn't even like each other any more. They both said they loved Elizabeth, and presumably they both wished her well, and were sorry that things hadn't turned out the way that people always hoped they would turn out when they were young and had a baby girl.

And if things weren't normal and if Father and Mother had actually spent the week deciding something so utterly non-normal as whether Father should divorce Mother for adultery and desertion or whether Mother should want Father to be a gentleman and go off to Brighton with a lady and pretend to spend the night with her so that a detective could say that Father was committing adultery, then that was about as non-normal as things could get.

Elizabeth stood up full of resolution. So why on earth should she, Elizabeth, pretend that things were normal? Why should she be the only one of the three of them acting as if nothing had happened? She was going to please herself now. Everyone else seemed to be acting as if they lived as individuals. So, what did *she* want to do, because whatever it was she was jolly well going to do it.

She didn't want to run away to Kilgarret. First there would be too much trouble, too much upset. Auntie Eileen would have to cope with Mother and Father, both writing and telephoning and perhaps even coming over the Kilgarret. Anyway, Aisling might not want her now, Aisling seemed very busy for the summer with her friend Joannie Murray and all these friends of Joannie's, the Grays who lived in a big house with stables outside the town. Perhaps it wouldn't be the same with Aisling, and she'd be in the way. It would be hard at the convent too. Sister Catherine would want to know why she was back, the nuns wouldn't understand about divorce and Mother going off with Harry Elton, and even less about Elizabeth running away. Uncle Sean? He always liked her, perhaps he would just say that it was a further sign of the decaying English empire that their marriages couldn't even hold together. But would it be fair to ask them to pay for her? It would cost money to have her. And perhaps Father would be so cross he wouldn't send any.

No, going to Kilgarret would hurt too many people. And it wouldn't work. She couldn't go and live with the Harts; they wouldn't agree, it would be too strange to move a few streets away. It would cause too much talk. She didn't want to live with Mother and Harry because that would be saying she approved of what they were doing, and she did not. Anyway they giggled too much and made jokes that left her out and then said, 'Sorry Darling'. But she would not live in this house clearing up dirt and rubbish and trying to look after Father and cheer him up, getting no thanks and no love in return.

Elizabeth went to her desk and got a pad of paper. Then, very carefully, she wrote three letters.

Mother, Father and Harry
You have all said that you want the best for me. Thank you. I want the best for you all too.

I do not think that coming back to a cold, dirty house with no explanations from any of you is the best for me. I do not think it is even half-way towards the best.

I am going back to the Harts. I shall tell them that you would like another week to make up your minds about the future. I shall return again next Saturday to see what you have all worked out.

I am about to begin my last two years at school; at the end of these holidays I will need somewhere to live where I can study and have peace and freedom from worry. I would prefer to live here in Clarence Gardens with Father, but I am not going to clean the place up so that it will be fit for us. It is like a pig-sty. If you decide that this is where I shall live please make arrangements to have it cleaned, and tell me what you intend to do about laundry from now on. I do not mind doing the cooking for Father and myself, but if I am going to study hard I will not have time to stand in queues for things, so there should be some other arrangement made about shopping.

I am sorry to sound so business-like about this, but I have been shocked and hurt, sitting here realising that nobody is giving any though to what is going to happen next.

You will all say that I am upset. I am. I have taken fifteen shillings from the piggy bank because I think if I am going to ask the Harts if I may stay another week I should give them a present. That's something nobody ever thinks of either.

When I come back next Saturday around three o'clock, it would be nice if you were all here. It will not help matters, it will only make them worse, if you come to Mrs Hart's house to discuss it there.

It's been going on for months. It can wait another week.
Elizabeth

She found three envelopes, and addressed one to Father. She left it propped beside the dirty milk bottle.

Then she walked to the lodging house where Mother still stayed and dropped it in the door. Then she squeezed the third envelope in through a slit between the door and the side of Harry Elton's van which she saw parked near the lodging house. It fell on the floor where he would see it. Hitching her bag up on her shoulder she headed towards the Harts' house. Monica saw her coming and ran to the door, delighted. With a wry sort of a smile Elizabeth thought that Aisling would be proud of her.

Elizabeth woke the following Saturday with the taste of dread in her mouth. There had been a message, a note slipped into the Harts' house late on Sunday night. Nobody had seen who delivered it. It has been as brusque as Elizabeth's own letter.

You are perfectly right, nobody has been business-like, and it has taken you to show us. George, Harry and I will be happy to make plans with you next Saturday. You can reassure the Harts that it will all be solved by then.
Violet

Elizabeth thought with a pang, as she read and reread the note, that she must indeed have grown up suddenly if Mother was referring to Father as George and to herself as Violet.

Throughout the week she had accompanied Monica absentmindedly on various outings with the unsuitable boyfriend; they went to the cinema a great deal and Monica and Colin kissed while Elizabeth stared at the screen. Monica had said that Elizabeth should say her parents had sent the fifteen shillings for entertainment money for the girls. Mrs Hart had thought this very reasonable, and indeed generous. Mr Hart had grunted and warned them not to stay out too late and not to injure their eyes by being too close to the flickering screen.

Now it was time to go home and face what had to be faced. Elizabeth washed her hair and sat in the garden while it dried.

'You have a beautiful head of hair,' Mrs Hart said approvingly, 'it's like silk.'

'That's very nice of you, I think it's a bit wishy-washy,' Elizabeth said.

'No, in fact women try to dye their hair your colour, flaxen, you're very lucky.'

Mrs Hart was shelling peas. Elizabeth started to help her. 'You're very helpful,' Mrs Hart said. Monica was up in her room reading a movie magazine and working out a complicated method of meeting Colin next.

'I always get on with other people's mothers better than with my own,' said Elizabeth sadly.

'Everyone does,' Mrs Hart said cheerfully. 'It's the law of averages, isn't it? If you see someone too much you learn to hate them. Monica hates me, Mr Hart would hate me if he didn't go out so much. People shouldn't see each other too much. It leads to trouble.'

'That's a bit depressing isn't it?' Elizabeth stopped with the peas in the pod open and ready to fall. 'I mean, there's not much point in love and families and friends if you're going to get tired of people when you see a lot of them. . . .'

'It may be depressing,' Mrs Hart said, 'but it's the truth. Look dear, haven't you got the living proof of it in your own house this afternoon?'

Even the front garden looked neater as Elizabeth crossed the road to 29

Clarence Gardens. She had her own key, but lest she catch people un-awares she decided to ring at the door. It was just ten past three, she had dawdled on the way in case it looked *too* business-like to arrive spot on time. With a lurch of her heart she noticed Harry Elton's van parked outside the gate.

Father answered the door.

'Welcome home, dear,' he said. 'How are all the Harts?'

'Oh, they're fine,' Elizabeth said. She left her case in the hall, hung her school blazer on the hall stand, and noticed with a quick glance that the place had been cleaned. The carpet was swept, and the paintwork had been wiped. So far so good.

In the kitchen, Mother and Harry sat at the table rather awkwardly and stagily; for the first time since the whole business had begun they seemed ill at ease and self-conscious.

'Here you are,' boomed Harry in a falsely cheerful voice.

Mother stood up. She was twisting a handkerchief in the way she did when she was upset.

'How nice you look darling, your hair is lovely.'

'Thank you Mother, hello Harry.' Elizabeth was so accustomed to jol-lying everyone along and pretending that nothing was amiss that she almost fell into the role again. She had to steel herself to remain aloof rather than creating some bustle and air of business to tide over the awk-wardness around her. She stood very deliberately waiting for the next move.

It came from Mother.

'We've made some tea. It's cooling a little, shall we make some more?' She was awkward. It wasn't her kitchen any more. She looked to her husband. 'George? What do you think?'

'I don't know. Would you care for some tea Elizabeth?' he asked politely.

'No thank you, we had a late lunch at the Harts,' Elizabeth said, bouncing the ball right back to them. Time could not be spent with ket-tles, artificial activity could not be generated.

'Well, it's not my place really, but won't you sit down, my girl,' said Harry. Mother darted him a nervous glance and Father a resentful one.

'Thank you, Harry,' said Elizabeth and took the proffered chair.

There was silence.

'Monica all right is she?' Mother asked.

'Oh fine,' said Elizabeth.

Father cleared his throat. 'We did have discussions during the week ... er ... we faced the things that had to be faced, and ... er ... as you requested we are all here. You see.'

George stopped. Elizabeth looked at him levelly. 'Yes Father.'

'And it's only fair that you should be brought into the discussion and your views ... sought ... on aspects of what we discussed.'

Elizabeth remained silent.

Mother took over. 'It hasn't been easy, you'll know yourself some day that the big things in life are not easy to discuss, and they cloud everything else. But as you pointed out, we were all ignoring the little things as well. So, what it boiled down to is this. . . . Your father is very generously going to give me evidence, let me divorce him. He will agree to do this because it is a courteous thing to do, and a gentleman's attitude. I do not deserve it, since as you know I am the one who is at fault. In return I shall ask your father for no allowance of course, no settlement. Harry and I will start again as if I were a girl with no stake, no belongings. I shall keep my clothes and some small pieces of china and furniture. Your father will employ a woman, whom I shall find, to come twice a week to do the laundry and cleaning. I have already cleaned out the entire kitchen and cupboards and listed what brands we buy . . . used to buy. It's all there.'

Elizabeth raised her eyes and look approvingly at the cupboards, which had even had a new coat of paint.

'Harry has dug the back garden. From now on if your father doesn't like working it himself he could give some as an allotment. Plenty of people do that. There is a back entrance so you would not be disturbed. . . .'

'We should wait and see how it turns out, perhaps you might enjoy doing it now that the basic stuff has been done.' Elizabeth stood up and looked out at the tidied squares and the cut-back briars and thorns. Harry must have worked all week on it.

Harry spoke. 'I've been able to get you a stove, an oil stove for your room. Vi was saying you would want a place to study on your own so that George could have the wireless on.'

'That's nice,' Elizabeth said.

'And I got a bookcase, a small bookcase at the second-hand shop, it fits in nicely under your window,' Father said eagerly.

'Thank you.'

'There are new curtains too. Very luckily exactly the same size – they were changing curtains in the family hotel where I'm staying so I took the opportunity. They're blue, like the bedspread. . . .'

'Thank you very much.'

A silence.

Mother said, 'Does all that seem suitable darling? I mean, I know we're talking about inessentials, but you know, for the moment, the sort of nuts and bolts.'

'Yes, Mother, I think that's fine.'

'Your mother wants to know whether you will go on living here with me or whether you want to tell us what you would prefer.'

'I'll go on living with you Father, if that's all right. And if we're both fairly tidy and don't make demands on each other I'm sure we'll get along just fine. I think you should go out more, Father, in the evenings. Go to meet people, or to play cards. I won't be much company in the evenings, I'm going to study, and it would be dull for you if you didn't go out a bit.'

'Yes, yes, of course, of course.'

'Mother, will you and Harry be nearby, will you want to come around and see us?'

'Well, no dear, that's what I was going to say, darling. Actually, your Uncle Harry and I . . . I mean Harry and I, are thinking of going north. It won't affect your visiting us in the slightest. If there's a chance that you'll come to see us you'll have the train fare right away. . . .'

'Even sooner,' said Harry.

'And our home will be your home. But for a lot of reasons, if it doesn't seem too harsh we thought. . . .'

Elizabeth looked at Mother helpfully, but did not finish the sentence for her.

'We thought a new start. . . . and a clean sheet . . . a fresh start. . . .' Her voice trailed away.

Harry butted in. 'And, as I said, you only have to ask – you don't even have to ask – once we get settled you just turn up, any day any night. It's as much your place as this is.'

Father gave a kind of snort – it might have been a cough.

'Thank you,' Elizabeth said.

'So that's about it, I suppose,' Father said. 'Unless there's anything else you want to discuss.'

Elizabeth's voice was very calm. 'No, that's fine, really. I think that covers everything. Have you all discussed everything, I mean, there's nothing more you have to clear up about arrangements and money and divorces and everything . . .?' She sounded as if she were talking about a shopping list. Detached, anxious to help, efficient.

'No, I think that side of things is all . . .'

'Sorted out. . . .' Father finished for Mother. She gave him a little smile and he half-smiled back. Elizabeth's heart nearly burst. Why couldn't they make the smiles last, and maybe they would all burst out laughing and Harry Elton would go out and drive away with a wave and it would all be perfect.

But that didn't happen. Mother picked up her bag and gloves, looked proudly around the kitchen that she had decorated in order to leave it with a clear heart. Harry pinched the small geranium on the window sill.

'Give that a lot to drink, Elizabeth, thirsty little devils, geraniums.'

Father stood politely holding the door open for the man who was taking his wife away. Elizabeth walked out to the van.

'I'll write in a week,' Mother said.

'Great,' Elizabeth said.

'I mean it, you know, whatever home we get will have a room for you, Elizabeth, we'll put blue curtains in that too,' said Harry.

'I know you will, thank you, Harry.' Elizabeth shook his hand. He gripped her around the elbow as well as shaking hands; he was very eager to give her a hug but didn't dare. . . .

Mother didn't look to see whether Father was at the door or not.

'Oh, I wish things were different.' Her eyes were full of tears, she looked very lost and young somehow. 'Oh if you knew how . . . how I wished that things could be different.'

Elizabeth sighed. Mother blinked away the tears.

'I'll say no more now. I'll say it all in the letter. Bless you my dear, dear Elizabeth.'

'Goodbye Mother.' Elizabeth touched Mother's thin cheek with hers, Violet held on to her, shaking.

'Say it in a letter, that's best,' Elizabeth said. Wordlessly, Mother got into the van and waved.

They were gone.

Father was standing at the kitchen table. 'We'll take it in turns to wash up after meals,' Elizabeth said. 'You do this one, I'll do supper. I'm going up to my room now.' She managed to get out without breaking down. She grabbed the bag she had brought back from the Harts' and ran up the stairs. She closed the door and threw herself on the bed with its new blue bedspread. She stuffed the pillowcase with its new blue frill into her mouth to muffle the sobs. She cried until her throat was sore, her ribs ached and her nose was so stuffed up she could hardly breathe. If she had taken the pillowcase away from her face the sound that came out would have been like a long lonely wail.

Aisling thought that Elizabeth was extraordinary to have been so worried, in case something would happen to her Mam and Dad, and then when it did happen she turned out to be as cool as a cucumber. She had written a very unworried kind of letter which had been more about new curtains and fresh painting in the kitchen than it was about what it felt like to be in the middle of a broken marriage. Mam had been very insistent that Aisling did not talk about it.

'Can't I tell Joannie? Please?' Aisling had begged. 'You see I've told her up as far as the bit where she got to calling Mr Elton "Harry", like I suggested, and Joannie will want to know what happened next. It's not fair to tell someone the story and then leave them hanging without knowing the end.'

Mam had laughed and said all right, but not to broadcast it around the town. If Elizabeth came back to see them she mightn't like to hear that everyone in the place knew of her private family matters.

'Do you think she'll ever come back?' Aisling wished she would. But she wished she'd come soon, otherwise there would be too much to catch up on, too many things to explain.

'Would she come back here, do you think, and start school again here in September?'

Mam thought not; she said she had written to Elizabeth and suggested it as a possibility; but Elizabeth had replied that bad and all as things were she would feel worse if she deserted her father entirely.

'I don't know why she writes such things to you,' grumbled Aisling, 'she only told me about the blue curtains.'

'She told me about those too,' Eileen looked worried. 'I think she was very upset by the whole business. . . . You know all of them doing up the house but for the wrong reasons.'

'Um.' Aisling was vague. 'Mam, would Mrs White, you know, Elizabeth's mother . . . would she technically be in mortal sin and everything, living with Mr Elton? I know she's not a Catholic, but she was at a Catholic school with you . . . and she was baptised . . . and it could be a sin.'

Mam ran after with the tea towel she happened to have in her hands and started to belt her around the legs. . . . 'Will you go away you stupid idiotic child and stop bothering me about sin! Sin, sin and more sin . . . what nonsense you all talk.'

But Mam was laughing. Laughing at somebody breaking their marriage vows . . . Mam was hard to fathom sometimes. . . .

'I wonder where they did it?' Joannie speculated as they both rubbed Vaseline on to their eyelashes with the narrow bits of combs, flicking them upwards.

'Did what? Who?' Aisling concentrated intensely but the lash wouldn't bend. 'The best I can do is to make these look like spikes. Why do yours bend? Are they made of weaker fibre or what?'

'I think they're naturally curly, I have a feeling they might be.' Joannie examined her eyelashes, pleased. 'No, I was talking about the couple, you know, Elizabeth's mother and that man . . . where did they make love?'

'I never thought of that. His house maybe?'

'But he didn't have a house remember, always in lodging houses. They couldn't go there. Maybe they went to hotel rooms for the afternoons.'

Aisling thought about that. 'I think you have to stay in a hotel once you book in. I don't think you can leave at teatime and say that's enough. Maybe they didn't do it at all, maybe they only held hands and necked.'

'Oh, don't be silly!' Joannie was very cross. 'Of course they did it, wasn't adultery mentioned and all? I mean, necking isn't adultery. Anyway you'd never leave one man and go off with another unless you'd done it with the other. Stands to reason.'

Aisling didn't agree with this. She put down her mirror and hugged her knees as she sat on Joannie's bed. She looked around the big room with its windows down to the floor. The Murrays' house was one of the best houses of Kilgarret. Eamonn always said, 'Off to your friends the Rockafellers?' when she went to Joannie's house.

'I think you've got it all wrong, Joannie,' she said seriously. 'I think you think that most of the world is much more interested in doing it than they really are. Elizabeth and I used to say we'd never mind if we never did it as long as we lived. . . .'

'Ah, but that was ages ago . . . I bet you feel different now.'

'No I don't,' said Aisling with spirit. 'I really mean this. I think it's something everyone goes on about and makes a big thing out of and nobody likes it at all. It's love people want. That's different to doing it.'

'They're meant to be the same.' Joannie's round face was puzzled. 'Didn't you listen when Sister Catherine said that love was the highest expression of doing it – or was it doing it was the highest expression of love? Remember, we nearly choked trying to keep straight faces in class? It was a scream.'

'Sister Catherine never talked about doing it!' Aisling was amazed at the very idea.

'No, she didn't use those words . . . she said something about the high something of married love resulting in the creation of children . . . if that's not doing it what is?'

'Yes, I remember. But honestly, I think it's the love bit that people want, that's what all the songs are about and the films and the poems, not all this other thing.'

'But the other thing is lovely!' Joannie said.

'How do you know, you're only going on what people say.'

'Well, David's done it.'

'He never has.'

'He says he has.'

This was electrifying news.

'What did he say it was like?' Aisling was so excited she nearly fell off the bed.

'He says it was perfect pleasure . . . and that I'd love it,' Joannie said smugly.'

'That's no description. *Perfect pleasure*, sure that's no help at all, and of course he wants you to think you'd love it, then you would go all the way with him. . . .'

'Well, then we'd know anyway . . . we'd not be sitting round and talking about it and guessing.' said Joannie mutinously.

'That's true mind you,' said Aisling. 'But would you mind?'

'I'd love it,' said Joannie.

They both whooped with laughter.

'Then you must. That's definite,' said Aisling.

'Well, why won't you?' Joannie was anxious at being thrust into the role of trail-blazer.

'Well, use your head! How can I? You can't go off and knock at someone's door. Hallo I'm Aisling O'Connor and my friend Joannie Murray would like me to sample sexual intercourse with someone to give her courage before she does it with David Gray, so may I come in and shall we take our clothes off now?'

'I didn't mean that.'

'But what else could I do, *you're* the one who has a fellow and *you're* the one who's fellow says it would be pure pleasure for you, and *you're* the one who's mad to try it. I'm only just being a supporter that's all.'

'I'd never do it, I'm only talking about it. I'd be terrified of having a baby. Anyway, David's only asking me because he expects me to say no. Nobody with any sense would say yes.'

'Because he'd leave you once he had got his way do you mean?'

'Well, yes, and anyway he wouldn't be able to trust me would he? You see if I did it with him, then what's to stop him thinking I'd do it with anyone else?'

'There has to be a flaw in that, somewhere,' said Aisling. 'How does anyone ever get together with anyone else if that's what they all think?'

'They get married first silly, then it's all right,' said Joannie confidently.

'But what about the *pure pleasure* one, the one who did go the whole way?'

'That was in south Gloucestershire, when he was on holidays. They all do, there, apparently it's a different kind of way of going on, it's not like here.'

'Well, why didn't he do it with lots of people if it was going on all round him?'

'Aisling O'Connor, you deliberately pick holes in what people say. It's impossible to talk to you,' said Joannie.

'I'm just interested, that's all,' said Aisling. 'Everyone else seems to think being interested in things is unhealthy. I'll never know why.'

Joannie's family liked having Aisling around the house; she was so bright and funny, they thought. Everything Aisling said seemed witty and entertaining when she said it at the Murrays' table. It seemed self-centred and showing-off according to Mam, Eamonn and Maureen when she said it at home. For the first time, she began to realise that in the Murrays' house she was a treat, but at home they had had enough of her. Perhaps that was why everyone liked Elizabeth so much in Kilgarret. Because she was a treat. When she went back to her own place it had been awful. Anyway it was just as well that the Murrays did like her because things at home were very depressing. Donal's illness had left a shadow of terror on Mam. Every time he coughed she would glance at him, while pretending not to.

The day that Father Kearney had come with the extreme unction had been dreadful. One of the nuns had come first to prepare the room and Donal for the sacrament. Da had been very annoyed at that and said that nuns were interfering busybodies and how could a child like Donal need to be prepared for anything? Mam had held Donal's hand all the time and smiled. Peggy had been crying at the door and Mam had thought she had a cold and said she should go down and sit at the fire rather than stand there in the draught. Father Kearney said that the sacrament worked in one of two ways: it brought back health and strength, or it gave comfort to the sick person to make a happy death. Eamonn had said something under his breath about covering your bets and Mam had nearly murdered him afterwards. Told him to keep his heathen beliefs out of a sick child's bedroom.

Anyway, Donal was better; he had to be careful never to catch pneumonia again and Mam seemed to think that pneumonia was like an enemy outside the door waiting to come in. Aisling felt it was very peculiar of God to keep sending bad fortune to people who could bear it least. After all, Sean hadn't been a bad person, he had been a good person who had believed in a cause, and God had let him be blown up, and Donal was by far the nicest of the whole family and God kept giving him whistling chests and bouts of pneumonia on top of his weak lungs. Maureen and Eamonn were awful and they were both as healthy as bullocks. God had no sense of fair play. Mam worked hard and was up till all hours and did she get any holiday or nice clothes? No, she didn't. Aisling herself had worked like a slave at school this year and what had she got? Any reward? Any thanks? Just a grudging admission that she had come to her senses at last and made an attempt to catch up on lost time. Mrs Murray said that there was a line about 'Whom the Lord loveth He persecuteth'. They found it eventually and Aisling said that the Lord must be simply mad about her because He persecuted her from morning to night with awful hair, straight eyelashes and demon nuns. Mrs Murray and John, who was Joannie's brother, a clerical student, thought that was very funny. Aisling repeated the remark at home in case Mam might find it funny and it would make her laugh. Mam said it was blasphemous and that there was great danger that Aisling was becoming a show-off.

Aisling liked talking to John Murray when he was home on occasional weekends from the seminary. He told them things about their trainings which were meant to be secrets. He told the enthralled Joannie and Aisling that sometimes they had lessons in manners so that when they were priests they wouldn't make eejits of themselves and bring down the respect of the clergy by eating with their knives and shovelling the food into their mouths with their hands. Aisling thought this was uproarious, but as usual got no enthusiasm when she told the tales at home.

'If that young Murray is cracked enough to go joining the priests when he has all that big family business to have a share in then he's even more cracked to be telling tales about how daft they're all inside there,' said Dad.

Mam was naturally annoyed at the disrespect Dad showed for the church, but she was also annoyed with John Murray. 'That place is like his family now, you don't go round telling secrets about the family. It's disloyal.'

Aisling remembered a few small acts of disloyalty when she had made the Murrays rock with laughter by imitating Dad coming in from work and being like a sultan asking for water to wash himself, a clean towel, his slippers, and the best chair ... without words. He didn't have to speak, so well were his little impatient gestures known; and whoever was handy – Peggy, Niamh or Aisling herself – would run to fill the needs. He never made these little signs at Mam. It was like a pantomime and Aisling had caught it very well. She reddened thinking how cross they would be if ever they knew how she had parodied the nightly routine. But she didn't feel disloyal spending most of the summer in the Murrays' house. It was so sunny and it had a big garden that went down to the river. If you wanted to sit in the sun you took out a deck-chair, not a folded rug or one of the kitchen cushions to put on the step of the yard like at home. There were always cakes and biscuits in the Murrays' house that went back into tins after meals, not like at home where once a thing was out it was eaten and that was that.

Joannie's romance with David Gray came to a head when school started. He didn't have anything to do until October and he begged her to skip school, so they could go off for the whole day together. Joannie, tempted and almost weakening, realised the dangers, even though Aisling agreed to cover for her.

'I could say to Sister Catherine that you were taken bad on the way to school, and I had to take you home.'

'She'd not believe the daylight from you,' said Joannie honestly if ungratefully.

'Well anyone she would believe the daylight from wouldn't do it, that's the whole problem,' said Aisling.

David's blandishments proved too much. He was going to pack a picnic hamper he said, and some cider. He had a loan of a car they could have the whole day, go off to some place in the mountains or by the sea. Joannie decided to risk it. She thought her best chance of success was to leave Aisling out of it. Reluctantly Aisling agreed. She was still considered – grossly unfairly – to be a trouble-maker; there was no point in creating suspicion for Joannie.

It was by great luck a day when the Murray house would be empty. Mrs Murray was going to Dublin, shopping, John would not be back from the seminary; Kate, the married daughter, would not call; Tony, the other brother, was in Limerick learning the trade in a wine merchant's, he would not be back. Noreen, the Murrays' maid, was on holiday, she had gone to her people in Wexford. It was the one day in the whole year that Joannie would have an alibi.

Twenty minutes into the first lesson, which was Christian doctrine, Joannie stood up and said she felt sick; after some time in the cloakroom she came back and said she felt awful, and could she go home? Sister Catherine looked round the class for a girl to accompany her; her eye didn't rest for a second on Aisling, who was amongst those waving an enthusiastic hand to be the companion. 'Mary Brady, you go with Joannie, and when you have her safely delivered there, come straight back.' Sister Catherine had chosen the class goody-goody, the Child of Mary, the most reliable and honest girl in the school, whose intention of becoming a nun and joining the order the day she left school was known to everyone. Wistfully Aisling looked out of the window and saw Joannie Murray setting off on her adventure. She found it very hard to concentrate on the Acts of the Apostles.

When Mary Brady came back, eyes virtuously downcast, Sister Catherine asked was everything all right.

The innocent accomplice explained that Joannie had seen her mother and waved to her at the window and she had gone in and was fine. Sister Catherine thanked Mary for her help, Mary smiled, and Aisling O'Connor sighed a sigh of pure envy.

A mystery always hung over the details of that day. Like how the whole idea of the picnic came to be abandoned so early, and what the cider had tasted like, and why they decided to drink it in Mrs Murray's bedroom. And it was never clearly explained why Tony, who lived with cousins in Limerick, had come home unexpectedly, and why he had been so upset. The combination of all these things had been a confusion Aisling had never known.

David Gray was forbidden to come near the house again by Tony. There had been great threats about how the Grays would react if they had been told the circumstances. Joannie spent what she always called the worst hours of her life begging Tony to believe that it would not help if Mummy were informed. Mummy went made over things, and she would never go to Dublin for the day and shop again if she was given a confused account. Tony had said, 'In Mummy's bedroom, of all places, of all places. On Mummy's bed.'

Aisling only heard it in fits and starts. She had called round to the Murrays' as arranged at seven that evening when the picnic should have been finished and shortly before Joannie's mother was meant to return from Dublin. Instead of exciting details and perhaps a glimpse of David fleeing into the distance . . . Joannie sat red-faced at the kitchen table with Tony. Lord, he must have been them coming back from the picnic. Oh Lord, what a desperate bit of luck. Joannie sounded funny and distant.

'Oh Aisling, it's not such a good time, I'm having this sort of chat with Tony. . . .'

'Sure. . . .' Aisling was puzzled. But she took the message. 'Hallo Tony, you back for a holiday?'

'Sort of,' Tony grunted. He was the one of the family she knew least. He was the eldest, nearly twenty-eight now. He seemed to have got good-looking since she had seen him some months ago, or maybe he was good-looking because he was obviously in a very bad temper. People got good-looking when their eyes flashed and their jaws got grim. Aisling had discovered this from reading and from the films.

'Right, I'll be off, will you come round to my place later or . . . what?' she asked Joannie.

'Aren't you going to ask her how she feels, or was the whole school in on this?' Tony enquired.

'Yeah, sure, that's what I came round for, to know are you all right? Maybe it's flu, Sister Catherine was. . . .'

'I'll see you tomorrow,' Joannie said.

'Right,' Aisling said huffily, and swung out. Next day at school, Joannie, still red-eyed, had given substance to the belief that she hadn't been well. In fact, Sister Catherine was moved to wonder should she have taken another day to make sure she had recovered. Apparently she was saved by the skin of her teeth; Tony had seen sense, she had promised not to get involved with anyone, least of all the Grays. She had tried to explain to Tony that they were doing nothing only fooling around, but he had got into a worse humour at everything she said.

'And were you only fooling around?' Aisling asked eagerly. Joannie was distant.

'That's not the point, the point is that he came back.' She had a look of such disappointment on her face that Aisling decided not to pursue the technical details, they could wait.

'Why did he come back anyway?' she asked.

'He's got fed up of Limerick, he came back to ask Mummy could he start working in our business here, you know take over himself sort of. He says he knows everything, and he got restless yesterday and drove back to talk to Mummy about it. Oh dear God, why couldn't he have got restless today instead of yesterday? Tell me God, why did you let him get restless yesterday?'

'I suppose to prevent you from committing a mortal sin,' Aisling said seriously. When you thought about it, God was very devious.

Tony Murray moved back to Kilgarret that autumn. It seemed to take him a long time to forget what he regarded as a great transgression, and a sign of his little sister's weak moral character. Since Aisling had cunningly been freed from any complicity in what had happened, she was not regarded with suspicion and she could come and go as she wished. Aisling wondered would Sean have felt the same and been so difficult about it if he had been alive. But then the thought of being with anyone on Mam and Dad's bed was so unlikely, and the house being empty ever was so unlikely, you couldn't really compare it. Anyway, the thought of going all the way seemed even less likely than ever now that Joannie, who would have been her only companion in that field, was virtually under lock and key.

The nuns had given Mam and Dad the depressing opinion that Aisling was not of a scholarly frame of mind. Like Maureen, she would probably be more successful in work where no great further study was required.

'Don't ever let Maureen know they said that about it not being a studying kind of a life,' Mam had said. 'The poor girl is demented by all those books on anatomy and physiology. She'd go up to the school and go for them if she were to know that. . . .'

Aisling didn't mind one way or the other. The school suggested that she went to the local commercial college also run by their nuns. Here she could learn shorthand, typing, commercial English and book-keeping. It sounded better than going back to do the sixth year and study for her Leaving Certificate. Joannie was leaving anyway and going to a school in France for a year. It wasn't a finishing school, it was a French convent where they would learn to speak French perfectly, and do sewing and cooking. Tony had been very keen on the idea and Mrs Murray thought it seemed sensible too. It would make a lady out of her. Mam had smiled when Aisling had told her that.

'That's why I was sent to the convent in Liverpool, and look what happened to me. And that's why poor Violet was sent there too; Ladies indeed.'

'You're much more of a lady than Elizabeth's mother,' said Aisling loyally.

Mam was pleased but she pretended not to be. 'We don't know what's going on in Violet's mind,' she said.

'Well, at least you didn't break up your marriage and go off and live with someone in sin and pretend it was all Dad's fault.'

'No,' Mam said thoughtfully, 'at least I didn't do that.'

Dad wasn't pleased that the nuns had said Aisling was not academic. He had been in a bad humour anyway and the news made him worse. While the door was still open Aisling heard him complaining bitterly.

'Fine lot of children we reared. The one couldn't wait to go and throw his life away for the British, another is meant to be in a job that doesn't need much brain work. We were told at the time that it was the divil and all getting her into that hospital.'

'Will you stop that . . .' Mam interrupted.

'I will not stop. I've Eamonn standing like a corner boy in the shop with a crowd of thick louts in and out looking for him, Donal is so sickly the Lord knows what we'll make out of him, Niamh is a spoiled madam and the only one we had any hopes for, those bloody nuns say, "she's not academic, she's not the studying type". Well what was she with them all those bloody years for . . .?'

'Sean.' Mam's voice was stronger.

122

'Now, what are you putting on that face for? Things are not all right. What are you and I breaking our backsides working for, what's the whole thing for, Eileen, if the children aren't going to get on, and do better than we did and . . .?' Dad's voice was a bit shaky but he shouted. 'I mean if there's any purpose in the whole thing isn't it that the children will do well . . .?' Aisling didn't hear what Mam said because Mam had banged the door shut very firmly.

Elizabeth wrote when she heard that Aisling was going to the commercial college. She said she had a memory of it being a second-best sort of place.

> . . . I know I sound preachy, but is there any point in going there if it's not the place that will give you the qualifications? Yes, I can hear Sister Catherine's voice too, but they're right. It's something like having the right clothes and implements to climb a mountain. And isn't life like a rotten mountain most of the time? I think you should go back to the convent and do the awful old stuff and get your Leaving Certificate, and then go to the commercial college, because once you had the exam, you'd be safe. Or that's what I think.

Aisling had thought about it. In a way Elizabeth was right. In a way it would be marvellous to cock a snook at the nuns, to put her finger to her nose and say, I got my Leaving and you told my Dad I was an ignoramus. . . . Yes, in a way. But it would be so hard, and she was miles behind, miles. And she couldn't bear being with all those creepy ones who were brainy and who would think she had ideas above her station. And she'd look so silly crawling back and saying that she had been wrong not to have worked harder. It would be admitting that all her antics up to now had only been an act. No. She was going to go to the commercial school. She would get a good job from there, she'd do the kind of work she liked doing, not learning rivers and kinds of soil and trade winds in geography, and all the terms of the treaties and the lists of the penal laws, and all the endless, endless things in history.

At least typing and book-keeping would be new, and shorthand, and she would start equal to everyone else, and this time she would work and come out top of the whole year . . . then she'd get herself a great job with maybe a bank manager or open an insurance office. And then that yellow-faced Sister Catherine with her thin whining voice wouldn't be able to make sarcastic remarks, and Dad wouldn't feel that it hadn't been worthwhile to have her, and Mam would be delighted and say that Aisling had great spirit, and Elizabeth would write one of her letters and say she had been all wrong, that Aisling had done the right thing.

Aisling wished that Elizabeth were here. It was silly to have a best friend miles away in England studying in a blue bedroom instead of here in Kilgarret where she should be.

*

There were bridge classes two nights a week in the old WVS Hall. The fee of one and sixpence a night meant that only respectable people would attend, and it included tea and biscuits. Elizabeth enroled Father and herself as soon as she saw the poster.

'I don't want to learn to play bridge,' said Father.

'Neither do I, but we'd better. Let's look on it as some kind of survival raft.' After four lessons, they began to enjoy it.

One night as they walked home together, he said, 'Once you realise that none of it means what it says, it's quite interesting.'

'How do you mean?' Elizabeth was thinking about Aunt Eileen. She hadn't told her about the proposed bridge classes when last she wrote. Aunt Eileen would have approved of her being kind to Father but only wealthy Protestant people like the Grays played it in Kilgarret.

'Well when you say two spades, it doesn't mean that you have two spades. In fact it needn't mean any spades at all. It's just a code. It's a way of telling your partner you have a fairly reasonable hand in most things. . . .' Father was what might even be called animated. Elizabeth was about to tuck her hand into his arm, but she held back. If she did it once, then Father would expect her to be that kind of person always. They didn't touch each other. They were managing very well on this formal level. Better keep it like that.

'I know what you mean,' she said seriously, 'but then I think a lot of conversations become like that as you get older. Sort of code, not saying what you mean, and hoping everyone else knows the rules.'

Mother did write quite a lot as it turned out. Elizabeth had expected the rare and rushed notes which had come with a leaden sense of duty around them all the time she had been in Kilgarret. She didn't write much about life now with Harry, nor did she enquire about life in Clarence Gardens. Instead she talked of the old days, as if Elizabeth was a contemporary who might remember them with her. She talked about how they had been to tennis parties when she was young, parties where sometimes ten servants stood around with glasses of home-made lemonade which were poured from big glass jugs. Ten servants, standing all afternoon in the heat, while little madams and little masters flung their racquets on the ground or their sweaters and expected them to be picked up.

Elizabeth read these letters carefully. She didn't know whether Mother sounded wistful for those days, or if she was condemning their selfishness. Eventually she decided that Mother was belatedly trying to tell her something about her life, so perhaps the best thing to do was to reply in the same way, in generalities, telling little anecdotes. Elizabeth discussed the school and compared it to the convent in Ireland; she wrote about the odd people they met at bridge evenings; she sometimes enquired whether there was some way she didn't know of to make a cake without the fruit all sinking to the bottom, or how to let down a skirt without the hem looking awful. Mother sent her a cookery book eagerly and told her about putting a ribbon or a braid around the edge of the skirt and seemed very pleased to have been asked. Elizabeth tried to think of some household query each week.

She thought that Mother was lonely, she knew that Father was lonely, she felt that Aisling would have nothing to say to her these days and only wrote when Aunt Eileen wrote. She worried that Aunt Eileen was too busy and was only making up nice things to ask like she made up for Mother. She knew that Monica Hart thought she was a boring swot nowadays, no fun, and no use as a decoy for the various young men, since she insisted on staying at home and studying.

And she didn't even have the satisfaction of being a brilliant scholar after all this work. She just managed to keep at the top section of her form. Nobody considered her an outstanding pupil, it took her longer than it took the bright girls to understand what was being explained, but she worried at it like a dog at a bone. She would stand shyly beside the mathematics teacher who would look at her with exasperation.

'I've been explaining this all week and you kept nodding, why didn't you say you didn't understand . . .?' Then the explanation, quick and often impatient, but usually kind. It wasn't usual to find a sixteen-year-old who would stand humbly after school, hair falling over her face, and admit that she wanted to understand complicated things but couldn't. The teachers usually had the world neatly divided: either they understood and could do it and were a reward to you, or they didn't and never would and idled their way through the school years. Elizabeth fell into neither category.

The art master, Mr Brace, had a lot of time for her. She had been taught nothing at that school in Ireland, he told the other teachers in the staff room. He had asked her what she had done in art class and apparently it had only been pictures of the Virgin Mary, or scenes illustrating the mysteries of the rosary. The other teachers shook their heads absently. Irish convents were indeed full of all kinds of mysteries, but then Mr Brace with his liking for beer at lunchtime was not to be relied on for a factual description. The girls in the school called him Beer-Belly-Brace behind his back and complained to each other that he had smelly breath, but Elizabeth liked him. He explained things to her easily, as if she were on his own level. He used to ask her more and more questions about the convent school. His first wife had been a Roman Catholic but she had never mentioned the mysteries of the rosary. She, in turn, had never thought of perspective before Mr Brace explained it to her, and she flushed happily when he held up her still life as the best in the group. She even enjoyed his history of art classes, which none of the others even listened to. When he held up reproductions of the Old Masters, partly obscured by his dirty thumb-nail, she would look with interest at the picture rather than at Mr Brace's stomach or finger-nails and she would try to imagine a world of castles and palaces and people with strange closed faces because they were princes. She was very familiar with the Madonna pictures but wondered why they hadn't painted any of Our Lady of Lourdes; the school in Kilgarret had been full of Lourdes pictures.

'When was that?' Mr Brace had asked. 'I don't know about it.'

'Oh, it was maybe a hundred years ago, you know St Bernadette and all the miracles and the people being cured and all,' said Elizabeth.

'Well Raphael could hardly have known that in advance,' said Mr Brace. 'He wasn't around to know about the miracles, was he?'

Elizabeth reddened and determined not to speak again. Mr Brace was sorry for her and lent her some books on art history, and one of his precious books of reproductions.

'I get bad-tempered, and shout at people in class,' he said. 'Some day you'll be in front of a lot of kids and you'll be the same.'

'Oh, I won't be a teacher,' Elizabeth said definitely.

'What will you be?' he asked with interest.

Elizabeth looked at him blankly. 'I have no idea, but I suppose I'll think of something when the time comes.' Her face looked troubled. He was the first person who had asked her that question. Mother had never wondered what she would do and neither had Father. But perhaps a lot of people had to face this kind of decision alone. She tried to remind herself of what Aunt Eileen had always said to Aisling whenever there was a crisis or a cry that things were unfair. 'Self-pity brings tears to the eyes quicker than anything else.' Aunt Eileen would be proud of me, she thought from time to time as she walked by herself back to Clarence Gardens, her books under her arm, glad to be out of the big, tiled corridors in the school but not anxious to get back into the empty house.

Often she delayed and walked by the library. They had little exhibitions from time to time and it was nice to stroll around and examine their tables full of model buildings, or ancient Greek reconstructions. The librarian, Mr Clarke, was a kind man. He was an albino and he had very poor sight. He told Elizabeth that in fact he could see much better than people had thought, it just looked worse because he peered so much. He had got the job during the war and had built up the library so well, now nobody could take it away from him. He found art books for Elizabeth to read and, even more helpfully, he got her the prospectus and application forms from the local art college.

'I don't think I could really study art, could I?' Elizabeth asked him doubtfully. 'I mean, I don't know anything about it.'

'That's why people study things,' Mr Clarke said, his white head bobbing up and down excitedly. 'That's the point.'

Walking back from the library, she often stopped and examined the window of Worsky's second-hand shop, or rather, antique shop. There were lovely things in the window. She used to tell Mr Clarke about the funny little screens and wondered where they were made. Mr Clarke said she should go in and ask, the owner would be glad to tell her.

'But I don't have any money to buy anything, I can't go in can I?' Elizabeth was hesitant.

'Of course you can, that's what people like, even more than making a sale, to chat about beautiful things. . . .'

And of course he was right, Mr Worsky showed her the panelling in the screens, explained how lacquering was done, and it was all so much more interesting than anything she had ever heard at school. She looked up more books in the library and told Mr Brace about it after art classes.

If only Aisling were here, she thought a hundred times. She would make such fun of her three friends. Beer-Belly-Brace, the albino in the library and the old Polish refugee, Mr Worsky in the antique shop. But it was good to have three friends. And she was able to go to the cinema too, a lot of girls had no money for that, at least once a week she went to the balcony by herself, to the four-thirty show. She saw *Gone with the Wind* four times, and she quite understood why Ashley loved Melanie and not Scarlett. She had written that to Aisling and, as she expected, Aisling had disagreed. Aisling thought that Melanie was a wet, mopey, old baggage and she spoiled the story by being so good.

Other people sang songs about being sweet sixteen and just sixteen and the joys of being seventeen. But Elizabeth didn't join in much. She thought it was a long lonely apprenticeship, and the day she got the news of her scholarship to the art college, she hoped that the weary business of growing up was now over. Father said he hoped it would lead to a secure job; Mother wrote and said that a lot of Honourables were going to art school now and she might meet some. Aisling said she couldn't understand it, Elizabeth had been no good at drawing at school, but Sister Martin who taught drawing was pleased. Mr Brace said she was the first of his pupils to do so well, Mr Clarke in the library gave her four old art books which were considered surplus stock and inscribed them all for her. And Mr Worsky in the antique shop said that now she was an official art student she might even like to come and work in the shop sometimes.

She did get the job in Worsky's antique shop. She called in one Saturday, shortly after she had started at the art college and felt she was a *bona fide* artistic person. At the back of the shop, lost in a catalogue, stood a much younger man than Mr Worsky. Elizabeth's heart lurched, in case the shop had been sold. She hadn't been in for a few weeks.

'What can I get you?' he asked pleasantly. 'Or would you like to browse around a bit?'

He was very very handsome, he had a sharp face – that's what Elizabeth thought was the word you would use to describe it – sort of pointed features, and a lot of black hair falling over his forehead. He looked like a film star.

'Oh, I wanted to see Mr Worsky. He is still here isn't he?'

The young man smiled. 'Oh yes, of course he is, he's having something he hasn't had for a long time. A day off. I'm Johnny Stone, his assistant.'

'Oh yes, of course, he told me about you.' Elizabeth smiled with relief. 'But he described you as an old man, or I mean I thought you were much older. . . .'

'He didn't describe you to me at all . . . but you are very young and very attractive, if I may say so.'

Elizabeth smiled and blushed a bit. 'Thank you very much,' she said. 'You're very kind. I'm Elizabeth White and he once sort of, half-said that if there was extra work here on a Saturday morning he might consider me.'

'If he doesn't, he is a very foolish man, and Stefan Worsky is not that.'

'Oh good, then you're on my side,' said Elizabeth earnestly. 'Can you tell him that I've started now, up at the art college, and I'm doing several design courses, as well as history of art, and if it's all right I might call in one afternoon during the week and ask him if he'd really like me to help out on Saturdays. . . .' She looked around. The place was empty. 'It's not very busy, do you think he'd really need help?'

'It's early still,' said Johnny Stone. 'In half an hour the place will be humming. I could ask you to start this morning but that would be a bit pushy. I bet I'll see you next Saturday. I certainly hope to. . . .'

'I hope so too, Mr Stone,' Elizabeth said solemnly.

'Oh come on,' he said.

'I hope so too, Johnny,' she said, shaking his hand.

'That's better,' he said.

The engagement between Maureen O'Connor and Brendan Daly was announced in spring, and a September wedding was planned. It certainly came as no surprise to anyone; the surprise had been that they had waited so long. Their walking-out period had been considered long even by Kilgarret standards. Eamonn had heard a joke about them; he heard that Brendan had finally plucked up courage to ask Maureen and he had said, 'Would you like to be buried with my people?' He had thought it was great, and he kept telling everyone, until his father had told him to shut his big ignorant mouth.

'Isn't it bad enough having the girl being made a fool of by that brood of tinkers without having you laughing like a horse?'

Eamonn was stunned. He had no idea anyone was being made a fool of; he checked it out with Aisling.

'Apparently, by being seen with him or something, she was saying she was willing; by his not naming the day it looks as if he was taking a bit of time to make up his mind. They're all cracked in this town,' Aisling said absently. 'But what's the worry? She wanted him, she's getting him. That's the system.'

Maureen had been talking about the clothes for the wedding non-stop. Aisling and Sheila Daly were to wear pink. Pink was the right colour for bridesmaids' dresses. It was a pity about Aisling's hair, and the clash, but it couldn't be helped, Maureen wasn't going to change her whole wedding just because her younger sister had such extraordinary red hair. Aisling shrugged. She could always have Niamh. No, that wouldn't do, it would look as if there had been a row, it would give cause for gossip. Anyway Aisling and Sheila Daly were around the same height.

Occasionally, Aisling tried to ask Mam was Maureen being normal about this wedding, or was she a bit disturbed; but Mam wasn't giving any sensible answers. She said that a wedding day was something so special that people should be allowed to have any kinds of fancies they wanted. After the wedding day, being married soon settled down to ordinary things again, so that's why people let brides go into such states of excitement. No, Mam hadn't been able to go into a state of excitement herself because things were difficult in those days, there was less money, things were more chancy, people had to concentrate so hard on having a living, a stake in somewhere. Mam's family had lost any bit of money they ever thought they had; Dad's family had nothing. But this was now; things were far better than the terrible twenties. . . .

'But Mam, she's daft altogether, it's only old Brendan Daly. I mean it's only the Dalys she's marrying, you'd think it was the royal family. Do you know she asked me to get thinner for the day! To lose a bit of weight for the ceremony. I couldn't believe it.'

Mam laughed. 'Will you wear a corset and tighten it up a bit and tell her you've lost weight? That's what I'm going to do.'

'She asked you to lose weight too?' Aisling could hardly believe it.

'Yes, but I'm getting on for fifty years of age. I should lose a bit and anyway I've more sense than you'll ever have in your whole life.'

Aisling said she couldn't study her awful grammalogues and do her shorthand preparation after such a shocking discovery about her mother's lack of honesty.

'Go off and write to your friend then,' said Mam. 'Give Elizabeth my love, and ask her whether she might come over for the Great Wedding. . . .'

'That's an idea.' Aisling's face lit up. 'Will I tell Joannie about it too, she'll be home from France in September . . .?'

'No, better do nothing until the love birds have sorted out whether the Murrays are on their list or not,' Mam smiled.

'You are laughing at them,' Aisling said.

'I am not,' said Mam.

Elizabeth sent a beautiful present for Maureen's wedding. It arrived a good three weeks before the day, so there was plenty of time to admire it. It was a small, oval silver dish.

'It's what they call a bon-bon dish,' Elizabeth had written. 'But I don't think anyone has bon-bons to put in them, we certainly don't here. It would do for anything I suppose, maybe biscuits when you have your friends to tea, or bread even, if you were having people to lunch. It's extraordinary to think of you as a married lady. You're the first of my friends to become Mrs. I've sent a book on hallmarks too, so that you can work out what year it comes from and where it was made. It's quite interesting. I'm always turning bits of silver upside down and looking up their history. If they don't have these four marks then it isn't silver. It's a nice thing to know. I hope you'll be very happy, and if I get good grades next June, perhaps I could come to Kilgarret for a visit and see everyone, and you could have me to tea.'

Maureen was childlike in her enthusiasm. Elizabeth was the first person to have called her a married lady, she was the only one to make something special about being married.

'She's so educated, and interested in things,' said Maureen, busy learning all the hallmarks to blind the Dalys with this new sophistication. 'I wish you were more like Elizabeth, Aisling.'

'Oh people have always been wishing that,' said Aisling cheerfully, 'but it never does them any good.'

Secretly she thought it was a bit wet of Elizabeth to have written such a gooey letter to Maureen and she thought that looking up all these ridiculous names of towns and marks of sterling and makers was just *typical*.

Dear Elizabeth,
You said to write about the wedding, honestly I don't know what to write. The main thing is that it went without any disasters. Father O'Mara was drunk, but people stopped him making a fool of himself, and Brendan Daly was a bit drunk. He's my brother-in-law you know. I'll be able to say things I heard from *my brother-in-law*, but I don't think I heard anything from him. His sister Sheila, do you remember her at school? I'm not surprised if you don't, she was mousy then and she is mousy now. She normally wears glasses but she didn't for the wedding and she fell over everything, and her eyes were all screwed up trying to peer out. I told her she was better with them, but that was the wrong thing to say apparently. The speeches were endless, I looked really dreadful. I know I've thought I looked dreadful in the past but that was actual beauty compared to the bridesmaid dress. If ever you get over here I'll show it to you. Maureen said it could be changed and used as a dance dress. I said I wanted to keep it for the rest of my life as fancy dress. Another wrong thing to say.

I told you, didn't I, about sort of going with Ned Barrett? There's nothing to it, we go for walks by the river, and a bit of messing about, but nothing great. We go to the pictures and meet inside too. I don't think they'd forbid me to meet him but I couldn't bear all the fuss, and people saying 'You're next'. I don't want to marry Ned Barrett, I just want to practise on him. I was practising a bit down by the river on the corner near the boathouse when who came by but Tony Murray, you know, Joannie's brother. He gave me a desperate look. I think he thinks Joannie and I are sex-maniacs, because of the incident. Joannie's gone to learn a year's domestic science in a place where nearly everyone else is a lady or an Hon. That's how posh they've become. She says it's awful and she'd prefer to be at home. I've got an interview soon for a job, a *real* job, in Murray's. Mam says that if Joannie and I are friends then I'm stupid to go and work in the office for them and get a salary. It will change the relationship. I don't agree. Everyone's got to work somewhere. What are you doing? You never tell me properly.

Love,
Aisling

Dear Aisling,
I never tell properly! I tell you *everything*, you tell *nothing! What* incident makes Joannie's brother think you're sex-maniacs? Why did you look so awful in the dress? What was it like? How is Donal's chest? Is Peggy still there – you never mention her? What's Maureen's new house like? Is Uncle Sean's business going well, does Aunt Eileen still work so hard? Are you really fat or was that just a remark of Maureen's? There's so much I don't know. It makes Kilgarret all seem like a book I read ages ago about a place that's not there any more.

Anyway, to tell you properly about me. Well it's hard because you don't know what life here is like. If I said that Father looks much smarter these days and plays bridge three times a week, you wouldn't know what a change that is. It's as if Uncle Sean suddenly started going to tea parties or something. I get a letter from Mother every week. She and Harry have a shop. She keeps asking me to go and visit them and I'm going to go in November. Term has started in the art college. I didn't realise how lucky I was to have got a place. They made about a dozen speeches telling us we were the *crème de la crème* and that we must fight to keep our places, because there are hundreds outside waiting for one of us to be thrown out.

The others in the class are very nice. It's a bit different to the convent, there are hardly any girls. Imagine. I think Aunt Eileen is right about not working for the Murrays. Suppose you wanted more salary, suppose they wanted to sack you? Won't the other people who work for them feel a bit annoyed when you can go to their house and they can't? Anyway I don't suppose I know anything about it, it just doesn't sound too easy.

I've got a job too, on Saturdays. I work in the antique shop I told you about. It's terrific. I dust the china and the small pieces of furniture, and I fill in stock lists and help when customers come in. It's run by a super old man called Mr Worsky. He's Polish, he came over here just before the war. He has two full-time people. His old lady friend, who is sweet but she's almost blind, and an assistant called Johnny Stone. It sounds like a cowboy's name doesn't it? He's rather like a cowboy too. Very handsome. But not in the shop a lot, alas. He's prowling the country looking for antiques. Love to everyone. Do they remember me? Do they talk much about what became of me?

Elizabeth

VIII

Aisling did not get the job in Murray's. In fact her interview lasted three minutes. She had dressed up exactly as they had told the girls to do in the commercial college; neat grey suit, grey short-sleeved jumper and white collar. No jewellery, very little make-up.

With her gloved hand, she handed copies of her typewriting, short-hand and book-keeping certificates to Mr Meade, who had been running Murray's since Joannie's father had died. As long as most people could remember.

Mr Meade had left the room to study the certificates as if there was a possibility they might be forgeries. Aisling looked around the office. It had a high ceiling and a lot of bookshelves and cabinets of different sizes and shapes. Their pigeon-holes were bursting with envelopes and files, with loosely tied together bunches of documents. It was very untidy and dusty, she thought disapprovingly. Even Mam's little eyrie back in the shop was better than this. At no stage of their secretarial training had anyone told them about an office which seemed to have no proper filing cabinets, no spacious tables and desks for working at. There was one corner of the room which had great boxes with hundreds of labels spilling on to the floor; many of the labels were stained and probably unusable. Aisling's fingers itched to get at them.

The room smelled funny too, of spices, or teas or coffees, she wasn't sure which, because there was another waft coming in on top. A smell of drink . . . a bit like Maher's on a Thursday night. This must be from the wine downstairs, she thought. She wondered how they could be so successful when they were so disorganised. At secretarial college they had stressed that an untidy office was an inefficient office. But then Maureen had said that they spent months learning how to make perfect corners on beds when she was training as a nurse, and mainly they never did them unless there was a fear that someone would inspect them.

Mr Meade came back, and to his annoyance and to Aisling's surprise, Tony Murray followed close behind him. Mr Meade seemed nervous in the present of Mr Tony. Mr Tony seemed irritated to extremes by Mr Meade. The typing certificates were handed over.

'These seem to be in order, Mr Tony,' said Mr Meade. He had examined each piece of paper carefully.

'Yes, well she's been there a year, they must have taught her to type,' said Tony ungraciously.

Mr Meade looked put out.

'What makes you think you would like to work here?' he asked precisely.

Aisling was ready for that one. 'I've always thought it would be most interesting to work in a company that offers such variety,' she said, as if reciting lines from a play. 'Murray's is an old-established firm with a long history of business with continental Europe. There would be an opportunity for me to know about the wine trade, the tea blending, the whiskey bonding as well as high-class grocery trade.'

'You would be sitting in an office typing out bills and stock lists. How the hell will you learn the wine business there?' interrupted Tony.

'Well I will be close to it, connected with it sort of . . .' Aisling stammered. Tony had always been nice to her, courteous, even joky she thought. Why had he turned into this kind of hectoring figure?

It seemed to puzzle Mr Meade too. 'I'm sure that . . . er, Miss O'Connor, realises . . .' he began.

'Quit talking like a parrot, Aisling, what on earth do you want to work here for? It's the same work you could do for your mother over in the square. Why aren't you in there typing bills and stock lists instead of wanting to come here?'

Aisling's eyes blazed back at him in rage. If he was going to break the rules and make a mockery out of the interview, then so was she. She had played fair, worn gloves, kept her eyes down, answered politely. Now she'd answer him as he wanted.

'I'll tell you, Tony Murray,' she said, conscious of the shock on Mr Meade's face without even looking. 'I'll tell you exactly why I want to work here. Here I work in my own twin-set and skirt, in Mam's shop I'd wear an overall; here I'd get money from your family and I'd spend it as I bloody pleased, in Ma and Da's shop they'd be giving me money like pocket money and complaining and saying sit up, and stop fidgeting, and why aren't these done, like they say to Eamonn. In Murray's I'd be someone, I'd be that new Miss O'Connor in the accounts office, I'd meet people, I'd have a bit of class because I was good enough to be hired by the great almighty Murrays, and a friend of the family. That's why I thought I'd like to work here. Now you tell me why you don't want me . . .'

'Because you're a friend of Joannie, and we like you coming up to the house, and you're a splash of colour around the place, and I don't want to be paying you a wage packet every week. You stupid thick girl. That's why.' He slammed out of the room.

Aisling shrugged. 'Well give me those back, Mr Meade, I gather I haven't got the job.' She picked up her certificates, put them back in her envelope, peeled off her gloves and put them into her handbag. 'Thanks all the same,' she said shaking hands in a totally over-familiar way for a job applicant.

Mr Meade watched her swinging out through the shop. He had no idea why Mr Tony had behaved in that extraordinary way, but in his heart he was quite relieved. That little O'Connor girl, with her mane of red hair, could have been trouble. She might have been quite a disruptive force in Murray's, and they didn't need that.

Mr Worsky was delighted with Elizabeth White. She was exactly the kind of child he would have liked, solemn and alert. His two sons had been interested only in kicking a ball round the yard back in Poland, and wherever they were today they would never have been thoughtful and interested in beautiful things. She was polite and attentive, she had a little notebook where she wrote down what he told her about furniture. Once she had said that it was she who should pay him for his training rather than take money for her Saturday help in the shop. When she left art school she would love to work as a picture restorer, she thought, or an expert adviser on furniture. They spent happy Saturdays and sometimes both of them would sigh with impatience when a customer came in.

Johnny Stone liked the girl too. Mr Worsky could see that. Johnny would speak flirtatiously to her when they were examining porcelain or the inlaid work on some desk. Elizabeth never responded coquettishly, since she had never seen the remarks as admiration. In a kind fatherly way, Mr Worsky made a few tentative efforts to warn Elizabeth about Johnny Stone's charms and how successful they were.

'For a boy of barely twenty-one he has amazing *succès* with the ladies.'

'Oh does he?' Elizabeth sounded interested, rather than hurt.

Mr Worsky went on then, sure that he was treading on no hurt young love. 'Oh a proper Prince Charming . . . that is why he finds such wonderful things when he goes to people's houses. They let him in, they let him come and rummage in their back rooms and their attics. They let Johnny Stone do what he likes.'

'Marvellous for us that they do, isn't it?' said Elizabeth enthusiastically, and Mr Worsky was touched that she thought herself part of his little shop and relieved that she did not seem to have become a victim of the famous Johnny line of chat.

Elizabeth was too busy to think of romance. She envied other students at college who had less complicated lives to lead. She had to organise the food for the week, she had to balance books like Dora in *David Copperfield* – except that she did it swiftly. Father felt that money was trickling down a drain unless he could see neat columns of figures. The cleaning lady sometimes didn't clean too thoroughly since she felt it was infra-dig to be working for a chit of a girl in a house where the mother had hopped it. Why didn't the girl do the cleaning herself, she wondered. Elizabeth had to tread the careful path which would ensure a higher standard of work without the cleaning lady's dignity being offended to the degree of her putting on her coat and leaving them.

Then there was Father. His bridge playing had been so successful it meant that he had to play host to his group every two weeks or so. On these occasions Elizabeth made sandwiches, served tea and emptied ashtrays. She thought it was worth it because it paid dividends. Father was out at other people's houses almost every second night. She didn't have to feel guilty about him, she didn't have to talk to him, except to ask him about his game when he came home. His face would light up as he helped himself to a small tot of ginger wine, and he became almost animated describing how he had finessed a queen, or his partner had gone for a grand slam on no evidence whatsoever.

Father cared nothing about the Saturdays at the antique shop. He had warned her to be sure to see that Mr Worsky paid her on the nail, foreigners could be very decent but many of them could be highly unreliable. But Father never asked her how much she got, nor did it affect her allowance. Girls need their pin money, he was apt to say from time to time. Father didn't realise either how well Elizabeth ran his house for him. But by encouraging him earnestly to grow his own vegetables, she saved them a great deal of money, as well as using up Father's copious spare time at weekends. Elizabeth also gave drawing lessons to two little girls who came to the house and sat with their drawing books at the kitchen table while she did her weekly bake. She made bread, pastry, cake, a casserole and peeled all the potatoes that would be needed for the week, leaving them in water which she changed every day. She topped and tailed fruit, she pressed every left-over into something else. It was a three-hour session; and all the while she overlooked the two children, correcting their perspective, lightening their shading and neatening their calligraphy. Their mother, who had artistic hopes and no money, gave Elizabeth jams, bottled plums, chutneys and even candied peel, for their lessons. It worked very well, and Elizabeth ran Father's home very comfortably while keeping a good quarter of the money it should have taken, in her own little tin box upstairs. Even Aunt Eileen, with all her religion, could hardly have disapproved, Elizabeth thought . . . She really did earn the money and if Father had anyone else, even Mother, it would have been spent in areas where Elizabeth was able to save.

She didn't know why she was saving. Perhaps it was for flight like Mother, perhaps it was to set herself up in business like Mr Worsky. It might even be for a velvet dress. Johnny Stone had told her about a singer he had seen who wore a rose-coloured velvet dress and it had made her seem like a flower. She had blonde hair and a rose velvet dress; Johnny had said it was like heaven.

Aisling had been mystified by the whole afternoon in Murray's, when she had gone along confidently expecting to get a job. She was at a loss to explain it to anyone. Mam had been right of course, and so, at long distance, had Elizabeth. Joannie wasn't there so there was nobody to ask, nobody to discuss it with. From nowhere Aisling remembered a line from one of Elizabeth's letters saying the hardest thing about growing up is not having anyone to ask. Aisling had thought it was only because the White family had more or less disappeared, leaving Elizabeth on her own; but now she realised that it was more than that. There are some things you can't just throw on somebody's else's life. This was one of them. She decided that since she was all dressed up she would get another job instead.

She called first at the chemist and spoke to Mr Moriarty. She made her voice light and cheerful, she showed him her commercial college certificates, she thought she would enquire around some of the nicer places in town, she said. The Moriartys said that there was hardly any work that they and the young man who worked there couldn't do. She went to the insurance broker, the solicitor and the jeweller's. None of them needed anyone. They all complimented Aisling on how well she looked and said she was a sensible girl to want to work in her own town, and that something would turn up. The bank she knew didn't hire people from the town; they had to come from far away so that they wouldn't know people's business and gossip about it. The hotel had a receptionist, the two doctors had receptionists. The grain merchants were Protestants, and it would be too common to work anywhere else. Weary and depressed she came into the shop ten minutes before closing time.

'Mam can I have a word with you up in the eyrie,' she called.

'What is it?' Eileen lifted her glasses to see Aisling properly. She saw a tired and disappointed-looking child, very different to the bouncy figure who had set out just after lunch. 'Come on up here,' she called.

Aisling made the little flight of stairs and flopped on to a stool.

'Mam, I've been thinking,' she said.

'Yes, and what have you thought?'

'I've been thinking that you'd be nearing the end of your work here.'

'Oh really?'

'Yes, a woman of nearly fifty as you were saying . . . .'

'A woman of forty-eight so I am . . . .'

'Yes, but I'm a woman of eighteen and honestly, if this place is ever to be a success, the whole family had better try to pull together you know and . . .'

'Oh I see . . . .'

'No, you don't, you work too hard, everyone says so. When anyone says to you why don't you get someone to help, you always list the problems. Why can't I do it Mam? I'm trained, I have all my certificates . . . what do you think Mam?'

'Well, it's a bit sudden, child, I mean you never wanted to help out here when we were busy, or you never thought of working here before, so far as your father and I ever thought anyway . . . .'

'I didn't want to help out, Mam, that's the whole point. I wanted to work like a real person. You know, hours and wages and pulling my weight . . . you know?'

'Well, I'll have to talk to your father . . . it's a bit of a surprise.'

'Sure, Da will do what you say Mam, you know he will.'

137

'I know nothing of the sort. This is your father's business, he's very particular about who he hires. Maybe he might think you'd be a bit . . .'

'A bit what, Mam?'

'Well, young.'

'You mean flighty,' said Aisling mulishly.

'Yes, I mean flighty,' said Mam, simply.

'I'm not flighty any more, not if I'm getting a real salary, and could be sacked and all,' Aisling said.

'You changed your mind about Murray's, then?' Mam asked quietly.

'Oh yes, I went and had a chat, it was more of a chat, nor a normal interview. Tony Murray and I agreed it wasn't such a great idea . . . .'

'And you wouldn't rather work, say in the hotel or the chemist where you'd meet more people . . .?' Mam was gentle.

'No, the Moriartys would only have a living for themselves and the hotel has Judy Lynch.'

'And the insurance, or the bank . . .?'

'No, they have their own people. Now what I had in mind was building up this place, Mam, like a real big family business. You know, you and Da and Eamonn and myself all talking about the future, and maybe when Donal gets older, some not too tiring job for him . . .'

Mam was smiling. She seemed to find something funny.

'Well, it's what people do,' Aisling said crossly.

Mam reached over and took her hand. 'And what about Niamh, will we find her a job in this new enlarged family business?'

'I think Niamh had better marry some money and get us the cash to expand. Build on out the back,' said Aisling.

'I'll suggest it to her at supper,' said Mam.

Aisling snatched back her hand. 'You're not taking me seriously,' she snapped.

'I am, child, I am indeed . . . I'll have a word with your Da. If he says yes, when would you like to start?'

Aisling threw her arms around Eileen, knocking off the glasses which had been perched on her forehead. 'On Monday, Mam, and could I not have to wear a shop-coat like you? Could I wear my own clothes?'

'They'd get very dirty, love, that's why we all wear coats, the dust.'

'But Mam, I'd keep my clothes clean, I promise.'

'They'd be destroyed, you'd spend your whole salary replacing them. I'm telling you from experience. We'll get you a nice shop-coat, whatever colour you like.'

'But Mam, it doesn't look right, not after all that course and learning all the shorthand and the rest. A shop-coat.'

'You'd look beautiful in green; suppose we got you a couple of emerald green coats to wear over your clothes?'

'Would it look . . .?'

'It would look unusual, special, you'd be the most eye-catching woman in Kilgarret. You're a beautiful-looking girl, Aisling.'

Aisling didn't know what to say.

'For goodness sake, go on, Mam,' she said eventually.

'You are. Don't you know it? With all the titivating you do on yourself?'

'Am I nice-looking?' Aisling asked shyly.

'You're lovely, far too good for that Ned Barrett, but that's your own choice, I suppose.'

'Mam, how on earth do you know about Ned Barrett?' Aisling was stunned. 'Not that there's anything to know,' she added quickly.

'No, of course not,' said Mam. 'But when you're nearly fifty like me you have to go round imagining things . . . it passes the time.'

'I don't think I'm going to be one of those people who get seriously interested in men. I really don't.'

'Oh, I'm sure you're right, Aisling, one has a feeling about that sort of thing.'

'Mam?'

'Yes love.'

'If Da says yes, can people call me Miss O'Connor, can some people call me Miss O'Connor anyway?'

'I'll insist on it . . . from the start.'

Johnny Stone said that he would be very happy to take Elizabeth up to Preston. He was going to make a journey into the dark north for Mr Worsky anyway with the van, so why not have Elizabeth along for company? She could make calls with him, learn a bit more about the real and the fake, the kind of things that were beautiful and things that only looked good. What did Mr Worsky think?

Mr Worsky thought it was up to Elizabeth and her father. If they had no objection, then he would be delighted of course. To have two staff on the road for him was coming up in the world. He did not foresee any awkward entanglement, where the little solemn face of Elizabeth might become hurt and bewildered. The child was grown-up beyond her years already. She could handle a Romeo like Mr Johnny Stone.

Elizabeth did not discuss her transport with Father. She simply told him that she would use the half-term break from college to pay Mother the long-promised visit. Harry had sent money for her; no, she did not need anything extra, just the normal allowance was fine. She carefully arranged that the first night of her absence, Father's meal would be there. But after that for five days he would have to manage on his own. Then he might appreciate more how smoothly and efficiently she ran his house. She also left that week's housekeeping money for him in an envelope, knowing that it would not stretch in any way to meet his needs. She did not think that this was cruel. She thought it was sensible. Father was living a strange life between the bank and the bridge table, far far away from reality. It would be no harm to bring him down to a few basics.

Dearest Elizabeth,

Harry and I are so pleased, so very pleased that you are really coming. I wake up every morning and I say to myself it's only nine more days now. Harry wanted to know whether it was like this during the war, whether I counted all the days when you were in Ireland? I don't think it was the same. I knew you were safe and well and happy. I read those letters every week and I couldn't think what to write back, there was so little to say about our empty house and about the long, weary hours in the munitions factory.

Here it's different. I think of you at home in Clarence Gardens. I think of the kitchen, and of your Father . . . I can't imagine what it's like for you there now. I wish . . . in a foolish sort of way that I was there, because you and I could talk. You could tell me all about Mr Worsky's shop, and I could go in and see it; I am sure that George doesn't even know where it is. At least I did buy some fire irons there once.

I hope you like our place. Harry has worked until after midnight for over two weeks 'to have things right for Elizabeth'. I don't think I'm telling you this so that you will be prepared to make a lot of admiring noises. But perhaps I am. We never made many admiring noises when you were younger, and I remember that week when you came back from Kilgarret you said that everyone reacted more in the O'Connors' house than in school. I'm just rambling on darling.

Only eight and a half days.

Love,

Violet.

'Why does she call herself Violet?' Johnny Stone asked Elizabeth the day they set off. It was to be a two-day journey.

'When she went away with Harry she started signing Violet. It's funny but it seemed quite right somehow. I suppose she thought that if she wasn't doing the job of being mother, then she shouldn't call herself Mother.'

'My mother never did the job of being mother but she still calls herself that: ever your loving mother. I think I'll have to tell her that she should call herself Martha. You're younger than I am, I'll use you as an example. Listen, Martha old bean, I'll say, my friend Elizabeth's only eighteen and she and her mother use first names. The world's changing, old dear, I'll say.'

Elizabeth laughed. 'It's not as easy as that. I still think of her as Mother. I'm going to try to feel out the ground a bit when I meet her. She may like to be called Mother still. She may prefer not. I cheat in letters you see. Dear Both. I worked it out, it was affectionate but not specific if you see.'

Johnny saw. The signposts flashed by, the miles disappeared under the wheels of the old van. Elizabeth unpacked a picnic which they had to eat in the car, since April torrents and winds were howling around them.

They had two calls to make that day. Johnny and Elizabeth crawled around a disused summer-house and collected forty old pictures, some cracked, some so gaudy that Elizabeth couldn't see for the life of her what Mr Worsky would do with them. 'The frames, you silly,' hissed Johnny as they pulled wicker chairs and old cricket bats and croquet mallets out in their search.

The lady who owned the frames, and the summer-house, offered them tea and biscuits and was overjoyed at the small sum that Johnny gave her. Before they left she asked Johnny whether his young lady would like to use the bathroom. Elizabeth flushed, not at the mention of bathrooms but at the woman's mistaking her for Johnny's young lady.

'She's more my colleague than my young lady,' Johnny grinned. 'But seeing you blush like that, Elizabeth, maybe I'll change my mind.'

Elizabeth fled to the bathroom and tried to hide her red-cheeks by rubbing in some of the talcum powder that was beside the hand-basin.

Back in the van she launched an immediate attack.

'If those are really mahogany and really silver frames, you didn't give her nearly enough,' she complained.

'Dear girl. She was delighted with what we gave her. Delighted. She pressed my hand in thanks, she's going to have the roof mended. She's going to ask a local handyman to come in and paint her living room. Now is that happy or not happy? What do you want me to do, throw poor Stefan's money down the drain . . .?'

'But Mr Worsky wouldn't want to cheat . . . .'

'Seriously Elizabeth, that woman had those pictures rotting in her tool shed or whatever it was for years. Her husband had always meant to clean up. He never did. He never came back from the war either. Now what happens? We come down, we spend two hours cleaning up, tidying her old shed. You got a broom for heaven's sake. She has a tidy place to put her deck-chair, if it's ever going to stop raining in the next few years, she's got cash in hand to have a new roof, a new-coloured sitting room and a new hat. Now what's that but happiness?'

'It's tricking her. We'll get thirty or forty times what you paid. You gave her thirty-three pounds. The big gilt frame alone will fetch that. More even, if we do it up. And there's twenty-nine others. It's downright dishonest!'

'It's business, you stupid girl, and you look terrific when your face is all red like that. It's really peaches and cream. Typical English rose, you should do it more often.'

'Does it really look nice, or is that a cruel joke?' Elizabeth asked.

'Of course it's nice, whole fortunes are spent by women trying to get their faces to look like that,' said Johnny.

'I was afraid it looked a bit consumptive, you know, too much contrast,' Elizabeth said seriously.

Johnny laughed so much he had to pull the van up on the side of the road. 'You are totally beautiful,' he said affectionately. 'I wish the old bird back there was right and you were my young lady.'

'I'd be no good at being someone's young lady, I'm not ready for it yet. Life's too complicated, there are too many things to sort out.' Elizabeth was utterly sincere. There was no way that she was hoping to be contradicted.

'When do you imagine things will be sorted out?' asked Johnny.

'I expect when I've finished college and get a job, and when Father's learned to live on his own, or have a housekeeper or something . . . about three years I expect.'

'I'll have to come and apply to be your young man then,' Johnny said. 'If I'm not too old that is . . . I'll be nearly a quarter of a century.'

'Yes,' said Elizabeth consideredly. 'You'll probably have given up playing around by then. But I expect I'll find somebody.'

They stayed in the guesthouse that was owned by Mr Worsky's cousin outside Liverpool. The second call had been equally contentious. Johnny had offered an old man twenty pounds for three mirrors and a table. According to Elizabeth they would fetch over one hundred pounds in the shop. Johnny had walked down the steps to the van with her before he clinched the deal. The little old man peered anxiously out of the window, terrified they would leave without buying the pieces.

'Once again, Stefan Worsky pays for a shop, he pays me a salary, he pays you something, he puts the petrol in the bloody van, he pays for me to stay with his cousin, he spends hours of his time and his skill – don't forget his skill and training, which took years to come by – in doing up these tables and mirrors. Then, and only then, will he get one hundred pounds for them. Now that's what the world calls business. It's not a well-kept secret. It's what people know happens. Have I your permission to offer this poor bugger twenty pounds before he has a heart attack, or should we cancel the whole thing, break his heart, mine and Stefan's just because Madam White here thinks she knows how to run the world?'

Elizabeth burst into tears. Johnny paid the perplexed man twenty-five pounds instead of the twenty he had been quite willing to accept. In confusion, they bundled the furniture into the van while Elizabeth sobbed in the front seat. In silence they headed for Mr Worsky's cousin's house.

'Do you think we might have a half pint somewhere while the storms abate?' Johnny asked. It was the first thing he had said in eleven miles. Elizabeth nodded. She wasn't able to speak.

They sat in a pub and, red-eyed, she drank a brandy and ginger wine which Johnny said might be just the thing. He made no attempt to cheer her up, to apologise for his loss of temper or to enquire why she cried so long and so deeply.

The brandy warmed her and she had another.

Then, in a small voice, she asked him about Liverpool. Was it a big place, suppose she wanted to find a small place called Jubilee Terrace, would that be possible? Was it idiotic? During her second brandy she told Johnny about Sean O'Connor and how Aunt Eileen had always said that if ever she got anywhere near Liverpool, could she say hallo to Amy Sparks. It was such ages ago, five years. Of course, Mrs Amy Sparks and her son Gerry might be dead. But just because Aunt Eileen had once said . . . no, it was silly, Johnny mustn't listen to her, she was just being silly.

'We're far too early for Stefan's cousin, why don't we see if we can find it?' said Johnny.

Gerry Sparks had had a stroke of luck, he said, in that he was good with his hands. He was a watchmaker and he could do a lot of work at home. They fixed a tray on his wheelchair, and he could spread all the bits and bobs out on it and look through his magnifying glass at them. It was a real bit of luck that they discovered his skill in the therapy classes, because the legs hadn't taken. Not enough for them to grab on to, didn't manage to use the muscles from the hips like other fellows did.

Mrs Sparks was now Mrs Benson. She had remarried, as a sensible thing to do; she was able to look after Mr Benson, and cook his meals, keep his shirts nice and clean, he could give her his pension. They had sold his little house and made a tidy profit. They were so pleased to meet Elizabeth and her young man; they knew all about her. Eileen O'Connor, a wonderful woman, wrote a long letter every Christmas and she sent money to the church in Liverpool where they had held this Mass for Sean.

They talked about Sean. Gerry said he had been a great mate, he'd never had a mate like Sean before. Elizabeth said he had always been restless when she knew him in Kilgarret. But then she was very young and maybe she hadn't really been able to talk to him.

'I never knew a mate like him,' Gerry Sparks said again. 'Certainly never knew one since then.'

He looked down at his rug on the wheelchair.

'Of course, like this it stands to reason I don't make many mates these days.'

'Yeah, that's the trouble when you work on your own,' Johnny agreed, having deliberately misunderstood him. 'You don't have mates at work, you miss that. Of course, there are advantages working on your own. If you feel like knocking off an hour earlier or taking a long lunch you can do it.'

Gerry brightened up. Together they talked about working on your own, piece-work rate for the hour. Johnny even went out to the car and asked Gerry's advice about an old clock that he had picked up at a sale of work. 'I only bought it for the face, but I think the insides are like scrambled egg.' Gerry had his eyeglass out, and in minutes it was ticking. The small kitchen filled with pride until it burst. Elizabeth couldn't have imagined anything that would have brought more pleasure. Addresses were exchanged, if ever any work came the way of Mr Worsky which needed the touch of a craftsman it would be sent to Gerry Sparks.

In the firelight and under the dim centre-bulb the peaky face and bent back of Gerry Sparks was joined with the handsome young Johnny Stone. If they had met in Italy they might have been mates too. But of course Johnny Stone wasn't old enough to put on a uniform, and the year that he was just old enough they stopped fighting. Elizabeth and Mr and Mrs Benson seemed to exchange innocent, pleased looks about the conversation at the fire. But it was something that could never have been put into words.

Mr Worsky's cousin was not at all interested in their visit to a house in Jubilee Terrace, a small, poor little place. She was very interested in Elizabeth, a lovely young woman, just right for Mr Stone, and very right for Mr Stone to settle down, too, no more of the romancing.

'It's just as well I'm not your young lady,' said Elizabeth wearily as she climbed the stairs to her bedroom. 'Since we left London this morning, everyone has assumed I am and that I have a dreadful time with you.'

Could it really only have been this morning that she had said goodbye to Father? She hadn't given him a thought all day. Perhaps that's what happened to Mother. But then they were married, which was different. She wondered whether Mother would like to be called Violet tomorrow. She wondered whether Johnny would come in and call like he had at the Sparks's house. She wondered how Gerry Sparks got out of his wheelchair when he wanted to go to the bathroom, and whether she should try to stay awake and write to Aunt Eileen about the visit . . . .

There were three more calls on the way to Preston. Elizabeth said nothing about the prices offered to and accepted by a war widow, a clergyman and an elderly doctor. She helped willingly and cooperatively, she wrote things down in her little notebook and she scrambled under a bed in a loft with Johnny where their hands touched over some old silver-backed brushes. When they took them downstairs the old doctor said that he vaguely remembered them from his childhood.

'I'll buy them if you like,' Johnny said.

'Oh, they're filthy now, and the hair's all rotting. I'd be ashamed to sell them, I'll throw them out,' said the old man.

'They could be nice if we got them done up, polished you know, and new bristles,' said Johnny.

He caught Elizabeth's eye before she looked away.

'And valuable, Doctor,' he went on. 'We might be able to sell them for a lot more than we give you.'

The old doctor smiled.

'Well, I should hope so my boy,' he said agreeably. 'Otherwise what's the whole business about?'

Johnny celebrated his triumph by avoiding Elizabeth's eye.

When the signposts said that Preston was only five miles away Elizabeth turned to Johnny almost shyly.

'I hope you'll come and stay for supper . . . I don't think they'd have a bed for the night. Not if Harry's been making all this palaver over doing up the guest room for me, you know. But supper would be super.'

'Why don't I just see you in the door, say Hi to Harry and Vi and push off, arrange what time to pick you up on Tuesday and let the family get together as nature intended?'

'It's not the family, you know that,' Elizabeth sounded troubled.

'I know but it's enough strain on everyone without having a total stranger there sitting in on it.'

'But you're . . . you're very good at making chat and sort of helping things along. Please come in and stay.'

'Listen, I'll come in and see what I think. If I think it's better for me to go I'll toddle off, if I think I'm helping I'll hang around a bit. Will that do?'

Elizabeth nodded. He took her hand and patted it. 'You don't have, you didn't have any awkwardnesses in your family, you know with your mum who calls herself your-ever-loving-mother?'

'Awkwardnesses? No. Not really,' he negotiated the wet, slippy road. 'What do you mean exactly?'

'You know, like them being too loving or not loving enough. You know. Like them being not what you expected or wanted.'

'Oh no, heavens, no,' Johnny laughed. 'My mother would like me to live with her and have a small car and drive her to see her friends . . . but I don't like that as a way of life so I have no intention of doing it. None at all. My mother's father wanted her to stay at home and look after him, but she didn't, she ran away with my father. People do what they want to do. Once you know that and accept it you don't have any problems.'

'And your father?'

'He ran off with someone else, with two someone elses. He ran off with people every ten years or so, my mother was the second. He's frightfully keen on running off with people . . . .'

'And you don't see him?'

'Why on earth should I? He doesn't want to see me. Look, it's not like your case, these folk have been painting a room for you for ages. They want you to come, you wanted to come . . . where's the awkwardness? There's no lies or demands or emotions.'

'You hate that sort of thing, don't you?' said Elizabeth.

'Doesn't everyone?'

'I think you do more than most, you were very annoyed when I was crying yesterday. I could see it.'

'No, my dear, honestly, I wasn't annoyed. It's just, I don't know, I don't want to get involved in dramas and tears and heightened scenes. So I never do.'

'It's not a bad philosophy I suppose.'

'It has its drawbacks. People think I'm a bit cold or selfish or too flippant . . . but perhaps all these things are true . . . Heigh ho, Preston, jewel of the North, here we come.'

'Do stay to supper,' she said.

'If they ask me,' he promised.

The bedroom almost brought tears to Elizabeth's eyes. Only the thought of having Johnny see her once more with a red, puffy face held them back. Harry had bought expensive and hideous ornaments which stood on the shelf. 'Girls like pretty things,' he said proudly as he looked at them. The utility furniture had all been painted white and so had rather a nice little bookcase which used to have doors. Elizabeth could see the hinges but they were painted over too. The bed had a flouncy blue and white spread; pictures in what she would now think of as the most awful chocolate-box tradition in shiny new frames covered the walls. In those days of shortages Harry had painted everything in sight. The blue carpet went wall to wall and you could see that he had stitched scraps together to get it to fit properly. His face beamed with achievement.

Johnny spoke first. He was marvelling at the things that should be marvelled at, how perfect the paint surface was . . . were three? three . . . yes, he had thought there must be three coats. Johnny marvelled too at how cleverly the electricity work had been done, a light over the bed, another over the wash-hand basin. He praised the bright, clear colours which made it look so cheery even in winter. As he spoke, Elizabeth found her tongue to praise and thank and marvel. She left her bag on the bed and looked around her with gratitude that nearly made Harry crack apart, so broad was his smile. Spontaneously she hugged him, and when she saw the delight in Mother's eyes she hugged Mother too. It has been a peck on the cheek as she had come in the front door of the shabby little corner shop.

'Oh Mother, this is great,' she cried. Mother hugged her back. Over Mother's shoulder she saw Johnny nodding slightly and she knew she had been right to decide not to say Violet.

Johnny stayed to supper, the atmosphere growing more and more cordial. Harry was like a big child, he had grown fatter and more genial in the two years. Mother had become even thinner, if that were possible; she seemed nervy, she smoked a lot and her eyes looked huge in her thin face. She jumped up half a dozen times, nervous, anxious to please.

They both seemed pleased, in a childish and obvious way, that Johnny did not know Father, Elizabeth thought, in fact Harry went so far as to say, 'That's good, lad, we're the first to have a look at you, eh?' as if Elizabeth had taken Johnny there on some kind of tour of approval.

Elizabeth answered that one without any embarrassment.

'The reason that Johnny doesn't know Father is that Johnny is in Mr Worsky's and Father, as you said in your letter, Mother, hardly knows where the antique shop is.' She paused and, lest it appear to leave an opportunity for Father to be criticised, she spoke again. 'You would be amazed at Father really, both of you. He is such a bridge addict now. No worries about what to get him for Christmas, new cards or scoring pads, or little bridge ashtrays. And he meets people all the time. As soon as somebody new comes to the area, if they can play bridge he's met them in a week.'

'Fancy George having a whole circle of friends.' Mother was mildly amazed, as if it were a story about someone she knew a long time ago.

'They're not exactly friends,' Elizabeth was thoughtful.

'Of course they're friends,' interrupted Johnny, 'if he goes to their houses and they come to Clarence Gardens, what are they? Enemies? Honestly, Elizabeth, you want people to exchange blood from their arms like Red Indians.'

Everyone laughed.

'We did that in Ireland once, Aisling and I,' said Elizabeth suddenly. 'I'd quite forgotten.'

'Yes, well you see,' said Harry meaninglessly. He was trying to say something that would make that Johnny realise he was on his side.

It worked. Johnny put his arm around Harry's shoulder. 'Let the girls talk a bit, Harry, and you show me this workshop of yours, and if you come across any of those old weighing scales on your travels, you know the old-fashioned ones with brass weights . . .'

Mother lit another cigarette and leaned across to clutch Elizabeth's arm.

'Oh, my dear, he's so nice, he's such a nice young man. I'm simply delighted for you. I worried about that too . . . you know, as well as anything else. I worried that you mightn't have a boyfriend or a social life. You mention so little about it in your letters.'

Elizabeth signed. 'I suppose it's useless my telling you that he isn't my boyfriend. Really, until today and yesterday we've hardly even had a proper conversation. He's someone I work with on Saturdays. But I agree, he is very nice, isn't he? He's been great company, simply smashing on the trip. The time just flew by.'

'I know,' said Mother. 'That's what's wonderful about being with the right person.' They spoke of him a lot during the weekend, which was a good thing as it kept them off the topic of Father.

Mother felt guilty about Father, she felt guilty about walking out with no proper explanations.

'I don't think explanations would have done much good,' Elizabeth said several times, feeling years older than she had felt the day Mother left Clarence Gardens. 'Father doesn't listen much, I've come to think.'

Sometimes Harry spoke about Father too, in a worried tone. 'You're a grown-up young woman, Elizabeth, and I don't want to sound like an adult talking to a child . . . but your mother and I worry about you down in that house, it's not healthy for a child to live alone with a . . . well with such a remote man as your father. Now Violet won't hear a word against him, and I wouldn't speak one word either against a person's father but you have to agree that he's an odd fish, a cold person. He has no blood. A real cold fish. There's an art college in Preston . . . .'

'I know, Harry, but . . .'

'And we'd be no interference, I mean you've been having your own way, you could have whoever you liked into your own room . . . that's a fair offer. We'd give you a key, you could come and go. Violet's eyes light up now that you're here . . . and mine too. I think it's champion, as they say here, to have you in and out . . . .'

'You're very kind, Harry,' sighed Elizabeth, and meant it. And she also meant it when she said that Mother was marvellous to her and had been like the kind of elder sister you read about in books. But no, she must really stay where she was. And no, really, she wouldn't join the general outcry against Father. He had a life to live just like everyone else, and he lived it. If they didn't have much joy that was bad luck and circumstance.

They eventually stopped trying to change her mind. In her shiny new bedroom, Elizabeth lay awake at night listening to the strange sounds of a different city and wondered whether everyone else had to keep being kind to people and talking down to them. She wished that someone would make all the decisions for her, and consult her views and take her moods into consideration.

In what seemed like a totally separate part of her mind she wondered how Johnny was getting on, and whether he would come back with a rabbit for dinner as he had promised Harry he would.

The rabbit was a great success. Johnny had arrived when the shop was very busy. Mother and Harry were both dealing with children who spent thirty minutes trying to decide how to spend their tuppences and their sweet points. Tired women buying thin slices of pressed meat and packets of semolina, old men shuffling in for tobacco. Elizabeth had been reading in the kitchen when she heard the cries of welcome for Johnny in the shop. Harry rushed back in beaming like an idiot.

'He's here, he's here, and he didn't forget, he's got the rabbit. Hurry Elizabeth, there's a dear, get out the pot. Your mother will be in in a minute . . . .'

Elizabeth wondered how she could have ever feared Harry, or Mr Elton as she had called him then. How could she have thought him a sophisticated dangerous man, he was a big baby. She wished that he could be more cool, less excited, Johnny might think they were all very simple and overimpressed by him.

But no, Johnny seemed just as excited. 'I'm going to spend the night here, and we'll leave early tomorrow. Your mother's invited me. We'll have the best rabbit pie ever eaten in this country since before the war.'

It *was* the best rabbit pie that had been eaten in the country since the war. Elizabeth had made pastry, Johnny had gone to the pub for cider. They set a table and Mother made up her face. Johnny told them about how he had got the rabbit. The farmer who had been clearing out his furniture always offered people the chance to shoot a rabbit, because he was too old and arthritic to shoot himself, but he loved to go with another huntsman. Johnny had shot three, one for the farmer, one for his party and one, all wrapped up in wet grass at the back of the van, for Mr Worsky.

And they sang some songs, and Harry recited 'The Green Eye of the Little Yellow God', and Mother did an imitation of how the nuns taught them to curtsey, which was hilarious. Elizabeth was pressed for a party piece. She didn't have any, she said. Mother said that there were always songs in Ireland, that Elizabeth said people used to sing in Maher's. With her hands by her side she began:

Oh Danny Boy
The pipes, the pipes are calling
From o'er the glens
And down the mountain side
The summer's gone and all the leaves are falling
T'is you must go
Must go and I must bide . . .

Then they all joined in:

Oh come you back . . .
When sun shines in the meadow . . .
And when the fields are hushed and white with snow . . .
For I'll be there in sunshine and in shadow . . .
Oh Danny boy, Oh Danny boy, I love you so.

Every one of them, including Johnny, had a tear in their eyes. Oh God, thought Elizabeth, why do I have to wreck everything? Why couldn't she have found a cheerful song to sing, something that would have made people laugh like everyone else was able to do? Why did she have to pick the most mournful song in the world? The one party she had been to since she came back from Kilgarret and now she had to close it down by singing a sad song.

They were washing-up and scraping chairs and putting things away. Everyone was saying what a great night it had been. Mother fussed about sheets and blankets for Johnny, Harry said better be on the road tomorrow before six o'clock in order to avoid the worst of the traffic and the big lorries in the narrow streets.

Elizabeth didn't sleep, she kept jerking awake in the middle of a bad dream where Gerry Sparks from his wheelchair was holding her wrist.

'Why did you come to see me if you weren't going to marry me?' he cried over and over again. Elizabeth felt herself running away while his mother Mrs Benson and Harry shouted after her, 'You're always the same, you start things without thinking and you hurt people . . . .'

After their last afternoon call at an orphanage, where Johnny bought four boxes full of old cutlery, the rain became so heavy that they had to pull in to the side of the road. The windscreen wipers couldn't cope with the torrents hurtling at them. As they sat waiting for it to ease a policeman with a flashing torch came to the window.

'Road's flooded ahead, you'll never get past. We're turning back traffic already. You take your missus back to the town there, only a mile or two, you'll not get to London tonight.'

'Well, you're my witness. I did try to get you home!' Johnny laughed goodnaturedly as he reversed the car and was waved on by the policeman in the sheets of rain.

'What will we do?' Elizabeth asked. She wished she could take everything as casually and cheerfully as Johnny did. Already her mind was racing with problems. What would Father say when she didn't turn up? Should she telephone him now before he left the bank? What time would she get back tomorrow? How could she explain about missing her lectures? Might Mr Worsky think that she and Johnny were just having a good time flitting about the country in his van?

'Have a meal and find somewhere to stay I suppose,' Johnny said.

The small hotel had a fire and a bar. Johnny carried in their two bags and talked to the receptionist while Elizabeth warmed her hands over the flames. He came back and put his arm around her.

'We're in luck, they have a room.'

The woman with the large key in her hand looked at Elizabeth's gloveless and ringless hands.

'Do you and your wife care to go up now and see the room?' she asked with a smirk that made Elizabeth feel so angry she didn't even care about the red flush she felt creeping over her face.

'No, I'm sure it's fine,' Johnny said lightly, 'we'll have a drink if we may, seeing that we're residents, and Elizabeth wants to use the telephone.'

In a few minutes of merciful privacy, Elizabeth got through to the bank. Her father hated being disturbed at work for what he considered trivia. Brusque and irritated, he said that he understood, fine, fine, he'd see her tomorrow then. Goodbye. No regrets, no sympathy at her being caught by flooding, no enquiries about her visit to Preston, no hint that he might have missed her.

No way of knowing that his daughter had one of the major decisions in her life ahead of her in the next few minutes.

She stood longer than she needed, clutching the receiver in the dark little box, wondering what to do now. It must be her own fault, she must have given Johnny the impression that she slept with men and that it would be in order to book them a double room. If she was going to be adamant and refuse his suggestion, then the grown-up thing would be to do it immediately . . . the longer she left it the more awkward it would become.

Johnny was sitting at a table with a beer, and a shandy.

'I thought this is what you'd like,' he said, smiling up at her, hoping that he had made the right choice.

'Yes,' Elizabeth said. They were in a corner away from everyone. The chintzy little lounge bar of the hotel might fill up later with local ladies drinking port and lemon; through the door the bar with its dartboard stood dark and empty in the afternoon of winter. Nobody could hear them. There would be no public scene.

'Yes,' Elizabeth said again. 'A shandy's fine, but Johnny about the room. I must tell you . . .'

'Oh sweet Elizabeth, I was just going to tell *you*. It's got two beds, and it's half the price of two rooms, and she doesn't have two rooms. She said she had just one room left before I said anything so . . .'

'Yes, but . . .'

'So there wasn't a chance for me to say "May I consult the lady?"' He looked not at all upset, just as if he had had to explain something that was self-evident. 'And I'll turn my back when you're putting on your nightie and you promise not to peek at me.'

'But . . .'

'We'll be yards away from each other – we were only a few yards away from each other last night and neither of us got carried away.'

Elizabeth laughed in spite of herself.

'No, that's true,' she agreed.

'Well.' The problem was solved for Johnny.

Elizabeth looked into her glass. If she were to make further protests it would appear as if she thought that Johnny was hopelessly besotted by her and was planning to seduce her. Since he said this wasn't on his mind, it would be arrogant and even pathetic of her to keep up this insistence on a room of her own. But suppose, suppose that there was actually a game involved, and that her agreeing to go to the same room meant agreeing much more . . . .

Johnny said he had to telephone Mr Worsky, he'd be back in a moment. Did Elizabeth want to change? There was a bathroom at the end of the corridor apparently but if a bath was needed you had to ask the lady at the desk and she would get someone to turn on the geyser.

He was gone.

Elizabeth ran upstairs, and changed her blouse. She gave herself an icy wash and examined her face nervously at the bathroom mirror, which was speckled where the bits of mercury or silver had peeled off. She wasn't at all pleased with what she saw. Her hair was so straight, and so pale and colourless. It wasn't blonde like real blondes are blonde yellow-and-gold, it was white, almost as if she were an old woman or an albino. And her face. Oh Lord, why were some people's faces the same colour all over when her face was patchy with great pools of red and valleys of white?

With her hands on her waist she looked critically at what she could see of her figure. It was very awkwardly shaped, she decided. Her breasts were small and pointy, she didn't have that nice swell that sort of 'S' shape that made people raise their eyebrows at each other. In fact she looked like a tall schoolgirl instead of a woman.

With a mixture of relief and disappointment she realised that Johnny couldn't possibly have had any designs on her. Thank heavens she hadn't made a silly fuss.

They had fish and chips in the fish shop up the street. It had looked much more inviting than the hotel dining room even though they did have to run to it through the sheets of rain. They talked about what Mr Worsky would say to each item they had got, and what Elizabeth would do next Saturday in the shop, and why Harry and Violet didn't have any nice furniture, why it was all modern and new and cheap. They talked about Johnny's mother who *did* have nice furniture, but who wasn't warm and welcoming. She'd never put herself out to have a visitor to the house, she just expected her son to be there all the time and sniffed disappointedly when he was not.

Elizabeth told him about Monica and *her* mother, and the complicated lies she had to tell when she went off with chaps. Monica had to keep a small notebook so that she did not get caught out. Johnny said that he thought Monica was very silly; she should tell her mother straight out that she was going to live her own life and she hoped that they could all be friends while she was living it. Then all she would have to put up with was a few sniffs.

'It's different for girls, you see,' Elizabeth said.

'Yes . . . so they keep saying,' Johnny agreed.

They ran back in the rain, and because they had had an early start decided that they should go to bed. Or go *to sleep*, as they kept calling it.

'Do you think we should go back and let you get to sleep, you've a long day tomorrow, the drive back, the unpacking, then college?' Johnny said.

'Yes, I think I will sleep now,' Elizabeth said.

She sat on the side of her bed, the one where she had already put her blue nightdress under the pillow. There was heavy, purple-flocked wall-paper and a huge, ugly dressing table. A small, narrow wardrobe with no room for clothes stood filled with extra blankets and smelling of moth balls. There was one small, white chair; they would both have to put their clothes on that. Elizabeth examined her feet ruefully.

'They got awfully wet, I'll have to go and wash them.' They felt like two little blocks of ice after the cold water, and she had splashed herself all over as well just in case Johnny did . . . well, it would be awful to smell of fish and chips.

She put on her nightie in the bathroom and, peering left and right before she emerged, she decided it was safe to scamper back to their room. Johnny hadn't used the tactful opportunity to get undressed, he was sitting reading the paper on the ugly white chair.

Elizabeth hopped quickly into bed and held the sheets around her chin in an exaggerated imitation of someone shivering.

'I knew you'd try to have your way with me and make me come in and warm you up,' Johnny laughed pleasantly, still turning the pages of the paper.

Elizabeth felt her neck and face go scarlet. 'No, of course I didn't, I wasn't . . .'

He stood up and yawned. 'I'm only teasing you, sweetheart,' he said. He bent and gave her a kiss on the cheek. 'Here, have a look at this and become informed about the world.'

Grateful to have something to do while her embarrassed flushes died down, Elizabeth turned on her side away from him and tried to take in something, anything, on the sports page which was what she had opened . . . .

She heard the creak of his bed, and again, relief mixed with a curious sense of defeat swept over her. Naturally, of course, it would be ridic-ulous to *want* to make love, suppose she became pregnant, suppose it hurt and she were to bleed all over the hotel bed, suppose she wasn't able to do it, suppose he then turned aside and refused to have anything to do with her, which is what the nuns had told them in Kilgarret? If a man is allowed to have his way with a girl he will not respect her, he will have nothing more to do with her, he would not like his own sisters to behave in this way . . . .

'Shall I put the light out or do you want to finish the paper?'

She looked at him and smiled.

'N, I'm so tired, I can't really understand it, I think I'll stop fighting it and go to sleep . . . .'

He put his hand out of his bed and reached for hers. She gave it to him.

'You're a great little companion, it's been a smashing trip. Night love.' He turned out the light and turned over in his bed. Elizabeth heard eleven o'clock strike, and midnight, on the town hall clock, and some time before one the storm rattled against the windows so much that it woke Johnny from his even sleep.

'Hey, are you awake?' he asked.

'Yes, it's a horrible storm.'

'Are you frightened of it?'

'No, not at all. No. Of course not.'

'Pity,' he yawned. 'I hoped you were. I'm terrified of it, of course.'

'Silly,' she giggled.

He lit a match to look at his watch. 'Oh, that's great, hours more sleep.'

'Yes,' said Elizabeth. She could hear him sitting up, and swinging his legs out of bed. He leaned over and held her hand.

'Are you all right?' he asked.

'Oh yes,' she said in a little squeak. In the dark he stood up; she felt him sit on her bed. Her heart was nearly coming through her rib cage.

'Give me a little hug,' he said. She reached up and found him without seeing him. He held her very tightly.

'I'm very fond of you, you're a lovely little girl,' he said. She said nothing. 'Very fond of you.' He was stroking her hair and her back, in long strokes. She felt very safe. 'And you're very very lovely.' She clung to him even more tightly, he was moving her gently back on the pillow; soon she would be lying down.

'I'm not very . . .'

'We won't do anything unless you want to . . . if you want to we can do anything . . . .'

'You see . . .'

'You're very, very lovely,' he stroked on and on and she couldn't really find the right words. 'I'd like to be very, very close to you.'

'But you see . . .'

'There'll be no problem about that, I'll take great care . . . .'

'But I never . . . .'

'I know, I know, I'll be very gentle . . . but only if you want to.' Silence. He stroked her and held her to him. 'Do you want to love me, Elizabeth, do you want to be very close to me . . .?'

'Yes,' she said.

He was gentle, and it didn't matter that she didn't know what to do, he knew enough it seemed. It didn't hurt so much as it was uncomfortable. It wasn't all those piercing pains you heard about in giggled conversations, and it certainly wasn't all that soaring joy either, but Johnny seemed very happy. He lay on her, his head on her breasts and his arms around her.

'You're a lovely little girl, Elizabeth, you made me very happy.'

She held him in the dark, she pulled the covers over him and she heard the town hall clock strike two. She must have missed three, but she heard it again at four o'clock, and she thought of Aisling and how they had wondered which of them would be the first to Do It, and now Elizabeth had won. Or perhaps she hadn't won. After all, she didn't think she was going to write and describe this. It was too important, you couldn't put it on paper, it would sound disloyal and cheap. Instead of love, which is what it was.

IX

Dear Elizabeth,

That was a great book altogether, you always find marvellous present, you have so much imagination. I'm sending you this scarf . . . it's awful I know, but Kilgarret's a far cry from London and you know there's nothing to buy here. Mam and Daddy loved the book too, they said you were very clever to find all those old pictures of Ireland in one book. I love the old ones when Dunlaoghaire was still Kingstown . . . a lot of people, like the Grays and those, still call it Kingstown of course.

Honestly, there's not much to say about the way things are. You'd have to come over yourself and see. I don't *feel* nineteen. I always thought that when I'd be nineteen I'd be different, I'd be a different shape, my face would be thinner and more knowing. I thought I'd have a different life . . . and know a lot different people than when I was young. But it all seems to be more of the same thing.

Well, I suppose I have changed a bit. I can't stand that Ned Barrett near me. I think I've practised all he knows anyway and I'll have to find someone who knows a bit more. From my desk here in the office I can see the bus come in, and twice a day I look at it hopefully in case somebody exciting will step off and book into the hotel. Isn't that pathetic for a grown-up woman in the middle of the twentieth century? Do you remember this time five years ago when we were fourteen and I got my period on my birthday and you didn't, and we thought you were abnormal and Mam had to sort us out? I don't know that being over-normal has done me any good. I wish you'd tell me something about your own life and who you practise on and everything. I feel it would be hard to talk to you. Mam says that's ridiculous, it would take five minutes and we'd be cackling like young geese the way we used to.

It all seems a long time ago. Thanks again for the book. Joannie says the plates in it are so nice I could have them framed but I don't think so, it's nicer as a book. I hope it didn't cost a lot of money. The scarf seems a mean kind of present.

Love from Aisling

Dear Aisling,
I loved the scarf. No, I'm not being polite. Mr Worsky said it made

me look very glamorous when I wore it this morning in the shop. I never thought of getting anything red because my face gets so red when I blush I thought the two would clash. Perhaps I blush less nowadays. Anyway it looks super, and I wore it under a cream-coloured blouse and I thought I looked *très snob*.

Yes, it is hard isn't it, the letters? I don't suppose either of us really believes that the other would be interested in long details of what goes on each day. I am interested because I know Kilgarret and even though it's so long I can still remember it . . . and whose shop was next to whose shop. I don't know where your office is. Is it in the eyrie beside Aunt Eileen? It can't be, you wouldn't be able to see the bus from there, so where is it? I didn't know your friend Joannie Murray was back. I thought she was at a finishing school abroad. You don't mention Donal. Does that mean he's well again? You don't tell me anything about Maureen's baby, you just said it was a boy. You're an aunt.

Really, I'd tell you about things here, but you don't know Mr Worsky or his lady friend, who now asks me to call her Anna, even though she's about seventy, or Johnny Stone who's the nice partner now of Mr Worsky. He's wonderful fun. And since you never even met Father, I can't tell you about this simply awful woman who has designs on him. I'd love Father to get married of course, but this woman is the end. Father can't bear her and he doesn't know how to get her out of the bridge circle.

And Mother's letters sound a bit funny from time to time. She writes a lot, but odd kinds of things, all about the past. She even forgot my birthday. I'm not complaining, but it does seem odd, I mean, she has only one daughter. Aunt Eileen never forgets and she has five children and a grandchild.

College is smashing at the moment too. We have a lot of classes out in the open because of the weather . . . and it's so marvellous to go into a park, twelve of us with easels and all our stuff and set up like real artists to paint a view or a clump of trees. The others are very easy-going. I do have friends, like Kate and Edward and Lionel . . . I'm sure I've mentioned them to you in letters. Sometimes they have parties in Kate's flat. She has a whole three-room flat of her own, because her parents are dead and her guardian thinks that this is what people should have. Imagine!

But I don't go to many of the things people organise in college. I find the dances a bit dreary. I prefer just talking to people and about things I'm interested in, I suppose. I remember Aunt Eileen once told me that we have to pretend to be interested in some things out of kindness to other people. I do that with Father and Mother so I'm not going to do it in my own life as well.

I spend a lot of time in Mr Worsky's shop I suppose. I drop in after college, or I go down there on my bike after Father's supper. Now that Johnny is a partner there's a lot of changes and little improvements, and sometimes there are four of us because Mr Worsky's friend Anna (aged seventy I swear) joins in. It's a bit like a family I should imagine, and yet none of us is related to any of the others. Isn't that odd?

Love and thank you again for the scarf. It makes me look jaunty. That's what Johnny Stone said.

Elizabeth

Eileen always reminded the family of Elizabeth's birthday each May. She even organised separate birthday cards so that Eamonn, Donal and Niamh could sign them. This year Eamonn had mutinied.

'Mam, I'm far too old now to be sending silly cards with flowers and horseshoes on them to some woman in England that I can hardly remember.

'Elizabeth White was reared in this house with you for five years like a sister, and you'll remember her as long as I say so,' said Eileen sharply.

'But Mam, she's gone for years and years. I was only a child when she was here. I'm grown-up now, she'll think I'm sweet on her or something. It's ludicrous.'

'I buy the card, I post it. I remember the date. I'm asking you to put your great ham hand around a pen and write two lines and your thick ignorant signature,' snapped Eileen.

'It's just sentimentality,' grumbled Eamonn. 'If anyone knew this here, I'd be the laughing stock of the town.'

Donal wrote a long piece about how much he had liked the book of watercolours that Elizabeth had sent. He wrote so much that Eileen had to get him an extra piece of paper to add to the card. Niamh wrote a long garbled and almost unfathomable account of school life, studded with characters of whom Elizabeth would never have heard, nuns who were new to the school, friends who had been toddlers when Elizabeth left. Maureen wrote a lengthy description of Baby Brendan, or Brendan Og as he was called in that household to distinguish him from his dadda. Peggy put her name on a card and Eileen wrote a long letter describing the changes and the happenings in the small town. It was Eileen who told Elizabeth about Aisling's new office – just inside the door, a smart raised area where she was away from the herd but still part of it enough to join in if she wanted to. Eileen explained that Joannie Murray had come back from her finishing school and was waiting to go to Dublin for this marvellous job in a wine importer's. Because she was a lady of leisure, she used to come into O'Connor's Hardware and try to distract Aisling. But Eileen wrote with pride that Elizabeth would be glad to know that Miss O'Connor, as she was now called in the shop, had explained that work was work, and indeed young Joannie Murray$s brother Tony had come into the shop one day and said the very same thing.

It was Eileen who explained that they didn't see too much of Maureen and Brendan and little Brendan Og because the Daly family were very possessive and liked to be in charge. Eileen said that this would sort itself out later ... there were a lot of old women in that family, aunts and cousins, and the trouble was they hadn't half enough to do just looking after hens and turkeys so they wanted to own the new arrival body and soul. It would all change when Brendan Daly's other brothers and sisters married and had children, which would take the pressure off Maureen.

Eileen wrote that Donal's chest was still weak, that he had to be very careful of himself, not to get overtired or to catch a chill, but that thank God he was far better than they could ever have hoped at times and he was a grand, handsome fifteen-year-old. He was tall too, nearly as tall as Elizabeth had been when he had gone back to England when she was fifteen. He could reach to the top shelf of the bookcase in the sitting room without standing on his toes. Eileen wrote that Peggy was walking out with a very nice fellow called Christy O'Brien. He worked on a farm out near Brendan Daly's father's place. Eileen half hoped for Peggy's sake that a match would be made – Peggy was in her thirties and hadn't had any great chances – but selfishly she hoped that the Christy fellow would tire of her which would mean that Peggy would stay.

Elizabeth thought to herself sometimes that if she had to rely on Aisling as an informant about Kilgarret she might well believe that all life had ceased there the day she left.

The nuns had been wrong, Elizabeth discovered to her great relief. Johnny *did* still respect her afterwards. Not only did he respect her, he seemed to like her a lot more, and she felt grown-up and proud and confident with him. When they had driven back to London, still through sheets of rain, he seemed more cheerful and happy than ever. Watching his face as he drove, Elizabeth wondered how he could talk so easily and lightly about the funny old farmer who had let him shoot the rabbits, about the way they were going to have a bandage up the inside of the van to stop it leaking, and what Mr Worsky would say about the treasures they had ferried back. Elizabeth knew he must be thinking all the time about their making love and thought he was very cool and calm to be able to talk about other things. She was relieved at this too and talked cheerfully in return rather than dwelling on the events of the night before. This pleased him she could see, and from time to time he patted her hand and said, 'You are a little darling, you know?'

Nobody at college noticed that she had lost her virginity. Kate asked her had she had a nice weekend, and told her about an awful party where somebody had stolen neat alcohol from a laboratory and everyone had drunk it in lemonade and been very ill.

Father hadn't noticed any change in her either. He had been fussed and anxious because that tiresome Mrs Ellis had wanted to come around and help with the preparations for the bridge party and he had told her his daughter would be there. Now his daughter had turned out to be late home from the North, late back from college and was doing only the most perfunctory of suppers.

'But this is my night for entertaining. You always arrange sandwiches and . . . savories,' Father began to whine.

'Father, this is indeed your night, and you can make your own savories and sandwiches. I have biscuits, and a small amount of cheese there. There's bread in that tin, and butter in the larder. It's your night to do it.'

'But that's not what we agreed . . . .'

'How could anyone agree anything with you Father? Answer me that. How could anyone make any possible kind of bargain about anything? I have just come back from my first visit to your wife. Your ex-wife. The woman you married twenty years ago . . . and presumably you loved her then and she loved you. But what have you asked me about her? Not one thing. Mother could be lying in a fever hospital breathing her last for all you care. Mother could be wretchedly unhappy. She could be a million things. But no enquiry from you. At least she asked how you were, and Harry did, and they wanted to know how your life went on. But you don't have it in your cold heart to ask one question about them.'

She was near tears.

Father sat down. 'This is uncalled for,' he said, looking like a schoolboy who is forced to accept a punishment without knowing what the crime was.

'Give me the bloody bread and I'll butter it for you. I'll cut off the crusts, and I'll leave the tray ready . . . .'

'But you are going to serve it aren't you . . .?'

'You really are the limit. I never understood what Mother meant by a cold fish until now. I really didn't.'

'I knew that Violet and that man would turn you against me. I knew that's what they had in their minds when they made all that fuss about inviting you to stay.'

Elizabeth looked at him in disbelief and unexpectedly she began to cry. Through her fingers she tried not to see Father moving the bread away lest it become damp with her tears and unsuitable for sandwiches.

Mr Worsky noticed. He was the only one. He saw a change in Elizabeth and felt sure he knew the reason. She talked as if she were part of a family with himself and Anna Strepovsky at the head of it, and Johnny as the heir-apparent. Elizabeth talked as if she were marrying into a royal house. Stefan Worsky laughed to himself at his fanciful imagery but really that is what it was like.

'Mr Worsky, I wonder if you thought about having a new sign painted for the shop? You know we do lettering at the college and the teachers are always looking for a real job to do . . . I was saying to Johnny last night that something in gold leaf might be nice . . . did he tell you? No? Well I don't want to be intrusive with my ideas. . . .'

And another time.

'Johnny and I were going to paint the name of your shop on the car. Would you like that or do you prefer to be more discreet? Johnny bet me two shillings one way, but I won't tell you which he said.'

He had confided his suspicions to Anna Strepovsky but she had snorted at him and said he was full of imagination.

'It's typical of a man to think that because a woman looks happy it can only be because she has been pleasured by a man.'

Mr Worsky wasn't prepared to argue about principles and beliefs but he was prepared to wager any money that he was right about Elizabeth.

Elizabeth was full of worries about what would happen next. Whether Johnny might want to try it again, and if so where and when? And should she appear enthusiastic, or should she try to go along with the theory that the one night in the hotel had been an isolated happening? She wondered too about contraception. Johnny had said that he had looked after that side of it and there would be no danger. She wasn't ex-perienced enough to know quite what he meant but presumably it meant that there were no little sperms inside her which might prove fertile, because he had organised it so that they would be on the hotel sheet in-stead. Her face still burned at the thought of whoever had to make that bed next day, but it would have been so unromantic and wrong to have tried to wash the sheet herself at the time.

He had said to her that night that next time he would 'get something' and she had nodded peacefully, yet there had been no talk of a next time. But Johnny had been utterly delightful and had seemed overjoyed when she called in on her way home from lectures and even skipped the whole of Friday afternoon's classes to see how the new acquisitions looked once they had been polished and arranged for the Saturday business.

'I'll take you out to the cinema tomorrow night if you're free,' Johnny had said. 'And then you can come back to my place and I'll cook you a Johnny Stone special.'

She smiled back at him.

'I'd love that. Will it be rabbit?'

'No sweetheart, nothing as good, but it might be a Spam special. Will that be all right?'

She nodded happily.

'Oh, Tom and Nick won't be there. They'll be going away for the weekend,' he added casually, 'so we'll have the place to ourselves and we won't be interrupted by their larking about.'

'I see.' Elizabeth saw. And was happy at what she saw. She used her savings to buy a very pretty slip the following morning, she put a tooth-brush, toothpaste and talcum powder in her handbag and told her father that she was going to the cinema and to a party afterwards. She would possibly be very late. He accepted it with the same air of defeat that he seemed to accept everything. She had her own key so there would be no problems. Oh, and could Father leave the kitchen nice and tidy in case someone drove her home from the party and she invited them in for cocoa?

Father didn't even say he hoped she would have a good time.

Tom and Nick didn't go away nearly often enough. Tom worked in a motor salesroom and Nick in a travel agency. They were both flattering to Elizabeth and considered her to be Johnny's latest. A phrase which was beginning to annoy her. When it changed to Johnny's girl she began to feel more secure. They were forever making mockingly gallant remarks in front of her.

'If ever you grow tired of this lady Johnny, be sure to let me know. I could sure step into your shoes. . . .'

Each of the boys had their own bedroom in the big Earls Court flat. But even though it would have been perfectly feasible, it was never suggested that Elizabeth should stay when the other flatmates were there. It was something to do with treating her as a lady and protecting her reputation, Elizabeth thought. She knew she could have a great laugh with Aunt Eileen about such a double standard . . . but then remembering with a shock that of course she could have no such thing. Aunt Eileen would have disapproved strongly. Her wise tolerance, her almost boundless understanding for every kind of situation would not have included this. Elizabeth realised that Aunt Eileen would have spoken very directly.

'What you are doing is wrong. It's silly, irresponsible and wrong. God invented marriage for a very good reason. So that two people could work out the best kind of life possible together, protected by rules . . . by laws, by what the people around you agree is right. You and this boy are being very silly and playing dangerous games. If he really likes you as much as you think he does, and as much as you like him, then why doesn't he do the normal thing . . . why doesn't he tell you this, and tell your mother and father, and propose that you get married? Why does he sneak you in and out of his flat like a criminal, like a common girl . . .?'

Aunt Eileen never said these words, but they were as clear to Elizabeth as if she had. They were an amalgam of attitudes and other warnings and chastisements and all that had gone before.

But she shook herself firmly. She was a grown-up woman of nineteen. She lived in London, not a backwater like Kilgarret. She didn't have all the Roman Catholic fears about sin and modesty and immodesty and purity and impurity. People didn't think like that in the real world. Aunt Eileen was just old-fashioned. She was a great person but old-fashioned.

Sometimes Elizabeth was able to invite Johnny to Clarence Gardens, not that Father ever went away for the night. But there were always the afternoons. Johnny often did deliveries and had the van at his disposal during the daytime. Elizabeth was often able to sneak away from a lecture or a practical class. They surrounded it with excitement . . . a picnic lunch in the kitchen, a double bolt drawn across the front door just in case the impossible happened and Father came home from the bank before twenty-three minutes past six in the evening. Up to Elizabeth's bedroom where the bed was small but the light was romantic and some of the harsher blues had been replaced by a style of her own choosing.

Johnny had once made a gesture towards the more comfortable main bedroom by an inclination of his head, but Elizabeth without words was able to convey that this was not to be considered. She loved him so utterly now she felt that she could talk to him and understand him without either of them having to speak in sentences. He too was delighted with her warmth and responsiveness. She was a little darling in every way, he told her over and over.

Sometimes as they lay in her tiny bed on an afternoon with the curtains drawn and the companionably shared cigarette passed between them, she felt as if she had never know such happiness; but always she knew that there was a step over which she must not cross. She must not ask him to swear love to her, she mustn't ask him to tell her that he was going to be forever faithful. She must hint at nothing more permanent than what they had. That way he was happy and loving, that way no shadow crossed his face.

Sometimes he spoke of people who had broken the rules.

Tom had a girlfriend, a nice little poppet she had been, but an engagement ring had been high on her list of priorities, and she kept taking him home to meet Mother.

'Oh dear, I took you home to meet Mother,' said Elizabeth archly.

'Ah yes, but you didn't do it with a gleam in your eye,' Johnny had laughed.

He had bought awful contraceptives in little packets, things which looked totally unsuitable until they were actually put on, which seemed to be an irritation and a nuisance to him. Elizabeth wondered what she could do to circumvent this. She didn't want to rely on the safe period which she knew only too well was the method of contraception which had ensured such enormous families all over Ireland. Kate and some of the other girls at college had said that the safe period was a dangerous period. It didn't exist.

'But isn't there anything a woman can do?' she asked Kate, feeling foolish.

Kate said there were a lot of things and described them all very graphically but they seemed much worse to Elizabeth than the rubber contraceptives so she left things as they were. Johnny never seemed to think that there was anything else she should do so she supposed it was just what everyone else had to put up with.

He told her little more about himself in those intimate times. His mother he spoke of jokingly, he wasn't close to his brother either, he had not even the mildest wonder as to where his father might be, and whether any step-brothers or sisters existed.

When his mother wrote cheerful, inconsequential letters he seemed pleased and told Elizabeth some of the things she said. When she wrote about how lonely she felt and how hard it was to have two ungrateful sons, he just dismissed her.

'Querulous old demon,' he said without the slightest concern.

'Shall I ever meet her? Will you take me to see her?' Elizabeth asked once. It had been a mistake.

'What for?' Johnny began to frown.

'Oh I don't know, to tell her to stop being a querulous old demon and irritating her handsome son,' she laughed, trying to retrieve things.

It worked.

'Yeah, why not? We'll go some time,' said Johnny.

Father had given Elizabeth a jewellery box for her nineteenth birthday. He had actually gone to Mr Worsky's shop and asked Johnny's advice about a gift. He had met Johnny half a dozen times and believed him to be a nicely spoken young chap who was now a partner in Mr Worsky's business which-must-under-no-circumstances-be-called-a-second-hand-shop.

He said he would like a surprise gift and wanted to pay about thirty shillings or two pounds at the most. Johnny steered him towards an antique box saying it was a snip at thirty shillings. Father grunted that it seemed a lot to pay for an empty box but took it. Johnny put the extra nine pounds into the till so that Mr Worsky should not be cheated on the lovely carved casket, and he bought a little marcasite clip with a blue-bird in it as his own gift.

Elizabeth, knowing the value of the casket, was touched and amazed that Father had spent so much on her present. In no way did Johnny diminish the gift for her. Johnny had helped her to find the book of watercolours for Aisling also. Together they had looked through them and she had told him about the Wicklow mountains, and the river Slaney in Wexford and the old houses half falling down but beautiful with perfect Georgian doors, and covered with creeper.

'Perhaps you and I should go over and take a van each. Stefan would have to buy a new showroom when we came back. Hey, that's not a bad idea. Maybe we'll do that in the summer. We could take the van to the boat and then hire another van when we're there. What do you think? And we could go to see your friends, these O'Connors, you're always saying you wanted to go back. Hey. Why not?'

'Oh yes.'

'You're not enthusiastic, you've always said you'd love to go back.'

'Yes, no, I am.'

'Well then?'

'Sure, maybe in the summer some time.'

She was hesitant. She didn't want to say that she didn't want to go back like this. Back as a hustler going into people's houses and taking away their old treasures, into homes where she had been welcomed as a little refugee during the war. She didn't want to go now all grown-up and hard and sophisticated and knowing the price of things and making a profit. She could never say to Johnny that it looked shabby somehow to go back to Kilgarret with a chap but no Understanding . . . when Maureen had been having an Understanding with Brendan Daly, and the hopes that Peggy would have an Understanding with her Christy. But that's exactly what Elizabeth would like to have had now . . . an Understanding. She would like to know where she stood with Johnny and unless she did she would not like to present him to her other home in Kilgarret.

Everyone agreed that Aisling was making a totally unexpected success of her new job in O'Connor's Hardware. Much of it was due to the way that Eileen had paved the way for her . . . but Aisling never realised that. She assumed it had all been due to her own strength of character. Before she began as an employee, Eileen had insisted that there should be special quarters in the shop for both the children. Sean thought that this was ridiculous nonsense and told her so forcefully.

'But can't you see that they want to believe there is a real place for them there, that it's proper work? If Eamonn just thinks he's your dogsbody and Aisling thinks she's helping me out . . . what pride will they have in it?'

'What pride will they have? Won't they have the pride and satisfaction of having a business built up for them? That's what they will have. They won't be like half the children around here taking the emigrant ship. That's pride enough. No one asked you or me what pride we needed when we worked like dogs. . . .'

'Pride is the wrong word,' Eileen agreed. 'What I'm trying to do is to let them think of home and work as separate, so that they won't cheek you, or answer me back like they would if we gave them an order here in the house.'

Gradually she won her way, a corner was cleared, painted and a door put on it and it became Eamonn's office; it was explained over and over that it was important for local farmers to know where they could find Eamonn, and that he should always be called by his first name since farmers didn't go for the 'Mr' bit. Look at the way they all called Sean 'Sean'; but Eileen was 'Mrs O'Connor', similarly Aisling would be 'Miss O'Connor'.

Aisling's office had a brand new typewriter, a real office chair and proper filing cabinet for the ledgers, the dockets and the paperwork. It wasn't like Eileen's eyrie where paper poked from every corner. It was modern and efficient just as she had been taught in the commercial school. In fact one of the commercial college teachers even took her own class of girls to see Aisling's work place as a model of efficient filing, which delighted Aisling and annoyed every other past pupil deeply.

Her smart green coats and her bustling air of importance gave her the necessary authority. Poor Jemmy, whose wits had grown no stronger and whose strength had grown less, called her Miss O'Connor.

'I don't mind Jemmy calling me Aisling, he's known me since I was a baby,' Aisling confided to Mam on the first day.

'No, he's quite happy calling you Miss.'

'But Mam, you know with him being not all there, I don't want to be putting on airs for poor Jemmy.'

'No child, you're not. He's happy to do what everyone else does. Just be polite to him always, and especially in front of people. That's what really pleases him.'

Aisling remembered her mother always consulting Jemmy.

'Where do you think we might have put those new lampshades, Jemmy? You remember, the ones that came in last week.' Jemmy would stop sweeping the floor and say,

'Gor, I don't know Mam, maybe they're in the back.'

'I think you're right Jemmy, thanks a lot, that's where they must be.'

For years Aisling had been aware of conversations like these, mildly irritating, mildly mystifying. Why ask poor Jemmy? Now she knew why. Mam was much cleverer than she gave the impression of being.

For the first few weeks Eileen explained the complicated workings of their credit arrangements. She showed Aisling the wages book, the bank pass book, the ledger for supplies and the income tax arrangements. She listened attentively while Aisling worked out neater, clearer and more efficient ways of recording their daily administration.

Sometimes the errors, the gaps and the confusions seemed pathetic and elementary to Aisling.

'Oh Mam, can't you see, you've been doubling the work by not having an alphabetical index? It'll only take half the time to look them up now. I can't see why you didn't set one up. It'll only take a couple of days.'

Eileen agreed that it had been a serious lapse. She didn't say that she had little time to set up alphabetical indexes while she was running the shop with Sean, keeping an eye on customers, deciding who to give credit to and who to hurry for bills, pleading with bank managers for further overdrafts, running a house with a wayward maid and six children. Instead of listing all that she had to do, while any fool could have been working out an alphabetical system, she praised Aisling to the skies and said that maybe they should send to Dublin for a proper ledger book with alphabetical indentations.

'Why would we do that, can't I do one myself at home this evening,' Aisling said.

'No work home from the office. If you worked in Murray's or in the hotel we'd be mad with them if they got you to do work at home.'

'Mam you're great, but sure what else would I be doing?'

'You could be going out and casting a cool eye over the men of this town to see if there's any of them good enough for you.'

'Mam I've told you a dozen times, I'm not cut out for men, and even if I were, there's nothing in this town, it's the end of the barrel as regards men.'

'So you say.'

'Honestly Mam, if I think the time has come, I'll go up to Dublin and make an assault on the place, but there's nobody here you'd be seen dead with.'

Joannie said that there were great men altogether in Dublin. But it was hard to know what Joannie meant these days by great men. She said that they had cars and they wore suits and had coffee in places on Grafton Street and sat in Stephen's Green and went to the races.

'And what do they do for a living, like where do they go to work?'

'I don't know that they do,' Joannie admitted, the thought not having come to her before.

'But how have they got money? Are they rich men or what?'

'I think a lot of them are students, or they work for their fathers or something.'

'I work for my father,' said Aisling proudly. 'And you wouldn't find me sitting around in coffee shops talking to people all day.'

'That's because there are no coffee shops and nobody to talk to here,' said Joannie.

'I suppose you're right.'

Joannie was very unsatisfactory at explaining what she was up to. The days when they could giggle and find interest in the most trivial encounters seemed to have gone. Aisling thought it must be all Joannie's fault because she was being so deliberately vague and concealing about her activities. But then she thought Elizabeth too was being distant and wasn't willing to write openly in the way that they used to talk when she was here in Kilgarret. Perhaps that's what happened as you got older, you stopped giggling. Mam didn't have any real friends to talk to. Perhaps when you grew up you had to stop telling people things and begin play-acting. Look at Maureen, for example, stuck out with all those desperate Dalys. She couldn't really like it. She must hate all Brendan's awful sisters and aunts and the whole tribe. Friendships must only be for young people. Niamh had a friend now and they'd drive you mad, Niamh and Sheila Moriarty, screaming with laughter at nothing.

Look at Mam's friendship with Elizabeth's mother ... that hadn't lasted and Mam said they were the best of pals for years at school. It was probably a sign of being grown-up to realise that friendships weren't important.

'You don't see so much of Joannie these days. You didn't fall out?' Tony Murray asked when he came into the shop to buy a length of flex one day.

'No, heavens no, but she's busy. She's got her friends in Dublin you know, and she'll be going there. I'm tied up here all day working and there's so little to do at night. It's a terrible town, isn't it Tony?'

'You used to come up to our house and make us laugh with your tall stories,' Tony said.

'I suppose I've got a bit more sense than to be telling tall stories now,' Aisling said.

'That'd be a pity.'

He dropped in a lot, and always a few words but no dallying with Aisling. Eamonn said one night that he thought Tony Murray must be going half-cracked because he used to come in for lengths of flex or boxes of nails and not care what he got, or remember that he might have got the same thing the day before.

'He's in a kind of dream half the time I think,' said Eamonn.

'I think he's keen on Aisling' said Donal.

Aisling put down her fork and screamed with laughter.

'Tony *Murray* keen on *me*? Have a heart, he's as old as a bush. He couldn't be fancying me surely.'

Sean was reading the paper. 'Quit making fun of the customers and don't start getting stupid ideas,' he said without letting his eyes leave the pages.

'I'm not getting any ideas Dad, it's Donal. Hey come on, what makes you think that, Donal?'

'I saw him looking at you on Sunday at Mass, and he looked like people look when they're keen on someone.'

'What kind of look is that?' asked Eileen, amused.

'Like a sick bullock,' suggested Eamonn . . . .

'Like this,' said Niamh, clasping her hands and closing her eyes in a position of suppliance. 'Be mine, fair Aisling, be mine.'

'Or just pale and sick with internal anguish,' proposed Aisling.

'No,' said Donal. 'More looking at you during the sermon, and then afterwards when we were all talking outside, laughing at things you said and being over-interested in them.'

'You couldn't be over-interested in what I say!' said Aisling. 'In fact, most people are utterly fascinated by everything I say.'

'Jaysus,' said Eamonn.

'Stop that blaspheming at the table,' said Sean.

'And do you see anyone over-interested in what Eamonn's saying? Maybe you could spot a romance there too?' teased Aisling.

Donal took her seriously. 'No, but I wasn't really looking. I think some of the shop girls giggle and snatch his cap and run off with it after devotions on a Sunday.'

'Oh, is that why you're all so keen to go to devotions?' Eileen said. 'I thought it was for the love of the Sacred Heart.'

'It is a bit,' said Aisling, who liked dressing up and going to devotions herself. It was a social occasion, everyone hung around the church and talked afterwards.

'I see I'm demoted to shop girls, but Princess Aisling here has the eye of the merchant prince.'

Eamonn sounded mock gloomy, and everyone laughed.

'Wouldn't it be smashing if Tony Murray did fancy Aisling and they got married? We'd have lots more money and a gardener like the Murrays,' said Niamh.

'What would you want a gardener for? We've no garden, you eejit,' said Eamonn.

'What do you want fixing me up with Tony Murray of all people?' wailed Aisling. 'Isn't he an old man, he's nearly thirty for God's sake. It's Mam and Dad's generation.'

But of course when she saw Tony Murray next night at the pictures she flounced and giggled and gave him come-on glances just to test whether Donal might have a grain of truth in his suspicions. To her surprise Tony Murray seemed to love it.

'Are you going to be here tomorrow night?' he asked.

'Is that a piece of general conversation, or is it a request?' she giggled.

'It's a request,' he said simply.

'You mean you're asking me?'

'I'm asking would you like to come to the pictures,' he said, having been manoeuvred into it.

'Well now, I accept,' she said.

'I'll meet you here then?'

They looked at the poster . . . *National Velvet*.

'That's great.' There was a silence.

'It should be good,' Tony said.

'Oh yes, it should indeed.'

'Lucky the programme changed.'

'Well it always does on Thursdays.'

'So it does,' said Tony Murray and they parted.

Aisling giggled the whole way home, when she had caught up on Judy Lynch and Annie Fitzpatrick.

'I've got a date tomorrow night. Tony Murray's going to pay for me going in to the pictures.'

They were very impressed.

Aisling wondered why he didn't have friends of his own age, and hoped that he wasn't abnormal or anything.

She told Mam about it and said wasn't it a scream that Donal was right?

'Just because he asked you to the pictures doesn't mean he's keen on you, and from the sound of what you said to him it seems to me that it was you who suggested the whole thing,' said Eileen in an unexpectedly stern voice.

'Mam, what is it? What are you so cross for? I was only having a bit of a laugh.'

'I'm sorry.' Eileen very rarely apologised even if she had been sharp. Aisling was amazed by this. 'Yes, you're right, I did sound a bit weasel-ish.' She took off her glasses. She had been reading when Aisling came in, Sean had gone to bed already. Mam looked tired.

'I don't know. I suppose I think that sometimes you don't realise how attractive you are, Aisling my love. You really are a lovely girl. You could well turn a man's head, and you're too silly still, you'd get your name up with his and then make a mess of it all.'

'But Mam, I tell you, it's only a joke. He's ancient, he could be my father.'

'Love, he's eleven years older than you if that. He's a single man. He's looking to settle down. He's not interested in going to balls and dances up in Dublin, he's drinking with the lads. His mother is very keen indeed for him to be settled – he's just the right age for it. Now do you see what I mean? For him it may not be a joke, so I'm annoyed with you getting your name up with his, all to no avail.'

'But what's getting my name up? It's like as if the banns were being read, Mam. You're making a mountain out of a molehill.'

'It's such a small town Kilgarret, you don't know how people love a chance to gloat.'

'But Mam, what's there to gloat over? They can't say I've been thrown over by him can they, if I'm not the one who's serious about him?'

'No child, Of course they can't. Come on, let's turn out the lights and off to bed and stop all this nonsensical chatter.'

Dear Aisling,
Tell me more about Tony Murray. The last time he was mentioned in despatches was some incident where he found Joannie up to something which was never clearly explained either ... but I thought he was very old, you know, like an uncle. But you've been to the pictures with him twice in six weeks. Is it a romance? Does he Make Suggestions as we used to say? I wish you'd tell me, I can keep a secret anyway, can't I? I'm miles away in a different country.

Mrs Ellis, the dreadful woman who has designs on Father, is really doing her best. It's Father's fiftieth birthday and she keeps saying that she'd like to organise a little party for 'your papa's half century'. In order to put her off, I said that I was organising a quiet family dinner at home and she had to be satisfied with that. Is Uncle Sean fifty? Did you have any do for that? A family dinner isn't much fun if Father and I are the only family, but maybe when he knows I've chased Mrs Ellis away from him he'll cheer up.

I see a lot of Johnny. It''s hard to tell you about it really. I did try but I tore up the page, it sounded a bit like the pages of a mushy love story . . . when it's not like that in real life. I just like him a lot and he me . . . but we don't say I love you or anything. I could explain it more clearly if we met. You asked what he looks like. I think he looks a bit like Clark Gable but thinner and without the moustache. That sounds ridiculous but what I'm trying to say is that he's dark and very handsome, and people look at him a lot, but he doesn't seem to notice them. I'll tell you what happens about the party for Father. Love to everyone. I write to Aunt Eileen sometimes as you know, not secrets just ordinary letters . . . but I haven't for a while, everything's been so busy and complicated here. I hope she understands.

Love, Elizabeth

Dear Elizabeth,

Like Clark Gable, I don't believe it! No wonder you're being quiet about him, you don't want to share him. I don't know why it's hard to tell what it's like. I know we're not good at writing, but now I'll change all that. I'll try to tell you what Tony is like. He's very old, he's thirty and he'll be thirty-one soon. He's been at university but he didn't do his degree. He's been in Limerick learning the business and now he runs Murray's here. He seems very keen on me. I don't know why. He puts his hand on the back of my neck and squeezes it, which is awful and he kisses me in the car and tries to put his tongue between my teeth but I don't encourage it. I let it happen by accident a bit. I don't like it much anyway.

He tells me I'm beautiful which I like to hear, and he comes and talks to Mam and Dad a lot too, so now everyone knows that he's Interested as they say. Dad doesn't know what to do, he's out of his depth. It wasn't like this with Brendan Daly because Brendan and all the Dalys are old eejits as everyone knows. Tony Murray is what they call a catch here. Mam is very tight-lipped. She thinks I'm playing with his affections. Me! Aisling O'Connor playing with the affections of a catch who is as old as the hills, Anyway I don't feel much about him one way or the other. I'd like him better if he didn't look so silly, and pant and huff and puff so much in the car.

He certainly doesn't look like Clark Gable. He's fatter for a start. He's got black curly hair and he's sort of square-built. He's not bad looking but he's certainly not like Clark Gable. Now I've told you everything, can't you sit down and tell me everything? I didn't tear up pages even though that bit about kissing looks a bit yucky.

Dear Aisling,

I will, I promise. In about two weeks' time. I'll write everything. It's just that there's so much happening here. I'm very taken up. Two weeks. Everything. Gory details, nothing spared.

Watch out for it.

Love Elizabeth

P.S. Do you love Tony Murray in any sort of way?

Father said that he didn't really want any celebrations for his half century. Nothing much to celebrate, he said. This annoyed Elizabeth greatly.

'You're the only father I've got and you're going to be half a hundred. I think we should make a little fuss. Now here are the options: I can take you out to a hotel and buy a bottle of wine. I have a tiny savings account. I would be very glad to do that, Father. Or we can have all your bridge people here and make a party with some people from the bank too and one or two neighbours. . . .'

'No, no, the bridge people wouldn't enjoy a party if we didn't play bridge,' said Father.

'Right, it's just us,' said Elizabeth.

'But a hotel is very dear,' complained Father.

'Right, it's Saturday week. I'll ask Johnny to dinner here, and we'll have wine and high-class food.'

'That would be very nice,' said Father, relieved that there would be no need for him to do anything now except accept what was put in front of him. He was mightily pleased that he had managed to escape anything too festive.

'He's a nice chap, that Johnny Stone. He's good company. I'd enjoy him coming to dinner,' he said.

Yes, thought Elizabeth, everyone enjoys Johnny Stone's company. Now the hard part – asking him to dinner.

'You won't think I'm trying to cast a matrimonial net over you if I ask you to do me a favour?'

They lay wrapped in sheets on the floor of Johnny's flat, reading the Sunday papers and drinking milk with straws.

'Mm what . . . making noises like a woman trying to pin me down?' he asked, still reading the paper.

'No, far from it, it's just that one night Father's going to be fifty, and there's nobody he really likes . . . so I thought I'd cook a special dinner . . . a White special . . . and would you come to keep the conversation going?'

Johnny looked up. 'Aw, no love, I'd be butting in. It's a family thing, a birthday.'

'Hell, you know how family Father and I are . . . very little traditional family love in our house. And we'd look silly the two of us. No, we need an outsider to make it festive. Do come sweetheart. Please.'

Johnny shook his head. 'No, honestly, I'd only be in the way. I'm no good on the formal sentimental thing . . . you know that I even hate going home for Christmas with the Old Lady because she wants ceremonies and everything.'

'But you were super with Mother and Harry.'

'But that's different, honeybunch. That was just a nice evening that developed. Not being asked formally or anything, you know making a big thing.'

'Please Johnny. Please.'

He was reading the paper again. 'No, heart. I'd be out of place. I wouldn't like it.'

'Do you never do things you don't like?' her voice sounded rather sharp.

He looked up, surprised, 'No, not often, Why?'

'I do, a lot of the time, so do most people. Please Johnny, just one night to please me, and to make Father happy.'

'No, dearest, ask another of your friends. Ask someone else.'

It was settled. He was not coming. He would not do her the favour, he wouldn't even consider it or discuss it. He assumed she had other friends, people as close as he was. He assumed that Kate and Edward and Lionel were on visiting terms.

She had to accept this in Johnny or demand more. But she had just been shown the door had been closed. There was no more being offered. If she asked for more, she would get nothing, and what she had already would be withdrawn. She had seen Lily, a one-time girlfriend, come into the shop. She still liked Johnny, and Johnny was unfailingly charming but Lily had failed the examination at an earlier time and could not take it again. Lily had made scenes when Johnny refused to come to her end-of-term dance in college . . . let Elizabeth be warned.

'Right ho,' she said cheerfully, 'selfish bastard. Well, you'll miss a good dinner, that's for sure.'

She looked sunny and uncaring. There was no way he would know the hurt and rejection she felt. No way he could see from her laughing face that she had come to a depressing conclusion about her love for him. She knew now that it would have to be one-sided and full of pretence if it were to continue. Johnny wasn't going to meet anyone half-way or even a quarter of the way. You played the game in his territory and according to his rules.

She forced herself to read the paper with a smile fixed on her face. She knew he was looking at her.

'Come here, gorgeous,' he said, unwrapping the sheet. 'You're much too attractive a girl to be reading papers. You should be giving pleasure to a passing gentleman, so you should.'

She lay there happily and looked at the ceiling as his head lay peacefully on her bosom. He was dozing in the morning sun coming in the window. Soon they would get dressed and wander off to a pub on the river where he would get her a glass of shandy and they would eat their sandwiches.

She had passed the examination. She could have flounced off in tears, she could have begged still more and annoyed him, and she could have sulked, but he would have taken no notice and eventually he would have wandered off to lunch alone.

But no. Elizabeth had done none of these things and she had her reward here in her arms. He still loved her and wanted her. It was worth a few little sacrifices.

Tony Murray told Aisling that he would like her to think seriously about him one summer night when the car had steamed up with passion and pushing and advances and rejections and squirmings.

'I want you to know that I haven't ever met anyone else who attracts me as much as you do.'

'That's nice Tony, but I'm still not going to take off my bra,' said Aisling.

'I'm glad you're not. I know you aren't the kind of girl who would go with anyone, and I respect you for it,' he said, red-faced with exertion.

'Well, that's the way I am.'

She was puzzled because she had let him go much further than what she considered wise. Surely there had been times when she had gone far beyond the level that someone should go before marriage. After all, it was quite obvious even to someone as inexperienced as Aisling sadly agreed that she was that Tony was satisfying his base desires in all these grapplings . . . and the nuns had said that to be the instrument of that was leading a man into mortal sin.

Still, it would appear that Tony respected her.

'I'm finding it very hard to go on with these kind of . . . outings,' Tony said.

'Oh, I like going out with you,' Aisling said, deliberately misunderstanding him.

'No, I don't mean that. You know what I mean. I mean I like you so much I want to have you all to myself all the time. . . .'

Aisling decided that this was very near to a proposal of marriage. She looked at Tony's face for a moment, as if she and he were strangers.

He was attractive enough looking, she supposed. He had this thick-set neck, and nice dark eyes. Other girls had told her that he was handsome, she heard people refer to him as a fine man. She knew that Daddy would approve . . . 'You'd be doing well if you married into the Murrays, girl,' he used to say half-jokingly, but she thought he meant it. Mam had her reservations, but only because she thought Aisling was too giddy.

Well I am too giddy, Aisling thought to herself with sudden conviction. And I'm not going to be railroaded into something I'm not sure about. I'm not going to let him ask me and have to say yes or no. I'm going to put it off, I'm going to be clever for once in my life.

She kissed him lightly on the forehead.

'You're a very attractive man, Tony Murray, and you say such nice things you nearly sweep me off my feet. But you're a grown-up, you know what you're doing. I don't, I'm only silly and young and I've never been anywhere.'

He began to speak but she interrupted him.

'I'm going to see a bit more of the world before I let myself fall for you . . . otherwise it would be pathetic. Look, you've been to university, you've lived away from home in Limerick and Dublin. You've been to France and to Rome. The furthest I've been is Dublin and spent a night in Dunlaoghaire . . . and that was with the whole family.

'No, if I want you to think anything of me, I'll have to grow up a bit, not just be the silly provincial Kilgarret girl. Then you'll be made about me.'

'I fancy you now,' mumbled Tony.

Aisling had manoeuvred them to a sitting position as if by accident. This would mean that the fumbling and grappling could be considered at an end . . . .

'Yes, but wait until I'm sophisticated, then I'll be a magnificent prize,' she tinkled.

'I don't want you sophisticated.' He sounded mulish.

'You want me with a bit more sense and a bit more polish don't you? Come on. You'd love to have me a bit smart, not just plain ignorant like I am.'

'Where are you going to learn all this sophistication and to be smart and polished?' Tony grumbled.

And indeed Aisling wasn't sure how to answer that even though her brain was working feverishly on an answer that would satisfy him.

'Well, I haven't it all settled yet, but I'm thinking of doing a little travelling. Not going away permanently or anything, just broadening my mind, and seeing a bit of the world. I'm not even twenty yet, Tony. I may seem all right now but I could turn into one of those awful dreary women you see up at the church with nothing on their minds except what the priest said to them and what Mrs So and So was wearing.'

'You'd never . . . .'

'Oh but I might, I can see the signs of it in me already.'

Aisling had warmed to her cause now and felt she had the upper hand. It was time to leave the subject.

'But listen, I'll tell you next week where and when I'll be going off to see the world.'

He agreed with a grunt, and reluctantly drove her back to the house in the square.

Mother was up as usual.

'You're a bit late,' she said mildly and without much sense of disapproval.

'I know. We went for a drive after the pictures and he spent a lot of time talking.'

Aisling looked at herself hastily in the mirror to make sure her lipstick wasn't all over her face and that her blouse was buttoned correctly.

But Mam didn't seem to be inspecting her. 'I just waited till you came in,' she said, folding her knitting and starting to turn off lights.

'Well Mam, there's no need. You know I'm all right, and that nothing . . . that I wouldn't . . . that I'd always come home.'

'Of course I do, child, but in a way you're my oldest, aren't you? Maureen was away in Dublin at your age, and well, boys are different. It would never matter what time Sean or Eamonn came in.'

'I'm no trouble to you now am I? Nice, reliable assistant in the shop, walking out decorously with the town's best catch . . . and Mam honestly, I'm not such an eejit. I told him tonight that I was too young to be serious about anything. That I'd have to see the world first.'

Mam laughed. 'And where are you going to go to first in the world? Wicklow Town, maybe as far as Wexford?'

'I'll go somewhere Mam. It's just to let him know that I know my limitations in a way.'

Mam ruffled her hair and laughed again. 'You're an entertainment in yourself. No wonder Tony Murray's delighted with you.'

On the hall table was a letter from London. Aisling snatched it eagerly and took it up to bed. This was the promised letter from Elizabeth which was going to tell her everything. It seemed quite thick as well.

She took a glass of milk and a piece of cake from the kitchen first and sat down to enjoy the story.

But when she opened the envelope the letter was very short. What had made the bulkiness was a parcel of four five-pound notes, English ones with pictures of the King of England on them wrapped in tissue paper.

The letter was certainly not telling at all.

Dear Aisling,
Is it silly to remember things we did as children, or is it not? Do you remember, when we became blood sisters by mixing our blood in the bottle, we swore to help each other if one was in trouble.

I need your help now. Please, please come to England. I'm sending you the money for the fare. Please come now. You must be here for Saturday. It's Father's fiftieth birthday and I can't cope with it by myself. Please come. I'll tell you everything when you get here. Don't let Aunt Eileen know how urgent it is. Pretend that you just want a holiday. Please.

Elizabeth

Well, thought Aisling, isn't that the best bit of luck ever? A chance to see the world and broaden my mind not ten minutes after I started looking for one. It's fate.

Elizabeth hadn't noticed that her breasts were getting bigger but she had noticed that her period was very late. It was now three weeks overdue. It had never been more than four days late. She had deliberately put it out of her mind in the hope that it might have been nervousness, tension or any of the reasons which she had read in a medical magazine.

But on the Sunday night after Johnny had driven her home to Clarence Gardens and sped off again, she could no longer dismiss it. Twenty-one days. She checked the calendar again and even smiled ruefully since she knew that this is what so many nervous girls all over the world must be doing at that minute. Saying to themselves that it couldn't possibly be true, and it couldn't happen to them, and trying to get rid of the hard knot of fear and disbelief that was forming in their chests.

Elizabeth looked out the window and saw Father in the garden. For some reason his ineffectual pottering, his unsuccessful attempts to trail the honeysuckle over the wall, and his sense of bafflement because it lay on the ground and got tangled, seemed to her unbearably sad. He could be seventy she thought, not fifty. He looked so dull and beaten and as if he had always known he would never amount to anything.

If Johnny had been in that garden there would have been life and laughter. There would have been movement and experiment and sudden flashes of inspiration, and determined hammering of stakes into the ground. If Mother was here in one of her good moods she would laugh too and go at it with interest, and Harry would bluster and laugh and make some fun out of it. But Father looked as if he were already dead and as if everything he did were some kind of sad duty forced on him beyond the grave.

Poor dead Father, nothing to live for, nothing to hope for; even bridge had revealed untoward dangers with that terrible widow Ellis in pursuit of him. Elizabeth decided to put away the calendar and its message of despair and go down to the garden to help him.

He was surprised to see her.

'Oh hallo. Didn't know you were in.'

'Yes, I came in about an hour ago.'

'Did you have tea?'

'No, I'd have called you if I had made tea. No, I went upstairs to my room for a bit.'

'Oh I see.'

'What are you doing, Father?'

'My dear, what do you think I'm doing? I'm trying to do something with this wilderness of a garden.'

'Yes, but what in particular? If you tell me what it is, perhaps I can help.'

'Well . . . I don't think it would be any use . . .' he stood looking like an old bewildered bird.

'Are you weeding this bed?' she asked through gritted teeth.

'Well . . . it's so overgrown . . . you see,' he waved at it.

'Yes so it is. Shall we start weeding it now, then, Father? You start at that end, and I'll start here . . . and we'll meet in the middle.'

'I don't know if that would work.'

She controlled her voice with a great effort, by taking it down an octave from where she had been about to speak.

'Why would it not work, Father?' Each word equal emphasis, no sign of rage on her face.

'You know, knowing which are the weeds . . . and which are flowers . . . it's so difficult to see . . . it's so overgrown you see.'

'We could take this kind of grass out, *that's* obviously weed. Then we could look at it again and have a reassessment.'

She stood there looking at him hopefully. Could he not catch a little enthusiasm from her?

He shook his head. 'I don't know,' he said.

Elizabeth went purposefully to the little shed, and took out some cardboard. She folded it into a kneeling mat. She went to her end of the big flower bed and started to wrench big tufts of grass out. 'Hey, look, this is beginning to look better already,' she called out. But he stood there, unsure, unwilling to go along with this sudden outburst.

'Come on, Father,' she called. 'In half an hour we'll have made it look like Kew Gardens.'

He bent over and fiddled again with the honeysuckle.

'This isn't a weed, don't dig up this, this is honeysuckle.'

'I know Father, we're just taking grass. Come on. I'll be catching up on you if you don't start.'

'It's such a wilderness,' he signed. 'No one person could do a garden like this. Not anyone who has a full-time job like I do. Nobody could do a big garden like this without help.'

'You've GOT help,' called Elizabeth on all fours from the back of the flower bed. 'I'm helping you'.

'You see,' he said. 'It was allowed to get into this state, and now you need a man twice a week in it.'

Elizabeth worked on. It took her forty-five minutes. The sweat was rolling down her forehead and her clothes were sticking to her. She gathered up a mound of coarse grass, and packed it tightly wrapped in old newspapers into the bottom of the dustbin.

'The bin-men don't like grass clippings,' said Father who had fiddled for forty-five minutes with fronds of honeysuckle.

She sighed. 'They won't know what's in it Father, that's why I used newspapers. It could be dismembered bodies for all they know.'

He didn't laugh.

She cleared everything away and had a bath. A hot bath was meant to bring on a period if it was late. There were even stories of a hot bath bringing on even more than a period. Elizabeth felt almost faint when she allowed herself to think that. She patted her stomach, it was still flat. She must be imagining it. She really must have been fancying it. People's periods were always late. The world was filled with false alarms, all the time.

Father had set the table for their supper. It was sardines and tomatoes on toast. Elizabeth was determined to cheer Father up. It became a game almost like not walking on cracks in the pavement. 'If I don't walk on any lines then I will get an A for my essay.' Just like that, exactly the same reasoning. 'If I make Father cheerful and happy then it will turn out that I'm not pregnant.'

The garden was obviously the wrong area. His depression about the unmanageable jungle outside the door was not going to be lifted, no matter how much Elizabeth praised what had been done and agreed to do an hour every day ... his head still shook ruefully as if there were things in that garden that Elizabeth couldn't understand, forces fighting back against amateur part-time gardening. She couldn't really discuss bridge in case Mrs Ellis was remembered. Elizabeth tried it but it didn't work.

'Do you think she has hopes of coming to live here Father?' she asked as she trimmed the toast neatly and shook some dried herbs on the tomatoes.

'I have no idea what that woman thinks or hopes. She is a very common woman. It was a great mistake of Mr Woods to introduce her to the club. He was very badly advised, and utterly misled.'

'Why don't you all tell her to get lost then if she's such a nuisance?'

'Oh you can't do that. You can't tell someone not to come.'

'Why don't you start up different games then, without her? You know, just drop her casually if she's so coarse and common? I mean you shouldn't be forced to play bridge with someone you don't like. People don't have to do things they don't want to.' Johnny's attitudes and words tripped lightly and effortlessly from her, but Father didn't agree.

'But of course you have to do things you don't want to. That's obvious. Everyone has to do things they don't want to do all the time ... Oh Elizabeth dear, don't put any of those herbs and spices on my tomatoes ... I don't like them with that taste ... thank you ... no of course people can't please themselves all the time.'

'But if none of you like her, Father, and she got in by mistake, does that mean you have to put up with her forever?'

'Yes, unfortunately it does.'

Elizabeth had scraped the dusting of dried herbs off Father's tomatoes and when he wasn't looking put them back on again. She set the plates on the table.

'Tell me about when you were my age or a little older, like say in your twenties. Did people never do what they felt like then?'

'I don't know what you mean?'

'*You* know, when you were starting at the bank, Father. Was the world full of people doing what they wanted to do or is it a sense of duty . . .? one must do this, one must do that?'

'I don't really know . . .'

'But you MUST know Father, you must remember. You can't have forgotten what it's like to be twenty.'

'No of course not . . .'

'Well what was it like?'

'It was very depressing, that's what it was. Everyone just back from the war, so many wounded and maimed. Others swaggering, just like they were after the last show. Always making you feel that you had a featherbed life because you didn't get accepted for the call-up.'

'It wasn't your fault.'

'I know, but tell that to the boys in uniform, practically accusing you of hiding under the bed. All blow and bluster. I went on my eighteenth birthday down to the centre. My mother didn't want me to, but I went, I didn't wait.'

'Some people went even before they were eighteen, didn't they Father? Aisling's brother Sean, the one that got killed, he told me that.'

'I don't know whether they did or they didn't. I hope you're not saying I should have gone before the age. . . .'

'No, Father, I was only remembering something. . . .'

'Well, I went the very day, and volunteered for my country but they put me in a reserve because I wasn't strong enough. My spine was weak even then, that's why I still can't do that gardening. It's impossible you know to keep a place this size with one. . . .'

'Did you go out with a lot of other girls Father, before you met Mother . . .?'

'What? What do you mean?'

'I just wanted to know did you have a lot of social life, and much going out when you were young?'

'I told you, it was just after the Great War.'

'Yes, but we hear about the twenties, and the flappers, and all the fun. You know, people doing the charleston and having *thé dansants* and wearing those amazing hats looking like buckets. . . .'

'What . . .?'

'Oh Father, you know, you know the sort of image everyone has of the twenties.'

'Well I assure you that wasn't the image I had of it. That may have been for a few idle, irresponsible rich people born with silver spoons in their mouths. It wasn't for me or for the people I worked with.'

'But Mother was a sort of flapper girl wasn't she? She used to wear clothes like that. I've seen the old pictures, and she went to *thé dansants* she told me. In fact she often writes about them still, and how she used to go and dance to the Savoy Orpheans. . . .'

'But why all these questions . . .? what are you asking me all this for?'

'Father, I'm only trying to get to know a bit more about you . . . we live in the same house and I hardly know anything about you. . . .'

'Oh my dear, don't be so silly. This is utter nonsense.'

'No it's not. We live here together for years and years without my even knowing what makes you happy and what makes you sad.'

'I can tell you that these silly questions . . . what was it like all those years ago . . . makes me sad rather than happy. . . .'

'Buy why Father, why? You must have had happy bits when you were young?'

'Naturally.'

'Weren't you happy when you and Mother were in love, and everything?'

'Now I really don't think . . .'

'But seriously Father, when you and Mother were expecting me, you know, when Mother went to the doctor and got it all confirmed. What did you do? What did you say, did you celebrate or what . . .?'

'Please. . . .'

'No, it's interesting to me to know. I'd like to know. Did she come back and say, "It's confirmed, I am pregnant. It will be born in May" or what?'

'I don't remember. . . .'

'Father I'm your only child, you MUST remember!' Her voice was becoming shrill. She remembered to lower it.

'Try to think Father. It would please me.' He looked at her.

'I remember your being born,' he said eventually. 'But I don't remember the day I knew.'

'And were you pleased, or did you think it was a worry and a problem?'

'Of course I was pleased. . . .'

'No, you might have thought it was just another thing to worry about. Why were you pleased? Did you look forward to my being born, being a small thing in a pram . . .?'

'Yes, well of course I didn't know about what a baby would be like in the house . . . but I was pleased. . . .'

'Can you remember why you were pleased . . .?'

'Well I think I thought it would make Violet . . . make your mother more content. She seemed restless.'

'Even as long ago as then . . .?'

'Oh yes.'

'And did it make her more content?'

'Did what . . .'

'Did I make her more content . . .?'

'In a way, yes.'

'And what were your happiest times in those days, Father?'

'Really my dear, I don't enjoy this conversation. It's probing and it's too personal, and in a way it's impertinent. People don't ask other people those kind of questions.'

'But how are people ever going to know what people feel . . .?'

'They know enough my dear. It's not necessary to know everything about people.'

'You're not right Father. It's necessary to know much more than you want to know. You wouldn't mind if you knew nothing about anyone just so long as people behaved correctly.'

'That's not true.'

'Oh but it is true. I'm begging you. I'm reaching out and begging you to tell me about yourself so that I can tell you about me . . . and make you involved in what I'm doing and feeling. . . .'

'But I am very interested in what you do, and very proud of you. You mustn't accuse me of . . .'

'Did you ever talk to Mother about feelings, you know, and what you thought and what you wanted and how much you loved her . . .?'

'Elizabeth, really.'

'Because honestly, if you didn't, then I know why she went away. It was nothing to do with your not being good enough, or Harry being better. She probably went because she was lonely. . . .'

'And do you think that her fancy Harry Elton is a great philosopher? Do you seriously think he sits down and debates about the meaning of life like you want . . .? Huh, what a thought.'

'No I don't suppose for a moment he does. But he makes up for it by laughing and joking. The ideal thing would be to have someone who could do both, but I'm beginning to think there's no way you can have the best of both worlds. And Father, if you won't laugh and you won't talk then you're the very worst of both worlds. . . .'

Father stood up and his face was hurt and red. His face muscles were working and his hands were clenched at his sides. He had never looked more wretched and humiliated.

'Well,' he stammered eventually. 'Well, I must say, I don't know what I did to deserve this, I really don't. I was out there in the garden minding my own business, and you come home in a state. You come home and criticise the way I'm doing the garden, even though you never came out to give me a hand in it before . . . you criticise the way I spent my youth. You attack me for not being able to recall every second of your own life before and after you were born . . .' His voice gathered into a sob. 'And then, as if that isn't enough, you hurl accusations at me about hurtful things and upsetting times . . . and blame me for your mother walking out on her duty and running away.'

He had such pain in his voice that he could hardly get the words out.

'I really don't know what brought all this on. I can only hope that you had a tiff with your young man, and that I needn't expect this kind of performance again.'

Father had never before acknowledged that Johnny was her young man. His brain would never now take in the intelligence that she and this young man had been rolling around naked on a floor in Earls Court a few hours previously and that she was very probably carrying the young man's child, and that there had been no tiff and nor would there be one.

But the spell hadn't worked. Father was not cheered up, Father was far from cheered up. This must mean that she was indeed pregnant.

She stood up.

'You are quite right. I *had* a silly tiff. It is unforgivable of me to have taken it out on you. Quite unforgivable. I really apologise.'

Then she went upstairs, took some five-pound notes out of her savings box and wrote to Aisling.

X

Aisling had more adventures on her journey to London than she had ever been through in her life. She felt that she had been quite right to tell Tony Murray that she must go out and see the world.

On the boat to Holyhead, an extremely handsome man with his shirt open at the neck had bought her a brandy and lemonade, not heeding her protests that she wouldn't like it. Then he had taken her for a walk on deck, told her she was the most beautiful girl in the world, tried to kiss her, apologised, proposed marriage to her, and finally went into a corner and got very sick. Aisling, who had not realised that he was drunk, had her eyes wide and round in horror at it all, but was rescued by two university students who were going to get a holiday job canning vegetables and tried to persuade her to join them.

On the train going down to London she met a young Welsh school teacher who told her that he was going to live in London because he couldn't stand his village any longer. Everyone was trying to pressurise him to get married. He felt that he should see the world first. Aisling eagerly told him her own tale and how she was determined to see as much of the world as she could in two weeks, which was the holiday she had wrung from Daddy with difficulty. The Welshman was very scathing about the two-week element of it, he said it wasn't nearly enough. She should go for much longer. Perhaps they should even go to France on a boat. But that was too wild for Aisling, she explained she was coming to see her friend because of a crisis. Her friend wanted someone to help her on her father's birthday. The Welshman said that the friend sounded like someone from a madhouse. Sending money over to Ireland for someone to come to her father's birthday. After four years too. He put his finger to his forehead and turned it around in further explanation of how loopy he thought the friend must be. Aisling then felt resentful of him and returned to her book.

Even at Euston station a middle-aged man asked her if she was lost and said he would be happy to share a taxi with her. But Aisling was looking out for Elizabeth.

She had telephoned Elizabeth early the morning after she got the letter and said of course, she would come that very night. Elizabeth's accent sounded very English like the people in the films who said 'frightfully' and 'jolly'. She said that Euston was a huge place but there were no problems because if Aisling just stayed there at the barrier when she came off the train they would have no trouble finding each other.

'When I came over four years ago, I thought I'd been abandoned,' Elizabeth had said.

'Sure, weren't we only children then,' said Aisling, dismissing it.

Still Aisling's eyes roamed anxiously through the crowds and she paused to comb her hair so that she would make a good impression. She wished she had a smarter suitcase. This one which Mother had used years ago was far too shabby for her nice new turquoise summer coat. But it had been a matter of buying new shoes or a new suitcase and the shoes seemed more important.

She must have walked right past Elizabeth, eyes still roaming the crowd, darting here and there looking for the pale blonde fifteen-year-old but with a few grown up clothes on nowadays. Then Elizabeth pulled at her sleeve . . . .'

'Aisling?' she said, almost hesitantly.

Aisling spun round.

They looked at each other for a moment . . . as if the words and greetings and reactions had been blown out of them like air after a punch in the solar plexus.

They spoke at the same instant.

'Elizabeth, you saved my life by inviting me to come over. . . .'

'Oh, Aisling, you've literally saved my life. . . .'

Then they burst out laughing. And Aisling linked arms.

'Maybe we're Siamese twins that should never have been separated. Maybe we're going to go on saying the same thing at the same time always.'

'Maybe, maybe,' laughed Elizabeth. She tried to lift up the suitcase but it was heavy.

'What on earth have you in this, rocks?' she asked.

Aisling took it back. 'No, food from the land of plenty. They all went mad: cake for your dad's birthday, side of bacon smoked, oh and butter, all wrapped up in newspapers ten times and in a tin. I hope to God it's not running all over the case and destroying every rag I've got in it.'

Elizabeth squeezed her arm and Aisling saw with surprise that in Elizabeth's pale attractive face there were tears in the big blue eyes.

'In a million years you'll never know how glad I am to see you.'

'And me to see you. On the bus to Dublin I began to worry in case you'd have got all different, but you're not. You're thinner though. Is it the fashion or is it this country full of shortages?' She patted Elizabeth's flat stomach admiringly.

'There's none of you there. You're what they'd call a rake, in Kilgarret. I'm dead jealous.'

'Oh there's more than you think,' said Elizabeth and got a fit of helpless giggles which were so infectious that Aisling started to laugh too though she couldn't see why.

They stood under the big arch at Euston, unaware of the admiring and interested glances which were directed at the redhead and the blonde, both of them wiping their eyes and clutching on to each other with a mirth that had quite a lot of hysteria in it.

From the start Aisling got on well with Father. Elizabeth could hardly believe how well she handled him. Father had been only mildly interested to hear that the visitor was arriving and had helped to take some of the boxes and other bits of lumber from the spare room to stack them in the garden shed. Elizabeth had gone to great trouble to make the guest room look nice. She had picked flowers and even bought a mirror from Johnny in the shop.

'Staff discount,' he had said, halving the price.

'Hey, come on, we're not going to cheat Mr Worsky. . . .'

'When oh when will anyone realise that this is Worsky and Stone . . . I am a partner here, cherub, I am trusted and loved. I cheat myself if I give it to you cheap. . . .'

'I'm a worker here, Mr Stone . . . I don't want to see the business I have pride in go down the drain. . . .'

They laughed. Johnny was in great form this week. He was disappointed that they couldn't meet because of her preparations for the friend from Ireland, but he took it lightly.

'Is she pretty, the colleen?' he asked.

'She used to be super. I think I'm going to keep her well hidden from you.'

'Perhaps she wants a chap to show her the sights of London,' he teased.

'Perhaps, but I don't think so. The local lord or squire wants to marry her. She's coming over here to have a think about it.'

'Marry? What does she want to get married at her age for? She's only the same age as you,' said Johnny.

'I know, it's ridiculous,' said Elizabeth, lifting her voice right up with almost a physical effort. 'Perhaps she'll change her mind about it when she sees the delights of London.'

Aisling had loved the room, the flowers, the pretty mirror. She had marvelled at everything: the red buses, the red pillar boxes. The neat gardens, the rows and rows of houses – she couldn't believe so many people must live in one place.

They were having tea at the kitchen table when Father came in. At once Aisling went into the attack.

'You're never a man who's going to be fifty years, Mr White, are you?' she said before any introductions were made.

'Well . . . er . . . how do you do . . . that's right I . . . er. . . .'

'Father, this is Aisling,' said Elizabeth unnecessarily.

'Well, it's some kind of mistake I think. I tell you Mr White, my father is fifty-one and he looks ten, fifteen years older than you. I mean that now, not a word of a lie.'

Elizabeth thought Father would recoil from such over-familiarity but to her amazement she saw him almost preening.

'I'm sure that your father . . .'

'I don't have a picture of him or I'd prove it to you. Come on now and sit down Mr White. You must be tired after your day's work. Isn't this an astonishing country?'

Hiding a smile, Elizabeth poured a cup of tea for Father.

'Why is it astonishing?'

Aisling burbled happily on, telling of all the marvels she had seen from the train. Huge cities and big factory chimneys and miles and miles of fields. Nobody in Ireland knew that there was any countryside in England, they thought it was all cities.

Then she leaped up and unwrapped some of the foods. She brushed aside Father's worries about how she got them through customs.

'Don't you see this tin has "dinner service" written on it?' The butter had kept, the chicken was perfect, the side of bacon was put in the larder.

'But my dear, we must recompense you for all this. . . .' Father began.

Elizabeth ground her teeth in rage. Trust him, trust him not to understand friendship and generosity and presents. Trust him to think that this was something you paid for. But Aisling didn't seem a bit put out.

'Not at all. These are presents from Mam and Dad. Now of course there is a chance that I might go into the black market seriously now that I've discovered how easy it is to get things in. Then it would be a matter of payment.'

She threw her head back and laughed. Elizabeth thought she looked so lively and bright, she was like a coloured picture when everyone else was in black and white.

'Now, Mr White, what are we going to do for this birthday of yours? That's why I'm here.'

Father looked up in alarm. 'No, not seriously. . . .'

Aisling was quick to see the alarm reflected on Elizabeth's face. 'Heavens no, I'm only pulling your leg, but it is a coincidence that when I wanted to come and see Elizabeth . . .' she looked over his shoulder for confirmation. Elizabeth nodded enthusiastically. 'When I asked if I could come for a visit . . . that I also heard it was your birthday.'

His face cleared. 'Oh, it's silly for a man of my age . . .'

'Not at all, when Dad was fifty we had a great party, and Mam will be fifty next year and so we'll have a massive celebration altogether.'

'What did you do when your father was fifty?' asked poor Father. Elizabeth felt a wave of pity for him, he was like a lonely child.

But Aisling seemed to see none of this. She leant across the table, chatting as if she'd known him all her life.

'Well, it was a Thursday so we went to Maher's. We still do that you know, Elizabeth, and they often ask for you there. It's a pub. . . .'

'A public house, and you all went . . .?'

'Well, yes, we always go.'

'They're not like pubs here Father. They're half pubs and half shops. They sell groceries at one end and drink at the other.'

187

'Well I never,' said Father. 'You never told me that.'

Aisling told the story of an evening when Peggy came down to Maher's four times to say that the dinner was stuck to the roof of the oven but Dad wouldn't go home because everyone in the place had to buy a drink to celebrate Sean O'Connor being fifty. Eventually Mam had taken Donal and Niamh home and put them to bed, and they woke up again at eleven o'clock when Father and Eamonn had come in singing, and Mam said that was the last time they'd ever go along with this nonsense of having a dinner in the evening like the gentry, it only led to trouble.

Father actually laughed at the descriptions instead of wrinkling up his lip as Elizabeth had feared. Normally Father spent three minutes having a cup of tea before shuffling off. Today he seemed ready to sit in the kitchen forever.

'It's your bridge evening,' Elizabeth reminded him. 'Mr Woods isn't it?'

Reluctantly Father went off to change his shirt and spruce himself up.

'He's grand altogether,' said Aisling when he was out of earshot. 'You never told me he was a fine handsome man. I don't know what you go on about for in your letters, he seems a very peaceable sort of man to me.'

'You bring out the best in him. I only make him more miserable,' said Elizabeth.

'Oh I know what I'll do. Why don't I marry him? He's not much older than Tony Murray, and to tell you the truth I think he's a finer-looking man. Then I'll be your step-mother and you and I'll be related after all.'

Elizabeth laughed, delighted with the whole fantasy.

'Great, we could have the wedding from this house and the honeymoon in Kilgarret and I could come with you.'

'Yes, Westminster Abbey, no that's Protestant, what's the Catholic one called?'

'I think you're forgetting about the d-i-v-o-r-c-e,' Elizabeth spelled out. 'It might have to be a registry office job.'

'Oh it's off then. Forget it,' said Aisling.

You must tell me all about Tony Murray, every detail, every single thing.'

'I will of course. But what about Clark Gable, where is he? I thought you'd have him on a padlock and chain at the station. It's not all over or anything is it? Not when I've come the whole way to have a look at him. . . .'

'No it's not all over. But wait until Father's gone. I'll tell you the whole thing then, I don't want to be interrupted . . . and I don't want to have to break off if he comes in to say goodbye. . . .'

'Does he not know about Clark Gable then?'

'Oh he does in a way . . . but it's too complicated. Now tell me about Squire Murray.'

'That's a good name for him. Well, he's a bit of a cock of the walk you know, big fellow with the lads in the hotel. Wouldn't drink in Maher's or anything, but in the bar of the hotel of an evening. He's got a car, a Packard. Well, he runs Murray's, Eamonn says actually that he doesn't do much in it, and that it's their awful little pickasheen Mr Meade that runs it. But you wouldn't mind Eamonn, you see he and his friends would call Tony's lot the High and Mighty's – not as high and mighty as the Gray's and all, but that's different they're sort of Protestants with big houses. . . .'

'Does that still matter?' asked Elizabeth.

'It doesn't matter, it's just still there. Anyway what else about Tony? Well he started to try and pin me down on Tuesday night last, and I told him a pack of lies. I said I was going to have to see the world before I said anything like yes or no. I'd no idea on God's earth how I was going to travel, and didn't I come home that night and find your letter? Wasn't it like an act of God?'

Elizabeth laughed. 'In a way I suppose.'

'So after I rang you yesterday morning, and after I had an hour-long barney with Dad about time off, Mam supported me of course . . . I went up to Murray's and asked to speak to him. Ten o'clock and he wasn't there, and prissy-prunes Meade said that Mr Tony might be in around eleven. Oh, the life for some! I was going to write him a note but I thought I'd express it wrong, so I got a lift from the hotel out to his house. His Mam was there. "I'm afraid Tony's in bed," she said. "At a quarter past ten in the morning!" I said. That didn't please her. "He was out late and he's tired," she said. I got an awful urge to tell her why he was tired. Anyway, to cut a long story short, he came down in his dressing-gown. His Mam was sort of hovering around in case we fell on each other. But she went off eventually, and I told him that I was going off that evening.'

'Was he upset?'

'He was outraged. Why hadn't I told him? Why was I springing it on him? Why was I so juvenile? Why this, why that . . . but I was able for him, I really was. I spoke in a low throaty voice like they do in the pictures. I said that I was young and I thought I knew my own mind, but I had to be sure. I reminded him that nothing had been asked or answered and that it was better that way. He listened, a bit mournful, but he didn't interrupt. So I said I'd look forward to seeing him when I got back.'

'It was very good timing for you then?' Elizabeth said.

'It couldn't have been better. It really did save my life as I said at the station. I couldn't have said to you that I wanted to come over and I really didn't have the fare together. Hey, Elizabeth, I can't take the fare from you. Why did you send it anyway? I'll pay you back.'

'Idiot, look at all the food you brought. That's twice the fare.'

'Oh, okay, well anyway, to end up – I told him I couldn't stay any longer, the delivery man from the hotel was waiting for me and that I'd see him later.'

'He came out to the steps of the house, you remember it don't you? The big one on the river about a mile out of town. ⁻
'"When is later?" he shouted.
'"Later is later," I shouted back. I don't know what I meant but it sounded great. And then I got myself together and here I am.'
'And what do you really think of him? Do you really like him?'
'I don't know. Honestly and truthfully I don't know. I'm flattered by him, and I'm becoming a bit of a cock of the walk myself with others in the town thinking more of me for going out with him. But . . .'
'But what . . . I mean when the two of you are on your own. . . .'
'I like it when he tells me I'm attractive-looking, and I like it when he says what he'd like to do with me . . . if you know what I mean, but I don't like all the grunting when he's trying to do it . . . if you know what I mean.'
'Trying, what do you mean trying?'
'You know, him struggling in the car to get my clothes off and me struggling to keep them on, the usual sort of thing.'
'Oh,' said Elizabeth. 'Oh of course.'
Father came in to say goodbye.
'You'll knock them sideways at that bridge party, Mr White. Don't let them run off with you now.'
Father looked ridiculously pleased. They watched him from the window, fixing his tie and smiling to himself.
'Now he's gone, will you take out some kind of an alcoholic drink and tell me what it's all about. Tell me what happened.'
'What do you mean?'
'Oh anything at all, a sherry, a whisky . . . I even had a brandy on the boat. I'm not particular.'
'I didn't mean what drink. I meant what do you mean tell you what happened? Why, do you think something happened?'
Aisling was on her knees in front of a cupboard. 'This is the kind of a place you'd keep the drink.'
'No, silly, it's in the other room.' They walked in and in the corner cabinet there was a bottle of sherry with three quarters of its contents left. A half bottle of whiskey seemed to be untouched.
'I think we'll start on the sherry,' said Aisling firmly. 'If it's bad enough we may get to the whiskey.'
'It's bad enough,' said Elizabeth. 'Let's take the whisky with us as well.'

They poured the sherry into two ordinary glasses, great dollops of it.
'Cheers,' said Elizabeth.
'*Slainte*,' said Aisling.
'It's as bad as it could be,' said Elizabeth.
'Johnny Stone threw you over . . .?' suggested Aisling.

'No.'

'He turned out to have a wife and children?'

'No.'

'Well is it about him at all?'

'Oh yes, yes it's all about him.'

'I can't think Elizabeth, really. What is it? You sounded desperate in your letter, even though you look quite all right now. What is it?'

'I'm pregnant.'

'WHAT?'

'I'm pregnant. My period was three weeks late. I went to have a test and it's positive. I'm going to have a baby.'

'No.'

'Oh Aisling, what am I going to do? What on earth am I going to do?'

'You mean . . .'

Elizabeth had begun to cry now and there was no stopping her. Aisling moved over and put her arm around the shaking shoulder.

'What am I going to do, you've got to help me.'

'Shush, shush. You mean, you mean you had sexual intercourse with him?'

Elizabeth's hands came from her amazed face.

'Of course I had. How else would I be pregnant?'

'You mean lots of times? For ages or just once?'

'For ages. Oh since last spring.'

'And what was it like?'

'What was it like?'

'Sexual intercourse, what was it like?'

'Aisling O'Connor, I can't believe you. I've told you the most terrible tragedy, I've told you the worst bit of bad news anyone could have, and you ask me what it's like having sex . . .'

'I just didn't know you did, like that you had done it.'

'Listen to me, doing it is no problem, that's easy, it's what to do about it . . . that's the problem.'

Aisling recovered. 'Yes, I'm sorry I got side-tracked. It just seems to put you on a different side of the fence from me, the ones who know what it's like and the ones who don't. I feel so stupid telling you all about the silly things I was up to and assuming . . .'

'No, why should you feel stupid? I would never have either if it hadn't been for Johnny. With him it's normal, it's part of the way we go on. He never thinks of it as anything special, or people who Do and people who Don't. I would have been like you otherwise, it's just that I take my line from him.'

'I know.'

'But now it's true, Aisling. I can't pretend any more. I knew really for days, but I wouldn't let myself admit it. Then on Monday I went off to a doctor miles and miles away. I bought a ring in Woolworth's and I told him I was a visitor and I just wanted it confirmed.'

'And what did you have to do?'

'I took along a specimen of urine, I knew that, I had heard you had to bring what you did first thing in the morning for them to do a test.'

'Yes, I see.'

'So I put it in a jam jar, I didn't know what else to put it in. And he said that was fine. And he asked me to come back on Wednesday. So while you were driving round Kilgarret giving ultimatums to people, I was lying in a chair like a dentist's chair and there were stirrups in it where you put your feet and he felt inside me and examined my breasts and said that there was no doubt.'

'Oh God. Poor Elizabeth.'

'He was very nice actually. He said, "Congratulations Mrs Stone," and I tried to put on a pleased smile. But I bet he knew anyway. I said to him that my husband would be pleased, and I gave him his money, thirty shillings it was, in an envelope. But I bet he knew. He sort of patted me on the shoulder as I was leaving. He said, "These things often work out better than you think," I said I didn't know what he meant. He said, "Just remember that things often work out better than you think." So I said I would. And here we are.'

'Oh Elizabeth. Poor, poor Elizabeth. What a thing to have to go through.'

'Yes, but that's nothing to what other things I'll have to go through.'

'What did Johnny say?'

'I haven't told him.'

'When are you telling him?'

'I'm not going to tell him.'

'But you'll have to tell him some time.'

'No I won't.'

'You're not making sense. When you get married, when it's obvious that you're going to have a baby – you can't keep it a secret until it arrives can you?' Aisling looked puzzled. 'I think you're in shock over it all, I really do.'

'We won't be getting married.'

'Well of course you will, once he knows. Won't you?'

'No. He won't know.'

'But he's fond of you. He still fancies you doesn't he?'

'Oh yes.'

'And you fancy him.'

'Oh I do.'

'And there's no awful secret like him being tied up with anyone else?'

'No.'

'So all you have to do is to screw yourself up to tell him. Isn't that it? And he'll be a bit annoyed because maybe he didn't want to settle down yet. But he'll realise it might as well be now as later. And count your blessings you're in a place like this where people aren't looking at you and whispering and gossiping about you. Nobody's going to count the months you were married before Little Stone junior is born . . . Elizabeth why are you crying so much? It isn't that bad. All he can do is curse and swear a bit about the timing . . . isn't that all? I mean it's not as if it were your fault is it? You're not trying to trap him or anything. You both did it, so it's the concern of both of you.'

'No, no, it's my decision,' Elizabeth mumbled into her handkerchief. Her eyes were red now and her face streaked. Aisling was very concerned.

'Here, have another dose of this,' she poured some sherry into the glass with a slurp. 'How do you mean it was your decision? You didn't want to get caught did you?'

'No, now, it's my decision now,' snuffled Elizabeth. 'You see I want him so desperately. I've never wanted anything so much in my whole life. I'll die if I can't have him. I don't want to go on living if I can't have Johnny. . . .'

'Yes, well.' Aisling was startled at such strong words from Elizabeth. 'Well, you will have him, won't you? He's not going to say that he doesn't want to have anything to do with you. I mean if you work together and like each other, and you've been going out with him and . . . er . . . sleeping with him and everything. It's not just a casual thing that he's going to get out of . . . is it?'

Elizabeth had stopped her crying suddenly. 'Now, this is what I'm going to have to explain to you, and it may take all night. This is why I begged you to come over and why you are the best friend I have in the world. I'm going to have to get rid of it. No, please let me finish. I've decided that's what I must do, but I'm afraid. I really am, I suppose, afraid I'll bleed to death. I'm afraid I'll get an infection and die. I'm afraid it will hurt so desperately that I'll scream and scream and she'll stop. . . .'

'Who will stop?' Aisling's voice was a whisper.

'Mrs Norris. She's a nurse and a midwife and everything, and the place is scrupulously clean. That's what I heard.'

Aisling's glass of sherry remained poised in the air. 'You never mean . . . you can't possibly mean that you're going to a woman to have an abortion? To have her do an abortion on you?'

'It's the only solution.'

'And what does Johnny say about this? Does he approve?'

'Listen, he must never know. I know, I knew it would be like this. I've had to explain it aloud even to myself, and I can't understand it logically . . . but what I've got to do is make you believe that Johnny doesn't get involved in people's lives, in fusses, in things he doesn't want to . . . that's not his style. . . .'

'So you're going to get rid of his child in an abortionist's because it mightn't be his style . . . Come on, out of that.'

'Pass the sherry, it's going to be a long night.' said Elizabeth.

It was a very long night. They transferred upstairs to Elizabeth's room, lest Father should come in and want to continue the easy-going conversation he had enjoyed earlier on. They heard him come in and go to his room. Later they moved downstairs again and made soup and sandwiches. This was at four a.m.

By now Aisling's eyes were as red as Elizabeth's. And when dawn came in the kitchen window, she had made the following promises . . .

– that she would never mention to Johnny anything of this occurrence;

– that she would try to maintain a cheerful and non-curious atmosphere in Clarence Gardens;

– that she would accompany Elizabeth to Mrs Norris's house and stay as long as was permitted.

'I've given in on everything,' she said to Elizabeth blearily just before they traipsed upstairs again to bed.

'I used to think I was a strong character, but now I've gone along with all these things I don't agree with. I can't see why you won't have the baby, I am utterly certain he would marry you . . . I can't see why you wouldn't have it even if he doesn't marry you . . . if he sees you living happily and cheerfully here with the baby he'll admire you all the more . . . no matter how happy-go-lucky he is. If you are going through with this thing . . . then it's brave and courageous and I really can't see why you won't let him praise you and congratulate you for that . . . .

'But no, you're going to meet him next week as if nothing had happened. I think you're out of your bloody mind, and I think he sounds the most cruel, selfish bum who ever walked. . . .'

Elizabeth smiled weakly. 'No, he's just very honest, he says he only does what he wants, and now I'm learning from him. I'm doing what I want. The unselfish one is you, because you're going to help me even though you think it's wrong. You probably even think it's a mortal sin.'

'God, I've almost forgotten about mortal sin with all the rest of the drama, but you can bet your life that's exactly what it is, a desperate mortal sin on top of everything else.'

The days passed in a blur for both of them. There was the visit to the shop, the meeting with Mr Worsky, how delighted he was with Aisling and her hair, and her name. He made her write it down . . . a fairy dream . . . how beautiful. He called Anna from the back room. She marvelled too. They had both heard of Elizabeth's wonderful years in Ireland. Aisling's heart softened again when she saw how much the old couple did indeed know about Kilgarret, and her big family, and how her brother had been killed in the war.

Then there was the meeting with Monica Hart, who worked in a dress shop now. She wasn't a close friend of Elizabeth's these days but she was delighted to meet Aisling.

'You called a cat after me didn't you?' she said. Aisling looked at the rather scrawny girl in her black shop-dress, her frizzy hair and very orange lipstick and nail polish.

'Yes we did, it's there still. It's a big cat now and it's old and it belongs to Niamh my younger sister. When Elizabeth went back here it sort of was passed on to Niamh like old clothes are.'

Monica came and had a cup of coffee with them in her lunch hour.

'I never see Elizabeth nowadays because of Romeo in the antique shop. Have you met him yet?'

'No,' said Aisling, 'I haven't met him yet. He's away until this afternoon. I am looking forward to seeing him though.'

She spoke jokingly as if Elizabeth weren't there.

'Come on, Monica, tell me, is he as handsome as they say? Is he really as good as he's made out to be?'

'Yes, he's every bit as glamorous . . . he's a real heartbreaker . . . He's the kind of man that would have slaves if he were in a film.'

'Well, thank heavens life isn't a film,' said Aisling, looking meaningfully at Elizabeth, who looked away.

They did the shopping for Father's celebration meal on the following night. Aisling bought him a bright tie and handkerchief to match. Elizabeth got him a smart tiepin and cufflinks. Then they wandered back to the shop where a big van was now parked.

'Remember you promised,' whispered Elizabeth hoarsely.

'I remember,' said Aisling.

Johnny Stone bounded down the shop to meet them. He was so warm and welcoming that Aisling was totally taken aback. From the hours and hours of description that night she had assumed that he would be distant and superior, that he would talk in clipped tones like lords and aristocrats talked in the countless films they saw in the cinema in Kilgarret.

'Well, let me have a look at you. Stefan and Anna . . . those two were meant to be working on cataloguing the last lot of stuff I brought in . . . but no, oohing and aahing over the lovely copper hair. Come here, let me see it in the light. It's good, I grant you, it's real but it's not blonde. I like blondes. You know where you are with a blonde I always say.' He had an arm around each of them affectionately.

He had a beautiful strong face, not at all like Clark Gable, but much longer and leaner. He was a very attractive man indeed. Aisling thought that it would be very dangerous and exciting to have sexual intercourse with a man like that and tried to imagine Elizabeth doing so, but failed.

'Enough playing about, Aisling, you are very welcome to London. What can we do to make your visit a good one . . . what shall we do to make you remember us here when you go back to the Emerald Isle?'

Aisling bit down her nervous giggle. She felt an urge to say that since she was going to take part in a conspiracy, an illegal operation and the Lord knew what else she had plenty to make the visit memorable. But she remembered her promise.

'You'd be appalled altogether to know what I really want to do . . . I want to sit down and catch up on the last four years with Elizabeth. Everyone in Kilgarret wants to know what she's been doing, and I want to tell her all my adventures. . . .'

'I'm sure there are plenty of them,' said Johnny.

'There's hours of them, thank God,' said Aisling. 'They'll have us entertained night and day. . . .'

She liked him. He wasn't flirting with her. He was being charming, as he would have been to any new acquaintance. He was possibly the most charming and relaxed man she had ever met. She didn't envy Elizabeth, she couldn't understand a selfless, slavish love like that . . . but she did see that if you wanted Johnny Stone to stick around in your life then you would need to be fairly high on charm yourself. You wouldn't want to be unlucky or depressing or to get dragged down, nor to let any of these things rub off on him.

But she gave no hint of this as she smiled delightedly when he said he was going to take them both for coffee and cakes to celebrate her arrival.

The appointment with Mrs Norris was not until Monday morning, so the whole weekend had to be got through.

'Do you feel any morning sickness?' Aisling enquired on Saturday morning when she had brought Elizabeth a cup of tea in bed.

'Heavens no, I've read all about it. That wouldn't happen for ages yet. There's nothing really there you know, inside me I mean, nothing to make me sick. It's only a speck.'

'I see,' said Aisling.

'Not a person, a baby or anything.'

'No, of course.'

'Anyway,' Elizabeth changed the subject, 'you've no idea what a treat this is . . . I don't know when I had a cup of tea brought to me in bed. Let me see. Not in Mother's, no Harry did offer, but I got up. Not anywhere . . . the last time I remember was when we had measles in Kilgarret.'

'Lord yes, we were awful weren't we, and with my hair I looked like a mad thing. Imagine how poor Mam had to cope with all of us, and Peggy being in bed. Sometimes I don't know where she got the energy. . . .'

'You seem to get on much better with her now. . . .'

Elizabeth sat up in bed and drank her tea.

'Yes, I suppose it's normal in a way, I used to be very jealous of the way she could talk to you, but since I've gone to work in the shop, it's been different . . . and she's been very grateful when I do any little bit extra . . . she does ask about you you know, she sent all her love and said that if you had any worries to say she'd say a prayer for you . . . .'

'That was nice,' Elizabeth said with a note of regret.

'I could say it was special intention,' Aisling said. 'Then Mam could pray and Our Lord would channel the prayers somewhere else for you. It wouldn't be right of course for her to pray that you'd get over an abortion or anything. It would be flying in the eyes of God.'

'Oh my goodness, I know,' said Elizabeth apologetically. There was a little silence.

'You couldn't discuss it with your own mother? You said that you were getting along much better with her nowadays, like I am ... would she be able to help?'

'No, I think it would frighten her ... confuse her. She's not really able to cope ... look, there's her last letter, have a look at it ....'

'There's no beginning ... this isn't the start.'

'Yes it is. That's the way she writes nowadays. ...'

'And you would find it very hard in this ugly world, this modern ugly world, to know what it was like when I was a girl. We wore long flowing dresses ... very tight waists, and flowers in our hair. Always fresh flowers, perhaps four or five different gardenias a day ... just a little sign of a flower wilting and it was thrown lightly away ... what we had Elizabeth that had been snatched away from you was beauty ... so much beauty ... the lawns where we had spread out the thick white cloths and napkins were green velvet lawns ... not scrubland ... the men ... the young men going off to the war were so gallant and so brave. Their eyes used to dance ... they were light-hearted about their lives. "It will be worth it, Violet, if you send me away with a kiss ...."'

Aisling stopped reading.

'Oh God, but none of this is true is it? She wasn't old enough to send people away to the first war was she?'

'No of course she wasn't. It's all imagination ... there weren't dresses like that, there were no flowers ... no picnics on lawns. She lived in a house a bit like this and went to a couple of twenties parties and married Father. You see she's got it all mixed up with those romances and books she reads. It looks a bit as if her mind is going doesn't it? Isn't that the way it seems to you?'

'Well a bit, but it might only be for a while. You know, it could be only temporary.'

'Oh Aisling, what *would* I do without you?'

Then there was the birthday party, that stood out in fairly sharp relief. They must have worked hard to prepare a festive meal, though Aisling could not really remember the day whenever she tried to go back over the sequence of events. They must have gone shopping, they must have cooked, and set the table with paper they coloured themselves.

They put on their best dresses, Aisling in a cream colour which she was afraid looked dull and dreary, but everyone else said it did wonders for her hair so she believed them. Elizabeth wore a rose-coloured velvet. She had never forgotten Johnny saying that he remembered this blonde in rose velvet, but in fact she wondered whether the colour suited her. Sometimes she feared she looked wishy-washy.

Father had dressed up too, they heard him humming and even whistling in the bathroom while he was shaving.

'He never does that,' Elizabeth said wonderingly.

'Poor old devil, he's just dead lonely, that's all that's wrong with him. He needs a bit of attention.'

'But when I try to give him some attention and ask him about things and what he feels and what he used to feel . . . he turns purple.'

'Ah yes, but that's the wrong kind of attention . . . he only needs a superficial kind of attention . . . nothing too deep.'

'You've got awfully good at handling men,' said Elizabeth.

'Indeed I have not. If I'm so good at handling them why am I such an eejit with that Tony Murray? Anyone who could handle men would have him like an adoring lap dog. I'm just in a tizzy in case I lose him on the one hand, or in case I'm tied to him on the other. . . .'

'You're better than I am,' Elizabeth said mournfully.

'You're a different class of a person altogether, you're prepared to put other people before yourself . . . I never was and never will be. That's what Mam always said when I was young, and honestly I think it's the truth . . . I *say* Mr White, don't you look the real birthday boy . . . look at him Elizabeth . . . isn't he gorgeous?'

'You look smashing Father.'

'Thank you my dear, and so do both of you. Very attractive young ladies to share the festive day with. . . .'

He offered them a sherry, and they exchanged glances of relief that they had replaced the bottle which had been finished on the night of Aisling's arrival . . . .

They gave him their presents. He seemed very pleased and in a rare mood of participation he decided that he would put them on. It took a time for him to adjust the tie and handkerchief, and place the tiepin and replace his old cufflinks with the new ones.

There was a card from Mother. Elizabeth had censored it to make sure it had not contained anything fanciful or unstable which would upset everyone. But no, it said: 'I wish you happy years ahead and happy memories of the years that have gone before.' He was pleased with it and put it on the mantelpiece. There was a card from Mrs Ellis which was flowery and vulgar and they all laughed at it in a guilty way. There was a small packet which had an ounce of tobacco and a note from Johnny. 'Happy Birthday wishes from Johnny Stone to Elizabeth's father. I'm sorry it's so small but perhaps when you reach your full century rationing will have gone forever.'

'He's a nice young man,' he said, pleased. 'Have you met him Aisling?'

'Oh yes, I met him at the shop, but he and Madam here are having some kind of silly tiff so I didn't get to know him.' Aisling followed the rehearsed line.

Everything was defined as excellent. Home-made bread from Ireland, soda bread, wrapped up in butter-paper to keep it fresh, spread thick with butter, slice after slice of it with the soup.

'Hey, don't let's forget the main course. We must leave room.'

They ran backwards and forwards from oven to table. Flashes of rose and cream, giggles when they bumped into each other. Oohs and aahs at the smell of the bacon . . . every plate cleaned to shining because nobody had eaten anything at midday in order to prepare for the feast.

Then there was the cake. One candle not fifty, that was more reasonable.

They lit it and looked at him expectantly.

'Oh no, I'm not a child . . . this is a bit too . . . it's not really. . . .'

'Come on Mr White. A birthday's not a birthday unless you blow out a candle.'

'No, no that's for children . . . no.'

'Oh do blow it out Father, it's a celebration.' Elizabeth almost trembled as she spoke . . . her lower lip looked a lot like someone about to cry.

'Mr White, if you don't blow it out how can we sing "Happy Birthday", how can we do it?' Aisling looked so eager and excited in the candlelight.

'Well, it's a bit silly.' Father stood up and took a great breath like a child and blew out the candle. They clapped and sang 'Happy Birthday' and 'For he's a Jolly Good Fellow'.

'Right,' Aisling pushed back her chair a bit. It was as if the signal for entertainment had been given. 'Right, what are you going to sing for us? Mr White, you must have a fund of songs.'

Elizabeth looked alarmed. Didn't Aisling realise how little singing went on in this household? They weren't like the O'Connors, who would burst into 'Believe Me If All Those Endearing Young Charms' as soon as there was the slightest encouragement.

Father didn't sing. Flushing, she remembered how she had practically closed down the party that night in Preston by singing 'Danny Boy'.

'No, I'm not a singer personally,' he was clearing his throat.

'You surprise me,' said Aisling. 'I heard great sounds coming from the bathroom there. It wasn't a gramophone you had in with you?'

'Yes, you're trapped now Father,' cried Elizabeth, joining in the game.

'No, no, no,' but he was laughing, not irritated.

'Let me see, what would be your forte . . . music-hall songs? Light opera . . . Gilbert and Sullivan maybe . . .?'

'Yes, you do know some Gilbert and Sullivan Father. . . .'

'Not really . . . not to sing.'

Aisling had stood up already . . . 'Come on, I'll start you off –

'Take a pair of sparkling eyes,
Hidden ever and anon. . . .'

She made gestures as if she were conducting a choir . . . 'Come on can't
you . . . don't leave me on my own. . . .'
Elizabeth and Father joined in . . . .
'No, no, we'll start again, do it properly.

'Take a pair of sparkling eyes,
Hidden ever and anon
In a merciful eclipse
Do not heed their mild surprise
Having passed the Rubicon
Take a pair of rosy lips . . .

Take a figure trimly planned . . .'

Elizabeth watched open-mouthed as Father's voice soared on and on
with Aisling, who couldn't really remember the words, humming and en-
couraging and joining in on last lines. . . .
'I'm not sure if I had the right key, I think I went through about three
keys altogether,' he laughed apologetically.
'Nonsense, it was beautiful,' Aisling insisted.
'Now come on Elizabeth, what have you learned since you left Kilgar-
ret?'
'I don't sing much really.'
'Come on, of course you do. Weren't we always singing on our
bicycles back home?'
'That was different.'
'All right, wait,' Aisling ran out the kitchen door and came in wheel-
ing Elizabeth's bicycle.
Everyone laughed. The bicycle looked cumbersome and out of place at
the table which was full of dirty dishes and the birthday cake. . . .
'Now you have your bicycle, get up on it and sing.'
Elizabeth looked nervously at Father to see how he was taking it. It
was all so silly, so irresponsible and childish. All the things he said he de-
tested and there he was grinning like an idiot.
She leaped up and sat on the saddle . . . and pretending it was a horse
she started . . . .

'As I was going over the Cork and Kerry Mountain
I met with Captain Farrell and his money he was counting
I first produced my pistol, and then produced my rapier
Saying stand and deliver for you are my bold deceiver. . . .'

And because it was done with such gusto, she managed to get Father and Aisling standing up and shouting the chorus . . . .

'Wack fol de daddy o
There's whiskey in the jar. . . .'

Elizabeth remembered all the verses and they sang louder and louder until the last chorus was almost bellowed.

Nobody cleared the table, the night went on and on. Elizabeth remembered 'Bold Robert Emmet the Darling of Ireland'. Aisling remembered 'Greensleeves' . . . and as his fiftieth birthday was coming to an end Elizabeth's father remembered

'On the road to Mandalay
Where the flyin'-fishes play
An' the dawn comes up like thunder
Outer China 'crost the bay. . . .'

'That's a great one, I don't know that,' called Aisling, and Elizabeth saw Father throw his chest out and sing like she had never known him to sing before. For an instant she wished that Mother could see it and then she was glad that these things weren't possible . . .

Father even sang it twice, so well did it seem to be going down . . .

'. . . An' the temple-bells they say
Come you back, you British soldier
Come you back to Mandalay. . . .'

It finished off the birthday on a high and excited note . . . .

Sunday seemed a blur. They must have talked, but their minds were on Monday. And most of Monday was a blur too. Bits of it were only too clear, like the explanation of where they were going. Mythical friends of the O'Connors had been invented, people who lived now in Romford. Elizabeth and Aisling were going to spend three days with them. The warmth and bonds of the Saturday night had to be cooled and disengaged again. Elizabeth had to remind her father by her voice that he and she led separate lives. Aisling had to become distant instead of engaging. They left him confused and bewildered. But that was a small problem.

The guesthouse was very cheerful. It was run by a young woman who believed in plain speaking as she told them at the start.

'Now listen to me good. I don't know why you're here. I have no idea what you are doing in the area. I gather you want to stay and have a little peace and quiet because one of you has to have some kind of job done. Right, none of my business, I never asked, I don't even want to know your names.'

They looked at her fearfully.

She relaxed a bit. 'Well, just your first names, eh? And it's a nice big room and it's got a wash-hand basin, and there's lots of towels and a rubber sheet and anything else you might need to make you feel comfortable and I'm leaving you in a wireless too for company. There's only a couple of other people staying in the house, a couple of residents, you know, people who live here all the time. They keep themselves to themselves, and a nice couple of gents, travellers. They stay Monday and Tuesday. You won't be disturbed.'

'Thank you,' said Aisling.

'And I'll leave you a kettle, and there's a gas ring, so if you want to do for yourselves, you'll be on your own.'

'Do people often want to be on their own? I mean not able to face people, you know, feeling awful afterwards,' Elizabeth stuttered a bit.

The woman softened still more at Elizabeth's white face.

'No love, I tell you Mrs Norris is really nice. I've been to her three times. Well, don't look surprised my dear, it happens, life is life I say ... No, of course you won't have to stay in your room ducks, it's just nice to know that you have privacy if you do need it.'

'Thank you Mrs ...'

'I'm Maureen dear, just Maureen. You're . . .?'

'Aisling and Elizabeth.'

'Ashley, like in *Gone with the Wind*? I thought it was a man's name ... it's nice though.'

'Yes.'

'I'll show you the room now. Come and go as you like. Listen Ashley, I'll tell you a bit of advice, now take it from Maureen here. I'm in the know. Don't talk about it all too much, no need to talk about things, only makes them a lot worse. That's what Mrs Norris said to me first time and I always remembered it. "Don't talk and talk Maureen, what's done is done." Anyway this kind of thing's been happening to women since the beginning of time. Nature organised life in a very funny way, it seems to me. Even the ancient Egyptians used to have to cope with it and here we are in the twentieth century ... so you take my advice, don't let her chat too much, brood, wonder is it right is it wrong, was it wrong was it right. No good comes of it.'

'No, that's true,' said Aisling.

'Good girl, she's lucky she has a friend with her. Lots of them come on their own.'

Maureen was speaking as if Elizabeth didn't exist.

They went upstairs.

'Let's not even look at this room properly so that we won't remember it,' Elizabeth said.

'The room isn't important, nothing's important except that you're all right.'

'Do you wish I'd turn back even now? Be honest Aisling. Do you want me to change my mind?'

Silence.

'Answer me, I know that's what you want, I know that's what you think is right. So admit it. It's what you hope will happen. You're glad this place is so awful, you're glad that woman's so dreadful and sordid and . . . ugh . . . three times . . . you're thrilled because it makes it all the more squalid. You think it's weakening my resolve don't you?'

'Elizabeth stop it, for God's sake.'

'No, for God's sake you stop it. Stop sitting there with that prissy dis-approving look like an early Christian martyr forced to go through something unpleasant . . . I won't have it. Say it straight out – you want me to cancel everything at this late stage and go ahead and have this child, and get it adopted, or look after it. That's what you really want isn't it?'

Aisling took a notebook out of her handbag and began to write in it. She kept her head down as she sat on one of the beds writing.

Elizabeth paced around. 'But you do see don't you . . . that honestly a lot of your attitudes come from Kilgarret. I mean you've said yourself that everyone lives their lives in the shadow of the church. You are full of the notion of sin about it, and you believe all this stuff about souls and heaven and limbo. Well if it has a soul it will go to limbo and on the last day limbo souls might well get into heaven. And maybe we could baptise it while it's still in me. Had we thought of that? Aisling don't be so cruel . . . why won't you speak to me? Why won't you answer me?'

Aisling handed her the notebook. 'At the end of an eight-hour conver-sation on Thursday night, we agreed that if you had doubts or worries at the last minute that I was to say NOTHING. That was your greatest fear, that I would talk you out of it, or that you would look for an excuse. You made me swear that no matter what the provocation I would say nothing. Now for Christ's sake will you belt up.'

Elizabeth closed her eyes, and laughed until the tears came through her eyelids.

'You are marvellous, absolutely marvellous,' she said. 'How have I managed to live without you for all this time?'

'I don't know, you seem to be going to pieces all right' Aisling said, and magically it made them both laugh.

Aisling remembered that going up the steps of the house where Mrs Norris lived was worse than going to confession after her first ex-periences with Ned Barrett. Elizabeth said that it had the same unreal feeling as had hung around the place when Mother and Father had decided to separate.

Aisling said that she didn't pray and that Mrs Norris was a liar to say that she was on her knees in the parlour of the house when Elizabeth had gone upstairs. She said that Mrs Norris was a dishonest old cow to say that she had been crying and holding her rosary beads when she had been told it was all over. Elizabeth said that Mrs Norris must have heard some praying because otherwise how would she have heard the words 'Hail Holy Queen'? Mrs Norris wasn't a Roman Catholic. She would not have been able to make up a prayer like that unless she heard Aisling say it.

Maureen said that she was sorry she had mentioned rubber sheets if it frightened them. Usually she only said it just to reassure people, of course there would be no need for rubber sheets. It was all over wasn't it? And there, it hadn't been too bad now had it? And there was the rest of her life before Elizabeth wasn't there? She talked to Aisling as if Elizabeth was deaf and dumb.

And Elizabeth felt so well on Wednesday that they went to the pictures. The film was about a woman who had a child but had to pretend that the child belonged to her sister. Bette Davis played the part of the woman and together Aisling and Elizabeth watched her agony as she saw her daughter grow up but could never admit to being her mother. The film was called *The Old Maid*. It was a great weepie and the two girls blew their noses, wiped their eyes and ate liquorice allsorts like any two young girls on an afternoon out.

'You'd never think we had even more adventures than that would you?' said Elizabeth, and Aisling gripped on to her hand and held it tight.

'You would not. We're great, the pair of us,' she said.

The house in Clarence Gardens looked a bit dusty and unwelcoming when they came back. It needed the windows opened and fresh air to come through it. Elizabeth said that it was an oddly-shaped house. It seemed to trap a lot of dead heavy air all the year round. In winter it was cold and musty and in summer it was hot and musty. She wondered whether it had anything to do with the walls. Aisling said she wondered were they going to talk about the weather for the rest of her visit or could they have a normal conversation again? Elizabeth's father came in just then and said he was delighted to see them back, the place had been very empty without them. Elizabeth said to Aisling later that Father was even more of a trial when he was being interested in things than when he was not, and Aisling said that the divil wouldn't please someone as crotchety as Elizabeth.

Johnny too was pleased to see them back. He said that London had been very dull without them, nobody laughed, people retired early to bed. He hoped that the whole problem had been sorted out and everything was all right now. What problem, they had wanted to know, alarmed. Well, the whole question of marriage and whether it was a good idea or a bad idea or the only solution or the last refuge. They looked at him blankly. But Johnny had thought that was one of the main reasons that Aisling had come over in order to sort out her complicated love life. Heavens above it can't have been very serious or pressing if she'd forgotten all about it already. In his innocence he thought that this was what they had gone off to discuss.

Elizabeth took Aisling to see the college of art. It was the summer holidays but some vacation courses were under way so they could wander about. She pointed out the classrooms, the studios, the workshops. In one of the classrooms a boy stood posing for the life class naked. They could see him through the door. Aisling was astounded. Did Elizabeth have to draw naked fellows like that? Never! And put in everything? Go on. And girls too? Absolutely naked? But couldn't you learn how a person was made and their muscles and all even if he wore underpants? Couldn't you just imagine the mickey and draw it? Wasn't everyone's mickey more or less the same?

Around this part of the visit things began to get clearer for Aisling and she remembered that everyone at home would want to know all she had been doing in London. She had better see some sights. She thought too that she had better try to integrate Elizabeth back into the life she was leading before all this drama. She assumed that it revolved around Johnny and this is what Elizabeth wanted to return to. Aisling asked could Johnny take her on a spin in the van the next time he was going somewhere exciting. He thought this was a great idea and said they must all go off to the Tower of London just in case he decided to move Stefan's business down there! He invented a ridiculous reason why they should go everywhere that a visitor might want to see. He found a real reason to go to Brighton and Aisling clapped her hands with excitement to see a huge beach. They went for a swim and splashed each other for hours in the water.

'People won't believe that there's real beaches in England,' she screamed happily. 'Oh Aisling stop making the Irish out to be ridiculous. Of course they know there are beaches here.'

'No, they don't. They really don't. I never heard of anyone tell of an English seaside before. It's great so it is.'

Elizabeth and Johnny exchanged affectionate glances about her, and Johnny put out his hand to touch Elizabeth as Aisling swam off on her own.

'I miss you. I don't suppose that you could slip away for a bit, Nick and Tom won't be . . .'

Elizabeth smiled regretfully. 'Oh no, not while Aisling's here . . .'

'She wouldn't mind.'

'No, out of the question. It's not the kind of thing that I'd do, that anyone would do, when they have a friend to stay. . . .'

She made herself seem both firm and light-hearted about it. And Johnny understood, he laughed goodnaturedly.

'You're a good hostess, you keep all the rules. "The perfect hostess does not abandon the guest in order to satisfy carnal desires with Loved One."'

Elizabeth laughed happily. 'That's it, it's Rule Three.'

'Whatever you say, but when the guest has gone back to the Emerald Isle . . . I warn you I'll be insatiable.'

'Oh good,' said Elizabeth.

Mrs Norris had explained that no relations must take place for two weeks. By then, she said, things could proceed as normal.

'You know you really broke your promise about telling me what it was like . . . sex . . . making love . . . doing it,' Aisling said.

'Funny, I knew I was breaking my promise. The very first night I lay there and wondered had you in fact made love a long time ago and not told me, because there really is something very . . . I don't know . . . something so personal it would be upsetting really to try to describe it.'

'Now you're making it more mysterious than ever. I'll never know. You were my only hope.'

'But I told you, I was sure you knew and everything and weren't telling me for the same kind of reason. . . .'

'Holy God Elizabeth, how would I know in Kilgarret? How on earth would I find out about having sex the whole way with someone?'

'Well, I didn't expect to either . . . you make this sound like Paris or something. This is a London suburb . . . there's not much sin going on here either.'

'Have you forgotten what Kilgarret is like? Everyone knows where everyone is all day and all night. It's like being in a goldfish bowl. I mean, without even being like policemen or suspicious, people know what you're doing twenty-four hours a day . . . "I saw you down at the river the other night" . . . "Josy Lynch says she saw you in Moriarty's chemist". The whole town would know when you were having your period.'

'Or I suppose when you weren't,' said Elizabeth.

'Certainly, I don't know how I'd have organised what you had to do. There's nobody that would know.'

'But what do they do?'

Aisling said nothing.

'They must do something, it must happen.'

'Yes, but . . .'

'Oh go on. Tell me.'

'Well, either the fellow would marry them and the talk would die down in a year or two, or in a dire case the girl might go off to the nuns.'

'Up in the school? Never?'

'Oh Lord, no, not those nuns. Nuns in some country place. They run homes for unmarried mothers, and the girls sort of work there and earn their keep, then when the baby is born it's given for adoption and the girl comes back. She usually says she's been to her granny's. It's a know expression, going to your granny.'

'It must be a very lonely sort of thing to have to do.'

'Yes, it's not great certainly. The whole fear of it would put you off going the whole way, even if you weren't afraid of losing the boy anyway.'

'Are people still afraid of losing people by sleeping with them?'

'Yes, definitely. I wouldn't sleep with anyone if I had serious designs on them, because if I was serious about some fellow and did sleep with him, he might think I was a tramp. I'm not saying he's right, but that's Kilgarret law.j'

'And would you think he was a tramp, or a male tramp . . . or whatever we'd call it . . .?'

'No, that's different. You know about men not being able to control themselves, having this urge implanted in them by God. Yes, I do think it's true actually. You know the way they want to do it with everyone. That's God's plan . . . or nature's plan if you want to call it that, of seeing that the human race goes on. Men are made to do it everywhere and women have to take control of them and insist that they only do it within matrimony and that's society. . . .'

Elizabeth was rocking with laughter.

'You'd be marvellous as a nun, honestly you would, telling all the girls about the facts of life like that. They'd never recover.'

'But honestly isn't that what they told us, in different words?'

'Yes, very different words.'

'I know it sounds ridiculous and complicated but that is the way things seem to work in Kilgarret anyway if not in the rest of the world.'

'Do you blame all those nuns becoming nuns? I think I'd become a nun if I thought all those men were rampaging the town, made to do it everywhere.'

'Spiking their seed all round the place . . . waiting for unwary females . . .'

'Aisling *honestly*.'

'But that's it, it's just a game, and it's like bridge or poker or whatever, people who know the rules and only take the right risks.'

Aisling was distressed to see Elizabeth cooking the books.

'It's very hard for you to understand,' Elizabeth had explained. 'Uncle Sean wouldn't in a million years question what you spent or what Aunt

Eileen spent . . . there's no question of having to account for this and that. Father has the mind of a bank official who has to balance the books at the end of the day. He wants to balance the housekeeping too.'

'But you're cheating him. You're keeping money. If he finds out . . . he'd be so upset. Why don't you just ask him for more?'

'He's got a small mind, he thinks in small terms and small sums and petty accounts. He never checks whether a tin of Spam costs three shillings or it doesn't, but he does add the total up in front of me. Anything I save I earn, I don't steal his money, I just think of ways of saving it and then I keep what I save. That's all.'

Aisling studied the accounts. 'Yes, I see. But it's a bit petty on your side isn't it? It's not very generous . . . or the way people go on in a family.'

'This isn't a family, Father has never been generous. A big open heart like yours or Uncle Sean's or Johnny's he'd find frightening. He'd think that your household was on the brink of chaos because nobody knows exactly to the last penny how much it costs to feed and clothe you all. He'd never take into consideration that your mother feeds half the beggars that come to the door, and that she dressed and fed me for nothing for five years, and that she sends presents and gifts and has pence always in her handbag for anyone she thinks might need one. No, Father would be alarmed by that. He's alarmed by all the marvellous food you brought from Ireland. Three times he asked me should we pay you. I think I should have said yes, it would have calmed him down.'

'You talk about him very coldly, don't you? You used to want him to be nicer and happier and everything. You used to want him to change?'

'Oh yes I did. I used to think I could change him, that we could become like a picture of the Happy Family. "Mr George White, banker, and his only daughter Elizabeth, estranged wife in North of England but isn't it wonderful how well they all manage in their ways." But it didn't work. You can't change people, they go their own way . . . Johnny says there's more unhappiness caused in the world by people trying to change other people than anything else.'

'Does Johnny say that? Why?'

'Oh he gives examples. His friend Nick loves football, Nick's girlfriend Shirley wants to settle down, go and look at furniture in the shops. Shirley wants to change Nick, make him stop playing football; Nick wants to change Shirley and make her come and watch football. They fight about it all the time . . .'

'Well, if old Shirley's got to pound around buying all the furniture on her own, and let loverboy Nick play football . . . is that Johnny's solution . . .?'

'Something like that, yes, then they wouldn't fight. . . .'

'God, he's more selfish than I thought,' said Aisling. 'I'm sorry, I'm sorry it slipped out. I didn't mean it.'

Elizabeth's eyes filled with tears. 'He's not selfish. He didn't come to Mrs Norris with me because he didn't know, he'll never know. He didn't stop me going there because he wasn't told the situation. Now you can't say he's selfish not to have been divinely inspired, can you?'

Aisling apologised. 'I'm always saying the wrong thing, because I don't think before I speak. I don't understand things either . . . but that never stops me interfering. When I think of all those years you stayed with us and you never interfered or hurt anyone. You only patched up quarrels instead of causing them. I feel very thick and stupid coming in here . . . telling you how to behave to your father, telling you what your boyfriend should and shouldn't think.'

'Oh, but if you knew how I hate your going back. I don't know how I'm going to carry on without you. It's so lovely talking and sharing and knowing that you're interested in everything . . . I've missed that so much, I've had a big hole in my life. . . .'

'So have I. . . .'

'But you've a whole family . . . Aunt Eileen . . .'

'Yes, but not about the things we talk about, you and I.'

'I know.'

There was a silence.

'Letters aren't really any good are they? They don't explain much. I can't see Kilgarret through your letters, but maybe it will be better now that you know how interested I am in even little things. . . .'

'Yes, and now that I know all the cast over here . . . maybe you'll write about them properly . . . and not all this "nice" and "super" . . . .'

'And you must cut out all that "nothing much has happened in the last six months" bit.'

'Oh, I will, I'll keep you informed of every groan and grunt in the back seat of the car . . .'

'Aisling, I'll be so lonely without you.'

'Of course you won't. Haven't you got Johnny?'

Johnny took them both to the pictures on Aisling's last night. And to a fish supper afterwards in a big noisy place with marble tables and high ceilings and a great smell of vinegar and batter. No, he wouldn't hear of any contribution, this was his treat. Elizabeth beamed, glad to see his generosity and big-heartedness shown so obviously to Aisling.

'Anyway,' said Johnny. 'It's a goodbye present.'

'Gosh, I'll have to keep coming and going if I get goodbye presents like this all the time.'

'It's not only for you,' said Johnny easily. 'I'm off too. I'm going to take a train to the Mediterranean Sea . . . so it's a joint goodbye.'

'You're going to what . . .?' Elizabeth's face was red and then white, just like it used to be when she was new at the school and the nun had asked her a question she couldn't understand.

'We only arranged it today . . . Nick's got a few weeks off. He works in a car firm, Aisling . . . and his boss says business is slow if he wants to go now, he can have half-pay for five weeks and then a guarantee of his job back. He's jumping at it.'

'And you . . .?' Elizabeth looked horrified. She looked so shocked that Aisling knew instinctively that it was going to irritate Johnny.

'So you're going to jump at it with him, Johnny?' Aisling said hurriedly. 'What a marvellous idea. Can you take time off from work too?'

'Yes,' Johnny was eager. 'Stefan keeps asking me to take a break and now this seems too good to miss. Nick's getting the tickets.'

'When are you going?' Elizabeth's voice was a whisper.

'Saturday, or Friday if he gets a sleeper on the train before.'

'How great.' Aisling had to speak at the top of her voice to try to cover the look of hurt and the stony silence from Elizabeth. 'Is it the south of France or is it Spain . . . or where?'

'It's France, apparently there's a village that a friend of Shirley's was talking about . . . where you can hire a chalet or a tent . . . and you don't need much food in this weather. Shirley said it was meant to be smashing.'

'Is Shirley going with you?' asked Aisling, before Elizabeth could ask the same question in a hurt little voice.

'No, between ourselves, that's part of the reason for the sudden hop. Shirl has been very wearying about everything, and Nick wants a bit of a breather. Too much domesticity and the dangerous clanking sound of wedding bells being yearned for.'

'Oh, he's quite right to run then,' said Aisling. 'That's why I ran from Ireland. You need to put space between yourself and that sort of thing. Thank the Lord none of us have those kind of inclinations.'

She looked sideways at Elizabeth, praying that she would have recovered. She was amazed at what she saw. Elizabeth's face was back to normal and she was smiling broadly.

'Poor Shirl,' she said. 'I suppose I'll have to comfort her when you've gone. I'll try to get her interested in someone else.'

'Oh, I think he quite likes her, it's just that she's such a hanger-on. . . .'

'She's rather pretty. I'm sure she'd find it easy to get another chap. Perhaps we'll go on the prowl together when you're off in *La Belle France*.'

'Ah, but *you're* not to have another chap. You're not to be lost. Do you hear me?'

'Um yes, well I'll probably still be here. I'll be rather too busy to go out prowling, so we'll have to hope that I'm not swept away accidentally. No? I'll work with Mr Worsky and Anna, I might even be a partner when you come back.'

Aisling looked in amazement at Elizabeth's bright face. She was playing it so utterly right. Johnny was almost wavering. He was regretting slightly his decision to go, he was looking at her with enthusiasm and interest.

With a wave of understanding, Aisling realised that if Elizabeth was going to play the game by these rules it was going to be one long act from now to the very end. There could be no normal behaviour, no real reactions, no chance of saying what you felt, what you meant. It would be watching your step, planning your moves.

Elizabeth didn't cry when they got home, she would not admit her shock and upset. She was calm and measured.

'No, I refuse to get upset. I told you before he's what I want. I'll do anything to have him, anything. I've done so much already. I'm not going to lose it all by behaving like silly Shirley and whinging and whining because I'm not being taken along. . . .'

'But for God's sake, I know I'm not going to interfere, but wouldn't it be reasonable to say. . . .'

'I'm not talking about being reasonable. I really am much more like Mother than I thought. Mother wanted something more open and outgoing than Father and so do I. Mother wanted Harry, everyone would have said that it was an unreasonable thing to want . . . but Mother went ahead and she did what was necessary to get Harry and she got him and that's it. That's what I'm going to do. . . .'

'It's different.'

'Of course it's different because Mother was dreadfully odd by the time she did it . . . but the principle is the same. . . .'

Aisling said, 'I suppose I don't know what it's like to be so fond of someone that I'd do . . . well, do all you've done.'

'Oh, you will Aisling, Honestly you will some day be as fond of someone as I am. It sounds a bit . . . as if I were an old woman giving you old wives' advice . . . but you will find someone. And then just like they say in all the songs and the films . . . you'll know.'

'Yes, but once you do know, that's when the troubles seem to begin,' Aisling said doubtfully.

Elizabeth's father said that Aisling's visit had been like a breath of fresh air. Mr Worsky and Anna Strepovsky gave her a picture of a fairy woman in a forest and said she should have it framed back in Ireland, perhaps it had to do with her name . . . Monica gave her staff discount on a blouse she bought for Mam, and Johnny Stone kissed her goodbye on the cheek and said that some time next year he was going to take the van and Elizabeth to Ireland and do a tour of all the old houses which might sell their contents to him.

'I'll come with you if I'm not married to the Squire.'

'Oh, don't dream of marrying the Squire,' said Johnny.

Elizabeth clung to her at the barrier in Euston.

'I keep trying to fight down this awful feeling that I'll never see you again, that you'll go home and think of everything that happened here and you'll become revolted by it all. You'll cut me out of your life.

'I'll never cut you out of my life, I couldn't, you're part of it you silly old thing,' said Aisling. 'If it weren't so soppy I'd say I love you.'

'Well I love you too, I'll never be able to thank you. Never.'

The crowds on the platform swallowed up Aisling in her turquoise summer coat as she walked down the length of the long train. And when she looked back at the barrier there were too many people and she couldn't see Elizabeth in her grey dress waving and wiping her eyes with the corner of the red scarf which was meant to make her look jaunty.

XI

Elizabeth thought that it would be much easier to write to Aisling after the visit . . . but she found to her great disappointment that it was just as hard to explain, just as difficult to describe things. One set of restrictions had been replaced by another. It made her uneasy since she realised that she must assume Aisling was critical of Johnny. And yet Aisling had hardly said a word that could be interpreted as criticism. But then what she kept forgetting was that Johnny didn't *know* there was any reason for him to feel especially protective and loving and grateful to Elizabeth at that time. Johnny didn't know anything about the visit to Romford and the encounter with Mrs Norris, and he never would.

So the letters seemed strained, again. Elizabeth tried to write cheerful things about Father, but Father had never again been so cheerful since his fiftieth birthday. In fact at times Elizabeth wondered whether she had imagined Father singing all those songs. He never sang since, and she hadn't mentioned the night to him.

It was odd that Aisling was able to write without restraint. Sometimes she would urge Elizabeth to burn the letters once they were read in case they would be both hanged or Aisling put in gaol for pornography. Her descriptions of the ever-frustrated passions of Tony Murray were hilarious, and often apologised for by the phrase, 'But of course to a woman of the world like yourself all this must seem very amateur'. She asked questions too about Father and whether the awful woman who was after him was getting anywhere. She told Elizabeth to tell Stefan and Anna that she had enquired about old houses in Ireland and whether they might be bursting with antiques. The answer was yes, they might, but if anyone came over from England in a van to buy them from them they would immediately assume they were being robbed blind and would hold on to whatever they had.

She touched so lightly and so unsurely on the subject of Johnny, compared to everything else. The references to him were half-joking, guarded almost as if she had reread the sentence before allowing it to go. The rest of the letter was pure Aisling, sentences falling over each other . . . enthusiastic and maddening. Exactly the way she talked.

Aunt Eileen still wrote, cheery newsy letters, half-joking references to the handsome young man whom Aisling had described as being the best-looking man she had ever laid eyes on. Elizabeth found it hard to write about Johnny in any normal way so she wrote in an exaggerated style

saying that the Lord and Master had gone off to Scotland, or the Answer
to Hollywood had put up a new sign on the shop saying 'Worsky and
Stone' and spent most of his day out on the pavement admiring it. She
couldn't write to anyone that she loved Johnny Stone so much that her
heart was hurting from jumping up and down in her rib cage. That's the
kind of thing Aisling would have been able to say but then of course Elizabeth remembered ruefully, Aisling's heart wasn't jumping up and
down at all. It was staying exactly where it was, stationary and deliberat-
ing whether or not to lock itself permanently into Tony Murray's heart.

Tony thought that Aisling looked even better when she came back from
England than she had done before. He had found the days very long
because he had no idea when they were going to end. His mother, dis-
approving and hard to please about this as well as everything else,
became a severe trial to him. She had suggested that he might invite one
of the Grays to the tennis club dance. Heedless of his protests that he
didn't even know the Gray girl and didn't want to go to the dance with
anyone, and would like to be allowed to mind his own business, she
spoke on in a firm monologue which she believed was reaching him
because of its constant repetition. Not that she had a thing against the
little O'Connor girl, a charming child. Had she not always been made
welcome at their house when she was a friend of Joannie's, but such a
child, and so nice and so limited, and so young, and what a pity Tony
didn't extend his friends a little more. Why, Mrs Gray had been saying
only last week . . . Tony turned off his mind. He would often get up without excusing himself and leave the table, or walk from the sitting room
with its view down towards the river. No explanation, no apologies, just
one swinging movement into the car and a bold sweep down the drive.

Eileen O'Connor felt that the whole teasing game with Tony was going
on too long. True, Aisling was an attractive girl, true there were more
ways of getting your man than being available. And indeed it was a great
relief after the Maureen and Brendan Daly situation to realise that this
time the boot was on the other foot. Eileen and Sean had felt humiliated
by the delay in Brendan Daly's proposal. It was as if they had decided to
keep the O'Connors on a string. Now Aisling was doing the whole thing
in reverse and it was the Murrays who were dangling in uncertainty.

Any attempts to know what Aisling's intentions might be were skilfully diverted.

'Do you think it's worth painting your office? Will you still be with us
next year?'

'Of course I'll be with you Mam. Were you thinking of firing me?'

'No, but you know if you marry into the gentry you wouldn't want to
go on working here . . . you wouldn't have to work for a living.'

'Aw, Mam, the Murrays aren't gentry, they're as ignorant as we are.

Anyway I'd like to see someone stopping me from doing what I want to do and I want to work here. What colour will we get it painted?'

'Tony Murray wouldn't want his wife working in a shop Aisling, you must know that.'

'Then he can go and take a flying jump at himself. Listen, what about that bright orange paint that came in a while ago? With the doors white and me in my green coat I'd look like the Irish flag!'

She didn't seem to be the slightest bit serious about him, yet she did see him almost every evening. What on earth was going to happen? Time would tell.

Maureen thought that Aisling had become unbearable since her visit to London. She had become more cocky and more of a show-off than ever. All these stories beginning: 'When we were in Piccadilly Circus' ... and 'Elizabeth and I went for a fish supper in Elephant and Castle' ... just plain showing off. Not a present bought for the babies. A feeble excuse about rationing in England, that was nonsense of course. Hadn't the war been over for years now? Aisling was turning out to be quite poisonous, she even managed to make a jeer and a mock of things when she did deign to come to the house. Poor Brendan was most put out by her, and Brendan's mother had said she was in danger of becoming quite fast with all this careering around the place with Tony Murray and no intentions made clear on any side.

Joannie Murray came back to Kilgarret from time to time, full of the great life she lived in Dublin. She found things increasingly fraught at Riverside House on every visit. People were constantly taking her aside to explain the truth of the situation as if her time spent working in the capital city had given her a new sophistication and insight into the big issues of the Kilgarret day. As far as Joannie could see they all revolved around her friend Aisling O'Connor. Mummy used to walk up and down the drawing room clenching and unclenching her hands and saying that she had nothing against Aisling.

From Aisling she got no joy either. Aisling said there was no mystery. She was very fond of Tony and he seemed to be fond of her. No, neither of them had the slightest intention of doing anything drastic like getting engaged. They were young for heaven's sake. Tony wasn't young, Joannie reminded her, Tony was very old, he was over thirty. Aisling would only giggle and say that thirty was like a spring chicken these days. Then Joannie would repeat this kind of conversation to Mummy, and Mummy would become bad-tempered and accuse Joannie of holding things back. It was really very wearying to come home to Riverside House for weekends. Joannie did it less and less.

Sean was getting tired of people asking him when they would see the great merger of Murrays and O'Connors. One of these conglomerates, they were calling it with wheezy laughs, it could take over half the business in the east of Ireland, a firm that size. They were joking about a possible merger but they weren't joking about Aisling. People wanted to know. Sean was irritated both with the curiosity of the people who came in to him in the shop or drank pints with him at Maher's. He was even more irritated with Aisling.

From time to time he said she was making them all into a laughing stock with her carry-on. Aisling put on huge innocent eyes and said she didn't know what he meant.

Sean would fluff Aisling's hair roughly with his hand and say that the most atrocious thing in the world was to live in a small Irish town and be at the mercy of a lot of small-town gossips.

Elizabeth wrote about Mother. She had been right in her reading of the letters. Mother's nerves were indeed under a strain.

She was in hospital now, and half of the time she didn't know where she was. Harry had been distraught. He begged Elizabeth to come up and see them and to bring that nice young man Johnny who had been such a great fellow the last time. Naturally the nice young man had no intention of going to a house where illness, insanity and confusion would reign, so Elizabeth didn't even try to persuade him. She went by train.

Harry did not look the same Harry when he met her at Preston. He had big worried runnels in his face.

'I did my best for her, Elizabeth love,' he began to bluster as if there was a possibility that he might be blamed for what had happened to Mother. 'I never treated her badly. I tried to go along with whatever she said and wanted. There wasn't all that much money of course, you see there wasn't all that much business. . . .'

To her amazement Elizabeth found herself hugging Harry there and then in the station with passers-by looking at them. Hugging the man she had called that dreadful Mr Elton, the man who had come to steal Mother away all those years ago.

'Harry you old fool,' she said over his big shaking shoulder. 'Harry, you did everything for her. She loves you, she's crazy about you, what are you apologising for? Think what it would be like if her poor nerves had gone when she was in Clarence Gardens. Think how lonely that would have been for her.'

Harry's face was wet too.

'You're a great girl, Elizabeth,' he said. 'Really champion. I don't know how any of us would get along without you. . . .'

Mother was pleased to see Elizabeth, but only pleased in the same way as she was pleased when it was teatime in the war or when it was time to go to the basket-work section in Occupational Therapy. She looked tired and pale. She had very little interest in anything. Elizabeth searched for some subject to bring a spark back to her dead face. She remembered when she had thought that Mother had been over-excited, when she seemed twitchy and nervy, and responded and reacted like a little bird to everything, spreading unease and restlessness around her.

Elizabeth tried to summon up that uneasy life but with no success. 'I often read your letters, Mother, about the wonderful times you had back in the roaring twenties. It must have been great, all those *thé dansants* . . .'

'All the what, dear?'

'Well maybe I'm not pronouncing them right – dancing teatimes, I suppose. Remember you wrote to me about them, you used to go in a lilac dress, you told me, and there were orchestras, small five- or six-piece orchestras . . .?'

She paused. Mother smiled back gently and vaguely.

'Weren't there people coming over to the table you were sitting at, and saying they would be honoured if you would while away a weary afternoon, you know, fancy exaggerated talk . . .?'

Violet looked at her, nodding politely as if she were being told something she didn't understand.

'And remember the man who asked you your name and you said Violet, and he said violet dress, violet eyes and now named Violet, and he ran away and brought back six bunches of violets from a woman in the street, he had given her a whole ten-shilling note. You must remember, you often told me about it even when I was little, and you wrote about it again this year. It *did* happen didn't it?'

'Oh yes, dear, if you say so.' Mother was looking around for the nurse. In her eyes was the hope she would be rescued.

'But Mother,' Elizabeth shouted, 'Mother you're so young, and so lovely and your hair is all matted, why don't you let me wash your hair and comb it for you, let me give you some lipstick, you have such a lovely face, Mother . . .?'

'Nurse . . .' called Mother in a rising tone. An older woman with a face so lined it looked like a dried mud puddle cracking in the sunlight, said to Elizabeth, 'Don't excite her dear, don't try to take her out of here, she feels comfortable here, you'll see. She doesn't want to be upset and confused.'

Elizabeth turned on her. 'She only needs to be reminded of what she's like. She's forgotten what kind of a person she is, *that's* what's wrong.'

'I know,' said the old woman. 'But she's happy forgetting.'

Back in the shop Harry put a closed sign on the door as soon as he saw Elizabeth coming around the corner.

'There's not all that much business,' he said. 'How was she, was she pleased to see you?'

'Harry, take down that closed sign. People who want to buy their half 'pound of margarine must be able to do it.' She reversed the sign on the door, took off her coat and picked up the beige shop-coat that was hanging on a hook; it wouldn't fasten around her. It must have been the one Mother had worn.

'No, I want to hear, I want to know.' Harry was upset and red-faced.

'There's nothing *to* hear, Harry, I swear it. She didn't know what I was talking about. She seemed happy, the other old crones in the ward say she's happy, the nurse says she's happy. She doesn't remember who she is, that's the problem. She's forgotten how to be lively and it's as if the life drained away.'

Harry's eyes were swimming. 'Do you think it will come back, could she change again?'

'The doctor will talk to me tomorrow. He said he hadn't time today and he would only talk if I promised not to ask for miracle cures. I thought he was arrogant and patronising but I didn't say so. I put on a humble face. . . .'

'But what caused it? Why did Vi lose all the life in her?'

'I don't know, Mother doesn't know, and I'm very sure that pompous doctor doesn't know. But Harry, if you're going to be able to afford the bus fare up to the hospital, we'd better keep open. Now, here we go, who's this . . .?'

'Mrs Park, the window, meanest woman north of Manchester, buys one cigarette at a time and two ounces of butter.' The small woman in black came in. 'Hallo there Mrs Park. What can we do for you, do you know my step-daughter Elizabeth?'

'How are you Mrs Park, Harry was just mentioning you were a good customer.'

Mrs Park looked from one to another. 'Aye, well I'm regular, I come here to support local business. Mr Elton, can I have an ounce of that hard cheese, please, more from the middle, not the outside mind, and two Woodbines.'

'Having a party, Mrs Park?' said Harry and Elizabeth had to stuff the hem of Mother's shop-coat into her mouth to stop her laughing aloud.

The doctor sat opposite Elizabeth and explained about illnesses which were psychotic and illnesses which were schizophrenic. He said that Violet's was almost certainly the latter. It was a latent schizophrenia. Normally such a disorder would show itself much earlier. It was a young person's illness. Elizabeth nodded. She kept her scorn for the doctor's posturings out of her face. The self-important way he held his fingertips together and emphasised words as he spoke to the twenty-year-old daughter of one of his patients. She wondered whether he ever stopped showing off and acting.

'Excuse me, does that mean a split personality? Is it a question of Mother having two sides to her personality like you read about in novels . . .?'

This gave the doctor time and opportunity for a peal of laughter. 'Heavens no, my dear. That's a very silly lay person's idea. Dr Jekyll and Mr Hyde. No, it means the person is out of touch with reality, their grip on what is reality has gone. The imaginary, the non-real is just as living to them.'

'And how are you trying to cure Mother?' Elizabeth asked, her cool young voice cutting across the plummy tones.

'As we think best.' His own voice was sharper now. 'With sedation, with giving her a life of order and control where she can be observed and calmed when the forces of unreality become too much. There are new drugs, Largactyl has been in use now for two years and we are trying this on many of our patients.'

Elizabeth forced her voice to be polite and deferential. 'Oh, are you *experimenting* with this new drug on Mother? Let's hope it's a good one.'

'No, I am not experimenting. It is being used all over Britain. We are reporting our findings. In your mother's case the best we can hope for is, well, to be frank, that her life will be as tranquil as possible.'

'You mean it would be foolish for me to hope that she will ever come out of here? She's only forty-nine, doctor. Do I have to tell my step-father that he should regard her as here permanently?'

'You seem a much more adult person than . . .' he looked at his notes, 'than Mr Elton. I feel I can speak to you frankly. His reaction is to promise me that he will give her more time and more attention. And making me assurances that he will offer a better lifestyle. In fact from what I understand, she was quite content with him. He was an adequate provider and husband.'

'She adored him.'

'Quite. Well it's no avail making this kind of statement. What we have to do is to hope that she may occasionally be able to go home for visits for the afternoon, or even for a weekend. These drugs have been known to create very surprising respites, you know. Nothing is impossible.'

'Except to believe that Mother will be as she was.'

'Quite. That would be the folly and a road to disappointment.'

Elizabeth looked at him carefully. Perhaps he was not such a phoney and a fraud. He was, after all, warning her and had tried to warn Harry against false hopes. She stood up. 'I'll go to see Mother again. I'm very grateful to you Doctor, I will explain all this to my step-father, and I will try to make him see.'

'Thank you, Miss White, it's . . . er . . . a pleasure to talk to somebody so calm. It's a great help in this profession, as you must imagine.'

'Yes Doctor, I'm not really calm, but I am practical.'

'Quite. Oh, there's no point in your own father, her first husband, coming to see her. I mean you do realise that she doesn't actually take into account much of that section of her life?'

'No indeed, I wasn't going to suggest it, I'll explain it all to him too in case he thinks that there's anything he should do.'

'Good, good, well goodbye, Miss White.'

He went along his corridor, importance emanating from him. Elizabeth was glad she had controlled herself, and not behaved like many of the distraught relatives of his disturbed patients must have. She braced herself and knocked on the door of Mother's ward.

Mother had slept for eight and a half hours last night, the nurse told Elizabeth, but it was still a tired face that looked up and gave its gentle smile. Mother was sitting in a chair beside her bed with her hands folded in her lap. Her hair had been combed and tied behind her neck with a piece of ribbon. It made her look thinner than ever. She wore a cardigan over her nightdress.

Elizabeth sat down. She held one of mother's thin hands in hers for a bit and said nothing. Violet looked at her anxiously. She seemed to be waiting in case Elizabeth was going to start some unfamiliar pattern of behaviour, some tirade. It was hard to know if she remembered yesterday's upset or not. Nurse was hovering nearby arranging the flowers that Elizabeth had brought in a small vase.

'Oh Mother, wait until I tell you how funny Harry was in the shop yesterday,' Elizabeth began, and she gave a reassuring monologue of trivia. Violet looked less at Nurse. Nurse moved away. Mother left her hand in Elizabeth's, she smiled at the funny bits.

'So, anyway, I have to go back down to London tonight,' Elizabeth said in the same cheery voice. 'I have my final exams soon. Then I'll have to go out and earn a living, but I'll come back and see you in a month maybe, all right?'

'London?' Mother said wonderingly.

'Yes, to Clarence Gardens, and Father.'

'Father?'

'George, your old man, he sends you his best regards, says he hopes they're looking after you here.'

Mother smiled. 'That was nice of him, thank him, tell him I'm fine.'

Elizabeth gulped. 'Sure I will, and Harry's great too, he'll be in later today. He's a smasher, Harry. You picked a great one there, didn't you Mother?'

'Oh yes, Elizabeth, you see there was no question of it right from the start, I simply had to have Harry Elton. He was the only man I ever wanted.'

'Right, and you have him and he has you.'

'Yes.' Mother was beginning to withdraw into herself again.

'So I'll be off now, I'll write a long letter every week and if ever you want me, you only have to get someone to telephone and I'll come back on the next train.'

'Thank you.'

Elizabeth stood up. She was wearing a grey flannel skirt and a dark grey twin set. To liven it up she had pinned on a big artificial flower. It was a bunch of violets in purple velvet with leaves made from taffeta. It was all wound around wire and attached to a pin. Suddenly she took it off and pinned it to Mother's cardigan. It looked lopsided and out of place.

'Thank you,' said Mother.

'You're a good girl, you're a good daughter,' said the lined old woman in the next bed, the woman who had spoken to her yesterday.

'They'll take that away from her, it's got a pin in it. She may do herself a mischief,' said another with her hair in an Eton crop and a puffy face.

'It doesn't matter,' Elizabeth said. 'I'd like to think she had it for a bit anyway.'

Father listened impassively as Elizabeth explained about Mother's illness. He shook his head when it was suggested that the whole thing had begun long ago and had only come to the surface now.

'There was absolutely nothing wrong with your mother when she was here in this house. Nothing at all. Her mind got disturbed when she went up to that place with that Harry Elton and lived in poverty. She had everything she wanted in this house. I'm not going to hear stories that her nerves got bad in this house.'

Elizabeth sighed. 'You're probably right, Father, I just thought I'd explain what the doctor said.'

'We'll say nothing about it to anyone here. I'm a fair man and I'm also a compassionate man,' Father said.

Elizabeth didn't get the drift of his thinking.

'I could easily tell people here, people in the bank and in the bridge club that Violet had become disturbed. I could tell them that she had ended up in a home for the insane. But I won't do that. I'll let me remember her the way she was, I won't give them the chance to say she got her just desserts.'

'Her just desserts?'

'Oh yes, people here would say that she could have expected no better luck when she upped and left her home and her child without a care, that no good would come of it. But no, I won't tell them.'

'That's good of you, Father,' said Elizabeth, closing her eyes so that she would not betray her utter disgust at his petty, old-womanish, told-you-so thinking.

'No, it's just a fair attitude, that's all, it's letting bygones be bygones. Your mother caused us trouble, now she's having her own troubles. That's life, no point in having her punished further by telling all the people she knew here what befell her. Just let it be, I say.'

Sometimes Mr Worsky would read to Elizabeth from some German magazine articles and essays on designs. He translated them as he went along and she politely sat in the shop, leaning against some well-cared-for piece like the sideboard he would never sell or on the little piano stools that Anna had covered lovingly but in the wrong fabric so they were now completely useless.

Elizabeth sat in the sunlight and listened or half listened. Part of her mind took in his words, she heard enough to be able to smile at the little jokes, and to nod thoughtfully as he explained and elaborated.

Her heart seemed like a big piece of ice that had detached itself from an iceberg and was flowing slowly downstream. She thought of Johnny. She thought over and over that she had been right to keep any bad news from him and she wondered did everyone else keep bad news from him like she did? She wondered had anyone else aborted his child rather than lose him? And if they had . . . if some other young woman had gone up the stairs of a house like the house of Mrs Norris . . . then the poor girl had been through all that for no avail. Because whoever she was she hadn't kept Johnny.

She knew it was fanciful and foolish but she felt some silly comfort thinking that other girls must have made similar decisions. She couldn't be the only person in the world who had done such a thing for love.

There was this fear growing in her that it had all been a waste of time. Johnny had somebody else. Well, he hadn't really got somebody else, but there was the woman . . . the girl . . . the one that he spoke of, talked of. The one who came into the shop a lot. The high society woman they called her. He couldn't love her. He couldn't. He couldn't touch her and whisper to her . . . he couldn't share with her what he shared with Elizabeth. It was impossible.

Right, it was impossible. She would not believe it. She had been so sensible about everything so far. She must continue, she must close the awful holes in her mind which let these suspicions in. She must try to warm up her heart again and stop it becoming this cold, dead, frightened thing. Everything was fine, Johnny was fine, he loved her dearly, he always went on about it. And Stefan loved her. She tuned in again to his voice. She listened and half listened as he fought for words, and stumbled for translations of these which would be utterly useless to her in her examination. From time to time, Anna would remonstrate.

'Stefan, seriously . . . the child will not need to know that. . . .'

'Anna, you know nothing about what the child will need to know or will not need to know. She is studying design. I tell her about design, I tell her about European design, otherwise she will think that all Germans made were horrid, horrid steel tubes and hideous modern furniture. I tell her about Meissen china and of the pottery and porcelain of Furstenberg, of Nymphenberg, of Ludwigsberg . . .'

'Berg, berg, berg,' muttered Anna. 'Why care about these bergs and what they made and what they did? They destroyed your country and mine, the people from Furstenberg and Ludwigsberg, and you sit here in the sun and tell the child about what beautiful porcelain they made.' She stamped off back to her little quarters, face red, full of good will, fearful that Stefan Worsky should be thought to be foolish or a bore.

'Sometimes I think your mind does wander, my Elizabeth. Perhaps it is a boring thing I tell you.'

She lifted a Meissen plate and traced her finger over the mark. 'If it weren't for you, Mr Worsky, I wouldn't know whether this plate was a new batch from Woolworth's. Now i can read its history, I can read the story of everything here. It's like a new language you've taught me. And I always wanted someone to care about what I'm doing, you know Mr Worsky, I have so many people I know and not one of them knows what examination I will be doing on Tuesday. Only you and Anna. My father just knows the end is in sight, the great day when all this ridiculous, affected studying of art will be over and I can get a job. That's all he knows. And my mother has lost her mind. I didn't tell you that because Father has this notion that we are to tell nobody in London. She is in a mental ward now of a big hospital in Preston up in Lancashire, and she doesn't really know where she is. I went to see her, remember? But I didn't tell you.'

'Oh, my poor child.'

'And Harry, my big, simple, foolish step-father is up there doing deals with all kinds of people, the vicar, I think, and the doctors and the ward sister, saying that if she gets better he'll look after her better. He looked after her perfectly. She loved every minute with him.'

'Oh my dear. . . .'

'And Monica Hart has just got engaged to a Scotsman who wears a kilt, and she couldn't care if I was doing an examination in design or in plumbing. Aisling O'Connor is waltzing around her home town playing some kind of I'm-the-king-of-the-castle game with all the local gentry, so far as I know. She barely reads my letters, she barely writes any. Her mother, Aunt Eileen, knows it's an examination, but she thinks it's like school. She thinks everyone does the same, she asks about how many of them are going in for the exam, as if it was some huge thing that half the country was doing . . .' Elizabeth was walking around pacing through the furniture. She was more distressed than Mr Worsky had ever seen her. She came back and put her hand on his shoulder. 'So you see how much I appreciate you, and thank you and could never be bored by you in all my life. . . .'

'It is I who thank you, for putting all kinds of happy things into an old man's life and work. Sometimes I am long-winded and boring and I talk too much and I read you long-winded things. Anna is right. I am not sensitive.'

She knelt beside him and took both his hands in hers.

'*You*, not sensitive? Dear Mr Worsky, you are beautifully sensitive. Just now when I'm full of self-pity and listing off all my friends and saying how they don't know and care what I'm doing, you didn't ask me what about Johnny? You didn't say, what about your lover? Surely your young man knows? You didn't say that.'

'But child, Johnny is Johnny, we know that.'

'We do. Johnny is Johnny, and nowadays Johnny is being driven around London in a smart sports car by that woman from high society.'

'She will not last long, the woman from high society.'

'No, you are right, she will want more than Johnny will give her. One of these days she will say to Johnny that they are all going to a house party to meet Princess Margaret, and Johnny will say he's not coming, with no explanation. And the high society woman will sulk and throw him out of her sports car, and she will wait until Johnny telephones to apologise or sends her flowers and then she will forgive him. But what she doesn't know is that he will make no telephone call and send no flowers, there will be no apology.'

'Don't distress yourself.'

'No, that's what will happen, and she will burn with rage for a week and she will call around here, and she will buy something very expensive and she will enquire about Johnny. And we will tell Johnny and he will roll his eyes up to heaven and say Good Lord, and we'll all laugh.' She was still sitting like a child at his knee. He said nothing, but he stroked her hair very lightly. 'So Johnny doesn't know that it's Design Finals and you're the only one in the world outside the college.'

'And I know you'll do very well. If you do not do well there is no fairness in this world.'

'Well there isn't much, is there?' She looked up at him. He said nothing. 'Is there? Your wife dead, your sons lost, your country gone.'

'I have been more lucky than many Polish people. It is you who have had a share of hard times my child. There will be good times to come.'

'Will there? Johnny won't change, you know that.'

'Yes, I know it, what is good is that *you* know it. Now you have two very simple roads to go down. To take him as he is. Or to leave him and to find somebody else. Two clear roads with signposts. You are not lost with a false map.' She stood up and held out her arms. He made an uncertain step towards her. 'Now I give you one big hug and then we go back to preparing for these examinations. If I am the only person who knows you are taking them then I have all the more interest in seeing that you come through with waving colours.'

'Flying colours.'

'I only made a mistake to make you feel superior.'

'I believe you did.'

In July Elizabeth got a distinction in her examination results. The dean of the art college congratulated her, and offered her a part-time job teaching and she could do a teacher's training course at the same time.

Johnny had finished with the debutante. Not that it was ever admitted or acknowledged that there had been anything to finish. He agreed enthusiastically with Stefan that Elizabeth should be put on the payroll as an adviser and consultant and special buyer.

Father took a very dim view of all this. 'Does it mean that there is no end to the college after all? More time at a training college and back in those art rooms with students and still working in the antique shop? It doesn't seem that you've got very far.'

'I've got as far as I want to get, Father,' she said in a clipped tone.

'And is there any sign of this young man of yours asking you to get married? He's been around for long enough,' Father complained.

'There is no sign of either of us wanting to get married, Father, when and if there is, I will tell you.' Her tone was even more clipped, and she thought ruefully that for the first time for a long time she and Aisling were probably saying the same thing at the same time.

The summer went on. Harry wrote to say that Mother was no better and wondered if Elizabeth might come back again, just to cheer them all up. Aisling wrote to say that Tony Murray had got very drunk and almost had his way with her. In her engagingly explicit prose she explained that she was almost certain that penetration had not taken place, but was dead relieved when she got the curse a week later just in case something might have gone wrong. Monica Hart wrote from Scotland. She had eloped with Andrew Furlong because his mother and her mother had been so ridiculous and they had got married at Gretna Green, which wasn't a bit romantic, but wet and miserable, and Scotland was worse. Shirley wrote from Penzance to say that she was going to get married to a very nice fellow she had met in a hotel where he worked as a barman, could Elizabeth please make sure that Nick knew all about it? Elizabeth was to enthuse about how excited and happy Shirley was and if possible to imply that Guy, her fiancé, was actually a hotel manager rather than a barman. He would be some day, of course, so it wasn't really a fib.

And Johnny's mother died suddenly, and he went off to the funeral by himself. Mr Worsky and Anna sent one wreath, and Elizabeth sent another. He didn't want any of them to come. He returned in his usual form, brushing aside expressions of sympathy graciously and easily. Yes, it was all for the best, his mother had been old, she had dreaded the thought of living on beyond her time, she hated being on her own, her best was behind her. He and his brother thought it was all for the best.

He took Elizabeth out to a restaurant for dinner on the night he came back and the waiter brought them a free drink.

'It's to celebrate the birth of the new little princess,' the waiter said. Princess Elizabeth had had a baby girl that day.

'I'm sure she's delighted,' said Elizabeth. 'First a boy and then a girl. Just right.'

'Just right for Princess Elizabeth, who has a fleet of servants and all the

225

money in the world, but not right for my Elizabeth who has no money and no time.'

'Absolutely not,' said Elizabeth, raising her glass to drink to the health of the baby with a brave smile and a defiant wave of the blonde hairs out of her eyes.

Elizabeth enjoyed the teachers' training course. She thought it had very little to do with real life, since the high principles of education were not nearly as important as being able to think on your feet and cope with children and students. She taught two mornings a week in the college, and two afternoons a week in a local primary school. She felt she could write a book herself, and she would say that it was exactly the same problem with seven-year-olds as it was with seventeen-year-olds – keeping their interest and keeping them quiet. Johnny suggested a whiff of ether in the classroom.

Elizabeth had paid two visits to Preston during the summer. Both had been very gloomy. Harry's spirit seemed to have collapsed, and he was wallowing in guilt.

'You used to be the life and soul of things before, you used to be great fun always, she said so,' Elizabeth said to him eventually in desperation. 'Can't you capture any of that back for yourself? I mean it's not as if it was all that long ago, it's only six or seven years. . . .'

'I can't remember anything except how much I wanted to do the best for Violet,' he said, looking like a big, sad baby.

'It's no use, that kind of love, you've got to be cheerful. Suppose she were to get better and come out, what would she have to come out to? She won't want to come here and see the place run down and you like an old sad sack.'

It worked. He didn't become his old self, but he became something more like it than he had been for months. Elizabeth explained to the nurses and the doctor that she thought it might be a sort of therapy to give Harry some hope that things could return to normal, and they agreed. Without telling him any lies they encouraged him to think that a home visit would be likely.

Elizabeth sat and watched Harry telling her silent, abstracted mother about his plans for her return, and saw Mother pat his hand from time to time. The hospital had removed the pins and wires from the artificial violet and had sewn it to her cardigan. It must have been washed each time the cardigan was washed because it had faded from its hard purple to wishy-washy mauve.

Johnny was distressed about Mother. She only mentioned it to him after her third visit. 'Why didn't you tell me? That's awful for you going up there to all that. It's not like you to run off like that. You did tell Stefan some time ago. I asked him.'

226

'Oh, well, no point in telling you.'

He looked hurt and a little annoyed.

'What are you playing at?'

'I swear I am not playing at anything. I mean it, my love. Why tell you sad things? You've often told me that you don't want to hear gloomy things, or problems, or low, bad things that depress you.'

'But darling, if your mother, if Violet's been taken into a mental home, that's big. Why didn't you . . .?'

'Because there was nothing you could do.'

She looked at him clearly. It was obvious she was indeed playing no games with him. He put his arms around her.

'You're very dear to me, funny face. You know you are the only woman I'll ever love properly.'

Elizabeth smiled at him. 'And I love you, Johnny,' she said.

XII

'Would you say that your romance with Tony Murray was passionate?' Niamh asked Aisling one evening as she sat at Aisling's dressing table and tried on bits of costume jewellery.

'No, more an animal attraction I think,' said Aisling without looking up from the letter.

Niamh giggled. 'Seriously, some of the girls at school were wondering, Anna Barry said it was more a question of a suitable match. Not passion.'

'Jaysus, it's far from a suitable match, it's about the most unsuitable match in Kilgarret from all the buzzing that's going on,' said Aisling.

'Mam would kill you if she heard you take the Lord's name,' said Niamh prissily.

Aisling looked up. 'And she certainly wouldn't like *you* putting on lipstick. Take it off at once and leave that stuff alone. It's mine. I work hard and I spend long hours earning the money to pay for it.'

'If you married Tony Murray, you wouldn't have to work any long hours. You could go to Dublin like his Mam and buy clothes there and three lipsticks at a time.'

Aisling didn't answer.

'I don't know why you don't marry him, you could lose him you know. Even though everyone says he's keener on you than you are on him.'

Aisling still read her letter.

'But they say you'd better not push your luck too far. He was seen with one of the Gray girls, you know, the one who was at school in England. She had a face like a horse once, but it's got a different shape now. Anthea or Althea, you know. He was having coffee with her in the hotel. Honestly. So I thought I'd mark your card, you know, if ever there's a chance of me being a bridesmaid I don't want to lose it.'

Aisling looked up. Her face was very pale. 'What? What are you saying?'

Niamh was shocked. 'No, nothing, I don't know if he was really with her or not, you know, it's just Anna Barry and all those, their sisters tell them gossip. I'm sure it's all made up. . . .'

'Oh my God.'

Niamh was frightened now. She scrambled off the chair where she had been kneeling. 'Listen, I said there was nothing in it, I was only repeating eejity old things, Aisling, it's all *right* . . . sure don't you know he fancies you like mad? Aisling answer me . . . don't you know . . .?'

'It's Elizabeth's mother, she's . . . she's tried to kill herself and Harry . . . my God isn't that desperate. . . .'

Niamh was open-mouthed.

'She's in a mental home . . . oh, I don't know whether Mam told you or not, she doesn't tell you things sometimes . . . anyway, Harry . . . he was sitting talking to her quite normally, and she said she wanted him to cut off a trailing string from her cardigan with his penknife and when he took it out of his pocket she grabbed it and stuck it into him first and then her. Oh God, isn't that terrible.'

'And did she kill him . . .?'

'No, but he had to have eleven stitches, and now she's in a different ward, almost a cell I think, and she can't have normal visitors and she thinks there's going to be another war . . . and she says she couldn't live through another one. Oh why do all these bloody things happen to Elizabeth . . .? It's so unfair.'

'Did Elizabeth go to see her?'

'Oh yes, she's been up there in the north of England for a week. She's written from there, but she's probably back in London by now. There's nothing anyone can do, and she's spent a week on her own going from the one hospital to the other and back to the little shop on her own at night. Did you ever hear of anything so awful?'

'But her boyfriend . . . would he go up and help her? Why isn't he there . . .?'

'Because he's a real beaut, that's why, he's the cat's pyjamas, that fellow, there'll be a good reason why he could never be involved in any trouble . . .'

'I thought you liked him, you said he was smashing-looking. . . .'

'He looks like a Greek god. That doesn't make him any help though.'

'If these kind of things happened to you, I bet Tony Murray would stick by you . . . God forbid, if Mam want mad and stabbed Dad.'

'Niamh will you shut your stupid face and go away?'

'I'm just telling you to count your blessings that's all . . . that's all. I'm being sensible, I'm being grown-up. It's you, you're the one with the silly face . . .' Niamh left the room in confusion.

Aisling sat down and tried to decide, would Tony Murray be any use in a crisis? Well, there was no point in pretending that he would be a tower of strength but he would certainly be there. He might not know the solution or even be able to suggest a plan, but he would be standing there solidly with his face cross and scowling, which was the way it got when he had to cope with something unpleasant. He was definitely sympathetic rather than unsympathetic too. Aisling sat and thought it all out. Whenever she had been upset about Donal's bad chest he had patted her on the back and let her cry. She had sobbed that she thought Donal might not be able to breathe during the night and might die, and Tony had considered this with a cross face and said no, it wasn't likely. Tony wouldn't run away to Dublin or back to Limerick or over to England if there was any crisis.

Very deliberately, Aisling combed her hair, and put on a little green eyeshadow. She drew a line behind her eyelashes which she normally only did when she was going to a dance. She put on her best blouse and her new shoes, she got out the pale turquoise suit that she had only worn once to Mass. Then she scribbled a note to Mam who had gone on one of her rare visits to Maureen and Brendan.

Mam,
I'm leaving you Elizabeth's letter to read, isn't it really desperate news? Maybe we might ask her to come over here for a bit of a rest. I'm going up to Murrays' for a bit now. I'll be home later, before ten. If you haven't gone to bed we might have a bit of a chat. I hope all the Daly Ogs weren't too exhausting. By the way I gave out to Niamh and she'll probably be sulking. She's too pushy for twelve in my view, but then I suppose I was too.
　　Love,
　　Aisling

Dear Aisling,
You're right, it's like acting a part in a play, isn't it? Writing to congratulate you and wish you every happiness. But I mean it, I mean it so much. I hope that you will be happy every day and every night and always. I am so looking forward to meeting him, but I know, and presumably Tony knows, that it's never going to be as you hope. You've probably bored him to death about me, and all our adventures, and he will be disappointed. And I of course can't see and won't see in him all the things you love, so I too will be acting a bit. But isn't it marvellous? You are so good in the middle of all your excitements to write so long about my problems, but why should you feel guilty about all your good news coinciding with Mother's decline? That's what it is now, there's not any real hope, and even Harry knows it. He's fine again, and there's an awfully nice social worker who cheers him up. He's so very very kind; that's the one good thing that's come out of all this, at least I've uncovered the sheer kindness of Harry Elton. Remember how terrified of him I used to be? Stefan Worsky sends you his love and so does Anna. They are utterly delighted, they want photographs and long descriptions. Johnny sends you a card, I'll put it in the envelope. And of course I'll come to the wedding, try to keep me away. Of course I don't want to be a bridesmaid, I understand all the business about Protestants officiating at sacraments. I bet your explanation is not at all sound, but I know the thinking of Rome so there's no panic. It's nice of you to ask if Johnny would like to come too but I think I'll just refuse for him without saying anything. I'd prefer to come back to Kilgarret on my own. Only three

months now, and you'll be a Mrs, but for me, the most exciting thing is that I'll see you all again. My accent is not posh by the way, over here it's considered very middle class.

I'm so pleased, Aisling, and so very very happy and hopeful for you:

Love,
Elizabeth

Hi Aisling,
Elizabeth tells me you settled for the Squire. If he turns out to be a mistake come back here and we'll show you a good time. Happy days.

Johnny Stone

Mam had told her to try to pay a bit more attention to Maureen.

'But why should I pay her any attention?' wailed Aisling. 'She's never done criticising me, I'm too forward, I'm too backward, I've shocked Brendan's aunt, I've scandalised them all, I've stood on Patrick's toys. It's a catalogue of complaints as soon as you get in the door of that place, why should I give her a bit more attention?'

'Well, she's feeling a bit in the shadow. There's more fuss about your wedding than there was about hers, she's tied down with three small children miles out of the town and all she hears is the excitement over your big day, your wedding dress . . .'

'Well, she doesn't hear it from me, I'm never blowing about things now am I?'

'Of course you're not child, but can't you be generous, try to put yourself in her position? She's feeling a bit matronly and it would be nice if you brought her back into things. Just a bit.'

'It's a long old cycle Mam, and for nothing at the end of it.'

'In a few months you can drive your husband's car up there, so don't pity yourself too much. Take her a pot of gooseberry jam from the kitchen. And tell her I'll be over tomorrow.'

Mam was right. Maureen did seem in a very low spirit. She was surprised to see Aisling sailing up to the door on the bicycle.

'Well now, to what do we owe the honour of this?' she asked sourly. Brendan Og had jam all around his face and his feet were filthy from waddling around the yard. The twins in their pram set up a great wailing at the arrival of a new distraction. Aisling thought they all looked revolting and the worst advertisement for marriage that you could find, but she knew by now that you could criticise everything except children.

'Hallo, pets,' she cooed insincerely. She still didn't know which one was which. 'Patrick and Peggy, say hallo to your old Auntie Aisling, will you? Of course you will.' She turned to Maureen. 'Aren't they gorgeous?' she said, hoping that God wouldn't strike her dead.

'Oh, they're gorgeous to you passing by once in a blue moon,' said Maureen. 'They're not so gorgeous when you have to live with them morning noon and night. Here, Brendan Og, come back at once. Don't *dare* to walk into the house with all that mud on you. Did you want something Aisling, or were you just passing by?'

Aisling gritted her teeth. How could she be passing by? Once you had cycled the three miles to Daly's, where else was there to go? Wasn't Maureen becoming an old sourpuss? But she remembered Mam.

'No, I thought I'd come out and have a bit of a chat with you. You know, married woman and all. Maybe you could set me straight on a few things.'

Maureen looked at her suspiciously. 'I thought you knew more than any of us about how life is lived,' she sniffed.

'Come on, Maureen, come on, I show off like we all show off but what do I know, living at home with Mam to deal with everything?'

'True, you've had it nice and sheltered. Still it's into a sheltered life you'll be going now. I suppose the Murrays are laying on a maid to welcome you back from the honeymoon. . . .'

'You can't be serious, Maureen, you're having me on? Don't you know what kind of a woman my future mother-in-law is . . . She'd give you a pain in the bottom . . . .'

Maureen was thawing a bit. 'Oh well, they say that Ethel Murray is a bit grand all right. . . .'

'She's dreadful. You're dead lucky here, I mean Brendan's mother is fine, isn't she? You always have her around the place or you used to.'

'She's not that great shakes either, between ourselves. Come on in, and I'll make some tea. Brendan Og, I'll give you the belt across the legs if you kick up any more of that dirt against the door. I don't know what we have that great clutch of hens for, they don't lay all winter, I'm sick to death of feeding them, another of Mrs Helpful Daly's ideas. Wait till you hear the half of it . . . .'

Eamonn refused point blank to be an usher.

'I'll have no talk about it, Mam, not a word. If the fancy Murrays think for one minute that I'm going to dress up in a hired fancy dress and ask people we've known all our bloody lives are they for the bride's side or the groom's side of the church . . . they've got another think coming. I'd be the laughing stock of the town . . . there'd be a crowd from Hanrahan's pub crowding the church just to have a laugh at me.'

'They wouldn't get in, it's *my* wedding,' said Aisling with spirit.

'They'd have to get in, it's the House of God . . . everyone gets in,' said Eamonn.

'Just one day, as a favour Eamonn, just four hours, five at the most, then you can go back to your friends in Hanrahan's. Please?'

'Crowd of idle layabouts in Hanrahan's pub anyway,' said Sean.

'You weren't ever in there Da,' said Eamonn.

'I wouldn't want to go in there when I see what comes out. Listen here, Eamonn, the wedding is for your mother and sister, it's got nothing to do with us. One of these days some half-witted girl will agree to marry you and her unfortunate brothers and father will have to dress them-selves up like buffoons, and what's more, spend a great deal of money on a meal and a lot of a nonsense . . . so will you not shut up and do it – it's one of those things like cutting your toe-nails, no-one likes doing it, but it has to be done. . . .'

'Dad I'll not do it, I'll leave the town, I'll leave home. You can't ask me to do it, not to please anyone. Mam, take it seriously. Suppose I asked you to walk around the square here, seriously now, in your knickers, would you do it to please me, Mam, of course you wouldn't, you'd say it was making a fool of yourself, and making yourself look ridiculous in front of your friends, no matter how much I wanted you to do it. . . .'

'Eamonn keep a clean tongue in your head, don't dream of speaking to your mother like that.'

Suddenly Aisling interrupted. 'No, I think he's right, he'd hate it, he'd not be able to do it. Why ask him to?'

Eamonn looked up nervously, sensing a trap.

'No, I'm serious, Eamonn, I thought you'd look nice in a suit. All kinds of old gobdaws much worse-looking than you, look terrific when they're dolled up, they'd make you look at them twice. But no, what you said is right. If you wanted Mam or me to dress up like Red Indians or something for your wedding we wouldn't. No, forget it. We'll get some friend of Tony's to do it with Donal. The trouble is most of Tony's friends are about a hundred, but that doesn't matter, he must have some youngish friends.'

Eamonn's mouth was open, a combination of relief and disbelief. 'God, Aisling, I won't forget it, I really won't. Mam you understand, don't you?'

'Don't be a baby,' Aisling was very cold. 'You've got your way, don't look for a pat on the back as well. You're off the hook. I have to go and face that battle-axe of a Mrs Murray and explain why we need another usher.'

'What will you say?'

Aisling looked at him innocently. 'Well, what you said, that your friends from Hanrahan's would come into the house of God and make a disruption for some reason, and that four hours is too long, even though poor Donal's going to stick it.'

'Don't tell her all that . . . it's making an awful clown out of me . . . don't put it like that.'

'But what other way can I put it? Tell me. I can't say that you're sick, otherwise you'll have to go to bed. I mean I have to tell the truth, don't I?'

233

'What will she say?'

'She'll be livid, like she is about everything. She'll say that's all she might have expected, and that's what's so bloody unfair, because she's constantly expecting rotten things and everything else is going marvellously. Daddy's booked a great wedding breakfast, and paid for extra waitresses during the meal, and Mam has got everyone gorgeous clothes and I've behaved like an archangel I'm so good, so the old bag has nothing to complain about. Still, I do think you're right. If it's that awful for you, and if they're going to invade the church, then you're right not to do it.'

'I didn't say they'd invade the church . . . some of them mightn't even hear of it until it was over.'

'No, Eamonn, if it's as bad as that you'd better not. Here Mam, throw me over my jacket, I'll go and talk to the old demon and get it over.'

'Oh I'll do it, I'll do it,' Eamonn shouted. He left the room deaf to the protestations and assurances.

'Oh, you're learning fast,' Mam laughed. 'Go on now . . . you've won that battle, you probably have quite a few more to fight before the big day.'

'You're right, Mam,' signed Aisling, thinking of Tony. He had been very irritable last night. Since they would be married in five weeks' time why couldn't she take her hand away and give over all this modesty bit? What difference did five weeks make one way or the other? Aisling couldn't think but she had a feeling that somehow it would make a difference and she felt that it would be like giving up on some game if she were to give in now.

And Maureen had blossomed a lot with Aisling's visits. She, in turn, began to get an unexpected and not at all welcome idea about how lonely Maureen's life must be. Mam was right to have urged her to share the wedding with her elder sister. Maureen was obviously very short of excitement out in that dreary place. It was neither farm nor private house . . . a big awkward building almost on the side of the road with four acres stretching up behind it. No crops, only a few geese, a donkey, hens, a sheepdog and the other farmers using the land as grazing. Maureen's attempts to make a garden had been ridiculed by the Daly clan, but her new-found ally, Aisling, seemed to regard this as a challenge.

'You don't understand, they think in terms of getting value out of the land, they'd think a garden was a stupid town idea, you know, ideas above my station. You can't eat flowers. . . .'

'But act the innocent, the flowers sort of grew . . . don't be telling them that you're planting a garden, do the work when there's no one around. I'll help you, I'll bring out a few plants and seeds, sure Dad has them in the shop, I'll say it's for a present for you. You can blame me.'

'God, Aisling, you're learning fast, you'll be well able for the Murrays.'

'I think I'll need to be.'

Indeed, Mrs Murray had been surprised to discover that the O'Connors were held in much higher esteem than she had believed. An established business in the town and well thought of. All the children bright and able to give account for themselves, except perhaps for the brother who hung about the doorway of Hanrahan's public house on Saturdays or at closing time of an evening. Aisling was well-spoken and would look presentable as a bride. There were even those who described her glowingly and said she was one of the most attractive girls in Kilgarret. It wasn't what she had hoped for, but then Mrs Murray sighed and realised that she hadn't got a lot of the things she had hoped for. Joannie was vague and mysterious about her life in Dublin and threw tantrums and caused scenes if any criticism was suggested. She invited no friends to stay, and seemed to need an unending allowance to supplement what she earned with the wine importers. She had developed no sense of business and saintly Mr Meade said that he didn't think she had any commercial leaning towards running the family firm.

A priest in the family was consolation, and John would be ordained next year. But somehow she had hoped that her son might be a short-cut to understanding and help; she had hoped that John would have words of consolation and open up brighter paths for her to believe in when things were bad. But in fact he was still her son, complaining when Tony took all the hot water for the bath, saying that Joannie was loud and on his last visit he had been disappointed with the front of Murray's saying that it looked shabby and run down. He said that his father would not like to think that the place was being neglected and this had managed to annoy every single person who heard him say it. Mrs Murray had expected a priest in the family to smooth down troubles, not to add to them. But at least John had been helpful about the honeymoon and had said Tony and Aisling should attend a papal audience, where they would get their papal benediction personally from the hands of the Pope. Mrs Murray had told a lot of people about this, it was one of the high spots. She had said to Tony that sometimes she woke up in the middle of the night and thought about it. Her son kissing the ring of Pope Pius XII, actually there in the same room as him. It used to send a shiver down her spine. Tony had said that he agreed, the Pope did look a bit spooky; he'd probably send a shiver down anyone's spine. Mrs Murray had been extremely upset.

Aisling certainly seemed to know how to manage Tony, though. She had said to him quite firmly that his wedding suit was too tight.

'It's all right when I hold myself in like this,' Tony had said defiantly.

'But you won't, you'll fall over, you're holding your breath,' she said.

'I'm not going on any diet, I'm not giving up drinking pints just to fit into a wedding jacket better,' he said, scowling at the thought.

Aisling laughed. 'Did anyone suggest you should? What a stupid idea, just to look well on one day. No, I don't think you should dream of losing a stone to fit into it, no, get him to let it out and you can be grand and comfortable.'

Tony gave up drinking pints for a month. Anyone could stay off the beer for a month, a few scoops of gin and soda to keep body and soul together. He lost the stone in three and a half weeks. Mrs Murray marvelled at it. She felt sure that this is what Aisling had intended when she was dismissing the very idea of it. She was a proper little madam that one.

Two weeks before the day Aisling and Tony walked out to see how the new bungalow was getting on. Aisling said she wanted to time the length it took her to walk from home. At a leisurely pace it was ten minutes.

'That's grand,' she laughed. 'If you hit me a belt over something I can be back in town and have a posse rounded up in no time.'

Tony looked hurt. 'That's a stupid thing to say, I'd never hit you . . . you're like a flower,' he said.

Aisling was touched. 'It's only my sense of humour. You're right, it was a stupid thing to say. That's nice of you to say I'm like a flower. Will we grow lots of flowers? I like delphiniums and lupins . . . we never had any room for them back in the yard in the square.'

'You can grow whatever you like,' Tony said expansively.

Aisling felt that Mam was right, Maureen had a lot of things to put up with. Imagine having to hide flowers from those pig-ignorant Dalys. She put her arm in Tony's as they walked through the unfinished house. Tony had been annoyed because the plumbers hadn't completed last week. Aisling wished that there weren't so many windows and opportunities for her mother-in-law to cluck over them and interrogate her about curtains not even ordered, discussed or thought about.

Suddenly he turned at her as they poked disconsolately into the half-finished kitchen cupboards filled with wood shavings.

'It'll be grand you know.'

'Oh, I know, sure there's ages of time, I mean we'll be four weeks in Rome . . . that's six weeks altogether,' she said, trying to be cheerful.

'No, I don't mean the house, the whole thing, you know, being married?' He looked eager. And pleading.

Aisling felt very old. 'Of course it will be grand. How could it not be, aren't we the best-matched pair in the whole town?'

'I love you Aisling,' Tony said, without any attempt to touch her.

'Then I'm really very, very lucky,' Aisling said. I am, I really *am*, she told herself.

Johnny was annoyed that he hadn't been invited to the wedding, but Elizabeth was cool and firm. It was tempting, very tempting to take him with her. The handsome Johnny Stone would steal the show, he would be proof that little shy Elizabeth White had done well out in the big world. He would be so charming too . . . even Aunt Eileen would fall for him. She could imagine him sitting on a high stool with Uncle Sean asking about the business and really wanting to know. In a flight of fancy she even saw him in the convent parlour. That he would be a success was never in doubt . . . but she felt it would be wrong. And, anyway, even more important, it was Aisling's day, not hers. Johnny would be a distraction, he would take from the bride and groom.

But she didn't tell him that.

Aisling was jumping up and down outside the glass partition. Elizabeth had to wait until her suitcase came off the plane and it seemed like a very long wait. Aisling kept making mouthing sounds and sign language and pointing her finger in the direction of the door and making a face. Elizabeth resigned herself to understanding nothing. She thought Aisling looked magnificent in her navy blazer and a green kilt. She even flashed her large engagement ring through the glass partition and mimed that the diamonds were too heavy for her hand to support. The prospect of marrying the Squire in a week's time certainly hadn't tamed her, Elizabeth noted with relief.

Eventually the case arrived and she was out, she was hugging Aisling like a schoolgirl after a hockey match. Within minutes they were away.

They had timed it well. Eileen had just come in and was having her customary cup of tea in the kitchen . . . the tea that divided the working day in the shop from the working day at home. Between mouthfuls she was instructing young Siobhan, the new maid who had replaced Peggy, on how to set out the salad.

'Don't throw it all together in the dish, Siobhan, lay the lettuce leaves out in lines and a bit of ham on top of each one, and then a bit of tomato on each one. No, give it here to me, I'll do it. Niamh, move your school books, they've no business here, they'll get covered with food. Move them do you hear, up to your room. Is Donal back in yet?'

At that, the door opened and Elizabeth entered. Aisling was behind her, laughing and holding a suitcase in each hand.

Eileen put down the cup and stood up. This tall, slim woman, this girl with the beautiful scarf draped around her shoulders, with the elegant gold pin and safety chain pinned on her lovely cream-coloured dress . . . Eileen could hardly believe it was the child with the cut knees, gawky on her bicycle, nervous and anxious to please, flushing and stammering . . . this was a different person altogether.

She stood at the door looking across the big kitchen and then she ran, she ran like a child and threw her arms round Eileen and squeezed her so tightly her breath nearly stopped. She smelled of expensive soap or talcum powder, but she shook and trembled as much as she had ever done when she lived in the house.

'You're just the same, you're just the same,' were the only words that Eileen could hear as she clung to the thin girl who gripped her so tightly. Eventually she pulled away and there were tears pouring down the pale face, she took out a handkerchief with lace on it and blew her nose hard. 'This is terrible. Here am I trying to make a good impression on you and I nearly suffocate both of us and then I start to weep all over my careful make-up. Can I go out and come in all over again?'

'Oh Elizabeth . . . thank God you came back to us . . . thank God you didn't change.' Eileen held her hands almost as if they were about to dance a reel together. They smiled at each other foolishly.

'Mam, you never make that kind of fuss over me,' Aisling complained in a mock-hurt tone, but laughing in order to lighten the intensity.

'Nor me . . .' Niamh said in genuine envy, tongue-tied by the apparition in the cream dress and the scarf . . . she was as open-mouthed with amazement at Mam's welcome as was Siobhan who stood with the lettuce and cooked ham in her hands gaping at the mistress with astonishment.

'The uniform looks much better on you than it did on us,' Elizabeth said hastily, feeling that Niamh needed some attention. 'Has it changed or something?'

Niamh looked pleased. 'No, but we're allowed to wear our own blouses now so long as they're not *loud*, as Sister Margaret would say. . . .'

'She *never* says it still?'

'She never says anything else.'

Elizabeth sat down on the kitchen chair and stretched her arms. 'Oh, if only you knew . . . if you had any idea how marvellous it is to be back. . . .'

The homecoming was even better than she expected, even in her best dreams. The bedroom was the same, the two beds with their white candlewick bedspreads, one on each side of the white chest of drawers. The same statue stood on the mantelpiece, a bit more chipped around Our Lady's cloak, but the same one, certainly. The Sacred Heart Lamp burned still at the little oratory on the landing, the rooms were a bit smaller and the stairs a little narrower but the place hadn't *shrunk*. Perhaps because it was such a genuinely large house by anyone's standards, she thought. And shabby. Had the carpet always been so torn, and escaping from the stair rods? Did the wallpaper peel and have big brown damp stains long ago or had all this happened recently? And did any of it matter? The place just welcomed her from every corner, it seemed.

Aunt Eileen and Niamh walked beside Aisling as the house was toured and even Siobhan followed at a distance, dazzled by this girl with the English accent who seemed to be so much part of the house.

And Donal ran up the stairs two at a time to see her. He was tall and thin and so white it was as if someone had rubbed chalk on his face. He had thin and almost blue lips and when he smiled and laughed his face looked like a thin skull. Elizabeth bit back the tears pricking her eyes. She had hoped he would look like his brother Sean but he didn't resemble him in any way.

'Do you think I grew up well, Elizabeth White?' he asked self-mockingly.

'You're terrific, Donal, you always were,' she said.

'Do I look gaunt, though, and bony?' his voice was light but she could hear the pain and worry.

She touched his forehead and melodramatically lifted a lock of hair that was falling in his eyes.

'La, sir, fie, Donal O'Connor you do seek for compliments, but if you must have them then you must. You look like a poet, you look like an artist. You look a bit like that picture of Rupert Brooke or maybe even Byron. Now, will that do you? Or must I flatter you more?'

He smiled a great smile and she knew she had said the right thing before Aunt Eileen squeezed her affectionately.

Uncle Sean came in as they were investigating the new kittens which had been discovered that morning in the bathroom.

'This is Monica's daughter, Melanie, and these are her first kittens.' Niamh was full of pride.

'Oh, a *Gone with the Wind* period, I imagine,' Aisling laughed.

'I wish I'd had a sister,' Elizabeth said suddenly.

'Hadn't you me, wasn't I better than a sister?' Aisling demanded.

'Yes, but you weren't there all the time.'

'I was there when you needed me.'

'Indeed, I'll never forget it.' Their eyes met.

'Where is she, where is she?' Uncle Sean had got older, much older than Aunt Eileen. He seemed to be full of extra hair, sandy hair in his nose and his ears and on the back of his hands; she hadn't remembered that. Or was it because Father had such smooth, hair-free, almost polished skin?

Uncle Sean was almost embarrassed by the elegance of her until she hugged him hard.

'Faith, and I couldn't keep you in pocket money these days by the look of you, isn't she a picture, Eileen, isn't she like a fashion plate?'

'Oh no, Uncle Sean, don't say that, you don't like fashion plates!'

'I love them, I just don't know enough of them. Eileen, give over this notion of having tea here, I think I'll take Miss White down to Maher's for a few quick ones and then maybe a dinner in the hotel. Wouldn't that set the town talking? Sure they wouldn't know who this posh young one is and they'd think I was a great old spark. What do you think of that?'

Elizabeth played along. 'Nonsense, they'll remember me well, and they'll say there's that Elizabeth White who spent years and years taking from the O'Connors and now she's doing it again.'

Eileen said seriously, 'Don't ever even say that as a joke, Elizabeth child, you were as much part of this family as any of them. The pity was that we couldn't have had you longer . . . but you'd not have turned out as well. I used to miss you as much as I missed my Sean.'

That was new too. When Elizabeth had left Kilgarret Sean's name was not spoken aloud in the house.

XIII

Elizabeth sat between Aunt Eileen and Maureen in the front left-hand seat of the church. Eamonn and Donal were at the church door guiding the guests to their seats. Niamh, as bridesmaid, was at home still with Aisling and Uncle Sean; about now they would be getting into the car which was already waiting in the square. Uncle Sean was pacing the sitting room like an animal in a cage and his hair looked odd since he had had too violent a haircut the day before. Nobody had commented on it, but Aisling had whispered to Elizabeth that he managed to make himself look like a convict, which would undoubtedly add to Mrs Murray's pleasure when she saw the wedding pictures.

Elizabeth looked across again at Tony as he knelt with his head in his hands, more from a hope of escape than from piety. He had what love-story writers would call a florid charm, Elizabeth thought; he had a high complexion and there always seemed to be sweat on his forehead. He was a big stocky man, and looked older than he was. If Elizabeth had been asked to guess she would have said closer to forty than to thirty. He had seemed uneasy on the three occasions they had met, but she excused him; so was she uneasy. She was very conscious of saying the right thing, the thing that would make her seem like a friend, an ally, rather than a rival. She had found herself talking about the weather, and the journey over from England and the journey down from Dublin.

Then, Tony must be nervous, it was a big day for him too. No wonder he had sweat on his brow, no wonder his mind hadn't been on their conversations. No wonder he half-sat, half-knelt, with his hands over his face, while his friend, Shay Ferguson, the best man, roamed the church with his eyes and winked twice at Elizabeth when he caught her eye. Shay was even older than Tony Murray and much fatter. He was a confirmed bachelor, and Elizabeth remembered that he had been one as far back as her own time in Kilgarret. Shay and his brothers sold agricultural machinery and they had often been in Uncle Sean's shop. She had always thought of him as being Uncle Sean's age; it was a shock to think of him as a friend of Tony's. Odd and uneasy-making. It was as if Aisling were being handed over to older, coarser men in some way. Elizabeth gave a little shiver and pulled herself together.

She whispered to Aunt Eileen.

'Can I say something or are you praying?'

'I'm only pretending to pray. Go on.'

'Are you happy or are you sad? Your face is hard to work out.'

Aunt Eileen smiled. 'I'm happy really. It took Aisling so long to make up her mind, you know that too. She didn't rush into it. He's a good man. I think he'll be able to look after her. No, I'm not sad. I'm mainly happy. There's your answer.'

Aunt Eileen smiled during her conspiratorial whisper. She looked very attractive, Elizabeth thought. Much, much nicer than Mrs Murray. Aunt Eileen had a lovely pink and grey coat and dress that matched. It had been bought in Switzer's in Dublin five weeks ago and tried on a dozen times while shoes and handbag and hat were matched to it. The great thing about Kilgarret was that you could always take home things like shoes and handbag and try them out in comfort and then decide what you wanted to buy. Aunt Eileen had a little rouge on too. Aisling and Elizabeth had tried to get her to wear more, but she said she looked like a Dutch doll. Her hat was a smart grey one and the battle to make her wear a pink rose in it had been lost.

'I'm a woman in her fifties. I'll not wear decorations like a Christmas tree,' she had insisted.

Maureen looked tense and unhappy. In the daylight and in the church she thought her shot taffeta dress looked cheap and flashy. Certainly her mother-in-law had managed to plant the idea in her mind this morning. Mrs Daly had looked at the changing colours that had pleased Maureen so much and sniffed. Wouldn't a nice two-piece have been more suitable? She would have thought that a wedding needed something a little formal. And those little shoes, they looked like slippers. Was Maureen really going to wear them? Oh well. Maureen looked with envy at Elizabeth's outfit. A lemon-coloured skirt and jacket with a coffee lace blouse underneath. It looked so right for a wedding. And on her hat she had coffee and lemon ribbons. Now why hadn't Maureen thought of something like that? Maureen pulled at the wide taffeta skirt and got no more pleasure from watching the colours change in it when the light changed. She had thought this was its best feature when she had tried it on and had spent ages admiring it secretly in the bedroom. Now she hated it. Even her hair was wrong. It looked flat and drab though she had washed it and pinned it up last night. Why hadn't she insisted to Brendan that she wanted to join the party back at home when Mrs Collins and the little shampooing girl had come up to do Mam's hair and Aisling's and Niamh's and even Elizabeth's? Brendan had said it was mad to waste money and time; why hadn't she been firm?

Mrs Murray smiled over a few times. She looked harsh and sharp, Elizabeth thought; but perhaps that was only because she had heard so many tales about her during the week she half expected the woman to look like the devil incarnate. Her navy outfit seemed to be all points and edges. Sharp reveres on the jacket, sharp edges on the handbag, pointed toes on the shoes, peaky brim on the hat. Beside her stood Joannie, who had only come home the night before. Joannie hadn't changed much in nine years, Elizabeth thought. Still stocky, and legs planted wide apart when she stood. She had freckles and a handsome sort of face, like Tony but better-looking. She wore a white dress and coat . . . which Elizabeth had always heard was bad taste. Somewhere in her store of knowledge she had the information that you never wore white to a wedding, in case you might upstage the bride.

But of course, Joannie Murray wouldn't have a dog's chance of upstaging this bride, even if it had been in her mind. Aisling was going to knock them sideways when she came in.

Elizabeth had actually gasped when she saw Aisling in the dress. It did everything that a wedding dress could do, and you got the feeling that Aisling never wore any other kind of clothes. Elizabeth knew that Aunt Eileen said that the wedding dress could cost whatever Aisling wanted to pay for it. When Aunt Eileen got married it had been a drab and poor affair, in a dress borrowed from a cousin. Aunt Eileen's own family, with notions of being genteel, had no money and they were disappointed that she was marrying Uncle Sean, who not only had no money but hadn't even notions of being genteel. The wedding ceremony had not been colourful. Then although nobody admitted it aloud, the wedding of Maureen and Brendan had been so masterminded by the Dalys and what they would like and what they wouldn't like, that the O'Connors seemed to do nothing but pay for it. This time Aunt Eileen dug her heels in, and she knew she had an ally. Aisling was not afraid of the Murrays, Aisling would do it right.

Together they had gone to Dublin on the bus, they had spent a morning looking at materials and an afternoon looking at patterns. Then, armed with ideas they went in to the dress designer in Grafton Street who made dresses for the best. She knew she was not dealing with country hicks here . . . they were informed, this mother and daughter. They were also happy to pay a deposit in advance. The dress designer became enthusiastic about the tall, auburn-haired girl with the bright face. It had been a labour of love. Nobody but Elizabeth knew how much it had cost. Maureen had been told one sum, Uncle Sean had been told another. Mrs Murray had not been told anything, despite her discreet probing about where it was being made and what it was like. Only when Elizabeth saw it on Aisling did she realise that it was worth every penny just for the sheer impression that Aisling would make on all their minds. The dress was satin. Heavy white satin, and not sateen which was all they had seen in Kilgarret for many a wedding. It had a full skirt which seemed to billow out and make her waist tiny. The long tight sleeves came down in little points, vees below her wrists and on to her hands making her arms more slender than they could possibly have been. The neckline, another vee, had little seed pearls to pick it out.

The satin looked so rich and cold it could have been marble. On any other girl the dress might have been deadening, it would have made another face seem wishy-washy, Elizabeth thought, a thinner paler girl would have looked like a doll in the dress. Aisling looked like a star.

Mrs Moriarty's sister played the organ, and somebody must have nodded to her because the organ stopped its rambling, gentle notes and gave a burst that startled everyone in the church; but they were standing up in a trice and Tony, his face red from the marks of his hands, stood more quickly than any of them. He looked over at the bride's side: both Aunt Eileen and Elizabeth smiled at him encouragingly. He gave a scowl which turned into a sort of smile. It was endearing in a funny way. Eamonn and Donal had slipped back into the O'Connor pew and they all shuffled a little to leave room for Uncle Sean when he had given Aisling away.

He looked sweet, Uncle Sean, Elizabeth thought, staring ahead of him with a rigid glance as if he were going to be executed, watching each foot as it went in front of him in case one of them might escape. Both his elbows were squeezed into his sides as if he were carrying precious documents that might fall. Aisling's arm might well have been squashed flat but there wasn't a sign of it on her face.

Far from the nervous, demure bride, shy because all eyes were on her, she was utterly in control; she smiled left and right seeing the admiration and even the shock of how well she looked. The church in Kilgarret hadn't seen a bride like this in a while. Her hair was the best decoration she could ever have planned; it escaped deliberately in bronze curls and ringlets, a flash of rich colour in the middle of all the white. The walk up the church took forever, Elizabeth thought, and then they were at the altar. Uncle Sean handed her to Tony, and loosening his collar stepped in beside Aunt Eileen. The bride and groom moved inside the altar rail and up the steps. The dress was so perfect that you could see Aisling's figure to the best advantage without it looking at all revealing. That was the cunning of the thing, that's why the woman in Grafton Street hadn't charged too much.

Aunt Eileen leaned over in front of Elizabeth and caught Maureen's hand. 'Here we go again,' she said. 'Just like your wedding all over again isn't it?'

Maureen's face brightened up a lot. 'Yes, I suppose so,' she whispered eagerly. 'Of course, I couldn't have known, being up there in the altar myself.'

'It was just like this,' Eileen hissed back firmly.

Elizabeth saw Maureen's face relax into a pleased smile as the congregation sat down and watched Anthony James Finbarr Murray take this woman, Mary Aisling as his wedded wife.

'In all the years I never knew Aisling was called Mary,' Elizabeth gasped to Maureen.

'It's a saint's name, you eejit,' Maureen whispered. 'She couldn't be baptised Aisling, it's not the name of a saint.'

'I never knew that,' Elizabeth said, settling down for the rest of the ceremony.

At the hotel, a room had been reserved for the bride's family. This had been regarded as the most ludicrous of a series of ludicrous expenses. The bride's family, after all, lived a thirty-second walk across the square from the hotel. They had all the rooms they wanted there. But no, the management said that it was included in the whole price and he begged them to avail of it. There was no refund if they didn't. And anyway they would find it a great assistance. Maureen was complaining that the light in the shop where she bought the taffeta dress had been faulty. Eileen said that she looked like a very elegant, smartly-dressed young woman and she was to stop whinging and whining. Aisling had taken off her white stockings and had one foot in the handbasin.

'The bloody shoes are too tight, Mam, I knew it.'

'Are you doing the right thing, Mrs Murray, bathing them? You might make it harder to get the shoes back on.'

'Janey, Aisling's Mrs Murray,' said Niamh, who was examining what she deeply suspected was a spot on her chin. 'Imagine, my sisters, Mrs Daly and Mrs Murray. . . .'

For some reason this cheered Maureen up. 'You'll be Mrs Somebody too, Niamh, you mustn't worry,' she said kindly.

'Of course I'm not worrying, Maureen you old eejit, I'm only fifteen. I'm not even old enough to get married if they were all after me.'

'Will Mrs Murray want to come in here and powder her nose?' asked Maureen, looking at the door nervously.

'Well if she does she can powder it outside,' Aisling said, drying her feet. 'This is for the bride's family, it says so on Daddy's estimate. It says no wicked mothers-in-law permitted.'

'She looks very well in that navy, doesn't she? Ethel has always had great taste,' Eileen was trying to be just.

'Oh Mam, she looks like the wrath of God, and you know it . . . her face is like a flour-bag, it's so white.'

'Don't blame the woman for her appearance, now Aisling.'

'Listen to me Mam,' Aisling stood in one stocking, hopped over to her mother and put her hands firmly on Eileen's shoulders. 'Now hear this, Mam, you're not talking to bold, difficult Aisling O'Connor any more, since half an hour ago you're talking to young Mrs Tony Murray . . . and by God if I want to call old Mrs Ethel Murray a hideous old bag, which is what she is, I'll call her that all day long.'

'Well you're going to have a fine easy life ahead of you if you go on like that, young Mrs Murray,' said Eileen. 'Here hold on to me and put on your stocking, we should be downstairs already. . . .'

'It's all going awfully well, isn't it?' Elizabeth said. 'Aren't you pleased with it all?'

'I hope so. There's three things I wish were over . . . this reception, all this awful losing virginity thing and bleeding and screaming . . . and I want to have got myself in the position where old bag Mrs Murray is afraid of me rather than the other way round. . . .'

'There won't be bleeding and screaming, you always exaggerate. . . .'

'No, I'm sure there won't. I think the battle over Ma-in-law is going to be worse than sexual intercourse . . . come on, let's hit the reception. Where's Niamh? She's meant to be standing beside me like an acolyte catering for my every whim, but she's picking her spots in front of every mirror she finds.'

Tony was waiting at the bottom of the stairs; Shay Ferguson was there with a large whiskey in each hand.

'Give her a belt, Tony, let her know that your Missus can't keep you waiting.'

'It's a rural witticism,' Aisling said over her shoulder to Elizabeth.

'You look gorgeous, gorgeous,' Tony said.

'You look lovely yourself,' Aisling said to him.

Elizabeth relaxed. She took Niamh by the arm. 'Since they're paying compliments . . . you look lovely too . . . and there are probably more people looking at you than at Aisling. She's out of the race now, you're still available . . . the only glamorous girl in the competition. . . .'

'What about you Elizabeth . . . you're not married yet?'

'Ah no, but I'm in love,' Elizabeth said in an uncharacteristic burst of information. 'I have the look of a promised woman about me.'

Elizabeth remembered something. She hadn't thought about Johnny for two days. She had thought she would have him in the front of her mind all during the wedding, that every moment she would wish it was the two of them going through the ceremony, with family and friends and all the promising to love and honour and obey and everything. But she had never even thought of him. What did it mean?

The hotel sitting room was transformed. All the chairs and sofas had been pushed back against the wall and four waitresses stood with trays of sherry glasses. There were minerals on the trays too for those who didn't partake. Elizabeth looked with interest at the scene . . . she hadn't been able to stare properly in the church in case she was being disrespectfully, but here it was perfectly acceptable. Some of the older women she recognised immediately. Mr and Mrs Moriarty from the chemist . . . how tall she had grown, how elegant she looked . . . any hope of seeing her take the plunge? . . . how well the Moriartys looked, how little they had changed . . . how much Donal liked working in the shop . . . .

Mrs Lynch, Berna's mother . . . oh yes, she remembered Elizabeth well, 'How pretty she was, ah well, that's what came of a nice life with no cares over there in England, as for herself, nobody knew the troubles she had seen . . . and her poor husband, the doctor, the Lord have mercy on him, did Elizabeth remember him? Well the poor man had gone to his reward five years now this June. Yes, wasn't it dreadful, the best husband and father a family ever had, his poor liver had been weak, a dreadful death he died. No, Berna wasn't married yet, but she worked in Limerick and had a boyfriend . . . .'

She was trapped then by Joannie. 'How much did your suit cost?' Joannie said. No word of greeting, no amazement at not having met for nine years, no expression of pleasure at the wedding or of admiration at the bride.

'*They* seem awfully happy,' Elizabeth said on a slightly rising note, to see what Joannie would answer.

She looked over at Aisling and Tony ruminatively for a few moments. 'Well, I don't know what took them so long . . . they've been walking out together for as long as I can remember. I suppose they'll be all right but I don't know what they want to live in this one-horse town for.'

'I don't know, but of course Aisling likes Kilgarret, she likes being near her family . . .'

'She must be off her head,' said Joannie.

'They're a very nice family. Of course, I was utterly devoted to them when I lived here. I still am.' Elizabeth's voice was slightly sharp but not nearly as sharp as she felt. How dare Joannie Murray dismiss the whole O'Connor clan with one ignorant remark?

Joannie noticed the sharpness. 'Oh no, I'm not saying a word against them. I'm just saying I couldn't live here . . . I don't know what I'd do with myself all the time . . . and you know there was murder altogether because Aisling wanted to go on working in the shop . . . did you know that?'

'In whose shop?'

'In her own, in the O'Connors' store. Imagine, a married woman working there with all the farm implements?'

'Aunt Eileen has worked there for thirty years, she's a married woman.'

'It's different for Mrs O'Connor, she's the family.'

'And Aisling's the family, isn't she?' Elizabeth was bewildered.

'Not any more . . . she's a Murray now . . . she can't do what she likes any more. The Ma will see to that.'

'That sounds very depressing I must say.'

Joannie shrugged. 'What did I tell you, this is a depressing, hick town.'

Uncle Sean was looking at his glass of sherry as if it were a glass of poison.

'I don't know how people drink this stuff, Molly,' he said to the waitress, whom he had know since she was a baby.

'Sure, wasn't it what you ordered yourself, Sean . . . two kinds of sherry.'

'I didn't expect to be having to drink it,' he laughed.

'Yerra, why don't you take a glass of the orange instead, it would be more refreshing?'

Elizabeth laughed at him.

'Go on, Uncle Sean, all the best people are drinking orange . . . look, the bridegroom is even drinking it.'

247

Uncle Sean looked over at Tony. 'Well, by God, that's a turn-up for the books. Your man normally has a fierce thirst on him. I'd say he has a drop of something in it . . . he's looking far too cheerful.'

'Oh Uncle *Sean*, don't be so unromantic. It's his wedding day! No wonder he's looking cheerful.'

'No, he's unnaturally high-spirited. I'll bet you ten shillings he's got something in it.'

'Well I won't take you on, it would be a highly disruptive thing to go around sniffing people's orange juice. Isn't it all super, Uncle Sean . . . aren't you delighted with it all?'

'I am, child, I am. And if you'll come over here and marry an Irishman I'll give you a wedding like this too . . . but we'll have none of this sherry.'

'That's lovely of you. I bet you would give me a wedding, but rest assured I won't call on you. Save up for Niamh's instead.'

'Sure who'd have Niamh? She's a desperate terror.'

'You used to wonder who'd have Aisling, and now look at her.'

'Men are terrible fools, Elizabeth. I often thank the good Lord that he guided me to make such a sensible choice myself when I was a young lad. I was a lucky man to get so fine a wife as your aunt.'

She walked with him over towards Aunt Eileen who had been making faces at them.

'I think it's time to move them in to the dining room. Sean, will we get them going? Ethel Murray's looked at her watch three times.'

With a surprising vehemence Elizabeth said, 'Don't dare to do anything to please Ethel Murray, Aunt Eileen, you're worth twenty of her, a hundred and twenty of her. You move them into the dining room when you're ready, not before!'

The place names had been checked, and double-checked, by Mrs Murray that morning. The seating plan had taken a lot of working out. Who exactly were the Halleys, she had asked Aisling. Were they the kind of people you could place near Father Riordan? But now it had all been finalised. Uncle Sean's pleas that he couldn't talk to Mrs Murray all through the meal had been ignored, as had Joannie's request that she sit at the end of a table where she didn't have to talk to anyone. All the grapefruits were already in place in their little glass dishes, each with a cherry-half on top. There were two glasses beside every plate. The Murray family had contributed a dozen bottles of champagne, and this would be used for the toast. There were teacups at each place too and jugs of milk and bowls of sugar on the table. The wedding cake was on a side table. There had been a lot of discussion about this, too. Mrs Murray said she believed it should be on the main table, Aisling said that if it were on the table the bride and groom wouldn't be able to see anyone. Maureen said that of course a wedding cake must be on the table, it was the tradition, and Aunt Eileen said that if Aisling would like the wedding cake kept in the back yard that was fine. Miss Donnelly in the hotel had said that the side table was a good idea and the whole table could be carried over for the cutting ceremony so that there would be no danger of the cake breaking.

In little hesitant trickles they moved into the dining room. Some of them exclaimed at how nice it all looked, others raked the table for their own place names before saying anything at all. Immediately people discovered their own name they snatched up the name on either side of them. 'There seem to be two women sitting together here,' called Mrs Halley disapprovingly, finding herself sitting beside Brendan Daly's aunt.

'There are more ladies amongst the guests than gentlemen,' hissed Miss Donnelly, annoyed to hear the complaints beginning before people sat down. The buzz of conversation had died down as people came in to the dining room, a silence almost like the respectful hush of a church came over them. Elizabeth was hoping that she might be between Donal and Eamonn. She knew that neither of them wanted to make conversation with uncles or priests and she herself felt a bit at a loss. But the endless negotiations had put her beside Shay Ferguson on one side and Father Riordan on the other. Half the people had settled into their seats, and some of them, like the Halleys, had already begun to eat the bread and butter when there was a loud cough.

Father Mahony, the elderly parish priest who had married Tony and Aisling, was clearing his throat.

'I think, if we're all settled,' he said looking over his glasses disapprovingly at those who had the daring to set down, 'I think that it's about time to say grace.'

Red-faced, the unlucky people trapped in their seats shuffled and scrambled to their feet again.

'Bless us, o Lord, and these thy gifts, which of thy bounty we are about to receive. . . .'

'Amen,' they all said and blessed themselves firmly. It was a signal for conversation as well as for eating. The grapefruits were attacked, more sugar was requested across the table. Slowly the buzz rose . . . how well Aisling looked, quite like the pictures you saw of the Honourable Lady this and that in the Dublin papers. And wasn't she lucky to make such a match? Elizabeth could hear some speculation about how strange it was that Aisling had married so well, while Maureen, who had the better education, had only married into the poor Dalys. She hoped that they would change the subject or lower their voices before Maureen stopped her own conversation and might overhear them.

Shay Ferguson was a tireless talker. He swivelled his head left and right, entertaining Elizabeth on his right and Joannie Murray on his left.

'Amn't I well placed now, between two spinsters of this parish? Huh, huh?' he said roaring with laughter.

'Jesus Christ,' said Joannie, and so he looked for a better reaction from Elizabeth.

'I'm not strictly speaking from this parish . . . though I often feel that I am,' she said pleasantly.

'Is that what you feel, is that all you feel?' he said.

'I beg your pardon?' Elizabeth asked politely.

'Never mind,' said Shay. 'When are they pouring the drink? Murrays are providing buckets of drink you know.'

'I think the Murrays are offering champagne for the toast, but the rest is being given by the O'Connors, the red and white wine,' Elizabeth retorted, anxious that this should be understood even by someone as loud and insensitive as Shay Ferguson.

'Yah, well, where is it? They should have it poured by now.'

She turned to Father Riordan.

'You're not a Catholic at all, they tell me,' he said.

'No Father, that's right, my parents were both Church of England.'

'And in all your years here in the convent up with the good nuns, and with a good Catholic woman like Mrs O'Connor you saw nothing to convert you to our faith? Isn't that a sad thing. Isn't that a lack in us all somehow?'

'Oh, I wouldn't say that, Father. I did learn a great respect and admiration for the Catholic faith. . . .'

'Sure, respect and admiration are no use if you're not going to be able to bow the head in humility and say I believe. That's what the church is about you know. Bowing the head in humility.'

'Yes, I suppose it is Father,' said Elizabeth dutifully. To herself she thought that Father Riordan had it all wrong. Whatever the Roman Catholic church was about it seemed to have little to do with bowing the head in humility.

The waitresses must have heard Shay Ferguson's plaintive pleas for wine. They began to dart in and out between people's faces with a 'Red wine or white wine?'

'I'd prefer a drop of whiskey, just a very small drop,' said Father Riordan.

'I'll go and investigate, Father,' said one of the waitresses.

'That you, Deirdre, good girl,' he said.

Deirdre, anxious to please the parish priest, went to whisper a word to Aunt Eileen before filling the wine glasses of Elizabeth and Shay Ferguson. The best man's face was not a pretty sight.

'Mother of Jesus, where has that one gone?' he said to Elizabeth. 'Did you send her off for something or what?'

'You'll survive for a few minutes.' Elizabeth smiled, trying to placate him and thinking what an unpleasant manner he had. She hoped for Aisling's sake that he wasn't a close friend of Tony's. It was hard to know. He must be fairly close if he had been chosen as best man. Tony's friends were spoken of very rarely . . . he was always said to be at the hotel with a crowd, or off with 'the lads' somewhere. Presumably Shay was one of 'the lads'. Elizabeth looked around the room to see if she could identify any of the others.

It was a big horse-shoe table, and people sat close together because the hotel dining room had never been built with the thought of entertaining seventy-three people to a wedding breakfast. The spaces between the guests and the wall were very narrow and the waitresses were now squeezing awkwardly through with their plates of chicken and ham and salad. Elizabeth couldn't see what she might identify as Tony Murray's friends, there didn't seem to be many men of his age in the company. Still, perhaps numbers had to be kept down because it was a family wedding.

'It's all very well for you,' Shay burst in on her thoughts. 'You don't have to make the speech. I have to read telegrams . . . and make a witty speech.'

'I'm sure you'll do it frightfully well,' she said.

'Frightfully, frightfully . . .' he imitated her accent. 'Yeah, that's what it will be, a fright. . . .'

He turned and called over to the bridegroom. 'How are you, Tony me old divil? Eat up! That's right, need all your strength for later. . . .' Mrs Murray looked up from her conversation with Father Mahony and frowned, but Aisling smiled at him. Shay was encouraged. 'That's right, Aisling, feed him up, and plenty of red meat . . . when you get him home not chicken and ham but red meat!' He laughed, delighted with himself, and at that moment the long awaited wine arrived. He drained the glass in a gulp and before the waitress had got to Joannie, he held it out for a refill.

'That's better,' he said to Elizabeth, and belched.

When the jelly and cream was finished, the teapots had been refilled and the wine waiter from the bar had come in to open the champagne, there was much whispering with Uncle Sean, who shuffled to his feet and said, 'I'd like you to know that the Murray family have kindly provided this excellent champagne for you to charge your glasses . . . when the time comes.'

Shay put his hand on his heart and said to Elizabeth, 'God he gave me a fright there, I thought the old clown was about to lose the run of himself and make a speech.'

There was no point, Elizabeth thought to herself, in saying that she didn't like to hear her Uncle Sean called an old clown. Anyway it was nearly time for the speeches. But first Father Mahony had to say grace, so they all shuffled to their feet again before settling back, chairs pushed back a little.

Shay read aloud the seventeen telegrams, stumbling over names, getting some of them so wrong that nobody knew who he was referring to.

'Who would they be, Jean and Jilly MacPherson,' Father Riordan asked Joannie, leaning over Elizabeth and behind Shay's chair to make himself heard.

'Oh, he means Joan and Jimmy Matterson, you know from the bakery, he just can't read.'

Then he said that the etiquette book told him he must praise the charm of the bridesmaid, so he would like everyone to consider the charm and beauty of the bridesmaid praised. He was sorry to see his old friend Tony Murray get hooked, trapped into the terrible penal servitude of matrimony but if he had to be caught at least his new wife was a fine-looking woman. He said that he hoped it wouldn't be long before the Murrays had another wedding and their lovely daughter Joannie would get married. He said the hotel had done a great job on the wedding breakfast, and that it was grand to see Father Mahony in such good spirits . . . and so many more of the clergy able to attend. It was typical of the Murrays to send over some vintage champagne . . . but they were known as one of the most generous families in Ireland. He told a story about a Kilgarret man who was in Dublin and was walking home . . . he found the road lined with tombstones he said . . . all Dublin men of different ages but from the same family. They were all called Miles from Dublin; there was the Miles from Dublin who was twenty-five and then some way further along the road there was his brother who was thirty. People explained it to each other and the laughter and clapping went on a long time.

Uncle Sean said a few words too, only to introduce Father Mahony he said. It was a privilege and a consolation for Kilgarret people to know that Father Mahony was there to baptise them when they came into the world, to say their Mass and give them the sacraments during this life and to see them out of it at the end with his blessing. It was a very happy occasion today that he was here to bless the marriage of Aisling and the fine young Tony Murray . . . he, too, would like to thank Miss Donnelly and everyone in the hotel for serving them so well . . . and now if Father Mahony could say a few words . . . .

Father Mahony said a great many words . . . he remembered Tony when he was at the Brothers' before he went off to the Jesuits, he remembered Tony's brother John . . . soon, thank God and please God, to be Father John . . . a fine, fine young recruit for the priesthood . . . he remembered the daughter of the house Joan, and he felt sure too that any day now he would be joining her in marriage . . . but of course there was all the time in the world. He remembered Mrs Murray, as brave in widowhood as she had been strong in marriage. Father Mahony talked about Murray's and the place it had as the centre of Kilgarret . . . there could hardly be a town without it. It had employed so many and looked after them so well . . . and been a pillar of what a Catholic community life should have . . . a good family business, run on Christian lines.

He did speak about the O'Connors too. Elizabeth wondered whether she was becoming over-sensitive when she felt that he didn't pay them as many compliments as he had paid to the Murrays. It was the O'Connors who were holding the wedding, it was their daughter who was the bride, they were four hundred per cent better people than the Murrays . . . But then it was Tony's turn. He stood up, red-faced and perspiring. Elizabeth felt a wave of sympathy for him and a hope that he would make a good speech.

'Good man, Tony,' called Shay. And then in an aside he said to Elizabeth, 'Jesus, he really is a good man, he must have had five gin and oranges before he even got in here . . . and the wine has been flowing up at their end ever since. . . .'

Tony was getting through his speech, but only just. He looked down after every second sentence to his written notes. He thanked Aisling's parents . . . but had to consult his notes to remember their names. He hoped he would make her a good husband. He read a list of relations whom he was glad to see, and he read them even more haltingly than Shay had read the telegrams. He thanked his mother for all the help and encouragement she had been, he said he looked forward to seeing Rome with his new wife and, if possible, if all went well, please God, going there again next year for his brother's ordination. He wanted to thank everyone for their useful gifts. He hoped they would all enjoy the wedding. He sat down abruptly, and when the clapping ceased there was an uneasy silence. Elizabeth saw Mrs Murray looking at her watch yet again, Shay was fidgeting. She noticed Aunt Eileen lean over and say something to Uncle Sean who stood up again.

'Would it be in order to ask Father O'Donnell to sing us a verse of a song . . . we all know what a beautiful voice he has.' This was greeted with great clapping and cheers.

Father O'Donnell had already arranged his face and his hands and he sang 'Bless This House', and then 'I think that I shall never see a poem lovely as a tree', which was not nearly as successful. As if he knew that he had lost his following, Father O'Donnell said that a little bird has asked him to sing one last song which was a special favourite of the bride and groom. His true clear voice soared again into 'Danny Boy', and a strange unexpected pricking at the back of Elizabeth's nose and eyes began. She looked over at Aisling, who smiled out of her veil and red curls. She had told Aisling about the time she had sung 'Danny Boy' for Mother and Harry and Johnny . . . Aisling had said it was only natural . . . everyone cried when they heard 'Danny Boy'.

With a blur in her eyes Elizabeth looked around the room. Everyone's face looked up at the young priest as he sang, and you could see that a lot of effort was going into keeping their expressions unmoved. There was a sense of rescue almost when it came to the last chorus and everyone joined in . . . .

Oh come ye back, when sun shines in the meadow,
Or when the valley's hushed and white with snow,
For I'll be there in sunshine or in shadow
Oh Danny Boy, Oh Danny Boy I love you so . . . .

And they wiped their eyes and they sniffed and they took great slugs of their tea or their wine, and they clapped, and Elizabeth smiled again at Aisling, blinking back the tears, and thought that weddings are quite emotional enough without introducing a song like that into them.

Aunt Eileen said that her feet had grown twice the size and that they were going to have to cut the shoes off her when they got home. Uncle Sean said that his throat was closing over from all that sweet wine and that only a couple of pints would open it again. Eamonn had been formally released by Aisling. He shuffled and said it hadn't been that bad and since he had been here for so long he might as well wait and see the send-off. Around the horse-shoe table, with the name cards scattered around on the floor and the children racing up and down, relatives sat in small groups and discussed other small groups.

Shay Ferguson had scooped up two very large whiskeys which he carried in one hand together with a glass of water held precariously by the little finger. He made a noise like an advancing train. 'Hoo, hoo, out of me way, I've got to get the bridegroom ready for the long journey ahead. . . .' Tony was changing from his wedding finery into a less formal suit in the back of Miss Donnelly's office.

Maureen was annoyed because Brendan wanted to go home.

'Why can't he go on his own and you come later?'

'Oh, it's easy known you're not married, Elizabeth . . . where one goes the other goes, that's the rule in marriage.' Maureen had two red spots on her face, caused by wine and emotion.

'There's no problem in your getting a lift home, go on let him go on his own . . . then you'll both be happy.'

'No, that way neither of us will be happy. If I go at least one of us will be happy. You go and distract him, talk to him about something, any-thing, will you?' Maureen looked upset. Elizabeth decided not to fight the matter on principle. She went over to Brendan, who was standing fid-geting at the door.

'Where's Maureen? Really and truly she's very selfish. My poor mother's been looking after Brendan Og since the breakfast is over. I can't understand why people want to hang around for instead of going back to their own homes. . . .'

There was a noise behind them, and together Aisling and Tony came out into the hall. From the dining room the women converged and out from the bar with pint glasses in their hands the men came. Aisling wore a suit which, she told Elizabeth, must be described as aquamarine,

because it was in fact green but a lot of people thought green was unlucky. She had a tiny pill-box hat too which was covered with the same
fabric. Her hair was piled up and tied in a chignon.

'She looks like a film star,' said Maureen in naked admiration. Maureen had appeared from around a corner to savour the moment.

'She looks very old, she nearly looks thirty,' said Donal. 'A glamorous
thirty,' he added, seeing Maureen's face. That didn't help. 'Not that
thirty's really old, you know,' he said.

Eileen walked behind them proudly as they came to the hotel door.
She saw Ethel Murray standing on her own and with an effort she went
over to stand beside her.

Elizabeth saw Mrs Murray smile quickly with surprise and then
arrange her face in its normal, slightly quizzical, expression.

'Ah yes, Eileen, the moment has come.'

'Don't they look very happy, isn't it great to see them setting out like
this?' Mrs Murray nodded. 'He's a fine man, Ethel, apart altogether from
the grand family that Aisling's marrying into . . . Sean and I are very glad
she'll have a good man to look after her. He's a good, kind man.' Aunt
Eileen squeezed her arm, and the two of them walked out to the foot-
path. Elizabeth stood a little withdrawn from the crowd. She looked at
the stranger, Aisling, in the pert little hat. Somehow it was much more
alien than the beautiful wedding dress which had been hung up carefully
in the hotel room under sheets of tissue paper pinned to cellophane.
Later Aunt Eileen would collect it and hang it carefully at home until the
bungalow was ready to house it.

The crowd was shouting encouragement. Shay Ferguson was hardly
able to stand as he banged on the roof of the car. 'Come on with you,
come on . . . it's nearly within your grasp, Tony, stop wasting time . . .
don't let her ardour die down.'

'Goodbye Aisling . . . good luck,' called Maureen, tears in her eyes.

'Where did she get that suit? It's very well cut,' Joannie was asking
around her.

Aisling kissed Uncle Sean goodbye, and Mrs Murray, and then Aunt
Eileen. Tony was shaking hands, holding everyone else's hand in both of
his.

'Goodbye, thank you, goodbye, thank you,' he said to everyone.

He came to Elizabeth. 'Goodbye thank you,' he said.

'I hope you'll both be very happy, Tony,' she said. 'Very happy and
give each other great . . . great happiness,' she finished lamely.

'Oh, I'm sure we will,' he said awkwardly.

Shay Ferguson was at his elbow. 'Well if you won't, Tony Boy, it's
hard to know who else will . . . what? Give her *lots* of happiness, and get
on the road huh?'

Elizabeth was crimson with rage at being taken up in such a loud and
coarse way when she was trying to be completely sincere . . . she *did* hope

that Aisling and Tony would give each other a lot of happiness . . . some people did, like Eileen and Sean, and like Mother and Harry for a while, but some people definitely didn't. Why had that great vulgar Shay Ferguson been there to overhear her?

Aisling seemed to sense her distress from the other side of the crowd. She rushed over and caught her by the arm. 'Tell me it wasn't all too appalling, tell me that there was a bit of style in the way Aisling O'Connor had her nuptials?'

Elizabeth held her and the two stood as if frozen for a moment. 'It was a beautiful wedding, it was simply beautiful. I've been listening to them. Nothing as classy and as . . . well as outright colourful and glamorous in Kilgarret ever before.'

'Elizabeth, will you come back again? Please, when things are more settled down and there isn't all this Twentieth-Century Fox stuff going on?'

'Yes, of course, I'll come back. Go *on*, Aisling, they're calling you.'

'And I'm right, aren't I . . .?'

'What?'

'I'm doing the right thing? It will be fine . . .?'

'Not now, Aisling . . . go.'

'You're my best friend. . . .'

'And you're mine . . . Go.'

The cheer was enormous when she got into the car and Aisling's smile was almost as great. Shay had put a big cardboard notice on the back of the car with the word 'Honeymooners' scrawled on it. Tony had tried to take it off but Eileen had said he should stop when he was outside the town. The car with its badly made notice revved up and drove off . . . but to everyone's delight it did one lap of the square before taking the Dublin road. Total strangers who had just come in on the afternoon bus cheered too. And then they were gone.

Part Three

1954–1956

XIV

People had told them to be sure to get a hotel on the north side of Dublin so that they would be on the way to the airport when they had to set out in the morning. Aisling had said to Elizabeth that most friends and relations assumed that they were going to be so weak from the night of passion that they would hardly manage to drive to the airport at all. Maureen had said that there was a guesthouse she knew of which was actually only a mile from the airport. Dad had said they could do worse than go the the cousins in Dunlaoghaire. There would be no bad feeling because they had been sent a wedding invitation but business was brisk and they couldn't be gone for a whole day. Dad had said that he heard they had the place much improved now, with carpets in all the bedrooms, wall to wall, and because they were family they'd get a cut.

Aisling took no notice of them and had written to the Shelbourne Hotel in Dublin, booking a night's accommodation in one of the best double rooms for Mr and Mrs Murray. In fact she had paused and reflected for a long time when she reread the words Mr and Mrs Murray. She remembered for no good reason all the whispered plans with Elizabeth years ago, years and years back when Elizabeth lived in Kilgarret. They would only marry for love, they would marry young men who roamed through the town, not awful businessmen who lived there. In those days Aisling had said suddenly that Elizabeth had a wider choice of business families because being a Protestant she could marry the Grays, and Elizabeth had complained and asked what was the point of learning all about contrition and grace and angels if she was still going to be considered Protestant at the end of it?

Being Mr and Mrs Murray wasn't part of that plan. But then neither was having an abortion because Johnny Stone couldn't be told that his attempts at contraception had failed. Aisling wondered what Elizabeth did nowadays to make sure that it never happened again. Aisling sighed a happy sigh. Thank God she wouldn't have to bother with that. If she got pregnant it would be fine, she'd have the baby, and the next one, and Main would help her look after them, and maybe Peggy would come and help her a bit. And Tony of course. She sighed again.

Tony looked over at her, and put his hand on her knee.

'Are you happy, Missus?' he said, imitating some of the old shawlies who always called people Missus even though they knew their names as well as their own.

'I'm very happy, Misthur,' she mimicked back.

'Great, so am I, and in in time we'll be in Dublin and we'll have that drink I've been thinking about, at the back of my mind.'

'Yeah,' said Aisling absently. She wondered would he have the drink in the bar of the Shelbourne or would they have it sent up to the room? In films drinks came in ice buckets on trolleys. They might even have that.

'It's grand to be back in the old Shelbourne,' Tony said when the car had been safely parked and the porter had taken their cases. 'Now for that drink. Right?'

'Great, said Aisling. To her surprise they walked right through the hotel and out again once he had signed the book. It had been curiously disappointing – she thought he would hold her hand and they would giggle. But no. And now where were they going?

'You wouldn't want to drink in here, it's too posh a bar, people with accents and notions of grandeur. We'll go to a real bar.'

Aisling had peeped into the bar, it looked marvellous. It had mirrors, and waiters in white jackets. There were one or two elegant women there and she thought she looked the match for them in her aquamarine suit and little hat. But no, they were almost running away from Stephen's Green and on Baggot Street. Suddenly they were in a bar which wasn't as nice as Maher's and not quite as seedy as Hanrahan's. But it had that sour smell of beer and stout that you get when a place is full of spilt glasses and barrels not properly cleaned.

'You don't drink in places like this in Kilgarret,' she said, 'you drink in the hotel. Why won't we drink back in the hotel? It's nicer.'

'I can't go into a bar in Kilgarret or I'd have everyone in the town asking me for a loan of ten shillings, or travellers from the business coming up and trying to buy me a drink and tell me how they should be promoted. That's why I have to drink in the hotel. But here it's all right, no one will know who we are.'

Aisling looked around her. Men with caps on barely looked up from their pints, a group of young fellows near the door laughed and jeered about something. The table was covered with dirty glasses and overflowing ashtrays.

'Oh come on back, the bar in the Shelbourne has drink too, it's much nicer,' she begged.

But Tony was at the counter. He indicated one of the tables with a nod of his head. 'Gin?' he asked.

She heard him order a large gin, a large Power's and a pint of Guinness. She looked with distaste at the table and the barman sent a man around to clean it. The man was a bit slow, like Jemmy back in the shop. He kept looking at Aisling as he wiped the ash and rings of beer. His cloth was so greasy the table didn't look much better after his efforts. Aisling saw an evening newspaper and she picked it up smartly. She put two pages on the table and two on the chair. Now she would only get newsprint on her, she thought angrily. At least it would be better than God knows what other dirt.

'That's grand,' said Tony, coming back to the table with the drinks. He saw no criticism in her improvements. 'Well, here's good luck to us,' he said, rising the pint first and then having a swallow of the whiskey before Aisling had even touched her gin. 'As you said we're a fine pair.'

A man with the red nose of a drinker and a shabby, crumpled suit that might once had been a good one leaned over and said to Tony as he might have addressed a regular in the pub, 'And what has yourself and your lady-friend all dolled up on a Saturday evening?'

Tony was delighted. 'I'd like you to know that's no lady-friend, that's my wife,' he said and roared with laughter.

The man peered at Aisling. 'Aw, well, it doesn't do any harm to take the wife out now and then, I always say. Were you at the races?'

.No, we were at a wedding,' said Tony winking and leering and looking so stupid that Aisling wanted to get up and walk away. With a jolt she realised that she couldn't do that any more.

'Oh, a wedding. Was it near here?' the man wanted to know.

'No, down the country. Two real country bumpkins.'

The man laughed. 'Oh, nothing as bad as a culchie wedding I always say. They can get desperately pretentious down in the country.'

Tony's face was all smiles. 'I could go along with you, I could lead you on and make a fool of you . . . but you look too good a man to do that to. It was our own wedding. Now what do you make of that?' and he sat back beaming.

The man, his eyes dulled with drink, knew something was expected of him. He stood up and shook hands with both of them. 'My sincere congratulations and my warmest felicitations. Under normal circumstances I would be the first to offer you a . . .'

Tony seemed to understand the man's predicament as if he had been inspired by the Holy Ghost. This was a man who was about to offer them a drink to celebrate their wedding but had no money. This was a drunk, a pathetic shambling drunk, exactly the kind of man who would want to borrow ten shillings from Tony back home, a man with extravagant promises. Maybe a civil servant once, or a clerk somewhere. Aisling raged inside and her gin and tonic tasted like acid. Tony was at the counter. The man, their new friend, wouldn't touch Power's, he was a man who drank Bushmill's, never touched any whiskey only Black Bush, he said. Funny how many good things came out of the North when you stopped to think about it.

Aisling decided to turn her mind off. She blotted Tony and this man out, she fixed a smile on her face and she worked out what she would have for dinner. She planned her menu, she planned the bedroom scene, where she would wear her new cream nightie and lacy dressing-gown which had to be called a negligee – it was never going to be called a dressing-gown when you considered how much it cost. She planned how she was going to come into the room having undressed in the bathroom . . .

she had been delighted that they had got a bedroom with a bathroom attached. Otherwise she would have had to walk down the corridor in her negligee. She planned that after it had all happened they would lie there and talk about the future, and Tony would say that he was glad they had waited for their wedding night.

In the middle of all this she heard Tony's voice and felt his elbow nudging her.

'You're very silent, Ash, is everything all right?'

'Oh yes,' she smiled,, and he went back to his conversation and she went back into her mind. The next morning they would drive to the airport and she wouldn't be a bit afraid of the plane. After all, a grown-up, married woman who would have had sexual intercourse by that stage . . . naturally she wouldn't be as eejit and gormless as other people.

She got another nudge.

'Gerry knows a great pub altogether, a known pint house, I said we'd go and have the one there.'

'Will we not be a bit late for dinner in the hotel?' she said, the frostiness plain even to the man who drank Bushmill's whiskey.

'Well, maybe old son another night . . .' he began.

But Tony Murray had felt no frost. 'Nonsense, tonight's the night, we might never find you again in this city, two culchies like ourselves.' He laughed loudly. Aisling got up obediently and Tony put his arm around her shoulder.

'Didn't I get the best girl in Kilgarret, Gerry?' he asked the drunk.

'Tony, you got the very best,' said the drunk firmly.

There was no dinner in the Shelbourne; the time spent planning whether to have melon or grapefruit or soup as a starter had been wasted. At closing time, Gerry had told them where to get chips. He wouldn't have any himself, he had kept his money for the last bus, but anyway, money or no money, he often found that he didn't fancy food after a few scoops of an evening. He shook their hands and wished them the best. He was no drunker than when they had met four hours earlier. He seemed no redder in the nose, no more dulled in the eye. Aisling was hardly changed either. She had accepted no more gin, only glasses of tonic water. And in the last pub they didn't have any so she had just sat there with nothing in front of her and her mind closed. Now, chips finished, and Tony laughing like a schoolboy, they walked back through the city. In her handbag was a key to one of the most expensive hotel rooms in Ireland; they had money and planned to have had a dinner for the two of them. But instead it had been bar after bar. Five of them, counting the first place. In the hall the porters looked at each other and smiled behind Tony's back as he fumbled for change.

'There's no need for a tip now, they've not done anything for us,' hissed Aisling.

'I'd like to give them a tip, it's my money, it's my wedding night,' stumbled Tony, swaying. 'It's my bloody wedding night, I'll give as many tips as I please.'

The porters thanked him. He gave one a half crown and the other two shillings.

'Fight it out between you,' he said.

'Goodnight, sir, thank you,' they both said, and Aisling tried to support him as he staggered making them a mock courteous bow.

'Leave me be, woman. She's the same as all of them you know, can't wait to get me upstairs,'

The porters smiled, embarrassed for Aisling whom they could see was sobbing. And humiliated. The older porter took pity on her.

'Mam, let me go ahead with the key,' he said. And as Tony staggered along the corridor, the kindly man said to Aisling, 'If you knew how many honeymoon couples we get Madam, and the men are always scared out of their minds. I think we men are definitely the weaker sex. I've always thought it.'

'You're a very kind man,' Aisling said.

'Nonsense, you'll be the happiest couple in the world, never mind.'

Inside the bedroom Tony was all smiles.

'Come on, let me at you,' he said to Aisling.

'Let me get my suit off me first,' said Aisling. It was filthy already but she didn't want it torn.

She hung the jacket on the back of a chair, and folded the skirt, she stood before him in her slip and her blouse.

'You're lovely,' he said.

'Hold on a minute,' she said. 'Can't I get out my lovely new negligee? I want to put that on. Please.'

'All right,' he said. He sat down in a velvet armchair, suddenly, as if the strength had gone from his legs. Aisling opened the suitcase she had packed so carefully with the dinner dress she had intended to wear on top, the negligee and nightie set underneath and the washbag with flowers on it beside that. She slipped into the bathroom and washed quickly. She would love to have soaked in a long bath but she was afraid that he would not want to wait as long as that.

She looked at her face, which seemed to her tired and drawn, pulled her long hair back and tied it loosely with the cream ribbon she had bought specially for the occasion. She put on more perfume ... and rubbed a little rouge into her cheeks. She looked better now. Oh God, may he not be too drunk. Please God, may he not hurt her. Please. After all God, I did wait until I got married, a lot of people don't, a great many people don't. I kept my part of the bargain God, please let him not be too rough with me. She went into the room and twirled around so that he would get the full view of the negligee.

Tony was asleep in the armchair. His mouth was open and he was snoring.

Aisling took off the negligee and hung it carefully on one of the hotel hangers. She switched off the light in the bathroom; took the extra blanket which had been left in the wardrobe and put it over Tony. She raised his head slightly and slipped a pillow behind his neck. She loosened his shoes and took them off and she put his feet on another pillow. She had seen someone do that in a film once, where a man had gone out and got drunk over this woman and when he came home she took his army boots off and put his feet on a cushion. It had seemed a lovely thing for her to do in the film. But of course in the film he had been crying and saying he loved her. He hadn't been snoring like Tony Murray. Her husband.

Dublin airport
Just a quick word to thank you for being such a support and help. Don't leave another million years before you come back to Kilgarret. Everything in Dublin super. Roll on Rome.
   Love from
   Aisling Murray

Hotel San Martino
Another picture for your collection. This is the Holy City or the Eternal City as we called it at school. It's very very hot, and there are an awful lot of poor people, much poorer than you'd see in Wicklow, and lots of the Italians have no religion. There's a bank called Sancto Spirito. Imagine having your savings in the Holy Ghost Bank! The hotel is beautiful and there's an old-fashioned life you can see through. Tomorrow we see Il Pappa. Tony sends his love, or he would if he knew I was writing to you.
   Love,
   Aisling

Hotel San Martino
There were a hundred people there, and we were introduced to him. Signor e Signora Murray d'Irlanda. It was unbelievable. I still don't believe it happened. Every time I see pictures of him, I keep saying to Tony . . . he met US. Still very hot. I roam about and look at ruins quite a lot, you'd be proud of me. We have meals in restaurants on the side of the street, not inside at all. Just like those pictures you see in Paris. The wine is very cheap and we drink it with every single meal. Except breakfast.
   Love from
   Signora Murray

It's got even hotter. Everyone else in Rome is golden and sun-tanned, but because of my awful colouring I just burn. So I've bought a parasol. Remember we used to have toy parasols once?

Tony doesn't want to go out in the heat, so we see a great deal of indoor things. I went to the catacombs. The poor martyrs, didn't they have an awful time for their faith when it's so easy for us? I'm quite looking forward to seeing Kilgarret where it's cool and green ... and wet, I gather from Mam's letter.

Love, Aisling

Mam, thank you very much for writing here. Nobody else did, I expect they didn't think it would arrive. You're an angel to tell me the bungalow is so far ahead. Thank God we won't have to stay with the old bag ... I'll have to put this card into an envelope now, won't I? Everything is smashing Ma, and as I said in the other card, thank you and Dad a million times. I hope the wedding didn't exhaust you and leave you broke or anything. I'm so looking forward to being home. I must try to remember I live with Tony now rather than saying goodbye to him in the square and running up to you and Dad like I used to. Tell the boys thanks again too and Niamh. Wasn't it great that Elizabeth came over for the wedding, and didn't she look marvellous? I've sent her a few cards from here. It must be very lonely for her back in London, I was thinking.

Love from your Married Daughter, Aisling.

'She looked utterly enchanting ... here, I have the pictures.' Elizabeth sat on a desk with her feet on a chair and opened the wallet of black and white pictures. She had been given this camera by Johnny for her twenty-first birthday and it had never been taken on a serious outing before. Now she had twelve pictures of Aisling's wedding, ten of them perfect she thought, and two spoiled. Stefan and Anna pored over them.

'Hasn't she become slim since she was here?' Stefan said.

'Look at her beautiful dress,' said Anna.

'Is this her mother, a handsome woman ... ' Stefan looked at Eileen and somehow Elizabeth felt her two worlds grow closer.

'And her husband, this Tony, he is handsome is he not?' Anna had spread the pictures down on the desk. 'And who is this man, the one who has his hand on your arm?'

'That's his loathsome best man ... a frightful fool.'

Stefan and Anna laughed.

'No, seriously ... really dreadful. I hope for Aisling's sake he's not going to be a family friend.

'And who is the sad lady?'

'That's Tony's mother. She did smile a bit, but I don't think anybody caught it. And that's Tony's awful bad-mannered sister, Joannie, and that's his rather wishy-washy brother who's nearly a priest ... oh, and that's Donal, the young brother who used to be delicate. Look at his laugh, isn't he marvellous ... and that's me looking silly with my hat. ... '

You look beautiful. Elizabeth,' said Anna seriously.

'Oh she does. Tony pulling a face . . . it was just before they got into the car to go to the hotel. He was still very edgy at that stage . . . he got better later on. More relaxed.'

'You don't think they are good enough for Aisling, these people?' Oh Stefan. I never said that. No they're the high and mighty in the town, honestly. Like the squire, as Johnny used to say.'

'But you do not like them . . . listen, this Tony he is edgy, his brother is wishy-washy, his sister she is bad-mannered, rude, his mother she is weepy, his best friend is frightful . . . of course you don't like them!'

Stefan laughed. Elizabeth looked at him, almost speechless.

'I didn't mean . . . ' she began.

'But it's not a crime not to like the people that your friends marry. I am sure if my sons are married I would not like their wives. Anna here does not like the family that her sister married into. They live in London, she never sees the family, but she meets her sister every month. So. It's not unnatural.'

'I never even said it to myself. I didn't even know I didn't like them,' said Elizabeth, grinning mischievously. 'But you won't tell them, and you'll never tell Aisling if she comes over here again. Because I don't really dislike them. . . . Listen, I won't delay you any more. I just collected these from the chemist and I wanted you to be the first to see. I'm off home now.'

'Johnny should be back next week, then it will all be fun and bustle here again,' Anna said with the air of someone trying to introduce a comforting note.

Elizabeth saw Stefan frown at her.

'Now, Anna, Elizabeth knows all Johnny's movements better than we do, in Brighton and Hove, and back on Friday . . . we don't have to tell her what he's doing.'

Darling Stefan, like Aunt Eileen, a diplomat, always wanting people to be given their dignity, never wanting to score over others. How great it had been seeing him looking at Aunt Eileen and saying she was hand-some. Wouldn't it be wonderful if Aunt Eileen came over here . . . or was that silly? Oh God, oh God, from Stefan's face it looks as if Johnny has a new woman. Of course she hadn't known that he was coming back on Friday. Thank God for Stefan and his refusal to admit that anything was wrong between Elizabeth and Johnny. Sometimes she thought that if it weren't for Stefan she would have lost Johnny forever.

Father was politely interested in the photographs.

'Which one is Violet's friend, he asked first, and Elizabeth thought that this was a good sign. Usually he refused any opportunity to bring Mother's name into the conversation.

'That's Aunt Eileen there,' she said proudly.

'Nice, nice, yes she looks a very presentable woman. Of course, she'll be glad that Aisling has married and married well.'

'Yes, Father, she is glad. I think she's very glad.'

'Well, of course she's pleased, dear. Her daughter married and set up. Safely off her hands, with a home and a future of her own. It's what every parent would want.'

Elizabeth looked up, amazed.

'Is it what you want for me, Father?'

'Of course.'

'What?'

'Of course I want you to marry and settle down. What else can I want for you?'

'And are you not glad that I'm happy as I am? That I have work which interests me, teaching and working in Worsky's, and that I have Johnny around . . . ?'

Father said nothing.

'Because I am fine. Really. To be utterly honest, I wouldn't like to be marrying someone like Tony Murray, someone sensible. I prefer to be the way I am. I mean it. I'm not just saying it to cover a broken heart. . . .'

'You're your mother's daughter, I'm afraid, Elizabeth, and that's what worries me. She had a fine home here, and a family and a social life and what did she do, she went off with a fly-by-night black-marketer, a man who made his money out of other people's suffering . . . she went off with him, flighty and thoughtless and ended up losing her mind. So do you wonder that I worry when I see that feckless side of her in you?' Father said all this quite calmly; there was no twitch in his eye, as there used to be when he became upset. It was as if he believed it all now like a story that had happened to someone else. That poor Harry was a black-marketeer. Harry!

She kept her voice as calm as Father's. If she was going to be able to talk to him, she must follow his lead. She must let his own dead objectivity be in control.

'Yes, I do see that, I can see now why you might be worried. But honestly, things have changed. It's the fifties now, not the twenties and thirties. Things change. Women really are interested in their work. And men, some men are simply not interested in settling down.'

'Yes, well. I would of course prefer you to have a proper life and be looked after. I mean, what's the point of having children if you're going to be worried that they don't settle down?'

Elizabeth hid her amazement. She decided it was time to end the conversation lightly.

'Yes, you may be right, and one of these days I might actually surprise you, throw over Johnny Stone and find a suitable husband . . . then we'll have a wedding like this. Here, look at Tony's mother, now she's a widow and you're divorced – what do you say we make a match there . . . ?'

Father looked seriously at Mrs Murray's gloomy face. 'She looks perfectly pleasant . . .' He peered at the picture. 'But she has other children . . . I don't think I could take on the responsibility of any more. . . .'

This was the nearest thing Father had ever made to a joke that Elizabeth could ever remember. She was still laughing when the telephone rang: it was Johnny.

'How was the poor sacrificial lamb? Did she go through with it?'

'Oh hallo, Johnny, yes, she went through with it. The whole ritualistic sacrifice. Marvellous, it was. Hymns and priests talking forever. I have some smashing pictures . . . your camera was a great success.'

'Oh good. Listen, I'm sorry I wasn't around. I don't know what Stefan said, or if there was any explanation when you got back . . . ?'

'What? No, don't worry, Stefan gave me your message.'

'He what?'

'He said you said you'd be back on Friday. How's it all going?'

'Well, plan's changed a bit, I think I'll come back tonight. I really only rang to know how the land lay . . . if you felt like coming round to the flat tonight?'

'Oh sure, that would be terrific. About eight all right?'

'Well, I'll be back by six if you could. . .'

'No, I've a few things to do here . . . see you at eight. Have you got any food . . . or shall I get some?'

'I'll get a bottle of wine . . . could you rustle up something? You sound very cheerful I must say . . . the wedding didn't make you all gooey and broody?'

'Who me? Listen, you're talking to Elizabeth White, my friend.'

'Yes, I know and I'm looking forward to seeing her tonight. I missed you, funny-face.'

'I missed you too, Johnny,'

Ethel Murray had said that she was going to be in Dublin anyway on the day that Tony was expected back. She was half-wondering would she go to the airport to meet him? Eileen had thought that was a poor idea.

'I suppose you're right, Eileen. You always seem so sensible about things,' Ethel Murray said grudgingly. They were talking outside the church where they had both been delivering flowers for the procession. Already people were busy decorating the float for the statue of the Sacred Heart. The women walked to the gate of the church in a companionable silence. 'I never knew you were so business-like, Eileen. I suppose you didn't know I was so . . . well, so alone and so dependent on my children, did you?'

'Ah, we're all dependent on our children, we'd be no use as parents if we could just produce them and forget about them, would we?'

'But yours are no problem to you. They don't run as far away from you as they can get, like mine do.'

'Haven't you a big handsome son coming back next week to live down the road from you, woman? And better still, hasn't he the eyes in his head to marry my daughter?'

They laughed. And Eileen wondered again why people thought she had no problems with her children. Eamonn and his father rowing worse than ever; Maureen expecting yet again, going to be tied down still more to the Dalys; Donal coughing and wheezing and pausing to catch his breath. Niamh was too pert for her own good. And Aisling. Eileen wished she knew why Aisling's cards had upset her. Sean had thought that the child sounded in great form. But she never said anything about being happy.

There had been an arrangement before they left for Rome that Tony would leave the car keys under the seat and Joannie could use the car for the month that they were away. As soon as they got on the plane for the return journey Tony began to regret this.

'It was sheer madness, I don't know how I got talked into it.' His face looked upset and hurt as if it had been a plot which he had recently discovered, instead of his own plan made long, long ago.

'You said it would be a saving, we wouldn't have to pay for a whole month's parking at the airport, and Joannie could have the use of a car while her own is being fixed.'

'Yes, but that's the point, did we ever hear the full story of why hers is being fixed?'

Aisling laughed. 'We probably never will. Stop worrying about it and look at the clouds. Imagine, these are the things that ruin whole crops on people and spoil people's weddings and picnics, and don't they look harmless from up here?'

'Yes, isn't it a mystery all right. You know, if she's burned out the choke on that car . . . or driven it into the ground, I don't know what I'll do to her. God almighty, Aisling, that's a new car. That's a car with only a thousand miles on the clock. I should have had my head examined before I gave in to the lot of you over it.'

'Tony, you suggested it, for God's sake, I'm not going to sit here saying yes dear and no dear. It was your bloody idea so shut up about it will you?'

Tony looked at her and laughed suddenly. 'Very well, I'll shut up about it. No, I can't imagine you saying yes dear and no dear. It doesn't fit into the picture. . . .'

'It didn't fit into the promise. And you won't yes dear me, like poor Mr Moriarty does to his wife. We must be equals in the yes dearing and no dearing. Or better still abolish it.'

Tony laughed again. 'You look so funny when you get all hot and bothered laying down the law. Fair enough: no yes dearing or no dearing in our house. Ever.'

'Won't it be very exciting to see it? I wonder what it will look like. Mam said that they had the drive down and all. . . .'

'Tony. Shut up about the car. It will be grand to have our own home. Won't it?'

He took her hand. 'Yes, it will all be fine there, everything will be fine at home. It's only natural that things should be a bit . . . I mean, shouldn't work out exactly right . . . when people are abroad . . . but in our own home. . . . In a person's own home is should all be grand.' He was red and embarrassed, his face working as he spoke, moving from a scowl to a pathetic little-boy look. Aisling deliberately misunderstood what he was talking about.

'Yes, of course things will be great when we have our own food. . . . I mean, we never promised to eat Italian food until death do us part or live with that kind of traffic screeching around us. No, what we were thinking about was life in Kilgarret. And that's going to be grand. Don't we know that?'

But he had begun, and he was not going to be turned aside. 'No,' he whispered. 'I meant about the other. The other thing. Bed, you know. All that side of things will be fine too when we settle down at home, in our own place. You know?'

Aisling was utterly light-hearted about it. 'You mean about us not doing it right yet? I think nobody does it right for a bit, I think we have to practise like playing tennis or riding a bicycle. I mean, we don't have anyone to teach us. Nobody has. So they all pretend like mad that they know by inspiration. I bet we'll be just as good as anyone at it in a couple of weeks and then we'll imply there was nothing to it!'

'You're a great girl,' he said.

'Isn't it right, though? I mean it makes sense,' Aisling said and they dropped the subject to talk about Tony's mother and how she must not be encouraged to drop in casually into the new house. Then they relapsed into a silence for a while and Tony looked in front of him. Aisling stared out of the window, and wondered did Tony think he should go out drinking by himself still like he had before he was married and go to the pictures other nights with her? If so, did he expect her to sit at home and wait for him? Doing what? Doing bloody what? Calm down, she told herself, no point in getting all upset about something that hasn't even happened and may not happen. Think about something else. Aisling looked out at the clouds and thought about the time she had asked Elizabeth what it was like having sex. Poor Elizabeth had been so distressed about the abortion and the whole situation she hadn't been much help but she hadn't said anything about it taking a long time to learn it. She had sort of given the impression that it was something you did. But of course she was hopelessly loyal and devoted to that Johnny that she wouldn't even admit that he had had to learn how to do it like anyone else. Or perhaps Johnny had practised on other people, Of course, that was it. That was why it had been so easy for them. And probably Mau reen and Brendan Daly had been years and years learning, it was amazing that they had managed to have Brendan Og so soon. Very soon in fact. It must have been a mistake. She shrugged. There were obviously secrets in everyone's marriage. She was never going to tell anyone about that awful night in Dublin with the drunk, and making fools of themselves in the Shelbourne Hotel in front of the porter. And she would never tell anyone about the times Tony had cried and she had cried in the Hotel San Martino in Rome. You didn't tell those things any more than you told things like Da hitting Eamonn in the middle of Sunday lunch one day and Mother standing up with a bread knife to keep them apart. It had shocked everyone so much that nobody ever mentioned it again, or even thought about it.

Dear Aisling,

I'm so happy that you are home again and settled into the new house. It sounds very exotic to be writing to you as Mrs Murray in San Martino Lodge instead of Aisling O'Connor, 14 The Square. Was it your idea to call it after your honeymoon hotel or was it Tony's? It's so marvellous to have been back to Kilgarret because now I know where everything is all over again. I had thought that the bungalow was on the other side of town completely – for some reason I thought it was on the Dublin road. Now that I can place things you simply must write and tell me all there is to be told.

You won't have the excuse of being busy, a married lady with nothing to do but tend the flowers all day. I know it's not comparing anything with anything, but my earliest memories of Mother before the war, before I came to Kilgarret, were always of her sitting at a writing desk writing letters. And now I can't think who they could have been to. Aunt Eileen said she only heard from her very rarely, so it's another mystery.

Mother, since I spoke to her, is well. By which they mean she is peaceful, she is so heavily tranquillised now and under such sedation that she doesn't know who anyone is, or where she is. I went up to Lancashire last week just to make sure. She is like a baby, a toddler really. Very thin and smiling. It's as if she were a shell. Father won't hear about it. He did mention Mother of his own accord not long ago when I was showing him your wedding pictures – weren't they super? – I had hoped he might be beginning to talk more about things, but no. Having scared me to death by saying that he had always hoped I would marry and settle down, he then went back to his normal uncommunicative self.

Oh, the reason he scared me by advocating marriage was that since he had endured such a poor experience of it himself I was surprised he wanted to see others enter into it. It's quite different in your house. I'm not at all surprised your parents are so happy about you getting married, they had so much themselves out of the whole married state. Anyway, I said to Father quite openly that Johnny and marriage were two separate notions and if I wanted one I couldn't have the other.

I was quite surprised to hear myself saying it, and in a way it was quite good for me. Because even to you I never admitted it openly did I? And you and I have talked about everything. I feel suddenly as if I cheated by holding back something. I didn't mean to. I think it was superstitious magic ... if I didn't admit that Johnny is a hopeless passion in the worst sense then maybe it might not be true. Suppose I went on behaving quite normally, maybe Johnny would come round.

But it's a release somehow to know that the little hints, the veiled enquiries, the polite wonderings don't matter any more. I am now able to admit to myself that there isn't going to be a fairy-tale ending. No bells ringing like they rang for you ... well, we wouldn't go anywhere with bells even if Johnny did want to get married. It would be a registry office. No huge happy family smiling, because there isn't one. No wedding presents and honeymoons on the continent. Johnny is the new generation. Or so I have decided to believe. the generation that wants no commitment, no ties, no promises. It won't tell any lies because there will be no need to lie.

It sounds a bit futuristic, but funnily, since I have decided to accept things like that, Johnny and I are much happier. I didn't actually spell it out to Johnny of course, men don't want things spelled out. But really for the past weeks things have never been better. He insisted on coming up to Preston with me. He even came to see Mother. He said she was like a broken doll. He was marvellous with Harry, and when he went out to get a half dozen light ales – Harry lives with a couple of neighbours now – Harry said to me, 'When's he going to make an honest woman of you?' I was able to tell Harry truly and without all that awkwardness that it wasn't on the cards.

Listen, you'll never write to me again if I keep pouring my heart out to you. But you used to complain once that I was too buttoned-up in my letter-writing. So here's the full whoosh of the waterfall.

Tell me every single thing about the honeymoon and I'll burn the letters. Tell me about the Pope, the coming back to the bungalow, how Aunt Eileen and Uncle Sean were ... they'll miss you a lot, you know – but you do know. And about Mother-in-Law Murray. Things are great here but I would like to be there too sometimes. Oh, for the chance of a private plane and lots of money.

Love to you and to Tony,
Elizabeth

Dear Elizabeth,
Of course it's all great, it's just as good as I had hoped it would be.
The house is very easy to keep clean – no horrible, dark corners. Of
course, that means no nice corners to hide the dirt in either. I give
it a huge going-over on a Thursday. Ma-in-Law comes for tea on
Thursdays. I was very firm. The first week she was dropping in
every second day and so I used to pretend I was going out. And I'd
leap on my bicycle and say to her why don't we fix a definite day for
you to come? Poor old cow, I'm sorry for her in a way, but she's
a bore and a snob and one who Does Things for Show. Burn this
letter.

And what else? I've got an awful cookery book with things about
filleting fish in it and stock and steamed puddings. None of the
things I like. I enclose two pounds; could you buy me a nice one
and send it to me? You know, something a bit sophisticated.
Nothing about cod and nothing about boiled mutton. I can smell
them as soon as I read the recipes.

Not that Tony's hard to please. He eats anything. He actually
eats very little, I think, considering that he puts on weight easily.
No breakfast, just tea. He has lunch at the hotel with Shay and
some of the lads, and then home here about eight. He says he has
his dinner eaten in the middle of the day so it's only tea and brack
really. But at the weekends I'd like to be able to cook something
nice.

You said that I'd have all day to be writing letters now. I thought
you were right. I was going to write to you twice a week, but it's
odd. Nothing much happens to write about and still the nothing
that is happening takes up a lot of time. I never find myself at a
desk like your mother did writing letter. The time goes. I don't
know where. When I think of all I got done in the days I worked
with Mam and Dad: a full job, dressed up to kill, books read during
my lunch hour, home and helping Niamh with homework, or
Mam with making something in the kitchen, then dressing myself
up again after tea and out to the pictures with Tony and a bit of a
court and home – and maybe in those days sitting down and writing you a long letter before going to bed. But now there's no
energy, no activity and no time.

Maybe it happens to married women to keep them sort of
weighed down so that they won't run off and do anything foolish.

I've been five months married now and honestly I can hardly list
one thing that has happened. I just feel everything's an awful
effort. That's why married women are such desperate bores. Stay as

273

you are with your Johnny, you're better off. I don't mean I'm miserable or anything.

Perhaps I'll feel better next week and write some real descriptions of things to you.

Love, Aisling

Dear Aisling, I'm writing this note immediately to you. I got your letter today and something occurred to me. Perhaps you are pregnant! Couldn't that be it? Not that I'm a great expert on the matter but I did read a lot about it in books at that time, and remember that pregnancy brings lethargy. Go on, you might be Momma. I'll write no more, I'll just wait to hear. Do write back, whatever, won't you? Love, E.

Dear Elizabeth. No I'm not. I got the curse the morning your letter arrived. Thanks all the same. It seemed a reasonable thing to suppose. I'll write next week. Love. Aisling.

Dear Aisling, Johnny and I are in Cornwall on a holiday. This is the hotel writing paper. It's simply beautiful here, the sea is so wild, it's very foreign, like being abroad.

I didn't hear from you for a few weeks. I hope everything's all right. I become very stupid and oversensitive as we all know, and maybe I'm just being silly, but when I didn't hear from you and when I remember your last letter, which was a bit curt and short, I wondered if I'd said anything to offend you. I rushed off that note about the possibility of your being pregnant. Perhaps it was crass, I don't know. It seemed to me like an explanation for you being under par. I always thing of you as being so bouncy and full of life. I always think of you as writing letters too. Please write and re-assure your

foolish friend Elizabeth

Dearest Foolish Friend,
No, of course I wasn't being curt, of course you weren't being crass. We're too young to be curt and crass, that's only for old ladies and not for friends anyway. No, the problem is that I don't write as well as you. I give all the wrong impressions. Sister Margaret said I once described the school picnic as if it were the Pope's funeral. If I try to describe ordinary everyday things I bring everyone down. No wonder you thought I was depressed and unlike myself.

So, the news cheered me. Everything is great, really great. I'm so happy all the time, Tony is very devoted and loving and we've struck a bargain. In return for my entertaining his maternal battle-

274

axe for tea and scones (made by Mam but pretended made by me) every Thursday then he'll come home for the end of it, drive her back up to her house, go in and have a drink there, and make out it's as if he never left home. She shows him the cracks and the leaks and the damp and he forgets all about it. Then he comes back to me. We go to Maher's for a drink with Dad and Mam and then we have dinner at the hotel. Every Thursday. Remember what a treat it was to have a drink there once? Maureen is apparently pea-green again over the hotel business ... but honestly I can't spend my whole life trying not to make her jealous. I did tell you she's having another baby didn't I? She looks awful most of the time. If she'd cheer up I'd go down and collect her and take her out places, but God, she's so bloody weepy. When I come with the car to see her, isn't it fine for me having a big car under my backside? When I come without it, isn't it a marvel that those who have cars don't drive them? I'm not a bad driver now, but I hate reversing, in fact if I'm in the square I drive the whole way round in order not to have to turn.

Now, foolish friend, do you believe I'm cheerful and not curt – and please write when you come back from your Cornish love nest to

your inarticulate friend,
Aisling

The college principal asked Elizabeth if she would like to give some adult art classes after Christmas. She said she thought that would be nice but wondered whether she would be able to do them.

'You're silly, darling girl,' Johnny had said. 'These poor sods by their very nature know nothing about art. There's no fear of setting a genius on the wrong path as you might do with kids, or running into a bunch of know-alls, among the students. No, the adult-ed people will be a push-over. Lonely old men and women filling in their evenings. They'll be dead grateful for anything you teach them.'

Johnny was both wrong and right. Lonely old men and women they were not, but dead grateful they were. It was a new venture, a course of twenty lessons over ten weeks. Elizabeth gave her object-painting classes on Tuesdays, and on Thursdays the principal lectured on the history of art. It was an attempt, he said, to try to share a little culture on a wider level.

'We could arrange visits to galleries in the summer if this is a success,' Elizabeth had offered, and the principal had looked at her with new approval.

Some of the adults were young women, often in secretarial and office jobs. They seemed shy and timid and Elizabeth found herself having coffee in the college coffee shop with groups after the class ended at 9.30.

Once or twice Johnny had looked in to collect her, flashing a smile of such charm that the entire group felt better for his having been there.

'Do you think you could take them on a tour of the galleries if I set it up next term?' she asked him one night. 'They really do want to know about art, but they're nervous to ask, they feel awkward, they think the world's divided into Arty People and Non-Arty.'

'Well, it is,' said Johnny.

'I don't believe that,' Elizabeth said.

'I am, you are, your Pa is not, my mate Nick is not. It doesn't matter, it's like being English or Greek, or being tall or short. It's just the way things are.'

Elizabeth was silent. She thought of the men and women who came to her Tuesday class. Perhaps it was just a bit of silliness pretending to open doors to them. But she thought that they really were learning something and several of them had said that they knew now what to look for when they saw a painting; before this they had thought it was a closed world.

'You can learn anything,' she said definitely.

'Sure,' Johnny said easily, 'of course you can learn anything – but you can't learn to *be* anything. You can't change yourself. You can add a few facts and bits of information, but it doesn't change the person.'

'You're very dismissive,' Elizabeth said.

'I find them boring, duck, that's all. The job's a nice one for you, it earns you a few more shillings, respect of Big White Chief and it makes you happy . . . but a crusade which I'm going to join, it is not.'

But in the summer term the principal said there was too much happening for him to set up another course, so Elizabeth was to feel free to do one herself. She printed little leaflets and offered a series of eight visits to the art galleries, each to be followed by a short discussion and coffee. She charged enough to pay for the art gallery entrance, and someone to serve tea and pass biscuits. She said it was 'Art for Everybody' and they even interviewed her for a local paper. 'I don't believe that the world is divided into the artistic and the non-artistic,' she was quoted as saying. Stefan put up advertisements for her and so did her friend Mr Clarke in the library. She told Stefan excitedly that if twenty people registered she would have enough to make it pay; anyone over that would be a bonus. On the day of her first lecture there were fifty-four students. She was ill twice during the afternoon in anticipation of it. But by seven o'clock she was standing talking to the curator at Late Opening Night, assuring him of cooperation, publicity and indeed increased revenue.

Stefan had lent her a wonderful set of little library steps which she carried under her arm and climbed on so that people could see her whenever she stopped at a painting.

The first time she climbed the little steps Elizabeth felt almost weak. Her voice started and it sounded faint and pathetic like a kitten. She had to clear her throat and begin again. This time it was not much better.

How could she have assembled all these people, over fifty of them, and set herself up to take their money and make speeches at them? It was monstrous. Then she told herself firmly that it was exactly the same as she had been doing while in the college, they were the same kind of people, anxious to know more . . . anxious to have other eyes show them what to look for in a painting. Their blurred faces sharpened a little and she grabbed at the courage . . . this time she found her voice, firm and strong, this time she knew that she mustn't think of how preposterous it was for Elizabeth White to have such notions about herself. This time she must just get on with it and tell them what had to be told.

Long before she had settled them down with cups of tea for the discussion, she knew it had been a roaring success. She had suggested some books that they might like to read about painters and great paintings before next week. Shyly she had said that when she was a schoolgirl she had been encouraged to read about art by a librarian and an art teacher; and that many people believed it was not the same as being an artist, but it certainly let you know what being an artist was like. She said reluctantly that she could not accept people's friend's, husbands, wives or neighbours next week, that the numbers were rather too large already but that perhaps later they might consider having two separate sessions.

Elizabeth was longing to discuss her triumph with someone; but Johnny had said he would be out of town for the night; no explanation, but possibly pique that she had started this scheme in spite of him, Elizabeth had thought. Father would have no interest, Stefan would be in bed and asleep, the keys to his beloved shop under his pillow. Elizabeth began a letter to Aisling telling her all about it. But she stopped after three paragraphs. It was almost the end of April. She hadn't had a letter from Aisling for . . . it must be months now. No, she had written at Christmas, of course, and after it to thank her for the old-fashioned tray-cloths, saying that Ma Murray went yellow with being impressed when she saw them. There had been a brief mention of Maureen's new baby, and of Donal being in the chest hospital for three weeks for observation, but he was fine again. Elizabeth had heard from Aunt Eileen the usual inconsequential things which Elizabeth loved to read. But there had been no word at all from Aisling since January. Months ago. Elizabeth tore up the letter. Aisling couldn't be interested in hearing all her silly tales, could she? If Aisling were interested she'd have written. Some sort of letter.

'What are you going to do for your birthday?' Mam asked Aisling at the beginning of May. They sat together companionably in the kitchen with a sense of achievement. Mam had said she had been meaning to tidy the drawers in the kitchen dresser for three years and Aisling had said they should do it now and give it an hour – not a minute more. They found old letters which Aisling put in a paper bag marked 'Old letters for Mam

277

to drool over later and to say how sweet we all were when we were young.' They found string and buttons and coins. Aisling had them into string bags and button boxes and money boxes like a flash.

'You're a great little worker,' Mam had said. 'I'm surprised you're not working like a beaver up in that new house.'

'Sure, it's all done there, there's nothing to do,' Aisling had said, lining the drawers with new paper. 'Now, Mam, you can fill them all up again with rubbish and I'll come round next year and tidy them up for you.'

They laughed at the role reversal and opened a tin of shortbread to eat with the tea.

'My birthday, I don't know. I'd forgotten all about it,' Aisling said.

'Well, that's a big change. I remember you and Elizabeth like two little puppies planning birthday treats from April on. I wonder does she still make a fuss of it?'

'We're too old Ma, the quarter of a century . . . not much to be crowing about.'

'You always did before,' Eileen said, letting no anxiety into her voice. 'I remember this time last year in the middle of all the plans for your wedding you suddenly stopped and said that you didn't like your birthday being overshadowed.'

Aisling laughed. 'Nor did I in those days, I suppose. Very carefree, nothing to worry about. Birthdays were big happy things.'

Eileen knew she was treading very gently. 'And what has made you less carefree may one ask? A car, no less, and able to drive it like a mad woman; a grand man who thinks the world of you and will buy you whatever you set your heart on; a honeymoon where you met the Pope, a house that's the talk of Kilgarret, and in and out of me as if you were never gone . . . and us all delighted to see you. Tell me what's not carefree about that sort of a life?'

'Mam,' Aisling leaned forward, her eyes troubled. Eileen prayed that Niamh wouldn't come bouncing in with screams and shouts about homework and exams.

'Yes love?'

'Mam, some things are a bit hard to put, you know?'

'Oh I know, I know,' Eileen gave a mock sign to take some of the tension out of the conversation. 'When I was trying to talk to you and Elizabeth when you were teenagers I remember searching high and low for words . . . but I could never find them. . . .'

'Yes, it's a bit like that. I wanted to ask you something . . . tell you something . . . is it all right?'

Eileen looked at her. She was too old to take in her arms yet her face was just as young as when she came home with a broken schoolbag or a note of complaint from Sister Margaret. Eileen didn't want her to blurt anything out too suddenly . . . something she might regret having told.

'Child, you can ask me anything. Anything, and you can tell me anything too. But I'll tell you something about telling. Often people are sorry they told things, they feel they let an outside person in on some secret and very unfairly. Then they resent the outside person . . . do you know what I mean? I wouldn't want you to grow away from me because you told something that shouldn't have been told. . . .'

'Then you know?' cried Aisling with a face full of horror.

'Know? Know? What do I know, how can I know anything? Aisling, be reasonable. I don't even know what you're talking about. I was only giving you a sort of general rule about confidences.'

'You don't want me to confide in you, is that it?'

'God, girl, you're very prickly. Listen I'll tell you something. When your Dad and I got married, I remember this bit always and I'll never forget it. Well we didn't have a honeymoon or anything, just a weekend in Tramore in a guesthouse, and neither your father not I were able to talk about the whole business of being in love or making love or anything, you know, we just did things . . . not talked about them.'

'I know,' said Aisling miserably.

'So there were some of the things about making love and all that when your father started them . . . well, I didn't know whether this was all right or not. You see he would only have been told about it from ignorant men working on the farm with him when he was a lad . . . his mother was dead, God rest her, and then he'd only have heard more things from ignorant fellows when he was serving his time in that hardware store. . . .'

'Yes, Mam?' Aisling was sympathetic and sorrowful.

'So I didn't know whether what he wanted to do . . . whether what we were doing was right or whether it was a sin, or what. Now, I had nobody to ask. Nobody in the world. I couldn't ask my mother in one million years. She was as strict then as she had been when I was a child. To her I still was a child. She died five years later . . . and you know, Aisling, I wasn't much older that you . . . but I never had a real conversation with her. Then Aunt Maureen was a nun, and she wouldn't be much use, and your Aunt Peggy and Aunt Niamh were in America and I couldn't write off to them and ask for advice . . .'

'So?'

'So I never asked anyone. I just went ahead and did the things I thought were right and a few of the ones I didn't, and didn't do some of the ones I didn't like, and that's the way it always was. Now, some might say I was wrong not to have asked openly something that a girl had a right to know . . . but I was always glad that I never, sort of, betrayed us if you know what I mean. It was very intimate. It may have been silly, but it was between your father and me and to talk about it diminished him and us.'

'I see,' said Aisling.

'So. I'm just saying that if it's something that's really personal it's probably no harm to keep it to yourself for a while in case you could work it out.'

'I have Mam.'

'Yes. I'm sure you have. But love, we're talking about thirty years ago in Old God's time when we're talking about me. Suppose when we're talking about you and it's something like . . . oh, let me see, like is it all right to have the woman on top and the man underneath . . . well, the answer is yes, of course. Do you see what I mean? I'm trying to gauge how personal it is to you.'

'It's more personal than that, Mam.'

'I see. I see, child,' Eileen sat still. Then, 'I'll always listen, I'll always be here, but if you tell me don't run away then and be sorry you told me . . . that's what I don't want.'

'I'd never do that.'

'You might. Here, since I'm confiding so much I'll tell you more. I never let Maureen tell me anything bad about Brendan Daly. Never.'

'Then it must be hard to have a conversation with her, she rarely talks of anything else, except when she's giving out to me,' said Aisling.

'No, when she starts I turn it into an attack on the weather, the house, the mother-in-law, anything except Brendan, because, you see, she is very fond of him most of the time . . .! and if she was feeling all lovey-dovey with him and then remembered she had told me he was the great-est criminal walking free from gaol, she'd feel she had to be defensive.'

'I don't know, I'm trying to give you an example, child. I'm not saying it's the same thing. You couldn't dislike Tony, he's a great fellow, and he'd give you the earth.'

'Yes.'

'So I'm still here . . . you can tell me anything. I just pointed out all those things in case . . . well, just in case. . . .'

'You're very good, Mam. I never realised when I was young how good you were.'

'You're still young. And I'm not good. I'm full of self-preservation. Maybe that's what I should teach you instead of how to make scones. Anyone can be a good listener. It's easy. All you say is, "Go on, go on, tell me. Yes. No. Never." That's easy. It's hard to be a wise listener.'

Sean was tired that evening and for once it was only the two of them for supper. Niamh was meant to be doing her homework with her friend Sheila; Donal had gone to his book-keeping classes. Eamonn had announced he wouldn't be home, a few of them were going out for a walk in the country.

'That's nice for him to get a bit of air these nice evenings,' Eileen said.

'Cock fighting, that's what it is, a crowd from Hanrahan's have arranged it. They think the rest of us are blind eejits and don't know. I'd like to ring Sergeant Quinn and tell him where it is and have the lot of them caught. It's a very cruel wrong thing that . . . grown men throwing pound notes and ten shilling notes on the ground watching two animals tearing each other to bits.'

280

'I suppose Sergeant Quinn knows well it's on,' Eileen said.

'I suppose he does.' Sean was reading the *Irish Independent*.

She felt very lonely and foolish at the end of the table with nobody there, only a husband behind a paper.

'Aisling was in today, for a long time. There's something troubling her.'

'What right has she to have something troubling her? Hasn't she got all she wants for the rest of her life? Look at me, stuck in that shop with a mad man of a son who's only a laughing stock. She's not stuck in there with people so thick that Jemmy is the brightest of them some days.'

'Oh, Sean, will you stop it, put down that paper, and stop pitying yourself? Stop it now. Haven't we done a lot for ourselves and the children, and really and truly if it's as bad as all that why don't you sell it?'

'Ah, quit talking rubbish, there's no sense in you talking like that.'

'Listen to me, I helped you build it up, I'm nearly fifty-five years of age, I'm tired, I'm very tired too when I come home in the evening. But today I came home early, so I don't have the financial worries and burdens of the shop on my shoulders, I have a new worry about Aisling. That's what I wanted to talk about, not let loose on myself an avalanche of complaints about everything from Eamonn, to tax men, to the rain in the yard, to O'Rourke's bullocks breaking the door. They broke the bloody door two years ago – you were paid for it, can it be dropped from the catalogue now?'

Sean laughed. 'I didn't mention O'Rourke's bullocks this evening.'

Eileen laughed too. 'That's because I didn't give you time to . . . but it's quite reasonable if you want to sell the place, quit. If Eamonn's such a layabout and on his way to the gallows, well he'll go won't he, and he won't need the shop after our time, and Donal will be a chemist, and Niamh will marry . . . so what have we to do it for? I ask you? Why is that rubbish?'

'I'm sorry. You're perfectly right. It's just a manner of speech. I only complain because I'm tired.'

'I really want whatever will make you peaceful, so I'm just pointing out to you that there are alternatives. Don't think you work ten hours in here a day for necessity. It's only because you choose to.'

'That's true, that's true. I must stop flaring up over nothing. It's bad for the blood pressure as well as being unfair on you. What's ailing Aisling?'

'I don't know, she began to tell me and she stopped.'

'Oh, I suppose she had a row with young Murray, she'll get over it.'

'No, it wasn't like that.'

'Ah, she's well able for him, probably gave him a telling off about all that beer he puts away. You know Aisling can be a bit of a boss. I wonder where she can have inherited that?'

Eileen didn't laugh as he had expected.

'Maybe she's starting a child? You remember how cranky you always were when you were carrying them? That must be it.' Sean looked pleased.

'No,' Eileen was definite. 'No, I have a feeling that that may be the very least likely explanation in the whole world.'

Johnny had to take more notice of the course eventually because it had been so successful. Elizabeth had managed to hit just the right note – informative. Already there was talk of another course to follow this one.

'I'll really miss it you know, when it's over,' she said to Stefan. 'Only two more and that's it, then it's the summer and people all go away. It's a bit flat.'

Why don't you have a party to round it off?' Stefan had said.

'But where? The thought of having any kind of gathering in Father's house. . . . 'You could have it here,' Stefan said suddenly. 'This is a huge room – you could have a hundred people here, if we pulled back all the furniture. It would be very nice, it would be a very good setting.'

'And it would be an advertisement for your business, Stefan,' cried Anna excitedly. 'Think, all those people who like art to come at once into our shop.'

'Perhaps it looks too commercial . . . perhaps people might think that was behind it,' Stefan said, his face falling.

But Elizabeth was thrilled. 'It's a wonderful idea, I can't think of anything I'd like more. I did make a lot more money than I thought, so if I were to buy some bottles of wine and offer it around . . . it would be a nice gesture. But Stefan, it would be too much trouble . . . moving everything back against the wall. . . .'

'Well, you can help, and Johnny. . . .'

'Oh Johnny.' Her face was anxious. 'I don't think he would approve. He doesn't think much of the art classes, you know. I think he'd say it was a waste of effort.'

'Well he can say what he likes. I am not dead yet, I am still the senior partner. I say there is to be a party and a party there will be.'

'And my sister, she will come to help pass the glasses of wine,' said Anna.

'But Johnny. . . .'

'Leave Johnny Stone to me.' Stefan smiled encouragingly. 'You are not afraid of Johnny Stone, you are a director of this little company are you not? Johnny borrows things from the store like the chandelier when his posh friends have a party and he brings it back. Do you object? No. Do I object? No. Johnny will be very happy to help. It will be the first time that either of us has done anything for you in all your years of working here. Now go away and plan it all.'

'Oh Stefan, thank you.'

'And no apologies, excuses or anything to Johnny, mind.'

'I understand.'

'I hope you do.'

She had never been directed so firmly by Stefan about how to behave towards Johnny, and she knew he was right. If she were to be full of explanations and excuses, Johnny's irritation and scorn would grow greater. How wise of Stefan to warn her. As she walked home, a fleeting stab of annoyance about Johnny went through her. Why did everyone have to be so careful of him and walk around him as if he were an unexploded mine? Stefan was right, she *was* a director, even though that was only so that the shop could be a business and claim tax relief, and Johnny *did* do whatever he liked with the place and nobody commented, and, true, Stefan was *not* dead yet and if he wanted to give a party for Elizabeth and her art group so he damn well *would* give it.

Laughing aloud at her resolution she turned in the gate of Clarence Gardens and almost bumped into Father.

'Heavens, Elizabeth, you're talking to yourself. You really are,' he said in alarm.

'No, Father, I'm only laughing to myself, that's quite different, it's almost respectable.'

'It's what mad old ladies do coming into the bank. They talk to themselves and mutter. Old spinsters, it's awful to see them. Really Elizabeth, don't be silly about it. It looks quite dreadful.'

'Father, you're going to have to face it. I *am* a mad old spinster, a quarter of a century old . . . why shouldn't I talk to myself? But this time I insist I was only laughing.'

'Well, there's a letter from your mother's friend, on the hall table. I'm sure that will stop you laughing.'

Father went on gloomily out through the gate, head bent and sighing. Oh God, what could be wrong? Harry didn't write letters. Please, please let Mother not be worse, please let Mother not need her this week when she was going to have the party in Stefan's. Please.

. . . I got to thinking I never laughed or had a good time since Violet got unwell, only the time you and young Johnny came up here. And we had such a good night that evening, and I got a pain laughing, that I began to think you both enjoyed it too. So that makes what I am going to ask a bit easier. Could I come and have a holiday in London? And could I stay in Johnny's place? You see, I can't obviously go near George, I know that, fair's fair. And I don't have enough readies for a guesthouse, and I'm not too steady on my pins and I'd be happier with someone I knew. . . .

Dear Harry,

I'm sorry I took two days before replying to your letter, but I had to work things out, and here's what we're going to do. You're to come

283

down next weekend, on the train and I'll meet you at the station with a taxi. It's not possible to stay in Johnny's flat because apparently there are a lot of people there at the moment. It's like Clapham Junction. But you *are* going to stay with Stefan Worsky who is my boss in the antique shop and his lady friend – well, she's about a hundred but she's still a lady and a friend – her name's Anna. They are doing up their room for you. I wish I had a house of my own Harry, and I'd paint a room like you once painted one for me. . . .

She posted the letter grimly and patted the top of the red letter-box as if it had done her some kind good deal by accepting the letter. It wouldn't know any more than Harry would ever know the two days of drama that had preceded its posting.

She had just shown Harry's letter to Johnny without comment and then, without pleading, she had asked coolly, 'Well, what do you think?'

'Oh Jesus, the poor old sod,' Johnny had said.

'So can he come, or can't he? I've got to write back.'

'Oh Eliza, Eliza, a holiday, the daft old fellow wants to come and spend a holiday with me. I can't have him . . . really and truly. . . .'

'Right.' she said, 'I'll tell him that.'

'Put it nicely . . . put it sort of diplomatically, you know.'

'No, I don't know.'

'I mean, don't say it badly, get round it, and tell him we'll take him up West one night he's here, and he can tell us what it was all like before the war, he'd like that. He's a nice old fellow.'

'Yes he is. And he obviously likes you too.'

'Don't blackmail me, Elizabeth, I'm not having it. I never ask you to take on any lame ducks for me ever, do I?'

'No, no indeed.'

'So, I'll be glad to see him, but there's really too many people passing through here to make it sensible for him to come and stay.'

'Right.'

'So what will you do?'

'Go to hell,' she said calmly. 'What I do has nothing to do with you.'

'Oh dear, dear. A temper. Look, Elizabeth, you're becoming very odd, sneaking behind my back to get Stefan to organise a party for the art lovers . . . trying to make me turn my house into a convalescent home for ailing step-fathers. . . .'

'Why don't you go all the way and say ailing step-fathers stabbed by mad mothers . . . that would round it off neatly.'

Johnny looked stricken. 'Look. I'm selfish and low. I didn't mean it. I'm very very sorry. I say it with all my heart. I am very sorry I lashed out like that.' He looked at her levelly. He was sorry, she could see that.

'That's all right,' Elizabeth said.

'What?'

'You said you were sorry and I accept your apology, I said that's all right.'

'Well. . . . ' Johnny was nonplussed, he had expected her to rush into his arms or to continue being upset. The calm reply seemed to bewilder him. 'Well . . . that's generous, and you know you're my lovely funny-face, don't you?'

'Yes, indeed I do.' She gathered up her handbag and gloves. She was leaving.

'Why are you going away? You are still upset, I said I was sorry.'

'I know, my love, and I said that it was all right. I'm not upset. I just have a lot of things to do. Arrangements to make. I'll see you.'

'When?' he asked.

'Soon.'

Stefan sat silently and listened. She finished the whole tale. 'I won't start apologising and begging and everything. I'll just ask you yet one more favour. Will you have him?'

'Yes, of course,' said Stefan.

Henry walked very slowly and though he pretended his stick was just an ornament, he needed it to lean on.

My mother did that to him, Elizabeth thought. My poor mother who loved him more than anything in the world did that to him. Left his insides so weak that he can't even walk properly down a platform.

She hated Euston. Mother had sent her away from Euston, she had come back as a grown-up and met Mother, the thin stranger, here. She had waited for Aisling to come that time, the time when she was so frightened, and she had seen Aisling off again when it was all over. No, she preferred the airport really. Big stations made her sad. And Harry's face looked pathetic. Nonsense, it didn't look pathetic. It looked fine. It was only because Elizabeth knew all that happened to Harry she thought he was pathetic. To himself and to everyone else he was not, and must never be.

Harry was the life and soul of the party. He suggested that he sit at the door and give people little names to wear on their lapels. He would write these out himself in his funny curly script. Elizabeth thought that this was quite a good idea, but feared that it might look too business-like.

'People are always a bit shy coming into any kind of gathering,' Harry had said. 'By the time I've got their names sorted out for them, they'll be so relaxed they'll be asleep.'

And of course he was right. People were delighted to talk to the cheerful man who hadn't an ounce of shyness or self-consciousness. He hunted for their names happily in the display in front of him, he complimented the ladies, he pointed the gentleman towards the table where the drink was being dispensed, he answered questions about the place, questions which many of the guests would never have put to Elizabeth.

'No, this is not Miss White's own shop, she does help out as a consultant and I do believe she is on the board of directors. . . .'

'Yes, Miss White is my step-daughter. I'm very proud of her. I am glad you like the art course, I'll certainly pass that on to her. . . .'

'Yes, it is a nice shop, isn't it, and I believe it does very well. It's run by a great friend of mine, Stefan Worsky . . . that is him over there, the elderly gentleman . . . and that's his assistant and manager, Mr Stone. Mr Stone's a card, you'll enjoy talking to him. . . .'

Elizabeth had no idea whether or not Johnny would come to the party. She had been deliberately vague when Harry wanted to know, and Stefan with his sharp old eyes had asked her nothing but obviously knew nothing either. Johnny was busy, she had explained to Harry. But Harry said no matter how busy Johnny was he would be able to come to the night of Elizabeth's triumph.

Johnny had even bought Stefan, Harry and himself buttonholes to wear for the part. Elizabeth couldn't believe it when she arrived, Harry at the door sitting up at a high desk and wearing a huge carnation; Stefan with his flower, examining the glasses to make sure that they were shining. . . . And Johnny – she still felt a tightness in her chest when she looked at him. He was so handsome in his dark suit and a cream shirt and the jaunty flower in his buttonhole. He stood smiling with welcome and she realised with a start that at the end of the gathering perhaps two dozen of these people would go away pleased and warmed by Johnny's personality. They would never know he dismissed them as amateur dabblers, as poseurs who wanted to learn the jargon of artistic conversation, they would only think he was a marvellous man to talk to. And he would never reveal to anyone, man or woman, that he was Elizabeth's lover, or that she was in any way special. That sort of thing didn't come into Johnny's conversation.

She saw him talking to the Clarksons, a middle-aged couple, both short-sighted, eager and intense. Both their faces were a study in concentration as Johnny explained something to them. He made no move to talk to the two attractive-looking girls among the guests, Grace and Susannah. Elizabeth knew Johnny well. He didn't need to make any move to talk to them, he could bide his time talking to the Clarksons, it would not be long before Susannah and Grace managed to find their way to Johnny. That's the way it worked.

Elizabeth looked around and smiled as she saw Henry Mason and Simon Burke. They were so funny, those two. They had been in the art course from the very beginning because their office was near the art college. She had been slightly surprised when they joined, somehow she had thought that they would both have had plenty of things to fill their leisure hours. . . . She imagined they would have gone to lunches with people who had big gardens sloping down to rivers, and they would have passed cocktail sausages and drinks to jolly girls.

They were always the first to laugh if she made any little joke, they had walked her back to her office several times when the coffee evenings were over and it was time for her to put away her notes and pointers and lists. Now tonight they had come early and had been very helpful at the start, making sure that the conversation kept going.

Simon was a big, rather flamboyant man, though how anyone could be flamboyant in his city suits she didn't know, but there was a hint of waiting to escape. It was as if he had only dressed up in fancy dress for this life . . . but in another world he would have been a troubadour, a sultan, a cowboy. She giggled to herself at the idea . . . and caught Henry's eye. He was nice too, Henry. Tall and pale, his fair hair always seemed to fall into his eyes. He was possibly taller than Simon but he didn't stand in such a shoulders-flung-back way as Simon did. He used to finger his tie a lot when he had talked to Elizabeth in the beginning, but she noticed he didn't do that any more. It was a mannerism she supposed, like the way she used to shake her own hair out of her eyes. She used to do that a lot, the O'Connors used to imitate her, it had irritated Mother even further back than that. And once or twice Johnny said she still did it and it made her look like a schoolgirl again. Henry Mason had a patterned tie on tonight, he must have changed it especially to be more festive for the party. She thought that was nice.

Elizabeth liked them, and particularly Simon who had an endearing streak of self-mockery. He had enquired whether any of her friends could start an Instant Music Appreciation class, and a Learn to Love Literature course; then he would feel ready to face the twentieth century.

Elizabeth had often seen Henry and Simon chatting to Grace and Susannah and had wondered whether or not the class was acting as a lonely hearts club, one of the many things that Johnny had suggested it might be.

'Henry and I would like to take you to dinner, will you come out with us one evening?' Simon was smiling at her.

'With both of you? Elizabeth asked, amused.

'Yes, I said I'd been thinking of asking you out to say thank you for the marvellous course, and Henry said the same so we agreed to do it together if you were willing. That way we could take you somewhere splendid. And that way you wouldn't be afraid of our ulterior motives . . . not if there were two of us.'

'That's true, I'd feel safer certainly,' Elizabeth said gravely. Simon smiled. He was a very pleasant young man. Why couldn't she set her sights on him rather than that man with the crinkly smile and the dark hair who was standing there effortlessly delighting both Grace and Susannah, and who now was shaking Henry Mason warmly by the hand and including him in the group. How simple it would be if she didn't have this ridiculous chain attaching her to Johnny. Then she could look at Simon flirtatiously and allow herself to become interested in him and his uncomplicated life.

Harry and Stefan had wondered whether anyone should make a little speech. They consulted Johnny and sought his advice about what should be done.

'It would be nice to mark it for Elizabeth,' Harry had said. 'And the people here obviously think a lot of her.'

'Yes, to round it all off there should be a few words,' Stefan had said.

Johnny looked at Henry Mason. 'Can you do it? It should be someone from the course. I don't want to butt in, you could say something that everyone would relate to, and you know the people. Elizabeth would like that.'

'Oh do, Henry,' squeaked Grace.

'I'm not very good at speaking in public,' Henry began.

'This isn't public, this is your group, friends now more likely, I'd say. Go on, just a few words. I'll call for hush.'

Elizabeth was startled to see Johnny clapping his hands. Her heart leaped in that anxious way it often did when Johnny did things. Oh, he wasn't going to say anything awful about it being time to go home, was he? Please no.

'Ladies and gentlemen, forgive me for interrupting you for a moment, but a lot of you have said that you would like somebody to express on your behalf thanks to Elizabeth White for all she has done to open doors into the world of art for you. . . .'

Elizabeth nearly dropped her glass. Oh Johnny darling, darling Johnny, he knew how much it meant to her and to everyone there. He was not cruel and dismissive. He stood with the eyes of everyone in the room on him and he was going to make a little speech about her. Her face went red and white and red she could feel the burning come and go. She saw Harry and Stefan looking pleased and proud . . . oh she would never be able to thank Johnny enough for this.

'. . . so on your behalf I have asked one of the long-standing members of your group, Mr Henry Mason, to say these words to Elizabeth from you all, Henry, the floor's yours. . . .'

The red went from Elizabeth's cheeks again. Johnny was smiling and pointing at Henry and everyone took their eyes away from him reluctantly and looked at Henry. But Elizabeth didn't. With a glassy smile she looked at Johnny's face as she heard Henry's stumbling clichés . . . debts of gratitude, never spared herself, interesting and stimulating talks . . . he stuttered and repeated himself and all the time Johnny Stone's face watched him with a pleasant, alert expression and when Henry finally ground to a halt it was Johnny who led the clapping and the cheer for Elizabeth.

Her heart felt like a heavy weight and there was a choking sensation as if she had swallowed a hard crust of bread which would not go down.

Dear Elizabeth,
This is a picture of the beach in Brighton and the pier. But in fact
we do not see much of it since play begins at 8.30 in the morning
and there is only one hour for lunch. It is very interesting to meet
so many bridge players from all over the country. Our club did
well on Day One but we were allowed to slip behind yesterday. I
find it all a very good change. I am glad you persuaded me to come
here.
  Regards, Father

Dear Elizabeth,
I am sending you two pounds ten shillings and an advertisement I
cut out of the *Sunday Express*. Can you ever do me a great favour?
Can you buy this strapless bra for me and send it to me? Mark the
envelope old clothes so that the customs men don't open it, and
could you put in an old blouse or cardigan or something you don't
want so that I can tell Mam that's what you sent? The bra costs
forty-five shillings and the extra five shillings is for postage. I'm
size thirty-four and if they have different cup sizes, which they
may have, I'm kind of middle cup. About average. Thanks a
million, and don't tell anybody.
  Love, Niamh

Dear Elizabeth,
Henry and I wish to take you up on your promise to have dinner
with us. Will Saturday week be all right? Can you telephone us,
either of us at the office (telephone number above), to say if this is
suitable and where we should collect you? It's probably best not to
leave any message in the event of our not being here. Efficient to
the point of obsession they are about work matters, but private
lives are wisest not entrusted to them.
  We look forward to hearing from you,
  Simon Burke

Dear Miss White,
Thank you very much for the kind donation you sent to the hospital. I have to inform you that the general opinion was that flowers
would not be a suitable gift for your mother, Mrs Violet Elton, to
receive considering her present state of health. Accordingly we
went along with your alternative suggestion and have bought a
floral arrangement for the Day Room of the ward. We would like
to express our thanks to you for both the gift and for your understanding of the nature of your mother's illness.
  P. Hughes, Hospital Secretary

Hallo Funny-face,
I've arranged to collect no less than six Welsh dressers before I come back! Now how about that for a working holiday? And you thought I was just sunning myself in Bangor. Remember that girl Grace Miller who was one of the people in your art course? She turned up here out of the blue, so we show each other the Mysteries of Wales ... and wish you were here.

Home soon.
Love always, Johnny

Roma. Anno Sancto.
There are millions and millions of people here, which is bad enough but those millions include *Father* John Murray ... yes, he's made it ... and Mother-in-Law Murray and Joannie Murray who, between ourselves and the whole postal system, has become almost insane ... and also the lovely young Mr and Mrs Tony Murray, toast of the continent. I dreamed last night you and I had had some awful fight. We didn't, did we?

Love Aisling

XV

Maureen said several times to Mam that it was unusual for Aisling to be so long in getting pregnant. 'It's not as if she had any reason to wait about, Mam.' No indeed, Eileen had agreed. 'And, Lord knows, there's plenty of money in that house, a nurse could come home with her for three months like the Grays have whenever a child is born. It can't be the money or anything.' She found Mam unresponsive. 'Not of course that it's my business or anything. It's not the sort of thing you feel you should bring up talking to someone . . . even your own sister. You know, you never like to say anything.'

'Oh I'm glad to hear that,' Mam had said.

'It's just that Brendan's mother was asking me yesterday was there no sign of a baby and I didn't know what to say to her.'

Mam had looked up suddenly and with a flash of bad temper she had shouted, 'Why don't you tell old Ma Daly to go and take a running jump at herself all the way down the road to the lake and right into it!'

'Mam!' Maureen had cried in shock.

'I'm sorry, it's the time of life. I'm going through the menopause. Why don't you go past your mother-in-law's house and discuss that with her too?'

Maureen had looked shocked. 'Well, I must say Mam, I don't know what I said to bring all that on me.'

Mam had relented. 'I know you don't. As I said, I'm becoming a bad-tempered old woman. Will you have a cup of tea or would you be afraid that I might pour it over your head?'

Maureen laughed, relieved. 'Oh mam, you're an awful eejit at times. You're worse than Niamh with your antics.'

Niamh was delighted when the parcel arrived from Elizabeth. It had been waiting on the hall table and she snatched it away and ran up to her bedroom to check the contents. There it was, boned and firm, standing proudly as if it were a part of a woman's body, waist-length strapless bra in white satin. And with it a lemon chiffon blouse. The letter said nothing about the bra at all, it was the kind of a letter you could show to Mam easily. Wasn't Elizabeth cunning, she must have been accustomed to doing all this kind of thing for years with Aisling, of course. There was a book of the reproductive organs which Aisling had among her other books but with a different cover on it. Perhaps Elizabeth had sent that in the old days. She tried on the bra: it made her stick out very naturally. Now she could wear that dress with the little bootlace straps, as they were called. She had told Mam that the dress was worn with a bolero and

Mam had said that was fine. But she had no intention of wearing the bolero. Anna Barry and her brother were going to have a party at the hotel at the end of August. Everyone had been looking forward to it. Niamh had washed her hair every four days with Sta-Blond shampoo. She had this feeling that if she went to quite a lot of trouble secretly she would burst upon an unsuspecting world. That's what Aisling had done at her wedding last year. Nobody had known how good-looking Aisling was until that day, and now even if she hadn't combed her hair and just wore her old gaberdine raincoat streeling open, she still had the name of being beautiful. It was odd but true. Once people decided you were beautiful then you remained beautiful for the rest of your life.

Niamh was going to wear a pony-tail at the start of the evening with a plastic clip on it, and then as the night went on she was going to take off the bolero and let her hair fall loose and when she was dancing people would notice her suddenly. She had thought of nothing else but the party since the school holidays began. She was waiting for the results of her Leaving Certificate and if she got three Honours Dad was going to let her go to university. The first of the O'Connors to go to college. She had prayed herself into a near coma for a while.

Mam had wanted her to work in the shop, but Niamh had been very unwilling. She was afraid that if she once got into O'Connor's she might never get out. She saw herself sitting for years in the little glass office that used to be Aisling's and had been empty for a year since neither of the new assistants had worked out well. She thought that if her Leaving Certificate results were not good she would do typing and book-keeping in the morning in the secretarial college and work in O'Connor's during the afternoon. Aisling had said she would have no need for shorthand in the shop. How dare Asiling interfere, why couldn't she live her own life now and be grateful for it? It was what she had wanted wasn't it? Why was she always down with Mam and filling Mam up with stupid ideas like Niamh working in the shop? What was she going for walks with Donal for? Why couldn't she let Donal find friends of his own? Niamh thought that Aisling was just as mournful as Maureen in a way. God, the whole business would put you off marriage forever.

Donal was disappointed not to get any letters or postcards from Rome. 'Aisling wrote three letters the first time she went,' he complained.

'Ah but she has the whole family out there now and the ordination and everything, she's on her toes,' said Sean. 'The girl can't be rushing off every minute to write letters home.'

'You'd think she'd send even one, to let us know how she's getting on,' Donal grumbled. 'The place is very dead without her anyway.'

Eamonn was finishing his supper hastily, he thought he saw his mother looking round for rosary beads and the suggestion that since they were all gathered they might say it early tonight.

'Isn't it amazing that she doesn't seem to be gone, not like Maureen? I mean we see as much of her as we ever did. She's getting no value out of being married at all.'

The return from Rome was fretful and exhausting. Father John was full of names of priests in this order and that order, and of those who had come to the ordination and those who hadn't. Aisling thought he sounded like an old woman. Mrs Murphy sounded like a very old woman indeed. She seemed twenty years older than when they had left Ireland, the noise and the heat and the crowds had been very wearing. Aisling had felt sorry for her and had fanned her in the evenings beside an open window while Tony and Joannie went out on their regular four-hour search for a restaurant, coming back plastered both of them with the intelligence that the restaurant in the hotel was as good as anything they had seen in their travels.

By the time they arrived in Dublin Aisling had decided that enough was enough and made a clear announcement as they were collecting their luggage. 'Tony and I are staying in Dublin tonight, we'll come down tomorrow.'

'Oh, I'll stay with you and the three of us will go down in the morning,' Joannie said eagerly.

'No, we're getting a lift with friends,' Aisling said firmly.

'You haven't got any friends,' Joannie said.

'Don't be childish,' Aisling snapped. 'Mrs Murray, we'll help you into the car and see you off all three of you. We'll be home tomorrow night, and ready for the first Mass on Sunday.'

'Well yes, the least you could do.' John was huffy and annoyed at being taken by surprise. They moved awkwardly towards the car, as disparate a group of five people as ever you saw. Aisling wondered what other people made of them.

Tony, who had slept the whole way home, was now awake and ready for an evening on the town. He went along smoothly with the notion that they had business to do, people to see, arrangements to make, and brushed aside the irritated squeakings of disbelief about why it hadn't been mentioned before, and who they could be meeting on a Saturday morning. . . .

'Where are you staying then?' Joannie asked, hoping to catch them out.

'With my relations in Dunlaoghaire,' Aisling rattled back. 'Tony hasn't met them yet, it will be a nice opportunity.'

'That's right, looking forward to meeting them,' said Tony, and Aisling threw him a grateful look.

'Well then, we can drive you there, no point in leaving you to get taxis ten miles into town from here, ten miles out of Dunlaoghaire, is there?' Joannie's voice was silky. She felt sure she had trapped them somehow.

'That's a great idea,' Aisling said sunnily, and somehow the hour and three quarters through rush-hour traffic was endured.

Then they were at the guesthouse. Aisling jumped out first and ran to the door; in case there was going to be confusion she wanted to try to have a head start in sorting it out.

'Aisling child, how grand to see you,' Mam's cousin Gretta Ross greeted her. 'Did you bring your fine husband for me to have a look at?'

'I brought him to stay for a night if that's all right,' she said quickly.

'Honoured we are, and delighted . . . where is he . . . ?'

Gretta went out to the car and shook hands with everyone while Tony was unloading the boot.

'Isn't he as handsome as they all said?' she said. 'I'm delighted you were able to come to me at last.'

The rest of the Murrays went unwillingly, having refused a cup of tea because John said he must drive on and get them home at a reasonable hour. He gave Gretta Ross his blessing which she asked for and Aisling noticed with a vicious delight that Joannie seemed quite put out to find her suspicions unfounded.

'You're very good Gretta, I just wanted to get away from them all for a bit and have an evening on our own, if you get me.'

'I'm delighted to see you child, and very pleased you thought of coming here. Come on now, we'll shift these bags up to the room on the right of the stairs up here, it's nice, it looks out at the harbour. Yes, and have a bit of a wash or a lie down and please yourselves, I've a lot of things to busy me. You might like to go out and have a nice walk, go off up Killiney hill or somewhere and look down at the view. When you get back there'll be a plate of cold chicken – help yourselves. It'll all be there in the dining room for you. I have about twelve in for supper tonight so I'll not be able to entertain you anyway!'

'God, that's great isn't it?' said Tony when he'd shaken out a clean shirt for himself and given himself a wash. 'That was sheer genius on your part getting rid of them all like that. I'd had all I could take and you probably had too.'

'Yes, I was afraid if we went back to Kilgarret we might never get away tonight.'

'You're a genius I say, I can't say it too often. Now will you put on your clothes like a good girl and come on and we'll head off somewhere and have a drink. I'm parched.

Aisling put on a clean dress and combed her hair. 'I want to talk to you Tony, which is why I kidnapped you.'

He looked hunted. 'All right, all right. We'll talk in the bar.'

'No. It's not about anything that can be talked about in a bar. Take your choice. Here or we'll go for a walk.'

'What is it, what are you playing at?'

'Just what I said. I want to talk to you. We have to talk.'

'Oh God, not now Aisling, not now when we're knackered from the journey . . . huh?' He looked at her appealingly.

She said nothing.

'Well if it's quick say it here, and then we'll go out. Isn't that fair enough?'

'It's not quick,' she said.

'Can't we find a nice quiet bar like two normal human beings and sit in a corner and you can tell me then? Wouldn't that do?'

'No.'

'Why in God's name not?'

'I don't know what you mean.'

'Of course you know what I mean Tony. I want to talk about how drunk you've been all the time we were in Rome. There wasn't a day that you didn't get maggoty.'

'Oh, you don't want to talk, you just want to nag. I knew there'd be a catch to it. Now why didn't you say I want to have a nice nag at you, Tony, instead of pretending you want to talk?'

He seemed pleased that he had identified the problem. He even gave a little smile, a nervous smile.

Aisling's lip trembled. She seemed to have difficulty in keeping calm. But if she wasn't careful the whole thing would slip away as it had slipped away before. She forced a smile on to her face.

'No, honestly, it's talk, really.' She smiled brightly, hoping to get some kind of a response. She didn't.

'No seriously it's talk, you know, me saying something, and you saying something and neither of us shouting . . . so that we can . . .'

'So that you can nag me,' he repeated triumphantly.

'I don't nag you.'

'You don't hell.'

'I don't. When did I last nag at you?'

'You're always nagging at me, sighing and groaning and throwing your eyes up to heaven. If that's not nagging I'd like to know what on earth is.'

'Please Tony, just tonight, just this one night. Not a bar, not a night on the jar, just a conversation. I swear I'll not say one word more about your being jarred. Honestly.'

'Well what do you want to talk about drink for if you're not going to mention getting jarred?' he was puzzled.

'I was going to talk about why you drink so much, and whether this has anything to do with . . . well with us . . . and what we don't have . . . and what we don't do.'

'Ah ha, that's it. Psychology. Analysis. A psychiatrist's couch. Lie down on this bed Tony, and tell me all your deep feelings. Why do you need a pint? I need a pint because I godamn want a pint and I'm going to go out and have one, now are you coming with me or are you not?'

'An hour. I'll reduce it to an hour. Please.'

'All right. After we've been to the pub.'

'No, before. Once we get to the pub, you'll start us talking to old hangers-on and fools and there won't be any chance *to* talk.'

'I won't I promise, I won't draw anyone on us.'

'No. Because when you do it will be too late. The night will be gone.'

'I can't talk in here, it's choking me. . . . ' Tony ran his finger around under his collar. 'Come on Aisling, stop playing about like a child.'

'Suppose I were to go and get us some whiskey? Could you talk here then?' She looked pleading.

'What do you want to say? One hour, mind. It's seven o'clock now. By eight we're to be in a bar.'

Aisling slipped downstairs and out the door. She remembered that there was a bar around the corner from when she had last stayed here. Her sense of direction was good. In no time, with the half bottle of Jameson carefully wrapped by a mildly curious barman she was back in the bedroom.

Tony had laid down on the bed again. She poured two large amounts into the toothmugs that stood on the handbasin.

'Your health,' he said, almost draining his.

'We are afraid to talk to ech other about what's worrying both of us,' she said.

'Go on,' Tony said with a mock wave, as if giving her the floor.

'We've been married for fifteen months and we haven't consummated this marriage. That's what we don't talk about.'

'Oh.' Tony looked stricken.

'Now, I don't know anything about anything, really. But I think it's the kind of thing we might have to go and see a specialist or somebody about, and I wanted to discuss it with you.'

'A specialist. . . . ' Tony was amazed at the word. 'A specialist in what might we ask?' In ramming himself into people? Is that what we're to look for? Would one of those leery Italian waiters have done? Why didn't we think of it then? Wouldn't that have been a great one to ask? He might even have been a free specialist. We mightn't have had to pay him a penny. In fact he might even had paid you. . . . '

'It's very hard for us to talk about this anyway, but, God almighty, you're not going to make it any easier by shouting and mocking at me before we even begin. . . . '

'No, I'm very sorry, let me go back, a specialist, have you found one? Is he perhaps waiting outside the door?'

'Tony.'

'No, go on. Go on, let me not interrupt you. You wanted to talk. Talk on.'

'It's not easy for me to talk, it's a hard thing to talk about.'

'Ah yes, but it's a very easy one for me to listen to. . . . '

'We can't go on ignoring it, we've ignored it for months now. It doesn't work for us, I don't know why, maybe it's something I'm not doing right – that's what I mean about advice. I thought all I had to do was lie there. There must be more I should be doing and I don't know. Please can't you see how awful all this is . . . ?'

'But it's you who want to talk about it, my dear Aisling.'

'And I'm trying to. I was wondering was it the drink?'

'Was what the drink?'

'Could it be because we both drink so much that we don't manage to do it right, that it doesn't happen for us. . . .'

Tony's voice was cold. 'But how could that be a serious suggestion, my dear Aisling, you hardly drink at all?'

'You're making me say it, aren't you? Listen, before we were married, you were mad to . . . you couldn't stop yourself, you said. You told me that it was cruel to you not to let you. Remember? Remember? In the car. In the orchard. Remember? You seemed to think that it was easy . . . like . . . and nothing to it. . . .'

There was a silence.

'And because you used to want to so much in those days and everything . . . I was wondering, I was wondering could it be because you drink a lot more now than you used to then? Perhaps that's what is complicating things and making it all so difficult.'

'Is that your own conclusion or have you discussed it with assorted people and come to this view as a result of a conference . . . ?'

'Oh Tony, may God forgive you . . . who could I have spoken to about it?'

'I don't know, you spend a great deal of time out of the house, how do I know where you are and what you're discussing?'

'I only go out when you go out drinking. If you're going to be home I'm always there, and then I only go down to Mam's or over to Maureen's. I'd prefer to be at home with you . . . but you're never there. . . .'

'I though you weren't going to nag, I remember you saying something about this not being a nagging session.' Tony reached over and filled his tumbler with whiskey.

'Well, what do you think we should do? I mean this seriously, please take it seriously. Do you think we should go along like this trying to pretend it doesn't matter? Isn't it better to face it and discuss it? We're meant to be great friends, you and I, we used to be. Now we can't discuss anything. I feel if we could discuss the bed thing . . . we'd go back to being able to talk about everything else and you wouldn't run off on me down to Shay and the fellows, and I wouldn't be left alone. . . .' She stopped and looked at him, his lower lip was trembling. He said nothing so she went on. 'Because you know how much I like you and love you, and how you're the one I want, and you're my Tony . . . and it's just ridiculous our pretending that nothing's wrong and that it doesn't matter. . . .' She got up and sat down on the floor and laid her head on his lap. He parted her hair and twisted it in his fingers.

'You always say it doesn't matter . . . you know when it happens . . . when it doesn't happen . . . you often tell me that it's not the most important thing in the world . . . so I thought it didn't matter all that much to you, now you say you've been pretending, that it does. . . .'

'Of course it's not the most important thing in the world . . . but, not being able to talk about it . . . that's what's so dreadful, and I feel sure that there's something simple we don't know. If we read books, say, together. . . .'

'I've read books,' Tony said.

She raised her head. 'And what do they say?' she asked.

'They say it's nervousness and inexperience, and that people get over it.'

'Well,' she tried to smile.

'And they say that the partner should be nice and consoling and say it doesn't matter. I thought maybe you'd read books too.'

'No I hadn't. I meant it, it doesn't matter.'

'Then why are we sitting here agonising over it?'

'Because it matters in a different sense. It doesn't mater in the night at that minute when it matters to you . . . but it matters in long term . . . my not being able to give you all that pleasure, you know, and children . . . ' she stopped.

'Yes?' he said.

'Well I suppose we might talk about whether there is any way of making it work . . . and if we decide there isn't then there's a possibility that we might both be happier if we didn't try, seeing as it upsets us. And we might adopt a baby.'

'Are you serious?' he asked.

'Well, yes. If you're not feeling deprived and missing that whole side of life, and if I didn't feel that we kept on failing to do something then we might both be much happier and we could choose a boy or a girl and carry on from there?' She was kneeling now on the floor smiling up at him, as if she were suggesting they make just trivial plans.

Tony stood up. 'You can't expect this to be a serious discussion can you, when you come up with preposterous ideas like that?'

'But why is it?'

'Utterly ludicrous . . . didn't you hear what I said? If you want the whole thing spelled out, which a more sensitive person might not want, then let's spell it out. I told you the book said it was temporary, get it? And normal? See? And nothing to be ashamed of? Right? And it passes. And it's due to inexperience . . . because unlike all these fast people and sophisticated people you obviously admire so much I am inexperienced. I didn't sleep around with the whole world. I only slept with you. . . .'

He stopped for a swig from the glass.

'And, if I might add, words from your own mouth, there's not much for the woman to do, is there? I mean you said it yourself, just lie there and wait. So I think we've covered most angles now, don't you ... or would you like to announce in tomorrow's paper that ...'

'Please. ...'

'No, you had your talk, I can have mine ... you have told me you didn't mind, then you told me you did, now you tell me you don't care if we never do it. ...'

'Tony. ...'

'Listen to me ... you have told me you have read nothing at all on the subject, but you think a specialist might help us; you think that you are doing everything such as there is to do correctly and that I am not; you tell me you would like to abandon the whole purpose for which marriage was invented so that I can bring up some other man's son. There's only one thing you said which is right ... only one thing. ...'

'What's that?' she whispered.

'That you're not going to be drunk tonight, and I am. I am going to be very drunk indeed.' He poured the last grain of whiskey into the mug and drained it. He turned the bottle upside down in the wastepaper basket. He smiled at her, a very forced, unreal smile.

'So, would you like to join me, Madam? You are my wife after all, and a wife's place is beside her husband ... as well as underneath him.'

Aisling stood up. 'I suppose this was our only chance of talking about it ever ... wasn't it? And we messed it up.'

'So shall we sally forth then?' Tony asked.

Aisling decided in two seconds' reflection that it would be less worrying to go with him than to lie there in terror of his lurching home and waking Gretta Ross and her twelve house-guests.

'Let's sally,' she said.

'That's better,' said Tony, and he looked quite happy again.

Simon and Henry had behaved like a parody of the Western Brothers where one would begin a sentence and the other would finish it. Elizabeth thought that they were great company, when they took her to the smart French restaurant. They had even brought her an orchid to wear on her dress. Simon said that Henry knew a great deal about wine so they would have to sit back and listen to a lengthy discussion with the waiter.

Henry laughed. 'Simon is so ignorant about wine that once someone asked him would he like red or white and he said, 'Yes please.'

When Henry laughed he looked younger, Elizabeth thought, less stooped, less conscious of himself, less awkward. He was really at his ease tonight ... mocking himself, letting Simon mock him. Sometimes he had looked rather anxious and ... yes, awkward. Perhaps it was because he was so tall, his elbows and his knees seemed to stick out a bit at angles. You felt that if he fell he might break into small pieces. Or if he stood up suddenly that he might knock everything over. And yet that was unfair, he wasn't at all clumsy, he only looked as if he might be.

Tonight his fair or light brown hair looked well. He must have washed it before he came out. It was soft and shiny. His sandy face looked eager and enthusiastic. He had pale eyebrows and his eyelashes were very light too. If he had been a girl he would have darkened them, Elizabeth thought. Wasn't it silly the way girls always felt they had to change their faces, and men didn't?

There was nothing wrong with Henry Mason's face, nothing that he should change. It wasn't very definite, that was all, you had to look hard at it to remember it.

They complimented Elizabeth on everything, on the success of the course, on her knowledge of paintings, on the marvellous party. They complimented her on what a nice house Clarence Gardens was, and they both said they liked her hair pulled up in that little pony-tail effect.

'I think it's rather mutton-dressed-as-lamb, I'm much too old to get away with that teenage hair-style,' she had said deliberately.

It worked. They both cried out that she was not too old, she was very young, and it suited her perfectly.

Elizabeth thought that it was all great fun and rather silly and wondered whether other people went on like this all the time.

'I had a postcard from grace Miller, you know . . . ' remarked Simon, 'she's in Bangor. Apparently you're quite a matchmaker, Elizabeth, she met that chap at your party. You know Johnny . . . from the antique shop . . . and he suggested they motor up there. Quite the love of her life he is now, apparently.'

'Yes, fast mover, Grace, isn't she?' Henry said admiringly.

'And so is Johnny Stone,' said Elizabeth. She felt the food sticking in her throat. Motoring up to Bangor with Grace, or turning up out of the blue – which was true? Was Johnny lying . . . he never needed to? Was Grace lying . . . why should she bother to?

Henry was saying something. 'Oh I say, I'm pleased to hear you say that. I was afraid that he was your chap. Something your step-father said that evening. . . .'

Damn Henry to the bottom of hell, how dare he let any information about Johnny out of the net? He should have known it was something you didn't talk about. 'Oh, what on earth did he say?' she asked lightly.

'Nothing specific, I just thought that he was – you know . . .'

'Oh heavens, everyone loves Johnny . . . it's like loving fine weather . . . it would be churlish not to be delighted with it, or him. Now enough about that Romeo . . . tell me how you two Romeos escaped all these predatory female clients who must be stalking you through the Inns of Court. . . .'

They both laughed hugely at this and things were back on course. Elizabeth allowed herself a small excursion in her mind back to Johnny. It must be Grace who had told the lie. Johnny did not need to lie, or if he had then it was serious with Grace and that's why the first real untruth had been told.

*

Mother died in November. She had a massive heart attack, they told Elizabeth on the telephone, very quick and in many ways a merciful relief. It had happened during the night and Mother had known no terror or anxiety about it. The kind voice said it must be thought of as the best solution.

Elizabeth stood in the cold hall of Clarence Gardens. It was Father's bridge night, she had answered the phone. It rarely ever rang for Father anyway. She had been thinking about Mother at the very moment the bell had sounded in the hall, because she had been in the middle of making a Christmas present list. She had paused to think about Mother and how sad it was that all she could now do for Mother was to send a gift to other people in the same hospital. It was very anonymous, it was like sending money for the black babies when they were in the convent back in Kilgarret – you wished you could see the black baby getting a present.

Now there was never going to be any kind of a present for Mother again. Harry had been told apparently and was very emotional but he would telephone later. Perhaps Elizabeth and Harry or one of them could telephone the hospital again in the morning to discuss the funeral arrangements. They were sorry to have to tell her such sad news but hoped she would see it as a very happy release for Mrs Elton.

From the front room came the sound of laughter; she even heard Father's tone in it. Father who had laughed so rarely in that room where his wife had sat at a little desk and written letters was laughing over a game of cards with people that he hardly knew while Mother was lying dead in a mortuary chapel in the North of England. Elizabeth would not now rush into the room and throw herself into Father's arms and they would not weep for her. Once they must have wept or been near to tears over Elizabeth . . . when they knew she was expected, when she was born, when she said something endearing as a toddler. They must have looked at each other and smiled or held hands then. What had happened to make it end up like this?

She thought of Mother that day at Euston. She thought of her with her eyes searching through all that grey crowd to find her child, and the slow look of disbelief when she saw the grown-up daughter. She thought of Mother throwing her head back laughing that time when Johnny had brought the rabbit to Preston for dinner, she thought of pinning the violets on her cardigan, she remembered Mother shaking her head dismissively about Miss James back in the first school. She remembered Mother crying outside this door the day she went off with Harry, big tears falling down her face as she had said that she wished things were different . . . those were her words . . . she wished things were different.

The Hardcastles had agreed when she asked them not to bring Harry to the telephone. 'Tell him I'll come up overnight. It doesn't matter what time the train gets in, I'll take a taxi to your house. Can you leave the key somewhere for me, I won't want to wake the whole house?'

'Well love, just put your hand in the letter box, it's on a string. There'll be a flask of tea for you, and rugs and you turn on the electric fire as soon as you get in. You're a good lass to come so quickly.'

'Tell him that Mother would like him looking smart and well and he's not to have red eyes when we go up to that hospital tomorrow,' she said. She rang the station. Dear God would something good happen sometimes at Euston? She wrote a note to Henry Mason to explain why she wouldn't be able to meet him the following day. She also asked him to let Stefan, the art college and the school know. Henry was very reliable, he would do that efficiently for her.

Then she wrote a note to Father ... she left it in his bedroom in case some of the bridge people might help him to wash up. She didn't want him to have to get the news in front of strangers, and she certainly did not want to be there herself when he reacted. She carefully mentioned the name of the hospital again, just in case he wanted to send flowers. She said that she would be gone for a few days. Finally she went into the bridge room and waited courteously until the hand was played.

'Ah, tea?' Father was pleased and surprised.

'No, not yet, it's all ready in the kitchen of course, but, sorry to interrupt you, I have to go away suddenly. It's all a bit complicated. I won't delay everyone here now explaining. I left you a note upstairs. . . . ' She smiled brightly around at the four people and left briskly. At the end of Clarence Gardens she saw a taxi and hailed it. She dropped the letter to Henry through the letter-box of the big house where he had a flat. It was a methodical house, like Henry himself. They would sort out the letters for the various tenants and leave them in neat rows on a large hall table. He would make all those other calls for her. She had listed the telephone numbers.

She thought she saw him at the window upstairs as she leaped back into the taxi, but it would take too long to explain everything, and the letter did it better. She would see him next week.

She slept in fits and starts on the train, her head lolling awkwardly so that she woke up with an ache in her neck twice. She rubbed it, trying to ease the cramp.

'Would you like me to do that for you?' said a man opposite her. He had been eyeing her since she got into the compartment. Elizabeth was glad that two other men sat in the far corner. She would not like to have been alone with him.

'No thank you,' she replied crisply without any hint of amusement at his suggestion.

A little later the extra coat, the black coat she had brought with her for warmth as well as for mourning, fell from her knees to the floor. The man picked it up and settled it around her lap with a lot of unnecessary patting and fondling.

She opened her eyes coldly and looked at him. 'Get back to your seat and take your hands off me,' she said.

He laughed.

She looked for support to the other end of the carriage. The other passengers were gone. They must have got out when she was asleep.

'Come on now, the way you were sitting, I thought you'd like a little company,' he said. He was confident. He was really awful, Elizabeth thought, a full face and thick lips . . . she could barely look at him he revolted her so much.

'I do not want company,' she stated. 'And if you believe I do you are wrong, and you are attacking me and I shall pull this cord.' She had stood up and placed her hand on the communication cord. . . .

He looked alarmed. 'Don't be such a fool. Sit down. I didn't mean any harm.'

'Get away from me. Go over to the other side of the carriage. Now.'

Fumbling and picking up his attaché case he moved.

'Now stay there. One more move and I'll pull the cord, and you can make your explanation to the train guard and the police.'

'Don't be such a bloody idiot . . . I wasn't doing anything. . . .'

'And you won't do any more,' she retorted.

He picked up his newspaper and in the dim light of the compartment pretended to read. Elizabeth sat down, fixed her clothes around her, so that the coat kept her legs both hidden and warm.

'Are you the nervous type then?' the man asked, relieved to see Elizabeth's hand at a safe distance from the communication cord.

'Will you *shut up*?' she shouted at him.

'I certainly will, crackpot. Cracked prim and prissy old maid.'

'That's it,' Elizabeth said, pleased.

The week passed in a blur. There were only ten people at Mother's funeral, and that meant only seven apart from Harry and Elizabeth and the nice Nurse Flowers. Elizabeth had taken a small bag with Mother's Effects, as the hospital had called them. She thought that they would upset Harry too much, and even she felt she wouldn't be able to look at them yet. The chaplain had been kind, his words were all about Going Home, and Laying Down one's Head, and Peace. Harry snuffled beside her.

'Violet wouldn't want peace, she hated peace, she wanted a bit of a good time,' he whispered to Elizabeth.

'I think these padres have it all wrong,' Elizabeth whispered back to him. 'Perhaps heaven is full of good times, and Mother's having the time of her life.'

'Not yet,' said Harry, picking holes in this idea. 'Not until after the resurrection and all.'

'Sorry,' Elizabeth apologised, 'I keep getting confused with the Catholics, I think they go there immediately, or maybe I've got it mixed up.'

'Poor Violet,' Harry sobbed. 'Poor little Violet. She wanted so little, she wanted so bloody little . . . and she never even got that.'

Elizabeth stood in the rain under Mr Hardcastle's umbrella and wondered about love. Mother had wanted a great deal, she had wanted much more than anyone else of her time had got. It had been impossible to please Mother. Yet when you boiled it all down all she had ever wanted was Harry. He hadn't given her any great wealth or good times, he had given her a hard life in a small shop. And while she still had her mind she had been happy there. No wonder Harry saw her as simple and easy to please. Father saw her as totally selfish and demanding . . . and people like Monica Furlong's mother had always thought that Violet had to have twice what everyone else in the world had, and that included two bites at the cherry in terms of marriage. Aunt Eileen had said that Mother had been such fun at school. Oh Lord, in all the fuss she hadn't written to Aunt Eileen. She must do that as soon as possible. Perhaps Aunt Eileen might even write a letter to Harry. Though strictly speaking she might prefer to write to Father. What the hell, let Aunt Eileen decide.

There were endless cups of tea with the Hardcastles. There were assurances that Harry's allowances and the rent he got from the little shop were more than enough to cover his board. There were plans made for Harry's next visit to London, and telegrams of sympathy from Stefan Worsky, and Anna, from the art college, from the school, from Henry Mason and Simon Burke, from one or two other people on the art course, whom Henry must have alerted. There was no message from George White and there was no message from Johnny Stone.

The night before she went back to London Elizabeth and Harry went out to have a meal. The restaurant was starting to decorate itself for Christmas and it looked far more festive than either of them felt.

'I say it over to myself that it's no different than it has been. But you know I always thought she'd get better, I thought one morning she'd wake up and say, "Harry. how ridiculous," and it would all be all right. Now I can't think that any more. Did you feel that?'

'Yes,' lied Elizabeth. 'Yes, I did.' She wondered why she had explained Mother's illness to Harry so carefully, she marvelled at his inability to accept what he couldn't bear.

'So you're not to worry about me down there in Fun City,' Harry said.

'No, I won't worry. I'll think of you a lot . . . between your visits.'

'And how's my mate Johnny?'

'He's fine. Fine,' she said. They were both subdued anyway, her tone was not out of character with the way they were talking, but he caught the slightest hint.

'I don't want to pry . . . ' he began.

'You don't ever pry, Harry,' she said.

'But I was wondering like. . . when he didn't come with you . . . whether anything . . . if it was all like it always was. . . .'

'No, it's not like it always was. You're quite right.' She looked at the table cloth for a long time. Harry said nothing. 'Well, I mean he's like he always was, and always will be. But I don't feel the same.'

'Ah, you've not gone off a fellow like Johnny? One in a million, that Johnny.'

'It's hard to explain. You see he doesn't have any really special feeling towards me . . . you know, like you had for Mother . . . he doesn't see him and me as any sort of unit. I didn't understand it for a long time. . . .'

'But you always said he wasn't the marrying type . . . you knew that. . . .' Harry was clearly very disappointed to see the end of Johnny in his life.

'Yes, but I didn't understand how light his hold on me was. I've been going out for the past few months with that chap Henry, you remember you met him at the party, the solicitor.'

'Oh yes, he made the sort of speech,' said Henry without enthusiasm.

'Yes, he and his friend Simon Burke, they've been very kind to me . . . and I've grown quite fond of Henry actually . . . and we go to the theatre . . . and we go to art galleries, and oh, I don't know where else . . . he's cooked me supper in his flat, and I've had him to supper in Clarence Gardens when Father's out, and once when he was there . . . and do you see – Johnny doesn't mind a bit. Not a bit . . . ?'

'Well, are you only doing it so that Johnny will get jealous. That's a bit silly isn't it. . . .?'

'No, that's not it, it's just that it would never have gone so far if Johnny had showed the slightest annoyance, he hasn't. He's quite happy if I say I can't meet him on Saturday because I'm going to the Old Vic with Henry.'

'What did you expect him to say?'

'I don't know, I didn't expect expect him to be so indifferent . . . I asked him straight out. . . .'

'And what did he say?'

'He said, "You know me pussy cat, I don't tie people down," and of course he pointed out to me that I didn't make a fuss when he took other ladies out so he certainly wasn't going to come the jealous lover bit. I told him that I hated him going out with other women and that I wanted him to come the jealous lover bit with me. He said I'd picked the wrong man for those kind of antics.'

'Well,' Harry said, nonplussed. 'He spoke fair and honest, didn't he?'

'Yes, but that's all there is to it, all there'll ever be. The love . . . the hope and all that. It's all on my side, don't you see? There's nothing giving on his . . . he doesn't need me.'

'So do you see him still?' Harry looked fearful in case his friend Johnny was being mislaid in a welter of confused female attitudes.

'Oh, I see him, I see him at Stefan's, I see him sometimes on a Sunday morning . . . we go and get the papers and go to bed for the morning – I've always thought of that as our time. . . .'

'And Henry . . . doesn't he think . . . ?'

'I don't go to bed with Henry. But I'm very fond of him, he's afraid to tell me that he's serious about me in case I tell him I prefer Johnny. I know it sounds ludicrous, but that's the way it is. So we're all walking on tightropes . . . except Johnny.'

'I'm sure it will turn out for the best.' Harry patted her hand.

'Oh yes, I'm sure it will,' Elizabeth said thoughtfully. 'But as in almost every walk of life, it will have to be Elizabeth White who makes the decision, what is for the best. Nobody else will.'

As it happened Aunt Eileen had heard about Mother because Aisling had telephoned Clarence Gardens one night for a chat and Father had told her why Elizabeth was away. Father had not wanted to hear about the funeral. Elizabeth said she would tell him about it if he liked, but he said no, that Mother had died for him a long time ago.

'I got a nice note from your Mother's friend, Aisling's mother,' he said in a surprised tone. 'Very sensible and to the point. There's one there with an Irish stamp for you too, she must have written to us both. Nice note really, not a lot of nonsense.'

Elizabeth wondered what Aunt Eileen had said that had pleased Father, because she knew it could be nothing like the great outpouring which she had received herself. Eileen remembered all the good bits of when Mother was young, and how Mother had written when Elizabeth was born and said they had never seen such a perfect baby in the hospital, and how Eileen had laughed because they had never seen such perfect babies as Sean and Maureen in Kilgarret either. Eileen begged her to remember the good bits of Mother and put aside the sad bits: that's what she did with Sean, she always remembered him laughing and enthusiastic and giving her flowers for a birthday, and being absorbed in a book. She never remembered him fighting with his father, sulking, or worst of all being blown to bits by a mine. Try to think of her mother as someone very like Elizabeth herself, half earnest and practical and half flighty – not as a figure in a mental home. Not that.

Eileen added that Aisling had seemed in very poor form these days, just between themselves. And if there was any possible chance of Elizabeth rushing over for a visit, then it might be a wonderful time to do it. It would cheer Elizabeth up after all the sadness, and certainly Aisling's face was never known to be long when her friend was round. Elizabeth would be very discreet and not mention this, wouldn't she?

It was tempting but it wasn't possible. Time to make up at the school, at the college, at the shop. No, there was no way that Elizabeth could go to Ireland. As she was thinking that she might telephone Kilgarret the telephone rang. It was Johnny,

Would she like to go and hear a bit of skiffle or was that too loud and cheery after all she'd been through? Elizabeth said she'd love it. She'd meet him at the skiffle club, it would be just what she'd need, take her mind off things.

'Was it dreadful, funny-face?' he asked.

'Very bleak. Yes,' she said.

'I know. I didn't write or send a wire, meaningless really. Just prefer to remember her as a very glamorous doll. That's what she was when I saw her.'

'Right. True,' she said.

'Old Harry all right? Must have been a bit of a relief in the end for him? Seeing as she wasn't going to get better?'

'I'm sure you're right.'

'Well, I'll see you at nine.'

'Great,' she said.

The telephone rang again. It was Henry.

'I know you won't want to go out and be jolly and cheerful, but if you liked I could cook you a meal, and we could just sit and talk about it,' he offered.

'No,' Elizabeth said slowly, 'no, it's lovely of you but there's something I have to do.'

Henry was apologetic at once. He should have realised it was too soon to intrude. He would give her a couple of days.

'I'd like to come tomorrow if you're free,' she asked.

He was delighted, he would come and pick her up. Call for her. That was nice. Johnny didn't call for her. She said she was looking forward to it.

She had a slight headache when she met Johnny at the club. He said he knew how to cure that and he asked for a coffee with some rum and a stick of cinnamon in it. Oddly, her head did feel a little better.

'How does it work?' she asked.

'It burns the headache away,' Johnny said, taking her cold hand and leading her over to a group of people at a table. He seemed to know them all. She was introduced to them by first names and she wondered which woman he fancied now. It was possibly the small giggly one but she was married to the man beside her, surely. He had his hand on her shoulder and she wore a wedding ring. What difference did it make being married? Anyway the romance, if it was one, would not last long. Johnny held her and she leaned against him as she drank her spicy coffee.

'It's nice that you're back, pussy cat,' he said stroking her neck. 'Are we going back to the flat later?'

'Yes, definitely,' she said. She must have imagined the speaking glances between them, Johnny and the small giggly woman.

She lay in his arms, and he sighed happily. She realised that this was the only reference to her sad pilgrimage to Preston – vanishing off to the other end of the country – no soothings, no sorrow, no consolations. Johnny didn't like thinking about sad things, so he never thought of them. He had told her that years and years ago. Simple, wasn't it?

She had a slight headache again the next night when Henry called for her, but she didn't mention it. She was afraid he might want to call off the evening, or that he would suggest an aspirin and some hot milk, which would be so dull compared to what Johnny had thought up. He had come in and talked to Father for five minutes. Just enough to include Father, but not involve him. As Elizabeth fetched her coat she heard Henry saying, 'I'm afraid I don't know the form, Mr White, about extending condolences on the death of an ex-wife – but I'm very sorry that Elizabeth's mother has passed away.'

Father seemed able to deal with formal kinds of conversation like this, he probably had a lot of it in the bank. 'Thank you, Henry,' he said. 'Elizabeth's mother had a very uneasy and disturbed life. It is to be hoped that she found peace at last.'

'Indeed, indeed,' Henry said respectfully. Elizabeth allowed them a few seconds of silence before she came in.

'Well, we're off now, I won't keep her out too late, Mr White,' Henry said. Elizabeth felt that this is what other girls must have had, ten years ago. She had missed out on it. She never knew any courtship, boys coming to the house, dates and having to be home at certain times – it made her feel very young and happy for some silly reason.

Henry had everything ready for the meal: a tin of tomato soup in one saucepan, and four scrubbed potatoes in another; on a grill-pan he had two small lamb chops and four halves of tomato. A tray was set with a little jug of mint sauce and bread and butter already arranged on a plate.

'It's just simple, but I thought it would be nice for you not to have to cook for yourself,' he said. He looked innocent and almost afraid that she wouldn't approve of his preparations.

Elizabeth's face broke into a great smile of delight. 'How marvellous to be waited on like this. You *are* thoughtful and kind.'

Henry flushed with pleasure. 'I just wanted you to sit back, after all you've been through. Tell me about it.' He poured her a glass of wine and sat down in front of his gas fire in the sitting room. He sat on the floor opposite her.

'Tell me what happened . . . you left here on the train. . . .' He looked at her, interested in her and what she had been through. The sympathy on his face was genuine. He really did want to know all about it. Slowly she began to tell him . . . and when she told him how small Mother was, like a little shrivelled doll, and how much Harry had cried, Henry's eyes filled with tears ... and then Elizabeth's eyes filled with tears and she wept on Henry's chest beside the gas fire for a long long time. They both blew their noses loudly and Elizabeth went into the bathroom to dab her eyes with cold water and Henry began his laborious preparations in the kitchen and guarded the lamb chops against burning with furious concentration.

Henry had a married sister, Jean, who lived in Liverpool, that was where he was heading for Christmas. His parents had died when he was still young. His father had died the night before he was to join up in 1940 and Henry had been only fourteen. His mother had lived a life of terror and constant anxiety over the war. And then, just after VE day, she too had died suddenly. Henry always remembered the war as taking both his parents away – he could never understand why people looked back half-affectionately to all the solidarity and matinées during those years. He had no nostalgia, a schoolboy with a mother whose nerves were on the point of snapping; it was by no standard the best time of his life.

Yes, he was very fond of Jean, she was a nurse and she had been wonderful to him when he was starting to study law, she had helped support him and given him money for his fees and indenture costs, and she had tided him over until they had sold the family house and had some money of their own. Jean had married Derek and they had one small son. He was called Henry too. Henry was going to get him a train for Christmas.

It all sounded very safe. Henry would take the train to Liverpool and Derek would come to meet him: then they would collect the Christmas tree together and take it home. Young Henry would be asleep; the three adults would decorate the tree. Henry didn't seem to know whether he got on very well with his sister and brother-in-law or not. He didn't even understand the question. Jean was his sister, he went there for Christmas. That was that. Elizabeth felt a little foolish about her questions ... they sounded like an interrogation. She had hoped that he might say that he and Jean had always been great friends, that they had laughed at the same things, and that he liked Derek enormously. Elizabeth had wanted to hear that at Christmas they sat, Jean and Henry, and remembered the good things about their mother and father, that they told each other everything and caught up on the year's happenings as easily as if they had only been separated a week.

If she had brushed with a Christmas like this, it would somehow make her own a little better. She and Father had weathered many a festive season together since Mother had left home, but it was never easy. Father would grow more and more morose as the build-up to Christmas Day continued, and by the time she carved the chicken he would be positively sepulchral. Elizabeth had learned how to cope with this: she just chattered pleasantly and inconsequentially as if she hadn't noticed any gloom or lack of reciprocal chatter. Then the dishes were washed, and they built up the fire and listened to the radio. She did not even know what Johnny had planned for Christmas; it had never included helping her to enjoy herself, and it never would. Johnny had no family – many people might think it normal that he should come for his Christmas feast to Elizabeth and her Father. But Johnny didn't do things that depressed him. He would let her know casually; might be Scotland like it was last year. Six of them had rented an old crofter's cottage and had spent four glorious days, walking and exploring the Highlands, and eating and drinking in front of a log fire. Elizabeth was wan with envy when she heard about it.

As it turned out Johnny went nowhere for Christmas because he got a bad attack of flu; it coincided with one of his little dalliances, and an Italian girl, who fancied herself as a Florence Nightingale, patted his brow and handed him drinks of water. Elizabeth called to the flat on Christmas Eve. In no way did she let the bewildered Francesca know that she was a long-standing love of Johnny's. She behaved calmly and kindly as if she were visiting a friend. She ignored the long white dressing gown on the back of the bedroom door, she never let her eyes fall on the clothes thrown over the bedroom chair, the make-up on the dressing table or the look of embarrassment on Johnny's face.

'I just came to wish you Happy Christmas, and Stefan said you were in bad shape so I did what they do in books – I've brought you some beef tea . . . ' She laughed happily. And after a moment, Francesca laughed too. Johnny managed a smile. 'So, Francesca can you perhaps heat this up . . . it's meant to do magic things . . . but let's not question what. If it's an old wives' tale, let's just believe it.'

Francesca scampered into the kitchen happily to find a saucepan.

From his fevered face Johnny's smile still looked good. 'I didn't know you'd come over, I thought . . . I thought. . . .'

'I know, you thought I'd be discreet. It doesn't matter.'

'What?'

'It doesn't matter. I think the worst has passed now, it will get better after this.'

Johnny reached out for her hand. 'It will change, I promise you, it won't always be like this.'

She patted his hand and stood up. She was very good at misunderstanding conversations, she had been doing it deliberately for years. She insisted on believing they were talking about his bout of flu. 'You're absolutely right, it will change, tomorrow even, it will have lessened. Of course it won't always be like this. . . . ' She blew him a kiss from the door. 'Happy Christmas, Johnny, oh, and Francesca . . . ?'

The tousled head appeared from the kitchen. 'Oh . . . you go Eleezabett. So soon?'

'Yes, I just wanted to say *buon natale*. That's it, isn't it?'

'*Si, buon natale.*' Francesca was delighted. As Elizabeth walked down the familiar stairs she could imagine Francesca sitting on Johnny's bed spooning him the beef tea, saying how nice Eleezabett was. And she could imagine Johnny impatiently changing the subject.

Henry came back three days after Christmas. It had been very pleasant, very quiet, very seasonal. Why had he come back so soon, Elizabeth wanted to know? If it was so nice there why had he not stayed until the weekend, until New Year's Eve?

'Because I missed you,' Henry said simply. 'I wanted to see you again.'

Henry wondered if Elizabeth would like to go to dinner with him on New Year's Eve.

'Let me cook a dinner for you instead?' she suggested. 'Father will be away, there's a New Year bridge gathering, he's very excited about it.'

Henry had brought a bottle of champagne and Elizabeth had one already cooling, so they decided not to wait until midnight. They could drink one now and one then.

'You know I'm very fond of you, I've become so very, very fond of you,' Henry said at one stage.

'I'm very fond of you too,' Elizabeth said.

'The problem is I don't know quite . . . where I stand . . . you know.'

Elizabeth looked at him, puzzled.

'You know I'm aware, of course, that you are very friendly with Johnny Stone . . . but I don't know how. . . .'

Elizabeth still looked at him and said nothing.

'You see, I don't want to be foolish and hope that you might be interested in me, if this chap, if there's something . . . so I hoped you might tell me what you think.' He looked so hopeful and eager, and almost dreading her reply. Elizabeth had never known such a sense of power in her life, but she did not get any enjoyment from it.

'It's a long story . . . ' she began.

'Oh, I don't want to know about the past . . . that's got nothing to do with me . . . heavens, no. It's just about what you feel now . .. what you want.'

'I don't love Johnny Stone any more,' she said. Her voice echoed in her head. It was true. Henry's face faded from her, she just thought of that fact. She did not love Johnny. It had happened without her knowing, for the love she always carried around for him had gone and she hadn't noticed it disappearing, it was only now that someone asked her where it was that she became aware that it was missing. She smiled at Henry as his face came back into focus. 'That's true,' she said simply.

'Well, is it possible that you might in time love *me*?' he was hesitant, unsure still. 'I don't want you to feel I'm rushing you or demanding you give me an answer, but if you thought that. . . .'

'But I do love you already,' she said.

Henry was so delighted he looked like a big child. Up to now he had kissed her lightly on the lips when he was leaving her, now he pulled her towards him and kissed her for a long time.

'I think you are the most wonderful person in the whole world. You are such a beautiful girl . . . I can't believe you might love me,' he said happily as he looked at her proudly.

'You're very good to me . . . no wonder I love you,' she said.

'Will you marry me? Can we get married some time in the New Year?'

She sat up from his arms, startled. To Henry love meant marriage, to most people love meant marriage. Henry was anxious to give up all his other chances, close down any alternative options and live with her, Elizabeth White, for the rest of his life. That's what he was aching to do. And she wanted it too. She wanted to be safe and happy and to look after him. She wanted the two of them to be together and plan things and share things. Yes, she would love to marry Henry Mason.

'I'd love to marry you, Henry Mason. Of course I will,' she said.

Sean had never found conversation with Ethel Murray easy: she was one of those women who spoke so firmly that there seemed nothing to add after any of her statements. He would have escaped her this time, only Eileen was in bed. She hadn't been herself over Christmas – she said it was all the rich food. And there had been too much work in the shop coming up to Christmas. She had determined that they would find a good girl in the New Year and pay her a proper wage. She had agreed, had said he would enquire around immediately after the break.

Ethel Murray called unannounced. She wore gloves which she fiddled with and she seemed very ill at ease. They talked politely about how they had all got over Christmas, the nice new priest and what a grand voice he had, just what the choir needed. They remarked that the world had come to a bad state when the poor Pope had to spend his Christmas broadcast on the wireless talking about the danger of atom bombs.

Finally Ethel Murray managed to get to the point. She wondered whether Sean and Eileen might have any . . . well, any information about how Tony and Aisling were getting on. It was as simple as that.

Sean was astounded. Weren't they getting on fine? Had there been any trouble? He had heard nothing – what was she talking about? Had there been an incident? Ethel Murray's face revealed that she had talked to the wrong person. She tried to back-track but now Sean was even more upset than she was. Let her say it straight out what was on her mind.

What was on Ethel Murray's mind was Aisling's announcement during the Christmas lunch that she intended to ask her father for a full-time job back in O'Connor's in the New Year. Her Mam was tired and overworked and a woman in her mid-fifties who should have a rest, and Aisling had nothing to do all day so she might as well fill in the time somehow. Tony had said nothing, but then poor Tony had been a bit under the weather.

There must be something wrong, and hard enough it was for Ethel to broach this to Sean and Eileen she thought she would do so in confidence . . . and ask their advice.

Sean was moved by her distress, and even more so by her bewilderment. It was not often that you found Ethel Murray not knowing what to do. He calmed her down, he insisted they both have a seasonal nip of whiskey, he said he wouldn't disturb Eileen now, but they would talk about it in the near future. He apologised for his own short temper, and she patted him on the knee with her gloved hand. He thought to himself that in her day she mightn't have been a bad-looking woman at all.

Eileen was back on her feet and up at nine o'clock Mass on New Year's Day. She met Aisling just as they were coming out the door. Aisling's eyes lit up.

'Oh Mam, isn't that great that you're well again, come on, get into the car and I'll give you a spin back home – or better still, come up to me?'

'I'd like that, give me a bit of peace – but hold on, let me tell one of them where I'm going or they'll have a search party out for me.' Her eyes went through the crowd coming out into the cold morning, calling Happy New Year at each other. She saw Donal, well wrapped up. 'Tell them I've gone up to Mrs Murrays' house for breakfast. Let them eat on their own without me,' she called.

'Fat lot you'll get to eat up in the Murrays' house, I'll tell them to put yours in the oven,' Donal called back good-naturedly.

'He's only making a joke of you Aisling,' said Eileen, tucking herself into the car.

'He's not far wrong,' Aisling said and she revved up and headed for the bungalow.

Eileen was shocked to the core by the state of things. The sitting room was filled with dirty dishes, there were glasses on the table, crumbs on the floor. The gleaming kitchen which had been such a cause of envy to poor Maureen was a sorry sight. The oven was thick with grease, saucepans half rinsed but not cleaned stood around, cornflakes were scattered, the sink had not been emptied. It looked filthy and uncared for.

'Child, you're mistress in your own house, but in the name of the Lord would you not make an effort to keep the place a bit better?' Eileen was aghast, she had to move a dirty dishcloth from a chair before she could even sit down.

'But Aisling . . . you can't live like this . . . you can't possibly. Where's Tony now, is he still in bed?' Eileen had lowered her voice.

'He didn't come home, Mam, he'll be home around lunchtime, to change his clothes and go off down to the hotel. . . .'

'But where on earth is he?' On New Year's Eve, were you all alone here? What happened to him?'

'Oh, I suppose he slept where he fell, in Shay Ferguson's or one of those places. He sometimes sleeps in the hotel too, I'd have thought you'd have heard. . . .'

'No, I heard nothing. Nothing.'

'So I sat here last night by myself. And I boiled some potatoes – that's that saucepan – he often feels like a few potatoes when he comes in with a feed of drink . . . then it got later, and I thought, well, he's not coming home, so I'll cook something for myself. . . . So there was some bacon there and I began fry it with onions and it burned and that accounts for that pan. And that's yesterday morning's scrambled eggs which he didn't touch, and that . . . I don't know, I think it's milk for something.'

Eileen felt a wave of nausea flow over her.

'How long have things been like this . . . ?'

'Oh, I don't know. Let me see, I've been married for one year and seven months . . . or is it seven years and one month. . . . ? About that long. . . .'

It was this dreamy self-parodying behaviour that snapped Eileen out of her shock.

'Do you have hot water in the taps?' she asked crisply.

'What?' Aisling was surprised.

'Is the immersion on? They'll expect me back in the square in an hour's time or an hour and a half. This place is to look right by then.'

'Oh Mam, it's not worth the. . . .'

'Shut up whining and complaining – get started. . . .'

'Mam, I'm not going to do it, neither are you.'

'You're not crossing the door of my house again, you little slut, unless you get up off your backside this minute and get your place into order.'

'It's my place Mam, you said so.'

'My God Almighty it is, and when you think of all the people who would love it, would make it into a little palace, but no, Miss High-and-Mighty-Aisling always has to know better than anyone else in the world. What your sister Maureen would give for a kitchen like this – I saw her face, you know. Think of Peggy out in a bothan on the mountain. What would she give for a house like this? But God didn't see fit to give it to people who would appreciate it, he gave it to a self-pitying snivelling slut – yes, Aisling, that's what you are. . . .'

Aisling was shocked. Not a word about Tony, not a speck of comfort, not a motherly arm around her shoulder about the terrible nature of men. Instead a lecture worse than any she had got when she was fourteen. Almost as a reflex action she stood up. Mam had taken off her coat.

'Hang that up somewhere it won't get covered in filth, and get me an apron or an overall . . . oh all right, get me one of your rags of dresses that cost pounds in Grafton Street, and I'll put that on over my good outfit. Hurry up!' She had found trays hidden away somewhere. 'Keep clearing the sitting room, go on, keep them coming.'

'Mam, I don't want you to wear yourself out. . . .'

'I'm not letting any outside person know the way I brought my daughter up. Do your hear me? Move!'

With a hysterical giggle Aisling thought that they must look like one of those old speeded-up films where the cops and robbers were running jerkily in and out doors.

'The sitting room's clear, Mam,' she called.

'I didn't hear the Hoover,' Mam shouted back.

They had it done in an hour and a half. Mam had opened all the windows to air the place.

'We'll get pneumonia,' complained Aisling.

'Better than diphtheria from the dirt there was in the place,' Mam said.

Bins had been filled, floors had been cleaned. Mam had left five saucepans soaking in soap powder, with instructions that they were to be scoured in a few hours' time. She had opened the door of the bedroom and closed it with a bang.

'You have about an hour or two before you expect your husband home. Get in there and clean up that room, take the sheets off the bed and make it properly, I'm coming back this afternoon to see you and I want to see the place perfect. Open those windows if you want to before you drive me back home, it might clear the place up a bit.'

'You're coming back, Mam?' Aisling said fearfully.

'Certainly I am, you invited me for a cup of tea, and, I don't know whether you noticed or not, we never had it. So I'm coming for it this afternoon. And I wouldn't like to drink it from a teapot that's all tarnished either. I got no silver teapots for my wedding, but if I had they'd be shining.'

'Tony may not be here Mam, I don't think you realise how bad it is.'

'I don't think you realise how bad it is,' Mam said grimly and put on her coat to leave.

Tony came in at midday. He looked terrible, Aisling thought. His suit was crumpled and had stains all over it as if he had vomited and it had been only superficially cleaned. His eyes were swollen and puffy. He smelled of drink even across the room with the draughts coming through the open windows.

'Happy New Year,' she said.

'Oh Jesus, I knew you'd be sitting here waiting to nag me,' he said.

'No, I'm not actually, I just said Happy New Year, and I've tidied the place up. Did you notice?'

He looked around suspiciously. 'Yes, yes, it's grand,' he said uncertainly. 'You've done a great job. I'd have given you a hand. . . .'

'No, it's fine. And look,' she led him to the kitchen, 'shining isn't it?'

'Yes, great.' He was worried.

'Now look at the bedroom, that's all tidied too.'

'Oh, Ash, you've done a grand job. Is someone coming?' he asked suddenly.

'Well, Mam may come in for an hour this afternoon, that's all.'

'Ah yes . . . well, that's grand for you. I may not be back actually. Shay and a couple of the others . . .'

'I'd like you to be back, Tony.'

'Now, what's this, what is all this? Some kind of court? Is Tony to be paraded in front of the O'Connors and put on trial? Is that it?'

'On trial for what, Tony?'

'I don't know, you tell me?'

'No, you tell me. I mentioned no trials, I just said I'd like you to be here when my mother comes to tea, that's all.'

'She hasn't bothered herself to come up here for a good bit, why should I be at her beck and call?'

'She's been sick in bed for one thing, and she was here this morning for another.'

Tony's eyes narrrowed. 'Here already? Did you tell her where I was?'

'How could I have done that, Tony, since I didn't know and still don't know where you were . . . ?'

'There was a session in the hotel, it wasn't sensible to drive back, a few of us stayed. . . .'

'Yes.'

'It was New Year's Eve . . . you know, excuse for a bit of a celebration.'

'Yes I know, I heard the bells in Christ Church, they played them on Radio Eireann at midnight. It was lovely. Smashing celebration, I thought to myself.'

'Oh Ash, I should have . . . but you know, you're not all that keen on the crowd . . . listen, I'll make it up to you.'

'Good, be here at teatime. Around four o'clock.'

'No, that's not fair, stop tricking me. Stop it. I've made my arrange-ments. I've got to go out. Are there clean shirts?'

'There are nine clean shirts.'

'What do you mean, nine? What are you playing at?'

'You asked me, I'm answering. The laundry comes every Wednesday. I give him seven shirts, he gives me seven shirts, that's the way we work it. It's called the miracle of having money.'

'I really don't know what's wrong with you, Ash, I don't. You have everything you want here . . . why are you always so bitter?'

'I don't know, I really don't. It must have been part of my nature.'

'So now it's sardonic is it? Sarcasm.'

'Mam isn't well. She's not looking well at all. I'd like to go back to the shop and work there to help for a while.'

'Is this what the confrontation was going to be about? I don't want it. I don't want my wife working back in her parents' shop.'

'I don't want my husband drunk as a fool, falling around the town making eejits of us both. I don't want to live here alone as if I were a widow. Your mother has more company than I do. There are a lot of things I don't want, Tony Murray, and I put up with them.'

'Now, I'm putting my foot down. I'm a married man and I won't be made little of by my wife going back to her job. Through pig-headed stupidity.'

Aisling stood up. 'And I'm a married woman and I won't then be made little of by my husband saying that there's nothing wrong with us. There is plenty wrong with us. We have not managed to have sexual intercourse yet. After a year and seven months, that is not normal, Tony. And for the last six months we haven't even made the effort. It is not acceptable to me that I sit here and take orders from someone who is pig-headedly stupid enough to maintain that everything's fine.'

Tony looked at her, his fists clenched.

'So what about a bargain?'

'What kind of bargain?'

'You get your way over my job. I'll agree not to go back to work. And I get my way over the other business. We go to Dublin and see a specialist. There are specialists. We can be helped.'

'A crowd of Americans, most likely, or worse, Irish fellows who've been in America, asking a lot of personal questions, getting their kicks that way . . . telling you to lay off the drink for a year . . . telling you to describe this and that. You're not getting me up there. I'm telling you that flat.'

Aisling looked cold. 'So, I go back to work in O'Connor's.'

'Yes, you win, you get your way as usual.' Tony looked at her with his face curled into a scornful look. 'That's right. Play dirty. Get your way at all cost. Do what you like.'

Aisling didn't even bother to argue. Her shoulders slumped and she said almost to herself, 'Oh that's totally wrong, I haven't got my own way. I haven't won at all. But I don't suppose anyone on earth will believe that.'

Dearest, dearest Elizabeth,

I can't tell you how pleased I am with your news. You must have thought that Mam and I were drunk yesterday when you phoned, we'd been sitting here talking and it had got dark . . . and when the phone rang it sort of brought us back to reality with a bump. I hope we sounded as happy for you as we are.

I know I was crass when I thought you meant that you were going to marry Johnny. You see I hadn't really heard of Henry, except very briefly. Now you must sit down and write me a long letter about him, give yourself headings like we did at English class back at school – no I'll give them to you: a) why you like him so much; b) what you talk about; c) what you laugh about; d) where you are going to live; e) what kind of wedding and where; f) do you sleep with him and if so is it nice; g) what did Johnny say?

Love from us all,
Aisling

XVI

Everyone seemed eager to know what Johnny would say. Even Father. He wasn't in a position to say anything for some time since Francesca had swept him off to her aunt's restaurant – somewhere – and she and Auntie were feeding him with home-made minestrone and building him up again. Or that was the message that Stefan seemed to gather from the telephone call. Stefan was pleased but slightly fearful at Elizabeth's announcement. He admired the ring, the single diamond which Henry had bought as soon as the jewellery shop opened the next day. He could have got Henry an antique ring at half the price, something much more beautiful but naturally he made no mention of it. Neither did Anna. Their congratulations seemed flat to Elizabeth, it was almost as if they were looking over their shoulders . . . expecting a fully-recovered Johnny to come in and overturn everything.

Fathers said that he was pleased, he offered his congratulations to Elizabeth as if she were a stranger, a customer at the bank rather than his only child. He said that he liked Henry and hoped they would be happy. Then immediately he asked where Elizabeth would live, and what would happen to him for the rest of his life? He asked it flatly and not at all accusingly. Elizabeth had the answers ready. She thought that they should arrange for someone to rent her room at a low cost and that whoever the tenant was – perhaps a student, or a teacher – she should cook Father a meal each evening. Father said it would have to be looked into. Perhaps in the bank, it might not be thought, well, proper, to have a woman living under the same roof. Elizabeth kept her temper: yes of course it would indeed have to be looked into, but then of course there might be no need for it. Father was still a young man in his fifties, he was well able to look after himself. Elizabeth would she could be glad to show him how to make simple meals, and even when she was married she could come from time to time and do some baking for him. At no point in the conversation did Father say he would miss her, and she did not say she would miss him. Father put on his anxious face for a while and said that it all did seem for the best, and he hoped there would be no problems, no trouble.

'What kind of trouble could there possibly be, Father?'

'Well . . . the other young man, Johnny Stone . . . do you not think he may have had expectations? After all you have been seeing him for years and years. It's not unreasonable for him to have expected. . . .'

'Nonsense,' Elizabeth said quickly, 'I know I have been going out with Johnny and I'm very fond of him . . . but that's different – Johnny's not a person who settles down. He had no "expectations" as you call it.'

318

'What does he say about you going to marry Henry?' Father asked dogggedly.

'Nothing, he doesn't know, he's away.'

'Aha,' said Father.

Harry's letter was muted in its warmth. Oh, he had all the right words but there was nothing behind them. There were three pages of Harry's great sweepy handwriting. Elizabeth had a little bet with herself about whether he would mention Johnny on page two or page three. Probably two, she decided. She won her bet. She threw the letter on the floor in a rage and then had to go and pick it up. Damn Johnny Stone, why did he make everyone think he was right? Why did he have to cloud her marriage even now? She knew that Johnny wouldn't mind if she married Henry, but nobody else knew this. Why did everybody take his side?

She told Henry Mason no lies. She said she had been Johnny's lover, that he had been the only one, that she had loved him for a long time but recently, over a period of a year, she had begun to realise that it wasn't any real relationship, it was an elaborate series of pretences and attitudes. Henry found this an entirely satisfactory explanation.

He had had one affair in his life too. It had not been so longstanding. It was with Simon's sister; Barbara Burke was one of the first girls he had ever met, he met her at tennis parties, she was terribly good. She had found him endearing he thought, but she was very impatient with him, if he didn't win the tennis match, catch the waiter's eye quickly, find a taxi in the rain, she sighed and he felt that he was very inadequate.

Henry had become determined to please Barbara . . . and he had succeeded: for a year they had an affair and she did not think he should be patronised and patted on the head. It had been a very happy time, and Henry had wanted them to get married. But Barbara had said they were far too young. Henry had been afraid that Simon might have thought it was a poor show having an affair with his sister and not making an honest woman of her.

Anyway, it had all been for the best, because Henry began to realise that he was in fact involved in a complicated business of pretending that he was happy doing things when he certainly was not. He had to make such an effort all the time. Barbara became so impatient when he forgot things that he had a little notebook where he wrote things she said down. She accused him of not being aware of what was happening so he used to note headings in his book of things to talk about. When she was away and he telephoned her he had a whole list of things to say beside the phone. Then it dawned on him that this was no way to live. He explained it to Barbara, and she didn't believe him she thought it was all a game; but he assured her that the real Henry would bore here to death in two minutes . . . she only liked the rehearsed and constantly-aspiring-to-please Henry. Barbara never really understood what he meant but the romance ended.

What had happened to her? Oh, she married a doctor, a very successful chap called Donaldson. They all met from time to time – there had been no bitterness. In fact Henry would like to invite them to the wedding if that would be all right? Of course it would be all right, after all Johnny Stone would be invited to the wedding as well.

'I wonder what he'll say when he hears we're getting married?' said Henry.

Stefan had obviously decided that it was not up to him to tell Johnny the news. So when Elizabeth came into the shop muffled up against the cold January winds, he still didn't know.

They hugged each other, she exclaimed at how well he looked. Italian soup must put strength into a man certainly, she laughed. Stefan went on polishing a candlestick that didn't need to be polished, looking carefully the other way.

'And what have you been up to?' Johnny said. Johnny never discussed his dalliances, there had been the slightest little frown at Elizabeth's reference to Italian soup.

Stefan had started to polish more earnestly than ever, and began to move unwillingly towards his own little office. Elizabeth had taken off her coat and long woolly scarf, her gloves and her knitted hat.

'Lord, that's better, I was beginning to feel like an Egyptian mummy. What have I been up to? Didn't Stefan tell you? Henry and I decided to get married. Look, here's the ring . . . you must wish us luck. . . .'

'You and Henry decided to do what?' said Johnny, holding her hand with the ring on it; he didn't even notice that Stefan had scuttled off into his office.

'Get married, some time at the end of the summer, if there ever is a summer, so now isn't that a surprise?'

'You can't marry Henry. It's . . . it's ridiculous. . . .'

'What on earth do you mean? Of course I'm going to marry Henry. It's exactly what I want to do, I'm delighted to marry him, he is exactly the right person for me to marry, and I think I'm right for him too.'

'Funny-face, is this some kind of silly joke?'

'Johnny, of course it's not. I wouldn't make a joke about something like this. . . .'

'Well, that's what I thought, but you're not serious?'

Elizabeth sat down on a carved hall chair. 'I don't know why you keep saying that.'

'What the hell did you expect me to say? Well done, how clever, here's to the bride and groom?'

'Something like that, yes.'

'Oh don't be so stupid.'

'But you like Henry, you like me . . . why aren't you pleased?'

'I had this silly idea that you were my woman. That's all.'

'Of course I'm not your woman, you would hate to think of a tie like that. You've never wanted one. Last summer when I asked you if you had any objections if I went out with Simon or Henry you looked surprised. "What objections can I have, pussy cat? You're your own person." Those were your words. . . .'

'Yes and I meant them. But marrying one of them. Marrying Henry when my back was turned. . . . Oh, come on.'

'I didn't marry him, I'm going to. If you were here I'd have told you. It wasn't when your back was turned. he asked me on New Year's Day and you weren't. . . .'

'Oh spare me the sordid blow-by-blow account, for heaven's sake,' pleaded Johnny.

Elizabeth shrugged. 'It's impossible to please you,' she said.

'You don't try very hard to please me, do you sweetness? When my back's turned going off to marry a twitching solicitor.'

'He is not a twitching solicitor. God, how dismissive and cruel you are. Henry never says anything except nice things about you . . . why do you have to be so hurtful about people?'

'He might say less nice things if he knew what I had been up to with his future bride.'

'He knows.'

'You never told prissy Henry about. . . .'

'You are not to call him names. I told him that you and I were lovers for years, since I was eighteen. I know about his past. We're not fools, but we don't go over and over it with relish. . . .'

'You are serious. You are going to marry him.'

'Of course I am. Can't you be happy for me, for us, instead of being all bitter and cruel? Can't you?'

'But I'm not happy, I'm not happy to have my lady love going off to marry someone else, let's not be idiotic. Why should I be?'

'I'm not your lady love. I'm one of them.'

'The main one. For me . . . and I was the only one for you wasn't I?'

'Yes.'

'So why can't things be as they were?'

'They can't, it was nonsensical. I was pretending I didn't care that you had other girls and that you didn't want to settle down, but I did care, and I'm sick of pretending.'

'You should have said. . . .'

'If I had said . . . you'd have left me years ago, you left all the others who said, didn't you?'

'It's rather drastic though, isn't it? Going off behind my back and getting engaged to someone else.'

'Wish me happiness?'

'You're making the greatest mistake in your life, choosing him rather than me.'

'You wouldn't have me if I chose you. "Free as the air," another of your expressions. . . .'

'Ah yes, but what we had was super. I thought we got the best of each other and none of the tedium – no valleys, all peaks.'

'A bit unnatural though, as a permanent way of going on, wouldn't you say?' Elizabeth spoke without guile; she was even surprised at being able to talk in this way to Johnny. Her heart didn't race any more, she didn't try to find the right phrase, the good approach. She wasn't eyeing him nervously in case his expression might change.

'Dear Lord, homespun philosophy already.' But Johnny was laughing. 'Right, if you've got such a puritan ethic, you want the bad times and the whole business, then you're going to get it. And I wish you well. And I wish you happiness. Of course I do, of course I do.' Johnny took her by the shoulders and pulled her up to face him. He kissed her gently on each cheek. 'All the happiness in the world. You're a lovely, lovely woman. He is a really lucky man. Hey, Stefan, you old humbug, come out here and give me an account of yourself. . . .'

Stefan appeared nervously from the office where he and Anna had been peering through the slit they used in case there was any shoplifting.

'Stefan, you're a fine watch-dog. While I was away getting my strength back, look what you did. You let that solicitor walk off with my lady love behind my back. And now we've got to wish them well. . . .'

Stefan and Anna burst into smiles of relief. So would Henry, Elizabeth realised, so would Father, and so would Harry. Johnny had decided to get over his pique. The wedding could go ahead.

Elizabeth had a letter from Jean, Henry's sister, welcoming her to the family. Simon Burke was so thrilled he had a drinks party at once in his flat, which was much more elegant and stylish than Henry's place. His sister Barbara was there, wearing a small hat made of smooth feathers shaped to fit her hair-style, a fur stole and a very expensive dress. Her husband, the doctor, looked considerably older than her, greying, a little paunchy and very charming.

Barbara embraced her and wished her every happiness. 'Henry tells me you're so kind,' she purred. 'That's what he needs, lots of kindness.'

Simon kept up a witty act about how he was the loser in some contest. It had always been the same, he complained, hand on brow in mock despair. When either of them wanted something it was always Henry who got it first. That flat with a view over the park? Henry got it. The office upstairs in the solicitors' firm, the one with the big desk? Henry had got it. And now Elizabeth, their beautiful art teacher. Henry had got her. Henry flushed with pleasure and disclaimers about his success. Elizabeth thought Simon was a very good friend, because actually neither Henry's flat nor his office were as good as Simon's.

After the party, Henry and Elizabeth walked in the crisp night air arm in arm and chatting companionably.

322

'Isn't Simon marvellous? I don't know how he does it, just assembles people and pours them drinks, a few little savouries ... and it's a party. ... ' Henry sounded admiring and envious.

'Wait until we have our own place, we'll give parties like that all the time,' she said, struck at how quickly he had been echoing her own thoughts.

'I'd love that,' he said, his face lighting up. He stopped under a street light and kissed her. 'We'll have great times,' he said.

'Sensational times,' she said.

'Would you come home with me now?' he asked. He had been about to take her home to Clarence Gardens; she had argued that it would take him too long, the journey there and back, but he insisted always on seeing her to her door.

'But it's in the other direction,' she said, confused. 'If I were to go back with you and then go to Clarence Gardens. It would take all night ... oh, I see.'

'Yes, I want you to stay with me,' he said, face full of hope.

'Why not?' she said suddenly.

They lay in the narrow single bed sipping mugs of hot chocolate. Henry had got up and made them and brought them back to bed.

'It's not a very comfortable bed.'

'It's fine, it's friendly,' she said, laughing.

'Yes, well, when I was getting furniture for this place, I thought it might be rather overoptimistic to get a double bed, you know. Tempting fate.'

They laughed together.

'I feel I've been with you always,' Henry said.

'So do I,' said Elizabeth.

'It's just right, somehow,' he said.

Elizabeth laid her head on his shoulder, 'You are the dearest and most loving man in the world, I can't tell you how happy I feel.'

'I was afraid ... I thought that maybe ... you know, I was worried that. ... '

'I don't know what complicated process is going through your mind,' said Elizabeth, who thought that Henry might be about to look for some reassuring comparisons, 'but whatever it is I want you to know that I feel safe and happy and loved ... and you are my man forever and ever.'

Henry sighed with happiness and content.

Johnny and Elizabeth did the books for Stefan once a month. They had always treated themselves to an evening out when the figures were finished. It had become a little ritual.

'I suppose all that is a thing of the past?' Johnny said casually when they had put away the ledgers. 'Home to my gloomy tomato sandwich for me.'

'Well, I'd like to go out to supper, we usually do, don't we?' Elizabeth said.

'But what about Faithful Henry?'

'What about him?'

'Won't he mind?'

'Why should he?'

'Good,' said Johnny. 'Hang on, I'll get the car.'

'Is good to see you Mr Stone,' said the waiter in the little Italian restaurant. 'I was afraid you an' the young lady had a quarrel, you no come here.'

'No quarrel. She's going to marry another man. But we haven't had a quarrel.'

'You make a joke, Meester Stone.' The waiter looked confused; he knew that somehow Johnny was making a fool of him.

'Shut up, stop embarrassing people,' she said. And after that they relaxed and talked about Stefan and the amazing woman with all that old glass who came in to sell it to him bit by bit, and how Anna was jealous because she thought the woman must secretly hanker after Stefan. They laughed over the contents of a house which had been offered to them, where nothing was more than five years old ... a brand new bungalow with modern furniture, which had, not unnaturally, displeased its owners.

Johnny's flat was nearby.

'Can I presume this eminently reasonable man's tolerance will include your coming home for a nightcap?' he asked elegantly.

'I never checked, but mine doesn't,' she said lightly.

It was cold and windy in the street.

'Well, goodbye then, my little chick,' he said and kissed her on each cheek.

Elizabeth didn't know why she felt so furious as she struggled against the wind and rain to the bus stop. After all, Johnny had very rarely driven her home to Clarence Gardens, nor collected her either. But here was something calculated. You don't come home to bed with me so you are left out in the cold and rain. She caught the last bus and did not feel at all in the mood for a chat.

'Coldest weather we've had for years, said the conductor.

'Yes,' said Elizabeth, telling herself she had no right to fell so angry with Johnny. He was sticking to his rules, it was she who had changed the pattern.

'Not been a day as bad since 1895, did you know that?'

She smiled at him, it didn't hurt to be pleasant, she told herself. 'Where did you hear that?'

'It was in the papers, you must have been up in the moon, or in love, if you didn't see it. Was it in love?'

'That's right,' she laughed.

'Well, he shouldn't let you come home on buses alone at this time of night. Next time you see him, tell him that from me, won't you.'

'Yes I will,' said Elizabeth wondering how it appeared that almost everyone in the world, including strange bus conductors, thought that she was in love with Johnny.

. . . If I stop once I'll never start again and you are right, you make all the running, you tell me everything and I'm the one who is buttoned up. So. What do I do all day? Now I work back in O'Connor's again, and I'm happy. What used I to do all day? Cry, wander around the house, cry more. Wash my face, go in and see Mam. Come home. Wait for Tony.

What do we do when Tony gets home? Well that depends. If he comes home before midnight we usually have words. That's not often. He is drunk, and bad-tempered, and the reason he has come home is because no better alternative presented itself. No party with Shay, no session at the hotel. He says I am nagging and I am, I say he is a drunk and he is. Then we go to bed. But most nights he does not come home while I am awake, I go to bed at midnight usually. Or he doesn't come home at all. We do not entertain people. I used to have his mother to tea but the pretences are over now, even with her. We are not invited to other people's houses. Tony may be invited to other people's houses, at two a.m., but if so he doesn't tell me, and I don't think he remembers.

What's next now, sex. I think Catholics are allowed to talk about it, that is if they have it. I haven't even known what it is like so I'm in a poor position to discuss it. Our marriage had not been consummated. We have never done it. Not once. I don't know why I think it's because Tony is impotent. It may not be that, it may be that we just didn't get round to learning about it properly at the start, and then Tony became such a drunkard that he couldn't manage it anyway. But there it is. You ask me do I enjoy sex, I don't know, I'm sure I might. Everyone else seems to. Do I intend to have children? Well there's no rule saying that a star couldn't appear over Kilgarret and another miracle happen, but so far the Holy Ghost hasn't arrived with any messages for me.

Mam isn't at all well. She won't admit it, but she has some very bad days where she looks very yellow and not well. She says it's the weather, or the change of life or indigestion. But I wish she'd see a doctor. I want everyone to see doctors, as you can see. Dad's fine, overworked, he's glad to have me back. He picked rows with Eamonn over nothing; I wish to breathe a word against Tony and they all shut up. Maureen's looking like a woman of seventy – she's not thirty-two yet, and honestly she's like an old woman. The Dalys are a crowd of devils really. Niamh is home about every second weekend with a college scarf and a smirk on her that would drive you up the wall. She and that friend of hers, Anna Barry, think they're the cat's pyjamas just because they're at UCD. I said to her very cattily that we could all have gone to UCD if we'd wanted to and that she was making herself foolish going round pretending she was intellectual and a genius. She said, truthfully of course, that none of us had the brains to get in there, and I must say it's very galling that snotty little Niamh is the one who's going to be a graduate. You were right all those years ago, I should have, I should have – but then there are so many things that I should have, and more important things that I should not have done. And Donal's fine. Did I tell you that the Moriartys are terribly pleased with him, and he's almost like a medicine man in there behind the counter? I heard a woman coming to consult him about ointments the other day – wouldn't have Mr Moriarty at all, had to speak to the young gentleman in the white coat who cured her baby the last time. Donal loved it, of course.

Things will not get better. They will only get worse. I am expected to cover up for Tony's drinking. If he doesn't look well in public, people blame me, I swear it. I'm not being a good wife to him, not looking after him. Do you remember that Doctor Lynch years ago? I honestly do remember people said that it was his wife's fault because she was a sour-puss and she didn't give him a good home. She's dead now but I'd like to go up to the churchyard and dig her up and apologise to her for ever having thought such a thing.

I'll certainly come to your wedding. I hope Tony won't, I don't think Mam would be able for it, or Dad to give the time, I think it would fuss Maureen to death, but she might like to be asked to show off to the Dalys. I'd hate Niamh to go, she's had far too much in life already without being invited to a smart London wedding. Donal would adore to go, he would love it. So please make sure to ask him.

I'll post this before I reread it and decide that I am mad –
Love, Aisling

They found the dream flat. It was on the top floor but that didn't matter. They were young and strong, they told each other, and if ever the funny little lift did break down, they could manage the climb. It had big rooms with high ceilings, a huge living room and dining room opening into each other. 'For our elegant dinner parties, Mr Mason,' Elizabeth had laughed. A huge bedroom with bathroom attached. 'For endless weekends without getting out of bed, Mrs Mason,' Henry had said, putting on a music-hall leer. There was a big kitchen, and three other rooms. A study, they agreed, a guest room and a nursery. When the regulation boy was followed by the regulation girl they would think again: either change the study or move to a house with a garden.

'By that time you'll be the senior partner . . . we can probably have a weekend cottage as well,' Elizabeth said teasingly.

They held hands in the spring afternoon and walked around their new home. Henry had been opening and closing doors happily. 'I do hope so,' he replied soberly.

'We are going to be ridiculously happy here, you and I,' she said.

After the terrible letter from Aisling Elizabeth had held herself back with an effort. She wanted to telephone, she wanted to write back an outpouring of sympathy. She was even tempted to find an excuse for a visit. But something made her feel that Aisling should have a cooling-off period. So she replied with a mildly sympathetic note about things seeming to be bad, but perhaps they were not quite as bad as they sounded. Elizabeth said she would wait to hear more news before agreeing that life was as black as Aisling seemed to think.

This appeared to have been the right course. A few weeks later there was a very cheerful letter. Tony had taken the pledge. He had gone to some priest in Waterford who was a marvellous man for getting people off the drink. This priest had been a two-bottle-a-day man himself once and now he was marvellous. He even offered Tony a drink while he was talking to him, and Tony had taken one but refused the second. He had agreed that it was ruining his life. He had come back to Aisling like a lamb. There had been no plans to have the other matter investigated, but now that the drink problem was over perhaps that would sort itself out. Aisling sounded very happy. She said that Tony had been paying far more attention to his work and that there were a lot of things that needed to be done to Murray's. They were both happy and busy again, and looking forward to coming to London for the Wedding of the Year.

'I brought that girl up very nicely. Look at the fine letter she's written,' Eileen showed it to Sean with a pleased smile.

'It's from Elizabeth, I thought it was from Niamh.'

'Niamh!' Eileen snorted. 'That one, it's very few letters we get from her unless she wants something . . . no, this is about her wedding.'

'You're not suggesting we go across the whole way to England for it now are you? Holy God, Eileen you get tired enough coming back up here from the shop, and there's no way I could find the time, no it's not possible.'

'Read it you clown,' she said affectionately. 'She knows all that, that's what I mean, didn't I bring her up nicely, she's a credit to me.'

Elizabeth had written that she and Henry were so looking forward to a good representation from the O'Connor clan, but she wasn't going to insist that the grown-ups came. They'd have to talk to Father all the time for one thing and that would simply not be worth coming over to London for; whatever virtues Father had, small talk was not amongst them. She said she didn't want to interrupt Niamh from her studies, she knew Eamonn would have it, but perhaps Donal and Maureen might like to come . . . she was looking for their views on this.

'Well, that's very sensible of the girl,' Sean said. 'Maybe Maureen would like to go, would Brendan go with her? It might cheer the pair of them up. I don't know whether Donal would have much interest though. . . .'

'Donal would give his eyes to go . . . we'll see about Maureen. I hope the child has a nice day for herself. I would go, I would really, but I get that tired if I do anything. . . .'

'Ah, stay where you are Eileen, and don't worry about the tiredness, it's been the divil of a summer, everyone's exhausted with the heat.'

It had been a divil of a winter too. Eileen had been tired for over a year.

Maureen thought about the invitation for a long time. Brendan didn't want to go, but there was nothing to stop her going on her own, he said. No, of course it wouldn't be too expensive, she must go if she really wanted to. No, they could easily find the money. Yes, he had been putting a bit by – what for? Well for a bit of a holiday for them all next year, Maybe a house in Tramore for two weeks.

Now a house in Tramore wasn't really a holiday, it would mean that Maureen would have to cook and clean and clear up for the family plus Brendan's mother and his aunt. That wasn't exactly what Maureen thought of as a holiday. A slightly rebellious streak came to the surface.

'Yes, It would have been nice, but if you're sure you don't mind we have the money I think I would like to go to London. It's the rest, you see, as well as the change, no four children to look after for a few days.'

Brendan did some rapid thinking. 'Oh you must go, that's definite. I hadn't fixed it about a house in Tramore. We could consult of course, maybe if we all went to a guesthouse for a week instead . . . what would that be like? There'd be no cooking or anything for you in a guesthouse. But if you're dead set on going to London. . . .'

A week in a guesthouse, now that was a proper trade-in. That was worth losing the wedding over. Maureen wrote a long letter to Elizabeth and thanked her warmly. She said that Elizabeth had always been very generous to her, and she still had the beautiful bon-bon dish which she had sent her for her wedding all those years ago. She said that another reason why she was sorry to miss it all was that she would love to have seen what an atheist wedding was like. Now she would never know.

Elizabeth had booked a restaurant room for the reception. It would have been far nicer to have had the group to lunch at home, but so many things were against it. Clarence Gardens, Father, Father and Harry. Neutral ground was far better.

Mrs Noble in the restaurant had never met a bride as composed and business-like as Elizabeth. Here was a young woman with whom it was a pleasure to do business, she said several times. She had suggested a charge of thirty shillings a head. Elizabeth had pointed out that through this wedding she would be introducing a lot of possible clients, her husband's guests would include lawyers and businessmen, and on her own side she would have the artistic world. Mrs Noble might see fit to reduce the price in the hope of making new contacts.

Mrs Noble thought not, she thought that thirty shillings was a good price.

Elizabeth pointed out that Mrs Noble might take into account the bottles of sparkling wine which would be ordered on top of the regular rate; on each of these bottles Mrs Noble would make a profit.

Mrs Noble said that she might just make a small profit on the whole undertaking if she were to charge a guinea a head. At this stage both women smiled and shook hands, and Mrs Noble threw herself whole-heartedly into making the occasion a success.

Elizabeth confided that she was paying for this herself: there would be thirty guests, and she paid in advance. She did not want a sit-down meal, she wanted people to pass through constantly, offering drinks and the hot sausage rolls, the plates of chicken and ham, the wedding cake and the coffee. Mrs Noble seemed to understand.

'Will it be a bit difficult?' she asked sympathetically.

'A bit.'

'Second marriage is it? Divorces and exes and so on?'

'No, only one divorce, my Father, my step-father will be here . . . but there's not an easy mix . . . or maybe everyone thinks that.'

'Everyone thinks it dear, but hardly anybody says it, that's why you're streets ahead.' Mrs Noble was positively motherly. 'We'll give you a great day dear, just you see.'

'I'm looking forward to meeting Aisling, I've met all the other people you like . . . Harry, Stefan, Johnny, Anna. Aisling's a funny name though.'

'It means a dream or a fairy woman in a dream. I forget now, I just think of her as that name. I never heard anyone else have it. I hope you'll like her. But it really won't matter if you don't.'

'No, I wasn't trying to be hurtful, I mean that before she got married, she said she hoped and hoped I would like Tony and that he would like me. And, well, to be truthful we didn't all that much.'

'Well that's not your fault. Tony's a drunk isn't he?'

'Yes, but Henry can I ask you, however excited and relaxed and friendly we all become, let's not say anything about that. . . .'

'Darling girl, of course I wouldn't. . . .'

'I know, I know. It's just that I've told things to Aisling that she has never told to a soul, and I want her to think that I've respected all she said too.'

'But telling me doesn't count.'

'Not to me it doesn't. I tell you everything, my love, but it would hurt Aisling if she knew I'd breathed a word. Anyway he's cured now, he doesn't touch a drop she says, we'll have to get Mrs Noble to serve some lemonade.'

'An Irishman who doesn't drink. There's a turn-up for the books!'

'Henry that's *exactly* the kind of remark I'm afraid you might make!'

'Oh, don't be an idiot darling, of course I won't. I tell you I'm looking forward to meeting them.'

'Aisling will know Father, and Stefan and Anna – and Johnny of course. From her last visit.'

'Oh did you know Johnny all that time ago?'

'Yes, I knew Johnny when Aisling was over here last.'

'What are you going to wear to the wedding?' Maureen asked Aisling.

'Do you know, I'd never given it a thought,' Aisling said. 'I'm very glad you reminded me. We might stop in Dublin and get something. And I'd better get Tony respectable.'

'Isn't Tony always respectable?' Maureen sounded envious of the ability to buy clothes if they were needed.

'He is not. When he was on the jar he used to look like a pig when he came home sometimes, half his suits are ruined, you know.'

'Aisling, don't talk like that about your husband.'

'Maureen, you know Tony used to be pissed six nights out of seven, I know it, why pretend it didn't happen?'

'Oh I don't know. It sounds very coarse the way you put it.'

'It's a lot more coarse taking it all for granted that he should come home maggoty drunk. No, he's fine now, thank God, and please God, while we're at it, it will last. But I'd be very hypocritical pretending to my own sister that my husband wasn't in the horrors of drink until a few months ago.'

Maureen was uneasy. She didn't like this way that Tony was being discussed. 'He's very good to you Aisling, don't ruin it by being too high and mighty. He lets you go on working in Mam and Dad's, though what you want to for I'll never know.'

'I love it, it's something to do, I earn good money which I put in the post office. Elizabeth taught me about saving. She was always very good, you know. That time I went over to London to see her she told me it was mad not to have. Do you know, all the years she lived with us in the square, she used to be mortified because Mam and Dad gave her pocket money . . . ? They never gave it a thought, but she was embarrassed every week, she told me that. And she was only a kid of ten or eleven or whatever.'

'She's very nice, I hope she'll be happy. I do wish I could go to the wedding, I really do. . . .'

'You know I'd give you the money,' Aisling said eagerly. 'Go on what else am I saving for except things like this? I'll give you the fare. Please take it.'

'I can't, it's not really the money, it's the fact of going . . . you don't know Brendan.'

'He keeps saying you can go.'

'Yes, but. . . .'

'Why not tell him you won the money on a horse . . . ? Then he wouldn't mind you having it, he won't be able to say that your sister gave it to you. Let's look up a race and see what won and say you had five pounds on it.'

Maureen screamed with laughter: 'I had five *pounds* on a horse . . . oh, Aisling, will you stop! He'd have me taken off to the county home in five minutes!'

Simon said that it looked as though they had timed their wedding to co-incide with a war – things looked very dicey in the Middle East. Elizabeth told him to stop being a scaremonger. Henry began to look anxious when Simon spoke like this.

'Well, it makes sense, Henry, Nasser knows what he's at, and the French troops aren't all sitting in Cyprus for the good of their suntans are they?'

'But there's not going to be a war. I mean, they wouldn't – or if they did, we wouldn't – would we?'

'We need the Suez canal, it's as simple as that. Britain didn't stand by in 1939 and let people walk over Europe, it's not going to stand by now. Mark my words, everyone's ready for it. . . .'

'Oh I don't think. . . . ' Henry looked so distressed that Elizabeth decided it was time to interrupt.

'No I don't think either, and I read the newspapers just as thoroughly as Simon. Neither of us has confidential chats with Anthony Eden, but nothing is going to happen. People are not ready for it. It's only ten years since there's been a war, nobody wants another one. Come off it Simon, just because you want to remain a gloriously free bachelor there's no need to start rumours of wars once any other bachelor is wise enough to go and get himself married. . . .'

'Were you always so sharp and witty, even when you were a little girl?' asked Simon, teasing.

'No,' said Elizabeth, 'No I was very mousy actually.'

'Oh, come on, we'd never believe that,' Simon said.

'I can't imagine you mousy, a beautiful blonde like you,' Henry said.

'Really I was so timid and shy. I was for ages, I got a bit less mousy at Kilgarret, I think. But it was only when Mother left home that I stopped being . . . so . . . well, so much part of the wallpaper.'

'I suppose we should all be pleased that she did leave home in a way,' said Simon.

Henry frowned, that might be going a bit too far. But Elizabeth didn't seem to think so.

'Yes, it's odd, I do think that more people benefited by Mother leaving home. Even Father. They wouldn't have become any happier, only more miserable had she stayed. I never thought that I would hear myself saying that, I cried so much when she left I thought my eyes would fall out of their sockets . . . my face ached with crying.'

'Oh Elizabeth, my poor Elizabeth,' Henry said, reaching for her hand. 'What a terrible thing to do to a child . . . poor Elizabeth.'

Simon looked upset too.

Elizabeth wondered what she had said that sounded so sad. It had all been true.

Ethel Murray had sent a hundred pounds to the priest in Waterford in order that his good work could be continued. She thanked him warmly and said that her son's cure had been miraculous. To her great annoyance the priest had sent back the hundred pounds. 'It's very kind of you and I know you meant well,' he had said in his letter, 'but I would prefer you to give this money to some charity in your own town. I didn't cure your son, your son isn't cured any more than I am, he has only agreed to stop drinking if he can. Please realise that if he does go back to drink again it's not because he is an evil man or uncaring, it is because the lure of it is too strong to resist. I am afraid every day when I wake up that I may be drunk by night time.'

Mrs Murray was very piqued; she showed the letter to Aisling. 'He'd have done better to have kept it, I suppose, and just sent you a thank you note. He's being too honest.'

'But he's being far too pessimistic. Tony's marvellous – he's totally cured now. It's a miracle. I'm afraid to say to you Aisling that I thought one time that he was really dependent on the bottle.'

'Well, he was,' Aisling said, surprised that Mrs Murray seemed to think that it could have been otherwise.

'Oh no dear, he was not. Doesn't the fact that he hasn't touched a drop for over six months prove that he couldn't have been dependent on it?' She smiled triumphantly.

Mam had been pleased when Tony gave up drinking; pleased but not surprised.

'I always told you that you were exaggerating your problems, child. Now that he has a nice clean house and a civilised wife to come back to, isn't he grand?'

'I don't think it had to do with the nice clean house, Mam, though I am grateful to you for all your help that day.'

'I was doing it for myself, not for you. Do you think I wanted Ethel Murray going around the town saying I'd reared a tinker?'

'He's not looking forward to the wedding at all, he's said, oh, a whole lot of times, that it's nonsensical going to a wedding when you can't drink. . . .'

'Well, can't you go on your own . . . ?'

'I could and in many ways I'd prefer to, but you know that priest said I shouldn't let Tony slip out of normal life. There wasn't any help for him in just turning into a hermit.'

'And he'll enjoy it when he gets there.' Mam sounded hopeful.

'He doesn't enjoy anything much, he sits there, you know, and he's not a reader, Mam, he wouldn't sit in a room peacably and read like you and I would do, he doesn't even read the paper with energy the way Dad does. He sits there looking in front of him.'

'Well, I suppose you talk to him, presumably you don't sit in silence.' Eileen sounded a little anxious.

'Oh I talk, it seems a bit empty though, he's thinking of Shay and the lads and the laughs. There's no centre to his days now.'

'With the help of the Lord when you have children that will all change. If you knew what it does to a man – your father, now, when Sean was born, I remember it well back in 1923 – he was like an eejit running round with him in his arms and playing games. He'd got a bit used to it when you came along and the others but he was thrilled with the lot of you. Tony will be just the same.'

'Mam, I've tried to talk to you about this, but you always change the subject. There won't be any children.'

'Now, you are not to say that, Mrs Moriarty was ten years married before she. . . .'

'I could be married a hundred and ten years. Mam . . .'

'I tell you . . . you don't *know* . . . now you'll say I'm just being a Holy Mary about all this, but the Lord does take an interest in every single one of us . . . and he knows when the time is right. Look now at the way Tony doesn't drink any more, it could be that the Lord was waiting until all that had been sorted out. . . .'

'Mam, I beg of you, don't talk to me about what the Lord is waiting for or not waiting for, what I am waiting for is to have a normal sex life with Tony. We don't have one.'

'Dear, dear, dear, now what is a normal sex life, as you call it? There's far too much written in books and magazines nowadays, it's only making people uneasy . . . is mine normal, is hers normal? What's normal in the name of the Lord?'

'I suppose having sexual intercourse is normal, Mam?'

'Yes, well, that's what we're talking about.'

'Not in my case we're not.'

'Well, maybe all this drink and giving it up took a greater toll.'

'Not ever, Mam, not once, not once since we got married.'

'Ah no, no Aisling, you're not telling me that?'

'Yes, very simply that's it.'

'Bur why ever not . . . what . . . ?'

Aisling said nothing.

'I don't know what to say,' Mam stopped.

'Nobody knows.'

'You haven't been discussing it with people, surely?'

'No, I mean Tony won't talk about it, I don't know what to do. I did write once, oh ages ago, and told Elizabeth about it, but she didn't really refer to it again, except to say it would probably work out all right.'

'And it will,' Eileen grabbed at this slender thread. 'She's quite right, it will. You're a sensible girl, and you won't be the type to take this . . . well, take it wrong, you know.'

'Were you going to say I'm not the type to take this lying down?'

Aisling laughed mischievously.

'I was, as a matter of fact,' Eileen said and they both laughed for a moment.

It was the moment that Dad came into the kitchen. 'Well, that's cheerful. Will you share it with me? I need a laugh after dealing with that thick brother of yours.'

'Dad if I told you what we were laughing about you'd drop down dead on the floor, so I won't,' said Aisling.

'Listen, I'm off home. Mam can I take that cake of soda bread for our tea?'

'You cannot. Make your own.'

'Oh Mam.'

'Take a quarter of it. Easy now, that's a big quarter.'

'Oh, there's nothing as hungry as a man that's given up the drink.'

'Go *home*, Aisling.'

'All *right*, Mam. I'm going.'

Aisling sat between them on the plane. Every pocket of air, every little lurch seemed to go through her like an electric wire. She had Donal trembling on one side and Tony shaking on the other.

'Nothing to worry about,' said the air hostess. 'Just a little turbulence. Captain says it will only last for a few minutes.'

'Yes,' said Tony, 'but will we last for the few minutes?'

The air hostess smiled. 'Of course we will. Can I get you anything, a drink?'

'No thank you,' said Aisling.

'Yes, can you get me a large Power's?' said Tony.

'Tony, no please . . . ' she began, but the air hostess had gone.

'Just for the journey, God Almighty what kind of gaoler are you? Just to steady my nerves until we're on the ground.'

'Please, Tony, anything, an aspirin, I've got a sleeping pill, you have that, and a cup of tea, please. . . . '

'Oh shut up, Ash, shut up for God's sake. . . . '

The hostess had brought a little tray with the miniature bottle on it and a glass of water; she smiled at the three of them.

'Only one of you having a drink? Nothing for the rest of you?'

'Please take it away, please,' Aisling said to her. 'My husband isn't well, he's not supposed to drink.'

The girl looked bewildered, she looked from the man to his wife and back again, not knowing what to do. She looked at Donal for some kind of middle road. Donal was embarrassed. He knew that Tony didn't drink these days and he had heard tales of his drinking in the past. But really, Aisling was behaving disgracefully in public. Imagine saying that Tony couldn't have a drink.

'Aisling,' he hissed, 'stop making a scene, for heaven's sake – let Tony have a drink, one isn't going to kill him.' Tony had his hand out; he took the drink and paid for it. Aisling said nothing. She didn't speak at all to either of them for the rest of the journey, not even when Tony pressed his little bell and asked for the same again.

As they came through the customs at Heathrow, Donal said sadly, 'Are you going to keep this up the whole time, Aisling? It's going to spoil the visit for all of us.'

'Too right,' said Tony.

'It's my first time abroad, please Aisling, get back into a good humour otherwise it'll all be desperate.'

Aisling's eyes filled with tears. 'I am a selfish cow. You're quite right. Tony I'm sorry I made a scene on the plane. I really am.'

Tony was surprised.

'No, you're both right. I behaved badly. You said you only wanted a drink because of flying and I had to be so rigid I said no. I'm very sorry. It's over now, is it?'

'Yes, well of course,' Tony said.

Donal relaxed. 'I'll say one thing about the pair of you, when you have a row you make it up handsomely.'

Aisling gave Tony a peck on the cheek. 'Now that's to prove it's over.' She picked up a case purposefully. 'Now, which way to the bus? We've got to show Donal O'Connor London.'

Tony and Donal followed after her as she walked with her little case in one hand and over the other arm, wrapped in cellophane paper, her wedding outfit, the wild silk dress and coat in the striking lilac colour that everyone in the shop in Grafton Street said was sensational. Please God may he not have another. Lord if you *are* looking after us, as Mam seems to think, will you look after us very carefully just at the moment? I have the feeling that we need a lot of attention.

The papers were full of Suez, much more so than at home. Donal said they seemed to be taking it very seriously. 'Do you think they will send a force out there?' he asked Tony.

'Who?' said Tony.

'The English?' said Tony.

Oh God, thought Aisling, oh God. I know this, I know this path, I've been down it before.

People stared as they ran across the room to embrace each other. The girl with the glorious red hair and the green dress had leapt up from the table where she was sitting; she and the pale, blonde girl in a kilt and a black polo neck jumper, who had left the man she was with, held each other away for a moment and looked with delight, then hugged again.

Only then did they remember the introductions. 'Aisling this is the man, this is the lucky fellow, Henry Mason.' He was tall and fair; he wore a very formal, dark grey suit, a nice sober tie, a nervous look in his eyes and a big smile waiting to break out.

'Henry!' Aisling said, 'you're beautiful. You're quite perfect, I'm delighted with you.'

Henry's smile did come out and it was a happy one. He seemed quite oblivious of all the people watching them and laughing at Aisling's over-effusive Irish greeting.

'And Tony . . . ?' he said courteously, looking at the man standing behind Aisling.

'Oh Tony had to go off somewhere, this is my brother Donal. Donal, salute Henry like a Christian now, before you wrap yourself around your beloved Elizabeth.'

'How do you do, and may I offer you my warmest congratulations,' Donal said shaking Henry's hand, then, as Aisling had encouraged him, he did throw his arms around Elizabeth.

'I'm so glad to see you, I'm so glad to see you. And if you wouldn't wait to marry me, well I'm glad you're marrying Henry.' It was very touching and bound them all together for an instant. Then Henry asked, 'Will Tony be back or shall we go ahead and order a drink?'

'Oh let's go ahead,' Aisling said lightly. 'Tony Murray's movements are very difficult to plot.'

Henry busied himself with a waiter and when he had ordered the drinks Donal asked him what he thought was going to happen in the Near East. 'Well, I think we should stay a million miles away from it all myself,' he began.

Elizabeth and Aisling sighed with happiness. They were free to talk, for hours if they needed.

'You must tell me what's expected of me at this pagan ceremony tomorrow. Do I have to deny God or anything?'

'Aisling, where's Tony?'

'On the piss, I don't know where. Forget it, forget him. Tell me what I have to do, do I have to answer responses? Imagine me as a witness at an atheist wedding!'

'Aisling, do stop calling it pagan and atheist, everyone there thinks they're Christians of a sort ... but look, about Tony, do you think we should ... ?'

'I'll tell you this about Tony, if we can drop the subject afterwards. When we checked in here around five o'clock he said he had to go out and do a bit of business. There *is* no business – we both know that. So I said, can you just take ten pounds with you, so if you decide to spend everything then only ten pounds goes. ....'

'And what did he say?' Elizabeth was horrified.

'He said I was mean-minded, low and suspicious and that I never gave anyone a chance, I always believed the worst of him and never the best. He deliberately took all his money and gave it to me except what he said was a tenner, but I could see was two tenners. Then he bowed and said, "Permission to leave, Major?" to me, and went out. That was just after five and it's eight now. No word, no message. There won't be. At best he'll come home after closing time, maggoty drunk; at worst tomorrow morning maggoty drunk. But I'll have him in shape for your nuptials. Now, please can we leave him and talk about tomorrow? Who's, going to be there?'

Elizabeth looked at Henry who was eagerly explaining why he was a Labour voter, and why Gaitskell was right and Eden was wrong. 'But you're a professional man, I thought you'd be a Conservative?' Donal was saying. Elizabeth smiled affectionately at them. 'Right, I'll make a list. ....'

There wasn't nearly enough time, not nearly, but it did seem sensible that Elizabeth should go home and get some sleep.

'Tell Tony I'm sorry we missed him, but we look forward to seeing him tomorrow,' said Henry courteously.

'Yes indeed.' They waved goodbye from the foyer.

'Let's go to Soho, and I'll point out dens of iniquity to you,' Aisling suggested.

'But aren't you tired?'

'I wouldn't sleep anyway.'

'Suppose Tony comes back.'

'Let him come back.'

They wandered around in the bright lights and the cosmopolitan crowds and the young men standing at the top of stairways that led down to strip shows. There were bookshops open late and at the back they had sections which had filthy books.

'How do you know all this?' Donal's eyes were out on sticks.

'Years ago, years and years – I was much younger than you – I came down here with Elizabeth and her boyfriend that time, Johnny. Johnny told us all these things, we couldn't believe him. But it's all true.'

'What happened to Johnny?'

'He's still a friend, you'll meet him tomorrow.'

*

337

Tony came in at one a.m. and the porter helped him to his room.

'I'm afraid there's a pound owing on the taxi,' he said apologetically.

'Thank you so much.' Aisling was icy calm. 'Can you give him twenty-five shillings, and can I ask you to have ten shillings please for a couple of drinks yourself tomorrow? Thank you very much for helping my husband home.'

'Thank you, lady.' The porter was pleased there had been no embarrassing scene. 'I'll give you a hand getting him on the bed if you like.'

Aisling accepted this willingly, and she took off one of Tony's shoes while the porter removed the other.

'Should we try to get him undressed?' he asked doubtfully.

'No, I have his good suit hanging up. You are kind.'

'You're a great little trooper lady,' said the porter.

Aisling got up early on the morning of Elizabeth's wedding. She went to the chemist and bought mouthwash, a bottle of eye lotion, some witch hazel and cotton wool. She ordered a pot of black coffee to be sent up to their room and then from the foyer she rang Elizabeth to wish her luck. She went up to the room and arrived at the same time as the coffee. She took it from the waiter before he could see the spectacle of a man in bed with a suit jacket, shirt and tie still on him. She ran the bath with luke-warm water and wearily pulled back the clothes on the bed.

'Up,' she said crisply.

'What? What?'

'Up. You can get as pissed as you like after the wedding, I don't give a damn, but for the wedding you will look right. Up.'

Tony tried to move. His head hurt him and he swallowed hard. 'How did . . . what happened?'

'You went out at five o'clock to do some business, the business took somewhat longer than you thought. It also seemed to cost you twenty pounds plus a pound for a taxi from Kilburn, which is where the business seemed to end up.' She was moving his feet, still in their socks, towards the floor.

'Ash, will you stop, let me rest.'

'No, I will not. Get up now and walk towards the bathroom, then start peeling off your clothes one by one and throwing them to me.'

He did it, like a slowly moving clockwork toy. When he was naked she handed him the first cup of coffee and kept them coming even though he gagged and said he could drink no more. She sat on the bathroom chair while he made feeble attempts to wash himself then she put a towel behind his head and told him to lean back.

'What're you going to do?' he asked fearfully.

'I'm going to mend your eyes,' she said. As he lay almost drifting off to sleep, she dabbed and soothed and patted his eyes, she soaked the cotton wool in cold water and, after half an hour, the swelling and blotchiness had improved greatly.

'Ash, I feel dreadful,' he said pathetically. 'It's just going to be this weekend, when we get back home again I swear I. . . . Just let me have a couple to get me on target again?'

'As many as you like. After the wedding. . . . ' She handed him his clothes, garment by garment, and with a hotel clothes brush she dusted his shoulders.

'You're a fine-looking man, that's the pity of it.'

'Ash, stop horsing about, get dressed yourself. . . .'

'I'm not horsing about, I'm saying the truth, you are handsome and now that you've lost all that weight you look very well. Very well indeed. Can't you take a compliment?'

'I feel dreadful, I'm not in the mood for play-acting.'

'Isn't that funny, neither am I? Now you still stink of drink – I don't know why, God knows you should have washed it out of you. Drink this.'

'For God's sake. . . .'

'Now.' She went into the bathroom to wash and she heard him frantically trying to open the bedroom door.

'Shit, the door's stuck,' she heard him say.

'No, Tony dearest, it's not stuck, I locked it,' she said from the bathroom as she shook on some expensive talcum powder. She had bought it at the chemist at the same time as all the medicaments; it had made the trip less depressing.

In the taxi on the way to the wedding Donal found them curiously relaxed. If he had been Aisling he would have been very cross indeed that Tony had disappeared last night. Aisling was very peculiar in some ways, here she was laughing in a very friendly way.

'So that's the bargain. Three drinks of your choice at the reception, and when we've waved them goodbye then you're on your own . . . you get miles away from the wedding party and do as you like, for as long as you like.'

'Why am I being sent away from the wedding party? That's a bit high-handed.'

'No, it's the bargain, you can drink yourself into a pig's mess like you did last night, you can slobber and pee in your trousers, as you also did last night, I noticed, but not with Elizabeth's friends, you don't.'

'Jesus Christ, what a boss.'

'Good, now that's settled. Donal, we're nearly there, that's Westminster . . . we'll come back here and see it when we've time tomorrow maybe, or Monday. Do you see Big Ben, now we know we must get the right time. It's a quarter to eleven, perfect timing.'

They got out at Caxton Hall, where the sightseers who came to look at weddings brightened up when they saw Aisling's fiery hair, her lilac outfit and her lilac and white hat. It looked like something glamorous.

'Is it a film star's wedding?' a woman said, pulling at Aisling's sleeve.

'No, I'm afraid not, it's a solicitor and an art teacher.' The woman was disappointed. 'But it will be full of glamour, stay around,' she said.

'I will,' said the woman, pleased.

Father looked very smart, he was wearing the buttonhole that Henry had brought the night before.

'Are you sure there won't be any call for me to make a speech?' he asked.

'None, Father, I told you over and over. Simon will make a speech, and that's it. Henry may say a few words, thank you for giving me to him, and for the reception.'

'Well, that's not right, I mean you paid for the reception. . . .'

'Yes, Father, but that's not the point. Anyway, you gave be board and lodging here, and educated me and everything, so in a way any money I saved came because of you and that's you paying for it indirectly, isn't it?'

'I suppose that's right,' Father was doubtful.

'Of course it's right.' She straightened his tie. 'How do I look Father, do you think I'd do?'

He stood away from her and looked her up and down approvingly. 'Oh yes, my dear, you look . . . ' he paused. Would he say she looked lovely, or beautiful, or neat? What kind of things had he said to Mother when she was all dressed up? 'You look very . . . *presentable*,' and he gave a little laugh to show that the word was a little joke.

She looked around the hall of Clarence Gardens and in the small mirror caught sight of herself in the cream wool dress and jacket, with the big orchid pinned to the lapel. She pulled the brim of her hat forward and fixed four hairpins in the ends of her hair so that they were guarded against the wind; the hair was meant to flick out not run wild, so she sprayed on a little lacquer. She would take them out when the car stopped at Caxton Hall. Henry was meeting her there with Simon. They had decided to go separately, to make it more formal in a way. And she wanted to have this last journey with Father so that he would realise that he was still special. He had been very silent about Harry coming to the wedding, so travelling to the ceremony with him alone might be some kind of gesture. Elizabeth gave herself a final check and had a last look at the house. In twenty years she had put very little of her own personality into it. It had always been Father's house. She hoped that the flat in Battersea would be different. Already she and Henry had found furniture and rugs and knick-knacks. All her clothes were there in the old-fashioned wardrobe they had bought, and Henry had moved his things in too. He left his own flat officially today.

Superstitiously they decided not to spend a night there until they were married. It would make it more significant they agreed, and laughed at themselves and each other for their silliness.

In under an hour she would be Mrs Henry Mason. Did every woman who got married go through this sort of unreality bit just at the last moment? She thought of Henry's face eager and expectant, and she smiled happily. After all the lonely times in this house, after all the upsets and uncertainties she was finally being rewarded. She was going to marry a man who was goodness itself. That was a phrase Aunt Eileen had used about people who were very kind. What a pity she hadn't been able to come, and she had forgotten to ask what was actually wrong with her. They had had too many other things to talk about. Aisling was so strong about everything; most women would collapse if their husband had disappeared on the rampage in some strange city. But Aisling took everything in her stride.

'My dear, I think we should . . . the taxi has been here for five minutes.' Father hated waste even though Henry had paid for the taxi.

'Right, come on, let's go and get me married and off your hands.'

'You were never any trouble to us. Your mother and I had no problems with you. Ever.' He said it with his back to her as he was double locking the door. Possibly the only compliment he had ever given her. She couldn't answer him because she was afraid she might start to cry, and anyway the people across the road, the rather prim and proper Kentons, were waving like anything. They had come out to see her go, and other neighbours had too. Elizabeth waved to them all, delighted, and Father smiled as they got into the taxi and went off to get her married.

It was much nicer and much more like a real wedding than Aisling had expected. The nuns had said that registry office weddings were mere formalities at the desk of a clerk or a lawyer – they had only been invented because British people had turned away from all religion, even their own. But this was very impressive, and the registrar was almost as good as a priest when he was asking them did they take each other for lawful, wedded husband and wife. Aisling had thought that it was all a matter of mumbling and writing things down in a book.

Simon, the handsome best man, was utterly charming. In a different way to Johnny, he was flowery in his speech, he paid extravagant compliments and told her that her loveliness had not been conveyed in any adequate manner, although to be fair, attempts had been made. Aisling thought this was great fun.

'You're the smooth elegant colleague,' she said triumphantly. 'Have you met my husband, Tony Murray?'

'I wish that you had met Tony Murray long after you had met me,' he said over-gallantly, bowing and shaking hands with Tony who looked very pale and not at all able to cope with such flamboyance at this time of the morning.

The ceremony passed in a flash and as they came out, and Stefan and Harry and Johnny organised the confetti, there was another wedding party waiting to go in.

Henry was smiling so broadly that it looked as if his face would break. Donal was busy taking photographs. Elizabeth looked so lovely, Aisling was amazed. She had always thought that Elizabeth was gentle and pale and blonde and pretty in a pastel way, but today she looked different; event though her outfit was pale she looked colourful. Her face was strong, her lipstick was bright, her orchid was dark purple, her hair looked bouncy, not wispy, her eyes were sparkling. Thank God she's having a nice day, thank God, after all the awful things that happened to her, Aisling felt. Who would ever have expected a day like this, with her stepfather cheering as well as her father, and Johnny Stone apparently delighted for her too? If anyone deserved a great wedding day it was Elizabeth.

Mrs Noble was waiting for them, a high-necked blouse, a cameo brooch; she almost made herself the unofficial hostess. In one minute she had decided that Harry and Johnny were her best allies and singled them out whenever anything needed to be done.

'Mr Elton, might I ask you to move that little group near the door down here towards the main body of the room, they seem to be a little left out. . . .'

And Harry was off like a terrier dog. 'Hallo. Might I introduce myself? I'm Harry Elton, on the bride's side. . . .'

Jean and Derek were shy at gatherings and were delighted with Harry; he introduced them to Stefan and Anna and only when a conversation about old folding draught screens seemed underway did he leave them.

Mrs Noble was vigilant. 'Mr Stone, can I suggest that you direct the waitress with the wine over there towards the rather sad-looking man?'

'That's the father of the bride, you couldn't cheer him up,' Johnny said.

'Oh dear, I see.' Mrs Noble felt she might have said the wrong thing.

'He's a widower, Mrs Noble. Now if you were unattached I'd say you might be able to cheer him up!' Johnny winked at her. Mrs Noble was delighted.

'You are dreadful, Mr Stone,' she said, patting her hair.

Johnny got the message though. Elizabeth's father did look like a wet week. Johnny went over to him and refilled his glass.

'Elizabeth looks lovely,' Johnny said.

'Yes, yes.'

'Very nice, this reception, very generous of you, Mr White.'

'Yes, well, indirectly, only indirectly.'

In desperation Johnny looked for someone to rope in. Tony Murray was nearby. Johnny filled his glass. He was a handsome fellow, this husband of Aisling's. 'Have you met Aisling O'Connor's husband, Mr White?' They had, and obviously hadn't found much to talk about then either. With relief he saw that Mrs Noble was organising the food on the tables at the end of the room and he was able to direct them both towards it. Tony Murray said he had to slip downstairs to make a phone call. Fine-looking fellow, but a bit restless, Johnny thought.

Aisling had taken down Harry's address and promised to visit him in

Preston. She was stunned to find herself laughing so heavily with the terrible Mr Elton who had come to take Elizabeth's mother away. After a while she even felt bold enough to tell him that.

'I know,' Harry was solemn for a moment. 'I think Elizabeth sometimes feels the same. She's such a good friend to me, but I think she stops now and then and puzzles over it all.'

'No, she always talks of you with great love,' Aisling said.

'Does she now? That's good to know, she's a great lass, I think of her as my own daughter. She always loved being over in your place too, mind. She said it was the best time of her life.'

'We are being polite to each other,' Aisling looked around for Tony; she couldn't see him, but he must be in that group which was moving to the food. 'Elizabeth;s very happy today, she's delighted with Henry and the whole thing. . . .'

'Yes.' Harry nodded, but his earlier enthusiasm didn't seem so marked now. 'Yes, I hope she made the right choice, she says she has, she says she has. I always thought she'd marry Johnny Stone.'

'Yes, well they both took long enough to consider that one, and it didn't work out at marrying each other did it?'

Harry laughed, Aisling was a great girl, he thought, a corker to look at too. 'Yes, but you see Elizabeth's her mother's daughter, there's a flash of Violet in her all the time. I hope this fellow will be enough for her.'

'Well, if he's not, let's hope that history won't repeat itself, and we won't see another wicked Mr Elton coming to carry her off in the future.' They moved towards the table and Aisling saw that Donal was having an animated chat with an attractive blonde, and she noticed with some relief that Tony had come in the door; he must have been to the toilet. He looked a bit better now, less pale and sickly.

Mrs Noble could whisper without even appearing to move her mouth. 'Mr Elton do you think we should discourage the waitress from passing any more wine to that rather stocky well-built man near the door? An Irishman I think.'

'Thank you,' said Harry, 'I'll see she passes him no more.'

A little later: 'Mr Stone, just before the speeches begin can I call your attention to that dark-haired Irishman? Over there.'

'The Squire,' Johnny smiled.

'Well, I don't want to say anything to Miss White, or indeed Mrs Mason as she must be called now, but he does seem to have a half bottle of spirits in his hip pocket. It may be unimportant but I felt you should know.'

Johnny stood behind Tony Murray for a while. Twice he saw the wine glass which had contained white wine until Harry had motioned the waitress away being refilled from a half bottle of vodka which now only had a third of the contents left. He did it very cleverly, with one hand, glass on the table, bottle out, cap off, filling down and bottle replaced in a moment; all the while Tony was looking innocently ahead of him, and with his other hand he was taking little puffs from his cigarette and waving across the room – but there was nobody returning his wave.

Simon was courteous, wordy, flowery and urbane. Those were the words that Aisling thought she would have used to describe him. He didn't say anything real about either Elizabeth or Henry, it was all little witicisms but people liked them – and indeed he said them very well.

The cake was cut, the champagne was produced, and toasts were drunk.

'Are you going to make a speech?' Aisling asked Elizabeth's Father.

'Oh heavens no, no, she promised, she said I didn't have to,' he looked worried.

'Go on out of that, she'd love you to say a few words . . . just a word or two, it would mean a lot.'

'I don't think . . .' he looked flustered.

'Tell them she was a smashing daughter, and she'll be a good wife and you're glad that everyone is here enjoying themselves and it's a happy occasion.'

'Is that all I'd have to say?'

'Certainly that's all. Go on now, slay them, knock them sideways.'

Father cleared his throat. Elizabeth looked up, startled. It had all been going so well, Father wasn't going to do anything absurd like saying it was over now? There were still five more bottles of champagne to be passed around.

'I'd like to tell you that I am not a good speaker, but I cannot let the moment pass without expressing my gratitude to you all for coming, my hope that you are enjoying the reception. . . .' A lot of hear-hears at this. 'And I would mainly like to say that I am very happy that my daughter, Elizabeth, is marrying such a splendid man as Henry Mason, I am sure he will make her very happy and I can tell him that if she is as good a wife as she has been a daughter, he will be a lucky man. Thank you very much.' It was so simple and unflowery, after all Simon's complicated and convoluted phrases, that it touched everyone. Glasses were raised again to the bride and Elizabeth had to concentrate very hard on the table cloth to stop the tears coming into her eyes. Fancy poor Father steeling himself to do that, he must have been practising it all the time. Who would ever have thought Father could have thought of just the right thing to say?

Harry had asked Mrs Noble if they could use the piano. She was most enthusiastic, so before Elizabeth was even aware that Harry was on the piano stool he had struck up 'For They are Jolly Good fellows', and everyone in the room including Father was joining in. Harry was in his element, he got them singing 'On Ilkley Moor Bah Tat', and to the cries of more, he had 'My Old Man Said Follow the Van.'

He played 'It's a Long Way to Tipperary'. specially for the contingent from Ireland, and then that turned into 'Pack up Your Troubles in your Old Kit Bag'.

'Another Irish song,' Stefan called. 'The Irish have the best songs.'

'I'll sing one,' Tony said.

'Oh my God.' Aisling turned round to see who could come to her aid. She saw Johnny not far away. 'He doesn't sing, stop him,' she said desperately.

Tony said, 'Do you know Kevin Barry?'

'No,' said Harry good-naturedly. 'But you start and I'll pick it up.'

> 'In Mount Joy gaol one Monday morning.
> High above the gallows tree.
> Kevin Barry gave his young life.
> For the cause of Liberty. . . .'

'Please Johnny,' Aisling begged.

'Hey what about some song we all know?' Johnny called out.

'No, let me finish,' Tony said.

'Let him finish,' Simon said. 'Can't cut a man off mid-song.'

> 'Just before he faced the hangman.
> In his lonely prison cell.
> British soldiers tortured Kevin
> Just because he would not tell . . .
> The names of those . . .
> The names of those . . .'

Tony looked around irritated. 'What comes next? Come on, someone must know?' Everyone looked blank.

> 'The names of those . . .
> His something comrades . . .
> And other things they wished to know . . .
> Tell us now or we will kill you . . .
> Barry proudly answered no.

'Ash you know the words, come on, you can hold the tune, join in.'

Aisling spoke clearly across the room. 'I can't remember them, I think you've skipped a verse, but, honestly, it's not a song for a wedding. Hangman, prison cells, can't you sing something more cheerful and we'll all join in . . . ?'

'It's important that we finish it,' Tony said doggedly. 'There's another verse:

> 'Kevin Barry you must leave us.
> On the gallows you must die,
> Wept his broken-heared mother

345

As she kissed her son goodbye. . . .'

Harry did a loud crescendo at that point, by way of ending, Johnny stated to clap; so did a couple of others and then everyone joined in.

Tony was very obviously not finished, but Harry had a louder voice. 'Right, we've had Ireland's turn . . . anyone from Wales . . . ? Come on, there must be someone from a Welsh choir . . . ? Or Scotland . . . ?' With the heaviest chords he introduced 'I belong to Glasgow', and Mrs Noble made sure that the remaining champagne was being poured among the guests.

Aisling said to Donal, 'Get him out, Johnny Stone will help you.'

'Aisling, I don't know. . . .'

'Right out of the room. If you want to do something to help I want him right out of here.' She saw Donal talking to Johnny and Johnny walking over to Tony. Tony was pointing back at the piano; Johnny was making a sign with his hand of a person who had a glass in his hand – he was asking Tony out for a drink. Tony gesticulated towards the bottle of champagne which he could see circulating. Johnny was shaking his head. He was indicating the stairs. Mrs Noble was with them. Whatever they were saying Tony was going like a lamb.

Harry in his role as compere was saying that as the humble pianist he had been informed that the bride and groom would leave shortly so could everyone join in a chorus of 'My Dear Old Dutch'? He had his arm tightly around Elizabeth's shoulder and she was smiling at him, Stefan was patting Anna on the hand, and everyone was joining in because Harry had a way of roaming around and catching your eye if you didn't sing.

Donal put his arm into Aisling's, and they sang together as Harry swept them back to the beginning of the song again.

'We've been together now for forty years
And it don't seem a day too much. . . .'

Aisling looked at the door; Mrs Noble and Johnny were standing there singing too. There was no sign of Tony. The goodbyes were being shouted. Elizabeth came over and held on to Aisling.

'Bless you for coming. It wouldn't have been a wedding without you.'

Aisling said, 'I remember saying the same thing to you in Kilgarret. Oh, Elizabeth I'm sorry, I'm so sorry.'

'What about?' Elizabeth's clear expression meant she didn't know what Aisling was apologising for.

'Tony. I'm so sorry, I don't know how he got that drunk, I watched him like a hawk. I'm so sorry he stood up like that and disgraced himself and us. . . .'

'Goodbye, Aisling,' Henry interrupted. 'Goodbye, thank you so much for being our bridesmaid, witness. You are good to have come all this way.'

346

'Thank you Henry,' Aisling fingered the little brooch with the pearl in it that Henry had given her. 'It's beautiful, I'll never forget the day.'

'Oh and say goodbye to Tony for me. I can't see him,' Henry said.

'I spend my time saying goodbye to Tony for people, I think I should say goodbye to him myself. . . .'

They all went downstairs in a happy troop, and clustered around the car. Elizabeth pecked at Father's cheek; she had given Harry a hug on the stairs. She was kissed by everyone and when Johnny kissed her very tenderly he said, 'You're the loveliest lady I ever met, I always said it and I always meant it. Be very very happy.'

Mrs Noble saw Tony and two men coming out of the bar where she had directed him; he had an arm around each of them. She blocked him from view by pretending great surprise. 'Hallo Mr Murray. Fancy seeing you here,' she said, while she could hear the taxi revving up.

'How do you know who I am?' Tony growled suspiciously; he felt he was being prevented from doing something he wanted to do, but wasn't sure what it was.

The two men who were being dragged with him said, 'Come on back in the pub mate, they close soon.'

'Yes, we'll all be in then, everyone's coming in, in a moment,' Mrs Noble said.

'Great,' said Tony, and re-entered just as the final cheer saw the taxi off. The crowd were dispersing on the pavement.

Mrs Noble drew Aisling aside. 'I thought I'd mention that he is in that establishment across the road Madam, if you wanted to know.'

'You're a brick,' said Aisling, 'I don't want to know. I'm going to take my brother off to the pictures. But thank you for telling me, and thank you for getting him there.'

'Not at all – a very high-spirited man, your husband.'

'Very,' said Aisling. 'Listen, what will you do when the pub closes if he tries to get back into your place?'

'I'll tell him the crowd moved on. I'll point him off towards . . . where would you like him to head . . . ?'

'I'd say the River Thames but that would sound a bit strong. Anywhere at all, he knows the hotel we're staying at so he'll end up there.'

'Poor Aisling, this must be so awful for you, and the last time you saw Elizabeth was your own wedding,' said Donal as they set off.

'That's right.'

'It must be sad for you . . . you know your wedding day turning out so great and now this so awful. . . .'

'Actually, Donal, my own wedding day turned out pretty awful for me too, but that's a long story and let's not tell it now.' She smiled at him and slowly his white, anxious face broke into a sort of a smile too, and they went off to buy an evening paper and see what film they would go to.

347

XVII

Donal told everyone that the very same day they came home from London on the plane the British started their war, they went off to Suez.

'It wasn't a real war, stop going on as if you were out in the front line,' Eamonn said. 'Sorry Mam,' he added suddenly when he saw Eileen's face.

'I wonder, when I'm dead and gone, will any of you remember you had an elder brother?' Eileen said.

'Oh Mam, of course we will.'

'Go on about the wedding.' Niamh was home for the weekend; she felt slighted that Elizabeth had not invited her, but Elizabeth was awfully stuffy and English in some ways. Fancy thinking that it might interfere with her studies.

'I've told you everything, it was like a service only no altars, no music and he wasn't a priest. And it was all in English of course, like Protestants anyway.'

'No, the bit after.'

Eileen sighed. 'Donal, show her the photographs. He took lovely pictures, and they got them developed for cost in the chemist. He's going to send copies to Elizabeth like she did at Aisling's wedding.'

'Janey, isn't her father a small little man,' remarked Niamh.

'That's not her father, that's Harry.'

'The husband?' screamed Niamh, in disbelief.

'No, her step-father.'

'God, it must have been very awkward having both of them there. Were there any scenes?'

Donal paused for a moment. 'No,' he said. 'There were no scenes.'

Aisling called on Mrs Murray a week after their return. 'Mother-in-Law, I think you'd better get in touch with that priest in Waterford again, sonny boy has broken out.'

'I wish you wouldn't speak in that flippant way, Aisling. We know it's not Tony's fault, the priest wrote it down in a letter. Try to be less . . . well, less jokey about it.'

'I think jokey is the only way to be about it. What should I do – sit down and weep over it?'

'No my dear, but if you tried to talk to him. . . .'

'I have tried, I try morning noon and night. I went down to Shay Ferguson and I said to him that Tony would actually prefer to be off the drink, and perhaps he could help him by not encouraging him. He laughed and said that Tony liked his pint and his jar like any other man, and wasn't it a pity that he was so hen-pecked. . . .'

Mrs Murray sighed. 'Oh my dear, I don't know what to do, I really don't. Will you stay and have some lunch with me . . . ?'

'No thanks, I'm on my way back to the shop. I only just ran up to you so that you'd know from me before anyone else. He's only been in to work twice, and that's just to get cash. Old Mother Meade is like a wet hen he's so upset.'

'Oh yes. Well, thank you Aisling, thank you. We'll just have to hope it passes over. Is it as bad as . . . before . . . ?'

'Worse, Mother-in-Law. Worse. When I gave him his dinner yesterday he threw one plate on the floor and the other plate at me. That's a new little refinement.'

'Oh Aisling, how can you talk about it like that?'

'Right, give me one other way of talking about it. Should I offer it up to the Holy Souls? Mrs M, the way I'm going I could get so many souls out of purgatory they'd have to close the place down. . . .'

Eileen announced that she was going to Dublin for a day or two. She had to do quite a few things and it seemed more sensible to stay the night, or even two nights. She had to get all the material for the curtains; no point in paying out that money unless you saw the actual stuff; she was getting a new winter coat, doing early shopping for Christmas, getting her hair cut in that good place where she went for Aisling's wedding.

Niamh asked her to stay. 'The flat isn't what you'd call posh Mam, or even tidy, but it's desperately handy for everything, you just have to walk along Baggot Street and Stephen's Green and you're in Grafton Street. . . .'

'No, no, thank you child. I won't settle in on top of you and your friends. I'll go to Gretta in Dunlaoghaire. It's nice to give her the turn.'

'Would you like me to come up to Dublin with you?' Aisling asked.

'What, and have the two of us away on the same day from the shop, are you off your head?' Eileen asked. Aisling noticed that they were coming to the end of those nice efficient ledger books which she had installed in the shop. You could only buy them in Dublin in that stationer's in Nassau Street. Why wait and get them posted? Mam could easily put two of them in her suitcase. She decided to ring Gretta in Dunlaoghaire.

'Your Mam here? Not at all, never heard a word that she was coming. I wish she'd let me know. Do you think she'll be turning up tonight?' Gretta sounded fussed and bewildered.

Aisling thought fast. 'No, it's all my fault, I looked at the wrong date on the calendar – it was next week she was going to go up. I'm very sorry, Gretta.'

'Well I hope she'll let me know, I'm very full around Christmas.'

'Oh, I'm sure she will, I'm sorry for getting it wrong. Goodbye.'

Dad had said that Mam rang last night, she was settled into Gretta's and everything was fine; she'd stay an extra day and be home on Friday.

'Mam, you're going to have to ring Gretta and talk to her,' Aisling said when she was sure she had the office to herself.

'What on earth do you mean?'

'I rang her when you were meant to be staying with her, and I caused all kinds of confusion. You'll have to put her straight, say you got it all confused and you'll be up after Christmas or something.'

Mam's face reddened. 'She said I wasn't there.'

'Where were you Mam, is everything all right?'

'Did you think I'd run off like poor Violet? Did you tell your father?'

'Mam, what do you take me for? If you'd rang from Dublin I'd have known you were safe; if you weren't with Gretta, well, there must have been a reason. Were you in hospital?'

'How did you know?'

'I couldn't think what else it might have been. Are you all right Mam?'

Eileen looked at her, smiling, 'I am, thank God, I'm absolutely fine. I'm all clear, and as sound as a bell, that's what they said.'

'But why didn't you tell us, Mam, why didn't you let me go with you . . . ?'

'And leave the shop?'

'Oh, to hell with the shop, Mam, when you weren't well.'

'But I'm grand now, I promise you, there were cysts, and I was afraid, and Doctor Murphy wondered . . . and we thought the best thing was to be whipped in and out just like that.'

'But why didn't you say Mam, why drag yourself round getting coats and curtains . . . ?'

'I didn't spend much time, just an hour, I picked the first coat I saw, and the curtains are fine, I knew that anyway,' Eileen laughed at her own cleverness.

'But you can't do that, keeping things to yourself.'

'Yes I can, and I'm not even going to mention it to anyone now.'

'Even though you're fine.'

'No, because every time I go out of the room people will think I'm off secretly to a specialist. . . .'

'What did they do to you, Mam?'

'I had an examination under anaesthetic, you know probing around, and just two cysts, both benign, removed easily. . . .'

'Poor Mam, poor Mam.' Aisling was hardly able to speak, she was so distressed to think of Mam all by herself in that hospital.

'But I'm fine, isn't that good news?'

'Are you sure, Mam, are you sure you're not being brave about that too?'

'No, that's different. I wouldn't be brave about that. If I was told that my days were going to be cut short I'd have to make plans for everyone. But they told me I was the healthiest fifty-six-year-old they'd dealt with for a long time.'

'And you really are fine?'

'Yes, my love, and I feel that years are taken off me now that I know that. You're a very good girl not to raise a hue and cry about it all. If ever there was anything else, I would tell you. I mean it.'

'Well, if that's a promise?'

'It is. Now I'd better go and calm Gretta down before she has the whole country alerted.'

Brendan Daly told Maureen that he had seen Tony Murray driving that car of his when he was in no fit condition. Maureen said that she had heard something about it herself.

'Well you'd better say something about it to Aisling, hadn't you?'

'What good will it do? It isn't Aisling who's driving dangerously.'

'I know, but she should be told, in case something were to happen.'

'I suppose she knows already, but I'll tell her.'

'Right. Now I feel I've done my duty. I heard in the creamery that he nearly lifted two people off the bridge the other afternoon.'

'Oh God, isn't he a maniac, wouldn't you think with all that money he could get someone to take him home, or stay in the hotel if he's had a few too many . . . ?'

Mrs Moriarty said to Donal that poor Tony Murray had been looking a bit under the weather recently; was anything the matter with him!

'I don't think so, Mrs Moriarty,' Donal had said, his face as white as his coat. He hated any implied criticism of Aisling.

'I don't like poking my nose into other people's business,' she began.

'I know you don't,' Donal smiled at her, 'you're a grand woman, you're not like all the old gossips in this town. People's characters are safe with you.'

Mrs Moriarty felt slightly disappointed, but she thanked Donal for the compliment.

'Anyway, it would be much worse if he was chasing the women,' she said out of the blue, and went back into her little room behind the shop.

Mrs Murray said that she had been wondering what was best to do for Christmas.

'Cancel it,' Aisling had suggested.

'Not very helpful, dear.' Mrs Murray was worried too, it was not fair to torment her with slick remarks.

'What would you like us to do, Mother-in-Law?'

'What do you think is best?'

'Will we have Christmas dinner at your place? I'll come and help you cook it. It might be more cheerful up there than in the bungalow, with all your family around. . . .'

'I don't know who will be here, Father John is helping with a Christmas liturgy in. . .'

'Wouldn't it be more Christian if he were to help with his own brother?'

'That's not the point, he won't be able to get away, two bishops and ten priests have been chosen, it's an honour.'

'All right, it's an honour. But we'll have Joannie, won't we?'

'I don't think so. I had a letter. I don't know where I put it, but she's not sure. She thinks that some of the girls in her flat. . . .'

'They're not girls, they're grown-up women, like Joannie, like me.'

'Yes, well, she calls them the girls, they were thinking of going to a house party they saw advertised in Scotland. . . .'

'Were they thinking that, by God? Isn't she a selfish cow?'

'Aisling please.'

'She is, Mrs Murray, a cow, a selfish cow. And what do that group of clowns want going to house parties for? Haven't they their own homes. . . .'

'You're not going to change things by calling them names.' Mrs Murray looked hurt and upset.

Aisling agreed that she was right. 'All right, Mother-in-Law, it's you and me for Christmas. Let's try to make it a good day.'

'And Tony, of course. . . . ' Tony's mother said.

'Oh, and Tony of course.'

Niamh looked very down at the mouth when she came back to Kilgarret from the Christmas holidays.

'It's Tim, this fellow, he's gone off with a really dreadful girl – she has nothing to recommend her, Aisling, she's a real Holy Joe, and she wears awful, long, straggly knitted cardigans.'

'Oh yes, Well do you think he's serious about your one in the cardigan or do you think it's just a passing fancy?'

'I don't know, but you know the *real* thing . . . I can't tell this to Mam, obviously . . . but I'm afraid he'll tell people about us . . . and you know, I don't want them to get the wrong impression. . . .'

'Tell what?'

'Oh, you know, about us, him and me, I wouldn't want people to think that I'd, well . . . with anyone. Tim was special . I'm not indiscriminate, and I wouldn't want him to tell people I was.'

'Do you mean you went to bed with him?' Aisling's face was round with disbelief.

'Well yes, he *is* my boyfriend. *Was* my boyfriend.'
'I don't believe you.'
'Well, suit yourself, Aisling, but don't go blabbing to Mam, she'd murder me.'

'It's very hard to know when Aisling's joking and when she's deadly earnest.' Elizabeth was reading the letter to Henry, who was pinning holly and ivy around the room.
'What does she say?'
'Oh, you know it's all about the horrific Christmas, three of them, rolling around a huge empty house.'
'I thought she had a big family.'
'Yes, but she's going to be with Tony's mother for some reason, alone. And Tony, she thinks, may have some difficulty in lasting the day with them.'
'Dear me, is he still very drinky?'
'What a marvellous word. Drinky. Yes, he is *very* drinky. It started at our wedding weekend and seems to have gone on since. Oh well, maybe another priest will cure him. Aisling is amazing, she never seems to be as upset as she should be.'
'Would you be upset if I was drinky and didn't come home?' Henry smiled down at her from the chair he was standing on.
'I'd be very upset indeed. So don't try it. And it you were very drinky indeed, which is what I think Tony is, then I'd leave you. I'd just go.'
'Why doesn't she do that? Leave Tony?'
'Oh, they don't do that in Ireland.'

Father managed very well without her. Elizabeth was pleased but slightly annoyed to notice this. Just as he had settled into a routine of life without Mother, so he did in a life without Elizabeth. He kept a little notebook in the kitchen, with the words 'Ask Elizabeth' on it. When the queries had been answered they were ticked, and sometimes the answers written down.
'Tea-cup stains,' he had written, and then beside it, 'I am only rinsing them. E says I should rub them with scourer inside and if stain bad try soaking in salt or soda.' 'Sour smell in sink.' 'E thinks it could be dish-cloths not properly washed and left to air.'
What a narrow and organised life he liked to lead. Everything in its little box, neatly ticked and docketed and filed away. He had been pleasantly surprised when she had invited him for Christmas, and suggested that he come and spend three days.
'That's very nice of you my dear. But stay? At night?'
'Well, why not Father? Henry would be very happy for you to come. And it would be nicer than flogging home all the way to Clarence Gardens.'

'That's very generous of Henry and of you. Shall I pack a suitcase?'

Sometimes she wanted to shake him until he fell limp from the shaking. He agreed eventually to spend Christmas night itself, but he would return home on Boxing Day.

'Nicer, really, to be in my own place,' he said.

Elizabeth had arranged a little holly for him and put the few cards he had received on the mantelpiece rather than leaving them on the table still in their envelopes.

It was good to work for a school and a college, Elizabeth told Stefan, they kept nice civilised hours, closing down well ahead of Christmas. Shops were a millstone, since people always wanted to buy at the last moment. She was arranging a table with a selection of items they had not sold. She made a card with beautiful lettering suggesting that people regard them as Christmas presents. Stefan had thought she was wasting her time; Johnny had said that people didn't come into antique shops to buy gifts at the last minute.

On Christmas Eve however they were all sold.

'I take my hat off to you,' Johnny said, generous as usual with praise. 'I never thought we would do it. Look Stefan, even those salad servers, we've had those for months. It was clever of you to think of doing those gift cards with the name of the shop. Not only is it good advertising but people will not feel so much that they're giving somebody something used or second-hand. With one of these little cards it becomes an antique. You could have been a great businesswoman.'

'I *am* a great businesswoman,' Elizabeth said.

'No, no, you're a wife, and before we know where we are you'll be a mother.'

Elizabeth looked at him in amazement. Not even Henry knew yet, she had only had it confirmed yesterday, and she wanted to tell Henry tonight as a Christmas surprise. She was indeed pregnant. She and the doctor had worked out that the baby must have been conceived on her honeymoon and would be born in June.

Trust Johnny Stone to have guessed.

There were Christmas drinks at the office. It was all very informal, the senior partner had said, but of course it was nothing of the sort. Everybody examined the wives critically, Elizabeth had known this without having to be told. She knew that she would be under a microscope. She was going to do him credit.

The hairdresser brushed Elizabeth's shoulders and together they admired the handiwork. She looked exactly right, she thought: white frilly blouse, cameo brooch, smart grey jacket, and grey and blue check skirt.

'Going somewhere nice?' asked the hairdresser who would be working until 7.30, she told Elizabeth, then after an hour's journey home she would start to stuff the turkey for her Mum.

'Yes, my husband's office are having a little party,' Elizabeth said.

'I'd love a husband and an office party,' the girl said.

'That's funny,' Elizabeth said, 'I used to think there was something safe about having a husband and office party too. It sort of lets you know where you are in the world.'

'You have a nice time, Madam, you look very well.'

She spoke when she was spoken to, she didn't want to seem pushy, but she answered clearly and directly. She told the senior partner about her art classes and how she also worked in an antique shop. When he said that he had a very old picture which had been in his family for years she expressed polite interest and murmured appreciation.

She parried Simon's flowery compliments very skilfully, she talked to other wives in a sunny way. From time to time she saw Henry straightening his tie and glancing at her proudly; he looked less tense and worried as the time passed – she even saw him laughing at one stage. How dreadful to have jobs like Father and Henry did where nervous people become more nervous. And no one could relax.

The senior partner was speaking to her again: 'Are your own family in the law, Mrs Mason?' he asked silkily. Around him people waited for her reply. Would she apologise, would she claim distant cousins who were barristers or solicitors?

'No, far from it, banking is my background. I've had to learn a whole new language. I never heard of precedents and injunctions and indentures . . . you may find this hard to believe, but a great deal of the world hasn't heard of them either!'

The senior partner laughed, and then so did everyone else. Some test had been given, and Elizabeth had passed. Soon she whispered to Henry that she thought it might be time to leave. They didn't want to look like hangers-on.

Simon asked them whether they would like a Christmassy nightcap, before he set out to Barbara's house for the festivities. Elizabeth steered them away from it. She wanted to tell Henry the news.

They sat for hours by the fire and talked about the baby. Henry said that he had to pinch himself to make sure he was awake. This time last year he had been on the train to Liverpool to stay with Jean, now he was a married man, and an expectant father. He put cushions behind Elizabeth, he insisted that she do no work next day, he would do all the cooking. They planned the nursery, the schools . . . they talked of the holidays they would all have together,

Names. They could have written a dictionary between them. Richard Mason, Susan Mason, Margaret Mason, Terence Mason. Henry's father had been called George, too, so that settled it: George Mason if it was a boy.

'Would you like to call it Violet if it's a girl?' Henry was solicitous and courteous.

'No, I think not. I think Father would be upset, you know, every time we mentioned her name. No, your mother's name . . . you told me, but I've forgotten.'

'Eileen,' he said.

Father was embarrassed, and delighted at the news. He seemed reluctant to hear about dates and missed periods and doctors' tests proving positive, but he was quite pleased with the notion of himself as a grandfather.

He had arrived bearing a bottle of sherry for their Christmas tree. He didn't even *know* it was mean, Elizabeth told herself as she unwrapped it and noticed that it was almost as cheap a brand as you could buy. They had bought him presents – nice playing cards in a fancy leather case, and a thick cardigan with leather bits on the elbows. But Father hadn't chosen anything for them.

'We should look on the sherry as an advance on last year. He never gave me any presents at all,' Elizabeth whispered when they were in the kitchen.

'Oh he must have. Surely?'

'I can't remember anything. No, he wasn't that kind of father.'

'I'm going to be a doting father, I'm going to buy everything in the shops for Little Eileen.'

'Or Little George. And I'll be a doting mother too. I won't run away from Little Eileen. . . .'

'Or Little George.'

'If they're all going to go off like prize eejits to some house party then let them go, Ma-in-Law,' Aisling said. 'There's no use in being martyred over it. Tell them you hope they'll have a great time.'

Mrs Murray agreed that it was better not to appear too dependent. So well did she follow these instructions that Joannie was moved to telephone and wish them a Happy Christmas. Aisling was in the house and answered the phone.

'I feel a bit of a heel, letting you cope with Mummy but, well, there is Tony, and the two of you can share it.'

'Oh heavens no, you mustn't look at it that way, we're going to have loads of fun here,' Aisling said.

'Yes, well, sure. Is Tony there?'

'Tony?'

'Tony?'

'Tony Murray? Your brother?'

'Oh, Aisling, don't be tiresome, what are you playing at?'

'Nothing, I just wondered why on earth you thought Tony might be here?'

'It is his mother's house and you're there, and it's coming up to Christmas. . . .'

'Ah no, none of those are reasons. No, no Tony, might be in the hotel. Or I believe he even drinks in Hanrahan's now, he's barred from Maher's, politely, of course, but barred nonetheless.'

'Oh, do stop this nonsense.'

'Nonsense is what it is, but there we are. Some people like to live like that, drinking what's left of their brains away. I don't and you don't but your brother – and my husband – seems to want it like that.'

'Can I talk to Mummy?'

'Of course you can, and listen, thanks a million for ringing up to say Happy Christmas, and have a great time at the house party. It's in Scotland, I believe.'

'Yes, anything to get out of this dump.'

'But you got out of this dump, you went to Dublin.'

'I meant Ireland.'

'I'm sure you're right, I'm sure Scotland's much less dumpish. Hold on till I get your Ma . . . Mother-in-Law, it's glittering Joannie just off to her house party, giving a little tinkle to wish Mama compliments of the season.'

Mrs Murray laughed at Aisling's affected accent. 'Well, it was nice of her to ring anyway, wasn't it?' she said later.

Aisling said nothing.

'It was,' Mrs Murray answered her own question.

Aisling said, 'I was just thinking of all those years when Joannie and I were inseparable . . . and I thought you were remote and sort of untouchable . . . and here we are, neither of us with a word left to say to Joannie but thrown together for Christmas. . . .'

'Not thrown together. . . .'

'We'll be spending Christmas on our own.'

'We won't be on our own.'

'We will if we're lucky.'

There was a do in the hotel on Christmas Eve. Aisling came for an hour.

'Your mother expects us for supper,' she said to Tony.

'Sure who wants supper on Christmas Eve, won't we be eating like pigs all day tomorrow?'

'Yes, but she still expects us.'

People were beginning to look at them. Tony's face got red. 'Well, you go on up there if it's making you fidgety. I'll come up later.'

'How much later? When will you come?'

'When I'm good and ready, in my own good time. She's *my* mother, it's *my* house. I'll go to it when and if *I* please.'

'Well said, spoken like a man,' said Shay Ferguson.

'Well said, spoken like an arse-licker,' Aisling said to Shay. People

357

thought they must have mis-heard, Aisling Murray looked so innocent and unmoved, could she possibly have said that? No, it must have been something else.

Shay was a dull red. 'Well, I suppose you'll be off now, Tony, this is the last we'll see of you this evening. . . .'

Aisling smiled at Shay. 'Heavens, you must be deaf, Shay, didn't you hear what Tony said? He's going to leave when he's good and ready, not before.'

Shay looked even more put out. He laughed nervously. 'Right, Tony, old stock, what'll it be?'

Tony turned round to say something to Aisling but she was gone.

She went to the bathroom in the middle of the night: it was four o'clock. Tony had not come back. On her way back to bed she passed Mrs Murray's door; it was ajar and the landing light was on.

'I'm awake, Aisling,' the voice said.

Aisling went in. 'Go back to sleep Mother-in-Law, being awake doesn't make any difference. The best thing is trying to sleep . . . because then you have less time to think of it.' She took the woman's thin hand and stroked it.

Mrs Murray's eyes were troubled. 'Of course, they may be back yet, maybe someone gave him a lift and they called into someone else's house.'

'Yes, that could be it.' Aisling was soothing.

'But on Christmas Eve . . . you'd think . . .'

'Maybe he went to the bungalow, maybe he forgot we were here; perhaps at this minute he's fast asleep in the bungalow, and he'll wake up in the morning feeling a right fool.'

Mrs Murray looked at her hopefully. 'Do you think that might be it?' she asked.

Aisling gazed at her, a thin, gaunt woman in her sixties: a widow; a son in the priesthood gone from her at Christmas; a daughter, half-crazed, gone looking for adventure on a package tour to a gathering of equally restless, lonely souls; and her pride and joy drunk in her home town, out doing the Lord knows what on the most sacred night of the year. Let her have an hour or two.

'I'd say that's exactly it, you know that car, it turns like a donkey automatically into its own yard. That's where he is.' She was about to leave.

'But when he sees you're not there . . . won't he . . . can't he . . . ?'

'He'll probably get into bed without turning on the light so as not to disturb me.' She didn't tell anyone that she slept on the small divan bed, the one that everyone else thought was a sofa. The lurch of Tony into the bed beside here, waking her and smelling of drink and sweat, was more than she could take. He had said nothing the first night she had slept there, when they came back from Elizabeth's wedding, so she had slept there ever since.

Aisling remembered from somewhere deep down in her mind something that Elizabeth's mother had once said. When things are worst, that's when you should spend a lot of time dressing yourself up. I wonder does it work? she thought as she got up in the Murrays' cold guest bedroom. She had not slept since she returned to her room. She had read instead. She had hoped it would distract her but it didn't succeed. It wasn't the author's fault, she thought, trying to be fair. No book could take her away from the never-ending whirlpool. Tony needed help; how could he be helped if he wouldn't listen? How could she get other people to help her to know what to do if *they* wouldn't listen? There had been no answer at four a.m. There was none now as she dressed for Mass.

She wore her good dark coat, and she spent time shining up her shoes and her handbag with face cream. Elizabeth's mother had thought that if you looked all right to yourself at least you didn't have that additional worry about looking like a tramp. . . . It saved you from self-disgust. She arranged her hair carefully, put on plenty of make-up and laid a mantilla on top of her red curls.

'Will we be late?' Mrs Murray fussed with her gloves: she too had dark circles under eyes, but unlike Aisling she hadn't shaded them away with liquid foundation and pressed powder.

'No, plenty of time, and we'll go by the bungalow in case sonny boy's there. . . . ' Aisling spoke cheerfully.

He was not there, but she prattled on what could possibly have happened, and soon they were at the church.

'Aisling, you'd think you were going to a dress-dance with all the pan stick you have on you,' Maureen hissed as they met in the porch.

'Happy Christmas, sweet sister, to you also,' said Aisling.

The sermon was about love; Christmas was the season of love – Father said they must put some love in their lives, not enough to talk about it, not enough to buy gifts, but give kindness and understanding. Let everyone look into his or her heart and see where they could give more love today.

I suppose I could decide not to kick him to kingdom come when he does get home, Aisling thought. That would be an act of love. But possibly superhuman. She looked at Mrs Murray's hands clenched in prayer, her eyes closed. Oh God, send him back sober just for today. Please. Not for my sake, I don't care any more, for his mother's. Please. God, you were nice to mothers, can't you give them a better deal? Look at Mam, all that business with Sean running away and being killed and all. And look at poor Mrs Murray, she's really praying. Now if that's not praying, God, what is? And I'll put half a crown in the poor-box. Five shillings. Please God, because it can't matter to you one way or the other, where Tony is, so why can't you send him home?'

On the way out of the church Donal sidled up to Aisling.

'Listen, Eamonn said that Tony was in some kind of a fight down in Hanrahan's last night.'

'Well, he's not home yet, so maybe he's still in it.'

'Not home, on Christmas Day?'

'I know. Did Eamonn say any more?'

'He said there was a matter of the barman taking away his car keys and Tony wanting them back.'

'He must have been bad if they took away his keys in Hanrahan's, usually they wouldn't notice there if you hanged yourself in the back snug.

'I don't know any more, I thought I'd tell you myself, you know, rather than your hearing it from someone else.'

'You're very good, Donal.'

'Will you do something for me, Aisling?'

'Sure, what?'

'Can you lend me a fiver? A five-pound note?'

'Of course I can. more if you want it. I've twenty pounds in my bag.'

'No, five is plenty.'

'Here you are.' Only her eyes asked the question.

'You see, there's the dance tomorrow night, Niamh's friend Tim is coming up from Cork, and he's always got loads of cash, and Anna Barry . . . just in case I ran out. . . .'

'Sure of course. Take another and buy champagne.'

'No, I have a bit already, it's just that I seemed to spend all my money on Christmas presents.'

'You did too, you're too generous.'

Donal shook his head. 'What's Christmas without presents?'

His car was at the bungalow when they drove there.

'Please, Mother, don't lose your temper or be cross with him.'

'No, of course I. . . .'

'It's just that I know how to deal with Tony when he's been out all night. He needs to feel that we haven't noticed, honestly.'

'All right, dear,' said Mrs Murray nervously.

Shay Ferguson was there too; he had a folded table napkin dipped in a water jug and was making ineffectual dabs at a cut on Tony's eye.

'Happy Christmas Shay, Happy Christmas Tony,' said Aisling, holding Mrs Murray who was about to run forward and see the extent of the injury.

'Oh, play-acting again, are you,' Shay said.

'No, just a seasonal greeting. What happened, Tony?'

'He had a bit of an accident with the car, he stayed up in my place last night.

'Are you all right, Tony?' Mrs Murray couldn't be stopped.

'Oh, stop fussing will you,' Tony said.

'Tell us about the accident, was it someone's wall sticking out, or someone's dangerous parked car?'

'I'm trying to tell you. The young Coghlan boy was out on his new bicycle wobbling and teetering over the road ... he nearly ran straight into the car with Tony and myself in it. Lord almighty. . . .'

'Is he hurt?' Aisling said.

'It's only a cut, I've been cleaning it, it was the mirror, the corner got him over the eye.'

'Not Tony, the child, the Coghlan boy?'

'He's all right, they shouldn't give kids bicycles, you know, silly kids who can't ride them. . . .'

'They shouldn't give cars to drunks, either, silly drunks who can't drive them.'

Tony tried to stand up.

'Take that back.'

'I will not, it's the truth.'

Shay said, 'Aisling, for God's sake, the man's hurt, stop picking on him.'

'I was not drunk. I'd been asleep in Shay's, I had nothing to drink today.'

'It's only nine forty-five, Tony, I wouldn't go boasting about that.'

'He was trying to get back for Christmas Day with you and his mother, quit attacking him.'

'Just tell me what injuries the Coghlan boy got.'

'His leg is ... well, I don't know if it's broken, they were getting Doctor Murphy when we left. . . .'

'You left? You didn't wait to see how the boy was?'

'Look here, get this straight. Tony did not hit the boy. You can look at the front of the car, there isn't a scratch. He swerved and braked in order to avoid him.'

'Where was this?'

'Outside Coghlan's.'

'Coming up the hill?'

'Of course coming up the hill.'

'But Coghlan's is on the right, if the boy was at his own gate he was on the right, *why was Tony on that side of the road*?'

'The child was all over the road. . . .'

'It's me that should get compensation, look at the cut on me.'

Tony had got up to examine his face in the mirror.

'Does he need any stitches do you think?'

'Was the child cut?'

'Only his hands and his forehead, grazes like kids get falling off a bike.'

'We'd better go down and see if he's all right.'

'Don't be silly, going back would be admitting liability, you know, the way people take up things.'

'So what are you going to do?'

'We explained to Dinny Coghlan, that the child had been staggering on the bicycle but that we'd not make a fuss about it since no one was too badly damaged.'

'And what did Dinny Coghlan say?'

'What could he say? He was pleased to see the sense of it.'

'The sense of it being that he works in Murray's.'

'Ash, what have you that sneer on your face for?'

'If you'd run over the child backwards and forwards you'd have made poor Dinny see the sense of something . . . if the boy's leg is twisted I suppose he'll see the sense of it for the rest of his life.'

'You're making a mountain out of a molehill, the boy's all right and so is Tony.'

'So as I said, Happy Christmas Shay. Are you off now?'

'I've no car. I came up with Tony in his to see him right.'

'Yes, for a man who was stone cold sober, it was nice that his friend should escort him back.' Aisling's face was cold. 'I'll drive you home Shay, no, no, it's no trouble. I'll take my car. Ma-in-Law, why don't you and Tony go on up to your house and I'll come back when I've dropped Shay at his place?'

There seemed to be no fault in these arrangements, even though they pleased nobody.

Shay smelled of drink as he sat into the car beside her. Pointedly Aisling wound down the window.

'You can be a cold, catty bitch,' Shay said.

'Yes.' Aisling concentrated on the road.

'He's the best in the world, Tony, you shouldn't be picking on him.'

'No.'

'Seriously. There's no reason for you and me to fall out. He's the best pal I ever had. I like him, you like him, why do we have to have all these barneys over nothing at all?'

'I don't know,' Aisling said.

'Well, you're very mute, you're singing very low compared to up at the house.'

'Oh Christ God, you are a stupid man.'

'No no no, for the New Year, now will we agree to differ and not be doing each other down, not fighting like enemies?' He looked at her, his big face foolish in the hope that she was going to shake hands and make friends. That the Christmas Spirit was going to soften her.

She stopped the car. They were nearly at the Fergusons' garage, where Shay lived with his father, his uncle and aunt. A big untidy house sprawling behind the garage as if nobody gave any heed or care to it.

'Tony is an alcoholic. he is drinking himself to death. He had almost eight months on the dry. Things weren't perfect but they were a hell of a lot better than they are now. He was lonely for the fun and crack with you. What kind of a friend were you to him then? Did you ever come up to the house when he asked you? Did you ever go out fishing with him, or taking a spin down to the sea during the summer?'

'It's not that easy to get off just at a moment's notice.'

'It's always easy to get off for a drink. But not for the best pal you ever had. You couldn't go for a bit of a walk with him.'

'I'd have felt silly.'

'He felt silly, he felt silly ordering red lemonade, or ginger beer. He felt silly in the long nights when he hadn't got you and the lads. But nobody would come and feel silly with him. That's friendship.'

'Ah, Tony's not an alcoholic. He takes a bit much, don't we all?' He'll cut down on it, in the New Year, we all will. And lose a bit of weight at the same time, two birds with the one stone.'

'Great, Shay. Great.'

'I mean it.'

'I know you do.'

'Pals then?' He held out a big hand before he got out of the car.

She drove home up the hill past Dinny Coghlan's house. Doctor Murphy's car was still outside the gate.

Mrs Murray had let Kathleen, the maid, go home for Christmas. 'In the old days we always had a girl, it's going to be hard coping,' she complained. But Aisling could see that she was pleased to have Tony to fuss over. All the hard bit, the long cleaning and chopping of vegetables, had been done by Aisling, and she had drawn the turkey and made the stuffing. She had got a plum pudding from Mam, one of the seven that had been made in the square, and she told Mrs Murray that it was her own making. The Christmas table was set for the three of them; Aisling had arranged crackers crossed at each place. She had sliced the bread very thinly and she had prepared half grapefruits expertly and put a glacé cherry on top of each.

'It's very festive,' said Tony, nodding towards the table.

'I suppose it is.' She didn't even look up. They sat opposite each other at Mrs Murray's well-banked fire. From the kitchen they could hear the clatter of dishes and the busy happy hum of preparations. There would have been no heart in the feast without the Prodigal's return.

Aisling couldn't think of one thing she wanted to say to Tony. She was weary of the time-filling tactics. The delaying moves which would put off his first drink of the day. Let him take it, let him swallow it. All she could do anyway was put it off by half an hour. She didn't want to talk any more about young Lionel Coghlan; if it was a boy old enough to have a bike it must be Lionel, Matty was too small. Her words with Shay Ferguson would soon get back to him anyway, changed, bent and slanted. No point in telling him of the conversation now.

And what point in recriminations, or investigation into the row in Hanrahan's? None of it would do any good.

'I got you a Christmas present, but I lost it,' he said.

'That's all right, Tony,' she said. 'It doesn't matter.'

'It does matter. I've said I'm sorry.'

'Okay,' Out of the corner of her eye she saw him stand up and move to the sideboard.

'Well, seeing the day that's in it,' he said, and poured a quarter of a tumbler of whiskey out. His mother came into the room at that moment. She saw the whiskey and gave an alarmed glance in Aisling's direction.

Aisling shrugged. 'Are you right, Mother-in-Law, will we sit down to the festive board?' She sat down and they said grace. And Aisling thought of all the Christmases she had had not a mile away from here. When the gathering around the table had been as exciting as the presents earlier in the morning, when everyone was in good humour and Dad would tell jokes, and Mam would say thank God to have had so many blessings during the year. She always said that – except for the year Sean had been killed.

Two years ago it had felt funny not to be having Christmas with the family, but she had cooked for all the Murrays and it had been such a flurry she had hardly noticed the time come and go. Last year Tony had come in drunk at ten p.m. and slept in the chair all night. He had been bad-tempered at his mother's lunch, but at least Father John and Joannie were there to share the burden.

This is the way it's going to be from now on. John won't come home. Joannie won't come back.

This is Christmas.

She smiled up at her mother-in-law and said that the turkey smelled smashing out in the kitchen; she was trying to finish her silly grapefruit so that they could carve it. And she held out her Waterford goblet while Tony filled it with wine.

Eileen said that they had a lot of blessings to thank the Lord for during the year. She closed her eyes for a moment, thinking to herself of the blessing that she alone knew. The fear that had been groundless. She thought of Sean and the shop. He had resigned himself to Eamonn now. He didn't come home with his forehead bulging over some small, confrontation. She thought of Maureen, who had been there this morning with the four children, the baby looking like a Christmas card with all his white fluffy wrappings, and Brendan Og turning into a lovely little boy. Eamonn was Eamonn, neither more nor less; at least the year had passed without his leaving the shop or abusing his father in public. Aisling, well she had her hands full with that Tony – and maybe she was exaggerating about the other business. Maybe she only meant that she hadn't had any pleasure from sex – that would be a normal thing to happen. And Donal, God bless him, didn't he look better this Christmas than any gone before? A grown-up man of twenty-two with a career and, as far as she could see, a girlfriend. It was Anna this and Anna that. And then Niamh, as pretty as Aisling without the striking hair, ten times more confident than Aisling at that age, happy as Larry now that she had her Tim back again. And she always included Elizabeth in her children; ten pages of a letter saying how happy she was and how their flat was like a little palace and it would always be a home for Uncle Sean and Aunt Eileen to visit though she could never make them a home as great as she had been given in Kilgarret. Wasn't it a wonder that Violet's child had turned out to be a closer friend than Violet had ever been?

Eileen thanked God for the blessings of the year.

They listened to the wireless after the meal, sitting around the fire eating the Christmas boxes of chocolates, some listening to the variety show, some doing the quiz in the paper.

Eileen dropped off now and then, after the big meal the heat of the room made her sleepy. Sean slept too, until the children laughed at him, with his glasses on, the paper clenched firmly in his hands and his mouth open giving loud snores.

'What's Christmas,' he said crossly, 'without a bit of a sleep?'

Mrs Murray's eyes closed too. Aisling slipped out to the kitchen and did the washing-up. She set a tea tray too and cut some of the Christmas cake. Mrs Murray was going to send squares of it to Father John and to Joannie.

Could it be still only five o'clock? It felt like ten. She came in quietly, it was too soon to wake Mrs Murray. Let the women sleep, she didn't sleep much last night. Tony can't have slept much either, in Fergusons'. His mouth was open, and he lay out in the chair by the fire. Aisling sat between them and looked at the flames making pictures and houses and palaces as she used to do when she was a child. A log fell out. It woke Tony. He reached out and poured himself a glass of whiskey. 'What's Christmas without a little drink?' he said.

Mrs Murray thought the clock must be wrong; how could she have slept all that time? Heavens, she must do the washing-up, oh dear, weren't they a marvellous pair, to do that, they shouldn't have. No, really, they shouldn't have done it.

A cup of tea was always nice after a big meal, the cake was moist, wasn't it? Was it as good as late year? It was hard to remember last year's but she thought this one was a bit dryer. Maybe not.

Tony was restless; he said he would prefer to spend the night in his own bed. 'I'd like to go back to the bungalow, Ash,' he said. 'If we're going to the races tomorrow I'll have to have a good sleep. I like to be in my own bed, my own room.'

His mother looked stricken. 'But that is your own room, your own bed, Tony, for years and years. If you can't sleep here where can you sleep?'

Aisling said nothing.

'Come on, Ash, you explain to her, I don't sleep well, I get headaches.'

'Not one night under your mother's roof.' Mrs Murray was becoming tremulous. 'You were the Lord knows where last night, and now tonight you won't even. . . .'

'I was not the Lord knows where, I was *you* know where, Ash knows where, I was with the Fergusons. God all-bloody-mighty will you stop making it a mystery, as if I was in Mongolia? I sensibly didn't drive home when I had a couple too many. Aren't you always asking me to do that? Well, aren't you?' He looked more upset than Aisling had ever seen him.

'Maybe Tony's right in a way, Mother-in-Law, that we should go back and sort ourselves out. Listen I'll be up tomorrow to see you and thank you for a marvellous day. That was a feast, a feast is the only word for it. Wasn't it Tony?'

'Very good, grand, grand,' Tony muttered.

'So we'll be off. It was a great Christmas mother,' she said, kissing the thin, tense face.

Mrs Murray squeezed Aisling's hand.

'Well, if you think . . . I don't know, rear a family and still it's a lonely day.'

'Well, they were fools not to be here for that spread, going to their monasteries and their house parties. Wait till I tell them what they missed.'

They waved goodbye and drove in silence through the dark wet countryside. One way back would pass the Coghlans' cottage. Aisling decided not to take it. Tony's face was set and hard.

The bungalow was cold and dark. She plugged in an electric fire and started to clear up some of the blood-stained table napkins which had been used by Shay for dabbing the wound.

'Will I light a fire?' she asked.

'What for?' he said.

'It might be cheery, were you going to sit down? For the evening like?'

'Ash will you stop *interrogating* me? It's like living with a prison warder. Do I ask you all the time where you're going, what you're doing?'

'I only asked you. . . .'

'You only asked, you only asked. . . . I can't hear this constant asking. I'm going out.'

'But where on earth are you going? Listen, Tony, there's drink here, plenty of it. Invite who you want in. Don't go out on Christmas night, please. There's nowhere open.'

'There's friends with houses open, friends who won't nag, nag, question, question.'

'Listen, Shay's not at home, you know he said they were going up to Dublin tonight, you're going to meet him at the races tomorrow. Won't that do?'

Tony had his coat on.

'Look, your eye has that terrible scab on it, if you knock it against anything it will open up and bleed, will you not have sense? I'll light a fire and we'll have a bottle of brandy. We'll sit by the fire like the old times.'

'What old times?'

'When we got married first. It's only a waste going out.'

'I won't be late, I'll be back tonight.'

'But where . . . ?'

Aisling went to bed eventually. It was cold, despite the electric fire. She wore a cardigan over her nightdress. She slipped into the small divan and took a book she had loved as a child, *The Turf Cutter's Donkey* by Patricia Lynch. She read it slowly, like she and Elizabeth had done, she remembered explaining the bits that Elizabeth didn't understand about cutting turf in the bogs. She thought of Elizabeth and Henry and their nice flat in London and Mr White going to stay with them. She remembered the way Henry had looked at Elizabeth during the wedding reception. Tony had never looked at her like that. Why had he wanted to marry her? Or anyone? Had his drinking pattern been started then, only she just didn't see it? Why had she thought that he loved her? She had never thought that she loved him. Not like people love in books. Not like Elizabeth had loved Johnny, or even Niamh was crazy about this medical student. She had never felt that for Tony. Maybe this was the punishment for marrying someone you didn't love. But how the hell were you supposed to know in Kilgarret what was love and what wasn't?

'I must have been mad to marry him. Quite, quite mad,' she said aloud. And somehow when she had said it, she felt a bit better. At least the situation had been defined. Aisling O'Connor married Tony Murray because she was quite mad.

Eileen was surprised that Aisling didn't go to Leopardstown to the races.

'You used to love going up there on St Stephen's Day,' she said, when Aisling came in to pick at bits of cold turkey around lunchtime. 'Leave that alone, there'll be no lunch if you keep taking the best bits.'

'I didn't feel like it, Tony thinks I'm eyeing him and watching him . . . which I am, I suppose. He keeps saying "It's only my second", when it's his seventh. I only annoy him and everyone else.'

'But shouldn't you be with him? Maureen told me she saw him this morning and he had a terrible cut on his eye. I'm not repeating things, now, to make trouble, it's just because you brought the subject up.'

'He braked hard in the car yesterday morning, just avoided killing young Lionel Coghlan, from what I can understand. The child was on a new bike. Lionel had bruises and two cracked ribs, Tony has a cut on his eyebrow which probably needs attention but he won't go near a doctor or a hospital.'

'Merciful Lord,' Eileen was shocked.

'Oh yes, the Coghlans keep saying, thank the Lord Tony didn't do himself any serious injury, and wasn't he marvellous to swerve and avoid Lionel, and Lionel is white-faced, in the bed there trying to say he was only playing with his new bike when this drunk maniac came round the corner at a hundred miles an hour. Well, Lionel's not saying that because he doesn't know how, but that's what he should be saying.'

'But Tony wasn't drunk in the morning, yesterday, was he?'

'He was filled with the night before's drink, he had no coordination, he was drunk.'

'Well, thank God that nothing worse happened.'

'Mam, what am I to do, will it be like this always?'

'You know he took the pledge before, lots of people take it after Christmas.'

'Mam do I have to stay with him? Couldn't I get . . well . . . an annulment or something?'

'What?'

'You know, I told you about the other business, I'd have no trouble proving that to any court.'

'Are you mad? Are you stark staring mad?'

'But I *can't* spend the rest of my life, Mam, I'm only twenty-six, I can't. . . .'

'Just tell me, what did you promise?'

'What do you mean, promise?'

'Up in that church, in front of all of us, what did you promise?'

'At the wedding, do you mean?'

'At the sacrament of matrimony, tell me some of the things you said. . . .'

'The words of the ceremony. . . .'

'Not words, Aisling, promise, a bargain, a solemn promise . . . what did you agree to do?'

'You mean better or worse, sickness or health. . . .'

'I mean that, and you meant it too, didn't you?'

'Yes, well. But I didn't know it was different. . . . It can't be counted.'

'Do you know what you are trying to do? Put aside the whole sacrament of matrimony. Oh dear, I didn't know it wouldn't all be sweetness and light. Sorry, let me start all over again. Is that what you think people should do? Is it?'

'Mam, I don't care what people do. I can't be expected to stay married to a man who doesn't want me in any way, who doesn't care whether I'm here or not. I cannot be expected to stand like an eejit beside him for the next fifty years, which is what you seem to think.'

'I do think. I certainly think that's what you should do, and will do.'
Eileen looked at the stricken face, eyes dark-ringed and troubled. 'Everything seems worse than it is at this time of the year, there's too much
fluster and too many expectations. . . . Don't be so dramatic, it will all
work out.'

'So you think, Mam, that no matter what happens, the only thing to
do is to stay with Tony and hope that things will get better and will all
work out?'

'Of course I do, that's the only thing *to* think, child. Will you come on
up to the fire with me and have a cup of tea? I was making a sandwich
for your father and myself – we'll all have a bit of lunch together. Will
you do that, he'll be delighted to see you.' Eileen was coaxing.

'No Mam, I think I'll go back to the bungalow.'

'No, stay here, you're cross with me now. You're in a kind of a sulk,
aren't you?'

'No, Mam, I'm not sulking. I asked you what you thought and you
told me.'

'But child, you can't have expected me to say anything except what I
did.'

'I expected you to say that there was a case for annulment. I think
that's what I expected, but you didn't.'

'We're not talking about technicalities. We're talking . . .'

Mrs Murray was surprised too that she hadn't gone to the races. They
had a cup of tea in the kitchen.

'That was a great meal you cooked, can I have a bit of the turkey?'

Ethel Murray bustled around happily getting plates and knives,
though Aisling only wanted to taste the skin and to please her by praising it all.

'I suppose he'll be all right at the races?' she said.

'Oh, I hope so . . . he's a hard man to fathom. Can I ask you something seriously? Not wanting a polite answer, you know?'

'Certainly you can.' But Mrs Murray looked worried.

'Would he have been better if he hadn't married? You know, he
didn't drink all that much when he lived with you, do you think if he
were single again, it might be . . . you know, like it was?'

'But how can he be single again, isn't he married now?'

'Yes, but try to think, suppose he wasn't, he hadn't. . . .'

'I don't know, I really don't. I don't think it would have made any difference, he does drink too, he drank before he got married and even
more after, but I don't think the marriage is the cause of it.' She took
Aisling's hand. 'You're not to reproach yourself, you do everything that
can be done, you're a grand little wife, if only he had the sense. . . .'

'No, you misunderstand me, I wasn't asking was I a good wife or a
bad wife, I was wondering did you think that Tony is really a bachelor at
heart?'

369

Mrs Murray looked bewildered. 'Well, I suppose there's a bit of the boy in every man. Is that what you mean?'

Aisling gave up. 'That's what I meant. Hold on, don't give me all that much. I'm going to Maureen's, I'll have to eat something there too.'

Maureen's house looked inviting and homely. Aisling wondered why she had always thought it was so bleak and dreadful. There was a big crib covered with cotton wool, the baby slept in a pram peacefully, Patrick and Peggy played with toys on the floor and Brendan Og read his new book.

'I'd have thought you were at the races, no ties, nothing to keep you at home.'

'Well I didn't go, I came to see you instead.'

Maureen said she would heat up some mince pies.

'I hear you saw Tony's face,' Aisling said.

'I didn't mean to go blabbing to Mam, oh God, now you think I'm talking about you all the time. Wouldn't you think Mam would have had the sense . . . ?'

'No, I'm not picking a row, I just wanted to ask you . . . do you think people talk about Tony a lot?'
'What do you mean?'

'You know, his drinking, fights down in Hanrahan's, him neglecting the business and all.'

'Oh Aisling, I never hear anything, I mean what would people say . . .?'

'I don't know, I was asking you. I wonder do they think he's in a bad way . . . do people think that he's the kind of man that . . . you know . . . should be . . . ought to be . . . ?'

'Aisling, what are you on about?'

'I don't think I'm the right person for Tony to live with.'

'But who on earth else would he live with?'

'I don't know, he could go back to his mother, or he could take a room in the hotel, or in Fergusons', they have rooms there, they were going to do them up once, I remember. Maybe they could do them up for Tony.'

'Are you feeling all right? What's this, some sort of game or joke?'

'No. I was just looking at alternatives.'

'And what would you do?'

'I could go back to Mam and Dad.'

'Aisling, you could *not*.'

'Why couldn't I?' Aisling looked genuinely interested. 'Just why not? That way everyone would be happy.'

'That way nobody would be happy. Stop behaving like a spoiled child just because you had a row with Tony and he went off to the races without you.'

'It's not that.'

'Well, it's something like it. When I think of all the things you have to be grateful for, it makes my blood boil. . . .'

'Like a drunken husband falling around the town?'

'So he drinks too much, you should look after him more, and anyway, look at how much worse it could be. Suppose he was after women, supposed he was like Sheila Moore's husband, or Brian Burns look at him with a woman up in Dublin as well.' Maureen stopped; Aisling's face looked very grave. 'Listen, you're only talking rubbish, you're not married as long as I am, you're new to it.'

'I've been married two and a half years.'

'When you have a child it will all change. . . .'

'If I were to tell you that side of it, you wouldn't believe it.'

'No, I know, Brendan's a bit the same, he says we can't afford another one, but when they're born he's delighted. He's made about the new fellow altogether. It would be the same with Tony.'

'I'm sure you're right. Let's not talk about it any more,' said Aisling.

'You're the one who brought it up,' Maureen said huffily.

'I know I did. I'm in a bad mood today.'

'I knew you were,' Maureen was triumphant. 'When he comes back from the races, make it all up with him, have a bit of a cuddle and forget whatever the fight was about. That's what people do.'

When Tony came home from the races it was one o'clock in the morning and he was in a blazing temper.

'How dare you go down to Coghlan's sympathising behind my back. How *dare* you go to that house. . . .'

Aisling had been asleep, she woke with a start. 'Tony, you're drunk, go to bed, we'll talk about it in the morning. . . .'

'We'll talk about it here and now. I was in the hotel. I met Marty O'Brien, a brother-in-law of Dinny Coghlan. He told me you'd been down at the house asking after the boy. . . .'

'Common politeness and a bit of humanity. Of course I did.'

'Behind my back.'

'Oh shut up, you stupid fool, you were propping up the bar in Leopardstown, how could I tell you I was going?'

'Don't call me a fool.'

'You *are* a fool.'

'And you're a thief, where's my money? I had a big roll of notes in my pocket. I didn't have it when I got to the races, only a couple of fivers.'

'It's in the drawer, Tony you know it is, I often do it when you're going out. It's in the top drawer where it always is. It's to save you spending foolishly or being pick-pocketed.'

'I don't want a bloody keeper looking after me like an animal in the zoo. Don't you *ever* do that again.'

'All right.'

'And another thing.'

'Look, whatever it is will wait till the morning. I've got to get up and do a day's work. Dad's opening tomorrow, so is Murray's by the way, in case it's of any interest to you. I'm going to our shop. I don't know whether you intend to go to yours or not . . . but I'm having my sleep!'

'What's that supposed to mean?'

'What?'

'If it's of any interest to me. Murray's opening. Of course it's of interest to me. I own it, don't I? It's my shop,'

'That's right. People keep forgetting.'

'What do you mean?'

'You're in it so rarely, and when you are it's to sign for fifty pounds. They see you coming and they say . . . here's Mr Tony, he'll need some cash . . . I've heard them.'

'Are you implying that I neglect my work?'

'Shut up and go to bed.'

'Are you suggesting . . . ?'

Aisling got out of her divan bed and began to strip off the blankets.

'If you won't let me go to sleep here, I'm going into the other room, let me pass.'

'Get back there, or back into the proper bed where you belong. Do you hear me?'

'Oh not tonight, Tony, I couldn't bear it, not tonight.'

He looked at her, his eyes blazing. 'What could you not bear?'

'Don't make me say it. I don't want to try tonight. Please, Tony, let me past you.'

'You're a vicious woman,' he said. His hand came out so quickly, Aisling didn't see it; caught her by surprise, across her jaw. The sting and the hurt jarred her whole body. He hit out again, this time harder. The blood came immediately from her lip or gums. She could feel it on her chin and falling on to her nightdress. She touched it and looked at her red hand in disbelief.

'Ash, oh, Jesus, Ash, I'm sorry.'

She walked slowly back into the room and looked at her face in the mirror. It seemed to be her lip that was bleeding but a tooth felt loose in her mouth so it could be that that was causing the blood.

'I could kill myself. Ash I didn't mean to, I don't know why I did it, Ash are you all right? Let me see – God let me see. Oh my God. . . .'

She said nothing.

'What will I do, will I get a doctor? Ash I'm so sorry. Tell me what to do and I'll do it. I'll do anything you say. . . .'

The blood was trickling on to her lap.

'Here, Ash, don't just sit there, you have to do something. Will I call someone?'

She stood up slowly and walked towards him. 'Go into the other room and go to bed. Go on. Now. Take these blankets.'

He didn't want to go. 'I'm so ashamed Ash, I didn't mean it, I wouldn't hit you for the world, you know that.'

She handed him the blankets and shamefacedly he went. She took the suitcase very deliberately from the top of the cupboard and began to pack. She wrapped a towel around her neck to catch the little drops of blood that fell from her lip. Very precisely and neatly she packed winter clothes and shoes. Underwear and jewellery. She took off her rings and left them in a conspicuous place on top of the dressing table. She took down a second suitcase, and she put in two blankets and two sheets. She collected letters and photographs and packed those too. After an hour she thought it was safe to open the bedroom door ... from their spare room came the sound of Tony's heavy breathing. He had split her lip but he could still sleep. She collected a few small things from around the house: a silver sugar bowl that Mam had given her, a teacup and saucer with huge roses on them that Peggy had come to deliver as a wedding gift.

She wrote a very short note to Tony. She told him that she was going to the hospital to have her lip stitched; she would say it was the result of a fall. Then she would leave in her own car and would not come back. There would be no point in asking any other family where she was because they would not know. She wrote a long letter to Mam; she said that she had tried every avenue, sounded out every opinion and nobody seemed to think that she could turn the clock back, so she was going to abandon the clock instead. She said that she didn't mind *what* cover story Mam used, whatever they wanted to say would be fine with her. Sickness, a new job, gone to visit a friend. ... But she thought it might be better just to say straight out that Aisling had not been able to live with Tony any more and had gone away. That way there would be no speculation and wondering about it. It would be out in the open.

She told Mam about her lip. 'I'm only telling you so that you'll know it wasn't idle fancy and selfish wishing for a happier lifestyle. I know too that there are women in this town whose husbands beat them, and women in every town. *But I will not be one of them.* I will not, and that's as definite as I ever was about anything.'

She said to Mam that she would ring her in a couple of days and the kindest thing of Mam to do was not to try to organise a reconciliation because there wouldn't be one. Only if Ethel Murray became difficult and began to cause trouble was Mam to tell her about Tony's violence. Otherwise better leave the woman a few illusions.

Her lip only needed one stitch. It was done by a young house surgeon whom she didn't know.

'Are you a student?' she asked him.

'No.' He was shocked at the thought, but she hadn't intended to insult him, she was thinking that she would never know about the dance that Niamh had gone to with Tim the medical student, and whether Donal and Anna Barry had fallen in love, and if Donal had been able to buy rounds of drinks with the fiver she had given him.

She knew two of the nurses and saw by their faces that they didn't believe her story of a fall.

'Come back during the week and I'll have a look at it,' the young doctor said.

'Sure, thank you very much,' Aisling put on her coat again and got into the car. She dropped the note for Mam into the shop, not into the house, she wanted Mam to read it in the peace of her eyrie when she got there early in the morning.

She took one last look back and drove out of Kilgarret on the Dublin road.

Part Four

1956–1960

XVIII

It had been the happiest Christmas that Elizabeth had ever known. Even in Kilgarret long ago she had felt a little separate, it wasn't quite her Christmas, she was comparing it with the ones she had known before and would go back to. This was her Christmas. Her husband, her father, and her baby starting to take shape. And in her home. It was as if she were being rewarded for all those other Christmas days, trying to console Father, trying not to worry about Johnny finding somebody new. Now it was all safe and as it should be.

Father had been happy to leave on Boxing Day; he wasn't at ease as a house guest. She had seen him nervously pacing in his dressing-gown with his sponge bag over his wrist.

'What's the matter?' she had enquired; he looked lost.

'I didn't know whether to go in or not, someone might have gone in the other door.'

'Father, I've told you a dozen times, if we go in one door we lock the other one so that no one comes in.'

'Very complicated way of having a bathroom,' he said.

Henry was looking over some papers in the dining room. Father and Elizabeth lingered over breakfast in the kitchen.

Was Mother ill much when she was expecting me?' Elizabeth asked.

'What? Oh. Oh, I don't know.'

'But you must have known, I mean, did she tell you that she felt groggy or what?'

'I'm sorry, I have no recall for all those details. I could never write a book – I wouldn't remember the interesting bits. . . .' That was Father making a little joke. Or trying to.

She felt a wave of sadness that he regarded the birth of his only child as a *detail*, but perhaps that was too harsh, maybe the whole memory of Mother was painful. She would ask no more.

'Imagine poor Henry taking work home for Christmas, I think he's too dedicated . . . I can't see the others doing it.'

'I think he's very sensible.' Father had a view! Elizabeth was surprised, she had expected a monosyllable.

'He's very sensible, the most important thing for a man to do is to get on top of his work. Once a man feels able for his work everything else falls into place.'

Elizabeth looked thoughtfully at him. 'It's not the most important thing, is it, Father? The most important thing is to get the most out of life, and give to people, you know, not just getting on in work.'

'I didn't say getting on, I said getting in control of it.' Father looked quite animated. 'You know in your world, in the art business it's not the same, there aren't the same pressures, not like law or the bank.' (Of course, it was all men together in the big, stress-filled business world, while silly women just dabbled in art.) Elizabeth didn't care very much about the argument, she was just glad to see Father lively, almost spirited for once.

'Do you wish you had taken work home at Henry's age?' she asked almost playfully. She wasn't prepared for Father's face.

'I tried to, my dear, I tried to advance myself, or even just keep up with my colleagues. I wanted to do evening classes when I first got married. I wanted to buy banking magazines and study them, I could even have sat for examinations in the Institute of Bankers if I had wanted to. But Violet never wanted me to do it. It was, let me see, *stuffy*, and *pathetic*, I think those were her objections. . . .'

'Surely not, Father? Mother would have been eager for you to do well.'

'But I wasn't doing well, I was just doing it to keep up, she knew that. *Petty little clerk* she called me sometimes. Once she asked me was I the office dunce that I had to have help to do a job that a child could do. Your mother could be very cruel sometimes.'

'But you could have gone on studying, couldn't you?'

'No, not really, not if it irritated your mother so much and made her so scornful . . . there was no point in making her angry. . . .'

Elizabeth hated the defeated tone in his voice. It was the voice of a weak man in a film – the coward who blamed other people for his own mistakes. She tutted sympathetically.

'You see, things come easily to you, Elizabeth, you're like Violet in that way. She was very quick, and inclined to be impatient with those who were not so quick. A lot of the world are not so quick . . . remember that.'

Was Father warning her, was he actually going so far, interesting himself enough in her well-being as to offer her some kind of advice? Far from resenting it Elizabeth was pleased. She regarded what he had said as nonsense, but the very fact that he said it gladdened her soul. She didn't want to break his mood, but he changed the subject himself.

'We were thinking of having a nice brisk walk in the park, Henry and I, and a beer and a sandwich at the pub afterwards. And then I'll push off back to Clarence Gardens.'

'You're very welcome to stay here, Father.'

'I'd like to have my things right for tomorrow,' Father said.

What possible things could he mean? He had been working in the bank for thirty-four years. What on earth could he have to get ready for the morning?

Henry came back from the pub glowing with the frosty weather, the brisk walk and the unaccustomed midday pints.

'Your father's got on a bus,' he said. 'He asked me to say goodbye and thank you again. I think he really enjoyed himself.'

'So did I,' Elizabeth said. 'And next year we shall have a six-and-a-half-month-old baby with us, isn't it unbelievable?'

Henry sat down by the fire and warmed his hands. 'I'll have to do a lot of hard work to provide for us all. But I'll enjoy it.'

'But sweetheart. I'm not going to give up work, not all of it. I'll keep on Stefan and the college, I'll give up the school.'

'Well, we don't know darling, we don't know,' Henry looked worried. 'We mightn't be able to get anyone to look after the baby, you may have to give up work altogether.'

'No. It's not necessary. We went over all this.'

'But whatever we do it will mean a cut in our income and you already earn more than I do.'

'Henry, I do not earn more than you do.'

'Count it up, the salary from the college, the salary from the school, the fee from Stefan, the art courses, of course you earn more than my salary.'

'I don't think it is more . . . anyway, it's not mine or yours, it's ours, isn't it?'

'Yes. but I worry, I'm not as light-hearted as you are, I'm not a believer in things turning up, I'm more of a plodder really.'

She tousled his hair and laughed at him and made faces at him and eventually she made him laugh at himself. But there had been a note of warning there in something he had said, it was uncannily an echo of what Father had said a couple of hours before.

How odd that she had never noticed before that Henry and Father very often thought alike about things.

'I'm not going to tell the whole world yet, but just a few friends,' Elizabeth had said when Stefan and Anna had kissed her and examined her complexion and said it was true that pregnant women did look more beautiful.

Johnny came in during the hugging and kissing, so he had to be told too.

'Well, isn't that fantastic? The new generation for Worsky's, eh? Make sure he grows up with a keen business sense . . . that's all we need in this firm. We've got flair and taste and bright ideas, but nobody who knows how to make real money. When young Mason goes to school impress on him that he's to be a financier. Do you hear me?'

They laughed. 'What if young Mason turns out to be a girl?'

'We'll wait for the boy,' Johnny joked. Later he spoke less lightly. 'I'm very happy for you, honey lamb, it's what you want, isn't it? This is really what you wanted all the time. Home, husband, kids. . . .'

'I am happy. I don't know whether I wanted it all the time, but I certainly want it now.'

'A little person no less. I'd quite like that.'

'You would?' She looked at him surprised, and with a catch in her throat like the old days.

'Yes, I often thought I'd like a kid, without all the marriage bit. Difficult though, some would say impossible.'

'Tucked away somewhere quietly with his mother, and you could call now and then and teach him things and take him for walks.'

'Yes, that sort of thing. Can't find the partners for such an endeavour.'

'Oh, I don't know, look harder, suggest it to people, it might work.' She thought to herself that he could have had it, exactly that, and the child would have been nearly eight by now.

Harry was delighted when she rang and told him the news. He said he would make a cradle, he used to be good at woodwork – but perhaps Elizabeth would have a fine cradle ordered already? On the spur of the moment Elizabeth invited him to come and stay for the weekend. She said she would send him his fare too because she said she wanted him as a consultant for the nursery.

Henry said he was delighted that Harry was coming, but was it not a bit much for Elizabeth's father to know that Harry would be a house-guest?

'Of course it's not a bit much, Father knows well that Harry is a great friend of mine.'

'But coming to stay,' protested Henry. 'It's almost saying that we don't think he was the villain of the piece, to put it very dramatically.'

'Well, I don't think he's the villain of the piece, I haven't thought that abut him for ages. Remember we decided that it may have been the best thing for everyone? Remember?'

'Yes, I remember,' said Henry, 'but I never thought it was the best thing for George.' Henry always called Father George when he talked about him. But when he was actually speaking to him he called him Mr White.

Simon had not been told about the baby because, well, that would be telling the whole office and it was all too soon to do that, wasn't it? Henry agreed readily. Elizabeth was marvellous at knowing exactly what things were like in there he said, she always knew little nuances and subtleties without being told.

'I think it's a bit like the staff room at school,' Elizabeth said.

'You say they're a lot of old women, in the staff room,' Henry protested.

'That's exactly what I mean,' Elizabeth said and laughed.

Simon called around on the evening after Boxing Day. Their office was closed until Monday, so in theory they had no work to do, but Henry had been working so much at home that there was little difference between this and a normal day.

Simon was full of his wonderful Christmas, Barbara had been a great

hostess, people had dropped in all day, there had been a permanent buf-
fet. Barbara sent everyone lots of love and hoped that the little nest in
Battersea was superb.

'I hope you told her it was,' Elizabeth said, jokingly. Henry still looked
slightly foolish when Barbara was mentioned to him, she wanted to relax
him.

'Yes, I said you had transformed Henry, that he was relaxed and lan-
guid these days. Barbara always thought Henry worried too much about
little things, and fussed about minutiae.'

'What rubbish, he's practically a beach boy,' said Elizabeth.

Henry laughed, almost an easy laugh. 'I certainly do think I've un-
wound a lot,' he agreed.

'You're perfect for me,' Elizabeth said, 'why don't you get another
drink for Simon while I go and tidy up all my old papers that I have
strewn in the other room?'

'Oh, was that your work?' Simon said. 'I thought old Henry had been
doing his eager beaver bit again.'

'At Christmas time? You must be joking,' Elizabeth said as she went
and tidied Henry's papers neatly into her own briefcase.

Father telephoned that night to say that there had been a message from
Ireland, it was from Violet's friend, Eileen. She had been very specific,
could Elizabeth please ring her at ten o'clock in the shop. Yes, that's what
the woman had said. Yes, he agreed, it seemed an odd time to telephone
anyone at business, but that's what she had said. Ten p.m. in the shop,
Kilgarret 67, and to tell Elizabeth that there was no accident, nobody had
died or was ill or anything.

'Whatever can it be about?' Elizabeth wondered.

'My dear, how on earth should I know, they are your friends. The most
important thing I was to tell you was not to ring her at home, not to ring
Aisling and to make sure you got the shop.'

'But why doesn't she ring me here? Did you give her my telephone
number?'

'I tried to, but the woman kept repeating to me that she couldn't make
any more calls, she was in a friend's house and was using the telephone
secretly. It's all a very odd business I must say.'

'So must I say, a very odd business,' Elizabeth said. 'Never mind, I'm
sure there's some innocent explanation, shall I ring you and tell you
about it?'

'No, no dear. Ten o'clock is somewhat late to disturb me. No, tell me
about it when I see you.'

Father hung up. Elizabeth realised that he had very little curiosity
about people. He didn't like many people enough to be curious about
them. She felt a horrible sense of panic. There must be something very
wrong indeed if she was not to telephone the house on the square, nor

Aisling, but to go through with this charade. Oh dear it was only seven-thirty now, she would have to wait two and a half hours. better persuade Simon to stay to supper, it would distract them.

'Hallo, is that you Eileen, Eileen can you hear me?' Elizabeth's voice sounded high and nervous after the endless clicks and spelling Kilgarret and talking to the exchange. It was now ten past ten and she had begun making the call ten minutes ago.

'Yes, child, are you all right?' Aunt Eileen's voice sounded just as usual.

'I'm fine, we're fine, but what is it, what's happened?'

'Have you heard from Aisling?'

'I had a letter from her just before Christmas. Why, what's happened to her?'

'No, she's fine, there's nothing wrong with her – she hasn't telephoned you?'

'Telephoned me, no, not for ages. No, I rang her when we got back from our honeymoon. What is it, Aunt Eileen? Please?'

'I'm trying to be discreet,' Aunt Eileen said.

'But aren't you in the shop, isn't this why I'm ringing you there?'

'Yes, but, you know. . . . ' Eileen's voice stopped.

'No, what . . . ? Oh, I see, yes, yes, of course, I see.' Elizabeth remembered the legendary curiosity of the Kilgarret postmistress, Miss Mayers. She listened in to the beginnings of conversations that she thought might be interesting and did spot checks on others until she got a good one to settle down with.

'I know what you mean,' Elizabeth said. She could hear the sigh of relief.

'Well, you know the problem that Aisling had, you know the problem like say your Henry?'

'Yes, I know what you mean.'

'It's over.'

'Dead?' gasped Elizabeth, shocked.

'No, no, wound up, like a business, you know.'

'Can't you tell me properly?'

'That's right, the line is very bad. So I was wondering if you had heard anything at your end. . . . '

'No, no, nothing.'

'You see I got notification of this, today, this morning in the office and naturally I would like to discuss it more.'

'Of course.'

'So if you are contacted you will urge that contact be made here, won't you?'

'Oh obviously, at home or at work?'

'At the shop around this time is good. Less questions asked, less people around.'

'I see, and does Uncle Sean . . . ?'

'Not yet. . . .'

'Who else . . . ?'

'Nobody . . . apparently.'

'And the . . . er . . . problem itself?'

'No word from there, no word at all. There's a car outside the home but that's all I know.'

'And do you know why, why now, and so suddenly?'

'An injury. . . .'

'Oh God. . . .'

'No, not serious.'

'But if it's done, it's done, you know what I mean, the contract broken, the business wound up. Why not, well acknowledge that publicly, as it were, it will all, have to sooner or later won't it?'

'That's what she said in her letter, but I'm hoping not.'

'But if it's as final as that, you know . . . ?'

'Child, business in this country is very different to business in your country . . . Violet and Harry's solution isn't open to people here.'

'But is there another . . . another? Lord, I'm so confused about the words, don't know which one I want. Does she have another problem like Mother having Harry?'

Aunt Eileen laughed. 'No, no, that's not it. But you see here there's no way of ending the problem, she'll have to come back.'

'I see.'

'You're very good, child. Do you have people there as you're talking to me?'

'Yes, Henry's here obviously and Simon, our friend . . . ' she smiled at Simon.

'They must be mystified altogether . . . I'll write to you tonight, and remember, when she gets in touch, what she's to do. . . .'

'But surely there must be a better way than all the code . . . ?'

'I'll arrange to go and talk to her – anywhere, in England if needs be, but she must ring me first to tell me that she wants me to.'

'You can't come over here the whole way for that kind of thing. You wouldn't even come for my wedding.'

'I know, and the last time I was there was to bury young Sean. I don't seem to have much luck with my trips to England these days.'

'Perhaps she won't contact me.'

'She will, that's the only thing I'm certain of.'

Aisling rang the next day.

'Where are you?' Elizabeth said.

'In Brompton Road, just opposite the Catholic church, at the terminal.'

'Are there taxis outside passing up and down?'

'Yes. I saw some.'

'Get into one fast and come here.'
'Will it cost a fortune?'
'Whatever it costs I'll pay it. Come here at once.'
'I look awful, you'll be shocked.'
'No I won't,'
'Is Henry there?'
'No, he's gone out to the library.'
'Thank you, Elizabeth, thank you, I don't know what I'd do.'
'Just get into the taxi ... tell me when you get here,'

She asked Henry if he would go to the library. 'That's a bit steep,' he said. 'Driven out of my own home.' He was irritated at being asked so sharply.

'I'm sorry, but it's important, if it was Simon coming here in a crisis I would do the same – clear out and let you have the place to yourselves.'

'Simon wouldn't do that, men don't,' grumbled Henry, packing his things obediently.

'I'm very grateful, very very grateful.'

'Well,' he said, not really mollified.

She went into the guest room and made up the bed. She laid out fresh towels. She thought that she hadn't told Aisling about the baby but she would have to, of course, when she came to stay. What a bit of bad timing, she wished she had told her and got it over with

She heard the lift coming up to their floor and she knew it was Aisling. Both Mr and Mrs Solomons across the landing went out to work. They would not be home at this time. Elizabeth steeled herself for Aisling's injuries. Aisling had her head down as she struggled out of the lift with her two suitcases. Then she looked up.

The whole side of her face had a black and purple bruise, at the corner of her mouth was a dressing held on with Elastoplast.

'Oh my God,' Elizabeth said. 'Poor Aisling. Poor Aisling.' They stood at the top of the huge curved marble stairway with the ornate little lift behind them; the door of the lift was still open but they didn't even hear the buzzing from below. They stood with their arms around each other and the cases on the floor, Aisling with her good cheek laid against Elizabeth's and they both kept saying over and over, 'It's all right. . . . It's all right.'

They kept making tea, pot after pot of it. The telling was not a litany of Tony's wrongs, rather a higgledy-piddledy kaleidoscope of life in Kilgarret. There were no plans, no strategies, no working out of the future. No regrets, or if onlys . . . Tony emerged as a man who should never have married anyone. Nothing was spared, but nothing was lurid in the telling. Aisling seemed to regard Tony's impotence as just one more reason why he was unsuited to marriage.

'He should have been a priest like his brother. Yes, I mean it.'

384

'But with his taste for drink, well, it wouldn't have worked.'

'I'm not being anti-clerical, but I think it would,' Aisling said. 'Look at the priest in Waterford that cured him that time, the two-bottles-a-day man, isn't he grand now? Priests are able to look after each other, if one of them goes on the jar the others help him, take over some of his duties, don't lead him into bad ways. They have no families to break up, drunken priests don't. . . . It's drunken married men that are the real pity.'

Elizabeth told of Eileen's phone call.

'I'm not going to do it, I won't meet her and have her lay the whole reasons out in front of me again. I'm not going to do it.'

'But you will ring her, won't you?' Elizabeth hated to see Aisling wince when she made some facial gesture as she was doing now. She was trying to put on a cheerful smile and it hurt her lip.

'Of course I'll ring her. I can't have Mam sitting there waiting in an empty shop – but it's not going to do any good.'

Henry came back home at six o'clock.

'Is she here?' he whispered in the hall.

'Yes, she's having a sleep, I said I'd wake her again at ten o'clock to ring her mother. . . .'

'Is she badly beaten up?' Henry was concerned.

'Just her face, it looks awful but she says it's only bruising and one cut lip which is swollen. It's a dreadful mess.'

'Her face?'

'Yes, that is a mess too, but I meant the whole thing. Everyone seems to think she should have gone along with him, you know, living with him. It's madness, he should have been locked up, for his own good.'

'So why didn't the family have him put away?'

'That family could see nothing wrong with him. I don't know, it's a mystery, but the desperate thing is that she had to run away.'

'In case he'd come after her and be even more violent, do you mean?'

'No, it would cause too much upheaval her going back to her own home, or so she says.'

'Perhaps it will all settle down again, when the first shock is over, maybe she'll go back?'

'She'll never go back to Tony, I know that, the question is can she go back to Kilgarret and not live with him? I think she can, the place isn't half as medieval as she makes out, but she's terribly upset . . . I said she could stay here for as long as she likes, was that all right?'

'Of course it was, you're very good to your friends.'

'She was always very good to me, very very good.'

'You mean having you as an evacuee in the family?'

'Yes, and a lot more.'

Elizabeth spoke to Eileen first.

'The injury isn't too bad at all, it looks very bad but it's definitely not serious and won't last.'

'Thank you very much child, and is there any problem about telephoning . . . ?' Eileen sounded weary.

'No, not at all, I'll hand you over in a moment, she's just having a cup of tea to wake her up, she's slept four and a half hours. But the meeting might be difficult – anyway I'll get her for you.'

Elizabeth and Henry went into the kitchen and closed the door when Aisling went to the telephone. Henry had said to her that she was to talk for as long as she liked. He had been uneasy talking to a girl with such a battered face. He tried to avoid looking at her as he spoke – which made Aisling hang her head even more.

'It will pass, Henry, today and tomorrow will be the worst. It will be gone by New Year's Eve.'

Now she stood speaking to her mother in the softly-lit hallway of the Battersea flat. Neither of them knew where Tony was.

'I haven't asked you to ring so that I can give out to you,' Mam said.

'I know, I know, Mam.'

'And I hear that, bad though it all was, it will go and leave no scar.'

'No, no, so the man said. I told him about the fall I had hitting the chair.'

'I see. I wish I could talk to you.'

'Well I rang you, Mam, when you said.' There was a muffled sound. 'Mam, are you crying, you're not crying, Mam?'

'No, of course not, of course not. I was blowing my nose.'

'Oh good.'

'Will you be able to come back?'

'To work and live with you?'

'No, you know what I mean.'

'Then the answer's no.'

'You could stay with me for a bit.'

'Permanently, or not at all.'

'But nothing's permanent, you know. Is Niamh permanent? Is Donal, is Eamonn? What's permanent?'

'It's longer that you want me for.'

'I'd have you forever, you know that, and so would your Dad. But . . .'

'But . . .'

'But it's not reasonable. You'd have to try to make a go of the other.'

'I have tried.

'Not enough.'

'How much do they want? I could have lost an eye!'

'There's no "they", Aisling . . . it's only you I'm thinking about.'

'There is a "they", Mam, there must be, otherwise why are we speaking this kind of pidgin English?'

'You know why, and that's different.'

'Leave me be, Mam, leave me. I'll ring you and I'll write to you. I'll write to the shop and it'll look like a bill. I'll put it in a brown envelope.'

'Child, don't start making arrangements as if it's going to be for a long time.'

'It is, Mam, it's going to be forever as far as . . . as far as the former situation was concerned.'

'If you'd let me talk to you, to both of you . . . I blame myself, I didn't know how bad things had got.'

'No, Mam, no, I won't sit around while short-term miracle cures are worked from Waterford, and the danger and threat of . . . of falling over another chair hangs over me. I won't do it.'

'I'll come anywhere.'

'I know, but you mustn't.'

'What can I do to help you, then?'

'I'm feeling better here, and calmer – by tomorrow night I'll be in a position to tell you more, or maybe the next day. It's a question of writing to people. I'll have to write to Jimmy Farrelly, for one thing.'

'Who?'

'Jimmy, about arrangements, finance and all – no, don't worry I only want very little, far less than I'm entitled to, but I'll work it out. Elizabeth's husband is a solicitor, he'll help me.'

'*No*, nothing like that, it's far too soon, too final.'

'I keep telling you, the sooner it's done the better. And I'll write to his Ma, she's very nice. Mam, I changed my mind about her a lot over the time, you know.'

'I know.'

'That's where you could really help, by being nice to her. She's kind of easy to distract, if you know what I mean . . . you can veer her away from the main point.'

'Yes.'

'And then do what's best for yourselves, you know . . whatever causes you the least problems.'

'Yes.'

'And that's all, really.'

'*Are you not forgetting anything?*' Eileen's voice was cold.

'No, what?'

'The other half of the bargain and the promise and the agreement.' Aisling said nothing. 'Did you hear me?'

'Yes, I'm trying to forget that part. I hope I will, but it's not going to be easy. Perhaps when my face is better I'll start trying seriously.'

'But. . . .'

'The best thing I could do is to forget all that. If I remember it I'd have to do something about it.'

'Will you be all right there?'

'Yes. Elizabeth's marvellous, Ma, marvellous altogether, and Henry too, they're so welcoming. They've got a grand room for me. I was able to sleep there like a baby. It was great. I really feel much better.'

'I'm glad, child. I'm glad you're with Elizabeth. I feel safe while you're with her.'

'Yes, well, I won't stay long, I'll get myself a place.'

'Not yet, not yet.'

'No, not this week. Will I ring you tomorrow, Mam, or the next night?'

'The next night. I'll ring you, I don't want Elizabeth's phone bill to be enormous.'

'What do you tell Dad you're doing in the shop at this hour?'

'I tell him the truth. I tell him I want to do a bit of ledger work when it's nice and quiet, and I do it too.'

'I wish things were different, Mam.'

'Goodnight, Aisling, God bless you. Go back to bed now. . . .'

Before Aisling spoke to Mam again Simon called; he was horrified to see the injury that Aisling had got when she had fallen over a chair. He was sad, too, to hear the unconnected fact that she had left her husband.

'He was the rather jolly bloke who sang at the wedding, wasn't he?' Simon asked.

'That was the bloke,' Aisling had agreed.

Johnny had called too, with a huge plant-holder for Elizabeth.

'Did the Squire beat you up?' he said sympathetically to Aisling.

'Yes,' said Aisling, 'but we say I fell over a chair.'

'Oh, definitely, that's what we'll say,' said Johnny. 'But I'd like to go and punch his fat stupid mouth in. I could see at the wedding he was a bundle of trouble.'

'Yes, he's a bundle of trouble,' said Aisling.

Elizabeth had been available all the time. 'You can cry, and I'll cry too, if you like,' she had said, 'but I think it hurts your face so try not to. We'll go on living a normal life around you, but any time you want me, tell me and I'll slip away from it.'

Shortly before Mam was to ring Elizabeth said to Aisling in the kitchen, 'I'm awfully afraid Father is about to enlist Henry as a bridge player. I can't bear the game, and Henry is so polite he might just go and learn it, to be courteous.'

'They get on very well, that's great, isn't it?'

'Yes, it surprises me all the time. Father was even saying tonight that he was flattered to think the baby might be called George . . . *Oh God.*'

'No, no, not really, why didn't you tell me? Why didn't you tell me? Isn't that wonderful! Oh, Elizabeth I'm so pleased. Isn't that marvellous? When, when did you find out?'

'Just before Christmas. I was going to tell you when things settled down a bit.'

The phone rang.

'It's a trunk call,' shouted Henry.

Mam told her that Ethel Murray had spent the entire day in the square, and Mam couldn't go to work. Donal was out all day at work and so were Eamonn and Sean. Niamh had gone to Cork with Tim. Ethel Murray had contacted the priest in Waterford, who had come to Kilgarret. Tony hadn't touched a drop of drink for twenty-four hours, he had told his mother, and the priest, and eventually told Mam that he had struck Aisling in drunkenness and he was extremely sorry. Everyone was delighted that he had taken all the blame so firmly upon himself. He acknowledged that the fault was all his. He begged Aisling to come back. He said that things would be different from now on. Mam sounded delighted as she regaled all this news.

'Isn't that great child, you were right all along,' Mam said. 'Now you can come home.'

Aisling waited until her face looked less frightening before she set out to look for a job and a home. It took ten days before the bruising had died down and the scar on her lip had become less vivid. During this time she scoured the Jobs Vacant, and Apartments Vacant advertisements with eager eyes. It seemed to her that most of what she would earn in a Sit. Vac. would have to go on an Apart. Vac. She had never appreciated the advantage of living at home in the square and putting a couple of pounds a week into the post office for Mam, she hadn't thought about the advantages of living in the bungalow bought by the Murrays' money. She couldn't remember any advantages living there. She had a year and a half's wages in her own post office book, all in her own name so there was no trouble filling in the forms which were sent off to the GPO in Dublin to withdraw the money. She was touched to the point of tears by all the offers of help she got. However had she thought that the English were cold? Stefan and Anna had offered her a room and part-time work if she was stuck. They invited her to a meal one evening and served her a funny strong liqueur that made her cough.

'You could become addicted to this stuff, you'll have me as bad as my husband,' she said.

'It is good that you can talk about it like that,' Stefan had said approvingly.

Elizabeth's father had been kind, too, even though Aisling felt there had been an undertone of disapproval. Mr White must see in her an echo of his wife's behaviour. In fact he seemed amazed that there was no man at the root of Aisling's flight. He offered her Elizabeth's old bedroom at a token rent until she got herself settled.

'I'm afraid I would not be much company for you,' he said. 'I'm a very private sort of person you know.'

Simon and Henry said they would ask a barrister friend of theirs to look up the legal situation for her. There would be knotty problems because of there being no divorce in Ireland for one thing, and the interpretation of the law of domicile for another. A wife's domicile was always judged as being in the country where her husband lived. But they were sure they could iron it out so that he would have to pay her maintenance. They seemed to enjoy discussing it as a technical problem as well as doing it on her behalf.

It was Johnny Stone who seemed to understand better than anyone that she really wanted to be finished with the whole business.

'Don't take anything from the Squire. You're a bright strong woman, you can make a living better than the Squire. If you go about fighting and haggling for his money this way and that way you'll never be shut of him. Wipe him out, start again.'

That's what she really wanted to do, but it was only Elizabeth who realised that wiping out Tony seemed to mean wiping out her whole life in Kilgarret as well.

Aisling went for long winter walks in Battersea Park with Elizabeth, talking about the baby; they read baby books to see what shape it was now. They said that they wouldn't make the mistakes with the baby that everyone else had made with them.

'I'll never make him feel awkward and stupid,' Elizabeth said. 'That's what Mother made me feel when I was little. I remember being so afraid of her when I came home from school, and so afraid of her fighting with Father.'

'I wasn't afraid of that.' Aisling remembered. 'No, we weren't made to feel stupid, and she didn't fight with Dad, but Mam was very set in her ways, what was right was right, what was wrong was wrong. She's still like that in a way. It makes things very sure and certain. It makes them too damn rigid. If Mam had been a bit more flexible. . . .'

Elizabeth didn't fully agree. 'I don't want to keep praising her out of some politeness, but she was utterly reliable. If you knew how important that sort of thing is . . . Mother was difficult, and then flighty, and then disappeared. Father was moody and weak and so much the underdog. Even before I came to Kilgarret and learned about prayer and sin I used to pray that they would be like a mother and father in a children's story book, yours were like that.'

'Well young George or young Eileen will be lucky. I'm becoming silly about the baby myself, and I'm falling in love with Henry, too, so you'd better move me out soon.'

Henry had indeed decided to learn bridge. 'It's only one evening a week,' he had pleaded to Elizabeth, 'I can go on the evening that you do the accounts with Johnny and Stefan. They have a lesson first and then a game, and then a discussion and then tea. . . .'

'But it's so awful there, remember, I went to one. Full of awful lonely people staring at the teacher thinking that if they learn this awful points system their lives will be transformed. I only took Father to one because he was lonely and had no social life. You're not lonely and you do have a social life.'

'I'd like to be able to play a hand of bridge with your father from time to time,' he said mutinously.

'If that's all it was, a hand with Father, it would be great. I'd encourage you like anything. But it's not a game for two, it's a game for four. Awful, awful people come to the house and they talk about nothing except the game and they demand teas with dainty sandwiches. . . .'

'Why don't you take it up again, and Aisling could learn, too? It would be super in the winter evenings.'

'Henry, we have each other for the winter evenings. Stop preparing for some long lonely session. We don't need to play bloody bridge.'

'Don't be so doctrinaire, Elizabeth,' Aisling said. 'I think he's right, and I will learn with him. I'm not a total beginner, Henry, I used to play a bit with Mrs Murray and Joannie and John when her children deigned to come home and see her. But they were all so busy talking about other things I don't think I concentrated properly. . . .'

Later, Aisling said, 'I hope you don't mind. but he was so eager, and it would be nice for me to play bridge if I'm going to live on my own in London. Better than shove ha'penny, I think, as a social skill.'

'Aisling, you are ridiculous, of course I don't mind, I'm delighted. I was just afraid Henry would become a fuddy-duddy. You know, like Father.'

'We'll make that bridge class go with a swing, Henry and I. Watch out for lively bridge players!'

Elizabeth laughed.

'It's great to see you laughing again, I thought you never would. Why can't you live on here when you get a job, instead of spending all that money on a flat? It would be marvellous.'

'No, it would ruin things. I'd feel dependent and you'd feel crowded. Where's Manchester Street? Is it on the way to Manchester?'

'No, it's not, it's very central – near Baker Street. You could never afford a flat in Manchester Street, could you?'

'It sounds nice, small and central. They had a minimum let of two years. Is that normal to you, or does it sound fishy?'

'I think people do it, but Aisling, you can't possibly sign a lease for two years. You'll be gone back long before then.'

'How many times do I have to tell everyone? *I'm not going back.*'

She got the flat and the same week she got a job, receptionist to three doctors in Harley Street. She was able to give Henry Mason and Elizabeth's father as references, and she told the doctor who interviewed her absolutely directly that she had recently left her husband in Ireland, and recently signed a lease for two years for a flat in Manchester Street. One act seemed to cancel out the other in terms of suitability.

'Am I to take it that the marriage is irretrievably broken down?' the doctor asked. 'I ask simply to ensure that you might not wish to disappear should a reconciliation take place.'

'No. It is completely over. I am reverting to my maiden name, O'Connor, and whatever else we can be sure of in this life we can be sure that I will not resume my marriage.' Unconsciously her hand went to the small scar on her lip.

The doctor smiled. She was an engaging girl and had perfectly adequate office experience.

'Will you be getting a divorce, Miss O'Connor?'

'There's no divorce in Ireland, doctor,' she said.

'I forgot,' he said. 'What do people do?'

'If they're lucky, the come over here and get themselves a fine job in a doctors' practice,' she said, laughing.

They told her she could start next week.

Johnny said he would help her settle in. She said she could afford fifty pounds out of her savings to make the place look nice. That was plenty, Johnny said. They would hunt for some nice bookcases in second-hand furniture shops, and he knew already where they could get her a pair of armchairs. . . . She spent most of the weekend with Johnny dragging her away from the windows of department stores where she was eyeing modern furniture with envy. She wrinkled up her nose at the kind of things Johnny was pointing out.

'We have old rubbish like that, rooms of it above the shop, and no one would touch it.'

'Have you really?' Johnny was eager.

'Oh yes, Mam would give it to you in order to get the place cleared out.'

'I always meant to go to Ireland and investigate that side of things. Elizabeth didn't want to go in the old days.'

'Didn't want to go?'

'I mean, not on business, she thought it would look a bit too sharp, a bit profiteering.'

'Why didn't you come? You could have come to my wedding.'

'I wasn't asked,' said Johnny.

Aisling thought quickly. 'No, that's right, you weren't – we were worried about numbers. You didn't miss much.'

'Elizabeth enjoyed it.'

'Yes, I enjoyed it too, to be truthful, as a wedding it was fine. It's just the marriage that was so rotten.'

'Yes, well, we won't talk about that any more. Look at this cane rocking chair. Do you think you could clean it up? And put a funny cushion on it here and another there? It would look super beside the window, and you could sit and watch the world of West One go by below.'

'It seems a disgrace to be buying this kind of thing when it's rotting at home.'

'OK. I'll drive you back to Kilgarret in the van and we'll fill up with second-hand furniture and leave. How does that suit you?'

'Oh stop that nonsense and let's buy this ridiculous thing.'

'If the Squire saw you carrying this up the stairs he'd have a fit,' Johnny said when they got it back to her flat and he was puffing behind with a table and an old tea trolley.

'If the Squire saw me now he'd probably find it difficult to remember my name. I gather his little burst on the dry didn't last very long. . . .'

Aisling wrote a long letter to Mam every week for five weeks, pages and pages going over all the reasons why she could not start again, and why it was unfair to expect her to do so just in order to please public opinion. Mam wrote spirited letters back explaining that public opinion was the last thing she was trying to please. If she had been trying to make an impression on Kilgarret, she wrote, she would have forbidden Eamonn to get in with that crowd living out in a wilderness with the Dalys; she would have forced Aisling to study and go to university and she would have had a coat of paint on the house in the square every five years. She did none of these things because they would all have been for show. What she did want was for Aisling to see that she had broken a promise made to another human being, and that the human being was making every effort; and all she had to do was to meet him half-way, or even a quarter of the way.

Then there was the letter saying that Ethel Murray had been taken into hospital suffering from high blood pressure, strain and her nerves.

Then there was the letter saying that Tony had gone back on the drink after three and a half weeks. His letters to Aisling had been returned unopened which was bad enough; but when Jimmy Farrelly called in to him and suggested that they organise some kind of settlement for Aisling that was the last straw.

Then there was the letter saying Ethel Murray was much better and sitting up with some colour in her face again . . . but she couldn't be told about Tony having broken his pledge until she was stronger.

And one day there was a letter in a typed envelope which Aisling opened because she thought it was from the solicitor.

It was from Tony.

Please Ash, please come back. It's only now I realise what it must have been like for you. I'll got to a clinic and get myself cured properly from the drink. I'll go to a hospital too in Dublin or in London and let them examine me all over to see why I can't do the sex act. I'll drive you to and from work every day, and buy a new record player that you once asked for. If you don't come back I will kill myself and for the rest of your days you will know that you could have saved me from doing that.

I love you and I realise I was a terrible husband but all that is over now and when all is said and done you are still my wife. And if you come home soon it will be better than it ever was.

Love, Tony

Dear Tony,
This is the only letter I am ever going to write to you so I urge you to believe what it says. I am never coming back to live with you. Never. I have no further recriminations, you know them all. I have every possible ground for an annulment of our marriage; if you would like this we can start proceedings. I understand there is a priest in the Archbishop's House in Dublin that we write to with the full details. However, at the moment I don't even feel that I want to do that. I have no intention of remarrying so we could leave the annulment side until one or other of us does wish to marry again.

I do not want you to write again making promises that you could or would not keep. I am not a higher person than you, there is no need to humble yourself. I am just as selfish – I left because I couldn't take the unhappiness any more. I am going to give you some advice, just as I would give advice to someone I only knew for a short time. For your own sake cut out drink because I think it's affecting your liver already. You have had pains that I think are the beginning of liver damage. I would try to take more interest in your firm, because very shortly firms like Murray's are going to be hard put to it to fight supermarkets and big chain stores. It would be wise to examine very carefully what you are doing and where you are going.

And lastly: mothers. Both your mother and my mother are worried sick about us. Yours is in hospital thinking that you've given up drink forever, mine is working in our shop thinking every time she looks across the square she will see me getting off the bus, coming back to start everything all over again. I'm writing to both of them, nice cheerful letters, but this is not a cause for hope, they are not to be allowed to think that I will come back, because I will not. I have started a new life. But they are both so good and have given up so much of themselves to think about their children it would be good if you could make it a bit easier for them by not threatening suicide or saying that your life is over. Because it is not. You have plenty of talents and when I remember all the times we used to laugh and go to the pictures and go for drives . . . you had a lot of happiness then. Maybe it will come back.

I am not going to discuss money or settlements or dividing up the contents of the house. I just want to wish you well genuinely, and to tell you that no promises, threats or entreaties will make me change my mind. Our marriage is over as definitely as if the annulment had arrived from Rome.

I wish things had been different for both of us.
Aisling

Bit by bit they realised in Kilgarret that Aisling had left Tony. Mam had been so vague and non-committal that Maureen thought Aisling must have gone to hospital with a miscarriage. As the time passed she suspected that Aisling was having fertility treatment.

Tony had been grumpy when people asked where Aisling was. 'Oh, wouldn't you know, gone off to Dublin and London to her friends,' was all he would say.

Donal, anxious to return the five pounds after the night out, had even called to the bungalow. He had met a wildeyed Tony asking had he any message from Aisling. In the bungalow itself he had seen all the blood-stained towels and cloths which had been thrown into a basket in a corner of the kitchen. 'What on earth happened?' Donal asked, his voice in a screech with fear.

Haltingly and unconvincingly, a tale of a row and provocation and a slight cuff on the ear was told. Donal stood up unsteadily.

'You're a great ignorant lout, Tony,' he said. 'Aisling's much too good for you, I hope she's begun to realise that at last.' Donal went back to Mam and saw by her face that she knew already. 'I won't ask questions, Mam,' Donal had said, 'but if there's anything I can do I will.'

'When we try to get them back together, maybe you'd talk to Aisling about how upset he is,' Mam had suggested.

'Oh, I wouldn't do anything to get them back together,' Donal said surprisingly. 'No, Mam, I've seen this coming for a long time. He behaved like a drunken bum in London, but we all closed our eyes to it.'

Eamonn said, 'The talk in Hanrahan's is that Aisling's run out on Tony – could that be true, Mam?'

'No, there's a bit of trouble but it'll sort itself out,' Mam said. But as the weeks went on Eileen's mouth became a thinner line and the sunny hopes that it was a matter of no consequence began to fade. When people asked about Aisling she shrugged and said, 'You know what young people are like these days, there's no knowing what they'll be up to next.'

The night that Tony came up to the shop and broke the window with a big stone he had carried from Hanrahan's back yard, Eileen was actually sitting in her eyrie. If she had been nearer to the window she would have been badly injured and possibly killed. A crowd gathered and the sergeant took Tony down to the station. Eileen said that it was to be overlooked; Tony was sent home in a squad car to the bungalow which was dark and cold. Eileen begged the sergeant not to tell his mother, it would upset her so much. Mr Meade arranged for a glazier to come first thing in the morning and fit a new window. Father John heard about it and wrote Eileen a letter which was meant to be soothing but in fact turned out to be an attack on Aisling for having deserted her marital duties. But apart from these happenings, life in Kilgarret was able to absorb the scandal of Aisling's flight. And a lot of people wagged their heads comfortably to each other and said that it just went to show that money and good looks don't necessarily bring you happiness.

The spring came to London and Elizabeth became much bigger. She said it was now impossible for anyone to get into the little lift with her and that when she and Henry came back from any outing he had to walk up the stairs. This was not quite true but her protruding stomach was very noticeable. She left the school at Easter and came home tearfully with a huge teddy bear the children had given. She had promised to return and show them the baby in September, she said that if it was a beautiful baby she might pop it up in the art room and they could all paint it. The children loved this idea but she knew it would never happen. Next September there would be a new art teacher who would hate this doting mother returning and looking for the limelight.

In the last weeks she felt she would never have been able to cope without Aisling. She had taught Aisling to cook more adventurously, surprised that she knew only the very basics.

'What would I have had to cook for? At home Mam always had a girl to cook for us, and when I entered married bliss it wasn't long before my husband decided he would prefer to drink his breakfast, dinner and tea rather than eat them.' Aisling shopped, and chopped vegetables and set tables while Elizabeth had rests and put her feet up. She found her legs swelling if she stood around too much. 'You do too much entertaining, what are you having Simon and his yukky sister and brother-in-law for?' She chopped bits of pork expertly and threw them into a casserole as she talked.

Elizabeth sat in the kitchen with her feet on a little beaded footstool that Johnny had found for her. 'You've no idea how much pleasure it gives Henry. He feels somehow that he's their equal if he can have them to dine at his home. . . . What are you *doing?*'

'The recipe says a little cider. . . .'

'But that's half a bottle you've put in.'

'That's a little, isn't it? A lot would be a full bottle.'

The baby was two weeks overdue.

'I feel unreasonably annoyed,' Aisling said as they sat in the flat looking out at the park one July day.

'Funny, I don't mind, I feel sort of dreamy and as if it's borrowed time . . . oh I do hope that there won't be anything wrong with it.'

'You'd have just as much love . . . or more, they say. But let's not start preparing for that sort of thing . . . Mam sent you her love by the way, in today's letter. And I got one from Dad, too.'

'What did he want?'

'That's what I wondered, but in fact it was just a chatty letter: your mother tells me that since we're not going to see you at home in Kilgarret the only way I can keep in touch with you is to write to you. . . . I think he always felt guilty when Mam did all that writing to poor Sean in the army and he didn't.' Aisling looked suddenly at Elizabeth, whose face was contorted in a kind of grimace. 'What it it?'

'That's the second time . . . oh, oh. . . .'

'Right, get your coat, the case is in the hall.'

'Henry, what about . . . ?'

'I'll telephone him from the hospital, come on.'

'Suppose we don't get a taxi . . . ?'

'Put on that smart summer coat. It was bought for great occasions like this. . . .' Aisling ran to the window and leaned out. Four stories below a taxi was passing by. The taxi driver heard the piercing whistle and saw the redhead waving from the window. 'We'll be right down,' she shouted.

He had pulled in outside the main door of the building when they emerged. Taking one look at Elizabeth, he groaned, 'Blimey, just my luck. Another mad dash to the maternity ward, and I thought I was going to have this gorgeous dolly all to myself.' He drove very quickly and Aisling held Elizabeth's hand and said babies were never born in taxis, first babies were always slow in delivering – people always thought that the contractions were faster than they were. 'You must admit,' she said to Elizabeth as they turned in the gate of the hospital, 'you really must admit that I'm very knowledgeable about childbirth for someone who has not even known the delights of sexual intercourse.'

Elizabeth was still laughing when they came to meet her in the corridor.

Henry arrived at the hospital, white-faced. In the waiting room he and Aisling hugged each other.

'They say it will only be a few minutes now. You're in time. You'll see the baby first. I was afraid I would.'

'It wouldn't have mattered.' Henry was stuttering with excitement.

The nurse opened the door.

'Mr Mason . . . ?'

'Yes, yes, is she all right?'

'She's fine, she's perfect, she wants to show you your beautiful daughter. . . .'

'Eileen,' said Henry.

'Eileen,' said Aisling.

Eileen was the most beautiful baby in the world. Anyone could see that. She was also the best-tempered.

'Did all those Brendan Ogs and Patrick Ogs look like this?' Elizabeth asked as she stared with adoration at the sleeping bundle in her arms.

'Nothing at all like this. They had red, bad-tempered Daly faces looking for notice and attention, and pushing their way on in the world at the age of one day. Eileen is gentle and well bred. You can see that. Look at her expression.'

They looked at the perfect little face and Aisling traced her finger lightly over the tiny hands with their little nails.

'It's impossible to think of her ever doing anything remotely bad, isn't it?'

'I suppose they thought that about us too when we were born.'

'Well, we didn't do much bad did we? We had a bit of bad luck along the way and we coped with it. That's all we did.'

'Yes, that's all we did. Are you listening Eileen? That is all your mother and your Aunt Aisling did.'

'I can't understand what you're having her christened for if you don't believe any of it.'

'It's so hard to explain. It doesn't mean that people want to believe all of it, it's just a nice tradition.'

'But it's a real thing, you know, baptism opening the floodgates of grace.'

'I thought you believed Protestant baptisms didn't count,' Elizabeth laughed.

'They do and they don't. They do if you can't have the real thing. After all you were brought up in the Catholic faith by me for five years.'

'I know, and it terrified me to death.'

'So this is only a social affair, is it?'

'Social and ceremony really. Ceremony and tradition – I think that sums it up.'

'Right. What kind of eats will we serve for ceremony and tradition? Roast beef of Olde England?'

'No, you idiot. Elegant hors d'oeuvres, things that can be eaten in one hand while champagne is clenched in the other.'

'Who will be there?'

'Most of the wedding crowd.'

'Will Harry come?'

'Certainly he will, I'm not going to put up with a lot of old-womanish nonsense from Henry and Father. Certainly he'll come. He can stay at Stefan's if that makes everyone feel better. No, he can't, he can stay here like he did the last time. And I won't have Father being brave about it, and noble.'

'You are marvellous Elizabeth . . . I wish there were somebody in Kilgarret who would smooth my path home like you smooth Harry's.'

'I've told you a dozen times . . . there's nobody keeping you away from Kilgarret except yourself.'

'So you say. Now let's think about food. Will we do it ourselves and say we got caterers?'

'Or shall be get caterers and say we did it ourselves?'

Dear Aisling,
I know, I know, I'm the one that didn't write to you. But I didn't
know what to say. Apparently even Eamonn sent you a birthday
card. I didn't know. I thought you were in disgrace. Anyway it turns
out that you write more letters than St Paul. So I'm sorry, I've been
away so much and so involved in other things that people didn't tell
me things. Eamonn knows nothing. Donal's like a lovesick calf,
Maureen spends her whole time giving out to me for even existing
so she's not any help, Mam always thinks of you as her pet and she
won't talk about you at all.
   Anyway, I didn't write to apologise or to whinge and whine, I
wrote because I think Mam looks *awful*. Nobody else will tell you
that in their letters because they don't notice. I only come home
now and then so I've seen an awful change in her. She's got very
thin, and looks kind of sallow. She doesn't eat much and sometimes
sits down suddenly as if she had a pain. I may be exaggerating it, but
I suddenly thought last night if it was me that upped and left and
nobody told me that Mam was looking badly, I'd feel very cross.
   I don't know what to say about the whole other thing, I really
don't. I suppose it's like when a love affair ends only worse because
there's all the fuss and bother. Don't tell Mam I wrote, she'd be very
annoyed, she gets sharp with me if I tell her she's looking badly. And
I'm not saying it to make you feel guilty so that you'll come home. If
things were bad you were quite right to go, and Donal thinks that
too. But you might be the one to persuade her to go to a doctor . . .
she listens to you.
   Imagine Elizabeth having a child so quickly, she must be dis-
gusted. I thought that there were no unplanned babies born in
England these days, she must still have her Kilgarret training rooted
in her.
   Love, Niamh

'Just enough to worry us to death and not enough to tell us what might be
wrong,' fumed Aisling when she read the letter. 'Ten months of silence
and then this. Isn't she really unspeakable?'
   'If it's such a village,' Johnny said, 'why can't you ask someone you
know and trust to go and have a look at her and tell you honestly?'
   'That's harder than you think, rumours start. . . . It's probably nothing,
Niamh sounds as if she just got the idea into her head and wrote it while
she was still thinking about it.' They were sitting in the Manchester Street
flat having little cups of china tea which Johnny said was an elegant thing
to do: he had shown her what kind of cups to serve it in and she had now
quite taken to the notion of sipping tea that smelled of perfume and which
you put no milk in.

'Yes, I'm sure it's all a bit overdramatic.' Johnny got up and stretched. Aisling remembered that Elizabeth had always said that about him. He didn't like to talk about unpleasant things.

'I'm sure you're right,' she said putting away Niamh's letter.

Johnny smiled, stretched again like a cat and sat down. What will we do tonight?' he asked.

'It's my bridge night,' she said.

'Oh tell them you can't go. . . .'

It was a big decision. She telephoned Henry and said she had to go out suddenly. Someone had tuned up out of the blue.

'Why didn't you say you were going out with me?' Johnny asked.

'I don't know,' said Aisling honestly. 'I just didn't.'

Mrs Moriarty wrote to Aisling a long reassuring letter; she had been into the shop, and though Eileen looked a bit wishy-washy the light there was never good at the best of times. She had made an excuse and called to the house in the square too. Eileen had been in fine form, full of chat about young Donal and Anna Barry. Not a complaint out of her. Mrs Moriarty had asked quite specifically how Eileen had been feeling and had discovered that she had been feeling in top form. Mrs Moriarty said that Aisling was a good daughter to be so concerned but she really mustn't worry. Mrs Moriarty said she would tell no one of the enquiry, not even Donal, who had become like a son to them. She ended by saying that she was praying that Aisling's problems and worries would be sorted out satisfactorily, and in the meantime, Aisling should rest assured that the Good Lord always looked after people in His Own Way.

Niamh wrote a short letter and said that Mam said she had been feeling a bit under the weather but she was much better now. She had been to Doctor Murphy and got some good tablets. And she did look a lot better.

I'm writing to tell you all this because it's silly to write and tell you the alarming news without writing back when the news stops being alarming. Thanks for not upsetting everyone about it. Or maybe you were too busy over there to be able to get in touch. I hear you work as a receptionist in some specialist's place. Tim and I will be going to London some time before Christmas for a weekend. Could we have a bit of the floor in your place? We've got sheepskin jackets so we won't need much in the way of bedclothes. I'll let you know nearer the time.

I hear Tony has gone off to England to learn more about the business. Diversification, is what Mrs Murray told Anna Barry's mother. Whatever that means. But of course you probably know all this already. I suppose you know that Donal and Anna are thinking of buying the ring. Or so I hear from other people. I find that the older I grow the less people tell you. Or maybe it's just Kilgarret. Or maybe it's just me. Look after yourself and see you in December for two nights, if that's all right.

Love, Niamh

Johnny took her to the ballet one night and to a little Greek restaurant another night.

'I never knew people had times like this,' said Aisling happily. 'What's it called again?'

'Retsina. It's a special way they have of making wine.'

'Have you been to Greece?'

'Yes, its terrific. I'm going to go again next summer. You should come with me. You'd love it, I thought the Squire would have taken you to the Greek islands. I thought that was the kind of thing squires did.'

'This squire took me to the pubs of Rome twice and that was it. So Greece is still to come.'

'It's a date,' Johnny said lightly.

'Can I pay for the meal tonight, you've spent a lot?'

'No, no, heavens no.'

'What can I do to repay you?'

'Ask me to supper in that tasteful flat that I practically furnished for you.'

'Of course. When?'

'Tomorrow?'

'Tomorrow.'

'Hallo, Elizabeth, is it a bad time?'

'No, no of course not. I'm just putting her into the cot, Conchita has arrived.'

'Oh yes, you're off to the college.'

'I hate leaving her actually, very boring and Mumsy suddenly. I thought wouldn't it be great if I could put her in a sling over my arm?'

'I don't see why not, in the art college they should be nice and Bohemian now. They'd accept it.'

'They might, but it's pouring with rain, she might drown on the way there. How are you?'

'I wanted to ask you something. It's a bit awkward. . . .'

'Go on, what is it?'

'Well, it's a bit childish, but Johnny asked himself to supper in my flat tonight.'

'Yes?'

'And I was wondering .. . I wondered did you mind?'

'Mind what?'

'His coming to the flat.'

'Heavens above, hasn't he been going to the flat since the day you found it, haven't we all? Why should I mind?'

401

'Well, just him and me, in case . . . God, this sounds silly, in case there was any lingering anything, you know?'

'I *see*,' Elizabeth said, emphatically. 'Oh, I *see*. No, Guide's honour, and cross my heart and hope to die, the coast is clear. . . .'

'And I'm not . . . ?'

'Treading on any broken hearts? No, not at all. Go ahead. With all the usual warnings.'

'It's nothing like that, it's just that . . .'

'I know, and you don't have to tell me, but if you do I won't mind.'

'There'll be nothing to tell.'

'Enjoy yourself.'

'I hope you don't mind my taking this extraordinary attitude.' Aisling was almost purple with embarrassment.

'Heaven, no, my dear girl, it's entirely up to you.'

'It's just I feel that by asking you to supper I sort of implied that the other was also . . . on the menu.'

'No no, shall we have another little drink instead?'

'Johnny, you're far too smooth, and like the hero of the film . . . why aren't you flustered like I am?'

'Darling girl, what is there to be flustered about? We were kissing each other very delightedly and I suggested that we might go to your bed and kiss further there, and you said you didn't want to, I said fine, let's have a little drink instead.'

'Yes, that's right, it's not a matter for getting flustered about.'

'You're very pretty flustered.'

'No, I'm not, my red face clashes with my hair. I'm best when I'm pale with anxiety. I once saw my face in a mirror when I was so anxious about something or other that Tony had done – I can't remember now – but I looked quite ravishing.'

They had a companionable drink and Johnny left before midnight.

'It was a lovely meal and a lovely evening.'

'I'm sorry about the other thing.'

'Don't worry about it, I'll suggest it from time to time – or better still, you do if it occurs to you. Otherwise we won't worry about it.'

'Are you going to get the tube back to Earls Court?' she asked.

He had his address book out. 'No, love, I think I'll go and call on a friend, it's early still.' He waved at a taxi and was gone.

She went up to her flat which smelled of food and cursed herself for being so stupid. Why could she not have said yes, she would like to have kissed him in her bedroom. Why could she not have learned about love making from a smashing lover like Johnny Stone?

'Nothing happened,' she told Elizabeth next day on the phone.

'You forgot to cook dinner?' Elizabeth asked.

'No I forgot to go to bed with him,' she said.

'He'll ask you again.'

Ethel Murray had never written a full reply to any of Aisling's long, warm letters. But she did reply when Aisling said she had heard Tony was in England, what possible course could he be doing in 'diversification'?

I had to say something, Aisling, when people asked me where he was, but in fact Father John was able to use his connections and get Tony into this very nice nursing home. They have a special Catholic chaplain there and Mass and confession for all the Catholic patients; others have their own services. I know I've pleaded with you long and often to see him, and I understand in a way some of your reasons for not coming back to Kilgarret, but now that he's in England, over in the same country, could you not go and see him? Make no promises, just go and see him. He's very bad, Aisling. Doctor Murphy here sent him for some medical tests and he definitely has a liver infection. So this is being treated as well as his craving for drink. That wonderful priest in Waterford has been a great support; he told me, and I believe him, that Tony did not mean to hit you that night, that they often do the very reverse of what they would do when sober. It's just their illness. I enclose the address in hope and prayer that you may find it in your heart to visit him. It's not near London, it's more in the North of England. It's near Preston.
Your loving mother-in-law Ethel Mary Murray

Johnny telephone and asked her if he could cook supper for her one night the following week.
'That would be great. What time?'
'Come earlyish, about seven say. That will give you plenty of time to catch a tube back home – if you want to.' It couldn't have been more straightforward, he could hardly have made it more plain.
She wore not only her best dress, but her good slip, and the only panties with lace on them. She even bought a new bra because she thought the one she had was grubby. She put a mouth-freshener and a small talcum powder in her handbag. Then she remembered having made all those preparations for her honeymoon and her heart became like a stone.
Johnny cooked some dish with rice: she couldn't identify what it was, it tasted like sawdust. The wine was bitter, yet she knew this was all in her mind. After dinner they sipped brandy by his fire and he played 'Unchained Melody' over and over on the radiogram. He kissed her several times . . . and said that they would be more comfortable in the other room.
'That would be nice,' she said weakly.
He helped her take off her clothes and kissed her again as she stood in her slip.

'You won't believe this, but I've never done it before.'

'I know, I know.' He was very soothing.

'No, you don't know. I've never done it at all. Not even when we were married. . . . ' She didn't dare look at him. 'That was part of the problem. He didn't, he couldn't . . . so I never. . . .'

Johnny folded her in his arms very tightly and stroked her hair. 'Poor Aisling, stop trembling, it's all right, it's all right.'

'I'm very sorry, I should have told you before . . . at my age it's ridiculous.'

'Poor Aisling.' He stroked her hair and held her to him. He was so nice and kind she could hardly believe it.

'So if you'd prefer us to get dressed and forget it, if it would all be a lot of work for you. . . .'

'Stop burbling, Aisling.' He stroked her hair still, she felt safe and happy in his arms. 'Whatever you like my sweetheart,' he said. 'If you'd like to stay with me, that's wonderful. If you want to go home, of course home you go.'

'I'd like to stay with you,' she said in a small voice.

'Then we'll just take it very easily, very gently,' he said. 'You're so beautiful Aisling, you're so lovely – I'm very glad to be the first.' He held her tight to him and she could feel his heart beating.

She was glad he was the first too.

She lay and looked at him as he slept.

It had been so gentle and natural and as if it had been meant to be like that always. In fact it seemed ridiculous to kiss and stroke someone without fitting exactly together with them like that. It has been so lovely to think she was giving pleasure only by welcoming him toward her.

To think how worried she had always been about this. She must have been very silly and immature. There was nothing awkward. No shame, no awful moment of when you did and when you didn't.

Suppose she had met Johnny years ago, years and years ago when it had all been groping and shoving and awkward and rough? Suppose she had always known this kind of loving, that it was there at the back of her mind? Then surely she would have been less hopeless. How great to have been able to love somebody properly, to have been part of this lovely man. If only it had happened to her long long ago, when she was a young girl.

Like it had happened to Elizabeth, she remembered suddenly. Then she looked at the sleeping Johnny and put that very firmly out of her mind.

XIX

Aisling found that being a doctors' receptionist was not very challenging. She welcomed the patients as they came in, settling them in the elegant waiting room with its highly-polished furniture and copies of *Country Life* and *The Field* on the huge table. She kept three immaculate appointment books, the card indexes and a detailed day by day book in three different-coloured pens, so that any of the doctors could look back and see what had related to him on any given day.

They were very pleased with her and each one of them told her separately that when she had taken two weeks' holiday at Christmas there had been utter chaos. The temporary girl had confused everything, and had not been able to follow Aisling's simple system.

'Maybe I've become an old retainer, a treasure . . . wonderful Old Miss O'Connor,' Aisling smiled.

They hastily assured her that she didn't seem at all old to them.

'They have absolutely no sense of humour, that's what's wrong with them,' Aisling said to Elizabeth and Henry as she was doing one for her impersonations. 'But I suppose if I was raking in all the money they are, I wouldn't have time for a giggle either, I'd be too busy counting it and gloating over it.'

'Do they make a lot?' Henry was interested.

'A fortune,' Aisling said firmly. 'I don't write it up, of course, they have a book-keeper – as well they might. I leave all the information there in the files: who came, what was wrong, what happened, what was prescribed . . . then they work out some enormous fees. They have two sets of books, one for the income tax and one for themselves. I know that because I saw the book-keeper working once. Funny little woman – she looks like someone's granny, not a fiddler.'

'That's very unfair of them,' Henry said. 'It's most unjust – if they make so much anyway why are they unwilling to pay taxes on it?' Henry was getting quite worked up about the doctors now.

'Henry, we're not going to cure the corruption in Harley Street – or any other street. As Aisling said, everyone's doing it. Just because we don't, it doesn't mean the world is like us. Here, take your beautiful daughter from me for a while; I must go and do some work on this year's art course or we'll not earn enough money to pay taxes on.' She smiled and handed Eileen over.

Henry took the baby absently, still looking upset. 'We earn enough money, I've had a rise. We manage. You don't need to do the art course this year.'

'But I *do*, Of course I do. We discussed it. Apart from liking it and wanting to do it, it really does bring in a nice little sum. . . .' She turned to Aisling apologetically. 'Why don't you and your chap Johnny join up, then I'd know I had two pupils anyway?'

Elizabeth had meant it as a joke, but Aisling answered her seriously. 'I was going to do just that, I thought it might educate me a little . . . but Johnny said I would only confuse myself and tie my already garbled brain up into more knots.'

Elizabeth laughed easily. 'Oh yes, I know, pathetic once-weekly culture-seekers . . . middle-class aspirations . . . *Readers' Digest* condensed art lessons. . . .'

Aisling burst out laughing. 'He told you he said all that to me?'

'Aisling, Johnny has been saying that for years. He has always been wrong but he never changes his tune. Still, suit yourself. You're missing the chance of a lifetime, isn't she, Henry.'

'What?' Henry was still annoyed. 'I'm sorry I wasn't listening.'

Elizabeth kissed Henry suddenly. 'If I hadn't had my art course,' she said, 'I'd never have found you, think about that.'

'Yes, but if you keep on having art courses, maybe you'll find another one,' Henry was almost good-humoured.

'That's the only reason I keep holding them, you know that!'

Aisling and Elizabeth pushed the pram through Battersea Park. Eileen was so wrapped up it was hard to see how she could get any benefit from the spring sunshine. Still, Aisling said, it was doing the grown-ups no harm to have a bit of exercise. As usual, they stopped at a bench for a cigarette.

'Undoing the good of the healthy walk,' Aisling would say, lighting up happily.

'Does Johnny not try to get you to give them up?'

'Oh, I smoke very little with him, one after a meal, and I'm forever brushing my teeth. He doesn't go on at me so much now. Anyway, it's only a phase, he'll go back on them.'

'No,' said Elizabeth, 'it's not a phase, everything he does he means. He won't go back on them.'

'It hadn't made any difference, between us, my being with Johnny?' Aisling asked.

'No, no, of course it hasn't. I mean that.'

'Yes, I know you said from the start . . . and I know you don't have regrets or anything. After all, it was you that gave him up.'

'Yes, in a way. . . .'

'Does it bring it all back, you know, the good bits, the start, when you see me with him, when I talk about it all? You see . . . it's the only thing I'm not sure about. . . .'

'About what, about me?'

'Yes, I know how you feel for Henry and Eileen and I know almost every corner of your life as you do mine . . . but I don't know about Johnny. If you cared for him so much once, how had it turned into a sort of joky friendship by the time I came over here?'

'Because that was the only way it could be. . . .'

'That's what I'm getting at. Do you regret it all, and wish that. . . . I don't know, wish that you and he were married and that it was all great?'

Elizabeth blew out a long breath of smoke. 'I'm being as honest as I know how, I'm not playing with words. But for me to wish that is a nonsense. It's like wishing for a square circle, or wishing that grass was blue instead of green. It's a nonsense because it could never have happened.'

There was a silence.

Then, 'After all that time, all that involvement, you still don't feel jealous or envious . . . or think that if you were free . . . ?'

'No. No. I do mean that and I want you to believe it.'

'I don't think I'll ever understand it.' Aisling said as they stood up to move on. 'But then you've been in love twice and I've never been in love at all.'

'Not even with Johnny?'

'No. I'm fascinated with him, but I'm not in love, not the way people are who would do anything for the loved one. I don't put him before me. . . .'

'You will,' Elizabeth said.

Dear Elizabeth,

I did what you asked and it wasn't a nice thing to do. The place is a real posh place for a start, very very pricey and they all speak with marbles in their mouths, the staff that is.

I said I was enquiring about Mr Murray on behalf of an intermediary who wondered whether his wife should come to see him. Oh, they wanted to give no information away. I gave details on the understanding that his family in Ireland were not to be told. I said I had met him at a wedding in London and would like to resume the acquaintance.

He was sitting in the garden, and a male nurse was beside him. He looked terrible. He's both fatter and thinner than on your wedding day, his face seems swollen and yet his neck looks thin and hangs in folds of skin.

He didn't remember me, I said we'd all met at your wedding. He didn't seem to recall that either.

So I said that I live nearby and maybe I might call in once or twice, and he more or less said suit yourself. Then the old biddy who runs the place sort of warmed a bit to me when she saw I really had met him. Anyway, she said he'd never come out of there. She didn't put it like that, Elizabeth, but that's what she said really.

It's worse than where your poor mother was because it pretends to be normal, yet they have these male nurses padding round beside the patients trying to look invisible. It gave me the creeps, and if it's all the same to you I won't go again. He's not a man, he's a shell.

Love to you, Henry and my lovely Eileen,
From Harry

'I asked Harrry to go and look at Tony for you,' Elizabeth said.

Aisling was startled. 'Why?'

'He's too big a part of your life to cut off and forget.'

'Surely you don't want me to try and go . . . after all you know and heared. . . .'

'No, no indeed, but I . . . we should know how he was.'

'And how does Harry say he is?'

'Like a shell.'

'Oh God. Like a shell.'

Johnny said they should go to Greece. He said she should ask for a month.

'Nobody gets a month off in my kind of job. I'm lucky they're going to give me three weeks. I had the two weeks at Christmas, remember, when we went to Cornwall.'

'That was last year's holiday, this is this year's.'

'Oh, but I couldn't take a whole month. . . .'

'September is beautiful in Greece. . . .'

'I'll ask, but I don't know . . . I don't want to annoy them either.'

'Look. I'll go for a month, you come for as long as you can. Right? That way there's no fuss.'

He was right, of course, but somehow it annoyed Aisling. She felt that she wasn't the whole reason for the holiday in Greece. She felt that Johnny would have been going anyway.

Father said that it was a pity Aisling had dropped out of the bridge classes, she had been very quick and would have made a good player. Elizabeth explained that she was going about with Johnny Stone.

'No!' said Father. 'Your chap Johnny Stone?'

'Yes, he used to be my chap, but not now, obviously.'

'Well, well,' Father said, 'I hope he treats her better than he treated you.'

Elizabeth felt a wave of resentment and irritation. She would like to have screamed at him. Yet she knew that to an outsider, it *was* treating a girl shabbily to have an affair with her for seven years and make no suggestion of marriage. And possibly, in many ways, it was shabby.

'Do you tell Aunt Eileen anything about Johnny in your letters?' Elizabeth asked.

'What could I tell her in the name of God?'

'You know, that you're happy, that you're seeing him – I didn't mean saying you were sleeping with him.'

'But Mam would be horrified to know I was seeing a man. I'm a married woman to Mam, still, you know. I couldn't tell her a thing about Johnny. Mam only sees romance as leading to the altar and while Tony's around there would be no way of going to the altar with Johnny, so Mam can't be told.'

Elizabeth felt that whether Tony were around or not there would be no way to the altar with Johnny but said nothing. I might not even be right, she thought to herself suddenly. Perhaps he is thinking of settling down, maybe he's had enough flings. Perhaps he might want to marry Aisling and have a child.

The thought disturbed her, and she was annoyed at herself for being disturbed.

But Aisling had told Donal about the affair. Donal after all had met Johnny at Elizabeth's wedding and had liked him. He also knew vaguely that he was the long-standing lover in Elizabeth's past. Donal was flattered to be told the secret, but his words of encouragement and enthusiasm were tinged with a caution that Aisling didn't like to read. Donal was now engaged to Anna Barry; she would do her B.A. Honours in September and they would marry in October. He would so much like Aisling to be at the wedding – but if she couldn't he'd understand. He was glad she was happy and having a romance with Johnny Stone, but he hoped she wouldn't get hurt. After all it was easy for Johnny to take advantage of her, new in London, fresh from a broken marriage. He hoped she wasn't being foolish. After all, he had used Elizabeth for a long time, and she had to throw him over in the end. He was sure it would all turn out for the best. Mam had been much better and was looking forward to the wedding, because the Barrys would have to organise it. Aisling and Tony's bungalow had been sold to a cousin of Mr Moriarty's who said that it was a marvellous labour-saving house. But Aisling probably knew that already. He hoped that she would make a lot of new friends in London as well as Johnny. Anna sent her love.

Patronising little sod, Aisling thought in a fury. Then she softened. It wasn't his fault, he was still a lovely gentle boy; he had just been steeped through and through with the values of Kilgarret. He was a little provincial; her smashing brother Donal had become a small-minded provincial chemist.

Johnny said they should go to Greece by train and ship. It would take nearly five days to get there and five days back. That was why they needed at least a month. Aisling hadn't asked the doctors yet, in fact she thought that she might send them a telegram from Greece with an imaginary ailment. She wondered would they travel as man and wife ... it hadn't occurred before. That cottage in Cornwall had belonged to friends of Johnny, so there had been no need for deception. Aisling had been lonely last Christmas. It was the anniversary of all her troubles and she was lucky to have found a marvellous man to whisk her off to the wild seas and peace of the countryside. But she had been lonely for earlier Christmasses, the ones in the square.

But a real summer holiday was something different. She could hardly wait for it. Elizabeth had been envious.

'I'm bright green, that's what I am. No, never did I go off to Greece with Johnny, or anyone. . . .'

'But he said he was always travelling. . . .'

'So he was, but without me. I couldn't go, there was Father, or there was Mother, or there was work . . . no wild roamings around Europe like you.'

'Perhaps you should have gone.'

'Perhaps,' Elizabeth cuddled Eileen, who always smiled at exactly the right time, as if on cue. 'Anyway, if I had gone, everything might have been different, and I mightn't have you . . . and that would have been *dreadful*, wouldn't it?'

'Elizabeth, you swore no baby talk!'

'So I did, but I forget. Anyway, I heard you cooing at her yesterday.'

'Ah, that was different. It's coming up to her birthday, everyone's allowed a few coos at a birthday.'

They had a cake with one candle, and they sang to her: Henry, Elizabeth, Johnny and Aisling, Simon and Father. Eileen put both her fat little arms in the air and waved. They were having a slice of cake when the telephone rang.

'It's for you, Aisling. It's your father,' Henry said.

Elizabeth stood up at the same time.

'My God,' said Aisling. 'It must be Mam.'

'It could be anything, don't panic,' said Elizabeth.

Side by side they went into the hall.

'What will we do?' Aisling asked.

'Talk to him, it may be nothing.' Elizabeth took Aisling's other hand as she picked up the receiver.

From the sitting room the birthday party saw them standing together in a shaft of sunlight. Both of them rigid as if waiting for a blow.

'Yes Dad. Of course you were right to ring, Dad. . . .

And when did they tell you?

And did they tell her, does she know?

Oh God. Oh dear God.

And how long do they say ... ?
Oh no, surely not, surely they must say more than that ... ?
And does she have pain Dad ... ?
Of course, Dad. Tomorrow. No, don't worry about that. I'll sort it out at this end. Tomorrow.'

The doctors had been very understanding. Aisling thanked her lucky stars that she hadn't asked them for the month's holiday; that would have marked her down as flighty. They might not even have believed the tale of a dying mother. She spent two hours writing out a very clear set of instructions for whoever would come from the secretarial agency to do her job.

'Choose an auld one like myself, don't get a flighty little thing,' she said to Doctor Steiner.

'How old are you? he said laughing.

'Oh, it's in my file, you know well enough, twenty-eight.'

'You had your mother a long time, compared to some,' he said gently.

'Yes, but I ran away from her ... that's what's hard.'

'Still, you're going back now, when she needs you.'

'Yes, and Elizabeth's coming with me, that's the best bit.'

Henry had been amazed when Elizabeth announced that she wanted to go to Ireland.

'You can't possibly go, what will we do with Eileen?'

'I'll take her with me.'

'You must be mad. Listen, darling, you're just upset by everything. You can't possibly take a year-old baby across the sea to Ireland to look after a dying woman.'

'That's not the way I see it. I want to go.'

'But work and everything. . . .'

'There's no work. the course has only one more lecture. One of the others will give it and tidy up. No college. No, it's all fine. We've booked the plane. . . .'

'You're going to take Eileen on the plane?'

'Henry, you come too if you like, you look as if we're all running away and abandoning you. . . .'

'No, no, of course you must go, I'm sorry, it's all come as a shock. I suppose I didn't realise how much she meant to you ... to both of you. . . . Aisling has been here for a year and more, and, not going back to see her, well, it' a bit sudden, everyone flying off at the drop of a hat.'

'It's not the drop of a hat. Eileen has cancer, everywhere, all over her. They opened her up and closed her immediately. She only has a couple of weeks to live.'

The air hostess said she had never seen such a beautiful baby and Eileen

411

had smiled, and Aisling and Elizabeth smiled wanly too. They were both very tired. Aisling had organised her work and her flat. And her social life.

'So I can't possibly go to Greece.'

'But when it's all over, you'll need a holiday – that's the very time to go to Greece,' Johnny had said.

'No. and anyway I'll have used up more than my holidays by then.'

'Oh, stop talking about holidays as if you were a schoolgirl, this is compassionate leave.'

'I'm sorry, you'll have to go to Greece on your own – unless you'd like to put it off until next year?'

'Well, you know best.'

There was a silence.

'I'm very very sorry, you know. You know how sorry I am.'

'Yes, I know,' Aisling had said. But he wasn't sorry enough to come to Ireland, or even to the airport.

'Never mind,' Elizabeth had said, reading her thoughts. 'He didn't go to my mother's funeral either.'

They hired a car at the airport and drove into Dublin. The city was filled with tourists, Americans and foreigners of every description. They blinked in the sunlight in the crowded streets.

'I don't know what they want to gather here for . . . full of noise and traffic. Why don't they go off down the country?'

'They like souvenirs and shops,' Elizabeth said. 'It's some kind of human weakness. When I used to take those tours to the National Gallery or the Tate, people wanted to slip away from the group and see the shops. I ask you. Often the same kind of shops they had in Dulwich or wherever.'

'Shay Ferguson was going to do up rooms near his awful garage, and let them to tourists. I wonder did he ever do it, now that his playmate Tony was taken from him?'

'It's going to be hard for you going back, you'll be an object of interest to them, won't you?'

'Honestly, Elizabeth, I couldn't give a damn. If they're such gossips and so low as to be more interested in me and my doings than in poor Mam, well let them.'

'I wasn't saying that, I was only saying that you'll have to be prepared for a lot of emotion. Worse than if you had been at home.'

'I know, I know. Thank God you came with me, you're so good.'

'She's nearly as important to me as she is to you.'

'I know, she'll be so pleased,' Aisling suddenly broke down. 'Oh, isn't it ridiculous that she's going to die, she's not old, she's not sixty, it's so unfair. . . .'

'Stop it Aisling, stop it now, you can't see where you're going, you'll kill us all, is that going to help?'

'No, you're right. I'm sorry.'

'We must be full of bravery when we meet her. That's what she'd want, isn't it?'

'Yes, that's what she'd want, to see us back in Kilgarret behaving very well and keeping everyone else's spirits up. That's what we'll have to do.'

They hadn't told anyone what time they would arrive and Dad didn't recognise the hired car as it came past the shop. But they saw him looking up; he looked old and stooped, his hair was straggly and his face was lined.

'Stop it, Aisling, remember why we came,' Elizabeth said, and the trembling in Aisling's lip stopped.

She got out of the car just as Sean was walking wearily towards the house in the square, and Elizabeth got out the other side holding little Eileen, who was fast asleep.

'Dad,' Aisling began. 'Dad.'

Elizabeth stepped in front of her. 'Uncle Sean,' she said, 'we've come back to show Eileen her namesake. We thought she'd like to see the baby and know that her name lives on. . . .'

That was when Sean broke down and right out in the square, where anyone could see, he sobbed like a child. They patted him and they blew their own noses and they offered him a big handkerchief which Elizabeth had seen sticking out of his pocket. Then he firmed up his shoulders and they went into the house.

'Can we have our old room?' Aisling asked.

'You can have what you like,' Dad said.

They went up and left their cases on the same beds that they had occupied as children, one on each side of the white chest of drawers.

They put the baby, fed and changed in her carry-cot, on the floor between them and sat down.

'Did we ever think in the years gone by. . . . 'Aisling said.

'No, but we never thought anything . . . it was all going to be so different, and everyone was going to stay the same age . . . we were just going to catch up with them.'

'And treat them like equals. . . .'

'And stay up as late as them. . . .'

'She's still asleep, Dad says . . . should we . . . ?'

'Yes,' said Elizabeth, 'let's go in now.'

'Take the baby?'

'All right. Brave, remember.'

'I'll remember. There's no point in coming home to weep, she doesn't want that, she wants . . . she wants. . . .'

'That's right. Come on.'

She looked tiny, or they had given her huge pillows. Mam was a big woman but everything, her head, her shoulders and her arms seemed to have been scaled down. The room was darkened, but you could still see the light through the flowery curtains, and you could hear the noises of the town, the bus revving up, children calling across the square, the clip-clop of a horse and cart.

Mam wore a cardigan, a pale blue one that Aisling remembered as one of her better ones. It had become a bed cardigan now. There was a missal, and rosary beads, on the bedside table beside all the glasses of water and bottles and medicines.

Her smile was without tears, her voice matter-of-fact. 'Well, I was right, I was right. Sean told me he had to make a phone call from the shop yesterday. A Sunday. He said it had to do with business. I knew he was ringing you, and he didn't want to tell me in case you didn't come. Let me have a look at you.'

'Oh Mam.'

'Merciful Lord, is that Elizabeth you have with you? The room's so dark. Come here, the pair of you, let me look at you.'

'It's the three of us. I brought her to see you. . . .'

'What do you mean, what are you saying? Who . . . ?'

'I brought Eileen to see her adopted granny . . . you're the only one she has. I thought she should have a look at you. . . . ' Elizabeth put the baby on the bed and little Eileen put up her hands towards the sick woman as if she wanted to be lifted. Elizabeth and Aisling stood motionless. The two frail arms reached out and lifted the baby with effort, and laid it against her breast.

'Wasn't that a beautiful thing to do, to bring her to see me? Oh, Elizabeth, I've always said you had more class than any of my own children. And much more than this rascal, who I love more than all of them put together.'

Then they moved to the bed and kissed her and they sat down beside each other so that she wouldn't have to keep turning her head to look from one to another. And sometimes she took Aisling's hand with her own thin ones, and sometimes she took Elizabeth's. She told them she was not afraid, and she knew that Our Lord was waiting for her. And that she would see Sean, and Violet and everyone, and she would watch down and pray for them all. She said that she worried abut Eamonn and his father, and what would happen when she wasn't there to keep the peace. She said it was a terrible pity that she wouldn't live to see Donal and that nice Anna Barry married, and what a tragedy for them, with all the plans made, and now a bereavement to hang over the wedding festivities. She said that Niamh was as bright as a button and would come to no harm, because she was able to look after herself better than any of them. It came from being the youngest of the family. She didn't worry much about Maureen either. Maureen was a Daly now, and she had settled down; the children were a great delight to her. She would always be a complainer: it was in her nature.

She told them that it was a great grace to be given a warning of your death, not to be killed in an accident or in a war. It meant you had time to take stock and to tell people things you hadn't wanted to tell them before, and set things right. She had even made a little will; not that she had much to leave, but a few personal possessions she wanted people to have. It was a comfortable feeling. She said nothing about Tony or Aisling's departure from Kilgarret. She said there was plenty of time. Doctor Murphy had said she would be well able to talk for a week or two. The trouble was she got tired easily.

She kissed the baby's forehead and let them scoop her up off the bed. Elizabeth held her child in one arm and held out her hand to touch Aunt Eileen's.

'I'll let Aisling come to you on her own . . . we don't have to be like Siamese twins,' she smiled.

Aunt Eileen smiled back. 'But you always were like Siamese twins, that was what was so wonderful about the whole thing, when you came here. Thank God it didn't die, when you grew up. I'm so glad you came back full of strength for me, you two fine girls. It's a great great help. You do know that.'

'Yes, Mam, it's the devil to try and keep cheerful but if it's what you want . . . well, you always get your own way.'

'No, I don't, you bold rossie, I never had my way over you . . . go on now, and let me sleep.'

She was still smiling as they closed the door.

It was very hard indeed to visit Mrs Murray. Aisling rang first to know if she would be welcome.

'Well, of course, you must come, if you want to,' was the reply.

It had been awkward, even when Mrs Murray tried to be warm. Aisling could not apologise for her own behaviour and Mrs Murphy could not forgive it. They were two women bound by a wish to be understood but a failure to understand.

'I believe that the home where Tony is staying is very comfortable.'

'How do you believe that, Aisling, if you haven't seen it?'

'A friend of Elizabeth's saw it.'

'Oh I see. And Elizabeth brought her baby over I hear.'

'Yes, they called her Eileen, Henry's mother was Eileen too.'

'That was nice.'

'How is Joannie?'

'About the same, the same really.'

And in the end when the conversation became almost too heavy to hand backwards and forwards to each other, Aisling said, 'I'm so sorry, about everything, Mrs Murray.'

'Yes. I'm sorry about everything too. Truly sorry.'

'I'll go back to my mother now.'

'And I'm truly sorry about your mother too,' said Mrs Murray. 'It's a very hard life that the Lord gives us here on earth.'

'And I gave it a lot of thought. It's not just a foolish dying woman's fancy, now.'

'No, Mam, I know that.'

'What could be better, you could live here and be mistress of this house, you'd have a girl to do all the work. You'd run the shop with your father, keep the peace between himself and Eamonn.'

'But Mam. . . .'

'There's no cause for you to be over in London working as a doctor's receptionist to people we don't know at all, and living in a poky little flat with second-hand furniture, and learning bridge, and going out to eat in foreign restaurants. That's no life, Aisling, no life at all.'

'But I'd be no good here. . . .'

'You'd be great, and I've come round to thinking that all the things you told me about your marriage mean you should ask for an annulment. You should try. Here you are, a fine young woman, and Tony, the Lord be good to him, hasn't his full senses. . . . The Church has to be understanding in cases like this,'

'I don't know if it's worth it, Mam.'

'You were the one who said it was worth it, and I didn't listen to you. After all, if you can prove that you never consummated your marriage, they'd have to say it wasn't a real marriage.'

'That's right.' Aisling looked down at the floor. Mam knew nothing of Johnny, nothing of any other love and interest in her life. Poor, kind, good Mam was trying to see that fate didn't deal her out of her entitlements. 'I'll be fine, Mam, I've . . . sort of settled into new ways, and I'm very happy. I'll be fine. I'd be better there than here.'

'I'll talk to you again about it, girl, I get tired so easily. Today I feel a puff of wind would blow me away.'

'Don't go away, Mam, please, please.'

'What good are you, Aisling, if you start to cry? Aren't we all worn out with weeping, my shoulders and chest are weary with crying.'

'It's only because we love you.'

'If you loved me, wouldn't you help me by being practical? Your father in here on his knees beside the bed . . . "I'll never live without you, Eileen, you keep us all going, don't die, don't die." Aisling, what kind of help is that for a dying woman? I want to know that he'll be all right, that he'll be able to look after everything, that he'll go on to an old age and let you and Eamonn run the business and give all the others their due out of it. I'd like your father to get the ground floor turned into a place for himself, with a bedroom and all, to save him all those stairs. Could you get Kearneys, the builders, in . . . ?'

Aisling stood up, eyes blazing. 'Right, Mam, would you like them to come this afternoon, or will we wait until the day after the funeral . . . ?'

Eileen laughed and her face looked years younger. 'That's more like it, my girl, that's it. That's the Aisling I used to know.'

'I don't know how I can be so calm with you, Eileen, we English are terrified to talk about death, and I sit with you casually talking about it all the time. . . .'

'I've always told you you're more Irish than we are. . . .'

'That's a great compliment, from you.'

'It's a compliment from anyone . . . will you send Aisling back? She's better off here. She'll become restless in England, it's not her place. . . .'

'She's settling there though, Eileen. I mean it, if you saw her place, she's made a little home out of it, much more than she ever bothered in the bungalow with Tony. . . .'

'Ah, it was all a very sad mistake that, wasn't it?'

'Yes, but she did the only thing she could have done when she left.'

'I don't know. I'm more of your opinion now than I used to be, but I'd like her to come home. Not only for Sean's sake and everything; I think she'll find that this is her place. In the end.'

'Maybe eventually, but I think she feels more free. . . .'

'My love, I know well she has a man in London. I've been that girl's mother for nearly thirty years, I don't have to be told . . .'

'Well, of course, I'm not sure . . . I don't really. . . .'

'Of course you don't, you don't know a thing. Now, tell me one thing – and this is the only thing – I don't want you to tell her that I asked. Is he a good man? Will he be reliable and it's hard to know whether he's a good man or not. In some ways he is very good, very good indeed. . . .'

Aunt Eileen sighed. 'So, it's your own young man is it . . . ah, well, well.'

'You have second sight.'

'When it's over, will you send her back here?'

'I'll encourage her to think seriously about it.'

'You are the only person who tells me the truth – everyone else tells me what they think I want to hear.'

'I wish my daughter had time to get to know you.'

'She'll do fine now with her own mother. God bless you child. I feel very very weary. . . .'

The next day the family were asked to come to the bedside. Father Riordan gave out the rosary and even Sean gave the responses. *Holy Mary, Mother of God . . . Holy Mary, Mother of God . . .* Maureen was crying and had her hands over her face; so was Niamh. Eamonn and Donal stood by the door with their heads bowed. Brendan Daly stood beside them. The woman breathed hoarsely, the sound and the drone of the prayers seemed to go together. Then her breathing got softer. The prayers went on and on.

Holy Mary, Mother of God, Pray for us sinners. . . .

Holy Mary, Mother of God, Pray for us sinners now and in the hour of our death.

'Goodbye, Eileen, thank you, thank you very much,' Elizabeth said softly. It didn't matter if Eileen heard or not. She knew

Peggy insisted on coming in to organise the house for the funeral. 'The mistress liked everything done right, the girl you have now wouldn't know what dishes to have out, and how things should be served.'

The kitchen was soon a hive of activity. Chickens boiling in a huge pot, bacon in another . . . Elizabeth looked on in amazement.

'How many people are they going to invite?' she asked.

'You don't invite people, they come. Surely you must have been at some funerals when you lived here?'

'I don't remember anything like this.' Elizabeth stared as more and more people called with mass cards, and sympathy.

'I'll have to go and help Dad cope with it all,' Aisling said. They had been sitting in their bedroom, as always, with the door open, aware of the activity of the house.

'Good, I'll settle the baby down and I'll come down too. Tell me what to do that would help.'

'Oh you'll know, talk, laugh, keep people's spirits up.'

'*Laugh?*'

'A bit, it's always a great help if it's not too solemn, it's unnatural with people making formal speeches.'

The undertakers took Eileen's coffin out at five o'clock that evening. The family followed slowly, heads down. All around the square people stood respectfully. Men had taken their hats and caps off. People blessed themselves as the coffin passed, carried by the four undertakers. People getting off the bus stopped to let the procession pass by and blessed themselves also. It wound up the hill to the church, where the bell was tolling in the most unsuitable way for a warm summer day.

They stood around the coffin at the back of the church for what seemed like hours and hours. The whole town of Kilgarret filed by one by one and shook their hands.

'She was a great woman.'

'She was a marvellous wife and mother.'

'You'll ll miss her, she was a fine woman.'

'She never had a hard word to say for anyone.'

'And this isn't the funeral you say?' Elizabeth whispered in amazement to Aisling.

'Of course it's not. Tomorrow's the funeral. This is just the bringing to the church.

Cousins and customers came back to sympathise with Sean, tea and sandwiches and whiskey for the men were served. People stayed until eleven o'clock.

The room where Eileen had slept and died had been cleaned and aired and the sign of illness had been taken away.

'Do you think Dad should sleep in that room tonight? What do you think?' Maureen asked Aisling.

Already she was in charge. Maureen was the eldest after all, but you'd never know it.

'Yes, of course he will. Didn't he sleep there all the time Mam was ill, in the little bed? And won't he have to sleep there for the rest of his life? Peggy has all the signs of Mam's illness gone, she's got a grand fresh bed, of course Dad'll sleep there. That's his room.' She went and took Dad by the shoulders and brought him upstairs.

'It's very hard to believe,' he said.

'I know Dad.'

'There's not much point in doing anything you know, in going on. I can't see any reason for doing anything, getting up, going to work. . . .'

Aisling looked at him, bent and much older than his sixty-odd and her not a day dead, and not even buried yet. She'd be thrilled to hear that kind of attitude. What did she work for all those years?'

'You're right child.' He straightened up. 'I'll go to bed now.'

'I'll look in, in ten minutes, to see you are all right. When she came back he lay, a lonely figure, in the big bed, with his pink and grey pyjamas buttoned up to his neck. There were tears on his face and he was looking straight ahead of him.

'She was a very good wife.'

Aisling sat on the bed and patted his hand. 'Weren't the two of you lucky that you had such a marriage for thirty-six years? Not many have that much Dad, try to see it that way.'

'I will, I will, I'll try.'

'What was the worst bit, do you think?' Aisling's eyes were red and sore. They sat in the bedroom with a large glass of whiskey each beside them.

'I think that old woman saying that Eileen used to give her food for the children when they were babies. I can see Eileen doing that so easily, with no fuss.'

'Yes, and poor Jemmy from the shop, I thought that was terrible. He kept wiping his nose with his sleeve and saying the poor mistress won't be back, she won't be back.' They both took a big gulp.

'If you think that's bad, Elizabeth, wait till tomorrow. That'll be terrible altogether.'

Elizabeth dreamed that Johnny came to Kilgarret and told them that Eileen wasn't dead, it had all been a mistake. Aisling dreamed that Mam had said she should marry Johnny and bring him back to Kilgarret to help Dad in the shop. They both woke up tired and slightly hung over. And now the funeral.

More flowers had arrived for the coffin, and this time there was a choir in the church. The family sat in the front right-hand pew. Elizabeth kept studying the little plaque in brass which was screwed on to the back of the seat that she leaned against. *Pray for the Friends and Relations of Rose McCarthy departed this life January 2nd 1925 R.I.P.*

She wondered would they arrange a plaque for Aunt Eileen and in years to come would some holy people kneel there in the church and pray for the friends and relations of Eileen O'Connor? She kept thinking about the plaque; it took her mind off the coffin with all the flowers on it which was only a few yards away at the altar steps.

Aisling had often wondered how people could bear the sadness of seeing a body go down into the ground. Why didn't they say goodbye at the gates of the cemetery and let the undertakers do the rest? But when Mam's body came to the churchyard she knew why. You had to go the whole way, and finish off the life with the person. she watched, drained now of all emotion, while they took the flowers from the coffin and laid them gently on each side of the grave, Then, tenderly and softly, as if Mam might still feel the pain, they lowered the coffin down. Then Dad took the first clay and threw it on top and the people moved away, to Maher's or to Hanrahan's or to the hotel for a drink. And a lot of them came back to the square where, this time, there were plates of cold ham and cold chicken and salad, presided over from the kitchen by Peggy, who never stopped crying all the time. Her tears even fell into the milk jug and she sniffed and said that if the mistress were alive, the Lord have mercy on her, she'd drop stone dead to see such carry-on in her kitchen.

They had been fifteen days away. Eileen had only lived ten days of the two weeks she had been given. Henry came to the airport to meet them. He was overjoyed to see little Eileen and swore that she had got bigger in the time she had been away. Henry was very sympathetic and when Elizabeth and Aisling told him about some of the scenes in Kilgarret his eyes filled with tears.

'Come home and stay with us,' Elizabeth said. 'Don't go home to an empty flat. It would be much better if you came back to us.'

'Yes, do,' said Henry kindly. 'It's too soon, you'll only fret.'

'No, honestly I'd really prefer it. I think I'd like to get myself settled in. Anyway, Johnny will probably be around, I'll let him know I'm back.'

'Oh, Johnny's gone to Greece,' said Henry. 'He told me last Friday, there was a chance of a group going on the Sunday so he went with them. He sends you both his love.'

'She seemed very upset that Johnny had gone to Greece without letting her know,' Henry said later.

'Yes, well, she's upset anyway for a start ... and he's very callous, Johnny, for another thing. Once you realise that it doesn't affect you, but Aisling doesn't realise it yet.'

'When did you realise it abut him?' Henry was diffident in asking, he didn't want to pry.

'Oh, I think I knew from very early on. But I agreed to live with it. Aisling has more spirit than I have. I don't think she'll accept things so easily. . . .'

'So what will happen?'

'The affair will end, and then I promised her mother that I would try to persuade her to go back to Kilgarret.'

'How precise women are,' said Henry.

Later still, when they had put Eileen back into her own cradle, Elizabeth said, 'You're worried about something. What is it?'

'I didn't mean to burden you the moment you came home.'

'I'm well home now. What is it?'

'It's so unfair, that's what it is. I don't mind the act itself, it's the sheer injustice I can't stand.' Henry looked very upset and Elizabeth was alarmed. 'I could see it happening, I told you, I told you, I said, I don't believe a word they say. I was right. I knew they were never going to hire a junior, it was too pat.' It was a complicated and troubled tale of office politics. There had been a vacancy, the most natural thing would have been to hire a young solicitor, somebody just qualified who would come in at the bottom and be trained in the general work of the practice. But that was not what had happened. Instead, a man of Henry's age had been appointed, a man who had come from Scotland specially – and you don't come all the way from Scotland without some promises, some understandings. He and Henry were going to share an office, he and Henry would deal with the conveyancing work – together.

Oh, the senior partner had made fine speeches about the work having grown, the need having doubled. But anyone with half an eye could see what had happened.

Elizabeth listened with her heart heavy. She had heard this kind of story before. Often. From Father.

XX

Johnny had a marvellous sun-tan when he got back from Greece, and his hair had grown longer. Stefan told him he looked like a proper teddy boy, but Elizabeth, who was in the shop, said it suited him.

'Tell me all about it . . . was the sea really as blue as it was on all those postcards you sent?'

'I'm awful, I didn't send any cards at all,' Johnny laughed, sounding not at all repentant. He told her some light-hearted tales of a minibus which had taken them all precariously to Greece and back; of Susie, who had driven it most of the way and who could speak Greek and catch fish with her hands. Susie. Elizabeth thought about the name. *Susie*. She wondered if it would sent little knife-stabs of pain into Aisling the way it used to do to her.

'How did it all go over there?' Johnny jerked his head. 'Was it harrowing?'

'It was terribly sad, really heartbreaking, but harrowing – no. They make much more of a thing of funerals than we do.'

'Oh, Irish wakes and all that.'

'No.' Elizabeth was annoyed.

'Sorry.' Johnny was puzzled. 'I don't seem to please anyone today, I telephoned Aisling to tell her I was back and she was very bad-tempered.'

'Well her mother *has* just died.'

'I know, but I said, would you like it if I come around and cook you some Greek food tonight?'

'And?'

'And she told me what to do with my Greek cooking, frying pan and all. I wonder if they were all listening in Harley Street.'

Elizabeth gave a scream of laughter. 'Did she really? Isn't she marvellous?'

'Bloody hell, marvellous? She's a madwoman.'

'What are you going to do about it?'

'I'll rethink my position.'

Perhaps that's what she should have done all those years ago? But then, thank heavens she hadn't. It would be far too exhausting to cope with Johnny's moods by having equally dramatic moods in return. No, it was just as well she hadn't been as fiery as Aisling.

Aisling refused an offer of dinner in a French restaurant, and a weekend trip to Brighton; she tore up his single rose with its fern and threw it out the window of her flat. After two days he waylaid her on the street going to work.

'Might I ask what all these tantrums are about?'

'Will you let me pass, please?'

'Aisling, I just want to have dinner with you. What's all the melodrama for?'

'Excuse me, you're getting in my way.'

'You went to Greece without me, you mean bum.'

'You wouldn't come with me ... you couldn't. ...'

'And so you went off on your own.'

'Well of course I did. We've no hold on each other, no tie. ...'

'No tie? We've no tie? We're *lovers*, for Christ's sake, surely that's some kind of tie ... ?'

People were beginning to look at them, amused. The handsome, tanned man and the angry redhead shouting at each other before nine o'clock in the morning – it brightened the day for passers-by.

'Aisling, do shut up. You do what you want and I do what I want ... that's always been the way. ...'

'Good, what I want is to go to work, let me pass, let me pass, or I'll get a policeman.'

'Don't be so childish. ...'

'*Officer!*' Aisling called at the top of her voice and a startled young policeman looked around anxiously.

'This man is preventing me going about my lawful business,' said Aisling pompously.

'Oh go to hell!' shouted Johnny.

'I feel so stupid, Elizabeth,' wept Aisling in the kitchen of the Battersea flat. 'I feel such a big hypocritical fool. Mam isn't dead ten days and here I am roaring and bawling over your ex-boyfriend and asking you ways to get him back.'

'Oh, it's easy to get him back,' Elizabeth said.

'What will I do? I'll do anything, anything.'

'It's easy, but it's unfair, you can have him back and play by his rules. He'll come back if you write him a jolly little note saying sorry for the prima donna act, have now recovered scattered wits. Why don't I serve you a delicious meal of Irish stew and Guinness, and you can tell me all about your holiday?'

'And will it all be all right then?' Aisling was drying her tears.

'Well, it depends on what you mean by all right. He may have to leave early, because he's had to see some friend he met in Greece ... that would be the pattern.'

'So I wouldn't have him back at all.'

'Well, if you play your cards right you will, the holiday romance will fade, or she'll want more than he can give ... and then if you're nice and sunny and not making demands he'll come back to you.'

'It's ridiculous, it's intolerable. Who could put up with that sort of behaviour ... ?'

'Well, I did for about seven years. For a quarter of my life, when you come to think of it.'

Simon called on Tuesday night when Henry had gone to a bridge class.

'You've just missed him,' Elizabeth said.

'I know, that's why I came.' Simon looked so relaxed and urbane that Elizabeth decided to play his little game with him.

'Now am I to take this as a frightfully indiscreet revelation of a forbidden passion for me, or are you arranging a surprise birthday party for Henry in the office?'

'Neither my dear, I wouldn't dare to aspire to the first, and as for the second, our stuffy office doesn't go in for birthdays. No, simply a lonely bachelor wonders where he cold possibly find a welcoming cup of coffee and a charming hostess. Thought comes unbidden to brain, wife of colleague, the lovely Elizabeth, and here I am.'

She made him coffee, he admired the sleeping Eileen, he made small talk abut Aisling, about Father, about the Worsky shop. Then he said, 'I'm rather worried about Henry at the office, this is really what I wanted to talk to you about.'

Every antenna was quivering. She did *not* want to hear this conversation, she did not like the way it was being done. 'Oh, anything about the office don't you think you should discuss that with Henry himself?' she spoke lightly but firmly. A lesser man might have got the message and retreated.

But Simon was insistent. 'No, it's not telling tales, and tittle-tattle just for the sake of gossip, I'm worried about his work. He takes too much time and gets himself into knots. . . .'

'Listen, Simon, I'm very serious, I know you mean well and that your motives are utterly honest . . . but you must understand that I cannot, I *will* not be drawn into a discussion about my husband's work in your firm. You and he are old enough friends. You've known each other forever. You can tell him far more easily than me what's wrong.'

'But this is just it – he won't listen to me.'

'Well, I do not want to hear whatever it is and to be put in the position of having to decide whether to pass it on or not. No, it is not fair and you will not do it to me. If I have a problem at work I speak about it to the person involved not to the husbands or wives. So should you.'

'I tell you, I have tried, I do this as a last . . .'

'Or if I find people not able to listen to a conversation I write them a letter . . . it's easier to list things in a letter.'

'Some people are so sensitive and thin-skinned, imagining insult and rebuff, that they would think a letter was a worse way of doing it.'

She smiled thinly. 'Well, I suppose if I were in that position I would do my best to find another way out, one that involved no conniving or disloyalty.'

'You are a magnificent person,' Simon said.

'So you really did come here to seduce me . . . ' she tinkled a laugh she did not feel, the conversation had given her a cold fear in her heart.

'Alas no, I don't dare risk further rejection – but if you had married me, what a pair we would have been! Together we would have conquered the world! Why didn't you marry me?'

'Let me think. Oh I know, you didn't ask me.'

Simon hit his forehead in a theatrical gesture. 'Oh, of course!' he said.

'And also because I love Henry very dearly, so I married him,' she said with a note of warning.

He took the warning, they talked a little more. Should they have a television? Simon was afraid that if he did he would stay in all night and forget to go prowling around in search of adventure. Elizabeth was afraid that she would sit glued to it all the time. He asked her if Aisling had any views on the new Pope, and Elizabeth said that Aisling's only comment had been that if he was a man of seventy-six there was no way he was going to be eager to annul her marriage for her. That was her only interest in popes these days.

'Has she given up her faith?' asked Simon, imitating Aisling's intonation.

'It's hard to know, you never know with Catholics. It seems to be much more part of them than you think. Even when they don't believe, they have something inside them that makes them think they do.'

'That's very deep, too Jesuitical for me. I must leave.' He left graciously, joking, waving flamboyantly as he ran lightly down the big marble stairs . . . never mentioning again the subject he had come to discuss.

Donal and Anna had put off their wedding until the spring. They thought it would be too overshadowed by Mam's funeral. Anna had come to work in the shop.

'What's a graduate doing in the shop?' muttered Aisling when she heard. 'She's got a BA, for heaven's sake, what's she doing rabbiting about with Mam's ledgers and my ledgers?'

'Why don't you go over and sort her out?' Elizabeth laughed.

'I might just do that,' Aisling was undecided.

'Will you go home for Christmas do you think?'

'I don't know, Johnny hasn't said anything, he may have a plan like last year.'

Elizabeth knew he had a plan but it wasn't like last year, it involved Susie. Still, it wasn't up to her, of course, to smooth the path for Aisling but she couldn't bear to see the naked disappointments.

'I'd say they'd love to have you back in Kilgarret, it's going to be a rotten Christmas for your Dad.'

'I know, but I don't want to arrange to go and then Johnny suddenly say that we're meant to be off to Spain or wherever. He's been talking a lot about Spain recently.'

Elizabeth knew that was right, she had heard him booking the holiday in Majorca for himself and Susie. 'You should ask him outright what his plans are, not just wait about, there's no point in everyone being messed around.' Her voice was sharper than usual. Aisling wondered should she talk less about Johnny to Elizabeth, it was impossible to fathom what her real feelings towards him were.

Aisling went home to Kilgarret, where she heard to her great relief that Mrs Murray had gone to spend Christmas in Dublin with Joannie.

'Do you know you car is still there?' Eamonn said to her. 'I'm surprised to see you coming off the bus. I'd have thought you'd have used your car. Had it in Dublin, you know.'

'My *car*?' It seemed like a different world: the cream-coloured Ford Anglia that she had been given by Tony to celebrate her learning how to drive. 'Where on earth is it?'

'It's back up behind the yard. Oh ages ago, the guards told Murray's it had been abandoned at the airport, and eventually someone drove it back down here, and Mr Meade said it should be left up here. Mam said none of us were to drive it. I could have done with it, but that was an absolute. *Aisling's car, the O'Connors will not drive round Kilgarret in the car Tony Murray bought for Aisling.*'

'Do you drink a lot Eamonn?' she asked him suddenly.

'What do you mean?' he was annoyed and bewildered.

'Well you used to, not like Tony but you used to get fairly pissed in Hanrahan's a lot.'

'No, I don't drink so much since you ask. I was getting a desperate beer belly on me, and, well, I'll be thirty this year. I thought I could get into the way of it, and after . . . after . . .'

'After the Tony business?'

'Yes, after that a few of us drew in our horns.'

'Okay, you can have the car.'

'What? You can't just say that, you can't give me your car.'

'I didn't know I even had it until two minutes ago, of course I can. But trade it in, will you, get something else. Everyone will remember it too well. I'll have the papers somewhere, I might even have them with me, I brought out a whole lot of papers to sort out. I'll give them to you tonight.'

'I'll never be able to thank you, God, a car, me.'

'It's all right, Mam would like you to have a car. I have a feeling that she would. It would make you more independent.'

'A car all of my own. I don't believe it.'

Aisling had to look away so that he wouldn't see how moved she was at his pleasure.

It was a strange, lonely Christmas, she felt she had grown away from them even in the few short months since Mam's death. They had all been bound together by the sadness and tension of Mam's funeral. Now it was different.

Donal was in Barrys' most of the time. Anna had been most successful at work. she sat in Mam's cyric at first but had the sense to realise that this upset people.

'My Lord, I thought it was Mrs O'Connor,' they would say. Anna organised her own office, she decided to call Dad Mr O'C. Aisling smiled at that. She had thought Mrs M was more affectionate than 'Mrs Murray' too. It was odd, this whole in-law bit.

'It will be nice for you to have Anna as a sister-in-law,' she said to Niamh.

'Yes. though it didn't work for you and Joannie Murray. You were great friends before you married her brother and then you didn't get on with her at all.'

'I didn't get on with either of them at all,' said Aisling and they giggled.

Dad was low and sunk into himself, it was hard to see what would cheer him up. She took him for a walk on Stephen's Day. They walked out on to the Dublin road, a lot of cars passing them going to the races in Dublin and people they knew tooting their horns. 'I wonder are they thinking that it's two years today since that bold strap ran out of the place and here she is bold as brass back again? But maybe they're not thinking about me at all, I might have to face that fact.' Dad's face looked gloomy; she felt he was only walking to please her, as she was to please him. 'Maybe we'll turn back now will we?'

He turned obediently and they faced down into the town. 'You're not to worry about us, Aisling, you know,' he said out of the blue. 'We'll all be fine, and you have your own life to lead.'

'I do worry.'

'Well, it's not going to do any good. Your mam is gone but she said to me before she went that nobody was to try and drag Aisling back from London, she'd come when she was good and ready.'

Aisling's eyes filled with tears. How well Mam had understood.

'But maybe I should come back, Dad.'

'No, not until you're good and ready. Your home is always here for you, but don't come back to look after us, we'll be fine.'

'I know, Dad.'

'And haven't you contributed to the peace of nations already by giving that lout a car for under his backside so that he can drive himself off out of my sight?'

'Dad, what a way to talk about Eamonn.' They both laughed.

'You know that I'd prefer to say a lot more, but seeing as it's Christmas, and I was at communion, there's no point in cursing and swearing.'

She did a lot of walking during her visit home. It was easier to think, walking. People nodded at her or stopped for a few words. Mainly they told her that her father was managing well enough and that young Anna Barry was being a great support. Nobody mentioned Tony or the Murrays. It was as if her marriage had never taken place.

She walked past the bungalow one day. It had bright new curtains. She wondered idly what had happened to all the furniture and what they had done with the fawn curtains when they put up these orange and white ones. the orange and white ones were nicer. They had done the garden too, the new people, cousins of Mr Moriarty, she remembered. She hoped they would be happy there. There was nothing wrong with the bungalow. She wondered who had wiped up all the blood in the end.

She walked to Maureen's house. Maureen was surprised and not altogether pleased to see her.

'What are you doing, lady of leisure?' she asked.

'I was calling to see you,' said Aisling, feeling she had had this conversation with Maureen a million times. She was tired of it. She remembered Mam saying that Maureen had been born a moaner and would be one for the rest of her days. Aisling turned as if to go.

'Oh, don't be so huffy, come on in and have tea. It's just that nobody knows what to make of you, that's the problem. Nobody knows what you're at.'

That was the problem all right.

Back in London after the holiday she discovered that Johnny had just come back from Majorca; it had only been a week's visit. Susie was not in sight. Elizabeth had been right about that. She found that the tree doctors were so happy to see her back – they realised that nobody could do their work like Miss O'Connor, she had indeed become indispensable – they said they would like to raise her wages and suggest that she have extra holidays if she would agree to stay with them for at least a year. Johnny had been right about that. She heard from Elizabeth that there had been some very awkward and embarrassing scenes at Henry's office because he had not got the expected New Year rise. Henry had become hysterical, and did what nobody ever did: he made his disappointment known in public. He had been highly overexcited and caused great alarm to everyone. Simon had been right about that.

'I don't know what more I can say. I can't tell you more clearly that we have enough, Henry, you and I and Eileen, we have plenty. We have more than almost anyone we know, can you not stop talking about the damn rise? It couldn't matter one fig.'

'Not to you, but to me it does. What have I been doing all those years? Why have I been slaving away and taking work home? Who has been more attentive to their work than I have, what other member of staff can honestly say that he has been as conscientious as I have?'

'But that's not the point. . . .'

'It is the point, that's what this office system is based on. It's not marks for being brilliant. *God dammit*, Elizabeth, it's not an American movie about lawyers, we're not getting a bonus for a rise for dramatic appearances in courts. It's just a system, when the work is done well and reliably, everyone gets a rise. Well, not everyone, but anyone who has done their part. . . .'

'Henry you're upsetting yourself for . . .'

'Of course, I'm upset, I didn't *get* a rise . . . can't you see what that means?'

'It means nothing, you're becoming hysterical. Last year you got one, your work was not out of the ordinary; this year you didn't, your work was not out of the ordinary for you. So what? We don't need their money. We have plenty.'

'You'll *never* understand. . . .'

'Apparently not, but I'd have some hope of understanding if you didn't shout.'

'I'm only upsetting you. I'll go out. . . .'

'Darling love, it's Sunday lunchtime. We're just about to have lunch. Why are you going out?'

'I'm upset, as you said, very upset, there's no point in upsetting you and Eileen.'

'I love you. I love you so much, I wish you wouldn't go out. You're not upsetting me, you're not upsetting Eileen. Look, she's smiling at you . . . why don't you take your coat off? Come back and sit down. . . . ' She had followed him to the door. He pressed the button for the lift. 'Please Henry, stay and have lunch, this is the way we always thought it would be, you know, when neither of us had a proper home, the two of us and a baby and whatever we wanted for lunch, not what somebody else wanted. . . . ' The lift was coming up. 'And I want you, I don't want you wandering down to the embankment and getting your death of cold, that would upset me much more.'

He came back and took her in his arms. 'You have a fool for a husband.'

'No, I don't, I have the man I love.'

'Eileen,' he called and she crawled from the sitting room, 'Eileen, you have a very foolish father, remember this always. But your mother, she's worth a million pounds.' Eileen smiled happily at them both.

'Will we have a joint birthday party? It'll be the last one before we're thirty?' Aisling examined her face as minutely for lines these days as she had done for spots long ago.

'That's a good idea. I'd like that. Any excuse is good enough for me.'

429

'Right, will we have it in your place, it's bigger?'

'No, the neighbours, they're difficult, and the stairs.'

Aisling looked up in surprise from examining her eyes.

'Yes,' Elizabeth said. 'Why do I think I can fool you? It's Henry. He's very unrelaxed these days, I think a party would fuss him.'

'Great, we'll have it here. Let's make a list . . . Old faithfuls, Johnny, Simon, Stefan, Anna, Your Pa?'

'No, for God's sake, let's not ask Father, not to something that's meant to be a bit of fun.'

'Elizabeth, you said he was much better. . . .'

'He is, but he's not jolly . . . let's not. . . .'

'Fine. Johnny's friend Nick is back living with him again.'

'Oh, Nick from the travel agency . . . ?'

'Yes, he's getting a divorce, his marriage went up the spout, he keeps saying . . . he's quite nice. And I can ask the girl in the flat below, Julia. . . .'

'Oh, I remember . . . the one that . . .'

'Yes. the one that Johnny was ogling. Well, if he does he does. I learned that from you. No point in trying to hide all the competition from him.'

'You learned pretty fast.'

'I was much older and sadder than you.'

'You're never really sad, Aisling, that's your magic . . . that's why Johnny likes you so much. I think he probably likes you more than anyone he ever met. I've never said it before because it seemed . . . well, intrusive, and maybe even giving you a false hope. But I've seen him and he listens to everything you say, and throws his head back, laughing. And he is delighted with all your bright ways. . . .'

Aisling looked embarrassed.

'Yes, I know, it does sound a bit flowery, but I know what I'm talking about. With me it was different. I was so young and so silly but I put on this great mask of independence for years. He admired my sort of gut-siness I think. But with you it's different. I think he'll stick with you. . . .'

Aisling stood up and stretched out her arms wide. 'Yippee. That's the best news I've heard yet. I'm never sure of him, not for one moment. Is that the only reason he's so important – just because people can't be sure of him?'

'I don't think it could be. Not unless he were really something to begin with. If he were empty and silly, half the world wouldn't be breaking their hearts over him so regularly.'

'Quite right. Now that you've told me this I think we'll strike Julia off the list. Why let her come up two floors just to break her heart over Johnny Stone when you and I know she's only wasting her time?'

Ethel Murray spent an hour sitting at the dining-room table and reading and rereading the letter she had written to Aisling. She would not send it, the girl would misunderstand it. The solicitor had told her she must make no remarks that could be taken up in any way and she must make no offers or promises. Did the letter give anything away or make any concessions? Who could be sure? She had wanted to write to the girl. But maybe it was wiser not. She was wracked with indecision. Why was there never anyone to advise her?

Eventually she tore it up and sent Aisling a telegram instead.

Regret inform you Tony Murray died peacefully today Requiescat in Pace.
Ethel Murray

'She couldn't go to the funeral. What on earth could she do? Standing up there at a dreadful little ceremony and from a hospital. I know what they're like, Mother died in a hospital. It was terrible, terrible. Just the Murrays there, not speaking to her. Standing in widow's weeds. Of course she couldn't go. It would be ridiculous.'

'All right, don't go on so, I just said that I would have expected her to go. You said yourself that the Irish were very conscious of attending people's funerals. That's all.'

'It's the way you said it, you were criticising her.'

'No I was not, but there are plenty of things I could criticise if I had a mind to. . . .'

'Oh, let's stop, Henry,' Elizabeth said wearily. They seemed to be rowing all the time these days. About nothing. Once she saw Eileen looking at her. She wondered had she looked at Mother and Father like that when she was nearly two? And had they worried about her or each other?

'I don't know what to say to you.' Johnny sat across the room. 'I don't know what I should do, sympathise or not

'They don't have a section on this in an etiquette book.' Aisling said. She looked pale and tired. She had been awake all night. The telegram had been so cold. They were cutting her out, keeping her away, when she never had any quarrel with them. Tears of self-pity had come in the night. What would have been the right course, wait until he fell down from drink or his liver gave out in Kilgarret? Perhaps she should have done so earlier. He could never have lived two and a half years drinking the way he had been when she left him. Perhaps Mam was right, she should have stayed. Now she had enemies, hostile people who sent her bitter telegrams, she had people who didn't know what to say to her. In Kilgarret and even here.

'He was very nice, years ago, Johnny,' she said. 'I'm not going to become all maudlin and start crying for what could have been. But when he was much younger, when he used to come round and take me to the pictures, and talk to Mam and Dad, he was nice then. And we used to laugh at the pictures, and even that first time in Rome . . . he was very, very nice. He wasn't always a bastard. . . .'

'I know,' Johnny was soothing.

'He hadn't a happy life, he never really liked working in the business, he didn't get on with his mother – they rubbed each other up the wrong way. And then I wasn't what he hoped either.'

'Well, he was a bit of a disappointment to you too, chicken, don't forget that.'

'No, I don't ever forget that. It's just, well, it's just such a waste, isn't it? Here he is, dead in Lancashire, and nobody loved him and he never had any real happiness – dead from drink before he's forty.'

'He was a loser, the poor old Squire,' said Johnny, and changed the subject.

At no time in the next months was it ever mentioned that Aisling was now a widow. She was now free to marry again. Aisling thought about it quite a lot. She thought that Johnny must have thought about it too, but it wasn't something you said soon after a husband died. Any husband, even an estranged one. Elizabeth believed that Johnny had never given it a single thought. If Tony Murray were alive or dead, good or bad, present or absent, Johnny Stone would still have paid the same attention to Aisling. Aisling was certainly Johnny's longest-lasting and brightest-burning romance apart from herself. In fact there were even fewer Susies and Julias than there had been. But marriage? Elizabeth was quite sure that this was never in Johnny's plans.

Simon got engaged, out of the blue, to a very pretty Welsh girl called Bethan. They announced it quite unexpectedly at a gathering in the Battersea flat. Aisling and Johnny were there as well. It was going to be a very quiet wedding, they feared. Bethan's parents were chapel, and very funny about drink and things, so the sooner and the quieter, the better.

In three weeks' time actually.

'Bet you she's pregnant,' Aisling whispered to Elizabeth when they were bringing things in from the kitchen.

'Obviously, but how cunning to catch Simon just at the right time of his professional life. He needs to settle down now, she's nicely spoken. It could have been any of a dozen of them. Clever little Bethan.'

'I wonder is Johnny at the right time?' Aisling mused, with a gleam in her eye.

'I don't think it would be wise to find out.' Elizabeth smiled. 'Johnny doesn't marry his pregnant ladies.'

'Some of them didn't give him a chance to decide whether he would or not. . . .'

In ten years that was the first time that the abortion had been mentioned.

*

432

Jimmy Farrelly, the solicitor from Kilgarret, had written to say that the Murrays had instructed a firm of solicitors in Dublin to handle the inheritance of Tony Murray. His letter was firm and to the point. There had been enough shilly-shallying during Tony's lifetime, Aisling must now decide to claim what was rightfully hers. The law said she was entitled to a one-third share in the business. Murray's Provisions and Vintners; the other two shares were owned by Joannie and Mrs Murray. She owned the bungalow completely – it had not been sold, as she had heard, it had been let to the present inhabitants. She might wish to come to some arrangement about being bought out of the firm, but it was only sensible for her own future to come to a realistic decision soon. The longer the whole thing was held in abeyance, the less likely it was she would get her fair share. Mrs Murray and Joannie had instructed their solicitors to disinherit Aisling on the ground of deserting her husband.

'I don't mind what you do, child, your mother would have known more about such things than I do. Do what you think is fair. That woman has had a lot of trouble, if she can be pleased in some fair way try to see it. You'll always have your share of this business, such as it is, after my time.'

'Oh Dad, stop talking about *your time*, and *after your time*,' she cried and hung up the phone.

Maureen said she should take them for everything she could. Otherwise they'd all be laughing stocks, everyone knew that Tony Murray was a drunk and a wife-beater. She had put up with a great deal too much. Take what she could. And to hell with their feelings.

Donal said it was hard to know, but living in a small town he felt sure that things should be worked out in a way that everyone could live peaceably together. It wasn't his affair, but he would urge Aisling to think of the future when she might want to live back in Kilgarret, and it was better not to have too many old sores to reopen.

Eamonn said that if she had to give back the car there'd be a problem because he had done a trade-in, and given fifty pounds of his own money to get a Cortina. But he could work it out.

Niamh wrote and said that since Aisling had asked their views she would be happy to give hers. If the law said the property belonged to the wife, take it. If she felt like making an act of great generosity to the dreadful Murrays, make it with part of the property, but one of these days Aisling would not be a dynamic twenty-nine-year-old, she would be an old bag. She should remember that, and be a rich old bag.

Aisling asked Johnny what he thought she should do.

'What would the Squire have wanted?' he said.
'At what stage?'
'When he was still sane.'
'I have no idea.'
'You must.'
'No, I haven't, in the lovey-dovey bit, of course, he'd have wanted me to have the moon.'
'Then take the moon, chicken,' said Johnny.

Jimmy Farrelly said it was very simple; he explained that Aisling was prepared to go into open court with a description of her life with Tony Murray and her reasons and justification for leaving him. She could produce witnesses from hospitals, and his own letters received almost three years ago. He said she was not unwilling to be generous about the business once any opposition to her right to inherit was withdrawn. Off the record he had told Mrs Murray that she would not press her share for the third of the firm, new deeds of association could be drawn up, dividing it between the two women, Joannie and Ethel Murray.

He said it had been electrifying; once they had heard she was prepared to fight it, all opposition fizzled out. Probate was granted, and Aisling inherited everything that had belonged to Tony Murray. His stocks and shares were transferred to her, the house was sold at a reasonable price to the cousins of the Moriartys, and that money was lodged to her account in England. She abdicated any right to a share in the business of Murray's, and she directed that Tony's car should be given to Mr Meade in the shop.

'God, I never knew anything happen so quickly,' Jimmy Farrelly said to his wife. 'Once those Murrays knew that Aisling O'Connor was prepared to fight it and tell about Tony they went down like a pack of cards. He must have had something desperate to hide, and he was the nicest fellow you could meet, when he was sober.'

It was all completed shortly before Christmas . . . and Aisling pointed out to Johnny that she was now a wealthy widow. 'You shouldn't pass me over, men like you are always on the lookout for wealthy widows.'

'But I haven't passed you over, I've found you and you're mine,' Johnny said, slightly puzzled.

'And when will you make an honest woman of me?' she asked, lightly teasing but in deadly earnest.

He stood up. They had been sitting on the end of her bed. He walked to the window and looked out. There was a light snowfall. 'You mean it, chicken, don't you?'

'Well, don't you want to?' She sat on the bed, her beautiful red hair falling down her back, and her turquoise dressing-gown making her look like a slab of colour against the white bedclothes.

'We *are* together, you *are* an honest woman, you've always been an honest woman.' He looked beseeching.

'I'd like to be your wife.'

'You are in every way, every possible way. This is better than being married.'

'How do we know, we haven't tried being married?'

'You have,' he said.

'To each other,' she said.

'It doesn't mean I don't love you. I do, very, very much, but I don't feel . . . I'm sorry – don't think me very weak. . . .'

'No, not weak.'

'What then?'

'I don't know. Mean, I suppose. Afraid to try it, afraid to take me on.'

'Ah, heavens above, Aisling, that's not true. I've taken you on. I'm besotted with you.'

'Why don't you marry me then?' she was begging. God, why had the script gone so wrong? She would lose him altogether. Elizabeth had warned her. It was too late. She was doing it all wrong.

'I've told you,' he said. 'Let's not change everything. Let's leave it.'

To her horror she began to cry; huge tears fell down on her dressing-gown. She couldn't stop. He didn't come over to comfort her. He looked embarrassed, at the window. 'It wouldn't be hard,' she pleaded. 'Nothing will change, we'll be the same as we are now. I promise. . . .'

'Well, why risk it? Why change something that's going so swimmingly? What's the point if nothing's going to change? People only make big decisions in their life if things are going to be better. . . .'

She couldn't laugh. 'Why could it spoil things? Lots of unlikely people are very happy when they're married. It doesn't have to ruin things.'

'Name me one or two,' he said.

'Elizabeth and Henry, just to pick our closest friends.'

'You must be joking,' said Johnny.

'They are, they are happy, aren't they?'

'Sweetheart, they are tearing each other to bits – if you haven't noticed that you are blind. Now, stop all this women's magazine stuff, clean up your face, get your butt into some nice clothes and I'll take you out for a drink. . . .'

'Go to hell.'

'Why? I'm being agreeable, pleasant and defusing a dangerous situation.'

'I've asked you to marry me, I won't be palmed off with a drink. . . .'

Johnny laughed. 'That's better.'

She managed a watery smile. And somewhere at the back of her head the humiliation of being refused in her proposal of marriage didn't seem so bad when she remembered what he said about Elizabeth's marriage. Maybe he was right. Perhaps marriage did destroy everyone. It could be nature's way of preventing people from enjoying themselves too much while on earth.

'But you have to come!' wailed Elizabeth, 'I really can't stand it on my own. I can't stand it. Not Father complaining and Henry complaining and Eileen grizzling. I'm in poor shape these days. . . .'
   'Oh, all right, I wanted to stay in bed all day. . . .'
   'You can't, it's immoral to stay in bed all of Sunday.'
   'Yes, you're right, what about Simon and Bethan . . . ?'
   'Oh, they won't come, too busy feathering the nest. You should see the place they've bought. Henry spends hours with a slide rule trying to work out how he pays for it on what he earns. . . .'
   'What about Johnny?'
   'Well, you should know more about him than I do, where is he?'
   'No idea. He went off a week ago, no word.'
   'Stefan thinks he's gone to Dover.'
   'Quite possibly.'
   'Tiff?'
   'No, misunderstanding really. I'll tell you later, Why must I get up – I'm nice and warm here in bed?'
   'You *must* get up, because you're my friend, and my husband, father and daughter will drive me mad. I don't need relations around me, I need a friend. . . .'
   Johnny was right, they were tearing each other to pieces. Not the kind of rows she used to have with Tony, much worse. At least the rows with Tony ended fairly smartly with his flinging himself out of the house. Here they disagreed over words. And what the other had said, or the other had meant.
   'Henry thinks that you were made to give back that share in the Murrays' business to them.'
   'I didn't say she was mad, I said that Aisling might have done better to wait a while, that in law the word "gift" is very precisely defined.'
   'I'm sorry, I thought you said, "Tell her she was mad". Those are the words you used.'
   'You totally misunderstood me. . . .'
   Elizabeth's father said nothing. He just ate his food, looking at the plate.
   Elizabeth burst into tears and ran out.

'You are picking on him, you know you are,' Aisling said. The lunch had ended by Elizabeth's apologising and a very grudging acceptance by Henry who wanted the whole subject re-examined. Henry and father had gone into the study, and Aisling and Elizabeth remained at the table picking at the apple tart bit by bit.
   'I know. I can't help it.'

'It's very bad, you usen't to be like that, neither of you. I'm very uneasy when I'm with you now, I used to love it. I used to feel that I was part of something nice and cheery. Not now.'

'Don't be so dramatic. It's just . . . it's just . . . well, a phase, I suppose. I'll tell you what kills me. I work hard, I go out and earn a living, I find a baby sitter, I teach her and train her to look after Eileen. After September there'll be a pre-school group. I set these things up, I entertain all his godawful friends. I make myself pleasant to people like the ludicrous senior partner and Simon's inane wife, Bethan, for him, and I wouldn't mind any of it, I'd do it all and more if there was any joy in him. There's no life or spirit or happiness. It's all as if we were going round with a great black cloud hanging over us.'

'Well, he is, obviously.'

'But how do I get rid of it? I've tried, Lord knows, I've tried. Am I supposed to get under it as well, make both of us wretched? Invite Eileen in too, depress her, let her think the world if full of insurmountable problems . . . ?'

'But you must have known. . . . ?'

'I did not know, and you're a fine one to tell me about what people must know and must not know, you married a violent alcoholic and thought he was the nice boy next door who would be a suitable match.'

'That's true enough.'

'Christ, Aisling, I'm sorry, why am I talking like that to you? You got up and came over here to help me, and I end up upsetting everyone and attacking you.'

'It doesn't matter,' Aisling grinned.

'I'm in such a foul mood. You see they're waiting for the senior partner to retire, and then it will all be fine. Simon and Henry move up to some other level. Both sorts of heads of sections, but separate from each other. That's all in the pipeline. Then this interminable bitching and complaining about people doing him down will end. Honestly, I know I sound as if I hate him, I don't, but there's such a wall of hedgehog spikes around him, I can't even see the Henry I love. It's as if he put on a suit or armour.'

'I know, I think I see.'

'Anyway, the light at the end of the tunnel is there. I'm only dragging you down with me, that's not fair.'

Aisling lit a cigarette. 'I'm fairly down anyway. I wasn't going to tell you but I will now. I asked Johnny to marry me.'

'You what? Oh no!' Elizabeth laughed. 'You're joking?'

'No. I'm not,' She sat silent for a moment.

'What did he say?' asked Elizabeth.

'You tell me.'

'He said, "Why spoil a good thing, we're fine as we are?"'

'That's what he said.'

'Well, you are fine as you are.'

'Except that he's gone, another Susie, I think, to punish me for being so foolish as to propose to him.'

'Oh dear me, Aisling.' Elizabeth's laugh had a slightly hysterical tinge. 'We really are a credit to our mothers and our upbringing, aren't we . . . ? I wonder if Eileen will make such a dog's dinner of her life? I wonder what we should do to stop her.'

'I don't suppose anything will stop her if she's as stupid as we are,' Aisling said, and they were both laughing when Father and Henry came huffily from the study and wondered if they might clear the table and have a hand of bridge.

Simon called once or twice at Manchester Street. Aisling was quite pleased to see him; Johnny had not returned from his dalliance and she was becoming increasingly humiliated at the memory of her own foolishness. She had made several weak and not very serious decisions not to see him again when he did return. Simon always brought a bottle of wine. The third time he called, he gave Aisling a very warm kiss, and she responded.

'Tut, tut,' she laughed. 'I mustn't play the merry widow while your poor wife struggles with a home and a nearly-born baby.'

'This is the time a man needs consolation most. In ancient Greece, young women and widows always thought it an honour to console expectant fathers, who were obviously anxious and uneasy and unable to find release with their wives.'

'I don't believe you,' Aisling said.

'I made it up, but it sounds good.'

Aisling giggled. It had been lonely without Johnny; she did not have the same draw towards visiting the flat in Battersea since Elizabeth's revelations about her problems with Henry. It was nice to be flirted with, and flattered. On his next visit he brought a bottle of sparkling wine and made an elegant pass at her.

'Heavens, I can't be had for false champagne!' Aisling said laughing. 'What do you think I am?' the next thing he brought a bottle of Moët et Chandon, and they drank it very quickly. Then they went to bed.

What does it matter, Aisling said next morning, he loved it, I didn't mind it and nobody's going to tell anyone else so nobody gets hurt.

Stefan told Elizabeth that he was going to retire. From now on he would only come in once a week. He and Anna would get a small place with a garden, they both loved flowers. His eyesight was failing, he no longer could see what he bought or what he sold. He wanted to know whether Elizabeth thought she would like to buy the business.

'But where on earth would I get the money, darling Stefan? We have hardly enough for ourselves. I need everything I earn.'

'I thought, with a rich lawyer for a husband, and a beautiful flat in Battersea, you were on the up and up.'

'No. You couldn't be more wrong. But, anyway, Johnny . . . won't he want . . . ?'

'I talked to Johnny. That's why I am talking to you. I had another idea, a different idea before I talked to Johnny. I thought perhaps Johnny and Aisling might now get married. Aisling has much money since her husband died. I thought that perhaps the three of you together could buy it and give Anna and me money for our last years. That's all we need. But I couldn't abide to have it go to people who would not love it.'

'I know. I know.'

'But Johnny tells me no, on no account must this be mentioned. He does not want to marry . . . I must never never say it to Aisling, it must not be brought up. Yet to me, whether they marry or not, it seems a good idea . . . Anna says so. She says Johnny is wriggling out of one more romance, and that I must talk to you, you and your husband, because Johnny has saved nothing.'

'Stefan, it's impossible. Don't retire yet. Leave it a little while. Things may change. Seriously, Henry is getting a new position in the firm at the end of the month. Next month Father retires from the bank. He may sell Clarence Gardens, we may all buy a different house and go and live together, Father with us. There may be more money. Can you hold on for a couple of months? Things will be better then.'

'I will hold on for a couple of months. I hope things will be better for you, dear Elizabeth, they are not well with you now.'

Bethan had a baby boy. It was born at two a.m. on a Thursday. His father, Simon, was in bed with Aisling at the time, but he was delighted when he heard the next day. Everyone had said it was amazing for a first baby to be born prematurely. Usually they were late.

Henry said that he was not going to consider having a party to celebrate the changes at the firm. It would look as if they were always finding an excuse for eating and drinking.

'I'm sorry,' said Elizabeth, 'When we got married first we both said that it was super to be able to have people round to our own home. It was one of the things we loved.'

Henry's eyes filled with tears. 'I know darling, I'm sorry, I wish I could see he world as easily and lightly as you do, but I can't, I worry abut things. *Somebody* has to worry. . . .'

'I don't see why,' she said.

Johnny called to Aisling's flat and saw Simon's car outside. He bounded up the stairs cheerfully. 'Hey, you two, let me in, I've got a bottle of pliska. It's a plum brandy, you'll love it!' There was no reply, which was funny because there was a light on – he could see it under the door, and he had seen it through the curtain from the street. 'Come on, are you up to no good?' he shouted. Still no reply. Johnny shrugged and went downstairs. Out on the street he looked up at the window and saw that the curtain had moved.

'I don't know why he can't know about me if I can know about him,' Simon said.

'Ah, but he's a serious contender for my favours, you're not,' Aisling laughed, not that her heart had calmed down again after Johnny had run down the stairs.

'You can't think Johnny Stone is a serious contender as a *husband*, can you?' Simon said.

'He has begged me to marry him, sitting on the end of this bed,' she said.

'And what did you say?' Simon laughed with her, not knowing whether to believe her or not.

'I said, why spoil what we have, it's good now, let's not ruin it.'

'Very wise, my dear, how sensible,' said Simon, putting his arm around her again.

'Won't Bethan . . . ?'

'She'll be busy with the baby,' said Simon.

'Things will be much better when I have the new job, there will be clear lines of demarcation in the office, people won't get on top of each other. . . .'

'If it's going to make all that much difference why wasn't it done ages ago?'

'Because the senior partner has always liked to keep the reins firmly in his own hands and leave the rest of us worrying and jockeying for position,' Henry said.

'Do you think there's any fear that your friend Aisling is two-timing me with your husband's colleague, Simon Burke?' Johnny asked Elizabeth at the antique shop.

'I never heard anything so ludicrous,' Elizabeth said.

'You'll never guess what Johnny came up with . . . he thinks you're having it off with Simon,' Elizabeth said on the phone to Aisling at work.

'Oh shit,' said Aisling.

'God, I'll be relieved when all that big fuss at your office is over. Elizabeth and Henry are like cats on a hot tin roof waiting for his new post, whatever it is.'

'What new post?' asked Simon.

'It's very good of you, and I know you mean well, Lord above, to use your own expression, I know you're doing it for the best, Aisling, but you must have got it wrong. . . .'

'I beg you, I beg you, come in today and have lunch with me. Bring Eileen. We'll go anywhere you say. I have to talk to you about it. I can't explain it on the phone. I can't keep saying how I know and what was said, it's too bitty. . . .'

'I've got the drift, and as I say, Simon's wrong.'

'Elizabeth, darling, he explained the whole thing to me, he's *not* wrong, Henry's got it wrong. . . . I'm only warning you for your own sake, I don't want to be one-up or anything. Christ, I didn't want to be told all this stuff in the middle of the night did I?'

'I know, and you are a good friend to pass it on.'

'I'm not a good friend if you don't take me seriously! Look, there's a queue forming here, I have to go. Please, please. One o'clock. Debenham's? Selfridge's? Where . . . ?'

'I can't come. Not today. I'll talk to you tonight.'

'Tonight he'll know.'

'You're exaggerating things, Aisling, you haven't heard every in and every out of all of this, I know, that's all there is to it.'

'I have to go. I'll ring again.'

'I may have to go out to meet Stefan. I'll talk to you tonight.'

Father telephoned Elizabeth – which was highly unusual of him. She wondered whether he'd thought of some little celebration for Henry, but Father never dreamed up little celebrations.

'Do you know if Henry is insistent on south of the river . . . ?' he asked without making any real greeting.

'What on earth do you mean, Father?'

'I'm looking for houses for us, as you know . . . but two likely ones are north of the river and I think he has his heart set on south.'

'Oh, I think you should look at the north of the river ones, too, Father.'

Elizabeth put her head down on her arms and cried. To be nearly thirty and to have all this to cope with. A father who couldn't make up his own mind about what side of the cornflake bowl he should face towards him; a husband who had managed to frighten himself into a panic all of his own making . . . when had things last been easy? When and where? And why would they never be easy again?

'Why you cry, Mama?' said Eileen.

'Mama's tired,' said Elizabeth.

'Mama go to bed,' said Eileen.

'Mama too busy,' she said.

The telephone rang again.

'Hallo, is that my step-daughter or my step-granddaughter?'

441

'Harry.' She had totally forgotten that today was the day he was arriving. Could she be having some kind of nervous trouble, she wondered suddenly? There was a time when she had held down three jobs, looked after Mother, Father and Harry at varying distances. Now she was hardly able to remember what day of the week it was.

'Harry, where are you?'

'I'm at Euston, you couldn't make it. . . .'

'No, couldn't do it, couldn't get a baby sitter. . . .'

'Never mind, darling, I hung around a bit, shall I come over now, or what? Do you want a spot of lunch out?'

She considered lunch with Aisling at a smart Oxford Street store. . . . that would be fun, Harry would like it, Eileen would giggle and get a lot of attention from people at their tables. . . . But no, it was too much effort, she'd never get Eileen ready. Let him come here. . . .

'Lunch here when you arrive,' she said.

'That's my girl, everything all right is it?'

'Why shouldn't it be?'

'You sound a bit fussed.'

'Can I speak to Aisling O'Connor, please?'

'I'm afraid she's gone to lunch, this is the book-keeper here – can I help you?'

'No, go back to the books.'

'I beg your pardon?'

Elizabeth hung up.

'Henry, can I beseech you not to make a scene in the office? Henry I am your oldest friend, you nearly married my sister. Will you listen to me? Listen to me. This must be discussed somewhere else. Every time a voice is raised, more office excitement is generated. We have to walk out of here calmly, do you hear me, *calmly*. As soon as we are out of reach of the office we will take a taxi to wherever we like, wherever you like. . . .'

'But. . . .'

'I'm gong to open this door as soon as I have your promise that you will be quiet. . . .'

'Yes. . . .'

They walked like marionettes out of the office. The eyes of everyone in the office followed them as they walked woodenly to the stairs.

Henry tried to think of somewhere to go but he couldn't remember the names of any bars. Or anywhere at all that he could go.

Simon tried to remember the names of places where they might not want to go again, because he knew they might never be able to. Just before he left he spoke to his secretary. 'Ring our wives, tell mine everything, tell his nothing.'

'Yes, Mr Burke,' she said.

*

Elizabeth never liked the women who worked in the office with Henry; there was a slightly know-all air about them. None more so than Jessica, Simon's secretary.

'Mr Burke said to telephone you, Mrs Mason, to say that he and Mr Mason have just gone out for a drink.'

'No, he didn't say why.'

"Or where. . . ."

'Just to let you know, I suppose, in case you were expecting Mr Mason home earlier or something.'

Aisling and Johnny went to the pictures, and he said he would say goodbye to her at the cinema because he was going to have an early night.

She telephone him an hour later and there was no reply from his flat.

Harry said that he found it a bit more tiring than he expected, the long journey, so he might turn in early. He went to bed sadly. Elizabeth was in poor health. Not like Violet or anything, dear me, no, but she was under a great strain, the poor girl.

He hoped that Henry was going to come home with good news about the job soon. But better leave the two of them to it. She hadn't stopped looking at the clock all evening: she was worried sick.

They were eventually refused any more drink at the pub and they went to have fish and chips. It helped. Or it helped Simon. It didn't really help Henry. He was still crying. At one stage he had taken a menu and listed all the good things he had done in his life. His conscientiousness, his honesty, his fairness, his refusal to do another man down, were all added up and set against the list of wrongs that had been done him.

'Where did I go wrong?' he whimpered. 'I did all the right things, I've done nothing wrong. Honestly, I've thought and thought. It's not my fault if. . .'

Simon was by now losing patience. Glancing at his watch he interrupted. 'Look, Henry, it's getting very late – oughtn't you to be going home? Elizabeth will be . . .'

'Elizabeth!' snapped Henry. 'That was a mistake. She's so busy with her arty job – far too busy to take any notice of my problems, she's no time for . . .'

'Henry, you're being ridiculous. For the last time, there is no conspiracy, Elizabeth is not. . . .'

'No time for Eileen, even. Only ever has time for Aisling. Irish tart. I know. Anything that moves. I know, I heard them talking. Not just Johnny. . . .'

'Go home, Henry. You'll feel much better tomorrow.'

'I'm not going home . . . I know where I'm going,' Henry smiled drunkenly.

'Where? Shouldn't you go home? Will Elizabeth . . . ?'

'To hell with Elizabeth . . . she doesn't understand. She snaps at me for nothing. I don't want to. . . .'

'Well if you're sure you can manage old chap . . . I must be going. . . .'

'I'm much better now Simon, I see what you mean – the whole thing needs to be handled with cunning, not scenes in the office, it's behind the scenes . . . isn't it . . . ?' he laughed foolishly.

'That's it,' said Simon anxiously, 'so you want a taxi. . . .'

'No, you head home .. . Ill go and dally . . . dilly-dally . . . I'll dilly-dally on the way.'

'See you tomorrow, Henry, bright and unemotional.'

'Bright and unemotional,' Henry muttered.

'Oh God, I seem to have a genius for attracting drunks. Henry Mason, I have never seen you drunk in you whole life . . . why tonight and why me . . . ?'

'I want to talk to you. . . .'

'Sure, you can talk to me, don't wake the house though. . . . ' Aisling struggled into her dressing-gown, and let him into the flat.

'You're undressed very early. Do you always go to bed before ten?'

'It's long after ten actually, but let's not worry about that, and I was tired. Right, will you have a coffee?'

'I'll have a drink. I gather you have a lot of drink here. You're a rich woman now, you can have as much drink as you like. . . .'

'I have one bottle of vermouth here, and it would make you as sick as a dog, but if you must, you must.'

'Why don't you have a drinks cabinet like rich people have . . . ?'

'Henry, you're very funny when you're pissed, because I had a husband who died a screaming alcoholic and I don't feel that I should indulge too much myself. . . .'

'That's what I came here for, to indulge. . . .'

'Well, if you want vermouth, but it's very sickly, I warn you.'

'Not vermouth.'

'Thank God, will we both have a cup of coffee then, and will I ring Elizabeth? Does she know you're headed to me?'

'How could she know I was here? You don't tell your wife when you go to see a whore. . .'

Elizabeth rang Bethan. 'I hate disturbing you so late – but is Simon there . . . ?'

Simon shook his head from the chair, his mother and father-in-law were there, and he was doing an imitation of a family man.

'No, sorry Elizabeth, I believe he's out with Henry. They must be out celebrating.'

'That must be it.'

'I hate telling lies and making a fool of her,' Bethan said.

'It's easier for her not to think we all know that he's gone out on a bender,' Simon said.

'But where is he?' Bethan wondered.

'Who knows? It's early still.' It was eleven o'clock. Simon poured another drink for himself quietly, and his in laws drank their cups of tea.

Johnny said that Virginia could certainly stay the night – he agreed that it would be silly for her to look for a taxi at this late hour. He put on the record player in his sitting room, and turned back the bed neatly in the bedroom so that it looked inviting but not too obvious.

Harry had a bad dream and woke up; he looked at the clock. It was only midnight, and he had been asleep for two hours. Oh well, a man of sixty-two must expect to feel a bit weary after the journey down from the North.

'Let's just say that you were very drunk, and why don't you go now, and I'll forget what you said?'

'What did I say?'

'You said I was a whore, but you didn't mean it.'

'I do mean it, I just want to know if I can join the group.'

'Oh, Henry, go home. You can't hold your drink . . . don't be silly.'

'Don't you dare call me silly.'

Aisling looked alarmed. She had a feeling that he was going to hit her, he was so like Tony that last night, yet he wasn't nearly as drunk.

'Come here. . . . ' 'He reached for her. 'Come here. If you do it with everyone else, why not with me . . . ?'

She leapt up and ran around to the other side of the room. 'I'm just asking you once more. I have not led you on, encouraged you in any way, to believe . . . I am your wife's best friend . . . this is idiotic, it is . . . what can I say it is . . . it's grotesque.'

'You like it with everyone else. . . . '

'Please, Henry, get it into your head . . . I have . . . I'm a lover, or whatever, of one person. Johnny Stone . . . nobody else . . . ' she faltered. Damn Simon Burke to the pit of hell, and her own stupidity – it must have been Simon who suggested he come here. . . . 'He's a good friend of yours, of all of us.'

'Oh yes, he is a good friend of yours, all right. I know that.'

'Henry, of course you know that – we all know that. Now, can you stop all this nonsense and go home?'

'A *friend* of yours, and a *friend* of Elizabeth's – how many other *friends* have you two had?'

'Henry, you know quite well that Elizabeth's affair with Johnny was over when she met you. It's you she loves, you great lump. . . . '

'But you met him years ago when you came to London first, you told me.'

She was becoming very tired of him indeed. How could she shift him? 'I met him when he was Elizabeth's boyfriend that time . . . the time of the trouble . . . the business. . . .'

'The business?'

'Henry, go away, you're being very tiresome, go home and talk to Elizabeth about it.'

'The business?'

'You know, Elizabeth told you everything, the time she had the abortion, that was when I met him first. But he. . . .'

'Elizabeth had an abortion . . . ?'

'But you *know* about all that Henry. Elizabeth told you. . . .'

'You are a filthy bitch. You are not fit to. . . . You whore. . . . I do not want you to. . . . Neither . . .'

'Get out. You know all this. Elizabeth said you know about each other's pasts. That's grand, I thought then, and that's grand I still think. But you're determined to pick a fight and you won't with me. I'm an expert in handling drunks.'

He got up and went out without saying a word. He went too quietly. She called down the stairs after him, he said nothing.

Johnny and Virginia were in bed when the phone rang. Johnny leaned over to answer it. It was a public call box.

'You're a murdering bastard,' a drunk's voice said.

'Who is that?' Johnny didn't recognise the voice, but the speaker was obviously drunk or upset or both.

'You let her murder the child. I know all about it now.'

'Who? What are you talking about?'

'Elizabeth,' the voice said and hung up.

Harry woke again. He wondered whether to see the doctor and ask for some sleeping pills. But no, this time there was a reason, there were voices outside his door.

'I don't care about the job, I don't care about it, if you were bloody sacked I wouldn't care. Why didn't you ring me . . . ?'

'You are a murderer . . . you murdered a child, I know about it.'

'What on earth are you talking about? Henry, come in and shut up. You'll wake Harry. . . .'

'You and he murdered a child. I know, everyone knows . . . you did, and you didn't tell me. I would never have married you if I had known, never.'

'Henry, keep your voice down. You'll wake Eileen. There, she's awake already. Now, come in from that door, stop swaying there, and tell me where you heard this ridiculous story. . . .'

446

'From your friend and helpmate, the Irish whore. . . .'

'I don't believe you are speaking like this. You've lost your reason.'

'Aisling the tart. I've had her, Johnny's had her, Simon's had her. I suppose if Harry wasn't so old he'd have her. By God, she's made up for her unconsummated marriage, hasn't she . . . ?'

'You were with Aisling tonight?'

'I was with precious Aisling.'

'You and Aisling . . . I don't believe you. . . .'

'Oh, I'm sure you'll discuss it in the morning, you talk about everything . . . I've heard you.'

'Aisling did not sleep with you. That I know. . . .'

'Why not? She sees fit to sleep with Johnny Bloody Stone. I rang him and told him.'

'You told him what?'

'I told him I knew he had murdered a child, with you.'

Harry tried to decide what to do. In a pub if people's voices got to this stage, it was time to step in. Interference was poorly regarded, however, between married couples. But he couldn't believe that this was happening. Henry must be mad. Murdering a child? With Johnny? Perhaps he should try not to listen. Impossible. He had to know what was happening. He had to be ready in case Elizabeth needed help. Perhaps he should call out. If he said, 'Hey up, what's all this?' maybe Henry would straighten his tie, and calm down, and come in or go away. Anything would be better than this business at the door. He could bear it no longer. He opened his bedroom door, just a crack, and then a little further.

The door out on to the landing was wide open, the light streaming in in a harsh triangle, Henry's face was working uncontrollably. 'You whore . . . you murderess . . . you're not fit to be a mother . . . I'm taking Eileen . . . now . . . you bitch. . . .'

'You're mad. . . . No, get out, leave me alone, God damn you. . . .'

'I'm taking my daughter away from you, you murdering . . . get out of my way. . . .' Harry had to stop them. He didn't care how embarrassed they were all going to be in the morning. He didn't mind admitting that he knew of their row, he pulled the door open. 'Hey, now. . . .' he began but the words were barely formed when he heard the muffled shout.

Aisling told herself that Henry *must* have known about . . . everything. Of course Elizabeth had told him about the whole dreadful business. She must have done. You do tell people things in intimate moments. She had even told Tony abut her early necking sessions with Ned at the cinema. He was just plastered, and half-crazed from not getting the job. That was all. He'd get over it.

447

Johnny told himself that there were lots of people in London called Elizabeth. He and Elizabeth had murdered no child. Certainly not.

Then there was silence. Nobody seemed to have heard. Elizabeth had closed the front door and bolted it. She remained frozen for a moment. Then she walked unseeing past Harry.

Harry stopped breathless. But almost immediately he heard Elizabeth's voice soothing little Eileen.

'It's all right, shush, shush. Don't worry. Daddy will be home soon. Everything will be fine.'

'Oh my God,' Harry said aloud.

The ambulance men left quietly. There was no need to rush to the hospital with sirens blazing. Henry Mason was dead. It was the porter who had gone up to the top floor to tell young Mrs Mason the news. She came to the door in her dressing-gown looking confused and carrying her little girl in her arms.

'What is it? You can't mean it . . . not possible . . . how did it happen? How could it have happened . . . ? He wasn't home. Did he fall? How could he have fallen? Can I see him? Henry? Henry? Henry?'

And there were cups of tea and the police as well. No, Henry hadn't come home, he was out having a few drinks. One of the secretaries had rung to say he would be late. He must have had too many. He wasn't used to drinking. Oh God.

'Elizabeth?'

'Aisling?'

'Don't move, stay where you are, I'll sit down beside you. . . .'

Aisling sat down on the side of the bed. She took Elizabeth's thin cold hand in hers. Elizabeth said nothing. Aisling rubbed the hand a little, as if to bring back the circulation. The clock was ticking very loudly. Outside there was a faint noise of traffic, and almost as faint was the hum of conversation from the sitting room. Harry was talking to the callers in a low voice, discouraging anyone from trying to see Elizabeth, noting all the offers of help. Eileen had gone to stay with friends who had a small child. Elizabeth's father had been and gone. Elizabeth had refused an injection to sedate her. She said she would be all right.

Elizabeth's eyes were not still, not for a moment; they darted all around, into Aisling's face and out of it. . . . Her head never moved, it lay on the pillow as if it was too heavy to raise.

'Can you walk? I think we should go out,' Aisling said.

'Yes, yes, that's what we'll do.' Elizabeth pulled her hand away and pushed back the covers. She was half-dressed. She moved to the chair and pulled on a blue polo necked sweater and a plaid skirt. She found a jacket in the wardrobe. She looked frail and ill.

'Are you sure?'

'Yes, you're right, it's just what I want to do. . . .' She slipped her feet into shoes and looked at Aisling trustingly like a child.

Aisling murmured to Harry, and in a moment they were out on the landing. Neither of them looked at the floor or at each other. They got into the lift and stood almost rigid as it went down. They walked, heads down and hands in pockets, out of the door and across the road. Their steps seemed urgent and anxious until they got into the park, then unconsciously they seemed to change their stride, into the stroll of park walkers, the slow gait of Londoners enjoying the grass and the flower beds instead of the traffic and the noise.

'What am I going to do?' Elizabeth asked eventually. There was a long silence, but Aisling had slipped her arm through Elizabeth's and they walked without looking at each other. 'I mean, what's going to happen?' her voice was very thin.

Aisling spoke slowly. 'You'll make a life for Eileen. You'll remember all the good bits and put the bad bits away. I think that's what people do.'

'Yes.'

They walked on, arms linked.

'It didn't turn out all that well for us . . . what was wrong with us . . . ?' Aisling said.

'What do you mean?'

'Well, here we are, Elizabeth . . . widows, both of us . . . only your Eileen to show for it all . . . for all the hope and the . . . dreams . . . you know.'

Elizabeth's voice had become stronger. 'Your Mam wouldn't like us talking like that . . . going over the past. . . .'

'No, she wouldn't.' Aisling was quiet for a moment. Then she spoke again. 'Mam always knew what to say . . . she used to say what I thought was the wrong thing . . . but it turned out to be the right one . . . I don't know how she found the right words . . . it was a kind of skill. . . .'

Elizabeth said, 'No, I don't think she even tried, I think the words were just there.'

'Yes,' said Aisling.

They sat down on a seat where they often stopped when they had taken Eileen out in a pram . . . and even before that, when Aisling had come to London first . . . in those days when she had just run away.

'It must have been very quick for him,' Aisling said.

'The policeman said that it would have been over in a few seconds.' Elizabeth put her face in her hands.

'Stop, stop.'

'No, I'm not crying, I'm just thinking about the few seconds. They must have seemed very long . . . it . . .'

'No, no, think of it like a dream, you know the frightening bit . . . then it's over. . . .'

'But in a dream you wake up.'

'Well, it was over for Henry . . . he felt no more then.'

Elizabeth stood up. 'Yes, I know.'

'It took Tony much longer to die,' Aisling said.

Elizabeth looked at her. 'I suppose it did,' she said.

'And look at all you did for Henry . . . look at it and remember all the good. You gave him a home, he always wanted one . . . you gave him confidence . . . all those things . . . he would never have got them from anyone else. . . .'

Aisling looked at the ground as she spoke. Elizabeth looked across the park.

'You made Tony happy too . . . ' she said.

'No, I didn't nobody could have, and I certainly didn't. I made him worse.'

'Don't look at it that way. . . . ' Elizabeth's voice was clear now, and strong as ever. 'You were what he wanted and he got you. . . . That's the only thing that gives us hope out of all this. . . If people got what they wanted. . . .'

'What can I do for you, Elizabeth? I'll do anything, anything, you know that. . . .'

'No, you rescued me . . . you did the rescuing years ago . . . if I hadn't a friend like you all my life what would I have had . . . Maureen, Niamh . . . Joannie Murray . . . some friends . . . they would have been, for all that happened. . . .'

'And we never fought . . . in all those years we never had a real row. . . .'

'I know, sometimes I think when you left Kilgarret first, when you came back here, I used to get annoyed because you were so distant . . . I didn't know. . . .'

'And I didn't know . . . when you and Tony were married at first and you sent these brittle letters . . . I was annoyed. But I didn't know.'

'What can I do for you Elizabeth, please . . . ' she asked again.

'Tell me what happens next. . . .'

'There'll be the inquest . . . and the coroner will say. . . .'

'Yes?'

'He'll say how he heard that Henry became upset and . . . and . . . went on a sort of drunken . . . well . . . batter . . . and then came home and then about the accident . . . and how he fell. . . .'

'And what will the coroner say?'

'I don't know. . . . I suppose he'll pass a vote of sympathy . . . isn't that what they do when you read about inquests? They say that they would like to extend their sympathy to the relatives and friends of the deceased. . . .'

'Like a sort of obituary?'

'I suppose so . . . something like that.'

'Oh.'

'And then it will all be over . . . and you'll have to start to . . .'

'Yes. . . .'

'Oh God, Elizabeth, I'm so sorry, I'm so very sorry. . . .'

'I know . . . I know . . . I'm sorry, I'm very sorry too. . . .'

The coroner's inquest was brief and formal

Aisling had read about inquests in the local papers back in Kilgarret. Mam had said that it was only a scourge and a torture to poor families to have the press reporters there, writing down every word and making it a thousand times worse . . . whatever awful sadness the people had already.

She looked around the small dusty courtroom. Two men were writing in notebooks, they might be press. They didn't look much like journalists. But nobody looked much like anything today. Everyone looked very odd as if they were playing a part in some play they hadn't rehearsed properly. That's what she felt anyway, and she felt sure Elizabeth must be thinking the same thing. It was odd, but for once it was hard to know what Elizabeth was thinking. Her face was like a mask.

Elizabeth's face was very still, but her thoughts were darting all over the place, she felt that she must run after them as if she were collecting marbles that had spilled from a box. She remembered there had been an inquest in the hospital where Mother had died. Yes, dreadful fuss and anxiety all over the place, doctors and nurses very upset. Nobody doubted that she had managed to get the glass to cut her wrists through great cunning that nobody could have foreseen. Nobody doubted that there could have been no blame attached to any member of staff. But they had hated the inquest. She remembered them telling her that. What good did it do they had asked, upset everybody and didn't bring back the poor old soul who had done herself in. She wondered had she ever told Aisling about that? Aisling looked very strong sitting there opposite her, her hands for once still on her lap.

What an extraordinary place for them both to be. A coroner's court. Harry Elton thought that the room was so small and shabby it must be only a temporary court. This wasn't like courts you saw in films, or the Old Bailey. This was just a dusty room. But of course it wasn't a trial, he told himself for the twentieth time, so there was no need to have a real court. It was only a tidying up of the bits and bobs of papers, that's all it was. If it had been necessary there would have been a real court. But not unless there had been a crime.

Simon Burke looked around, he could tell the titles of familiar law books just by their bindings. The place was a bit dusty. If he had been in charge of the place he'd have seen that it got a good going over each week. It never did any harm to give the Law some trappings, not make it seem like a storage depot in the back of some second-hand bookshop. He wondered what the others made of it. Aisling and Elizabeth so still, so pale both of them. He remembered the first time he had seen Elizabeth, he and Henry had seen her when they went to register for the little art course. Oh God. Henry. Poor bloody Henry.

Johnny thought he saw Aisling smile at him and he smiled back. But she hadn't been looking at him, she had only turned her head his way, her eyes didn't meet his. Lord, Lord, what a business all this was. It was unbelievable that they should all be caught up in an inquest. Henry's inquest no less. It was bloody ridiculous. Henry should be alive and well and going his own way, hitting the sauce a bit less. Incredible to look at both those girls . . . well women . . . Aisling and Elizabeth, and to think that both their husbands had more or less died from drink. The odds against that must be overwhelming. Poor old Henry, Lord this was a bloody awful business. Sooner it was all shut of the better.

Elizabeth thought, Aisling said it would all be very quick and formal. Please may it all be quick and formal. I can't stand sitting here. I can't stand it one minute more.

Aisling thought, it they don't start soon I'm going to crack. This is desperate, sitting here while he fusses about moving papers from one side of his bloody desk to the other. God almighty, get on with it can't you, it's meant to be a formality, a formal taking of evidence. Can't you get on with it you stupid old bumbler? Stop making yourself into a little tin god.

The coroner was now ready, everything on his desk was to his satisfaction. He was ready to hear the evidence. . . .

Evidence was given by the police, by the ambulance men, by the porter. Everyone spoke in flat, measured tones about what had happened, and what times it had happened. Only Harry Elton and Simon Burke were called to speak. Harry Elton, step-father of Mrs Mason . . . guest in the house. Heard absolutely nothing until the huge knocking on the door and the porter and the terrible news. Poor Elizabeth shattered. Dreadful, tragedy . . . happy family life. . . .

Simon had left him in an intoxicated condition at the corner of great Portland Street and Mortimer Street. No, he hadn't said where he was going to go. Simon Burke had advised him to get a taxi home, and he had said he would do that. No, Simon Burke had no idea where he might have gone after that.

Nobody called Aisling O'Connor, friend of Mrs Mason, to give any evidence.

Nobody asked Johnny Stone, friend and colleague of Mrs Mason, to describe the telephone call. Because no mention of a visit or a telephone call had ever been made.

So they sat in the coroner's court and said nothing until the verdict of misadventure and accidental death by falling down an internal staircase, after excessive alcoholic consumption, was recorded by the coroner.

And then they all came out into the sun.

The Lilac Bus

Nancy

Nancy was early, but then she always was, and she didn't like being seen there too soon. It looked as if you had nothing else to do if you arrived far too early for the bus home. The others all arrived rushing and panting and afraid they'd miss it, because if they missed it then they really did. Tom turned the key in the ignition at 6.45 and swung the Lilac Bus out into the road. That way he had them all home before ten o'clock and that was his promise. No point in going home for a weekend if you aren't in the pub by ten, that was his philosophy. It wasn't Nancy's but she was compulsively early for everything. It was just her way. She went into a shop that sold magazines and cards. She knew a lot of the cards by heart from studying them on a Friday. There was the big one with tears falling down it: 'Sorry I missed your birthday.' They had the country papers in this shop too but Nancy never bought one. There'd be a paper at home and she could catch up on everything then.

She examined her new perm in the big round mirror which was not meant so much as a mirror as a deterrent to shoplifting. It was set high on the wall and at a funny angle, or she hoped it was. Otherwise the perm looked very odd indeed. She stared up at her reflection anxiously. Surely she didn't look like some small worried animal with fuzzy hair and huge terrified eyes. That's what she saw in the mirror, but of course that's not what people down at her own level would see. After all, everyone looked silly from this point of view. She patted her head and had another pang about the perm. It looked to her dangerously like those old-fashioned perms that people like her mother got in Rathdoon. The summer perm and the Christmas perm. Frizz, fuzz . . . tight curls growing out into what looked like flashes of lightning or electric shocks as the weeks went by. The girls in the salon assured her that she was made to think this. She had got a modern perm, one of the newest on the market. Think what she'd have paid if she had to pay for it! Nancy had smiled grimly. Paid for it! At that price! Nancy Morris wouldn't have paid half

457

that price or a quarter of that price for a perm. Nancy Morris had crossed Dublin to go to a salon where she heard they needed people to practise on. *Models* was the expression, but Nancy was more realistic. They needed heads with hair and smart people like Nancy found out which were the big salons with lots of trainees and on what nights their classes and demonstrations were. She had only paid for two visits to a hairdresser since she came to Dublin six years ago. That wasn't bad going, she smiled proudly. Still it was done now, this perm, no point in peering up at herself and worrying. Better go across and get on the bus. Surely some of the others would be there by now, and it was well after half past six.

Tom was sitting there reading an evening paper. He looked up and smiled. 'Evening, Miss Mouse,' he said pleasantly and lifted her big suitcase up on to the roof rack with one easy movement. She got in crossly. She *hated* him calling her Miss Mouse, but it was her own fault. When she had rung to ask for a place in his minibus she had given her name as Miss Morris. Well, she was used to being formal on the phone – that was what her job was about, for heaven's sake. How was she to know that she should have said her first name and that he genuinely misheard the Morris bit. But it was very galling that he still refused to call her Nancy, even though he always called old Mrs Hickey Judy and she could have been his mother.

'It's light for such a big case,' he said pleasantly. Nancy just nodded. She didn't feel like telling him it was her only suitcase and she had no intention of going out and spending over a fiver on some kind of nylon holdall like the others had. And anyway she needed a big case: there were always things to take back to Dublin, like potatoes and whatever vegetables there were, and anything else that turned up. There was the time that her mother's friend, Mrs Casey, was getting rid of her curtains: Nancy bought them back and they were lovely in the flat.

She sat down in one of the middle seats, straightened her skirt under her so that it wouldn't crease and took out her glucose sweets. They had jars of them in the hospital, and they always told her to help herself. She didn't eat them normally but it was nice on a bus journey to have something; the others often bought barley sugar or toffees, but what was the point of spending money on sweets when they were there for the asking? She unfolded a newspaper that one of the patients had left behind in the waiting room. She got a lot of her reading material this way – people waiting for the specialists were inclined to be forgetful about papers and magazines, and there was rarely an evening she didn't have something to read. And it was nice to have a variety, she told herself. It was like a surprise. Mairead didn't understand. Nancy's brow darkened when she thought of Mairead. And all that had to be sorted out. It had been so unexpected and so unfair.

She held up the newspaper so that Tom would think she was reading and she went over it all again. Mairead coming in on Wednesday and walking round restlessly picking things up and putting them down. You didn't have to be a genius to know there was something on her mind. Nancy thought she was going to ask about the television again. They had a perfectly good black and white set which was a bit snowstormish now and then but usually got a terrific reception. What on earth was the point of paying out a fortune renting a colour set? And even a video: Mairead had once mentioned this as if they were some kind of millionaires. She had looked up from the telly, which was admittedly having one of its bad nights and you had to guess a lot from the soundtrack; but Mairead had wanted to talk about something much bigger.

'I've been thinking all week at work how to say this, Nancy, and I can't think of any proper way so I'll just say it straight out. I want to share the flat with someone else, and I am going to have to ask you to leave. In your own time of course, I'm not throwing you out on the road . . .' She had given a little nervous laugh but Nancy had been too astounded to join in. 'You see,' Mairead had gone on, 'it was never permanent. It was just what we thought . . . that was the arrangement. That was what we said . . .' Her voice had trailed away guiltily.

'But we've been sharing for three years,' Nancy said.

'I know,' Mairead said miserably.

'So why? Don't I pay the rent in time always and the electricity? And I contribute to the food from home and I got curtains for the hall windows and . . .

'Of course, Nancy, nobody's saying you didn't.'

'So why?'

'It's just . . . no there's no reason, can't we do it nice and easily now without quarrels and questions. Can't you just find another place and we'll still meet now and then, go to the pictures, you come over here one evening, me go to your place. Come on, Nancy, that's the grown-up way to do things.'

Nancy had burned with rage. Mairead, who worked in a flower shop, telling her what was the grown-up way to do things. Mairead who hadn't got one honour in her Leaving Certificate ordering Nancy out of her flat. Her flat. True, she had found it, and when she needed someone to share the rent her aunt Mrs Casey, the friend of Nancy's mother, had suggested Nancy. Where had Mairead got these notions and more important, why? Who did she want to share with?

The worst thing was that Mairead didn't seem to know or care, she just said she would like a change. At this point Nancy had turned off the flickering telly and had settled in for what she thought was going to be a heart-to-heart where Mairead would tell her all about some star-crossed love. But no. Mairead was busy looking at the calendar. Would we say just over a month, like the middle of October? That would surely give her time to find somewhere.

'But who will I share with?' Nancy had wailed.

Mairead had shrugged. She didn't know, maybe Nancy could get a bed-sit on her own. She didn't do much cooking or entertaining, a bed-sit might be just as good. But they cost a *fortune*! Mairead had shrugged again as if it didn't concern her.

The following morning Nancy was having her tea in the kitchen – she never bothered with a breakfast since there was always food in the hospital, and what was the point of being a receptionist for all these doctors unless you got some perks like a canteen and glucose sweets? Mairead rushed in late as usual and Nancy asked her had she forgiven her.

'Forgiven you, Nancy? What for? What in heaven's name for?'

'Well I must have done something, otherwise you wouldn't be asking me to leave our flat.'

'It's *my* flat and don't be such a clown. We're not married to each other, Nancy. You came in here to share my rent, now that bit's over. Right? Yes. That's all there is to it.' She was gulping down a bowl of corn-flakes and trying to pull on her boots at the same time. Mairead loved these boots; they horrified Nancy – they had cost a week's salary. For a pair of boots.

'What'll I tell them in Rathdoon?' Nancy asked solemnly. Mairead was startled.

'About what?' she had asked, bewildered.

'About us breaking up?'

'Sure who would want to know? Who even knows we share a flat?'

'Everyone: your mother, my mother, your aunt Mrs Casey, everyone.'

'Well, what do you mean what will you tell them?' Mairead was genuinely surprised.

'But your mother, what will she think? What will I tell her?'

Mairead had lost her temper suddenly. Nancy still felt a shock just thinking about it.

'My mother is a normal woman; she's like everyone else's mother, including your mother. She doesn't think anything. She wants to know that I'm not pregnant and I'm not on drugs and I'm still going to Mass. That's all any mother wants to know in the name of God, those same three things. In India mothers want to know that or Russia or wherever, and it may not be Mass for them but it's something. People's mothers don't give two flying damns about their daughters sharing flats with people and whether they get on well or whether as in our case they drive each other up the wall. They just want to be told the essentials.'

'We don't drive each other up the wall,' Nancy had said quietly.

'No, well, irritate each other. What's the difference. Why bother your head explaining and telling and reporting back. People aren't bloody interested.'

'Do I irritate you?'

'Yes.'

'How?'

'Oh Nancy, *please*.' Mairead was stricken. 'We agreed last night to be grown-up and not to have pointless rows and recriminations. We agreed. Now look what you're starting. Of course people irritate each other: I probably drive you mad. Listen, I must go.'

Nancy had a terrible day: she had looked at the prices of flats and bed-sitters and they were sky high. The further out you went they came down a bit of course, but she had to be within cycling distance of the hospital. There was no way she was going to spend her hard-earned money on bus fares. She had thought too about what Mairead had said. She couldn't think why she was irritating. She didn't smoke, she never invited rowdy people in like Mairead often did, people who brought a bottle of wine each and then went out for chicken and chips. She didn't play records loud – she didn't have any records. She did everything to help. Often she cut special offers out of the paper and collected vouchers for foods or detergents. She suggested often to Mairead that it would be cheaper to come home every weekend to Rathdoon because people spend a fortune at weekends in Dublin and you could live free at home. How had she been so irritating?

Even this very morning she had asked Mairead if it was definite, and Mairead had nodded wordlessly. Nancy had offered to let Mairead have the weekend to consider her decision but in a low soft voice, unlike her harangue of the previous morning, Mairead had said there would be no considering and she realised that Nancy would be co-operative and start looking for another place straight away.

She looked up at the sound of voices. Dee Burke had arrived; she wore her college scarf even though she had left UCD two years previously, and she carried a canvas grip which she threw up on the roof herself. Tom was laughing at her.

'You'll be a discus champion yet,' he said.

'No, it's to show you that women are genuinely liberated, that's all – besides there's nothing in it except a couple of pairs of knickers and some law books I'm meant to be studying.'

Nancy was amazed that Dee, who was Dr Burke's daughter and lived in a big house covered with creeper, could talk about knickers to Tom Fitzgerald in such a relaxed way. It didn't even sound rude the way she said it. Dee was a law unto herself though and always had been. You'd think she'd have her own car but she said that she wasn't earning much as a Solicitor's apprentice. Still Nancy would have thought that this minibus would have been beneath the Burkes. They were people of such standing in Rathdoon, they must find it strange that their daughter travelled with anyone and everyone. Dee never seemed to notice. She was friendly with everyone, with that tinker of a fellow Kev Kennedy that you'd try to cross the road to avoid, with desperate Mikey Burns and his dirty jokes. Dee was specially nice to Nancy; she came out and sat beside her and asked, as she often did, about Nancy's work.

It was quite extraordinary the way Dee remembered the names of the doctors she worked for and knew that one was an eye specialist, one an orthopaedic surgeon and one an ear, nose and throat man. She knew there was Mr Barry and Mr White and Mr Charles. Even Nancy's mother wouldn't know that, and as for Mairead she could hardly remember the names of her own bosses let alone Nancy's.

But then Dee was nice and she had great breeding. People like that were courteous, Nancy always thought and they had the manners to be interested in other people.

Rupert Green arrived next. He was wearing a very smart jacket.

'Merciful God, Rupert, is that Italian? Is that the real thing?' Dee asked, feeling the sleeve as Rupert got in.

'Yes it is actually.' Rupert's pale face flushed with pleasure. 'How did you know?'

'Aren't I worn out looking at them in magazines. It's gorgeous.'

'Yes, it's a second, or a discontinued line or something, but a friend got it for me anyway.' Rupert was very pleased that it had caused such a stir.

'Well, they'd need to be a second or something, otherwise your father would have to sell his practice to buy it,' Dee laughed. Rupert's father was the solicitor, and it was through Mr Green she had got her apprenticeship in Dublin. Nancy looked at them enviously. It must be great to have such an easy way of going on. It was like a kind of shorthand in professional families, she noticed, they could all talk to each other at the drop of a hat. She felt a twinge of annoyance that her father, long dead, had been a postman and not a lawyer. The annoyance was followed by a stronger twinge of guilt. Her father had worked long and hard and had been pleased to see them all do well at their books and get secretarial or clerical jobs.

Rupert went to the back seat and almost on cue Mrs Hickey arrived. Suntanned even in winter she looked healthy and strong and as if she might be any age. Nancy knew she must be in her late fifties, but that was only by questioning people and piecing it together. Judy Hickey worked in some kind of mad place that sold herbal cures and grain and nuts, and she even grew some of the things herself which was why she came home every weekend to harvest them and bring them back to this shop in Dublin. Nancy had never been to the shop; Dee told her it was marvellous, that everyone should go and see it just for the experience of it but Nancy took her position as receptionist to three of Dublin's leading consultants very seriously. It wouldn't do for her to be seen going in and out of some quack's shop, would it?

Judy went to sit beside Rupert in the back and Mikey Burns had begun to squeeze himself in to the front seat. Laughing and rubbing his hands he told them a joke about hairy tennis balls. Everyone smiled and Mikey seemed to be able to settle down now that he had told at least one dirty story. He looked out eagerly.

'Will I be lucky and get the beautiful Celia beside me or do I get Mr Kennedy? Oh dear, just your luck, Mikey, here comes Mr Kennedy.'

Kev sneaked into the bus looking over his shoulder as if he expected a guard to lay a hand on him and say 'Just a minute' like they do in films. Nancy thought she had never seen anyone who looked so furtive. If you spoke to Kev Kennedy he jumped a foot in the air, and he never said much in reply so he wasn't spoken to much.

And lastly Celia came. Big and sort of handsome in a way, though Nancy didn't admire those kind of looks. She often wore tight belts; as she wore them when she was nursing, she had probably got used to them. They made her figure very obvious. Not sexy, but it certainly divided it for all to see: a jutting out top half in front and a big jutting out bottom half at the back. Nancy would have thought she might have been wiser to wear something more floppy.

Celia sat in beside Tom: the last person always sat beside the driver. It was only twenty to seven and they set off with five minutes in hand.

'I have you very well trained,' Tom laughed as he nosed the minibus out in the Friday evening traffic.

'Indeed you have. No wee-wees until we're across the Shannon,' said Mikey looking round for approval, and since he didn't hear any he said it again. This time a few people smiled back at him.

Nancy told Dee all about Mr Charles and Mr White and Mr Barry and how they saw their private patients on certain days of the week and how she kept their appointment books and shuffled people around and how patients were often very grateful to her and gave her little presents at Christmas. Dee wanted to know were they well thought of, the doctors, and whether people praised them. Nancy tried to dredge examples but couldn't. She was more on the administrative side, she kept insisting. Dee wanted to know whether she met them socially, and Nancy had laughed to think such a thing was possible. That was the joy of being a doctor's daughter, you didn't think class distinctions existed any more. No, of course she didn't get involved in their home lives. Mr Barry had a Canadian wife and two children, Mr White's wife was a teacher and they had four children, and Mr Charles and his wife had no children. Yes, she sometimes spoke to their wives on the phone; they all seemed very nice, they all remembered her name. 'Hallo Miss Morris,' they would say.

Dee fell asleep when Nancy was explaining about the hospital switchboard which was very awkward and how they had been looking for a separate switchboard for the consultants for ages, but maybe things would get better with the new set-up in the phone headquarters. Nancy was a bit embarrassed at that. Maybe she had been rabbiting on, possibly she did irritate people by talking too much about little things; sometimes her own mother got up and went to bed in the middle of one of her conversations. Mairead might be right. But no, that couldn't be, Dee had been positively pressing her for details of her working life, she had asked question after question. No, Nancy couldn't blame herself for being boring. Not this time. She sighed and looked at the fields flying by.

Soon she nodded off too. Behind her Judy Hickey and Rupert Green were talking about someone they knew who had gone to an Ashram in India and everyone had to wear yellow or saffron. In front of her Kev Kennedy was half-listening as Mikey Burns explained a card trick with a glass of water. Mikey said that it was better if you saw it done but you could still grasp the point if you concentrated.

In front of them Tom was saying something to Celia; she was nodding and agreeing with it, whatever it was. It was very comfortable and warm, and even if she did lean over a bit in sleep and slump on top of Dee, well it didn't matter. She wouldn't have let herself doze if she were beside one of the men. Or indeed beside Judy Hickey: there was something very odd about her.

Nancy was asleep.

Her mother was still at the kitchen table when she got in. She was writing a letter to her daughter in America.

'There you are,' she said.

'All in one piece,' said Nancy

It wasn't much of a greeting between mother and daughter when the whole country had been crossed. But they had never been a demonstrative family. No hugging and kissing, no linking arms.

'How was the journey?' her mother asked.

'Oh, the same. I had a bit of a sleep so I have a crick in my neck.' Nancy rubbed it thoughtfully.

'It's great to be able to sleep on that road, with maniacs screeching past you in all directions.'

'Oh, it's not that bad.' Nancy looked around. 'Well, what's been happening?'

Her mother was poor at handing out news. Nancy would have liked her to get up, wet a pot of tea and come back full of detail and information. She wanted to hear the week's events and who had been home, who had been heard from, who had revealed what. But somehow it was never like that.

'Whatever happens? Nothing's been happening – weren't you here until Sunday night?' Her mother went back to the letter, sighing, 'Do you never write to Deirdre at all? Wouldn't it be a Christian thing to write to your own sister in America and tell her what's going on? She loves to hear little things you know.'

'So do I, but you can never remember anything to tell me!' Nancy cried in complaint.

'Ah, will you stop that nonsense, sure aren't you here the whole time? You only go up to Dublin for a couple of days in the week. Poor Deirdre's on the other side of the Atlantic Ocean.'

'Poor Deirdre has a husband and three children and a freezer and an icebox and a sprinkler in her garden. Poor Deirdre indeed.'

'Couldn't you have all that yourself if you wanted to? Stop grudging things to your sister. Have some bit of niceness in you.'

'I've plenty of niceness.' Nancy felt her lip tremble.

'Well stop giving out about Deirdre then, and go on, take a sheet of paper and put it in with mine. It'll save you getting a stamp and everything.'

Her mother shoved a writing pad across the table. Nancy hadn't even sat down yet. The big suitcase with the hard corners was in the middle of the floor. She felt this was a shabby welcome home, but she was also a practical person. If she scribbled off a page to Deirdre now, well it would save her having to do it some other time, and it would please her mother who might go and bring out some soda bread and apple tart if she was in a good humour. Nancy wrote a few lines hoping that Deirdre and Sean and Shane and April and Erin were all well, and saying she'd love to come over and see them all but the fares were desperate and it was much easier for them to come over this way because of the pound and the dollar. She told Deirdre about Mr White's new car, and Mr Charles going to Russia on this holidays and Mr Barry's wife having a new handbag that was made from the skin of a baby crocodile and had cost what you wouldn't believe. She added that it was nice to get back to Rathdoon at weekends because . . . She paused at this point. It was nice to get back to Rathdoon because . . . She looked at her mother sitting at the table frowning over the letter writing. No, that wasn't why she came home. Her mother was only mildly pleased, and if she wasn't here there was the television or Mrs Casey or the bingo or half a dozen other things. Sometimes on the long summer evenings, Nancy had come home and found the house empty and her mother out at ten o'clock. She didn't come home for the dance like Celia did, or Kev or Mikey on the bus. She had not got what you'd call friends in Rathdoon.

She finished the letter, 'It's nice to get back at the weekends because the Lilac Bus is really very good value and you'd spend a small fortune in Dublin over the weekend without even noticing it.'

Her mother was packing up for bed. No tea, no apple tart.

'I think I'll just make myself a sandwich,' Nancy said.

'Did you have no tea? Aren't you very disorganised for a high-up receptionist?' said her mother, who went to bed without a word of goodnight.

It was a bright sunny September Saturday. The tourists were mainly gone but here were always a few golfers around. Nancy wandered up the street with no plan. She could have bought a newspaper and gone to the hotel to have coffee, but apart from the money altogether she wouldn't do that. It was being uppity going in here sitting as if you were the type.

No. She saw Celia's mother washing the step of the pub. She looked older, her face was lined like that gypsy-looking Judy Hickey. She called out a greeting but Celia's mother didn't hear, she kept scrubbing. Nancy wondered was Celia still in bed or was she helping to clean up inside. Celia worked weekends in the pub, that's why she came home. Her mother must have made it worth her while, because it was a hard job to stand on your feet all weekend there after having stood on your feet as a nurse all week. But you'd never know the time of day with Celia, she was so tight with information or anything at all. It was odd to see her talking away to Tom on the bus last night; usually she looked out the window with a moon face. Not like Dee, who was so full of life and so interested in everything. Nancy often wished that things were different, and that she could call on Dee at the weekend, or go off somewhere with her. But she wouldn't dream of going up to Burkes. Not in a million years would she call on the house. The surgery was a different matter, that was the way things were.

She passed Judy Hickey's cottage and saw signs of great activity out in the back. Big packing boxes were laid all round, and Judy was wearing old trousers and had her hair tied up in a scarf. The house itself was shabby and needed a coat of paint but the garden was immaculate. It was odd that so many people watered and weeded and kept the birds off for Mrs Hickey, Nancy thought; she wasn't the kind of woman that you'd think people would like at all. She only went to Mass one Sunday in four, if that. She never spoke of her husband and children. They had gone away years ago when the young lad was only a baby; Nancy could hardly remember the time when there were children in that house. Anyway, up and away with the father and the two children and not a word out of the mother. She never got the court to give them back to her; people had said there must be some fine secrets there that they didn't want to come out, otherwise she would surely had gone to law. And for years her working in this shop which sold things gurus used out in the East and things that must be disapproved of, ginseng and all that. Still Judy Hickey seemed to have more friends than a few. Even now there were two of Kev Kennedy's brothers helping her, and last week Mikey Burns was there with his shovel. Young Rupert would probably have been in the team but his father was very sick and that's why he had been coming home every weekend.

Nancy sighed and passed on. A half-thought that she might help too had come in one side of her mind but flashed quickly out the other. Why should she dig and get dirty in Judy Hickey's garden for nothing? She had better things to do. When she got back home and there was a note on the kitchen table, she wondered what better things she meant. Her mother had scribbled that Mrs Casey had called to take her for a spin. Mrs Casey had learned to drive late in life and had a dangerous-looking old car which was the joy of her heart. It had brightened life for many people including Nancy's mother. Indeed there was talk of a few of them coming the whole way to Dublin in it. The plan had been that Mrs Casey and Mrs Morris would stay at the flat. After all, Mrs Casey was Mairead's aunt. Now there would be no flat and no Mairead. Nancy's heart lurched at the memory of it all.

And nothing for the lunch and no mention of when the spin would be over, and nothing much in the press or in the little fridge, nothing you could eat. Nancy put on two potatoes to boil and went across to Kennedy's shop.

'Can I have two small rashers, please?'

'Two pounds is it?' Kev Kennedy's father didn't listen much to people: he was always listening to the radio in the shop.

'No, just two single ones.'

'Huh,' he said picking two out and weighing them.

'You see my mother hasn't done the shopping yet so I don't know what she wants.'

'You can't go far wrong with two slices of bacon,' Mr Kennedy agreed, morosely wrapping them in greaseproof paper and putting them in a bag. 'She'll never accuse you of getting the family into debt over that.'

She heard a laugh and to her annoyance noticed that Tom Fitzgerald was in the shop. For some reason she didn't like him hearing her being made fun of like that.

'Oh, Miss Mouse is a great one to live dangerously,' he said.

Nancy managed a smile and went out.

The afternoon seemed long. There was nothing on the radio, and nothing to read. She washed her two blouses and put them out on the line. She remembered with great annoyance that nobody, not even her mother, had remarked on her perm. Paying good money for one of the newest perms. Well, paying money if she had had to: fortunately she hadn't. At six she heard the banging of car doors and voices.

'Oh, there you are, Nancy.' Her mother always seemed surprised to see her. 'Mrs Casey and I've been for a great drive altogether.'

'Hallo Mrs Casey. That's nice,' Nancy said grumpily.

'Did you get us any supper?' Her mother looked expectant.

'No. Well, you didn't say. There wasn't anything there.' Nancy was confused.

'Oh, come on Maura, she's only joking. Surely you've something made for your mother, Nancy?'

Nancy hated Mrs Casey's arch voice treating here as if she was a slow-minded five-year-old.

'No, why I should have to? There was no food there. I presumed my mam was getting something.'

There was a silence.

'And there was nothing for lunch either,' she said in an aggrieved tone. 'I had to go over to Kennedy's to get rashers.'

'Well we'll have rashers for our supper,' Mrs Morris brightened up.
'I've eaten them,' Nancy said.
'All of them?' Mrs Casey was disbelieving.
'I only got two,' she said.
There was another silence.
'Right,' Mrs Casey said, 'that settles it. I wanted your mother to come
back with me but she said no, that you'd probably have the tea made for
us all and she didn't want to disappoint you. I said it was far from likely,
judging from what I'd heard. But she had to come back, nothing would
do her.' She was half way back to the door. 'Come on, Maura, leave the
young people be . . . They have better things to do than getting tea for
the likes of us.' Nancy looked at her mother, whose face was set in a hard
line of disappointment and shame.
'Enjoy your evening then, Nancy,' she said. And they were gone. The
car was starting with a series of jumps and leaps.
What could Mrs Casey have heard, what did she mean? The only person she could have heard anything from was Mairead, or Mairead's
mother. What could they have been saying – that Nancy was irritating?
Was that it?

She didn't want to be in when they came back but where could she go?
She had arranged no lift to the dance: she would as soon be hanged as to
go out on the straight road and hitch all the way to the night entertainment which she wouldn't enjoy anyway. She supposed she could always
go to Ryan's pub. She'd be bound to know people and it was her own
home town and she was twenty-five years of age so she could do what she
liked. She put on one of her freshly cleaned blouses which she ironed
with great care. She decided the perm was an undoubted success and
gave herself a spray of the perfume she had bought her mother last
Christmas and set out.
It wasn't bad in Ryan's; some of the golfing people were buying big
rounds, shouting at each other from the counter: what did you want
with the vodka, Brian, did you want water with the Power's, Derek? Celia
was behind the counter helping her mother.
'You don't usually come in here,' Celia said.
'It's a free country and I'm over twenty-one,' Nancy said snappishly.
'Oh Jesus, take it easy,' Celia had said. 'It's too early for the fights.'
There was a phone in a booth and she saw Dee Burke making a call;
their phone must be out of order at home. Nancy waved but Dee didn't
see her. Biddy Brady who had been two classes below Nancy at school
had got engaged and she was celebrating with a group of the girls. The
ring was being passed around and admired. She waved Nancy over to the
group, and rather than sit on her own she went.
'We're putting a sum into the kitty each and then the drinks keep
coming and we pay for it until the money runs out,' said one girl helpfully.

'Oh, I don't think I'll be here all that long,' Nancy said hastily, and noticed a few odd looks being exchanged.

She waved at Mikey Burns who was carrying two drinks over to a corner.

'Have you any pub jokes?' Nancy asked, hoping he might stop and entertain them for a moment.

'Not tonight, Nancy,' he said, and didn't even pause. Mikey! Who would do anything for an audience! He was heading for the corner, a woman with her head down sat there, it looked like Billy Burns' wife.

Billy was Mikey's brother, the one that got the looks and the brains and the luck people said.

There was a bit of commotion behind the bar and Celia's mother seemed to be shouting at her. It was hushed up but Celia looked very anxious. One of the Kennedy brothers had stepped in behind the bar to help wash glasses.

Nancy felt a bit dizzy. She had drunk two gins and orange which she had bought for herself and two as part of Biddy Brady's celebration. She had had nothing to eat since lunchtime. She decided to get some fresh air and some chips in that order. She could always come back. She sat on the wall near the chip shop and ate them slowly. You could see the whole town from here: the Burkes' house with all that lovely creeper cut away from the windows so neatly. She thought she saw Dee leaning out a window smoking but it was darkish, she couldn't be certain. Then there was the Fitzgeralds' drapery, Tom's family's business. His two brothers and their wives worked there, as well as his father. They had a craft shop now attached to it, and they made up Irish tweeds into skirts for the visitors. Mrs Casey lived about a mile out so she couldn't glare at her windows and imagine her mother eating lamb chops and looking at television, counting the days with Mrs Casey until the *Late Late Show* came back from its summer break. When they had been planning the Dublin trip they had wanted Mairead and Nancy to get them tickets for the show, and Mairead had actually written and found out what the chances were. Nancy had thought it was madness of the first order.

It was chilly and the last chip was gone. She walked back to Ryan's and thought she would go in the side entrance and visit the Ladies' on the way. She nearly fell over Mrs Ryan who was sitting on the step.

'Oh, it's *Miss* Morris,' the woman said with a very snide little laugh.

'Goodnight, Mrs Ryan,' said Nancy a bit nervously.

'Oh Miss Morris, Miss Mean Morris. Mean as all get out, they say about you.'

She didn't sound drunk. Her voice was steady and cold.

'Who says that about me?' Nancy was equally cold.

'Everyone. Every single person who ever speaks your name. Poor Biddy Brady's crowd of girls, just to mention a few. You sat down and took a couple of spirits off them and walked off. That's class, Miss Morris, strong men have wanted to be able to do that and they're not.'

'Why do you call me Miss Morris?'

'Because that's what you call yourself, that's what you think you are. And by God that's the way you're going to stay. No man would take you on, Miss Morris, a mean woman is worse than a nag and a slut put together.

'I'll be off, I think, Mrs Ryan.'

'Oh I would, Miss Morris, those little girls in there have had a few drinks now and if you haven't come back to put a couple of fivers into their kitty, I think you'd be far better to be off.'

'Put *what* into their kitty?' Nancy was stunned.

'Oh, be off, Miss Morris, I beg of you.'

But her blood was up now. She pushed past the woman and went into the smoke and heat.

'Sorry, Biddy,' she said loudly, 'I went home for change, I hadn't my money with me. Can I put this into the kitty and I'm having a gin and orange when the round comes.'

They looked at her in disbelief and with some guilt. Those who had been the loudest against her were abashed.

'A large gin and orange for Nancy,' they called and Celia who was working alone with only Bart Kennedy to help her raised her eyebrows. Nancy Morris ordering large ones.

'They cost a fair whack nowadays, Nancy,' she said.

'Oh, for Christ's sake, will you give me a drink not a sermon,' Nancy said and the others all laughed.

They were singing 'By The River of Babylon, where I sat down,' but Nancy was only mouthing the words.

Mean, Mean, Mean. That was what Mairead thought, what she told her mother and her aunt, why she wanted her out of the flat, that's what Mrs Casey thought, that's what her mother had felt tonight, that's what the Kennedys' father had been jeering at in the shop. That's what Celia meant now, talking about the price of a drink. That is what Mrs Ryan, who must have gone stone mad tonight, meant, sitting on the floor of her own public house in the side entrance.

Mean.

But she wasn't mean: she was careful, she was sensible, she was not going to throw away her money. She was going to spend it on what she wanted. Which was ... which was ... Well, she didn't know yet. It certainly wasn't clothes, or a holiday or a car. And it wasn't on dear things to furnish rented accommodation, and it wasn't on going to dances or discos or to hotels with fancy prizes. And it wasn't on smart hairdressers or Italian shoes or fillet steaks or a stereo radio with headphones.

They had linked arms now and they were singing 'Sailing' and swaying from side to side. Mrs Ryan had come back and was singing with the best; in fact she was standing up in the middle of the circle and playing the Rod Stewart role with somebody's golf club as a microphone.

Celia was pulling pints still; she looked at her mother with neither embarrassment nor pride – it was just as if she were another customer. Tom Fitzgerald was talking to her over the bar. They were very thick, those two. Tears came down Nancy's face at Mrs Ryan's words. A mean woman. She wasn't at all mean. But if people *thought* she was, then she must be. Mustn't she?

Deirdre had once said she was a bit tight with money, but she had thought that was Deirdre being all American and accusing people face to face of things. Her brother in Cork had once said that she must own massive property up in Dublin now, what with her earning a good salary and paying hardly a penny out a week except her rent and the Lilac Bus. She had said nonsense, that it cost a packet to live in Dublin. He had pointed out that she had a bicycle and she got a three-course meal in the hospital at midday, and what else did she spend it on? The conversation had ended fairly unsatisfactorily, she had thought. Now she realised that he was saying she was mean. Mean.

Suppose people *really* thought she was mean? Should she explain that it wasn't meanness, and she was only making sure she didn't throw money away? No, somehow it was one of those things that you couldn't explain. It was either there, the belief, or it wasn't there. And so, unfair as it was, she was now going to have to go overboard the other way.

Tomorrow she would suggest to her mother that she take them both to a nice Sunday lunch in the hotel as a treat. It was too late to do anything about Mairead, there was no promising to be more generous or to spend more or whatever it was people wanted. And maybe she could get some posters of Ireland and send them to Deirdre's children. Happy birthday Shane or April or Erin from your Auntie Nancy in the Emerald Isle. And to the silent brother in Cork, some book about fishing and a pressing invitation to visit her when next he came up for the Spring Show.

It must work: look at Biddy Brady's party, they were delighted with her. But why shouldn't they be, she had put ten whole pounds into their bowl on the table. But it seemed to please them a lot and they were raising their glasses a bit crookedly and saying Nancy Whiskey and things to her that they'd never have said otherwise.

There was no sign of Mrs Ryan; she had gone out again after her party piece. Nancy would like to have thanked her. Because now she had a lot of problems licked. And the great thing, the really great thing was this: it needn't cost a lot of money. In fact, if she was very careful it need cost hardly anything. She could take a lot of those glucose sweets and put them in a box, say, that could be a present for her mother one week. And she could give as presents those paperweights which she got from the drug companies – sometimes you could hardly see the name of the medicine they were advertising. And wasn't it just as well she had told nobody about the rise in her wages. She had negotiated it herself quietly, so no one need ever know about that at all.

Dee

They often had a drink on a Friday night in the pub beside the office. Dee would only stay for half an hour. The Lilac Bus wouldn't wait, she knew that. She knew too that a lot of people in the practice were surprised that she went home every weekend. It was so far, and there was so much to do in Dublin. Wasn't she very dutiful? Oh no, she had denied, no. It was selfishness: she went home because it was peaceful, there were no distractions, she could study at home. But the law books that crossed Ireland in her canvas bag came back again unopened as often as not. Dee Burke spent much of her weekends sitting at her bedroom window and staring out at Rathdoon. Until it was time to go back to Dublin again on Sunday evening.

And of course her parents were pleased. She could get off the bus at the corner and walk up to the golf club, waving cheerily as the Lilac Bus went on into town. For every Friday night in human memory Dr and Mrs Burke were at the golf club, and if there was a birth or a death or something untoward in between, people knew to phone the club and the Doctor would take the call.

They had been surprised at the beginning of the summer when she began to come home so regularly. Surprised but glad. It was great to have company round the house, and Dee was always the liveliest of the family. They would jump up with pleasure when she put her face around the door on a Friday night to join them and whoever else in the club bar. Her father would get her a toasted sandwich and put his arm around her shoulder if she stood beside him at the bar counter. Her mother would smile over from the table. They were so delighted to have Dee home again. Sometimes her stomach rose and fell at their innocence and their kind welcome. What did people do when they didn't have the Burkes to go back to, Dee wondered? Went mad maybe? Went to discos? Got sense? Pulled themselves together? Oh, who knew what other people did? Who cared?

473

Tom Fitzgerald was quite handsome, she had never thought of it until tonight when he was laughing at her for flinging her own bag up on the roof rack. He had a lovely grin. He was an odd fellow – you could never get a straight answer out of him on anything. She knew nothing about him, nothing at all, and she had grown up fifty yards from him and his brothers. She didn't even know what he did for a living. She had asked her mother once.

'Don't you travel across the country sitting beside him? Why don't you ask him yourself?' her mother had said, not unreasonably.

'Oh, he's not the kind you could ask,' Dee had said.

'Well then, you'll have to remain ignorant,' her mother had laughed.

'At this stage of my life I'm not going to go into the drapery and ask personal questions to the Fitzgeralds about what occupation their son follows.'

Nancy Morris was sitting in the bus, first as usual. She looked different somehow. Was it a new blouse or her hair? Dee wasn't sure – she wouldn't ask in case Nancy would start bewailing the cost of everything as she usually did. And yet she was getting a fine big salary, so Sam had told her. Far more than any of the receptionists or clerks were getting in the Solicitors' office. Maybe I won't sit beside her tonight, Dee resolved, but she knew she would. Who else knew Sam, who else could tell her about Sam Barry and his daily life except Nancy? Imagine being able to travel home with Sam's receptionist every weekend. It was like having a bit of Sam with her. It took a lot of the loneliness away just to be able to talk about him. Even very indirectly, even if it meant talking about Mr Boring White and Mr Boring Charles as well. Because Nancy must never, never know that it was only Mr Sam Barry that she was interested in.

Nancy would talk for ever: she explained the routine and the kind of problems the consultants had, not being able to get beds quickly enough in the hospital, and all the complications of the Voluntary Health Insurance and the forms and people not understanding them. But she knew nothing about their lives outside the hospital. Nothing except what they told her and what the nurses told her, and that was little.

'Do their wives ever ring them at work?' Dee asked. It was like probing a sore tooth; she knew she shouldn't ask.

'Oh yes, sometimes they do.' Nancy was maddening.

'And what do they say?'

'They're all very nice, they call me by my name.'

That surprised Dee: Nancy was so unforthcoming and businesslike, you couldn't imagine anyone chatting to her.

'Oh yes, "Hallo Miss Morris" they say. All of them: Mrs White, Mrs Charles, Mrs Barry.'

So that's what she meant by calling her by her name!

'And has Mrs Barry much of a Canadian accent?'

'Gosh, Dee, you do have a great memory for them all. No wonder you're so brainy and going to be a solicitor. Imagine you remembering she was a Canadian. No, not much of an accent, but you'd know she was from over there. American sounding.'

Imaging my remembering she was Canadian? Imagine my being able to forget it! She doesn't know many people here; she's far from home, it's not as if she grew up here and has her own circle of friends; she needs time to make a life for herself, we have to wait until things settle down.

Dee could never understand the logic of that. If they were going to wait until Candy Barry settled into Irish life they were building up more and more trouble for themselves. Why didn't they settle her back into Canadian life, she wanted to know? Before she had become isolated from her roots there. Why? Because of the children of course, the two little Barrys, small clones of their father, five and seven. He wasn't going to let those go four and a half thousand miles away and see them once a year on a visit.

But what about the children that he and Dee would have together? That would be different. Wonderful but different. You didn't parcel away your two lovely sons because you were going to have a new family with somebody else. No indeed. Dee was immature to suggest it.

Sam used that word as a great insult. He said it had nothing to do with age. People younger than Dee could be mature and people much older than both of them would never achieve it. She didn't like the word, it seemed to mean whatever he wanted it to mean. Like when you're playing poker and the two is wild, the two can be any card you want it to be.

She didn't know why she asked Nancy about his work. She never learned anything new, but it was like seeing a photograph of some scene that you knew well; it was always interesting to see it again from another angle. The only bit she shouldn't have asked was about their wives ringing up. That had made her uneasy now.

Sam said that Candy never called him at work and yet Nancy Morris said she did. Nancy probably wanted to show off about how she knew them all. Boasting. She was in the middle of some complicated diatribe about the telephone system now. Dee felt her eyes closing. She slept and dreamed that she was getting her parchment from the Chief Justice and Sam was there congratulating her, and a photographer from the *Evening Press* had the three of them lined up and was writing their names down in his notebook.

Dee often dreamed that Sam was part of her life: she felt that this must signify that she was not guilty about him and that everything they had together was above board and out in the open. Not too much out in the open of course, but not hole-in-the-counter either. For example her flat-mate Aideen knew all about Sam, and met him when he called. And Sam's friend Tom knew too: he used to go out to meals with them sometimes. So it wasn't as furtive as you might think. Sam had wanted to know why her parents didn't cop on, but Dee had said it would never cross their minds, and anyway she had no romantic interests yet but would certainly fall for somebody highly unsuitable when the time came. Dee had pealed with laughter over this, and Sam had looked sad. She had stopped laughing suddenly and he had been very quiet.

'The future mightn't be perfect,' he said. 'Not for us: you shouldn't hope too much, you know.'

'The future's not going to be perfect for most people,' she had said cheerfully. 'But they have to keep hoping, otherwise what's the point of anything?'

That had seemed to cheer him a little, but he had been quieter than usual.

Dee wasn't sure why she came home so often now. Aideen couldn't understand it either.

'Sure if you're down there, he'll never see you. Can't he ring you here, if he has a free minute?'

True. But he was having less and less free minutes. Candy's parents were over from Toronto. They had to be shown round. One of the little blond boys had fallen off a bicycle and opened his forehead; he had to be visited in hospital, and looked after when he got home.

There was the family holiday on the Shannon, on the cruiser, and the hurried phone calls from coinboxes when he was meant to be buying drinks or going to the Gents'.

And recently there were times that weren't explained at all, but they were times that seemed to have no minutes in them all the same. It was easier in Rathdoon, he *couldn't* ring her here, even if he wanted to. Her father would recognise his name, the phone was in the hall, it would be hopeless. Perhaps that's why she went, because anything was better than sitting in a place where he could ring and didn't.

Aideen said she should fight harder for him, force him to leave that Candy. He had been so keen on Dee at the start that he would have done anything for her; now she had let him believe that he could have it both ways. But Dee thought she might want it both ways too. She didn't want a huge scandal, and having to leave her apprenticeship and end up half-qualified, half-married, half-home-wrecker and half-disgraced. Aideen said that was nonsense and that Dee's parents had been able to accept that her brother was living with a girl, so why couldn't they accept what she planned to do. Dee thought there was a lot of difference between Fergal living with his girlfriend when everyone knew that they would get married soon anyway, and her making off with a well known Dublin consultant and forcing him to abandon his wife and two little boys. It was a matter of degree. Aideen had said that was nonsense, it was all Sin and it was all not Respectable. So why not do it?

Why not? It wasn't really up to her any more: Sam was not nearly so ardent. In fact once or twice he had made excuses that seemed just like the things he had said to Candy on the phone a year ago. 'Sorry love, I tried, but it's useless, there's this meeting, it's the only time they can get all the people together. I pulled out last time. I can't be seen to do it again.' Very familiar. Frighteningly familiar. But was he making excuses to his young mistress so that he could be with his middle-aged Canadian wife? Or was there another young mistress? Someone even younger than twenty-three? Someone who didn't sigh and groan when he cancelled an arrangement? Someone who never suggested that Candy be sent back to Toronto?

Dee was remarkably calm about the possibility of a rival. She couldn't take it seriously. He really *was* a busy man, by anyone's standards; he worked long hours and there were still more people straining to see him. He had barely time for one relationship, not to mention two. To think of three would be ridiculous. Nobody could juggle that many romances and promises and endearments in the air. Nobody.

She was glad when they stopped, just for the chance to stretch her legs. Tom gave them ten minutes and not a minute more in the pub beside the garage where he filled up the Lilac Bus. The men usually had a half-pint each and sometimes Dee bought Nancy a gin and orange and Celia a bottle of Guinness. She would have a little brandy herself if her stomach felt cold and nervous. But tonight she felt all right. Sam was away on his conference.

He had rung her from the airport to say goodbye. He had said he loved her and that he'd see her on Monday night, late when he got back from London. He'd tell Candy the conference went on until Tuesday. That was fine, it was ages since he had been able to stay a full night, she would make sure that there'd be no confrontation and scenes. Just like it had been in the beginning.

They were settling back in the bus. Poor Mikey Burn, the bank porter, who was so nice apart from all his lavatory jokes, said that he felt much better now that he'd shaken hands with the wife's best friend. He said it twice in case people hadn't got it. Kev Kennedy still hadn't.

'You're not married, Mikey,' he had said.

Mikey looked defeated.

Dee said she mustn't sleep too much on the bus, it gave her a cramp in her shoulders, and Nancy said there was a great way of getting rid of tension in the neck: you had to hang your head down as if it was a great weight and then roll it around. Judy Hickey joined in the conversation unexpectedly and said that this was one of the principles of yoga and seemed greatly in agreement. Dee thought Nancy was put out by this, as if she didn't want to join up with yoga over anything.

He would be in London now, staying in that big posh hotel near the American Embassy where she had once spent a weekend with him as Mrs Barry. It had been so racy, and she kept thinking she'd meet someone from home as if anyone from Rathdoon would ever go inside a place

477

like that. He had said there would be a reception at 8.30 and they would all wear name badges. It would have begun now. She felt an urge to talk about him again. This would be her last chance since she wouldn't be able to mention him at home.

'I expect they go away a lot on conferences, professional sort of things,' she said to Nancy.

'Sometimes.' Nancy was vague. 'Not often. Of course they've all had their holidays in August, and you've no idea how hard it is to fix appointments; people don't understand that doctors, specialists, have to have holidays like anyone else. More than anyone else,' she added righteously.

Dee wasn't going to go down that martyr road; she wanted to hear about Mr Barry being invited to this very prestigious gathering in London. She wanted to hear what he said when he got the invitation, and she wanted to hear Nancy say that he was coming back on Tuesday, so she could hug that to herself like a little secret.

'Yes, but didn't you say one of them was off to a conference this weekend?' she said.

'No.' Nancy was puzzled. 'No, definitely not.'

'Maybe they'd go and not tell you?' Dee's heart had started to move in a very unacceptable rhythm.

'I don't think so,' Nancy was lofty. 'But anyway it wouldn't be this weekend, because I know where they're all going, as it happens. It's a big do. Mr and Mrs Barry – she's a Canadian you know – well, they're having their tenth wedding anniversary party tomorrow, and it's going to be a big barbecue. Mr Barry asked me to pray specially that it wouldn't rain.'

She didn't hear anything else for the rest of the journey home. But she must have managed to nod or smile or something because she certainly didn't notice Nancy looking at her puzzled or anything. She felt as if somebody had opened her throat just under the gold horseshoe he had bought her as a pendant that time in London, and poured in a jug of iced water. The water was freezing up again. Why? That was all she wanted to know. Why the elaborate lies? Filled with such detail, about the name badges, the names of Americans and French and Germans that he was going to meet? Did these people exist at all, or had he picked names out of a phone book or out of literature? Why? If he and his wife had such a good marriage that they were gloating publicly with a big babyish barbecue over the whole thing . . . then why did he need Dee as well?

She went over it all, from the very start, when they had met at a party on the day of a Rugby International. It had been a big lunch where people had been invited to pre-match snacks and most people had such a good time they had stayed on and watched the match on telly instead. Dee had felt guilty about their tickets and all the young disappointed hopefuls who could have used them and Sam had gathered up half a dozen and run out on the road and given them to the first crowd of passers-by he saw. They had looked through the window and laughed at the waving kids and the eager way they had run towards Lansdowne Road. She and Sam had laughed a lot that afternoon. Candy was at the other end of the room talking about recipes. When they were leaving, Sam had said, 'I must see you again,' and she had laughed a peal of delight, and told him it was pure Hollywood.

'I am pure Hollywood,' Sam had said, and somehow it had sounded endearing and nice. She had given him work and home numbers and he had called the next day. He had pursued her, yes, that wasn't too strong a word for it. *Pursued.* She had said she didn't want to get involved with a married man, and he said that he knew it was more pure Hollywood and pure corn and pure things-that-married-men-said, but actually his marriage was empty and a great mistake and something he should never have done but he had been in Canada and lonely and far from home, and that, apart from Dee altogether, he and Candy would undoubtedly drift their separate ways when the children were old enough to understand, and that he would be very gentle and careful, and that he would love her always. Now why would someone do that? If you loved one person and thought that they were smashing and lovely and fresh why would you then have big parties and hand-holding and a lot of bullshit with another person? What was the point? Or suppose you loved the other person and enjoyed being married to her for ten years and adored the two little boys and everything then why would you tell lies about being fresh and lovely and tell tall tales about conferences in London with name badges to someone else? It was beyond understanding, and Dee felt that something in her head was about to break with the effort of understanding. She bent forward a little. Tom's eyes in the mirror caught the movement.

'Are you OK, Dee?' he called

'Sure,' she muttered.

'Right, coming to your corner in five minutes,' he said. He must have thought she was car-sick.

'We're never home already?' She was genuinely shocked. She thought they were seventy miles from Rathdoon. 'You should try driving Concorde,' she said, managing a sort of joke for him.

'Sure that would be child's play after the Lilac Bus,' Tom grinned back at her.

She wondered should she go straight home and not get off at the golf club. But that would be worse, back to an empty house on her own. No, better join in and be with people who would talk and laugh and be pleased to see her.

She opened her bag and got out a mirror before she went in. Unbelievably she was not too bad, her face tanned from all those weekends at home, her hair straight and shoulder length – Sam said it was like an advertisement for shampoo, which was high praise. Her eyes normal looking, not wild. No, she wouldn't frighten her parents and their friends. In she would go and when they asked her what she'd have she'd say she had a stomach upset and could she have a brandy and port. Someone told her once that this was great drink and it cured every ill. Or most ills anyway.

They were delighted to see her as always, but they were bursting with news. They couldn't wait for the drink to be in her hand so that they could drink a toast. They had had a phone call from Fergal – what do you think, he and Kate had bought the ring, they were getting married just before Christmas, wasn't it marvellous? And Kate's parents had been on the phone too and they had all said wasn't it wonderful the way things turned out, and maybe young people nowadays were much wiser than their parents and didn't rush into things. Dee Burke raised her glass of port and brandy and drank the health of her brother Fergal and her new sister-in-law-to-be, Kate, and she wondered with her mother what they both would wear to the wedding. And the drink went down through that channel where there had been iced water before, and it sort of burned it with a fiery anaesthetic and she began to think that whoever said it cured all ills might have had a point.

But it didn't bring sleep. And she had to move gently if she moved at all. The big old house was full of creaks and bumps. If you went to the lavatory during the night you woke the whole house. It was considered courteous to arrange your functions so that you didn't have to. Her parents talked on long downstairs. They had been married for thirty years, she realised. They never made much of anniversaries and when her mother was fifty last year it had been very politely ignored. No showy barbecues for them, no public displays.

But that didn't matter. What was she going to do? Was she going to pretend that she knew nothing, let him lie on about London? No, that would be living out a total dishonesty. But then wasn't he prepared to do that with her? Some of the time. And with Candy some of the time. He didn't have this high regard for total honesty. How had he not known that Nancy would prattle about it? She had told him that she travelled home on the same minibus every weekend as his receptionist. But Sam didn't know that she talked to Nancy about the consultants, and Sam would never believe for one moment that Nancy would mention something as trivial as his party to someone who was not meant to know him. Would she ring him at home and confront him? What earthly good would that do? None.

She would try to be calm and wait until daylight. What was that thing you were meant to do to your neck and shoulders? She tried what she remembered of the instructions but it just made her feel worse.

An hour later she understood what insomnia was about. She had never understood why people didn't just turn on the light and read if they couldn't go to sleep.

Another hour later she laughed mirthlessly to herself about her lack of sleeping pills. There she was, a doctor's daughter, and another doctor's lover and she hadn't one little Mogadon to call her own. A bit after that she started to cry and she cried until she fell asleep at twenty to eight just as her mother was creaking down the stairs to put on the coffee.

She woke after one o'clock: her mother was standing by the bed.

'Is your tummy better?'

Dee had forgotten the so-called gastric attack to excuse the ports and brandy.

'I think so,' she said bewildered.

'If you're well enough, can you do me a favour? We've had another phone call from Fergal,' her mother paused expectantly.

'The wedding's off,' Dee said rubbing her eyes.

'No stupid, but they're coming this evening, about six o'clock. Can you run me into town, I'll want to get things.' 'Into town' meant the big town seventeen miles away. 'Down town' meant Rathdoon itself.

'What do we want to go into town for?'

'You can't get anything nice here, anything different.'

'Mummy, in the name of God, isn't it only Fergal? Why do we want anything *nice*, anything *different* for Fergal?'

'But it's Kate as well.'

'But hasn't he been living with Kate for a year? Are you losing your marbles or something, what would she want anything nice and different for? Can't we go to Kennedy's and get some ham or lamb or whatever we'd be having anyway?'

'Well if you don't want to drive me, you need only say so. I'm sure your father won't mind giving me a quick spin into town,' her mother was huffy now and annoyed.

'It's not a quick spin, you know it, it's seventeen miles. It's a bad road, it's jam packed with shoppers on a Saturday in there, we'll never get a parking place, the whole thing will take three hours.'

'Well, don't *you* worry about it, Madam: you're so busy you can sleep on into the broad daylight – I see what a demanding life *you* have. No, your father may be able to give up his one game of golf a week to take me.'

Dee got out of bed, and picked up a dressing gown.

'I'll have a bath and I'll take you now, but I want you to know that there's a grave danger you're going mad. Next week you'll be going into town to get something nice and unusual for me.'

'If you were bringing home a fiancé I'd be glad to,' her mother said. 'And by the way, do you never wear pyjamas or a nightdress or anything? Isn't it very peculiar to wear nothing at all in bed?'

'It's very peculiar Mummy – I'd say I'd be locked up if anyone knew.'

'Oh there's nothing like a smart aleck, nothing as lovely as your own daughter turning into a smart aleck,' said her mother and went downstairs happily to make a list.

Mrs Burke bought a new tablecloth and six napkins to match. Dee cast her eyes to heaven so often her mother asked her not to come into the next shop to be making a show of her. She was moved on three times by guards, hot harassed men who could never have dreamed that this is what it would be like when they joined the force. She saw a woman slap her three-year-old hard on the legs until he roared in fright and his father thought she had gone too far and gave the woman a hard shove. Marriage! Dee thought. Family life. If a Martian were looking at us, he would think we must be insane to run towards it like a crowd of lemmings. And it's all we want, everywhere: romantic books, *Dallas* on the telly, everyone we know. Nobody seems to learn any lessons on the way.

Her mother came out weighed down with parcels just as a guard was coming at her again; she dragged the parcels and her mother into the car with one movement.

'You're becoming very rough, Dee, very ill-mannered,' Mother said, annoyed and flustered.

'It's all this naked sleeping,' Dee said, smiling up at the guard. 'That's the cause of it, I'm certain.'

Half-way home Dee realised what had happened. That stupid Nancy had got the weekend wrong. That was it. Hadn't Sam said he'd be tied up with the family, *next* weekend. Imagine believing the daylight from Nancy Morris. She really was going mad, it wasn't just a joke she made to her mother, of course that was it. Nancy was fussing and filling in her appointment book and complaining about the cost of living and she hadn't heard.

The relief was immense: it was the joy of getting an exam, it was like going to confession, not that there had been much of that lately – it was like passing your driving test.

She laughed happily and her mother looked at her in alarm.

'Mummy, I was just thinking of the day I passed my driving test,' she began.

'Well I don't know whether you'd pass it if you had it to do again,' her mother said. 'You've been hitting those potholes at a great rate, your father wouldn't like his car to be belted about like that.'

'No, I was just thinking of the lovely feeling when the man said I passed. Would you like me to teach you to drive, Mummy, seriously?'

'I would not,' her mother said. 'And what's more I don't think I'll ever sit in a car with you again. Will you look at the *road*, Dee!'

'It's an open invitation. One lesson on a Saturday, one on a Sunday – sure you could drive us all to Fergal's wedding.'

She felt light-headed and happy. If she saw stupid Miss Mouse as Tom called her, she would have mown her down.

When Fergal and Kate arrived, Dee thought they both looked slightly touched. They wee a revolting mixture of over-talkativeness and utter wordlessness. They explained at tedious length how they had become mature in the last few months and both of them had developed this sense of their immaturity and lack of responsibility at exactly the same time. They wanted to make their commitment now in front of everyone, rather than shilly-shallying any longer. Doctor Burke, who looked as if he wouldn't have minded if they never married, nodded and grunted appreciatively. Fergal's mother gasped and pounced on every word, and reminded them of every detail of John's wedding five years before, every detail that is except the one that his bride was four months pregnant. Dee switched off for a little and thought of Sam in London. He had said there would be papers all of Saturday afternoon but that he was going to skip the official dinner. Together they had looked at an English newspaper and circled plays or shows he might see. She wondered was it a nice warm night in London as it was here. Then it hit her like a tennis ball coming suddenly into her stomach. He had asked Nancy Morris to pray for a fine weekend for the barbecue. *This* weekend. She wasn't able to eat the meringues which her mother had filled so carefully with a coffee flavoured cream to impress Fergal and Kate. She asked to be excused for a few minutes because she had remembered there was something she had to give Celia Ryan down in the pub.

'Won't it do later?' her mother had asked.

'No, she wants it now.' Dee was standing up.

'Will I come down with you and have a pint? She shooed Fergal away. 'What a thought, after all this lovely meal Mummy's got for you. No, I'll be back in a few minutes.'

'What does Celia want at this time of night?' Her father asked mildly. 'Won't she be pulling pints and trying to help that poor mother of hers to cope?'

'See you,' Dee called.

She ran up to her room for her handbag and swung down the road.

'Can you give me a pound of change for the phone, Celia?' she asked.

'God you're a great customer, if we had more like you we could open a singing lounge and have a cabaret on the profits,' Celia laughed.

'Piss off, Celia. I'll have a brandy in a minute, I just want to make a call to Dublin.'

Celia's level glance never changed, she never enquired whether the Burke phone was out of order, she just gave her the money.

'Could I get a call back in that box?' Dee wanted to know.

'Yes, I'll give you the number but I don't put it up – I don't want other people to know.'

'You're a pal,' Dee said.

'Barry residence,' said the Canadian voice she hadn't heard since the one and only time she met its owner at that rugby party which was only a year and a half ago but felt like a lifetime.

'May I speak to Mr Sam Barry, please.'

'Well, it's a little awkward just at this very minute. Who is this please?'
'It's Miss Morris, his receptionist.'
'Oh Miss Morris, I didn't recognise your voice, I am sorry. Sam is just getting the barbecue going, it's a very delicate moment.' There was a little laugh. 'Once the thing has taken we can all relax. Can I ask him to call you, Miss Morris, I assume it's urgent?'
'I'm afraid it is, Mrs Barry.' She sounded apologetic. 'It's just a short message, but I should speak to him. It won't take a moment.'
'Well, listen, I know he says that you are a rock of stability in a changing world, can I have him call you?'
'In the next half hour, if he could.' Dee gave the number that Celia had written down.
'Rathdoon, what a pretty name!' Mrs Barry was determined to be charming to the rock of stability. Or else she was so happy about the anniversary barbecue she was at peace with the world. Dee didn't wait to find out.
'Very pretty. Bye, Mrs Barry.' She hung up; she was shaking. She sat on a stool at the bar. Celia made it a large brandy but charged only for a small one. Dee made a move to protest.
'Nonsense, you're always buying me drinks.'
'Thanks.' She held the glass with both hands. Celia must have noticed the shake.
'They tell me your Fergal's engaged,' Celia said.
'Lord, that didn't take long.' Dee grinned.
'Oh, it's stale news, I heard last night when I came off the bus.'
'So did I: the parents are over the moon.'
'Well, they don't have to pay for the wedding,' Celia laughed.
'Celia, stop that, you sound like Nancy Morris.'
The phone rang. Celia refilled her glass wordlessly and Dee slipped into the booth.
'Hallo,' she said.
'A call for you,' exchange said.
'Miss Morris?' Sam asked.
'No, Miss Burke,' Dee said.
'What?'
'Miss Burke speaking. Can I help you?'
He wasn't sure. 'I'm sorry, I was asked to ring a Miss Morris at this number . . .'
'No, you weren't, you were asked to come in from the barbecue and talk to your mistress Miss Dee Burke. That was the message I gave your wife.'
'DEE, DEE.' He was horrified. There was actual fear in his voice.
'Oh, she was very nice about it, she got a pencil from her purse and wrote down the number. She said Rathdoon sounded a pretty place.'
'Dee, what are you doing?' His voice was a whisper.

'I'm at home for the weekend, like I told you I would be. The question is, what are YOU doing. Did they cancel the conference? Let's see, you were leaving the airport about four thirty – gosh, did they tell you at London airport or did you have to get into town?'

'Dee, I can explain exactly what happened but not here and now; what did you really say to Candy?'

'Oh just that, and she really did say that Rathdoon sounded pretty – ask her.'

'You didn't . . . but why?'

'Because I felt it was all so confusing, all this business of lies and saying one thing and everyone knowing it wasn't true. Everyone. I thought it would be easier not having to pretend so much.'

'But . . .'

'I mean she knows, Candy does, that you'll be spending Monday night with me, and so now you don't have to lie to her about that, and I know that you and Candy are having a marvellous tenth anniversary barbecue and that Mr Charles is there and Mr White and all your friends and they were all watching you start up the fire. She told me all that, so there's no pretending: it will be much easier from now on.'

'You didn't, Dee. You didn't really say those things to Candy.'

Her voice was very hard now. Very hard. 'You'll have to find out now, won't you.'

'But she said it was Miss Morris on the phone.'

'Oh, I told her to say that.' Dee sounded as if she were explaining things to a child. 'Much simpler for your guests; I mean I don't know what you want to tell other people, but we'll talk about it all on Monday, won't we?'

'Dee, please don't go, you've got to explain.'

'I have explained.'

'I'll ring you back.'

'Ring all you like, this is a pub.'

'Where are you going now?'

'I see the real Miss Morris over here in a corner. I think I'll buy her a gin and orange and tell her all about us. That will make it easier for me to ring you at work; you see, I couldn't before because she knew me, but now with all this new honesty . . .'

'What new honesty?'

'What Candy and I have been talking about.'

'You're a bitch, you told Candy nothing; this is a game, some vicious little game.'

'Hush hush, don't let them hear you.'

'Where will you be tomorrow?'

'I'll see you on Monday night, as arranged: come any time, straight from work if you like now that there's no need to hide things any more.'

'I beg you, tell me what you told Candy.'

485

'No, YOU must ask Candy that.'

'But if you told her nothing then . . .'

'That's right. you'll have walked yourself into it.'

'Dee,'

'Monday.'

'I'm not going to be blackmailed into coming round to you on Monday.'

'Suit yourself, I'll be at home then, if I don't get called away or anything.' She hung up.

'If he rings again, Celia, will you say you never heard of me and I haven't been in all night.'

'Sure,' said Celia.

She went back to the house. Fergal was explaining that there came a time in your life when you couldn't play any more – you had to face up to things.

'Jesus Mary and Joseph, Fergal, you should have been a philosopher!' Dee said admiringly.

'Did you have a drink with Celia Ryan?'

'I had two large brandies, mother dear,' Dee said.

'How much was that?' Fergal the man saving for a mortgage was interested in the cost of fun.

'I don't know; I only paid for one small one when I come to think of it.' There were sudden tears in her eyes.

'Dee, why don't you and I go for a walk for a bit and let the wedding talk go on to a crescendo here?' Doctor Burke had his blackthorn stick in his hand.

They walked in silence. Down past the chip shop and over the bridge and on to the fork in the road.

It was only coming back that there was any chat.

'I'll be all right, Dad,' she said.

'Sure I know you will, aren't you a great big girl and won't you be a solicitor one day, a fierce terror making them all shake in the district court?'

'Maybe.'

'Of course you will, and all this other stuff will sort itself out.'

'Do you know about him?' She was genuinely surprised.

'This is Ireland, child. I'm a doctor, he's a doctor, well a sort of one – when they get to that level it's hard to know.'

'How did you hear?'

'Somebody saw you and thought I should know, I think, a long time ago.'

'It's all over now.'

'It may be for a while . . .'

'Oh no it is, tonight.'

486

'Why so suddenly?'

'He's a liar and nothing else; he lied to her and to me – why do people do that?'

'Because they see themselves as having lost out and they want some of everything, and society doesn't let us have that so we have to tell lies. And in a funny way the secrecy keeps it all going and makes it more exciting at the start.'

'You know what it's like all right; I don't know how you could.'

'Oh, the same way as your fellow does.'

'DADDY. No, not you. I don't believe it.'

'Oh years and years ago. You were only a toddler.'

'Did Mummy know?'

'I don't think so. I hope not. But she never said anyway.'

'And what happened to the girl?'

'Oh she's fine; she hated me for a bit, that was the worst part – if she had been just a little bit understanding. Just a small bit.'

'But why should she?' Dee was indignant.

'Why, because she was young and lovely like you are and she had the world before her, and I had made my way and it was nice but a bit, you know . . . a bit samey.'

'She should have shook your hand like a chap and said, "No hard feelings, Johnny Burke, you'll be a treasured memory."' Dee was scathing.

'Something like that,' her father laughed.

'Maybe she should have.' Dee linked her father companionably. 'Because you're a much nicer man than Sam Barry will ever be. I think he deserves a bit of a roasting, actually.'

'Ah well, roast away,' her father said goodnaturedly. 'You've never listened to me up to now – there's no reason why you should now.'

Dee sat in her room and looked down at the town. She thought she saw Nancy Morris sitting on the wall near the chip shop, but decided that it couldn't be. Nancy . . . pay for a whole portion of chips . . . ridiculous.

Mikey

Mikey always said that you couldn't come across a nicer crowd of girls that the ones who worked in the bank. The men were grand fellows too but they were often busy with their careers and they wouldn't have all that time to talk. And one of the men, a young buck who'd be some kind of a high manager before he was thirty had taken it upon himself to say to Mikey that it would be appreciated if he watched his sense of humour since the bank ladies had found it rather coarse on occasions. Mikey had been very embarrassed and had said nothing all day. So silent was he that the nice Anna Kelly who was pure gold asked him if he felt all right. He had told her what the young buck said, and Anna Kelly had said that banks were stuffy old places and maybe the buck had a point: jokes were fine with friends, but God the bank, it wouldn't know how to laugh if you were tickling its funny bone for a year.

So he understood now and he never uttered a pleasantry within the bank walls again. If he met them on the street that was different; he could pass a remark or make a joke like anyone then because they were all on neutral ground. And he used to tell the girls about his family in Rathdoon, well, about the family that Billy and Mary had really. The twins with the red hair and the freckles and then Gretta with the pigtails and the baby, a big roll of butter with a laugh you could hear half a mile away. He told Anna Kelly that sometimes on the summer evenings when it would be very bright the twins wouldn't have gone to bed, and they'd be sitting at their window waiting till the Lilac Bus turned into the street and Uncle Mikey would get off. They collected stamps and badges, any kind of badges, and he had them all on the lookout for anything of that order so as he never went home empty-handed.

He was the only one of the bank porters who came from the country. The rest were all Dubliners: they used to laugh at him and say there'd have to be an official enquiry as to how he got the job. But they were a very good-natured lot, and there was great chat all day as they manned the doors, or wheeled the big boxes on trolleys where and when more money was needed or had to be put away. They delivered letters and documents up and down the street. They knew a lot of the customers by name and they got great Christmas presents altogether.

The Lilac Bus had started just when Mikey had needed it. His father was getting senile now, and it was hard on poor Billy and Mary to have the whole business of looking after him. But it would have been a long way to come back without Tom Fitzgerald and the little minibus that dropped you at the door. Imagine having to get yourself to the town by a crowded train, packed on a Friday night and maybe not a seat, and then after that to try and organise the seventeen miles home. It would take all day and all night and you'd be exhausted.

His old father was pleased to see him sometimes, but other times the old man didn't seem to know who he was. Mikey would take his turn spooning the food, and combing the matted hair. He would play the Souza marches his father liked on the record player, and put the dirty clothes in the big buckets of Dettol and water out in the back. Mary, who was Billy's wife and a sort of a saint, said that there was no problem to it if you thought of it all as children's nappies. Into a bucket of disinfectant for a while, throw that out, into a bucket of water a while and throw that out and then wash them. Weren't they lucky to have space out the back and a tap and a drain and all. It would be desperate altogether for people who lived in a flat, say.

And the nurse came twice a week and she was very good too. She even said once to Mikey that he needn't come back *every* weekend, it was above the call of duty. But Mikey had said he couldn't leave it all to Billy and Mary, it wasn't fair. 'But they'd be getting the house: what would Mikey be getting?' the nurse had pointed out. Mikey said that sort of thing didn't come into it. And anyway, wasn't it a grand thing to come back to your own place.

The twins told Mikey that there was never any fighting when he came home and Mikey was surprised.

'Why would there be fighting in this house?' he asked.

The twins shrugged. Phil and Paddy were afraid of being disloyal.

'Sure you couldn't be fighting with your poor old grandfather, he would never harm the hair of your heads,' Mikey said.

The twins agreed and the matter was dropped.

They loved Mikey around the house and he had a fund of jokes for them. Not risky ones of course, but ones they could tell anyone. Gretta even wrote them down sometimes so that she'd remember them to tell them in class. Mikey never told the same one twice; they told him he should be on the television telling them one after another with a studio audience. Mikey loved the notion of it. He had once hoped that he might be asked to do a turn for the bank's revue but nobody had suggested it, and when he had whispered it to that nice Anna Kelly, she said she had heard you had to be a member of the union to be invited, that only members of the IBOA were allowed to perform. He had been pleased to know that, because otherwise he would have felt they were passing him over.

He had his doubts about the Lilac Bus when he arrived the very first Friday. Tom Fitzgerald had asked them to be sure not to wave any money at him, because the legalities of the whole thing were what you might call a grey area. He did have the proper insurance and everything, and the Lilac Bus had a passenger service vehicle licence, but there was no point in courting disaster. Let them all give him the money when they were home in Rathdoon where it would be nice and calm. None of them had understood the ins and outs of it but they all agreed. Mikey wondered if people like Doctor Burke's daughter and Mr Green's son Rupert would fancy sharing a journey home with Mikey Burns the bank porter and the son of poor Joey Burns who before he lost his wits had been a great man for standing waiting till Ryan's pub opened and nothing much else. But Dee and Rupert were the salt of the earth, it turned out. There wasn't an ounce of snobbery between the pair of them. And Mrs Hickey, she was a lady too but she always seemed pleased to see him. Nancy Morris was the same as she always had been since she was a schoolgirl, awkward and self-conscious. Nothing would get her out of that, she'd be an old maid yet. Celia Ryan was another fish altogether: it was a mystery she hadn't married someone by now. She always looked as if her mind was far away, yet she was meant to be a powerful nurse. He knew a man who'd been in Celia's ward, and he couldn't speak highly enough of her. He said she was like a legend in the hospital.

Nowadays he enjoyed the journey home, after he had got over his shyness of the first few runs. He would tell them a joke or two; they weren't a great audience, not like Gretta and Phil and Paddy, but they did smile and laugh a little and didn't it cheer them up?

Sometimes he sat beside Celia and he would tell her tales of the world of banking. He told her of all the new machines, and the days of bank inspections, and how the tourists would drive you mad, and how in the summer you'd have a line half a mile long of Spanish and French students all wanting to change about £1 each of their foreign money. Celia didn't tell many tales of the hospital, but she often gave him helpful advice about his own father, all in a low voice so that the others didn't hear her talking about incontinence pads and velcro fastenings for clothes.

But tonight it was the young Kennedy fellow sitting beside him. There was something seriously wrong with that boy. His brothers Bart and

Eddie were the nicest fellows you could meet in the day's walk, but whatever had happened to young Kev he looked as if he had seen the Day of Judgement. You only had to address a civil word to him to have him leap out of his skin. Try to tell him a good story and he'd miss the point altogether. Mikey thought he'd teach him a few tricks that might be of use to him, to be able to do a trick in a pub. But the young fellow looked at him with the two eyes staring out of his head and didn't take in a word of it. In the end Mikey let him be, staring out the window as if the goblins were going to leap out of the hedges and climb into the bus after him.

Mikey nodded off. It was easy to sleep in the bus. The two girls behind him were already asleep, dreaming of fellows probably. Mikey dreamed that his father was well and strong again and had opened some kind of import and export agency in Rathdoon and that he, Mikey, was the manager and that he was able to give grand summer jobs to Phil and Paddy and Gretta delivering letters to people up and down the street. He often dreamed of the children. But he never saw a wife for himself in the dream. Mikey Burns had missed the boat as far as wives were concerned. Too nervous and eejity at the time he should have been looking for one, and now at forty-five he wasn't the kind of forty-five year old that would be in the race at all. Better not make a fool of yourself going to dances or picking up fast-knowing women in pubs and being made to look thick altogether.

When they crossed the river and were really in the West they paused for the ten-minute comfort stop, and the half pint to open the throat a bit. Celia came up to him quietly and put an envelope in his hand.

'That's for the bedsores: it's all written on it, keep him moving as much as you can.'

'Aw Celia you're terribly good, can I pay for this?'

'Are you mad Mikey? Do you think I paid for it? Dublin Health Authority would like you to have it as a little gift.' They laughed. She was very nice.

What a pity he hadn't found a grand girl like Celia when he was young and promising looking. After all, he had a grand well-paid job now, he'd be able to make a home for anyone. The reason he didn't really have one wasn't money, it was lack of interest. He couldn't be buying a place and furnishing it and getting tables and chairs in it all for himself. The room he rented was grand and comfortable and he denied himself nothing. He had a grand big telly and he had bought a mirror himself to fix to the front of the wardrobe – that way he'd go out properly dressed. He had a lovely radio beside the bed which was a lamp and a clock and an alarm all in one. When he went out to people's houses, and the Dublin fellows often invited him up to their places, he was always able to bring a big box of chocolates, a fancy one with ribbon on it. He was able to give a good account of himself.

But when he'd been a young lad, who were they except the sons of poor Joey Burns, and his mother had taken in washing and cleaned people's floors? It hadn't held Billy back: Billy strutted round Rathdoon as if he owned it, as if he were as good as any other citizen of the place. And wasn't he right? Look where he was now, he had all kinds of business interests, he employed five people in Rathdoon. He had the take away shop; nobody believed there was a need for it until it appeared. Half the families in the place ate Billy's chicken and chips on a Saturday night, and they had fried fish too, and hamburgers. And they sold cans of lemonade, and stayed open late to get the crowds going home from Ryan's, and Billy had put up two huge mesh litter bins at his own expense and everyone was delighted with him.

And he had an insurance business as well. Not a big one but anyone who wanted cover went through him – it could all be filled in quickly in the house. And he had some kind of a connection with a fellow who came to do tarmacadaming. If you wanted the front of a place all smartened up then Billy would get other people with their places facing the same way to agree and the man with the machine and the tar would come in and it was cheaper for everyone, and the place looked a king to what it looked before. A whole section of the main street looked really smart now, and Billy had got a tree planted in a tub and it was like something you'd see in a film. Billy had the brains and Billy never ran away the way Mikey ran off up to Dublin after his mother had died. Billy had stayed to marry Mary Moran who was way beyond anyone they'd ever have thought about. Or that Mikey would have thought about.

He was looking forward to being home tonight. He had a computer game for the twins' birthday. It was several cuts above the Space Invaders they had tried out once, and it could be plugged into any kind of television; he had been playing it on his own television all week but the shop assistant said it would work as well on a smaller set. The twins had their birthday on Monday and he was going to give them the game on Sunday afternoon. He would set up the room with the curtains pulled and pretend they were going to watch something on the television, and then would come the surprise. He had got a smart red girl's handbag for Gretta, even though it wasn't her birthday, because he didn't want her to be left out, and a yellow rabbit for the baby in case it might have feelings of discontent in its pram.

Mary would never let him near his father on the Friday night, she'd have a supper warm for him, or if it had been a busy day she'd run across the road to the family take away and get him fish and chips as soon as she saw the Lilac Bus pull up. She used to thank him so much for coming back to help with his father, and she'd tell him funny things about the children and what they had done during the week. They were back at school now so there would be tales of what divilment Phil had got up to and the threatening messages that came home about him from the Brothers.

Mikey was the second to get out. They would leave Doctor Burke's daughter up at the golf club entrance; her parents were always there of a Friday night and she'd go and join them. Then when it came to the end of the street the first drop was Mikey. He would take down Nancy Morris's huge suitcase which weighed as light as a feather and leave it inside the bus because she and Kev Kennedy would be next out, and Kev had nothing with him ever except a parcel which he kept under his seat.

Mikey advised them all to be good and if they couldn't they should be clever and if they couldn't be clever then they should buy a pram. He laughed happily and closed the door behind him.

There was no light in the kitchen and no meal on the table. There was no sign of Mary and no note either. He didn't mind not seeing Billy – his brother was usually up at the take away or in Ryan's doing some deal with someone. But Mary?

He looked in the other rooms. His father was asleep, mouth open, wheelchair near the bed, on the chair a large chamber pot, optimistic since the old man was never able to time things so accurately.

There was a smell of disinfectant mixed with better smells. Mary had big bunches of flowers round the room. She always said that she thought it cheered the old man up, and sometimes she had seen him stretch out and touch the flowers gently. He snored lightly, there was a night light, and a Sacred Heart lamp as well.

Then he went up the stairs quietly. The twins had bunk beds; their toys and clothes and books were all around. Phil slept in a ball with his fists clenched; Paddy was more peaceful, lying on his side. Gretta looked funny with her long straight hair brushed out. He remembered her with plaits for as long as she had been old enough to force her hair into them. She had a smile as if she was dreaming. She was a thin little thing, gawky and plain-looking but she had a smile that would tear the heart out of you. Even when she was asleep.

The door of Billy and Mary's bedroom was open: they weren't there. The baby round and soft like a cream bun lay in its cot near the bed. There was a lovely white lacy bedspread, and on the wall there was a picture of Our Lady in a field of flowers. It had a blue lamp lighting under it. It was called 'Queen of the May'. Mary told Mikey once that the day she and Billy got engaged he had won a competition at a carnival where you had to throw rings over things and he had chosen that picture for her because she liked it so much.

Mikey put his small bag in his own room which was neat as anything. She always had a bright clean pillowslip on the tops as if he was the highest quality coming for the weekend. Sometimes Mikey's mind went back to what the house had looked like in his mother's day when they hadn't any such style or time for it.

It was puzzling, but maybe she had gone to get him fish and chips. He waited downstairs and listened to the news on the television. And eventually he began to get worried. They never left the children all alone in the house, even though they were perfectly safe, but it was just the way they were. His anxiety increased. He walked across to the take away and to his surprise there was Mary serving. There were four people waiting for their order and only one of the young girls who worked there was behind the counter. They were working flat out.

'Mikey, Lord is it that time already?' She was pleased but flustered to see him.

'Will I get behind there and give you a hand?' He knew the way he had done it with them a few Saturday nights during the summer when they had been very busy. And the prices were on the wall.

'Oh Mikey, would you?' She was very grateful.

He hung up his jacket and took an apron from a drawer. In a few moments they had the crowd thinned, and Mary was able to draw breath again. She spoke first to the girl who worked there.

'Treasa, would you take off your apron like a good child and run up to Ryan's. Tell them that we're short-staffed tonight and we'll be closing early. Tell them if they want anything to come down in the next half hour for it otherwise they'll be disappointed.'

'Who will I tell, Mam?' the child seemed worried.

'That's a point – not much use telling poor Mrs Ryan these days. Let me see, if there's anyone behind the bar helping, like Bart Kennedy, anyone like that, someone who looks in charge.'

'Celia's home: she was on the bus, she'll probably have got behind the counter by now,' Mikey said.

'That's it, tell Celia.'

Treasa skipped off up the road, pleased to be out of the heat.

'Where's everyone?' Mikey looked around.

'Oh there's been a lot happening. I'll tell you all when we get back. Keep a brave face on it for half an hour more and then it will be done.' A trickle of people came in, and Mikey served them, and just as Mary had guessed would happen a great influx came from Ryan's pub. They were full of good-natured abuse about it being against the law of the land to close the chipper before the pub. Mary had laughed good-naturedly and said wasn't she going above and beyond the call of duty to let them know rather than have them going home with stomachs full of beer and nothing to soak it up.

She didn't want a portion for herself, so Mikey wrapped up his own choice, and when they had drained the fat, scrubbed the tops and swept up anything that could be swept into black plastic bags which were tied with little wires at the top, they crossed the street and went home. Mary heated a plate under the hot water tap, got out the tomato sauce and some bread and butter.

'Will I get you tea or would you like a drop of anything?'

They got a bottle of Guinness each and sat down.

494

'Billy's gone. Gone for good.'

He stared at her, fork half-way to his mouth.

'He went this day before lunch, he'll not be back. Ever.'

'Ah no, Mary. That's not possible.'

She took a sip of her drink and made a face.

'I never like the first sip, but it tastes grand after that.' She smiled a weak little smile.

Mikey swallowed and said:

'It was just a bit of a row, that's all. People have rows, they get patched up.'

'No, there was no row, there was no difference of opinion even.'

Mikey remembered the way the twins had said there was no fighting when he was around the place.

'But just a bit of a barney now and then, these things sort themselves out, really they do.' He was pleading now.

'No, I'll tell you it from the start to finish – there was no row. Back there early on in the summer we did have rows all right: he was very touchy, I thought, bite the head off you as soon as look at you, but he said that's the way I was too. The children even noticed us.'

'So what happened?'

'Well I don't know, honestly. But anyway we had a great summer, as you know, business was booming. He used to be tired but he was never cross any more, and what with the baby getting to be so grand – you know they're like divils for the first few weeks – anyway we hadn't a worry under the sun.' She stopped and looked away beyond him.

Mikey was silent,

'Eat up your fish and chips, Mikey, you can eat and listen.'

'I can't.'

She lifted the plate from him and put it into the oven very low down. 'You'll eat it later then. Today was when it all happened, and if I hadn't come back I wouldn't have known: I wouldn't have known at this moment. I wouldn't have known until the end of next week. And the whole of Rathdoon would have known before me.'

'Known what, for God's sake?'

'He's gone off with Eileen Walsh, you know the one we said was too good to be working in a chipper. Well, she was far goo good, she was only biding her time to go off with the owner of the chipper. That was the little plan. Could you beat it?' The voice was steady but the eyes were over bright.

'But it's only a fancy isn't it, it's a bit of madness. I mean where would they go, and what would they do? And how could he leave you and the baby and the whole family?'

'He's in love with her. That's the word: *In Love*. Isn't it marvellous? He was never *In* love with me; he loved me, of course, but that was different apparently.'

Mikey stood up, but he didn't know what to do so he sat down again. Mary went on with the story.

'I was meant to be going into the town. There's always a lift in on Fridays and I had a list of things we needed for the take away, not things we get from the suppliers, but stupid things, big ashtrays for example and a couple of tins of bright red paint – we were going to paint the windows to match the geraniums, can you believe? But to go on with what happened: You know old Mrs Casey who's only just learned to drive, well she was giving me the lift and as soon as we were out on the road beyond the golf club, didn't the engine splutter and make these desperate sounds.

'Ah well, I said to myself, there's my day in town gone for its tea. But she's such a nice woman, Mrs Casey, you couldn't offend her. I told her it was a blessing in disguise and I could get the things next week and maybe I'd go home and make an apple tart since Mikey'd be coming back on the bus tonight.'

A big lump came up in Mikey's throat.

'And I said to her to sit tight, I'd walk back and tell the Brennans in the garage to go out for her.'

Mary took another sip.

'It was a gorgeous day, and I picked wild flowers from the hedges, and when I came in there was Billy at the table with a whole load of papers all round him. And I was delighted because he was meant to have been gone for the day. So I said wasn't this grand and we'd have a bit of lunch the two of us – something we hadn't done in years – and I saw that there was "Dear Mary" on one piece of paper and on another and only two or three lines on each. And I *still* didn't know anything was wrong so I said "Are you writing me love letters at my age?" as a kind of joke. You see I thought he was just back unexpectedly and was writing me a note to explain that he'd been in.'

'Oh Mary, isn't this terrible,' said Mikey, believing it for the first time since the saga had started.

'And this is the awful bit: he started to cry, he started to cry like a child. Well, I nearly dropped dead – Billy Burns crying. I ran to him to try and put my arms around him and he pushed me away. And he was sobbing like a baby that's getting teeth, so I said to him to hush it down or his father would hear. I'd left the baby next door but your father would have been having a doze and it would have frightened the daylight out of him like it was doing to me.' She paused for a moment.

'Then he said about Eileen, and her expecting and all.'

There was a silence and the clock ticked and the soft snoring sound of the old man could be heard from the back room.

'And he said he couldn't face me, and he was leaving a letter. And I said that he didn't have to go now, not at once, that surely he could stay and we could talk about what was to be done. But he said there'd been too much talking and that was it, now he was going.' Mikey put out his big hand and patted Mary's arm hopelessly.

'And there was a lot of this and that, but funny no fight, no shouts or me saying he was a bastard or him saying he couldn't bear me any more, that I was an old nag or anything.'

'Well, no one could think that,' Mikey cried loyally.

'No, he said I'd been the best wife and mother in the world, and that he couldn't tell me how sorry he was, he was just heartbroken, he said. All the papers were to show me that the chip shop is in my name, and the thousand pounds in the building society is for me, and the name of a solicitor who'd be able to find him, who'd pass letters on.'

'And where does he think he's going?'

'To England. Where else?'

'And how will he earn a living for himself and this floosie?'

'She's not a floosie – Eileen a floosie? Billy would earn a living on the planet Mars, don't worry about that.'

Mikey was struck dumb.

'But the thing that upset him most was his father, your father.'

'Billy never gives much time to poor old Dad.'

'No, but he thought it wasn't just for me to be left with him – to have to look after an old man who isn't my own father. I said that Da was the least of the problems, what I wanted to know was how he could leave me, his wife, his friend for years and years, for fourteen years married, and a year before that mad about each other. That's when he explained all this *In Love* business.'

'What did you do?'

'What could I do? His mind was made up, he was leaving. He had a list of things he wanted me to do. There was a special sum of money left in one envelope that was for me to have driving lessons. I was to find out who taught Mrs Casey: whoever taught her could teach the divil himself. He was leaving the van. I was to ask Bart Kennedy to give me a hand and pay him a proper wage, I was to decide whether he should write to the children or not and what I should tell them, if anything. He thought I should say he had gone away for a bit and then they'd grow used to it.'

Mary stood up to get another bottle of stout.

'He had been packing his things too, it nearly broke my heart to see his good shirts stuffed in all creased, and he had forgotten all his shoes. I asked him to say goodbye to your father – he's been very clear the past couple of days, knows all of us – but no, he wouldn't. I said he might never see him again and he said that he'd never see any of us again. That's when I got a bit frightened about it all. I knew there's never any changing his mind. So I decided I'd let him go, without screaming and roaring and begging.'

'You let him walk out . . .'

'No, I said I'd go out and let him finish at his ease. I said he needn't bother about the letter now, he'd said it all, that I'd go out for an hour or two until he left. That he could leave all the insurance papers where they could be found, and the solicitor who would pass on the messages to him if there was anything we hadn't thought of. He was SO relieved: you should have seen his face – you see he was afraid there'd be this big scene. He said that maybe I'd be glad of the change too, and I said, oh no, I wouldn't, I would miss him every day of the year and so would his children, and on the days when his father was clear his father would miss him too. I wasn't going to give him the nice comfortable feeling that he was doing us any favours. And out I went. I crept along the back way and he finished his packing and put his leaving things out on the table, and your one came along in her car and he put the boxes and cases in and she kissed him just standing at our door and they drove off.

'When I came in it was all in neat piles on the table and a piece of paper saying "Thank you very much, Mary. All the best, Billy." So now you know everything, everything that's to be known.'

'Isn't he a callous bastard, isn't he the biggest most selfish . . .'

'That won't bring him back.'

'I'll bring him back, I'll get him back. He's not going to desert you, there's ways of bringing him back.'

'Not if he doesn't want to come back! Will you have your fish and chips now, they'll go all hard otherwise?'

He hardly slept all night; it was only when the dawn came that he fell off and it wasn't long after that the twins were in the room followed by Gretta carrying a cup of tea. That was always their excuse to wake him: it was called bringing him his tea in bed. Most of it was in the saucer and some of it was on the stairs but it was still an excuse. They were full of plans for the day. They'd come down and wait while he was feeding grandpa and changing him: they accepted that routine as part of life like sunsets or having to wash your hands before meals. They wanted to show him a new game that had arrived in Brophy's shop. It was a huge thing like a Space Invaders but it cost twenty pence a time and they could only have three goes altogether unless of course Uncle Mikey wanted an extra game. And Mammy had said they could go on a picnic in the afternoon because since daddy was gone to Dublin for a bit there'd be no work to be done around the house and no one coming in about Insurance who had to have tea. And hadn't he better get up now in case all the good went out of the day.

Matty felt the day was very heavy on his hands, that things kept happening as if he were outside looking in at all the things that were happening instead of being part of them. He saw himself feeding his father slowly with a spoon, he saw himself cutting crusts off the sandwiches for the picnic, and climbing for the blackberries. It was like playing a part in a play.

He was glad when it was evening and the children went to bed; they went easily because he had promised them the most monstrous surprise of their lives tomorrow. Something that he absolutely guaranteed they would never expect. He assured Gretta that it was something she could share too and that there was a small non-birthday present for her as well.

'I don't know what I'd have done without you and that's the truth,' Mary said. 'The day just flew by for me.' He was glad it had. He had arranged for two girls to help Treasa in the chip shop.

'Will Eileen not be in again?' Treasa complained. Her tone was guileless, she didn't know.

'No she won't, she's gone off somewhere; we'll get you these two young ones you've had in there before on bank holidays and high summer,' he said firmly. 'Mrs Billy and I are going to be down in Ryan's for a bit, so you'll know to send one of them down there if there's any problem, but a big bright girl like you, Treasa, you'll manage it. Don't you know it all like the back of your hand?'

Treasa was delighted with him.

'Oh go on, Mr Mikey, you and your Dublin chat,' she said.

'Are we going off down to Ryan's?' he asked her.

He was going to make a joke and say something about stepping out together or hitting the high spots but he felt it would have been the wrong thing to do. She looked up at him pleased and surprised that he seemed so eager.

'I'm not much company for you.'

'I think we should go out though, don't you? From the start like. No hiding away in corners, no crawling out when people think you've got two heads. Be out there from the word "go". After all YOU haven't done anything.'

'I've failed to hold on to my husband, that's a great crime around these parts.'

'Oh I don't think so; aren't they all stuck into television every night here? I think you'd have to do far more than that to be a disgrace.'

'I hate you to be involved in it, Mikey, you've been nothing but kindness itself, every weekend as nice as anything and look what happens to you: caught up in all the scandal, all the gossip.'

'There won't *be* scandal and gossip, and that's up to you to make sure of.' He heard his own voice in his ears. He thought it sounded very confident, very sure. Mary must have thought so too.

'You're a great help to me taking all these decisions, I'm like one of those things in films that just walk about not knowing what they're at.'

'Zombies,' he said.

'Imagine you knowing that,' Mary said.

'I see a lot of films,' Mikey said. 'What else have I to do?'

Ryan's was crowded. He put Mary in a corner and went up to the counter. Celia was going full strength and Bart Kennedy was giving her a hand. Mikey remembered his brother's instructions about paying Bart a

proper wage and bile against Billy rose in his throat. To be able to calcu-
late like that, to plan for her desertion, to deceive her so long.

'It's not like you to be short of a word, Mikey Burns.' Celia was standing in front of him. She must have asked him his order and he hadn't
heard.

'I'm sorry.' He had to force his sense of outrage down before he could
speak.

'Are you all right?' Celia's voice was concerned.

Mikey shook himself. He was full of brave words to his sister-in-law
about how SHE was to behave, now he must do the same for himself. He
could speak again, but he hadn't the heart for jokes.

He gave his order and carried the pint and the glass of Snowball across
to Mary. As he was passing young Biddy Brady's engagement party,
Nancy Morris of all people put her hand out as if to stop him. Wanted
him to come and tell them some funny stories. And he always thought
she was such a superior acting kind of a one, always looking in on herself
and never having time for other people. Well, Well.

'Not now, Nancy' he had said and he saw her face turning away
embarrassed. He hadn't meant to be so short with her, but honestly, *now*
of all times.

'Here we are' he said.

She had her head down looking at the floor.

'Look up Mary Burns, look up and smile.'

She looked up and gave a watery smile.

'That's marvellous but it isn't a patch on your daughter's.' She gave
one of Gretta's sudden grins, the kind of grin that split a face in half;
they both laughed.

'That's better,' said Mikey, 'now let's see what we'll do.'

They got out a writing pad and made out a list of things she had to do
this week. Ring suppliers – their names were all on some kinds of bits of
paper on various spikes around the office. Billy Burns hadn't kept any
books that would gladden the heart of a taxman but at least there was
some method in his ways. They wrote out a kind of notice which she
could give to anyone who called about insurance: 'Mr Burns' policies are
all being dealt with by the following office . . . ' followed by the name of
the solicitor's. She would give these to anyone with a laughing explanation that unfortunately as a mere woman she was never kept
informed of the Master's doings. It seemed fairly sure that he hadn't
absconded with other people's money, so his Book had been passed on or
sold to some other agent by now. The solicitors would know. They listed
the people they could call on to work in the take away, and how much
they should be paid. He went for two further pints and two further
Snowballs, and by that time they had covered every eventuality and worn
themselves out.

'I'll sleep tonight, I'm that exhausted,' Mary said, letting out that she hadn't slept the previous night.

'I'll sleep too: I'm less frightened,' Mikey said. She looked at him gratefully: 'You're very very good to me, but there's one thing you haven't mentioned at all.'

'What's that?'

'What about you? Will you still be coming home on the bus at weekends?'

'I'll get off the Lilac Bus before ten every Friday with the help of God,' he said.

'You're very different tonight, you're not always cracking jokes and making games out of things people say. I find it easier to talk to you, but hard to believe it IS you, do you know what I mean?'

'I think so,' he said.

'Like I want to ask you do you want to come home to Rathdoon even more than at weekends, but I don't know how to put it. If I say, will you come back altogether, it looks as if I want you to come back and look after us all and take it all on, and that's NOT it. And then, if I don't ask you, you might get the notion you're not welcome.'

'I've thought all that out too,' Mikey Burns said.

'And what did you arrive at?' She learned over the glass with its rim of froth. She couldn't wait to hear.

'You're still hoping in your heart he'll come back. That it's only a bit of summer madness. That it'll be all forgotten by the end of the month.'

'I'd like it, but I don't think it's going to happen,' she said simply.

'So, suppose I came home and settled myself in and Billy Boy came over the hill one fine day, where would that leave us all?'

'As we were, wouldn't it?' She looked at him enquiringly.

'No, I'd have to run away again, there wouldn't be room for us all in the one nest.'

'So are you not coming back to us? I always thought you had a great soft spot for us altogether.' She sounded sad.

'I'll come back for good if he isn't back for Christmas. That's the best way. That's the way to do it.' He looked proud of his deductions.

'It's your home,' she said gently. 'You were always as welcome in it as the sun coming in the windows.'

'You say that because you're like that. My brother Billy didn't say it, did he, when he was leaving. He told you to get Bart Kennedy and pay him a proper wage.'

'He did say it but I didn't repeat it. I didn't want to be making you think you had to do anything.' She looked troubled now.

'What did he say?'

'He said . . . ah it doesn't matter what he said. He made it clear he thought of the place as your house too.'

'I want to hear it.'

'Why? What does it matter? We know he hardly knows what he's doing: he's half mad these days, he couldn't string words together.'

'Well I'd like to know anyway, please,' he said simply but firmly. This wasn't the giggling, jokey man of last weekend.

'He said something like: "Mikey's not likely to settle down anywhere with anyone at his age, and he's very good to the old man, and the children love him. Maybe if he could find something for himself round here, he'd be in the place. Sure the house is half his anyway, he has a right to it." It was something along those lines.'

She didn't look at him, and he looked hard at the beermat which had a puzzle on it.

'Full of charm, my little brother, isn't he?'

'That's what he is: your little brother, don't ever forget that.'

'And would it suit you, Mary, if I were to be about the place?'

'Would it suit me? Wouldn't I love it, isn't it what I always wanted? There's always been a living for us all in that take away alone, you've seen the takings, and if we were working in it together . . .'

'Well then, I'll come back at Christmas, that's the best. I might even get myself made redundant up at the bank, and have a lump sum. Those fellows up in the bank, the porters, are fierce organised, you'd never know what kind of a deal they'd get for me.'

'And wouldn't it be dull for you, after Dublin?'

'No, don't I come home for nearly half the week as it is?'

'And maybe finding yourself a girl?' She was hesitant.

'I think brother Billy was right on that one, the time is past.' He smiled an ordinary smile, not a screwed up one.

Rupert Green passed the table. 'Did you see Judy Hickey at all?' he asked.

'No, I'm afraid we were talking, I didn't notice,' Mary said.

'She could be round the corner behind the pillar there,' Mikey pointed. Biddy Brady's party had linked arms and were singing 'Sailing' and Celia's mother was arriving with a golf club as if she were about to brain them but as they all watched horrified it turned out that she had no such intention: she was about to join in the singing, and was in fact calling for one voice only, her own.

'I've met everyone from the Lilac Bus except the one I set out to meet,' grumbled Rupert. 'Dee Burke was just flying out the door, Miss Morris looks as if she's had a skinful, Kev is cowering in a corner, and the rest of the cast is at the counter canoodling.'

'If she comes in what will I tell her?'

'Oh I'll find her, I have to tell her something extraordinary.'

Mary and Mikey looked politely interested.

He was gone.

'It's probably about some toadstool or mushroom; they're always talking about herbs and elderflowers and things,' Mikey said. Mary laughed and tucked her bag under her arm.

*

'Won't you want another man?' he said suddenly. 'I mean you're still young. Won't living with a brother-in-law cramp your style?'

'No, she said, 'No, I won't. I mean, even if I could have one and I can't. But I think I'm through with all that sort of thing. I think I just want a bit of peace and for the children to be able to grow up happily enough and for me to have a place here, you know, just like you said, not running away. That will do me.'

He remembered the dream that he had on the bus: the dream where there had been no wife but he was in charge of the children sending them on little messages up and down the street. He realised now there had been no Billy in the dream either. Some of the details were different, of course, but the central part was the same. He would be safe at home with them all. And there would be no demands made on him as a man. He could be just himself, and he'd be as welcome as the sun that came in the windows.

Judy

There had been four customers in the shop that afternoon, Judy had been taking note recently and writing it down in a little book. After lunch two students came in and spent almost half an hour reading books on herbalism and the art of home-made wines. An elderly man bought a copper bracelet for his arthritis and said that when the savages who came into his house and robbed him blind were leaving they pulled his copper arm band off in case it had been valuable. A woman with a tight hard face bought some Evening Primrose oil and asked could you dilute it with ordinary vegetable oil or baby lotion to make it go further.

It was a matter of weeks now before they had to close. Judy's heart was heavy as she walked toward the Lilac Bus. She was tired too, and not in form for a long drive to the West. She had been tempted to opt out. To go back to her little flat and have a long long bath listening to some nice music on the radio. Then to put on her caftan and her soft little slippers and lie there until the arches in her limbs and the build-up of a headache behind her eyes was gone. Fine advertisement I am for a health shop . . . she smiled to herself as she strode on towards the bus. Aching and creaking and bankrupt. No wonder people live such unhealthy lives if they see what good living leads to!

She hoped that Mikey Burns wouldn't be too loud tonight with his schoolboy jokes. He was a decent poor fellow but he was hard to take at any length. The trouble was that if you made no response to him he thought you hadn't heard and said it all again, and if you did manage a laugh he got encouraged and told you a few more.

She arrived just at the same time as Rupert: that was good, they could sit together in the back seat. It looked a bit standoffish if you were to keep a seat for anyone, but she really couldn't bear to be nudged by Mikey the whole way to Rathdoon or, even worse, to hear that solemn tedious little Nancy Morris telling her how to get free soap by buying toothpaste on a Wednesday or some such hare-brained scheme.

He was a good boy, Rupert: yes that was exactly how she would describe him if anyone asked her. Good. He was an only child of parents who were middle-aged when he was a toddler and who were old now that he was a man of twenty-five. His mother was sixty-seven and his father was seventy this year. But Rupert said there were no celebrations, his father was bedridden now and was failing by the week. Rupert said it was harder and harder each time he came home because he had this vision of his father as a hardy man with views of his own on everything, and then when he got into the big bedroom on a Friday night it was the same shock, the same readjustment – a paper-thin man with a head like a skull, with nothing alive except the big restless eyes.

Judy had known Rupert since he was a baby and yet she had only got to know him since the bus. He had always been a polite child. 'Good morning, Mrs Hickey. Do you have anything for my pressed flower collection?' Protestants were like that, she had always thought in her good-natured generalisations: pressed flowers, politeness, neat haircuts, remembering people's names. Mrs Green was so proud of her Rupert, she used to find excuses to walk him down the town. The Greens had been married for twenty years when Rupert was born. Celia Ryan's mother in the pub had whispered that she gave Mrs Green a novena to St Anne that had never been known to fail, but because of her religion she had delayed using it. The moment she had said it, Catholic or no Catholic, St Anne had intervened and there you were, there was Rupert.

Judy told him that one night on the Lilac Bus and he laughed till the tears came down his face. 'You'd better tell me about St Anne and what class of a saint she is. I suppose I should be thanking her that I'm here, or speaking sharply to her when times are bad.'

Judy often smiled at Rupert's quaint ways. He was wonderful company and the same age as her own son, Andrew, miles away in the sun of California. But she could never talk to Andrew like she talked to Rupert – in fact she could never talk to Andrew at all over the years. That was the legal agreement.

Judy wondered would you recognise your own child.

Suppose she went to San Francisco now and walked through Union Square, would she immediately know Andrew and Jessica? Suppose they passed her by? They would be grown man and woman, imagine, twenty-five and twenty-three. But if she didn't know them and they didn't know her, what was all the point of giving birth and holding a child inside you for all that time? And suppose they did recognise her, that something like an instinct made them stop and look at this fifty-year-old woman standing in the sunshine. What would they do? Would they cry 'Momma, Momma' and run to her arms like in a Hollywood film? Or would they be embarrassed and wish she hadn't turned up? They might have their own idea of a momma back in Ireland. A momma who was just not suitable. That's what Jack said he would tell them. Their mother hadn't been able to look after them – no other details. And when they were old enough to hear details and understand them, they would be given Judy's address to write to and she could send them an explanation if she felt able to. She never felt able to because they never wrote. For years and years she had been rehearsing it and trying out new phrases, like practising for a job interview or a school essay.

Little by little she realised they were eighteen, nineteen, twenty. Well old enough to ask about an unsuitable mother. Well old enough to be told. But no request ever came.

She didn't even write to Jack's brother after a while. Jack's kind big brother who had given them all a home on the West Coast of America but who had always tried to patch up the split. He had told her nothing in his letters except to assure her that the children were settling in to their school and that all was for the best.

This evening she wondered about them both, Andrew and Jessica – golden Californians now. Were they married? Very probably. Californians married younger, divorced sooner. Was she a grandmother? Very possibly. His name might be Hank or Bud or Junior. Or were those all old names? Why did she think it was a grandson, it might be a girl, a little girl in a sunhat like Jessica had been the day they took her away. She had a Californian clock in her mind always, ever since they left twenty years ago. She never paused and said, 'I wonder what time it is out there,' she always knew. It was coming up to a quarter to eleven in the morning for them. It was always that when she came round the corner to the Lilac Bus. And she didn't know if they were married or single, working in universities or as domestics. She didn't know if they were happy or wretched, she didn't even know if they were alive or dead.

She slipped neatly in beside Rupert on the back seat, passing young Dee Burke who had been looking so troubled for the last Lord knows when, it was amazing she hadn't cracked up. Past the odd young Nancy Morris. What a cuckoo in the nest that little one was – her mother was a grand little woman altogether, and Deirdre who had gone to the States was very nice, whenever she came back, full of chat. The brother in Cork was a nice lively fellow too. What had come over Nancy to make her so prissy or whatever it was she had become?

Rupert was wearing a new jacket which obviously thrilled him to the core. It just looked like an ordinary teddy boy jacket to Judy, but then she was the first to admit she knew nothing about smart clothes. Dee Burke had gone into ecstasies over it and Rupert had flushed with pleasure.

'It's a birthday present,' he whispered as the bus started, 'I'll tell you all about it later.'

She didn't want to hear all about it on the bus, not while her hip was aching and her head was throbbing, and that young Morris girl might well pretend not to be listening but was only two feet away from them. She felt old tonight. She was years older than everyone on the bus except

Mikey Burns and she was a good few years beyond him too. She was twenty years older than the young couple who had set up the health shop and who would be dismantling it within six weeks unless there was a miracle and they discovered the Elixir of Youth and bottled it in expensive but appealing packaging. Surely she was past all this rattling backwards and forwards across the country. Surely she should have some peace and settle down, in one place or the other.

She rooted in her big bag and gave Rupert a small parcel. 'It's Green Tea,' she said, 'just a little to see if you like it.'

His eyes lit up, 'This is what you make the mint tea, the proper mint tea with?' he said.

'Yes, a handful of fresh mint, a little sugar in a glass, and you make the tea separately In a silver pot if you have one and then pour it on the mint leaves.'

Rupert was very pleased. 'I'd been making it with tea bags since we came back from Morocco, and it tasted really terrible, but out there it was like heaven. Oh I AM grateful to you Judy.'

'It's only a little,' she said warningly.

'Look on it as a sample. If we like it we'll come in and buy kilos of the stuff and make your shop do a roaring trade,'

'It would need it.' She told him about the kind of trade they were doing. He was reassuring, it was the same everywhere.

He worked in an estate agency. Things were very slow. Houses that would have leaped off the books weren't moving at all. And there were shops closing down all over the place. But these things went in phases, he said. Things had to get better soon, the kind of people who knew about these things were confident, that's what you had to remember. Judy said wryly that the kind of people who knew about such things could probably still afford to be confident, they had so many irons in the fire. It was the rest of the world that was the problem.

They felt like old friends the way they talked. She asked him to come and advise for a bit at the cutting of the elderflower, and to help choose some of the dried rosemary and lemon balm for the little herb pillows she was making. Rupert said that for the Christmas trade she should make dozens of those and sell them herself to big shops in Grafton Street – they would make great Christmas gifts. Fine, Judy said, but what about her own shop, the shop she worked in? That's the one she wanted to help, not big stores which would make money anyway.

He told her about a politician's wife who had come into the auctioneer's and enquired politely about the location of her husband's new flat. Somehow they all knew that this flat was not a joint undertaking and that the wife was trying to find out. Everyone in the place had copped on and they all became vaguer and more unhelpful by the minute. Eventually the woman had stormed out in a rage. And they had drafted an immensely tactful letter to the politician pointing out that his nest had not been revealed but was in danger of coming under siege.

'Poor stupid woman,' said Judy. 'She should have let him install a harem in there if it kept him happy.'

'You wouldn't have let him do that, you'd have too much spirit,' Rupert said admiringly.

'I don't know. I let a man walk away with my two babies twenty years ago. That wasn't showing much spirit, was it?' Judy said.

Rupert gasped. Never had Judy Hickey mentioned the amazing happening that the whole town knew about in garbled versions. He had asked his mother who had said that nobody knew the whole ins and outs of it, and that Rupert's father who had been the local solicitor then also, had been very annoyed because nobody consulted him, and he was the obvious person to have been brought in on it. But there had been something from Dublin coming down for Jack Hickey and then documents being drawn up and Jack and the two children going to America and never coming back.

'But people must know WHY,' Rupert had insisted.

His mother said there were more explanations than there were days in the year.

She had been only six years married and twenty now without her man and her children, but she always kept the name Hickey. It was in case the children ever came back, people said. There was a while when she used to go into the town seventeen miles away and ask at the tourist office if you could get the lists of American tourists or just those with children. There was a while she would go up to the bus tours that sometimes came through Rathdoon and scan the seats for nine-year-old boys with seven-year-old sisters. But all that was long in the past. If it was so long in the past, why had she mentioned them now?

'Are they on your mind then?' Rupert asked gently. She replied as naturally as if she was in the habit of talking about them. She spoke with no more intensity than she had talked of the mint tea.

'They are and they aren't. We'd probably have nothing to say to each other at this stage.'

'What kind of work does he do now? He's not retired, is he?'

'Who? Andrew, he's only your age. I HOPE he hasn't retired yet.' She looked amused.

'No, I meant your husband. I didn't know whether your children were boys or girls.' Rupert felt he had put his foot in it.

'Boy and girl, Andrew and Jessica. Andrew and Jessica.'

'Nice names,' he said foolishly.

'Yes, they are nice names aren't they? We spent ages choosing them. No, I've absolutely no idea whether Jack Hickey is working or whether he is lying in a gutter being moved on by big American cops with sticks. And I don't know if he ever worked in California or whether he lived off his brother. I never cared. Honestly I never gave him a thought. It sounds like someone protesting, I know it does, but it's funny: I have

508

great trouble remembering what he looked like then and I never until this moment wondered how he's aged. Possibly got fatter. His elder brother Charlie was a lovely man, he was fat, and there was a family picture I remember, and the parents were fat.'

Rupert was silent for a moment. Such obvious indifference was chilling. You could understand hate or bitterness even. You could forgive a low fire of rage and resentment. But she talked about him just as you would about some minor celebrity who had been in the news one time. Is he dead or alive? Who knows, who remembers? On to another topic.

'And do the children, well . . . do Andrew and Jessica keep in touch even a little bit?'

'No. That was the agreement.'

If he was ever to know, it would be now. He inclined his head slightly to see if anyone else was listening. But no, Dee was fast asleep with her head at an awkward angle, and that awful Morris girl was asleep too. The others were too far ahead to hear.

'That was a harsh sort of agreement,' he said tentatively.

'Oh they thought they were justified. People used to think it was quite justifiable to hang a sheep stealer, don't forget.'

'Is that what you did?' he asked smiling. 'Steal a sheep'

'Would that it had been so simple. No no, I thought you knew, I thought your father might have told you. No, I was a dope peddler. That's even worse than anything, isn't it?'

She looked like a mischievous girl the way she said it. He felt she couldn't be serious.

'No, what was it about really?' he laughed.

'I told you. I was the local drugs person.' She spoke without pride or shame. Just as if she was saying what her name was before she was married. Rupert had never been so startled. 'You do surprise me,' he said hoping he was managing to keep the shock out of his voice. 'But that was YEARS ago.'

'It was the sixties. I suppose it is years ago, but your lot aren't the first to know about drugs, you know – the sixties had their own scene.'

'But wasn't that only in America and England? Not like now.'

'Of course it was here too, not in huge housing estates, and not kids and not heroin. But with brightish, youngish things, at dances, and people who just left College who had been abroad, and it was all very silly, and to this day I think perfectly harmless.'

'Hash, was it?'

'Oh yes, Marijuana, pot, a few amphetamines, a bit of LSD.'

'You had acid? YOU had acid?' He was half-admiring, half-shocked.

'Rupert, what I had was everything that was going, that wasn't the point. The point was that I was supplying it, and I got caught.'

'Why on earth were you doing that?'

'Out of boredom in a way, I suppose. And the memory was nice, not huge but nice. And there was a lot of fun too, you met great people – not dead-wood people like Jack Hickey. I was very stupid really. I deserved all that happened. I often think that.' She had paused to muse. Rupert mused with her for a bit. Then he spoke again:

'Were you doing it for long? Before you were caught?'

'About eighteen months. I was at a party and we all smoked something, Lord knows what it was called – I thought it was great, Jack had said nothing at the time, but when we got home he roared and shouted, and said that if this ever happened again, and what he'd do and what he wouldn't do.'

'Had he refused it then?'

'Ah you didn't know our Jack, not at all, he had passed the poor little cigarette with the best but he had kept his mouth closed and only pretended to inhale. He was sober and furious. Oh, there was a barney that went on all week, then the ultimatum: if I ever touched it again . . . curtains, he'd take the children off to America, I'd never see them again, no court in the land . . . you could write it out yourself as a script and it would be right, it would be what he said.' Rupert listened, fascinated. Judy's soft voice went on:

'Well, Jack was dealing with livestock. It wasn't like a farm, you know, the house then, it was like a ranch: there were only livestock – no milking, no hens, no crops, just beasts in the field – buy them, graze them, sell them. We had poor old Nanny, she had been my Nanny in the days of old decency and she minded Andrew and Jessica, I used to go here and there. Gathering material for a book on the wild flowers of the West. Gathering bad company more likely. Anyway, because I had my little car and because I went here and there what could be more natural than I go to Dublin or to London as I did twice to get some stuff for people. Others suggested it, I took it up like a flash.'

'It's like a story out of a book,' Rupert breathed admiringly.

'A horror story then. I remember it as if it was yesterday: acting on information received, warrant, deeply embarrassed Mr Hickey, a person of such importance as yourself, absolutely sure there's nothing in it, but have to apply the same laws to the high as to the low, and if we could get it all over as quickly as possible wouldn't that be for the best? Dear, dear, heavens above, what have we here, in MRS Hickey's car, and MRS Hickey's briefcase in the bedroom. And hidden away behind MRS Hickey's books. Well, he was at a loss for words and perhaps Mr Hickey could come up with some explanation?'

She was like an actress, Rupert thought suddenly. He could see the Sergeant or the Superintendent or whoever it was. She could do a one-woman show, the way she was telling the story, and it was without gesture or emphasis since it was being told in a low voice not to wake the others as the minibus sped through the evening.

'It took for ever. And there were people down from Dublin and there was a TD, someone I didn't even know Jack knew. And Jack said that the whole place was becoming too much for him anyway and he had been thinking about selling it for a while, but if there was this scandal then people would know he was doing it under a cloud and the price of the place would drop right down. They were all businessmen, even the guards, they could understand that.

'Then the documents. Jack was going to take the children to his brother unless I signed a sworn statement that I agreed I was an unfit person to act as their mother any longer. The Sergeant could charge me, as soon as Jack had the place sold, his plans made and was off to California with the babies. He begged me to think of the children.'

'He did that and yet took them away from you?' Rupert was confused.

'Yes, you see his point was that I was a drugs criminal, that wasn't a good start for any child: they'd be better without me. A deal had been done, kind wise people had seen extenuating circumstances, it was up to me to make the most of them.'

She looked out the window for a while.

'I didn't think it would be for ever. I was frightened, I was sure it would all die down. I said yes. He sold the place, well he sold it to that gangster, remember, who conned everyone and went off with a packet. Then the Liquidator or whatever sold it to the nuns and they made it into the conference centre. So now you know the story of the Big House and all the bad people who lived there until the present day.' He hadn't realised that she was once mistress of the big Doon House where she now lived in the gate lodge. Today the house had priests, nuns and lay-people coming to do retreats, have discussions. And sometimes there were ordinary conferences that weren't religious at all: that's how the community made the costs of the place. But it was usually a very quiet type of conference where the delegated weren't expecting much of a night life. Rathdoon could offer Ryan's Pub and Billy Burns' chicken and chips; people usually expected more if they came a long way to a conference.

'I had to leave Doon House within a month. But he tricked me in one way. Even with the slightest hint of a drugs offence in those days you wouldn't get into the States. They wouldn't give me a visa. And in order to make the distance as great as possible between poor Andrew and Jessica over there and their mad mother over here Jack arranged that I be charged with a minor offence: possession. It was a nothing, even here, and compared to what I could have been charged with, which was dealing, it was ludicrously light. But then the deal had been done, don't forget. And even being charged with possession kept me out of the States.'

There was another silence.

'Wasn't that a bad trick to play on you?' Rupert said.

'Yes. Yes. I suppose he thought like the people who burned people in the Inquisition . . . that they were doing the right thing. You know, rooting out evil.'

'It was very drastic, even for the sixties, wasn't it?'

'Will you stop saying the sixties as if it was the stone age. YOU were born in the sixties, don't forget.'

'I don't remember much about them,' Rupert grinned.

'No. Well I suppose you'd call it drastic; Jack would have called it effective. He was a great man for getting the job done.' She spoke with scorn: 'That's all he cared about. That's done, he'd say proudly. It was the same coping with me. But Rupert, did you not know all this before? I mean, I don't want to make out that the whole town talks of me morning, noon and night, but I would have thought that you must have heard some drift of it?'

'No, never. I knew that the children had gone away with their father and I think I asked why but I was never told.'

'That's because you're so nicely brought up! They're too well bred in your house, they'd never talk of other people's business.'

'I think my mother'd be glad if she knew about it. And it's not only us. I once asked Celia why you didn't have your children, and she said there was some desperate row years ago when judges were even worse than they are today. That's all, nobody knows about the . . . er . . . the smoke and things.'

'I don't know whether to be pleased or disappointed,' Judy laughed. 'I always thought people believed I was up to no good with all the herbal remedies, bordering on the witch doctor nearly.'

'I'm afraid people think that's very worthy, we'll have to make your image more villainous for you,' Rupert said.

'Oh for ages the unfortunate guards used to come and inspect my herb garden. I had a map of it for them in the end, and told them they must come in whenever they liked and that I would explain anything that looked a bit amiss. Then by the time I went to Dublin, they'd more or less written me off as a dangerous drugs pusher.'

'You mean you're in the clear at last, after twenty years?'

'I don't know: sometimes I see the imprint of heavy boots round the camomile beds. Eternal vigilance?'

'Do you hate Jack Hickey for it.'

'No, I said to you I never think of him. But you'd probably find that hard to believe, especially when I think of the children a lot, and to all intents and purposes I don't know them at all. They're strangers to me.'

'Yes,' Rupert obviously did find it hard to understand.

'It's the same with your mother, you know. Even thought she doesn't let on, she thinks of you every day up in Dublin, she is aware of you in a way that it's hard to explain.'

'Oh, I don't think so.'

'I know it, I asked her once, just to know whether I was odd. She said that when you were away at school it was the same and at university and then when you went into the company. She says that often in her day she pauses and wonders what Rupert's doing now.'

'Heavens,' he said.

'Not for long, just for a second, you know, not brooding. But I expect you don't pause and wonder what she's doing.'

'No, well I think of them a lot, of course, and since Father's been so badly and everything. I DO think of them of course,' he said somewhat defensively.

'Stop getting upset, I was only using you as an example. Even if Andrew and Jessica had lived with me until they were grown-up they might still be away and not thinking about me any more. It's the way things happen.'

'You're dead easy to talk to, I wish I could talk to my mother like I talk to you. She's much older of course,' he added tactfully.

'She is indeed, she could nearly be *my* mother too, but that's not the point . . . You can never talk to your own mother, it's the law of nature.'

She smiled and looked out the window, and when that Nancy Morris started talking sense for once about how to relax neck muscles she joined in. She was afraid that young Rupert Green had too much of the Meaning Of Life and the Wronged Woman's viewpoint. She decided to let him snuggle back into his expensive Italian jacket and dream whatever his dreams were.

She always got on better with young people. Someone once said she should have been a teacher but she said no, that would have been putting herself on the other side of the desk from them. But she had much more young friends than people her own age. Bart Kennedy, for example. She could talk to Bart till the cows came home, and she only exchanged the time of day with his father. Kev Kennedy up there in the front of the bus, he was another story: it was very hard going have a chat with Kev. He'd remind you of a young lad who'd been posted at a doorway to give a warning when the master was approaching. And she liked Celia and Dee, she thought, looking round the bus. And young Tom Fitzgerald, he was a great lad. You couldn't like Nancy Morris but she wasn't young anyway. Despite her years she was an old woman and always had been.

And the young people of Rathdoon had always been a great help to her with the things she grew in the small bit of land that Jack Hickey had given her twenty long years ago. She was DIFFERENT to other people, they told her: she didn't pass judgement on them all, she didn't tell them they should be married, or settled down, or more provident or less drinky. And even though they may have thought she was half cracked they came and helped her dig and pick and dry and pack.

She never found the house lonely, no more than the flat in Dublin. Not after all this time. She liked her own company, she ate meals at odd times, she would listen to music at midnight if she liked. In the flat she wore padded earphones and thought she must look like some ageing raver if anyone could see her, but it was a house with many bedsits and flats and you couldn't wake civil servants and people who worked in big office blocks by playing your music through their walls. She did not feel the need of headphones in the lonely little lodge that was all Jack Hickey gave her from the big house. There was nobody near enough to hear, and the birds seemed to like hearing concertos and symphonies. They came and sat on the fence to listen more carefully.

The first time Tom had dropped her there he said he'd wait till she turned on the light. She had been pleased. He had enough nature in him to make sure that she got in safely. But then he was like all the youngsters she knew nowadays, far more natural and a lot more decency in them than the bombasts of her time. Like young Chris and Karen who ran the health shop. They cared so much about it, they never wanted to be rich, to find a good line in anything which would be a snazzy seller and move quickly. They knew none of the jargon of the middle aged businessman, and because they *were* idealistic and simple about things they were going to go to the wall. Her heart was heavy thinking about them. Maybe over in California somewhere Jessica and her husband, if she had one, were starting a health shop. Suppose they were in difficulties, wouldn't it be great if some kind older person were to help?

Judy only had a life interest in her gate lodge, she couldn't sell it even if she wanted to. She only rented her bedsitter in Dublin, she had no savings. Once she had saved the fare to America and kept the post office book thumbed and touched so often it was almost illegible. She had it always in her handbag and would finger it as if it were the ticket to the States. But not now. And she would love so dearly to be able to contribute to Chris and Karen and their dream. Because it was her dream, that shop too. They could make her a director or some such nonsense. If only she had a small lump sum and a regular little subsidy for them instead of taking a small wage from their very sparse little till.

She told Rupert not to waste his weekend coming up to help her in the garden. He had come home to be with his parents and he might as well stay in Dublin if he didn't spend his time with his dying father and give his mother some lift by being in the house all weekend. She was very firm about this, even when he said he'd like the work and the exercise. There'd be plenty of time for all that later. Let him not waste the last months or weeks of his father's life digging and hoeing in a stranger's garden.

'You're not a stranger, Judy, you're a friend,' Rupert had said. She had been pleased at that too.

It was a bright sunny September Saturday. The place seemed to be full of activity. You got weekends when that happened, when Rathdoon seemed to hum with excitement and you got other weekends when not even a tornado coming down Patrick Street would shake them up. She saw Nancy Morris prowling up and down as if she was looking for lost treasure, Kev Kennedy was in and out of his father's shop with a face on him that made it clear the Mafia had put out a contract on him that morning. Every time you stepped out on the road there was someone driving into town that would nearly mow you down. Mrs Casey's ramshackle car with Nancy Morris's mother in it, Mikey Burns going round the place with a set face on him, either doing messages or taking his brother Billy's children blackberrying. He was preoccupied to a degree she had never known. She saw Celia too during the day driving a car with the intent look of someone in a rally. Her mother was beside her and the back of the car was filled with some kind of luggage under a rug. Tom Fitzgerald came in for a couple of hours to help in the garden, saying that since he hadn't had one single cross word from any member of his family or their spouses he felt things were too good to be true and he wouldn't risk staying in their company one more minute in case the whole thing would fall apart. She saw Dee Burke driving her mother to town, her face empty and sad, her mother talking away without seeing any emptiness at all beside her. Imagine anyone thinking the country was quiet. Some weekend she must ask Karen and Chris to come and stay – some bank holiday, if they were still in business.

Red Kennedy came in to help his brother Bart.

'Would these make a lot in Dublin?' he asked, looking at the little boxes of seeds.

Judy reflected: 'Not a lot, in a way, we're just the wrong size. If it were a one-woman operation selling them at the side of the road, yes, there's a living; otherwise it should really be huge nurseries and big chain stores and all that. Still we struggle on.'

But it underlined to her the fruitlessness of it all, and the waste of effort not just from her but from decent young fellow like Bart and Red, like Mikey last week and Tom Fitzgerald's nephews when they were home from school. Was it really fair asking them to help in such a doomed business venture. They never did it for money, there wasn't any, but even in terms of their enthusiasm was it wrong to take so much of that as well? She thought of Chris and Karen in Dublin, anxious and also anxious on HER behalf. They felt they owed her a place and a living because she had been so solidly supportive for them. How she wished that there had been a letter from a firm of American solicitors saying that the late James Jonathan Hickey of San Francisco, California had left her a legacy and that her two children were going to fly over and deliver it personally. She often had fantasies about the children arriving, but this was the first time she had thought about the money. Yes, she'd even take a legacy from Jack even if the children didn't deliver it. Anything to help Chris and Karen.

515

Soon she called a halt to the work. Judy's great success was that she stopped her helpers before they got tired.

There were huge glasses of her elderflower wine which some said was better and reached you more powerfully than anything that was pulled as a pint down in Ryan's. They sat on a wall in the sun and drank it, and the Kennedys went home.

It was dark in the small house and she felt well when she had washed the earth off. She lay out on her window seat with her hands behind her head.

'You look like a cat,' Rupert said as he came in. The door was never closed in summer, never locked in winter.

'That's good. Cats are very relaxed,' Judy said.

'Are you relaxed?' he wanted to know.

'Not in my head. My head is worrying about inessential things like money. I never worried about money before.'

'I suppose it was always easy to get it before.'

'Yes, well in the old days I told you how I got it, but since then I haven't needed it much. Now, I'd like to keep the shop open, that's all.'

Rupert sat down on a rocking chair that squeaked. He got up immediately and went for the oil.

She thanked him, but said his mother had a rocking chair, he should be sitting on that.

'There's nothing to say; I had to escape for a little bit,' he pleaded.

'Only a little,' Judy said.

'It's just that he tried to talk. He asks are there many houses on the market and things.' Rupert had a face full of pain.

'But isn't that good? He's well enough, alert enough to know. Kind enough to care.'

'And mother says that he really likes having me home. But it's nothing. Nothing at all.'

'Only if you make it nothing for them.' Judy lost her sympathy. She stood up and stretched.

'Listen to me Rupert Green, not one more minute of your father's time am I taking. I'm going for a walk in Jack Hickey's woods.' He looked hurt.

'Please boy, please. Think of all those years when you'll say if only I could have just sat there and talked about any old thing. And for your mother, please. I'll meet you and you can buy me a pint of that synthetic stuff they call chilled wine down in Ryan's.' He brightened up.

'Will you? That would be nice.'

'When he's asleep, when he's had some return from you.'

'I'm not THAT bad.'

'No, but he was nearly fifty years of age when you arrived in his life and he had to be woken up with your teething and your screaming and then you didn't come into his office: he couldn't put Green and Son. It's

Green and MacMahon. Go on, sit with him, talk about anything. It doesn't matter if it seems formal and meaningless, you're there, you're trying . . . that's all that matters.'

'And what time will we go to Ryan's?' He was eager.

'RUPERT! Will you give over, this is not a date. Ryan's is not a cocktail lounge, it's the only bar in Rathdoon, I'll be down there when I feel like it and you come when your father's well asleep and you've had a bit of time with your mother.'

'Around nine or so? he said desperate to be specific.

'Around nine or so,' she said resignedly.

She put on her boots. It was a long time since she had walked the woods. The three nuns who ran the ecumenical conferences and the diocesan seminars in the big house knew vaguely that Mrs Hickey in the gate lode had once lived in the big house. They were always polite to her and encouraged her to wander around if she ever felt like it. They were possibly relieved that the wildish looking woman in the gypsy style headscarves didn't take them up too often on their offer. She never went anywhere near the house but she had told them it was nice to be able to feel free to walk under those old trees and pick flowers. Sometimes she would leave a great bunch of bluebells at their door, wrapped up in damp leaves. She never rang or asked to be entertained in the parlour. It was an ideal relationship.

Today she walked more purposefully. She didn't just stroll following a whim or a line or young saplings. No, today she knew where she was heading.

It was still there in among the ivy covered trees. Wild now, but hidden from the most determined searchers because of that old fallen tree. It looked as if there was nothing beyond. She eased herself over the tree and stood once more in her own little marijuana grove. She saw the cannabis plants that she had begun twenty-two years ago, many dead, many seeded and wasted. Some living though, some needing only a little attention.

It wouldn't take her long to find a proper outlet in Dublin. It must be done well away from the shop, Chris and Karen must never know.

She felt as strongly about this as her husband had felt that Andrew and Jessica must never know.

She felt the old quickening under her heart. It would be exciting to be back in the business again after all these years.

Kev

Kev thought he'd never get away from the Pelican. The Pelican was in one of those good moods, very rarely seen of late, where he'd ramble on about people known only to himself. There was a cast of thousands in the Pelican's stories and the same people never appeared twice. Kev listened attentively because if you missed the bit where your man came in one day and your other man was already in there and your old fellow came out the other door then you lost the whole grasp of it, and the Pelican might easily snap some kind of a question at you to make sure you were on the ball.

Kev was only afraid of the Pelican; he was *terrified* of some of the others. But even though the Pelican was not the highest in the terror stakes Kev would have let the Lilac Bus go to Rathdoon without him rather than risk insulting this man whose big hooked nose was the cause of his name. You didn't mess with the Pelican, Kev didn't know much, but he knew that.

Fortunately the Pelican was hailed by someone more interesting and Kev was released; he sprinted round the corner. The bus was almost full. But he wasn't the last. Mikey Burns was rubbing his hands: oh please may he not have the quiz games tonight. Mikey was perfectly nice when he quietened down, but all this 'I say I say I say' like one of those comics on a music hall show on telly. And he was no GOOD at it, that was what was so hopeless, he always laughed in the wrong place. It would have been nice to sit beside Celia; that's what he liked best: she'd address about five civil sentences to him and then she'd leave him to his own thoughts, as she looked out the window. Or Rupert, he was a quiet fellow too, and not toffee-nosed or anything. Kev's brothers Bart and Red were always surprised that he didn't seem to know Mrs Hickey better. They were mad about her: in fact her Da was always saying that they'd go over to her place and dig her witch's brews in the garden and her lavender and her forget me nots and they wouldn't dig their own potatoes like men. Mrs Hickey was nice enough, but she had a disconcerting way of looking right through you when she was talking, as if she didn't want any small talk. Neither did Kev of course want any small talk, but he didn't want that dark intense face with those X-ray eyes looking at him either. He always got the feeling that she saw just a little bit too much.

Kev worked in security, well not real security with helmets and coshes and alsatians and vans with no hand signals. More like being a porter really or a commissionaire but it was called security. When anyone phoned down to the front desk to ask if a letter had been delivered by hand or if a visitor had arrived Kev answered the phone with the words, 'Hallo, Security?'

Once he had got a phone call from his father asking him to bring down boxes of some new potato crisp that had been advertised on the television and the place was going mad looking for it. Kev's father had been so entertained by Kev calling himself Security that he had threatened to telephone every day just for the sheer pleasure of it. Kev had told him anxiously that they had been told to keep personal calls down to the minimum. But he shouldn't have worried, his father wasn't going to waste good money on hearing the same joke over and over.

Bart and Red didn't know what he came home for every weekend. It wasn't that they didn't want to see him, they were just as happy that he was back as not. But why *every* weekend? That was what would fox you. And he didn't even go to the dance on a Saturday night. And he didn't have a crowd to drink with in Ryan's; he'd go in and out for a couple but he wouldn't have a session there. The Kennedys had little or no conversation with their Da who had a cigarette in his mouth and the radio on full blast from morning to night. It was unlikely to be for company.

Kev knew that he was a bit of a mystery to them. And to Tom Fitzgerald who had explained that the bus only made a profit if he could be sure of his seven passengers on a Friday. That's why he could do it so cheaply. You agreed to come on the bus every Friday for ten weeks, or if you couldn't you'd send someone in your place – not to Rathdoon of course, but part of the way or as far as the big town seventeen miles from home. Or if you could find nobody you still paid for your seat. That way it was half the cost of any other bus going that route and what's more it brought you to the door. Kev was getting out of the bus before ten o'clock and saying goodnight to Nancy Morris who lived across the street. He was home in Rathdoon safe. He would take a big breath of air and let it all out in a long sigh of relief. Tom often looked at him puzzled, and his father would nod welcomingly over the radio and tell him it was just coming up to the news. A mug of tea might be handed to him and a slice of shop cake cut. They had never known any other kind of cake, Kev and his brothers. Their mother had died long ago and even Bart, who could remember her, never knew her when she was well enough to make bread or cakes. When the news was over his father might ask had it been a hard week and were there any savages with crowbars in. He said there were more cases of violence in Dublin than there were in Chicago and he would never set his foot in the city again without an armed guard. Kev had tried to argue with him in the beginning, but now he didn't bother. Anyway, nowadays he was beginning to think his father was right.

Nobody at work knew where Kev went at weekends: they all thought that he was some kind of lay monk or something and that he went to do good works but part of the goodness was that you didn't talk about it. The kind old Mr Daly, one of the nicest people Kev had ever met, would shake his head in its uniform cap full of admiration.

'I don't know why they give out about the younger generation,' old Mr Daly would say, 'I really don't. There's that young Kev who works with us in the front hall, and he's off giving soup to winos and praying in front of the Blessed Sacrament, and teaching illiterates to read. Gone out of here like a bow from an arrow at six o'clock and we never hear hair nor hide of him until Monday morning.'

Kev had never told one word of this fabrication to Mr Daly or to anyone else. But having heard it, and seen that it was accepted he let it pass. After all if anyone came nosing around and asking questions, wasn't it better that old Mr Daly and John and the others thought he was with the Simon Community or the Legion of Mary rather than knowing he caught the lilac-coloured minibus as regularly as clockwork and sped out of Dublin and all its dangers every Friday night.

Just suppose for one sickening minute that Daff or Crutch Casey or the Pelican came round upset over something, well there was nothing they could be told. Nobody knew where Kev went at weekends.

He had always had this secrecy, even when he was a young fellow. He remembered Bart telling a total stranger in the shop that their mother was dead, that she had died in the hospital after two months and a week. Kev would never have given that information to a woman who had come in to buy bars of chocolate and ice cream for the children in the car. No matter how nice she had been, no matter how much she had praised the three young lads serving in the shop because their father was out getting the shed at the back built to hold the gas cylinders and the briquettes. Kev would have told her nothing and put his arm in his mouth which was a great way to stop having a conversation. But Bart and Red would tell anyone anything . . . Bart even told about the time when Kev was seventeen and he had tried to get Deirdre Morris, who was the much nicer sister of Nancy, to come into a field with him and swore it was to show her a nest of small birds.

Deirdre Morris had thrown back her head laughing, pushed him over so that he fell in the mud and had gone home laughing. 'A nest of small birds – is that what they call it nowadays?' Kev was shocked. To admit to such a lustful thing and even worse to admit to such a defeat. But no, Bart thought it was a scream, and that time that Deirdre had come back from America married with a baby called Shane, Bart was still able to laugh over it with her. And Red was the same, a demon dancer and he'd tell half the country their business, and about how they should have got an agency for tarmacadamming the place but his Da hadn't moved quick enough and Billy Burns had got it first. Kev told nothing. But then Kev had much more to hide

Celia arrived just after him and the doors were closed. They were off. Round the corner and through the open door of the pub he could see the Pelican holding a pint in one hand and a rolled up newspaper in the other. A rolled paper was a great thing for making a point, for emphasising something. And that was the Pelican's style. Emphasising things.

Mikey was unfortunately in top form tonight: tricks with matches and a glass, have them rolling in the aisles in a pub. Didn't poor Mikey realise that it was only drunks that suddenly started doing match tricks in a pub, or lonely people, or madmen. Not ordinary people unless they were all in a group of friends, and if you had a group of friends why would you need to do tricks anyway? He was explaining how to weight the matchbox; Kev looked out the window and saw the housing estates outside Dublin flashing by. Old Mr Daly said to him that any day now Kev would find himself a young woman and they'd save for a house in a place like that and there'd be no knowing him ever after. People like Mr Daly and Mikey knew nothing about the real world. There was Mikey going on about how you weighted the matchbox deliberately with a two-penny piece in it and it always fell over on the side you'd put the coin in, so you could bet someone that it would always fall on the side you said. Kev had looked at him vacantly.

'I bet you Bart or Red Eddie would love a trick like that,' Mikey muttered. Kev knew they would. They had the time and the peace of mind to enjoy it.

Kev never told Mikey that he was a porter too in a way. Well security really, but it was the same field. He never told any of them where he worked, except that it was in the big new block. You could be doing anything there, Literally anything. They had civil servants and they had travel agencies, and airlines and small companies with only two people in them, they had a board in the hall with a list a mile long of the organisations who were tenants of the building. Kev just said he worked there; when anyone asked him what he did, he said this and that. It was safer. One morning he was standing there in his uniform and he saw Dee Burke coming. She was going with some papers to a solicitor on the fifth floor. Mr Daly phoned up and announced her and Kev had sorted furiously on the floor for something so she didn't see him. Later he wondered why. It couldn't matter whether Dee Burke knew that he worked

521

at the front desk of the big new office block. She hardly thought when she went to buy her cigarettes at the Kennedy shop that their younger son was the chairman of some company up in Dublin. He didn't even want her to think he was in a clerical job. Why hide then? Wiser. Like not walking on cracks in the road. No reason but it just *seemed* the right thing to do.

Of course in a way it was all this secrecy that had got him where he was. If he had been a different type he'd never have got into this mess at all.

It began on his birthday, he was twenty-one. It was an ordinary working day. His father had sent him a ten pound note in a card with a pink cat on it. Bart and Red Eddie had said there would be great drink in Ryan's next Friday on account of it. Nobody else knew. He hadn't told Mr Daly in case the old man might get a cake and embarrass him; he didn't tell anyone back up in the house where he had a room. They kept to themselves a lot and if they heard him saying he was twenty-one they'd feel they had to do something for him. He didn't tell anyone up at the pigeons either. In the lofts they didn't have time for birthdays and such things. So that day nobody in Dublin knew that Kevin, youngest son of Mr Michael Kennedy, shop proprietor, and the late Mrs Mary Rose Kennedy of Rathdoon, had now reached twenty-one. He thought of it a lot all morning and somehow it began to seem over-important to him. Other people had records played for them on radio programmes, other people who were twenty-one had cards, lots of them, not just one. Dee Burke had a party in a hotel – he remembered hearing about it just a couple of months back; Bart and Red had been invited and Bart said he couldn't get into a monkey suit but Red the demon dancer had hired one and had a great time. And even his own brothers had bits of celebration. Bart and all his pals had a barbecue down by the river, those were before every Tom, Dick and Harry were having barbecues. They roasted a bit of beef and ate it between doorsteps of bread and it was gorgeous, and there'd been great singing and goings on. And when Red was twenty-one two years back there had been a crowd of them who had all come to the house for a few drinks and a cake then they'd got into a truck and driven off to the dance. But nothing at all for Kev.

It got in on his mind. He made an excuse to Mr Daly and said that he wanted to go out the back for a half an hour. He didn't feel well. Mr Daly was so concerned that he immediately felt ashamed. Those were the days before he had been a regular disappearer at weekends, before Mr Daly had assumed that he was an unsung and uncanonised saint.

He sat out in the loading as it was called, a place where vans could come with deliveries of paper, or messengers on those big motor bikes with speaking handlebars could leave their machines. He took out a cigarette and thought about other fellows his age and wondered why he had been so anxious to get away and why he had ever thought it would be any better. Four men were loading a van efficiently. A fifth was standing leaning on a crutch and staring around him idly. Into the can were going sanitary fittings, handbasins, lavatories, small water heaters. Without haste but with commendable speed they loaded.

Kev dragged on his cigarette. They must be getting new fitments somewhere upstairs, that looked like a big contract. Wait. He hadn't seen any of them come through Security, and everyone had to come to the front desk. Even if they went straight out the door again and were sent round to the loading bay. The rules said desk first.

His eyes took on the merest flicker of interest but it was enough to alert the man with the bent leg leaning so casually on the crutch.

'Not wearing a cap, didn't notice him,' he said out of the corner of his mouth.

A big man with a beak-shaped nose paused momentarily and then slid from the human chain which was stacking the fitments. He strolled over to Kevin whose stomach knotted in fright. He realised like a shower of cold rain coming down his gullet that this was a Job, these were five men taking fitments OUT of the new building, fitments that would turn up again in houses all over the city. He swallowed hard.

The Pelican walked slowly: he didn't look a bit furtive, nor did he look worried.

'Can I have a smoke?' he asked casually. Behind him the loading continued regular as clockwork, innocent as anything.

'Yes. Um.' Kev handed him the packet.

'What are you doing with yourself here?' The Pelican's eyes narrowed.

The question was perfectly polite. It could have been a gentle enquiry of any fellow lounger on a summer morning. He might even have added something like 'on this fine day'. But he hadn't. The Pelican and all of them were waiting to know what Kevin would say and Kevin knew that what he said now was probably going to be the most important question he ever answered in his life. 'It's my twenty-first birthday,' he said. 'And I got annoyed sitting inside there in Security and nobody knowing, so I thought I'd come out here and have a bit of a smoke anyway to celebrate.'

There was absolutely no doubt that what he said was true. You didn't need a lie detector or the experience of years with truth drugs to know that Kev Kennedy had given a perfectly accurate account of why he was there, and something about him made the Pelican believe that there was going to be no trouble here.

'Well, when we're finished here maybe we'll buy a drink at your lunch hour. A fellow shouldn't be twenty-one and have nobody know.'

'That's what I think,' Kev said eagerly, averting his eyes from the biggest and most barefaced theft from the building where he was meant to be part of Security. It seemed to be winding up now, the convoy were closing the doors and getting into the van.

'So, what is it? One o'clock?' the Pelican's nose was like a scythe so large and menacing did it appear, and his eyes were like two slits.

'It's a bit difficult at lunchtime, you see I only get forty-five minutes and I suppose you'll be moving on out of the area,' Kev's face was innocent.

'But where would you like your birthday drink then and when?' There was no area for argument in the proposal, only a small margin of latitude for the time and place.

'Well, wherever you like of course, and at about six. Is that all right?' Kev was eager. The Pelican nodded. He named a city centre pub.

'We'll give you a drink each, and as you no doubt saw there's five of us, so that's five drinks.'

'Oh, God, that would be great altogether,' Kev said. 'Are there five of you? I didn't notice.'

The Pelican nodded approvingly. He swung his way back to the van and in beside the driver who looked like a champion wrestler.

'Six o'clock,' he called cheerfully out the window.

It wasn't discovered until four thirty. A lot of offices on the first floor weren't occupied yet. Some people just assumed that the bathrooms were being refitted, and sighing had gone to other floors. It was only when one of the secretaries said she was getting dropped arches and told Mr Daly that it was an extraordinary thing to think that brand new cloakrooms should be redone within three months that any kind of alarm was raised. The broad-daylightness of it all staggered them. The guards were called, the confusion was enormous. Kev had difficulty in getting away by six. He was ninety per cent sure that they wouldn't be there. They could be walking into a trap for all they knew. How were they to know that they were dealing with Kev Kennedy who never told anybody anything? They might have assumed he would have plain-clothes guards drinking pints of shandy all round the pub. But just in case. And just in case they came back and dealt with him. After all they knew where he worked, he knew nothing about them.

They were all there.

'There was a bit of commotion at work, I got delayed.' he said.

'Ah, you would all right,' said the Pelican generously. He was introduced to Daff and John, and Ned and Crutch Casey.

'What's your real name?' he asked the man with the twisted leg.

'Crutch,' the man said, surprised to be asked.

They each bought him a pint and they raised their glasses solemnly and said Happy Birthday at each round. By the fourth round he was feeling wretched. He had never drunk more than three pints in Ryan's and never more than two anywhere else. Ryan's led you to be daring because even if you fell down you got home on all fours without too much difficulty.

Daff was the man like a wrestler. Kev wondered why he was called that but he decided it might not be wise. Daff bought the last drink and handed Kev an envelope.

'We were sorry to see a culchie all on his own with no-one to wish him a happy birthday, so that's a small present from Pelican, Crutch, John, Ned and me.' He smiled as if he were a foolish, generous uncle dying for the nephew to open the electric train set and begin to call out with excitement.

Kev politely opened the envelope and saw a bundle of blue twenty pound notes. The room went backwards and forwards and began to move slowly around to the left. He steadied himself on the bar stool.

'I couldn't take this, sure you don't know me at all.'

'And you don't know us,' Daff beamed.

'Which is as it should be,' the Pelican said approvingly.

'But I'd not know you, without . . . without this, you know.'

He looked at the envelope as if it contained explosives. There were at least six notes, maybe more. He didn't want to count then.

'Ah but this is better, this MARKS the day for all of us, why don't we meet here every week around this time, and if you've invested properly then you could buy us a drink, and slowly we could sort of GET to know each other.'

Kev's mouth felt full of lemon juice.

'Well I'd love to . . . sort of keep in touch with you all . . . but, honestly, this is too much. Like, I mean, I'd feel bad.'

'Not at all, you wouldn't,' smiled the Pelican and they were gone.

Every Tuesday he had met them; sometimes it was just a drink. Sometimes it was more. Once it had been a driving job. He would never forget it to his dying day. They went into a new block of flats and carefully unrolled the brand new stair carpet. They had heard that the fitting men were coming that afternoon so they had anticipated the visit by removing every scrap of it. The timing had been of the essence on that one. The expensive wool carpet had arrived that morning; there was only a four-hour period when it could be removed, and that meant watching the flats very carefully in case any untoward enquiries were made. It was all completely successful, of course, like all their enterprises seemed to be. Kev had taken a day off work for the carpet heist but the carpet heist had taken years off his life. He felt as if he had been put down on the street and the whole crowd coming out of Moran Park had walked over him. He couldn't understand how they remained so untouched. Crutch Casey told of horses that had fallen at the last fence. Ned and John were more dog people, they talked of evil minded and corrupt greyhounds who KNEW how to slow down through some instinct. The Pelican told long tales full of people that nobody knew, and Daff seemed to say nothing much but he was as relaxed as a man coming out after a swim about to light his pipe on the beach on a sunny day.

They never told him he HAD to join in, and they didn't ask him so much that he felt he should run away to America to escape them. Often he didn't have to do anything except what they called 're-sorting'. That night mean wrapping a whole load of Waterford Glass which arrived from a hotel before it got time to get out of its boxes, into different kinds of containers. Each glass to be held carefully and sorted according to type, wrapped in purple tissue paper in gift boxes of six. He became quite an authority on the various designs, or suites as they were called, and decided that the Colleen Suite was a his favourite; and that when he got married he would have two dozen Colleen brandy glasses and use them around the house as ordinary everyday glasses, or in the bathroom for his toothbrush. Then he remembered what he was doing and the fantasy would disappear. He would look around the garage and keep parcelling in the nice anonymous gift boxes. He never knew where they went, and what happened to them. He never asked. Not once. That's why they liked him, that's why they trusted him utterly. From that very first day in the loading area they thought he was one of their own, and it was too late now to tell them that he wasn't. The longer it went on, the more ludicrous it would be trying to get out.

On calmer days Kev asked himself what was so terrible. They never took from individuals, they didn't do people's houses and flats: it was companies who had to replace miles of red wool carpet, boxes of prestigious glassware, rooms full of sanitary fittings. They never did over old women, young couples, they never carried a weapon, not even a cosh. In many ways they weren't bad fellows at all. Of course they never actually went out to work in a normal way, and they did lie to people, with their clipboards and their air of being perfectly legitimate. And people did get into trouble after they'd visited places, like poor Mr Daly who'd been hauled in by everyone and though it was never said, the thought had been in the air that he might be getting too old for the job. And they stole. They stole things almost every week and by no standards could that be a thing that Kev Kennedy from Rathdoon wanted to be in. Or worse, caught in. It was unthinkable. They still talked about that young fellow who was a cousin of the Fitzgeralds and worked in their shop for a bit; he was given three years for doing a post office in Cork. The whole of Rathdoon had buzzed with it for months and Mrs Fitzgerald, Tom's mother, had said she hoped everyone realised that he wasn't a first cousin, he was a very far out one, and they had tried to give him a start and look at the thanks they got. Could you imagine what old Da would have to go through? And all Red's hopes of getting some gorgeous wife would go for their tea, and poor Bart was so decent and helpful, wouldn't it be a shame on him for ever?

But how did you get out? He couldn't live in a city that contained the Pelican and Daff and Crutch Casey if they thought he had ratted on them. There was no point trying to pretend that he had left town or anything. They knew everything: it was their business to know things, to know when deliveries were expected, when watchmen went for their coffee, when regular porters were on holidays, when managers were young and nervous, when shops were too busy to notice their furniture being loaded into private vans. They knew where Kev lived and worked; he wouldn't dream of lying to them.

But he got out of weekend work. That's when they did some of their bigger jobs, and he wanted to be well away from it. He told them vaguely that he had to go out of town. He had been going home that very first weekend after they met him and so it had seemed a natural continuation, not a new pattern of behaviour. He didn't say it was Rathdoon, he didn't say it was home, but they knew he wasn't lying when he was saying that he went out of town for weekends. Crutch Casey had said goodnight to him one Sunday night outside the house where he had a room, and Kev knew that it was just a routine inspection. He had been cleared now, even the Pelican whom he had met by accident just on the corner knew that he was leaving Dublin for the weekend – he didn't even bother to check.

But how could he get out of working for them mid-week? Some of the jobs were getting bigger and Kev was getting tenser. Once or twice Daff had asked him not to be so jumpy – that he was like some actor playing a nervous crook in an old black and white B movie. It was fine for Daff who didn't have a nerve in his body. Simply fine for him. Others didn't find it so easy. The very sight of a guard was enough to weaken Kev's legs, even the shadow of anyone fairly big was enough to make him jump. Oddly enough it hadn't made him feel guilty about religion: he went to Mass and at Christmas and Easter to communion; he knew that God knew that there wasn't much Sin involved. No Grievous Bodily Harm or anything. Bur he had never been much of a one for talking to God individually like you were meant to: he didn't feel like putting the question personally. And there was nobody else really BUT God when all was said and done because everyone else would have a very strong view one way or the other, and mainly the other. Like get out of that gang at a rate of knots, Kev Kennedy, and stop acting the eejit.

Mikey's poor kind face was there a few inches from him, Mikey Burns who'd be the kind of bank porter that would get shot in a raid, certainly not like Kev, the kind of security man who had become best buddies with the gang that had ripped off all the fittings from the place he worked. Mikey Burns sleeping with a little smile dreaming about something, jokes with glasses of water and coins maybe, and there was he, Kev, who had driven get-away vans and done watch duty and helped to reparcel stolen goods. Kev felt alien as he looked out at the darkening countryside. Lonely and guilty as hell.

His father told him after the news that Red had notions about a farmer's daughter and was going to bring her to tea during the weekend no less, and they were all to keep their shoes on, talk nicely and put butter on a plate and the milk in a jug. He said that he thought Bart might as well join the Franciscans and put on sandals and carry a begging bowl for all the good he was ever going to do with his life and his share of the business. When he wasn't digging up Mrs Hickey's foxgloves and hemlocks or whatever it was she grew he was helping Mrs Ryan in the pub to stand on her own two shaky legs and serving the customers from behind the bar and not a penny piece was he getting from either of them. He was surprised that Bart hadn't gone into Fitzgerald's shop and said that if they'd like someone to stand there and serve for a few days a week without wages he'd be happy to do it. Kev didn't know what to say to this. He nibbled a slice of cake and thought about the difference between people. There was Daff who had a nice big open face like Bart, organising the transfer of twenty microwave ovens from one warehouse to another by a deceptively simple scheme which involved Ned who was the most forgettable of them all going up with a sheaf of papers, an air of bewilderment and an instruction that they were apparently to go back to have something checked. And there was Bart Kennedy who had a big open face like Daff digging Judy Hickey's garden for her and helping Celia's mother to stay upright in Ryan's. God, what different worlds he moved in; Kev thought with a shudder at the danger of it all. 'Are you not going down to the pub?' his father asked.

'No, I'm tired after the week, and the long journey, I'll just go up and lie on my bed,' he said.

His father shook his head: 'I really wish I knew what brings you home, you do so little when you arrive, and you've lost your interest in football entirely. You could have been a good footballer if you'd put your mind to it.'

'No, I was never any good. You only say that because you wanted a son a county footballer, I'm no good.'

'Well what does bring you back here, what are you running from . . . ?' He hadn't finished but the cup was in pieces on the floor and Kev's face was snow white.

'Running, what do you mean?'

'I mean is it the violence up there or the dirt, or those blackguards roaming in tribes or what? Haven't you good wages and you're always very generous giving me the few quid here . . . but a young man of your age, you should be up to all kinds of divilment and diversions, shouldn't you?'

'I don't know, Da, I don't think I was ever much good at anything, football, divilment, anything.' He sounded very glum.

'Haven't you got a fine job in one of the finest buildings in the land, and you earn your own living which is more than those two boyos there – oh they're a great pair I have on my hands. One a sort of Martin de Porres going round the place giving half his cloak to everyone he meets, one a dandy who has the bright red hair nearly combed off his scalp and the mirrors nearly cracked in its staring into them. You're the best of them, Kev, don't be running yourself down.'

Kev Kennedy went up to bed without a word, and he lay there as the sounds of Rathdoon which were not very loud went past his window, a small window over the shop, which looked out on the main street.

Red's girl was coming the very next day it turned out, so they all had to do a spring clean on the back room. There were to be cups instead of mugs, a clean cloth was spread and bread was cut on a tray and then put on to a plate to avoid all the crumbs. They took ham and tomatoes from the shop, a bottle of salad cream and Red hardboiled three eggs.

'This is a feast, she'll marry you immediately,' Bart said when he saw Red looking speculatively at some of the frozen cakes in the cold food section.

'Quit laughing and keep looking round the room to see what it would look like to a new eye.' Red had it bad this time. Her name was Majella and she was an only child, she was used to much greater style than the three Kennedy brothers and their father could provide even if they had been trying seriously. But none of them except Red was making much of an effort: their father wanted to be in his shop, Bart wanted to get over to Judy Hickey and Kev wanted to go off down by the river where he felt nice and quiet and miles from all that was happening at this very moment to microwave ovens in a warehouse in Dublin.

Majella was arriving at five o'clock: her father would give her a lift, but he wouldn't call in, it was much too early for that yet. They did a deal, the brothers. Bart and Kev agreed to wear proper ties and jackets and have polished shoes. Red agreed to go over to Judy Hickey's and put in two hours because she needed it this weekend particularly and because it would keep him calm. There would be no bad language, eating with fingers and picking of teeth, but in return Red would not embarrass them by giving moon faced sick calf impersonations, nor would he ask them to delight Majella with stories of their exotic lives. When the bell rang to say that somebody had come into the shop they would go in order of seniority. Da first, then Bart, then Kev, then Da and so on. Red was not to abandon them to talk to Majella on their own.

She was a lovely girl with no nonsense in her and by the time they had sat down she was like part of the family. She said they must be great fellows altogether to have the butter on the place and the milk not in a bottle but in a jug. Whenever she went over to her cousin's place they were all putting their dirty knives into the butter at once, they needed a woman to civilise them. Red began to look like a sick calf when she talked of the civilising influence of a woman and he had to be kicked until he dropped it again. Majella said she was going to do the washing up and they could all dry, and seeing out of the corner of her eye that the dishcloths were not all they might be she called to Red to bring a packet of J-cloths out of the shop.

'Isn't it paradise to be here!' she said with a big smile at them all. 'Who could want anything better than a shop right off your own living room?'

They had dried up in no time; the big room looked better somehow than it had done for years. Majella said that maybe she and Red might go for a bit of a tour round Rathdoon now and get out of everyone's way. By half past six she had a blushing delighted Red firmly by the arm and was linking him on her own little lap of honour around the community she had decided to join.

'Oh there's no escape there, that knot will be tied, poor Red.' Bart laughed good-naturedly about the fate that could well be happening to his brother.

'Will you stop that nonsense: poor Red, my hat! Wouldn't a girl have to be half mad or have the courage of a lion to marry any one of the three of you.' He sounded very pessimistic indeed.

'Would you say she IS mad?' Kev asked interestedly. 'She was a very nice class of a girl I thought.'

'Of course she's nice, she's far too good for him: the thing is will she realise it in time?' Bart and Kev exchanged glances. Their father seemed to be torn between the delight of having the lovely laughing Majella around the place and the strictly honest course of action which was to warn the girl that his son was a bad bargain.

'Let her work it out for herself maybe?' Bart suggested and his father looked relieved.

Bart had a lot of sense, Kev realised, suddenly. He wasn't just a do-gooder and a big innocent. But he was the other side of the tracks now, he wasn't in the Underworld like Kev was, there could be no talking to him about the problem.

'Would you fancy an early pint down in Ryan's before the mob gets in there?' Bart said to him. Kev was pleased.

'That'd be the way to do it,' he said sagely. Their father had gone back to the shop and was twiddling the dial for the news.

They walked down the road. It was quiet – most people were in at their tea; the sound of the half past six news that their father was listening to back in the shop came from several windows. Down past Billy Burns' chip shop. Billy wasn't there today, Mikey and that bright little Treasa who worked there, no sign of the new girl Eileen, well she had always looked too good to spend her day lifting pieces of cod or wings of chicken out of a deep fryer in Rathdoon. They came to the bridge. Bart leaned over and looked at the river. They used to race sticks under the bridge here when they were kids, and there were always so many arguments about whose stick had won Bart invented a system of tying different coloured threads on to each one. It seemed very long ago.

'What's eating you?' Bart asked.

'I don't know what you mean?'

'I'm not the world's brainiest man but I'm not blind either. Tell me, Kev. Can't you? It can't be any worse when you've told me. It might even be a bit better. Like I'm not going to be saying aren't you an eejit or blame you or anything, but there's something terrible wrong up in Dublin, isn't there?'

'Yes,' Kev said.

'Before Red fell so much in love that he can't think of anything else, he and I were going to go up there one day on the excursion and try and sort it out, whatever it was.'

Kev gulped with gratitude at the thought of his two brothers taking on a heavy gang like Daff, the Pelican, Crutch Casey and their team.

'What did YOU think the problems might be?' he asked nervously, fishing to see had Bart any notion of how bad things were or was he still in a world like the playground of the infants' school.

'I thought it might be a girl you got into trouble, but it's going on too long for that. I thought it might be a debt – you know, poker or the horses – but you don't seem to have any interest in either.'

Bart's big innocent face looked puzzled. Kev drew a long breath. Well it seemed that Bart could take on that much anyway. What about the next step, could Bart listen to the story that had begun on his twenty-first birthday a year and a half ago, or would he run for the guards. Kev didn't know. Bart was shaping a stick and tying a bit of string round it.

'Here,' he said to Kev, 'Let this be yours: I'll beat you any day with my one.' They threw the sticks over the side and rushed across to see them coming through. Kev's stick was in front.

'Would you beat that?' Bart seemed surprised. 'I've been up here practising and I thought I had the shape of stick that ran best with the flow.'

Kev began to tell him, in fact once started it tumbled out of him: a mixture of names and commodities, Crutch Caseys and Microwaves, Daffs and cut glass, Pelicans and Axminster carpet. Kev had no starring role the way he told it, his only stroke of genius had been to go home every weekend on the Lilac Bus to avoid even more major crime in the city at weekends. He was in now and there was no getting out. Bart must know that, they'd all seen the films, they knew the plot. If Kev said to Daff that he'd had enough, thank you, he couldn't answer for the consequences but he knew it'd be awful. He didn't think they'd beat him up: they never used violence, he said almost pleadingly to Bart. But they would punish him. They'd send the guards round to his house or to work, or they'd send a note to Mr Daly accusing Kev of giving the tip-off about the cloakroom fittings that time. It was a nightmare: he was in it for ever.

He hardly dared to look at Bart during some of the confession, and once or twice he gave the odd glance and got the feeling that Bart was half smiling. Maybe he didn't understand the hugeness of it all. Once he was almost certain he got a smile and Bart had hastily put his hand over his face.

'So now, you see I'm caught entirely,' he ended.

'I don't think so,' Bart said slowly.

'But it's not LIKE here, Bart; you don't know, they're different to us. They're not our type of people.'

'But they must have thought you were their kind of person otherwise they wouldn't have pulled you in,' Bart said.

'But I TOLD you how that happened. I'm not a thief by nature, I'm fairly happy to work for my wages. Not very, but fairly. I'm not any good as a criminal.'

'No I don't mean their type as a thief, you're secretive like they are. That's what they liked about you – you're not a blabber about who you know, what you do: that'll make them think you won't blab about them.'

'Well I don't – haven't until now, that is.'

'So that's how you get out if you want to. Tell them you're in with another lot now. No hard feelings, handshakes, pints all round, and that's it.'

'Bart, you haven't any idea . . .'

'But you see, you keep up this hard man image with them except once or twice when you've had a fit of the shivers. You never try to talk them out of it, or discuss what they do with the stuff. They probably think you're a silent pro and someone has made you a better offer.'

'They wouldn't have such a high regard for me as that.'

'They must have a very high regard for you if they let you in on all their jobs. No, leave them as you joined them, with no chat, no explanations except the one they are owed. That you've got a new scene.'

Bart talking about scenes, Bart saying that these gangsters are owed an explanation – it was like the end of the world.

'I don't think I'd be able to go through with it.'

'You were able to join them, that was harder.'

'And should I give them back the money?'

'Give them WHAT?'

'My share, I mean, if I'm not staying on like?'

'Your share. You have it still?'

'Of course I do, I didn't spend any of it, in case . . . you know . . . the guards and everything and a court case and I'd have to give it all back.'

'Where is it?'

'It's upstairs in the room.'

'In Dublin?'

'No here, back at the house, Under the bed.'

'You're not serious.'

'But what else would I do with it, Bart? I carry it with me home and back each weekend in a parcel with my clothes.'

'And how much is it at all? Your share?'

'I'm afraid it's about four thousand two hundred pounds,' Kev said with his eyes cast down.

Eventually he raised his glance and Bart was smiling at him with pride.

'Isn't that the direct intervention of God?' Bart said to him. Kev would never have seen it like that; however confused his relationship with God was and however non-personal it had become, he couldn't imagine that the Almighty was delighted with such a sum of stolen money arriving under a bed in Rathdoon.

'This solves all our problems,' Bart said.

'When Romeo back there went courting Majella the only fly in the ointment was would we have enough to build on a bit at the back. We were afraid it would get a bit crowded with us all on top of each other, and we saw the very thing we wanted, a kind of ready-made extension that they dig foundations for and then sort of plant on top of. Do you follow?' ·

Kev nodded nervously.

'But Red and I were afraid you were in some kind of financial trouble and we'd better not get ourselves too far into a loan. But here you are, a millionaire. Now we can go ahead, and if you'd like to contribute a bit . . .'

'Yes, well of course I would but you think if I'm getting out of their gang I should *offer* them the share back?'

'What kind of criminal are you at all?' roared Bart. 'Won't they know immediately you're a ninny if you start a caper like that. You've got to consider that your wages, your share of the deal, now you're meant to be going on to a bigger one, you eejit: you're not meant to be giving them conscience money.'

'No.'

'And there's no way you can give it to the carpet people or the lavatory makers or the microwave people . . .'

'I wasn't in on the microwave – that's this weekend.'

'See?' Bart felt this proved some point. 'So what are you going to do with it, wouldn't building up the family home be as good as anything?'

Kev was astonished. No blame, no lecture, no accusation. Sheer hard practical advice, as if he knew the kind of people that Daff and Pelican were. Because when you thought of it that was EXACTLY the way to go about it. And then he need never see them again.

'I'll give it all to you tonight, Bart,' he said eagerly. 'Where will we say we got it? Like if anyone asks?

'You'll keep some of it, put it in the post office, but we'll say nothing to anyone, like you've been doing all your life. We'll get in touch with those people about the extension on Monday. What could be more natural than that country eejits like us would have money in a paper bag under the bed, they'll only be delighted – no VAT, nothing.'

Kev was stunned. Saint Bart, in the black economy.

'And thanks to your very generous donation, we'll be able to get the bigger extension, and there'll be plenty of room if Majella produces a brood of Kennedys.'

A stone fell off the bridge and into the water and Kev Kennedy didn't jump at all, and his eyes didn't widen with anxiety.

Rupert

He bought a packet of mints because Judy Hickey had told him last week that he reeked of garlic and much as she loved all good herby smells she didn't want to sit cooped up beside a porous sponge of garlic for three hours on a small minibus. Funny, Judy: if he had met her in Dublin, he would never have suspected that she came from home. She wasn't a Rathdoon sort of person. He had told her that once and she had retorted that neither was he – a thin, pale, artistic young Protestant: what could be more unlikely?

But she was wrong. There were handfuls of Protestants in every town in the West; they were as much part of the place as the mountains and the phone boxes and the small beautiful churches with hardly any attendance standing dwarfed by the newer Catholic churches which were bursting at the seams. No use explaining that to Judy, trying to tell her that she was much more unusual, dark and gypsy-like, living in a small gate lodge at the end of the drive from Doon House, growing herbs and working all week in a health food shop in Dublin. In another time she'd have been burned as a witch without any discussion, he had once told her. Judy had said gloomily that the way the country was going it could happen yet, so he shouldn't joke about it.

He smelled of garlic because he had eaten a very good lunch. He always did on a Friday; that was because he wouldn't be back again until late on Sunday night when it was the wrong time to have a meal. So Friday lunchtime was the only opportunity they could get to have anything approaching a relaxed weekend meal before he went back to Rathdoon for the weekend. Of course there *was* the rest of the week but it wasn't quite the same, as there was work next day, and anyway there was something about a weekend that gave you more time – more anticipation. He hated not having his weekends in Dublin. He hated going home on the Lilac Bus.

Rupert had never had an argument with his father in his whole life.

535

And he could remember only three differences of opinion with his mother. These went back to the time he was away at school and she had written three times to the headmaster to receive assurances that the beds were aired. He knew nobody else in the world who had such a relationship with their parents. Everyone else fought and forgave and loved or hated and stormed and railed or became fiercely protective. Nobody had this polite courteous distance based entirely on gratitude and duty. Nobody else who felt such irritation couldn't express it.

They didn't really need him, that was his whole point, and he wished them well, but he didn't need them either. So why should the pretence be kept up? It made it so much harder on all of them. Not only on Rupert – but maybe it was a little harder on him, he felt, after all their lives were ending. His hadn't really begun and couldn't begin as things were.

There hadn't even been a row when Rupert had decided to give up his law studies. He had been apprenticed to a firm in Dublin, begun his lectures with the Incorporated Law Society and at the same time read for a degree in Trinity. It wasn't a superhuman load – a lot of people did it easily – but Rupert never took to it. Not any of it. The bit he liked best oddly was the office. He was quite happy doing the clerical work, the part that Dee Burke, who worked there now said she hated. Rupert had made few friends in Trinity which surprised him; he thought it would be like school, which had been fine. But it was very different and he felt totally outside it all.

He had come home the weekend he knew he had failed his First Law with a heavy heart. He hadn't tried to excuse himself, he just apologised as if to a kind stranger, and his father accepted the apology as if it had been given by a kind stranger. They had sat one on either side of the table while his mother looked left and right at whoever was speaking.

Rupert said it was a great waste of his father's money and a disgrace to him in his profession. His father had brushed these things aside: heavens no, people often failed their first examination, there was no cause for alarm, some of the greatest lawyers claimed that they had never been showy scholars. No need for any regrets, it should all be written off as part of sowing wild oats, part of getting your freedom. Next year it would be more serious, head in book, down to it, wasn't that right?

On into the night Rupert had talked, saying that he wasn't cut out for it. It wasn't what he wanted. He didn't believe he would love it when he was in his father's office: he didn't love the office he was apprenticed to in Dublin, he only liked the more mechanical parts. He couldn't get interested in the theory of the law or the way it was administered. He was so sorry it had turned out like this, but wasn't it better that they should know now rather than discover later. They agreed logically that it was. They asked him what DID he want. He didn't know; he had been so sure that he would like Trinity, and like studying law, he had never given it much thought before. He liked thinking about the way people lived and their houses and all that. But wasn't it going to be very hard to try and get accepted to study architecture? his father wondered. He didn't mean study it, he didn't know, Rupert said desperately. He would get a job, that's what he'd do. His parents didn't understand this: they thought you had to have a degree to get a job, the kind of job Rupert would want. When he found the position as a junior in the estate agent's they said they were pleased if that's what he wanted. They didn't sound displeased, they sounded remote as they always had been.

His father was remote when he told Rupert that the time had come to get someone else into the office and that if Rupert were absolutely sure that he didn't intend to come into the profession he was going to offer a position to David MacMahon's son. Rupert assured him it would be fine, and got only a minor start when he realised that young MacMahon would have to be offered a partnership and the name of the office would be repainted to read Green and MacMahon. Once or twice they had asked him whether he had thought of coming back to Rathdoon and setting up his own little auctioneering business. There must be plenty of sites being sold and garages and people liked to keep things local. 'It might be no harm to get in before Billy Burns sets one up, he's started everything else in the town,' his mother had said, but firmly and politely he had assured them that this was not going to happen. He left them in no doubt that his plans involved staying in Dublin. This had happened on the day his mother had said that she wondered whether they should put a new roof on the house or not. Sometimes she felt that the one she had would do for their time and wasn't that all it would be needed for . . . ? Rupert had answered her levelly as if she had been asking no deeper question or making no last desperate plea. He talked of roofs and the value they added to houses and gave the pros and cons as he knew them, bringing himself no more into their plans than if he had been asked by a passing tourist.

His mother asked a bit coyly once or twice if he met any nice girls in Dublin. She didn't ask that any more. He must have given her some fairly firm answers, because he was only twenty-five, an age when you might be assumed to be still meeting girls. If people didn't know that you never met girls, you only met Jimmy.

Rupert's throat tightened just thinking of Jimmy. They had met for lunch this Friday; it had now become a bit of a ritual. Jimmy had no classes on a Friday afternoon: they had found the boys didn't study too well and had given them games or art or music. So Jimmy could jump into his little car and drive off to meet him. Rupert had noticed with an alarm mixed with pleasure that Dublin was becoming very slap-happy on Friday afternoons anyway, and not just in schools. At the office they did very little business and people seemed to be leaving for home – even if it was just the suburbs – earlier and earlier. If the noise in a nearby pub was anything to go by those particular workers of the world weren't going to do much to change it when they got back to their desks – if they got back. Still it was nice for Rupert. He could take a long lunch hour with no questions asked. They had found a restaurant that both of them liked (not easy as they had such arguments about food), and it was a very happy couple of hours.

Jimmy insisted that he go home every weekend; it was even Jimmy who found the Lilac Bus for him. Jimmy said it was a pity that they couldn't have weekends but it wouldn't be for ever, and since the old man had always been so undemanding wouldn't it only be right to go back to him now in his last few months? And it must be desperate on his mother waiting all week for him: of course he had to go. Jimmy wouldn't even let him pretend he had flu, not even for one weekend. He was very definite about it.

Jimmy was desperate about everything, it was part of his charm. He never wondered about anything or deliberated or weighed things up. And if as it turned out sometimes he was utterly wrong, then he was equally definite about that.

'I was all wrong about the man who invented those cats' eyes for the road at night. I was thinking about somebody totally different. I couldn't have been more wrong.' Then he would go ahead with the new view. But he had never changed his view about Rupert going home at weekends; that was an absolute.

Jimmy didn't have any home to go off to on a Friday. Jimmy's home was right there in Dublin. He was the youngest of six, and his two sisters and three brothers had gone exactly the way their father wanted which was into the newspaper vendor business. Some had pitches on good corners, others had roofs over their heads and sold ice cream and birth-day cards as well. But Jimmy's father was in the habit of saying gloomily, 'There's always one arty farty cuckoo in the nest, one who won't listen to reason.' Jimmy had been a bit of a pet when he was a youngster: they all encouraged him at his books, and then to university and into teaching in a very posh school. They made jokes about him being gay but it was never said straight out whether they believed he was or not. Anyone over-educated as they regarded him would have had the same abuse, the accusations of being limp-wristed, the mockery of his clothes, the vain search for an ear ring and the camp clichés from the television: 'Ooh Jimmy, you are awful.'

But he went there every Wednesday evening. They all called in on the small crowded house; they talked about rivals and which magazine would be seized by the censor as soon as somebody in authority had a look at it. They talked of how the dailies were doing and how there was no point in taking this magazine because it wouldn't survive to a second issue. They told each other how they had long narrow sticks and beat the hands off any kid stealing a comic. Jimmy would join in by asking questions. He always brought a cake, a big creamy one from the nice delicatessen where they often went. His family would have a communal coronary arrest if they knew how much the cake cost. His mother used to say it was a nice piece of cake even though the smallest bit soggy just in the middle. Jimmy would scoop up the bit where the Cointreau or Calvados had concentrated and eat it with a spoon. His brothers said it was a very fair cake, and reminded them of children's trifle.

It would be so easy to have a family like Jimmy's. They asked so little of him, they were so complete in themselves. If Jimmy were to disappear from their lives for ever, he would be spoken of affectionately, but if Rupert were to forgo just one weekend going home on the Lilac Bus It sould be a national crisis for the Green family. Sometimes he thought that this was very unfair, but Jimmy would have none of it.

'You're a difficult sensitive plant, Roopo,' he'd say. 'Even if you had my family, you'd feel threatened and anguished – it's the way things are.'

Rupert would laugh, 'Don't call me Roopo, it sounds like some exotic bird in the zoo.'

'That's what you ARE: like a dark brooding exotic bird that finds almost every climate too difficult for it!'

He had met Jimmy one great lucky day in the office. There was a picture of what they called a 'charming unconverted cottage' in the window. It was a bit far out too, not in the more fashionable direction and it could not be described as trendy, even by the most optimistic of those who wrote the descriptions.

Jimmy came in, slight figure in an anorak, wearing tinted glasses. He had blond hair that fell over his forehead and he looked a bit vulnerable. Rupert didn't know why he moved over at once to him even though Miss Kennedy was nearer. He didn't feel any attraction to him at that stage – he just wanted to see that he got a fair deal. He had been studying the picture of the cottage, and had an eager smile on his face.

Rupert had told him the good and the bad: the bad being the roof and the distance and awful boulders of rocks in what had been loosely called the garden. He told him the good, which was that it was fairly cheap, that it was nice and private, and that if you had any money now or later there was another building attached to it which was a sort of an outhouse but which could easily be made into another small dwelling. Jimmy listened with growing interest and asked to see it as soon as possible. Rupert drove him out there, and without anything being said they knew they were planning their future as they stood in the wild overgrown rocky ground around the little house and climbed the walls of the outhouse to find that the roof there was perfect.

'It's not handy for where you work,' Rupert pointed out, as Jimmy had said where he taught.

'I don't want to live handy to where I work, I want to live miles away. I want to have my own life away from the eyes of the school.'

Rupert felt an unreasonable sense of exclusion.

'And will you share it, do you think? That is, if you take it,' he had asked.

'I might,' Jimmy had said levelly. 'I have no plans yet.'

He bought the house. He had been saving with a building society for four years and he was considered reliable. The estate agency was pleased with Rupert: they had had the cottage on their books for rather too long. When all the negotiations were over, Rupert felt very lonely. This small smiling Jimmy was going to be off now living his own life in the wind-swept place. He would build that wall that they had discussed as a shelter, he would do up the second part of the house, paint it white, paint a door bright red maybe, grow some geraniums and get a suitable tenant. It would pay his mortgage. And Rupert would hear no more of it. Or of him.

He phoned on the Friday.

'Rupert, will you help me? I've lost all the fire for the place. I can't SEE it any more, what it's like, what's going to be so great about it. Will you come out and remind me?'

'Yes,' Rupert said slowly. 'Yes, that's what I'd love to do.'

He sat in a kind of trance all that Friday; if people spoke to him he only heard them vaguely. It was all so clear now: the confusions, the guilt, the hope that it would all settle down and sort itself out and that one day a woman would come along who would make him forget all this short-term stuff – which frightened him rather than making him satis-fied. But all the time knowing there would be no woman, and not really wanting a woman. But had he read the signs right? Suppose Jimmy was just a charming fellow with nothing on his mind but a good cheery chat with that nice fellow from the estate agent's? Suppose Jimmy said he had a fiancée or some married lady that he wanted to meet in secret. He drove out, noting that it would take him half an hour from door to door should he ever need to go that way again. Jimmy was standing at the gate. Waiting.

He knew it was going to be all right.

And it had been more than all right for three years now. They had done the two little houses up with such love that now they really *did* merit a glowing description on an auctioneer's books. But they would never be for sale. They were separate enough to pretend that they were two dwellings if it were ever needed. But it never was. When Jimmy in-vited his family out to see the place they all thanked him and said they must get round to it but they never arrived. Rupert didn't press his elderly parents to come to Dublin, and just showed them pictures of his part of the house. And of the garden. They made it all into a giant rockery and knew as much about alpines and rock plants as anyone for miles around. They had a big kitchen with a sink and work area on each side so that they could both cook if they wanted to. Every penny they had went into their little place. They had friends soon, people who came to dinner and admired or offered advice but mainly admired. It was so ideal and they were so happy.

That's why he hated leaving it at weekends. It was on Saturdays that they used to be most peaceful there, often shopping and cooking a meal – not only for Martin and Geoff or other gay friends but for the nice young married couple, who lived nearby and who kept an eye on their garden that time they went to Morocco. These were people to relax with. These and one or two people in the estate agency didn't have to have any pretences arranged for them. It was only in Jimmy's school and Rupert's home town that the acting was essential.

Jimmy said it was so ludicrous in the 1980s not to be able to say he was gay. And he would have at once if it were remotely possible. But no, apparently the boys' parents would think he had designs on them: they would think he was looking at them speculatively.

'I don't want any of those horrible ink-covered filthy ignorant kids,' Jimmy would wail. 'I want you, Rupert, my beautiful dark Rupert that I love.'

And Rupert would fill up with pleasure and pride that Jimmy could be so natural and open and say all that to him. He tried to say spontaneous things too but they came out with greater difficulty. He was a bit buttoned up as Judy Hickey had once said to him. He wondered often if Judy knew that he was gay. Probably. But it had never been the right time to tell her or to invite her out to see the rock plants and alpines that she would love.

Of course he could tell Judy Hickey: after all, she was a scandal herself in some way, wasn't she? There had been some really murky business years ago. She would be pleased to know there was another Great Secret in Rathdoon. But he could never tell Judy that one of the real reasons he hated so much leaving every Friday for these empty weekends was that he was so afraid Jimmy would find someone else. Or maybe even had found someone else.

At lunch this very Friday he had asked Jimmy what he would do all day Saturday, and there had been no satisfactory answer. Martin and Geoff were having people in for drinks – he would go to that in the evening. He'd mark exercise books, he'd try and fix up the hi-fi which had never been satisfactory. It was all very vague. Suppose, suppose, Jimmy had begun to like somebody else? His heart was cold inside like the unexpected bit you find when you take a loaf out of the freezer and it hasn't properly thawed. He could never tell anyone that fear. Not anyone in the whole world.

It was easy to talk to Judy. She told him about her little herb pillows;

541

he told her all the fuss over the TD with the love nest. They both laughed at that and for some reason that he couldn't quite see it brought her into talking about her own past. He was astounded at her story, a young wife and mother dealing in drugs all those years ago. And the husband doing deals with the law as if he was part of the Wild West. Imagine her not seeing the children, but imagine even more her getting supplies of LSD for the huntin' shootin' fishin' set! And hash! Jimmy would go wild when he heard. He could have listened for ever but suddenly she decided she was boring him and launched into chat with that half-mad Nancy Morris. She had also said that his mother thought about him every day. That couldn't be so. Mother thought about father, and the house, and the vegetable garden and the hens, but mainly father and how she was afraid that young Mr MacMahon didn't have the respect due to the senior partner and founder of the firm. Mother hardly showed any interest in Rupert's life in Dublin which was of course a relief, but it did mean that it was most unlikely that Mother would think about him every day. Surely Judy was being fanciful? She probably hoped no matter what she said her lost children thought of her every day. That was it.

Their house was small and white with clematis growing up over the porch. Jimmy thought that a Protestant solicitor's family would live in a manor house, heavy with creeper and inspiring awe among the peasantry. Rupert had said that only two houses had proper creeper. One was Dr Burke's, which was beautifully kept and one was the old vicarage, which was so neglected it now looked like a huge stone covered with ivy. They had a service each Sunday in Rathdoon in the beautiful church, but had no vicar, no rector, he came out from the big town seventeen miles away and had Matins in Rathdoon, and another, later Matins another fifteen miles down the road. Jimmy was fascinated, but Rupert had never asked Jimmy home to meet the family. Jimmy had asked him to his house many a time. Rupert had gone once and felt awkward even though nobody else had and they had all button-holed him about the price of property.

His mother was waiting just inside the door. That always annoyed him too and he got annoyed with himself over the very annoyance. Why shouldn't she wait to stop him ringing or knocking and disturbing his father's sleep. But it always made him think she had been standing waiting for his shadow to fall through the glass panels. He said goodnight with a much lighter tone than he felt, and braced himself. The soft leather of the magnificent jacket touched the back of his neck. It was Jimmy's birthday present to him. A few days early but Jimmy said it would cheer him up for the weekend, Dee Burke had been right, they did cost a fortune. Again the niggling worry: how had Jimmy been able to spend that much money even if it was a second? Put these doubts away, Rupert, he told himself firmly. Jimmy is good and true. Why pour vinegar on to it all with your stupid suspicions. Jimmy is at home tonight marking books and looking at television, Jimmy is not in a bar in town cruising someone. Why destroy EVERYTHING?

'He's very well, very clear,' his mother whispered delightedly.

'What?'

'Your father. He's very clear. He's awake; he asked several times what time would the Lilac Bus be in. Every time he heard anything change gear on the corner, he said 'Is that the bus?''

Rupert put his carrier bag down on the hall floor. 'That's great Mother, that's really great,' he said with heavy heart and went up the little stairs slowly to see the man with the head like a skull and the skin like cling-film. The man he had never been able to talk to in his life.

It was a sunny Saturday but his father's room was darkened and the dim light hurt his eyes. His mother was bottling fruit downstairs. Jimmy said Catholics never bottled fruit or preserved eggs – it was something their religion didn't go along with. Jimmy had told him more lies about Roman Catholicism than he ever believed anyone could invent. He had always been brought up carefully to respect it at a distance by his parents, and even though they thought it definitely held the people back they were impressed by the piety and the crowds going to Mass. His parents had gone to Galway to see the Pope. Jimmy said that his parents had made a small fortune the weekend the Pope arrived since the whole of Dublin wanted to buy every newspaper twice in case they missed anything.

Back at home in the cottage, Jimmy would be drinking freshly brewed coffee and reading the *Irish Times*. Then he might go out to the garden and do some transplanting: September was the month to move the evergreens if you wanted to change the plan a bit. But no, Jimmy would wait for him to come back for that. Maybe he would be puzzling over the hi-fi. Please may he not be driving into town just because he's bored; please may he meet nobody at lunch over a drink and smoked salmon sandwich.

'You're very good to come down every weekend,' his mother said suddenly as if she could read the homesickness for his real place written all over his eyes. 'Your father really does like talking to you. Do you notice that? Can you see it?'

Jimmy had begged him not to cross the whole of Ireland and then have a row. How could Jimmy understand that there were NEVER rows, and there never would be. Well, a coldness then, Jimmy would say. If you are going to go to all that trouble, it's silly to balls up your weekend: if you're making the gesture, make it properly.

'I think he *does* seem to like talking,' Rupert said. 'It doesn't tire him too much does it?'

'No, he plans all week what he's going to say to you. Sometimes he asks me to write it down, or just headings. I want to talk to Rupert about this, he'll say, and I write it down. Often he forgets what it was he was going to say about it, but it's there at the time.'

Rupert nodded glumly.

'Like he was going to ask you about those flats you sell in blocks; he was very interested in how they work out the leasehold. He said that there was never any of that in the conveyancing he had to do. But all he asked me to write down was "Block of Flats," you see, and then he couldn't remember last week what it was he wanted to say about them.'

'I see,' Rupert said, trying to sound more sympathetic than he was afraid he might appear.

'But this week, he seems very much brighter and more aware, doesn't he?' she was pleading.

'Yes, much more. Oh indeed. He was talking about this house here and what we would say if we had it on an auctioneer's books. I was giving him funny descriptions and he smiled a bit at it.'

Rupert's mother was pleased. 'Good, he hasn't smiled a lot. That's nice.'

'Why don't you have a bit of time off, Mother, when I'm here? Why can't you go into town, maybe, you'd like that. I can keep an eye on father and be here if he wants anything.'

'No, no, I want you to enjoy yourself,' she said.

'But really Mother, I mean I'm not doing anything anyway.' He shrugged. 'I might as well look after father and let you have a few hours to yourself.' He meant it generously, but he knew it had come out all wrong.

'But you're home for the weekend,' she cried. 'I wouldn't want to miss that by going off to the town. I can do that any day: Mrs Morris or young Mary Burns, Billy's wife, would sit with him. No, I want to get value out of your being here.'

'Sure. Of course,' he said, appalled at his own insensitivity. Jimmy would never in a million years have said anything like that. Jimmy would have brought life and laughter into the house the moment he got back. Jimmy. Oh Jimmy.

They had lunch, the kind of lunch that only his mother could serve: endless preparation and toasting of bread and cutting of crusts and spreading of cheese and slicing of tomatoes. And yet it was nothing – it managed to be both stodgy and insubstantial. If only she would let him cook. But then he had never asked her. Perhaps it might be giving something away to say that he could have made them a light and delicious lunch in a quarter of the time. It was his own fault like everything.

His father struggled all afternoon. And Rupert struggled back.

Sometimes his mother was there, sewing. She was always making little things for her sister who was married to a vicar and who always needed things for parish sales. His father would struggle and concentrate. His efforts to please meant that he could even be re-routed back to his own old days as a solicitor coming first to the town, when things were different and better. There was a time when his father had been happy to

ramble through the times gone by. But not now. It was as if he was deter
mined to show a guest in his eyes that he *was* interested in whatever kind
of strange thing the guest did for a living. All afternoon Rupert's soul was
crying out, 'It's all RIGHT father. Look, can't you rest: I have an okay
life and I wish you and mother well but why do we go through all this
meaningless chat? There is nothing to say any more.'

The sun was almost going down when he could bear it no more; he
said he had promised Judy Hickey he would do something for her and he
had better dash over to her.

'A brave woman, Judy Hickey – she held her head high in this place
for two decades,' his father said in a surprisingly strong voice.

'Yes, well, why not?' Rupert was defensive. 'She got a harsh punishment.'

'She took it, and she didn't run away and hide. She stepped down
from being lady of the manor and lived in the gate lodge.'

'And lost her children,' Rupert's mother added. 'That was the worst
bit.'

'Yes, well, I won't be long.' He felt he could breathe again when he
was out in the air; he left the square and went off towards the gate lodge
of the big Doon house.

Judy was lying curled up like a cat. She wasn't pleased to see him – in
fact she nearly sent him back straight away. She was like Jimmy really
but without the persuasive charm Jimmy made it seem reasonable; Judy
made it seem like a duty.

But she meant it: she got up and stretched and said she was going to
go out and walk in her husband's wood. Jack Hickey's wood she called it.
She said he should talk about anything, anything to show his father that
he was trying too.

But what could he say? He couldn't tell him that his heart was tearing
with the barbed wire of jealousy in case his male lover might have been
unfaithful. Then NOBODY could tell a father that about a lover of any
sex. But Rupert was worse off: he couldn't talk about his life, about the
beautiful gentians that he and Jimmy had planted and how the willow
gentian had burst into a whole pool of dark blue flowers last July and
they had taken photographs of each other admiring it. He found it hard
to talk about the garden without mentioning Jimmy because the two
were twined together, like the house, like cooking, like holidays and
reading and laughing and the things people did for heaven's sake.

Annoyed with Judy for being short with him, he walked home. He
passed the Kennedy's shop and saw a big handsome girl being ushered
in. The red-headed Kennedy boy, Eddie, was looking at her with a foolish
grin: they must be courting. She was very attractive; how simple life
would have been if only he had been born to court a big handsome girl
who would bring life and laughter into his quiet house.

Suddenly he thought of Jimmy in the house. Jimmy pausing at the door to touch the clematis and cup it in his hands with admiration. Jimmy saying to Rupert's mother that she should sit down and put her feet up and let her big ugly son and himself make the meal·for a change. Jimmy telling Rupert's father tales of the boys' school where he taught, and the fees and the extras and the awful school concerts. Jimmy walking casually down the road with him to Ryan's for a drink before dinner while the carbonade was in the oven. Jimmy would lighten their house better than any strapping girl from a well-to-do farm outside town.

'I was just thinking,' he said to his mother when she let him in the door again as if she had been hovering. 'Could I bring a friend home next weekend?'

After that it was easy. His mother said she was glad that she had got good notice because she would clear out the guest room. It had been something she had meant to do for a long time but never had the heart somehow. And his father said that it would be very interesting to meet someone who taught in that school because he had known a lot of people in his time who had been there and they were all united in never having a good word to say for it but having done extremely well as a result of being there.

Then a sudden shock. Suppose Jimmy didn't want to come?

'I hope he'll be able to make it; I didn't think of asking him,' he stammered.

'Why don't you ring him?' his mother suggested. His mother. Who made trunk calls as one might try to get in touch with another planet. Cautiously and without much hope of success.

'God, isn't that lovely to hear you?' Jimmy said.

'I'm ringing from home,' said Rupert.

'Well, I hope so. I did think sometimes you went off to exotic places without me, but I decided to trust you.' Jimmy's laugh was warm. Rupert swallowed.

'It's lovely here this weekend and I was wondering . . . I was wondering . . .'

'Yes?'

'I was wondering if you'd like to come down next week and stay, you know?'

'I'd love to.'

There was a pause.

'You would? You would, Jimmy?'

'Sure I thought you'd never ask,' Jimmy said.

Celia

Her friend Emer used to call it the Dancing Bus. All over Dublin people got on buses on Friday night to go home to great dances in the country. It had been a revolution, they said – culchies choosing to go home because the crack was better there than in Dublin. And they had the advantages of a bit of freedom in the city during the week and not losing touch with the home place either.

Celia laughed at the thought of her bus being a Sweetheart Special. She told Emer when they had cups of tea in the day room about the cast that turned up at a quarter to seven every week. Emer had sighed in envy. It sounded great, a nice spin across to the West, a weekend with no washing and housecleaning and trying to tell the three teenagers that there wasn't enough money for anything and trying to tell her husband who had been out of work for three years that there was plenty of money for everything. Emer had a sister married in the town that was seventeen miles from Rathdoon. Wouldn't it be lovely to go off there in a while? Oh Lord, she'd love it.

And so that's what happened. Celia had to work weekends, one in every four. So she gave her place on the bus to Emer. It had suited them all, and Emer said her family in Dublin were so grateful to see her back on a Sunday night that they never complained about anything, they just made her a coffee and said they'd missed her. Of course Celia did go to the dances at one time, and they were great altogether: you got a first-rate band to come to a place where the people drove in for miles and there would always be a big crowd. She used to dance with Kev Kennedy's brother, Red, sometimes, but she much preferred Bart, the eldest of the family. He was so solid and reliable. You never quite knew what he was thinking but he was always there. In fact you never had to ASK him to help, he seemed to know when it was necessary and turn up. Emer said he sounded a very suitable sort of man indeed, but Celia thought not. She said he wasn't interested in settling down and she wasn't going

547

to set her sights on another one who was a permanent bachelor. She'd had enough trouble getting over the first. Emer had sighed supportively and wondered why as a married woman she was trying to encourage others to join the club. It certainly wasn't what it was cracked up to be, and in many ways it wasn't much good at all.

But Celia only laughed at her. Emer was thirty-eight and sounded tough and cynical but deep down she would die for that handsome, whinging husband of hers and those tall rangy kids who got bigger and needed more clothes every time you looked at them. Celia wasn't going to be put off love and marriage by any of Emer's protests; it was what she wanted. Not urgently, not immediately, not at any price, but she wanted it sometime. Despite what she had seen of it in her own family.

She could hardly remember a day at home when there hadn't been some kind of a row. A lot of them were in public too because if the whole of Rathdoon was coming into the pub from eleven o'clock in the morning on, then they would have to be aware of the shouts and the disagreements and the sight of Mr or Mrs Ryan coming flushed with anger from the back room into the bar and serving a pint, only to disappear again and fight the point further. Celia had often heard that children grew anxious and withdrawn when their parents fought in the home. But that's not what happened to the Ryans. They grew up and went away, that was all. As soon as they were able to get out, out they got. Her eldest sister had joined a band of Australian nuns who had come to Ireland looking for vocations. Looking for very young vocations, since Celia's sister had only been sixteen. But the offer of further education had been attractive as well. She wrote home from time to time incomprehensible letters of places and things that were never explained. Then the boys had gone too. Harry to Detroit and Dan to Cowley in England. They wrote rarely, hard sorts of letters with a kind of graspingness they never had as youngsters – how a bar in Ireland must be a gold mine now. Harry had read in Detroit that Ireland was booming since the Common Market, and Dan had been told in Cowley that having a publican's licence in the West of Ireland was like having a licence to print money. These letters hurt Celia: there was much more than a hint, there was a direct statement that Celia and her mother were doing very nicely out of the family business, thank you. When she saw how things really were she felt she should laugh, but before she laughed she should weep.

Five years ago when her father died people said that at least one blessing was that Kate Ryan had always been more or less running the business single-handed and so there'd be no doubt at all that she'd be able to carry on. It wasn't like some establishments where the wife had always been in the background. No, poor Kate had been managing on her own while her husband drank down at one end of the bar with his own little circle.

And poor Kate had carried on for a good bit. In the summer she'd hire a young fellow to wash glasses and there was always Bart Kennedy to give a hand if things got very busy. No she was fine. There was no shortage of customers, and mercifully drink wasn't the kind of thing that came and went in fashions – people always loved drink. Apart from the first week of Lent, the custom was always steady and at weekends it was roaring. There was no opposition, and you'd never get another licence for a place as small as this. Rathdoon was unusual in that it had only one pub; other places might have had three. There had been talk once that Billy Burns was thinking of applying for a licence; he had been interested in buying a place about twenty miles away and asking to transfer that licence to Rathdoon, but nothing had come of it. Celia had been thinking about Billy Burns during the day for some reason. She had woken with that silly tune on her mind, 'Where have you been all the day, Billy Boy, Billy Boy?' and she thought it fitted Mikey's brother down to the ground. Mikey was such an innocent old eejit, and there was something a bit too smart about Billy. Nothing to do with his setting up another pub or not. In fact if he did that might be a solution to a lot of their problems. If her mother's pub went downhill due to legitimate competition that would be an honourable way out. If her mother drank Ryan's into the ground that was a less honourable way altogether.

But you couldn't say anything even vaguely like this to Celia's mother. Other people were hitting it a bit hard these days, other people were making fools of themselves and running up debts: there were men in Rathdoon who had big pores in their noses and red and blue veins in their cheeks from drink; there were women in Rathdoon who went into the big town seventeen miles away to do the shopping, but Kate Ryan could tell you that it was little shopping they did except half a dozen half-bottles hidden under the teatowels or whatever they bought as an excuse. Half bottles were easier to hide and they were easier to dispose of. Kate Ryan could tell you of those who came in at night for just one drink, Mr Ryan, and she had seen them topping it up from their handbags. They didn't want to be seen ordering more than the one. But Celia's mother would have no tales of a woman who didn't even have to hide it because she had it there on her own shelves, and she was surrounded by it as her way of earning a living for twelve hours a day.

It had been such a shock the first time she saw her mother drunk. Mam had been the one who didn't and Da had been the one who did. It was like left and right and black and white. To hear those slurred words, to have to cope with an inarticulate argument – Celia had been quite flustered and not at all the calm Nurse Ryan who could cope with anything on her corridor. The next day her mother had made great excuses, frightening excuses. It was food poisoning: she had eaten some of that chicken paste out of a jar, she was going to write to the manufacturers and enclose the label. Not only had it made her sick several times during the night but it had also affected her mind in some way. She couldn't re-member clearly, she couldn't piece everything together. When Celia said agreeably enough that the chicken paste might well have been bad but it was probably the drink that made her forget the night before, she flew into a rage, one of those real rows like there used to be when Da was alive. It was NOT drink. Could Celia kindly tell her what drink she was referring to? Had Celia seen her mother sitting down to have a drink even once last night? Celia shrugged. She thought it might have been just this one time. Let it pass.

Three weeks later she came home for the weekend, and her mother was mixing up the gin and the vodka, forgetting to take the money from people and letting the pints overflow while she went to deal with some-one else. It was then that Celia decided she had better book herself on to the Lilac Bus and come home every weekend that she could. This had been going on for a year now and her mother was getting worse and worse. And the really bad thing was that she wouldn't admit it, not for one moment. Not even to herself.

In the hospital Celia had seen dozens – more than dozens, probably hun-dreds – of people who were trying to help people who wouldn't help themselves. There had been endless conversations about old men who wouldn't go into sheltered accommodation and had set fire to their kitchens three times and old women who had broken their hips over and over because they wouldn't ask anyone to help them across a street. There were shrivelled anorexics who wouldn't eat, there were ashen-faced coronary patients who had insisted on doing overtime in stress-filled jobs and eating huge meals filled with cholesterol. There were women worn out with the fourteenth pregnancy, there were the mothers of the schoolchildren who had overdosed, there were the wives of the men whose livers had packed up despite a hundred arguments that alco-hol was poisoning them slowly to certain death. Always she had sounded sympathetic, always she had appeared to understand. But inside there was a bit of her which said that they couldn't have tried hard enough. If Celia had a daughter who was desperately unhappy at school and who had lost four stone in weight, she wouldn't hang around – she'd try to cope with it. If she had a father who couldn't cope, she'd have him to live with her. Only now was she beginning to realise that it was not to be so simple. People had minds of their own. And her mother's mind was like a hermetically sealed box in the vault of a bank.

Emer had been in high good humour: she had won a hundred pounds on the hospital draw. Each week they all had to buy a ticket for the building fund. It cost fifty pence, and they *had* to buy it – there wasn't any choice. Three hundred fifty pences added up to £150 and every second week the prize was £50 and every other one it was £100. It kept people interested and that small weekly contribution to the building fund was assured. Even if you were going to be on holidays you had to give someone else your stub. The winning ticket was announced on a Friday afternoon by number and you went to Wages to collect the prize. Emer was going to say nothing about it at home. Not one word. They would never hear. They would want jeans, they'd want a holiday, they'd think you could go on a holiday for a hundred quid. They'd want to go to Macdonalds every night for a month, they'd want a video. Her husband would say it should go into the building society, it should be saved in case he never worked again. No, much better to keep it for herself. She and Celia would have a night out next week. Celia had laughed at her affectionately. 'Sure,' she had said. 'People do what they want in the end, isn't that what you always say?'

She knew that what Emer would want despite all the protestations of independence and keeping the money to herself was totally different. She would want to arrive home this Friday night bursting with the news. She would want to send out for chicken and chips and plan endless treats which would indeed include jeans and a bit saved to please her anxious husband and a promise to look into the economics of a down payment on a video. That's what Emer would want and that's what she would do in the end. They both knew it.

And if Celia had a husband and kids she hoped that's what she would want too. Otherwise what was the point of the whole thing?

She was tired. It had been a long day. In other hospitals they worked twelve hour shifts: eight in the morning till eight at night. Celia thought she'd be ready to strangle some of the patients, most of the visitors and all of the staff if they had to have that routine. It had been quite enough to have eight hours today. A young woman had become desperately upset because at visiting time her brother, a priest, had said that he was saying a special Mass for her in their house. He had thought she would be pleased, she had thought that this meant it was the end. Then her husband told the priest that he had a neck to come in and upset the wife and there was a row of such proportions that everyone in the ward stopped talking to their own visitors and began to listen. Celia had been called. She pulled the curtains round the bed, she organised some light sedation, she explained in a crisp cool voice that the woman's diagnosis had been entirely optimistic, that nothing was being hidden from her or from anyone. She said that since priests had the power to say the Mass, what could be more natural than he would say one in the family home as a thanksgiving for her recovery so far and a hope that it would continue?

She also said with a particularly pointed look at the priest that it was a pity some people couldn't explain things sensibly without using voices laden with doom and ritual, and have some sensitivity about people's association of having Masses said with being very ill indeed. Then with a reprimanding glance at the husband she said that the whole point of a visiting hour was for the patient to be made more comfortable and happy and not to be plunged into the middle of a huge family row with accusations being hurled for the whole ward to hear. They were all younger than her except the priest, and he was probably under thirty. They took it very well and nodded their apologies to her and to each other. She drew the curtains open again and busied herself around the ward until she was sure they were all properly calm again. When the priest and the husband had gone she sat with the woman and held her hand and told her not to be an eejit: priests would want to say a Mass in a house at the drop of a hat. And after all it was their life. If they didn't believe it was important, who did? It was only the rest of the world, Celia explained, who thought that Masses and God were only brought in when all else had failed. For priests they were there all the time. She hit the right note exactly and the woman was laughing by the time she left the ward.

Would that it were going to be so easy at home.

Last weekend Bart Kennedy had let slip that he had been there several nights during the week as well as the weekends. She was alarmed. She and Bart never spoke of the reason for him being there. He never said that her mother was drunk, he would say she needed a bit of a hand. He never said that her mother had insulted one of the customers, he would say there had been a bit of a barney but it was probably all sorted out now. She had asked him to take wages for himself, and he had laughed and said not at all. He was helping out and how could he go and sign on if he was getting a regular salary? He assured her that he took the odd pint for himself and offered one to a friend occasionally but it was peanuts and couldn't go on. Emer wondered had he perhaps any hopes of marrying into the establishment, but Celia said that was nonsense – Bart wasn't the type. Nothing funny about him, mind you, but just one that would never marry. Don't forget, Celia knew all about those: she had served her time for five years on a hopeless cause. She could spot them a mile off now.

But enough: she wasn't going to think of that fellow any more. That was all behind her and at least the humiliations weren't known in Rathdoon. It was to another town that she had followed him hopefully at weekends, thinking that there was much more to it than there was, being there, being available. Eventually, because it seemed the one thing he was sure he wanted, she had slept with him. That was what he had called it but there was no sleeping involved: it was guilt for fear of discovery, and not very much pleasure for either of them. She hadn't lost him because she had been too easy to get; she hadn't lost him at all because he was never hers to lose; he had no intention of disturbing the very even pattern of his life by a wife and house and children. No, no, he would stay on with his parents while they lived and maybe with a sister later. There would always be girls – girls now and later women – who would believe that they had the secret and the key to unlock his independence. No, Celia could write a book on the Irish bachelor if she wanted to, but she hadn't time: she HAD to sort it out this weekend, otherwise she'd better leave the hospital and come home. It wasn't fair on everyone else in Rathdoon.

She was glad that Kev Kennedy was a little bit ahead of her. That meant that he would sit beside Mikey. Tonight she was not in the mood for Mikey's jokes; some evenings she could take a few and then turn to her own thoughts but there was too much on her mind, and Mikey was so easily hurt. It was good not to have this battle between offending him or going mad herself. She slipped easily in beside Tom the driver. He leaned over her and slammed the door shut.

'It's only twenty to seven. I have you all very well trained,' he said and they all laughed with him as the bus went out into the traffic and headed for home.

Tom was a fine companion. He always answered agreeably and gave long answers if he were in the mood to chat and short ones if he weren't The silences were companionable. He never talked to people behind because it distracted him and he liked the person sitting beside him to tell him if it was all clear on the left as they nosed on to main roads from side roads. Much nicer than the rest of the Fitzgeralds up in the craft shop, but then it was silly to expect families to be the same. Look at Billy Burns: he'd buy and sell Mikey a dozen times before breakfast. Nancy Morris – there was something wrong with her, Celia thought. She had a very fixed look, a look that really was fixed on nothing. Celia had seen it in hospital sometimes. Nancy was as different from that laughing Deirdre, her sister in America, as she was different to a Martian. And there was poor Kev, Bart's young brother behind her there in the bus. And possibly she was different to her own brothers and sister. At the thought of her own family her brow darkened. Why would none of them do a thing to help? How had it happened? She *could* write them a round robin: 'Dear Maire and Harry and Dan, Sorry to have to tell you but Mam is hitting the bottle worse than ever Dad did. What will we do? Looking forward to hearing by return from New South Wales, Cowley, Oxfordshire, and Detroit, Michigan, Your loving sister, Celia, Dublin.' That was the point: Dublin. It was only up the road as far as they were concerned, and she wasn't married, that was even more the point wasn't it? If she had been a wife then none of them would have expected her to abandon that and look after her mother, no matter how near she was. But being a nurse, an angel of mercy, helping the sick and earning her living . . . that would be written off.

And what's more they wouldn't understand, any of them. Maire would write from Woolowogga or wherever she had gone on a course – she was always going to ludicrous places on courses – and she would say it was Blessed to give and Blessed to help. Great. Harry would write from Detroit and say she must do what she thought was best as she was the one on the ground. He would add something about it being a nice tidy living for her, and probably put in a really sensitive bit about not wanting his share out of the family business yet. Dan would write, he might even ring from England: he'd encourage her like mad to go home, he'd say that nursing wasn't a REAL career or anything, and that it was all for the best. His bit of tact might be to hope that now she was known as the landlady of a pub in all but name perhaps Celia might get a few offers of marriage. She was only twenty-six, why had they written her off in three countries? She was their baby sister; she remembered them as big and strong and great fun, but in their letters and their rare appearances they were selfish and they were strangers. And they thought of her as an old maid.

'Do your family drive you mad? she asked Tom as they had just overtaken a huge dangerous-looking lorry that seemed about to shed everything it had on everything that was near it.

'Oh yes, of course they do,' Tom said. 'I mean that IS what drives people mad actually, families. It's not strangers in the street or the Bomb or the economy, it's always their relations.'

'Or love, I suppose, or lack of it?' Celia was impersonal, interested in talking about ideas. So was Tom. That's why they found their chats easy and never found their long silences threatening.

'Yes, love, but love usually involves some idea of family: you love someone, you want her to be your wife; she won't, you go mad. That's family. You hate your wife, you don't love her any more, you wish she'd fly off on the next space shuttle. That's family.'

Celia laughed. 'God you'd be great in one of those family counselling places with psychiatrists and all.'

'I'm always surprised they never asked me in on one,' said Tom, and they didn't speak for another fifty miles.

She was glad to get out and stretch. She had heard of other buses where they got stuck into a pub like this one for a real session and maybe it would be an hour and half before people got back on the road. But Tom Fitzgerald ruled his Lilac Bus very firmly, it was time to visit the Ladies' and a very quick drink. There really wasn't even time for a coffee because they always took ages to make it in pubs, and indeed in Ryan's of Rathdoon they wouldn't make it at all.

'What'll you have Celia?' Dee had a knack of getting to the counter quickest and an even better knack of getting served. Celia had a bottle of Guinness and a few words. Dee had never changed, not since she was a schoolgirl bursting with pride at her new uniform and coming into the bar to show it off to the Ryans. She had been everywhere to show it off, and everyone had given her a lemonade, or a bar of chocolate or even half a crown. Nobody had anything but good wishes for the doctor's daughter off to her posh convent boarding school. Dr Burke was part of every life and death in Rathdoon, nobody would have a jealous thought about his children and what they had. Who would deserve it more?

She slipped Mikey some ointment that they used up in the hospital to ease bedsores. She didn't want to let Dee see her in case it was thought that she might be trying to improve on the doctor, but Dee would prob ably never think that in a million years. She was a grand girl with a very infectious laugh, and of course she had the patience of Job that she could talk to Nancy Morris so animatedly about Nancy's boring job and her endless tales of Mr This the consultant. How did Dee put up with it and even look interested and remember their bloody names? The ten minutes were up and they were back in the dark comfort again.

She saw that Tom had tapes in the van; she had never noticed them before.

'Is that a player as well as a wireless?' she asked with interest when they were on the road again.

'Yes, do you wonder I have to guard this vehicle with my life? All I own is tied up in her,' he laughed.

'You don't play any, while we're driving?'

'No. I thought about it: everyone would have a different taste and I wouldn't want to inflict my choice on all of you.'

'Oh, it would have to be yours, would it?' Celia threw back her head of thick brown hair, laughing at him. 'Where's the democratic bit then? Why couldn't everybody choose their own, even bring one each week?'

'Because if I had to hear any more in my life, I think I'd drive off the road and into the deepest bog that would close over us,' he said.

'Let's have no music then,' Celia said agreeably and they drove on thinking their own thoughts. Celia was wondering what time she would catch her mother at the most receptive. There must be *some* moments in the day when the unfortunate woman was not suffering from a hangover or withdrawal or had got stuck into it again. There must be a time – late morning maybe – when she could ask Bart to man the place. Not that anyone came in much on a Saturday until it was well into lunchtime. She could always put CLOSED on the door, Father Reilly put closed on the presbytery for heaven's sake when he simply had to have an hour to him-self, or maybe it was for some poor divil that couldn't be disturbed. That was it, no more drawing on poor Bart. Anyway he liked to work with Judy Hickey during the daytime when she was home for the weekend. She could put CLOSED on the door for an hour or two, but apart from chaining her mother by both wrists and ankles how was she going to get her to stay and listen to the very unwelcome view that she was now in-capable of managing her own pub and must get herself into an alcoholic unit before it was too late? It was gone beyond false promises now, and assurances and little games. Celia had been present when a surgeon told a forty-two year old man last month that he had terminal cancer and had less than two months to live. This is what it felt like again. That sense of dread and half hoping the world would end before you had to say it. Of course it had turned out very oddly in the hospital; they had thought the shock might be intense and that was why Celia was there as part of a back-up. But he had been very quiet, the man, and said, 'And I never went to America. Imagine in my whole life I never saw America. Isn't it ridiculous in this day and age.' He had said that several times before he died; it seemed to disturb him more than death itself and leaving his wife and three young children.

Suppose her mother were to say something equally unexpected like that she had been wondering was this what was wrong with her, and she would like to go at once as a voluntary patient to some kind of place that would dry her out. Stop thinking like Alice in Wonderland, Celia told herself sternly. You're a grown-up, it's no use shutting your eyes wishing things would happen.

'There's a lot of rags tied to a bush coming up now. I think it's a holy well or a wishing tree or something,' Tom said suddenly. 'Maybe we should all get out and tie our shirts to it,' Celia said. They passed it, and indeed there were ribbons and what looked like holy pictures pinned on to it.

'I never saw that before, and all the times we must have driven past it,' Celia said, looking back over her shoulder. She thought she saw Dee Burke crying, her face was working in that sort of way a child's does to keep off the sobs. But Nancy Morris was yammering on as usual so there couldn't be anything really wrong.

'I never saw it before. Maybe it's a new saint; you know the way they get crossed off like St Philomena.

'Why DID St Philomena get crossed off, I wonder?' asked Celia.

'I don't know, maybe they found her out,' Tom grinned. 'I know my sister Phil was very annoyed indeed at the time, she felt it was an attack of some sort.''Oh yes, Phil, that would be her name. How is Phil by the way? I haven't seen her for a while.'

'She's fine,' Tom said shortly.

Celia went back to the tree for conversation. 'Are they pagan or are they religious, I wonder?' she said.

'A mixture, I think.' She was still short.

Celia thought about the tree. Wouldn't it be great to go there and pray to some saint who had a special interest in drunken mothers, leave an offering or whatever they left and then go home and discover that it had worked. Bart Kennedy would be serving behind the bar and her mother would be sitting with a packed suitcase and face full of optimism.

'See you during the weekend,' Tom said with a friendly smile.

She nodded. He had been a bit moody tonight, she thought. She didn't mind their stops and starts normally, in fact she liked it. But tonight she had wanted to talk. Actually what she had really wanted was

Emer. You could say anything to Emer and you knew she would think about it but she wouldn't bring it out again on every occasion and ask you how you felt about it. Emer would give you advice but not be annoyed if you didn't take it. 'Everyone does what they want to in the end,' she would say. She wasn't as specific when it came to knowing how to convince someone else to do the right thing. Or the best thing. Celia had long discussions with her over this. Did you wire the jaws of fat kids who were compulsive eaters? Did you have medical cards for smokers and only those who were certified as having good strong lungs and no trace of emphysema would be allowed to buy a packet – they'd have to show the card first. That would save life wouldn't it? Celia might suggest. Emer would shrug. Temporarily only: the child with the wired jaw would wait eagerly until the contraption was removed; the smoker would get the cigarettes somehow or smoke butts. But then why were drugs banned? Why not just sell heroin by the kilo in Quinnsworth and be done with it. Those who wanted to kill themselves would and there would be no drugs racket and pushers and people having to turn to prostitution or theft for it.

Emer said that drugs were different: they were poison, they killed. You wouldn't sell arsenic or strychnine would you?

What about alcohol: that killed, they had see enough rotted livers to know that; they could see the slow death around them. Emer said that if Celia felt as strongly as that she shouldn't own a pub, and she should have a temperance banner. Then they would both have a bottle of Guinness and talk about something else. But she was such a comfort, no wonder that her handsome husband and her three giant children were always waiting so eagerly for her to come home from work. And she wasn't a Superwoman either. There were bad time and low times in Emer's life as well as in everyone elses's. That's why she was so good to talk to.

'Goodnight,' she nodded, and added 'Thanks for getting us here.' She didn't want to be curt with Tom just because he hadn't been like Emer! That would be unfair.

'Best to the West, as Mikey would say,' Tom laughed.

'Don't encourage him – he has enough catchphrases already.' She went in the door and knew from the loud greeting that her mother called across the bar that it was going to be a long hard hour and a half. She put her bag in the kitchen, she hung up her jacket and came out quickly to stand beside Bart Kennedy who patted her on the arm and wordlessly began to pull the pints.

Her mother shouted for two hours when the pub eventually closed. She sat at one of the tables and hurled abuse as Celia methodically emptied the ashtrays and wiped the surfaces. She would NOT be patronised in her own pub, she cried, she would not have Celia coming off the bus and taking over as if she owned the place. Celia did NOT own the place and in fact the place would never be hers. She hoped that Celia knew this. She had made a will with that nice young Mr MacMahon in Mr Green's office, and she had said that after her death the pub should be sold and the money divided equally in four and shared out between Maire and Harry and Dan and Celia. So now. Celia said nothing. She washed the glasses under hot water first, then under cold, then turned them upside down to drain on a plastic grid: that way the air got at them from all angles and dried them without smears.

Her mother had a brandy bottle on the table beside her. Celia made no attempt to touch it. She just moved past her and locked the door. The place was now ready for the next day. She gulped a bit at the thought of the conversation she was going to have in the morning when the closed sign would appear on Ryan's door for the first time since her father's funeral.

'Aren't you going to have the common manners to say goodnight, Miss High and Mighty?' her mother called.

'Goodnight Mam,' said Celia as she went up the narrow stairs wearily to the small white bedroom with the iron bed. She lay awake for a while. Long enough to hear her mother stumbling up the stairs and hitting off the chest of drawers on the landing. She must have known it was there: it had been there for thirty-eight years, all her married life.

It was very sunny, too sunny. Celia woke with a jump. The curtains had been pulled back, and there was her mother with a cup of tea.

'I thought you might like this, after your week's work, and you must have stayed up late last night doing the glasses.' The voice was steady enough and the hand wasn't shaking as it passed the tea-cup and saucer.

Celia sat up and rubbed her eyes. 'You were with me when I washed the glasses,' she said.

'I know, I know, of course,' her mother was flustered, she hadn't remembered. 'Yes well, naturally, but thanks for . . . um . . . organising it all the same.'

There was no smell of drink but Celia realised that the must have had a cure, maybe a vodka. That's why she was able to cope. She had smartened herself up too, combed her hair and worn a dress with a white collar. Apart from her eyes which looked terrible, Mrs Ryan didn't cut too bad a figure at all.

This might be the time. Celia swung her legs out of the bed, and took a great swig of the tea.

'Thanks Mam. Listen, I wanted to say something to you. I've been trying to get a good time . . .'

'I have a kettle on downstairs; I'll come back up to you when I have a minute.'

She was gone. There was no kettle on. Celia got up and dressed quickly. She decided against jeans and put on a skirt and blouse with a big wide belt. It made her look more authoritative, more nurse-like in a way. There was no sign of her mother in the kitchen. Where could she have gone? There was a sound of scrubbing out the side entrance, and there was Mrs Ryan on hands and knees with bucket and scrubbing brush working away.

'I was noticing this last night: it's in a very bad way, we mustn't let the place go to rack and ruin around us.' She was sweating and puffing. Celia let her at it. She went back into the kitchen and made more tea. Eventually her mother had to come back in.

'There, that's much better,' she said.

'Good,' said Celia.

'I saw that Nancy Morris, a proper little madam that one. "Hallo Mrs Ryan" if it suits her, and wouldn't give you the time of day if it didn't. I pretended I didn't hear her. She has her mother scalded coming home every weekend.'

'I'm sure,' Celia said. Mrs Ryan's jaw dropped.

'Oh not like you. I mean it's grand that you come home, and you're such a help.'

'I'm glad you think so this morning It was a different tune last night,' Celia said.

'Oh you wouldn't need to mind me on a Friday night, the place gets so crowded and they're coming at you from all sides. I probably sounded a bit impatient, but didn't I thank you for doing the glasses, didn't I bring you a cup of tea in bed?' She was pleading now, almost like a child.

Celia took the bucket and the brush away from her gently and closed the door behind her. She lulled her to the table with soft talk. She didn't want the woman to bolt from the room.

'Of course you brought me a cup of tea in bed, and I *know* that deep down somewhere you are grateful to me for coming back and helping out, but that's not the point, Mam, not the point at all. You don't remember anything about last night, not from about nine o'clock on, that's what I'd say.'

'What are you talking about?'

'You were well gone when I arrived – that was before ten. You fought with a man and said he'd only given you a fiver not a ten. You told young Biddy Brady that you didn't want a whole crowd of her girl friends cluttering up the pub tomorrow – fortunately Bart got us out of that one. You spilled a whole bottle of lime juice and you wouldn't let anyone wipe it up so that the counter was sticky all night. You couldn't find the tin of potato crisps and you told a group who had come here for the golfing that you didn't give a damn whether you found them or not, because they smelled to you like a child's fart. Yes, Mam, that's what you said.'

Her mother looked up at her across the table. She showed no signs of getting up to run away. She looked at Celia quite calmly.

'I don't know why you are saying all this,' she said.

'Because it happened, Mam.' Celia begged her. 'Believe me, it all happened, and more and much more other nights.'

'And why would you make this up?'

'I didn't. it was like that; it will be like that again tonight, Mam, you're
not able to cope. You've had a drink already today, I can see. I'm only
telling you for your own good.'

'Don't be ridiculous, Celia.' She was about to stand up. Celia reached
out and held her there. Hard by the wrist.

'I haven't written to the others yet: I didn't want to alarm them, I
thought it might pass. I thought it was only weekends when you were
under a bit of pressure. Mam, you have to accept it and DO something
about it.'

'Others?'

'Maura, Harry, Dan.'

'You're going to write all over the world with these tales.'

'Not if you can help yourself first. Mam, you're drinking far too much,
you can't control it. What you're going to have to do is . . .'

'I'm going to have to do nothing, thank you very much indeed. I may
have had one too many sometimes and all right I'll watch that. Now will
that satisfy you? Is the interrogation over? Can we get on with the day?'

'PLEASE Mam, listen. Anyone will tell you, will I get Bart in here to
tell you what it's been like? Mrs Casey was saying, Billy Burns was saying,
they were all saying . . . it's getting too much for you here . . .'

'You were always prudish about drink, Celia, even when your father
was alive. You didn't realise that in a bar you have to be sociable and
drink with the customers and be pleasant. You're not cut out for a pub
the way we were, the way I am. You're too solemn, too sticky for people.
That's always been your mistake.'

There was no point in putting CLOSED on the door, she wouldn't
talk. The most she would admit was a drop too much on some occasions.
She denied all the scenes, she remembered none of the conversations.

People started drifting in around lunchtime. Celia watched her mother
accept a small whiskey from Dr Burke who had come in to get some
drink to celebrate his son's engagement. Celia wished that Dee's father
would lean over the counter to her mother and say 'Mrs Ryan, your eyes
are all bloodshot and there are big lines under them; for your health's
sake you must give up drink.' She wished that Father O'Reilly would
come down from the presbytery on a home visit and tell her that for the
good of her soul she must go and have some treatment and then take the
pledge. But doctors and priests didn't interfere enough these days maybe.

The phone box was way at the end of the bar, quiet and discreet. No
wonder half of Rathdoon made their calls from there rather than beside
the eager ears of the post office people.

Emer was just getting the lunch. They had all been to the pictures last
night on her winnings and tonight they might go again. Videos had gone

560

through the roof. even the kids realised that a video was out of the question.

'What will I do with her?' Celia asked.

'She doesn't admit it to herself?'

'No. I have her chapter and verse – what she said, what she spilled and broke, who she insulted. Not a word does she believe.'

'And you can't get support troops in.'

'Not really. Bart will be too polite and anyone else would be embarrassed.'

'I suppose you'll have to wait.'

'I can't wait any more and neither can she. It's terrible. There MUST be some way. How do people come to see things? Is there no way of hurrying it up?'

'Well, I did hear of a man who signed himself in for treatment the moment he saw himself on a video of his daughter's wedding. He had no idea that he was so bad until . . .'

'That's it. Thanks Emer.'

'WHAT? You're going to turn a video on your mother in Rathdoon? Have sense.'

'I'll tell you about it on Monday.' Celia was gone.

Mrs Fitzgerald invited her in. Yes, Tom was here. They were having a pot of coffee – would Celia join them? She felt they had been having a chat, that she shouldn't interrupt. She said she'd only be a minute. Yes he did have a small cassette recorder, and yes a blank tape . . . or a tape that he could record over. What was it – something from the radio? No, OK, it didn't matter. Look, it was easy to work. No, he didn't mind being without it until they were on the bus again. He was puzzled, but he didn't ask any more. She took it back to the pub.

There was so much clutter under the pub counter that the small tape recorder passed unnoticed.

Celia used it judiciously, half an hour on one side and half an hour on the other.

She even moved it out in her hand to be closer to her mother when the solo singing began and Mrs Ryan was screaming a tuneless racy version of a song which she hardly knew. She let it play for the insults to Bart Kennedy and for the bad language.

At one stage Tom Fitzgerald came into the bar, he saw his recorder and said 'Is that fair?'

'You have your standards, I'll have mine,' she snapped, and then much more wearily: 'She doesn't know, you see, she really doesn't know.'

'She's not going to like it,' he said.

'No.'

'When will you . . . ?'

'Tomorrow morning, I'd say.'

561

'I'll come in around lunch and pick up the pieces,' he smiled. He had a very, very nice smile.

Her mother sat stonily through the first few minutes. She railed with anger at the arguments and the bad language. Then she decided it was a fake and when she heard her maudlin conversation about what a great man her husband had been, tears of shame came into her eyes.

She folded her hands on her lap and sat like some timid employee waiting to be fired.

Out of the little tape recorder came the voice of Mrs Ryan as it called on Biddy Brady's engagement party to shut up and let HER sing. Tears fell from her closed eyes as the voice came out in its drunken, tuneless wail. Celia started to turn it off.

'Leave it,' her mother said.

There was a long silence.

'Yes,' said Mrs Ryan, 'I see.'

'If you wanted to, we could say you had pneumonia or that you were off to see Dan in Cowley. That would sort of cover it up.'

'There'd be no point in covering it up. I mean, it's only more lies isn't it? Might as well say what it is.' Her face was bleak.

'Sure you're halfway there, Mam, if that's the way you think – you're nearly better,' said Celia, leaning across the small dark tape recorder to hold her mother's hand.

Tom

He remembered the day he painted the Lilac Bus. It had been a sort of dirty beige before, and there was an exhilaration about pointing the spray can at it and seeing it change before his eyes. His mother had been appalled. It looked so vulgar and called attention to itself. That was about the worst crime in her book – attracting attention. The good went by unnoticed and understated; the bad were flashy and loud and painted their vans this silly mauve colour. Tom's father just shrugged. What could you expect? he asked his wife in a tone that meant the one thing he really didn't expect was an answer. Tom's father hardly ever spoke *to* Tom anymore: he spoke about him, in his hearing.

'I suppose that boy believes that money grows on trees . . . that boy thinks we should have the itinerants living in our garden . . . that boy feels that work is beneath him.' Sometimes Tom answered; sometimes he let it pass. It didn't really matter which he did. His father's mind was fixed anyway: that boy was a waster, a left-wing long-haired layabout. A purple minibus was only what you'd expect.

It wasn't what Tom expected. He just decided one day on a whim, one day when the washing didn't seem to be making the van look any better. And he LOVED it now that it was lilac-coloured: it had much more personality and more life. That was when he decided to go into the transport business. It wasn't *exactly* legal of course, but suppose they did have an accident: an insurance company would have a hard time proving that he wasn't driving seven friends home for the weekend. No money was ever seen to change hands in Dublin. He didn't stand at the door selling tickets as the bigger bus people did. They were the same people all the time, give or take one or two a month. It wasn't a moneyspinner or anything, he paid for his petrol and cigarettes out of it, that was all. But it did mean he could smoke as much as he liked and he could come home every weekend to Rathdoon, which was what he wanted to do. The Lilac Bus had made all this possible.

Tom knew all about his passengers' lives in Rathdoon, but very little about what they did in Dublin. He had thought of finding out where they all lived and dropping them home rather than leaving them in the city centre at ten o'clock on a Sunday night but something told him that they might prefer the anonymity of the city to be kept absolute; they mightn't want the others to see their digs or their rooming houses or their set-up. More than once Tom had noticed a small fair-haired fellow in tinted glasses in a car parked near where the bus began and ended its weekend run. He would wave eagerly to Rupert Green. Now Rupert very clearly might not want that known. It was only because Tom had X-ray eyes that he had noticed the car. And his eyes had sometimes caught Dee Burke slipping into a big car and the arms of an older man. The older man had never been mentioned by Dee or by anyone in Rathdoon, so it was safe to assume that he was a secret older man not a legit one. No amount of watching or guessing could tell him what young Kev Kennedy was so afraid of. It hadn't always been that way: he used to be a very nice young fellow, and the only one of that family to get up from the kitchen table and leave their father and their slices of bread and ham and the radio on from Goodmorning to Closedown. But for the past year or so he was in bits.

Celia lived in a nurses' house. Six of them shared a place which was apparently highly successful. They had two television sets, a washing machine and an ironing board always in position in the back room. Celia had said there was never a cross word exchanged in that house – it was an ideal way to live until they married and had homes of their own. Nancy Morris shared a flat with that nice bouncy Mairead Hely; how Mairead stuck it was a mystery. He had met her one night at a party and she told him that Nancy's newest trick was to watch out for food tastings in supermarkets and rush in before they closed and have paper cups of soup or bits of cheese on toothpicks and then to come home triumphantly to the flat and say 'I've had my supper.' That night, and it was about three months back, Mairead had said that she was gathering up her courage to ask Nancy to leave, but she couldn't have gathered it yet. Poor Mikey was so nice Tom would have driven home willingly, but he just laughed and walked to a bus stop with the never failing sense of good humour that was so hard to take. Judy Hickey took a bus the same direction and Tom often saw them talking together as he turned the Lilac Bus and drove off home.

None of them knew where his home was, that was certain. Long ago he had developed a gift for not answering direct questions so skilfully that people thought they had been given some kind of answer but didn't ask again. When Nancy Morris had asked him how much he paid a week for his flat, he said it was hard to work out, and that was that from Miss

Morris. Rupert once asked him which side of the city he lived, and Tom had said that he was sure Rupert must know the trends in what people wanted. He often thought that it was interesting looking at people in cinema queues for example and wondering where they lived; he supposed that if he were working in an auctioneer's like Rupert, he'd think it even more interesting. Rupert agreed and had talked cheerfully about the unexpected ambitions of a lot of the people who came into his office. He never again asked Tom where he lived, and he didn't sound as if he had been rebuffed.

Dee Burke had told him that her brother was living in sin and wasn't it monstrous that boys could get away with it and girls still couldn't really. She had asked him suddenly, 'Maybe you live in sin too. Do you?' 'I don't know,' he had said. 'I'm very confused about sin; they never explained it properly at our school, what about yours?' Dee had said gloomily that they never stopped explaining it at her school and they were all so sick of it by the time they left, they had hardly the energy to commit any, which might have been the aim all along. But she still didn't find out what his lifestyle was. And down in Rathdoon he was spoken of as the one Fitzgerald boy that didn't join the family firm, the only one who didn't want to build an empire. He did something arty up in Dublin. But in any gathering of three if his name came up there would be three different theories on what he did. It gave the lie to the obsession with gossip that small towns were meant to have automatically, Tom thought. There was Dee with her older chap, Rupert with his boyfriend, Kev with his gambling debts or whatever it was and no one back home knew a thing about any of them. Or about Tom. In Rathdoon only one person knew how Tom lived and why: his mother.

Nobody would guess that in a million years. His mother tutted with the best, sighed over his clothes and bus – genuine sighs. She really would have preferred a nice inconspicuous bus and more conservative clothes: nice neutral colours, stone-coloured trousers and brown jackets like her other sons wore. Suits, white shirts, restrained ties for Mass on Sunday. When his father railed about the young generation in general and That Boy in particular Tom's mother was gentle in her reproach. Anyone looking on might have thought she agreed with her husband. Who could have known that Tom was her lifeline?

She was a handsome woman, Peg Fitzgerald. Fifty-two, very well groomed; you never saw a hair out of place on Mrs Fitzgerald. She wore knitted suits, in lilacs or dark green, and a good brooch to tone in with whatever colour it was. In summer she wore lighter suits but they were the same colours and she had looked the same for years. She had three perms a year in the big town, and she had a shampoo and set every Friday morning of her life with little Sheila O'Reilly, the neice of the Parish Priest. Sheila didn't do much business in Rathdoon, but she never seemed to mind. She was always cheerful and if there were no heads of hair to deal with she did knitting instead and made a little out of that as a sideline. She wished there were more regular customers like Mrs Fitzgerald, who wanted their hair done the same way at the same time every week.

Mrs Fitzgerald was in the shop every day. The craft shop side of it had been her idea and was very successful. Any time a tour bus stopped there was a heavy electronic buzzing of tills in the Fitzgerald Craft Centre. There were shawls, lengths of tweed, pottery – a very wide range to suit all tastes. It was also the place where the whole of Rathdoon bought birthday presents for each other. Peg had difficulty persuading the family that it was a good idea, but now they looked at her with a new respect. She was a firm believer too that things should be kept in the family. When the boys married it was understood that their wives would work there. In fact one potential daughter-in-law broke off the engagement because she said all she would get from the marriage contract was to be an unpaid shop worker instead of the bank official that she was. Tom had thought that showed some spirit but the rest of the family including the jilted brother all combined in thinking they had a lucky escape if that was going to be her attitude.

From the outset Tom had said he wouldn't work in the shop; there had been no fight about it, only scorn. He had said reasonably he thought that it was better for his three brothers and two sisters if they *knew* from the word go that he would not be joining them. Then they could make their own plans without any question marks hanging over him. He decided this as long ago as his school days. But they had thought it was like being an engine driver and took no notice. What he would like to do was go to Dublin and live. Just live, not necessarily DO anything until he found something he'd like to do, and then maybe America or Paris or Greece. If you didn't have high living standards and want a comfortable house and a lot of possessions and rich food you could live very cheaply. They had thought it was a phase.

He had got a lot of honours in his Leaving, much more than the brothers who were well on their way to being merchant princes: expanding to other towns, opening new branches, developing their mother's much mocked idea of a craft shop in other centres all over the West. Tom was pronounced brighter than any of them by the masters who had taught all the Fitzgeralds, but he was adamant and very firm for an eighteen year old. He had all these bits of paper to prove he was educated now could he get on with his own life? He thanked his father as warmly as he could for the grudging offer of university fees, but still it was no. All he wanted was to be left alone. He wouldn't go to the bad, he would come home regularly if they liked so that they could see him and satisfy themselves that he was still normal. He would hitch. He would sign on for the dole each week, and NO that would not be an almighty disgrace in Dublin. Who would see him or know him for God's sake, and

NO it was not unfair, and there was at least bread and a roof for those who weren't rich. We didn't let them die in the streets today, stepping over them saying wasn't it a pity they didn't have the get up and go to find a good job and earn their living. NO, he did not intend to stay on national assistance for ever. And, YES, he was very grateful for the offer of a place in the family firm but we only had one life and that was not how he was going to spend his.

And wasn't it lucky that this is what he had decided to do? What on earth would have happened if he hadn't been around? It had been very easy to live cheaply in Dublin. For a while he lived with a young couple who gave him a bed and some food; they didn't have all that much themselves. He taught their children every evening, two nice bright little boys. He went over everything they had done at school and helped them with their homework. But he didn't really like it because he felt they should be out playing instead of doing more and yet more. They knew enough, he kept telling their worried young parents, they're fine: don't pack their heads with facts more and more. The parents didn't understand. Surely the best thing was to get a good start, to be in there with a better chance than the others? But they were only ten and nine, it was YEARS before they would need to be in there fighting the others for places and points and positions. No, the pale mother and father hadn't got on in their lives because they had nobody to guide them; they weren't going to let the same thing happen to the children. He left them amicably. He worked as a gardener for an old lady and slept in her garden shed for a year without her knowing. She never knew in the end, and he had moved his camp bed and primus stove long before the funeral so nobody ever knew.

He worked in a night club as a sort of bouncer. He was slim and not the typical bouncer material but he had a look in his eye that was as important as muscle. His boss who was one of the sharpest men in Dublin was anxious to keep him on, promote him even, but it wasn't the life Tom wanted. He left again amicably and before he left he asked the sharp boss what was good about him. He'd like to know just for his own record. The boss said he owed him no explanation if he was leaving but OK, Tom had a look in his eye that said he would go the distance. People didn't mess with him. Tom liked this reference just as he had liked the old lady saying he was a loving sort of gardener, and the nine-year-old boy saying that he made Latin so much more interesting than they did at school because there was none of this treating it as a language – more as a puzzle really. But these were not written references. Each new job had to be found on charm or effort; each time he had to go in cold.

He had a summer in Greece driving a minibus, not unlike the Lilac Bus, over mountainy roads, taking holidaymakers to and from airport and hotels. He had a summer in America working at a children's camp with seventy discontented youngsters who would all rather have been at home. He had a winter in Amsterdam working in a souvenir shop. He had a funny three months in London working in market surveys – going up to people on the street with a clipboard and asking them questions. He had a different kind of three months in London working as a hospital orderly; he found it harrowing, and his respect for nurses went way, way up. He had been on the point of telling Celia about those months, several times, but he never told stories about what he had done – it led to questions and questions often needed answers.

He didn't think of himself as a drifter, and yet for nine years, since he had left school, he had done nothing with any purpose or any permanence. Still, he wouldn't have missed any of it, not even those strange days in the hospital pushing elderly frightened people on trolleys through crowds, all speaking different languages, all the nationalities under the sun working in the hospital and coming in as patients. And now it meant that he could look after Phil, for he had no job to give up, no real lifestyle to interrupt.

Phil was the nicest in his family, there was no doubt about it. They all agreed on that, just as they all agreed that Tom was the oddest and the most difficult. Phil was the nearest to him in age: she was almost a year to the day older than he was. All the six Fitzgeralds arrived within seven years, and then the young Peg stopped producing a new baby every season. There were pictures of them all when they were toddlers and Tom always thought it looked like a nursery school rather than one family. But his mother had always said it was great to get it all over at once. You had a period when they all seemed to be unmanageable and then suddenly they had all grown up. Anyway Phil had always been his special friend, and in the great sixteen- and seventeen-year-old arguments about Tom not joining the firm Phil had been very supportive. She had been in the big town seventeen miles from Rathdoon learning shorthand and typing at the time, it had been agreed that she should work in the office rather than the shop. But she used to come home at weekends during her commercial course and encourage Tom to live his own life. She had a big round face, Phil had, and she was always laughing. Years ago he remembered her dancing with Red Kennedy and getting a lecture that the Kennedys were perfectly nice, not a thing wrong with them but she should set her sights a little higher. Phil had said indignantly that she wasn't setting her sights at Red Kennedy or at anyone, she was just dancing with him but there had still been a lot of head shaking.

Phil was what they called a fine girl in Rathdoon, Mrs Fitzgerald used to say that she'd slim down when the time came. Hadn't Anna, the eldest of the family, had a lot of puppy fat too. But Mrs Fitzgerald always thought that there was some kind of law which said that a girl needed to be nice and slim and attractive when she was thinking of choosing a husband and settling down. It was just the way things were. But Phil didn't notice some magical trick of nature: she remained plump and round-faced and never developed the hollow cheeks and small waist which were generally agreed to have been important when her sister Anna attracted and married the very suitable Dominic whose family made tweeds.

Tom had never thought she was too fat; he had told her that several times when he came home for the weekend. He said she must be losing her marbles to think she was a fatty, and cracked to think that she had no friends because of this.

'Who are my friends then? List them,' she had cried.

Tom couldn't, but he said he couldn't list any friends of his family for God's sake, he was away, he didn't live here. She MUST have friends. No, she claimed, she didn't. That was when meaning to be helpful he had suggested this Singles type of holiday. Everyone went on their own, there were no loving couples to start out with but hopefully plenty of them on the way back. Phil had read the brochure eagerly and decided that she should go on it.

'Don't tell anyone it's a singles special,' her mother had advised. 'It looks a little pathetic. Say it's an ordinary holiday in Spain.'

Tom never knew quite what happened, but it wasn't a success. Phil said that Spain was all right, and the weather had been fair, but nothing else. Later, much later, he heard that all the girls except everyone on the group charter had enjoyed a close physical relationship with one or more other person on the same group charter – again, everyone except Phil – and that there was no question of meeting people and dancing with them and talking to them and getting to know them. This was apparently a much more swinging type of holiday that some singles outings, and swinging meant going to bed with people, people who were total strangers.

But Tom didn't know all this at the time. Phil had come back quiet and non-communicative. He noticed shortly after this that she seemed to have lost weight, but he didn't say anything because he had been the one to tell her that weight wasn't important. If he admired her now, she would believe that he had only been kind before. Phil didn't go to the dance any more and she didn't go out to the sea with a crowd of girls like she used to. But to be honest, he didn't notice these things at the time, it was only afterwards he remembered it all.

Phil had come to Dublin on one of the day excursions by train from the town. It was a bit of a killer: the train left at 9 a.m, you were in Dublin at noon and then the train back was at 6 p.m. So it was some concentrated shopping before they all fell back with sore feet and bulging parcels to go home again that night. Phil always rang Tom if she went on one of these marathons, and he came to meet her at the station in his minibus which was a dirty beige in those days. She looked very pale, and said that she had been having really terrible pains like a knife on the train, so bad that the people in her carriage said she should go to a hospital or a doctor since she had been crying out with the sharpness of them. Tom looked concerned and just at that moment she bent over again doubled up with pain and letting out a long low scream, so his mind was made up. He drove her to the out-patients' of a hospital. He was quite firm. He got her seen before anyone by saying it was an emergency. As her brother, he signed the permission to operate for a burst appendix and he was there when she woke up to tell her that it had all been fine, and it was over and all she had to do now was to rest. Her troubled face smiled at him sadly. Their mother came up the next day with a suitcase of things that Phil would need, a lot of reassurance, sighs of how good God was to let it all happen when Tom was there to take charge, and messages of love, boxes of chocolates, bottles of lavender water from the rest of the family.

She was recovering quite well, Tom thought. Well, her strength was coming back quickly and he was very startled when one of the nurses said she would like to talk to him about his sister. Privately. She had made a report to the people who should know already, like the matron and the surgeon who had operated, but this was now something that must be taken further, through Miss Fitzgerald's own doctor perhaps.

He was alarmed. The nurse spoke reprovingly, as if poor Phil had been caught stealing in the wards. What was it? Well, the nurse had noticed she spent a long time at the lavatory, and she had asked her about constipation or diarrhoea. Apparently neither, but she was still in there for a considerable time, so the nurse had listened at the door. Tom felt his heart beating: what horror was he going to be told?

It was what the nurse had suspected. Vomiting, retching. Two or three times a day.

'What's causing it?' Tom cried. He had no idea what the tone of shock was all about. Why wasn't he being told this by a doctor?

'She's doing it herself,' the nurse said. 'Eating chocolates, biscuits, banana, slices of bread and butter. You should have seen the papers and the empty boxes. And then vomiting it all up.'

'But why on earth would she do that?'

'It's called bulimia; it's like anorexia nervosa – you know, where people starve themselves to death if they can. It's a form of it. They binge and gorge and then they make themselves sick to get rid of the food they've eaten.'

Phil does this?'

'Yes, she's been doing it for some time.'

'And did this cause her appendix to burst?'

'Oh no, not at all, that was something totally unconnected. But maybe lucky in a way. Because at least now you know and the family will know and help her try to fight it.'

'Can't you just tell her to stop. Can't we all tell her it's . . . it's revolting – it's so senseless.'

'Oh no, that's not the way, that's not what they'll say at all when she goes in.'

'Goes in where?'

'To a psychiatric hospital. It's a mental condition, you know, it's got nothing to do with us.'

The nurse wasn't quite correct. It did have a little to do with them because Phil was admitted to the psychiatric wing of that same hospital as well as all the therapy and group discussions on the psychiatric side. She had been very relieved at the beginning to know that other people did the same thing. She thought she was the only person in the world who had ever done it, and she felt a great burden of guilt taken off her shoulders. She never felt guilty about the self-induced vomiting: she said it was the easiest thing in the world. If you just put your finger in the right place down your throat it happened automatically. But she did feel guilty about stuffing herself with the food. Especially eating in a lavatory – that was the thing she felt shameful about. She wasn't ready at all to talk about why she did it. Tom was told that she would undoubtedly do it again and again before she was cured. Before she came back to reality and accepted that she was perfectly fine as she was. The help and support of a family at a time like this was crucial. If Phil was to see that she was a person of high esteem in her own family that would go a very long way towards helping her have a good image of herself again. The family, yes. But Lord God the Fitzgerald family. At this time.

Poor Phil couldn't have picked a worse time to call on them, Tom thought grimly. It was the very period that the newspapers were full of the case about the armed raid on the post office in Cork and the subsequent conviction and sentencing of Teddy Fitzgerald their cousin, who had worked in the business with the family. That had been a heavy cross. Then there was the infidelity of Dominic, the highly suitable husband of Anna the eldest. There had been many a tale of a relationship and finally the birth of a child which Dominic grudgingly acknowledged as his, even though it was born not to his wife but to one of the most unsuitable women in the West of Ireland, tinkers who had settled down and according to Mrs Peg Fitzgerald the only thing worse than a tinker on the road was a tinker who had settled down. So there was that disgrace. And there had been a few other things too, none of them as shocking but all of them adding up to a general family anxiety. It was the wrong time to hear that a member of the family was now entering on to a long period of psychiatric treatment and would need their support.

Mrs Fitzgerald made her point of view absolutely clear. There would be no talk about Phil whatsoever. This was final. Phil had recovered from her burst appendix, she had been convalescing, she had been visiting friends, she would come back shortly. Meanwhile they would get a temporary girl for the office. Mrs Fitzgerald would go to Dublin once a month to give this support that the hospital said it needed, Tom would go to see her as often as he could, and that was it. It would not be discussed; they had quite enough problems already without adding this one.

And what would it do to Phil's chances of getting a husband if it was widely known she had been in a mental institution? No more arguments.

Tom was sure that this was not what the doctors meant by family support: hushing it all up, making it into a greater shame than Phil already felt it was. He was certain that his mother's monthly visits – full of assurances that nobody knew, no one suspected, people had been fooled and hoodwinked, cover stories had been invented – were all the worst thing for his sister who would listen with stricken face and apologise for all the trouble she had caused. Sometimes his mother would reach out awkwardly and take Phil's hand.

'We love you . . . um . . . very much. You are much loved, Phil.' Then she would draw her hand back, embarrassed. She had been told by the psychiatrist that this was a good line to emphasise, but she recited it as if it were learned by heart. They were not a demonstrative family, they had never hugged or kissed each other. It was hard for his mother to reach out and say that to Phil. And bewildering for Phil to hear it, just before her mother gathered her gloves and handbag and started to leave.

He went to see Phil every day, every single day and he telephoned her on each Saturday and Sunday. His mother said that she would telephone except that there was nothing to say, but Tom found things. After all he knew her much better: they had been meeting each other constantly, and he was able to pick from a variety of things to say. He never felt as if he were talking to someone who wasn't well. He didn't talk down to her, he would never apologise profusely if he hadn't been able to ring or visit, just briefly. He wouldn't let on that he thought his presence was essential to her. He treated her as if she were as sane as he was.

They talked about childhood a lot. Tom remembered his as happy enough, too much talk about the business, a bit too much of covering over and not letting the neighbours know this or that, and keeping our business to ourselves. Phil remembered it quite differently. She remembered that they were always laughing, and that they had all been sitting round the table together talking to each other, though Tom said they couldn't have been. There would have to have been either their mother or their father in the shop. Phil remembered them going on great outings to the sea and picnics, Tom said he honestly could only remember one. Phil said they used to play games like I Spy and the Minister's Cat, and Sardines, where one person had to hide and when you found them you squeezed in like a sardine beside them. Tom said that was only at parties. But they didn't fight over the memories; they talked them over like an old film that you'd seen years ago and everyone could remember bits of, but nobody could remember all of.

They talked about boyfriends and girlfriends and sex. Tom wasn't surprised to hear that she was a virgin, and she wasn't surprised to hear that he was not. They talked easily and without guilt, sometimes for hours in the day room or in the garden, sometimes just for short times because

Phil was silent and withdrawn, or because Tom had to work. He was working in an auction showroom these days, helping to carry furniture in and out, put lot numbers on things and write them up in a catalogue. He had been thinking of moving on, but the hours suited him and it was near the hospital so that he could come and go easily. One of the other patients asked if Tom was her boyfriend. She had laughed uneasily and said she never had a boyfriend. The other girl had shrugged and said she was probably as well off: they were a barrel full of trouble that's all they were. She hadn't assumed for a moment that Phil COULDN'T have a boyfriend. It made Phil fell a lot more cheerful. She asked Tom what kind of girls he liked, and he said unusual ones, not people who talked about houses and engagement rings and the Future. He had a very nice girlfriend once but unfortunately she met a really dull guy and he offered her all this other business, security, respectability – and she came and told Tom straight out she was going to take it. Phil had been very sympathetic.

'You never told us any of this,' she said.

'True, but you never told us that you half fancied Billy Burns, even though he was a married man,' he said laughing.

'You dragged that out of me,' she laughed too. He thought it was all too slow, she MUST be better now.

He said this more than once to the psychiatrist and was depressed to hear that Phil was still not happy, still not at ease with herself and sure of her place in the world. They all thanked Tom for coming and said he was invaluable. Not only in his own visits but in the lifeline he offered back to Rathdoon. She never minded his going back home at weekends. In fact she like it because it brought her closer to the family and because he always brought back news of them all and, better still, a cheerful letter from her mother.

Every Saturday morning he forced his mother to write her a letter. He literally sat there while she wrote. He wouldn't accept that she had nothing to write about, and he refused to let her wriggle out of it.

'Do you think I'd be doing this, do you think I'd sit here every Saturday morning unless it was important?' he had shouted. 'She is desperate to know that we are fond of her, and that her place is here; she won't be ABLE to come back unless she knows this.'

'But of course it's here, naturally we want her back. For heaven's sake, Tom, you're making a big drama out of it all.'

'It is a big drama. Phil is in a psychiatric hospital and mainly because we can't let her know that she is important here,'

'Your father and I think that's all mumbo jumbo. She was never made to feel anything but important; we treated her with great respect, people loved having her in the office. She was always so cheerful, and she knew everyone's names: wasn't she the life and soul of that place?'

'Write it. Write it down on paper,' he would order.

'I'd feel stupid saying that to Phil. It's silly, it's treating her as if she's not all there. She'll know I'm only acting.'

'But you said you meant it, a minute ago.'

'Yes, of course I mean it, but it's not something you say, not something you write down.'

'Since you're not there to say it, you have to write it. Since you won't let her come home and be treated in the town where you'd only be seventeen miles away, where you could see her every day, then you're going to have to write it. Otherwise how is she to know, how in God's earth can she KNOW that she's important here?'

'It's not that I won't let her come back here. It's for her own good, to keep things quiet, to keep our business to ourselves.' He had heard it so often, maybe he would hear it for ever. Perhaps Phil would never get better.

He was in the middle of yet another Saturday confrontation when Celia Ryan came in. He was surprised to see her, and in a way relieved. His mother had been very hard to pin down today. She had escaped him in the morning by saying she was needed in the shop, and it was only when he brought her a cup of coffee and a writing pad that he could get her to listen. She had been going through one of her Phil-Must-Pull-Herself-Together phases. Tom felt a mad urge to ask Celia to sit down and explain to his mother her own first-hand knowledge of anorexia and bulimia, mentioning casually that Phil was in a psychiatric ward with the latter. His mother would probably fall senseless to the ground if he were to tell the family disgrace to Mrs Ryan's daughter. The temptation had only been a flicker.

Celia wanted a loan of his tape recorder, of all things, and a blank cassette. She wanted to record something. She seemed flustered. She didn't tell him what she wanted it for, but then he rarely told people anything, whether they asked him or not, so he couldn't fault her there. She said she'd give it to him on the bus.

'Terrible time she has with that mother of hers,' Mrs Fitzgerald said.

Tom nodded. He thought he didn't have a great time with his own mother but it was not in him to say it; he just wanted the letter to give to Phil on Monday.

'She'll probably marry Bart Kennedy, and they can keep an eye on the place that way,' Tom said.

'Bart Kennedy? Not at all. Sure nobody will marry Bart Kennedy, he's not the type that marries.' Mrs Fitzgerald was positive.

'Bart, a fairy? Go on out of that.'

'No, I don't mean that or anything like it. He's just not the kind of man who marries, you must see that. Maybe men don't notice these things: women do. Red Kennedy now, he'll be married within the year I'd say, I hear he's not courting. But Bart – not at all.'

'I thought that's what she came home for,' Tom said.

'She comes homes to stop that place going down the drain, that's all.'

'Really?' Tom felt pleased. He didn't know why but he felt a sense of relief.

He went into the pub that night and discovered why she had wanted the tape recorder. It seemed a bit sneaky somehow. Like taking advantage of the poor woman who was slobbering and messing around behind her own bar. Even more humiliating was the thought that Mrs Ryan's daughter was recording the tuneless singing.

'She doesn't know, she really doesn't know,' Celia said as an explanation when he had asked her was it fair. He imagined Celia trying to tell her mother about the excesses of the night before and Mrs Ryan brushing it away with that business-like cheerful manner she had when sober. It wasn't the kind of thing anyone else would say to her so she would be bound to believe that Celia was making it up at worst or at the very least exaggerating it.

'I'll come round tomorrow and pick up the pieces,' he said. She smiled back at him, a warm grateful smile. He looked at Bart Kennedy. Bart was pulling pints and laughing with the lads – he and Celia didn't have eyes for each other at all. Tom must have been mad to have thought it in the first place.

There were no pieces to pick up next day. Celia's mother had taken it very well. She was sitting in the back room while Celia and Bart dealt with the Sunday lunchtime trade.

'She's coming to Dublin. I thought it would be easier: I'd be able to get to see her.'

'When?'

'Tomorrow. I won't come back on the bus tonight. I'll wait and go with her. I've a great friend, a nurse in Dublin – she'll work for me tomorrow even though it's meant to be her day off.'

'Does she live in your harem of nurses?'

'Emer? Not at all: she's a respectable married woman with a family.'

'Would you work if you were married?'

'Bloody sure I would. Catch me giving up a job to cook meals and clean a house for a man. Anyway everyone has to nowadays. How would you have any life at all if you didn't? And nursing's fine, I'd hate to lose it.'

'How long will it be . . . ' he nodded towards the back room where Mrs Ryan sat waiting in a chair.

'I don't know. It depends on her – you know, if she wants to.'

'Doesn't it depend on her family too, and support?'

'Well there's only me; she can't have the beauties in Australia and Detroit and England, so she'll have to make do with me.'

'My sister Phil isn't well, she's got the same problem,' he said suddenly.

'I never knew Phil had a drink problem.' She said it without censure or shock.

'No, not that, I meant she has the same problem: she only has me in Dublin. She's got an anorexic thing, you know, but she does eat and makes herself vomit.'

'She's a better chance with that; so many of the anorexics die, it's desperate to see them, little wizened monkeys, and they think that this is the best way to be. But bulimia is very stressful, poor Phil. Isn't that very bad luck.'

He looked at her gratefully. 'Will they be any help, the ones who've gone away?'

'I shouldn't think so, will yours?'

'No. I'm beginning to realise it now. I kept thinking I could change them, but it's all head in the sand, pretend it isn't happening, don't tell anyone.'

'In time, in their time maybe. Not yours.' She was very gentle.

'Well they'll have to make do with us then,' he said. 'Your half mad Ma and my half mad sister.'

'Aren't they lucky they've got us,' said Celia Ryan and laughed like a peal of bells.

'I'll miss you going back on the bus tonight,' he said.

'Well maybe you might come and console me when I've got my mother in. And if it would be any help I could come and see Phil with you, if you'd like it, that is.'

'I'd like it a lot,' said Tom Fitzgerald.